SEVEN BRIDES FOR SEVEN TEXANS

LONESTAR BROTHERS

ERICA VETSCH   GABRIELLE MEYER   AMANDA BARRATT

LORNA STEILSTAD   KELI GWYN   VICKIE MCDONOUGH

SUSAN PAGE DAVIS

PROLOGUE

ERICA VETSCH

CHAPTER 1

"Quiet down, now." George Washington Hart put his hands flat on the dining room table and levered himself upright. "I have something to say."

Deep voices stilled and masculine laughter died.

Looking down the long expanse of walnut laid out in china, silver, and crystal, he surveyed five of his seven sons. Dark-haired, with either blue eyes or brown depending on whether they took after his late wife or himself, intelligent, strong, capable, God-fearing. Ranging in age from thirty-four down to twenty-three, they were strapping examples of Texan manhood. Everything a man could ask for in his progeny.

Except for one thing.

Not a one of them had seen fit to marry and give him some grand-children.

But all that was going to change, or his name wasn't George Washington Hart. After all, he wasn't getting any younger, and the doc over in San Antonio said the sand might be trickling through his hourglass faster than he thought.

"You boys have made me proud, and that's a fact. And like my father

3

before me, I always planned to give my sons their inheritance while I was still around to watch them enjoy it."

Eyebrows raised, and the boys looked at one another, and then back at him. GW turned to the portrait over the fireplace behind him. Victoria's lovely brown eyes stared down at him, and his heart jerked, the way it always did when he thought of his bride, gone from them more than a decade now. "Your mother, God rest her soul, would agree with what I'm about to do."

"What's that, Pa?" Hays, his youngest, asked from the far end of the table.

Crockett shoved Hays with his elbow. "If you'll keep your tater trap shut for a minute, he'll tell us."

"*My* tater trap? You've been talking flat stick through the whole meal. My ears are worn out listening to you," Hays shot back.

"Knock it off, both of you." Austin, the eldest, leaned forward from his seat at GW's left hand and sent them his best glare. "Go ahead, Pa."

"Thank you. Hey, Perla," GW called out into the hallway. "Bring our guest in."

The housekeeper led Harley P. Burton through the doors. The arrival of the lawyer had all the boys sitting up straighter, with the exception of Bowie, who scowled and leaned forward so his hair fell over his face. His shoulders hunched, and he put his elbows on the table, bringing his hands up and lacing his fingers together. He pressed his lips against his thumbs and went still.

GW shook his head over his second-born's insecurities. Wounded and captured at Gettysburg, Bowie had never gotten over the loss of his left eye or the black-powder burns that colored the left side of his neck and face. Always a taciturn kid, he'd become even more so over the years. Bowie was the one GW worried about the most once his announcement was made, though none of them would be particularly happy with his decision.

"Harley." GW motioned him over.

"Happy New Year, GW." The lawyer, rotund and jolly, shifted his satchel and held out his hand.

"And to you. Did you bring them? Any trouble at the courthouse?"

"No, it's all done." Harley looked around for a place to sit, and Austin hopped up.

"Take my seat, sir."

Harley nodded and eased his bulk into the walnut high-backed chair. The letters *SAH* had been carved into the wood by a master craftsman. Stephen Austin Hart.

Each of his sons, named after famous residents of the great state of Texas, had their own monogrammed chair and place at the table. His wife's idea when they finished building the house known as El Regalo, carrying on the tradition of naming Hart sons after famous Americans.

Now her chair and Houston's and Chisholm's were empty. Houston had left home years ago to make his fortune in California, and Chisholm was a Texas Ranger, chasing down outlaws, preserving the peace, and returning to El Regalo and the Seven Heart whenever he could. The last time they had all been together had been before the war, which was another reason for GW's decision. It was high time his sons remembered their roots.

Austin moved down the table and dropped into Houston's chair. The lawyer fussed with his bag, digging out paperwork and seven sealed envelopes. "Here you are, GW."

Now that the moment was upon him, GW hesitated. This was going to be like throwing a stick of dynamite into a chicken coop. It might rain feathers for a long time. He strengthened his resolve. In the weeks since the doctor had given him the long face, he'd been planning this. If his sons wouldn't get up off their pockets and see to their futures, then he would.

Fanning the seven envelopes out, he cleared his throat. "What I'm holding here are the deeds to seven parcels of the Seven Heart Ranch. One for each of you."

Austin smiled and nodded to his brothers. Travis and Crockett shared a look, and Hays grinned. Bowie sat like a statue, hands fisted against his lips, waiting.

"Now, before you all start turning handsprings, there's a condition to you receiving your share." GW tapped the envelopes into a pile. Harley smoothed his hand over his vest, pursing his lips and narrowing his eyes. The lawyer had laughed loud and long when GW had proposed his condition, but now that the time had come to unveil it, he looked as nervous as GW felt.

GW caught himself raising his hand toward his chest and stopped.

None of the boys needed to know about the heart condition that prompted his decision, nor how little time he might have left.

"I have decided to parcel out your inheritance, the land, the cattle, the assets of the ranch, to each of you equally, provided..." He paused for breath. "Provided each of you marries before the end of this calendar year and lives on his property."

Stunned silence greeted him as his words hung in the air.

Then everything broke loose.

"You can't be serious." Crockett shot up, skidding his heavy chair backward. "None of us is even courting anyone unless you count Hays, who is courting pretty much every woman he sees."

"Forget it. I am *not* marrying to order." Austin smacked his hand on the table. "I'll get around to finding a wife when I get around to finding a wife, and not a minute before."

Travis stroked his chin, questions in his eyes that made GW skittish. His observant and thoughtful doctor son might just guess at GW's motivation, and that was something he'd rather keep to himself. The last thing he wanted was his sons coddling him like some fragile baby. Or watching him like a ticking clock, waiting for the hands to reach midnight.

Bowie said nothing, but he turned his head slightly to take in each of his brothers with his one good eye.

"What about Houston?" Travis asked. "He isn't even here. Chisholm either." Travis and Houston had always been close, and they communicated frequently.

"So write or send telegrams. Maybe this is what Houston needs to get him back here from California." GW took his seat once more. There, the gauntlet had been thrown down. Now it was up to the boys to pick it up, if they had the guts.

Hays plucked an apple out of the fruit bowl in the center of the table. He bit into it, grinning as he chewed. "I don't know why you're all in such a flap. A whole year to find a wife? How hard can it be?"

FIRST COMES LOVE

GABRIELLE MEYER

To my brothers and their beautiful brides.
Christ & Sarah VanRisseghem
Brent & Angie VanRisseghem

CHAPTER 1

JANUARY 2, 1874
HARTVILLE, TEXAS

*J*ohn Coffee Hays Hart grinned as he looked at the stack of *wanted* posters he had just picked up from the *Hartville Herald*. They draped over his forearm, still warm from the press.

"What do you think?" Hays held up a poster to show his friend, Gage O'Reilly.

WANTED: A BRIDE FOR HAYS HART.

Hays's grin turned into a chuckle. "For once in my life, I'll be the first to accomplish something before my brothers."

Gage looked over the poster, his blue eyes shaded by the rim of his Stetson. "Do you think it'll work?"

Hays wiggled his eyebrows. "We won't know unless we try."

With Pa's ultimatum still ringing in his ears, Hays no longer had the luxury of waiting to find the perfect mate. Pa said that each of his seven sons had to be married by the end of 1874, or they would lose their inheritance—a section of Hart land. And the portion Hays would inherit was a beautiful spot along the Sabinal River. He had known it would be his since he was a child, and he wasn't about to lose it now.

He surveyed the bustling town of Hartville, named after his grandfather, Benjamin Franklin Hart. Dozens of false-front buildings extended from one end of the dusty street to the other, their gray weathered siding a testament to the hot south-central Texas sun. "Might as well begin at the church and work our way back to the mercantile. I aim to hang every one of these posters before I head back to the ranch."

They started walking toward the end of Main Street where the white clapboard church was the first building to greet people arriving from the south. Their spurs rang against the wooden boardwalk as they sauntered past friends and neighbors. Hays tipped his hat at Ruby and Julia Brown standing outside the telegraph office. "Morning, ladies."

Color bloomed in Ruby's cheeks as she batted her pretty eyes under the brim of her bonnet. "Morning, Hays."

Hays didn't take the time to stop, and the ladies' whispered giggles followed him and Gage to the end of the boardwalk.

"Why the rush to get these hung today?" Gage asked, glancing back at the Brown sisters. "You have a whole year to choose a wife."

"I plan to beat my brothers to the altar." As the youngest of seven brothers, Hays had never been the first to accomplish anything. By the time he was twelve, all but one of his brothers had left the ranch to either fight in the Civil War or start a life outside the 7 Heart Ranch. He'd grown up under the shadow of his brothers' successes. No matter what he did, it had already been done before.

"For once, I'd like my pa to look at me with the same pride I see when he talks about Austin's and Bowie's heroism in the war, Houston's success as a merchant in California, Travis's medical career, Crockett's work ethic, and Chisholm's job as a Texas Ranger." His voice became serious as he looked at the *wanted* poster again. "I'm going to be the first to marry and make my pa proud."

He'd also prove to his family that he was no longer a child.

Gage lifted his Stetson and ran his hand over his wiry blond hair. "I'll do what I can to help." As the best wrangler on the 7 Heart Ranch, Gage was a natural choice to help Hays lasso a wife.

They arrived at the church, and Hays handed the stack of posters to Gage. He pried four rusty tacks off a weather-stained advertisement from last summer and positioned the *wanted* poster in the very center of the board. He set the tack in place, pounding it with the flat edge of a rock he picked off the ground.

He made quick work of the second tack and was on the third when the front door opened. A young lady stepped out of the church, her green eyes filled with curiosity as she peered around the edge of the door. "May I help you?"

Hays stopped the rock mid-strike, his attention no longer on the poster, but on the beautiful stranger standing before him.

Gage quickly doffed his hat. "We're just tacking a poster onto the bulletin board."

She glanced at the board, as if seeing it for the first time. "Oh, I didn't realize there was a bulletin board. I thought someone was vandalizing the chur—" Her response was cut off as she bent forward and studied Hays's poster.

Hays backed up to give her a better view, his chest puffing out just a bit.

She stood straight, incredulity arching her eyebrows. "'Wanted: A Bride for Hays Hart'?" She glanced from Gage to Hays. "Who is Hays Hart?"

Hays leaned against the side of the building, his arms crossed. "I'd much rather know who you are," he said, affecting a drawl. "I thought I knew everyone in town."

She lifted her chin a notch—barely enough for Hays to notice. "I just arrived after Christmas." Her dark brown curls were gathered loosely at the back, and a white blouse was cinched with a red sash at her slender waist. A long black skirt came down to the tops of her polished boots. Everything about her was in its proper place—yet somehow she looked as out of place in Texas as a snowstorm in July. "I'm the new teacher, Miss Longley." She sized up Hays with one quick glance. "I presume you're Mr. Hays Hart?"

He grinned, knowing his dimples would flash, and hoping they would charm her as they had so many others. He lifted his hat and offered a grand bow. "The one and only."

She didn't look impressed. "Are you George Washington Hart's son?"

"Right again." He dropped his hat onto his head and tried to coax a smile from her—but to no avail. She looked more and more vexed by the minute.

"Does Mr. Hart condone this...this..." She indicated the poster with a wave of her slender white hand. "This advertisement?"

Gage lowered his head and allowed the brim of his Stetson to cover his face.

"As a matter of fact..."—Hays tossed the rock into the air and caught it with a flourish— "he's the one who suggested I look for a wife."

Her arms fell to her sides, a bit of bluster fading away. "I can hardly believe it."

Hays deliberately pounded the last tack in place. "I'm looking for a wife—and anyone can apply, whether they've lived here all their life or" —he winked— "they're new in town."

Her long lashes fluttered against her high cheekbones. "I can't allow you to post that here."

"I think that should be up to the pastor—and besides, this is a community board. It's been used for years to advertise anything and everything."

She straightened her back and looked every inch the schoolteacher. "As the pastor's daughter, I believe I can speak on his behalf. I know he'll insist you take it down."

"Well." Hays tossed the rock onto the ground. "Until he does, here it will stay." Something about the pure exasperation in her stance made Hays want to stay and tease her a bit more, but he had chores waiting for him back at the ranch, and there were still several dozen posters to hang. "Good day, Miss Longley." He wiped his hands on his trousers. "I do hope to see you again real soon."

One of her hands slipped up to rest on her hip, while the other pointed at the board. "Mr. Hart, I demand you remove that poster, or..."

"Or?" He waited, loving how the rosy tint in her cheeks made her eyes look even greener. So much about this woman intrigued him.

"Or I-I'll remove it myself—and any other poster you hang in town. It's unseemly!"

He lifted the stack off Gage's arm. "Don't worry. There are more where these came from."

She let out a frustrated breath, but he didn't stop to acknowledge it.

"That could have gone better," Gage said with a nervous laugh as they walked away from the church.

"Maybe." Hays glanced behind him and chuckled when he saw her taking down his poster. "Maybe not." He had never met a woman who responded to him the way Miss Longley had. It was a refreshing change.

He turned his attention back to the blacksmith's, already looking forward to the next time he'd encounter the new schoolteacher.

～

*E*mma Longley clutched the *wanted* poster as she watched Hays Hart cross the street. Of all the nerve! Who would advertise for a bride in such a distasteful manner? Was he serious?

"I see you've met my favorite Hart."

Emma turned at the sweet sound of her new friend, Constance Prescott. Connie stood in a black mourning gown and bonnet, a small Bible in her gloved hand. Her black eyes revealed the recent pain of losing her mother, yet her gentle smile showed her resilience. She came to the church every morning to pray, and the unexpected friendship was the one bright spot in Emma's short time in Hartville.

"If he's your favorite," Emma said. "I can't imagine what the others are like."

The edges of Connie's eyes crinkled as her smile widened. "They're all wonderful, but Hays and I went to school together, and we've been good friends for years. He may be a little unpredictable, but he's one of the nicest men in town."

"Nice?" Emma crumpled the poster. "He's arrogant and stubborn—not to mention improper. He's advertising for brides."

Connie brought the worn Bible up to her lips as she giggled. "Oh, Hays."

"You're not shocked?"

"When it comes to Hays, nothing could shock me." Connie lifted the hem of her gown and walked up the steps to join Emma. "He's the youngest of the Hart sons and doesn't quite fit in with the rest of them. They all tend to be serious—but Hays is different. I know you'll come to like him. Everyone does."

Emma stole a glimpse across the road, unable to keep her gaze off the handsome man. "I don't see how."

Connie smiled at Emma and then opened the front door. "Are you getting settled in the school?"

Emma followed Connie inside the building, happy to change the subject. "It hasn't been easy." The church also served as the schoolhouse for the children of Hartville. The winter term would begin in four days, but it was almost impossible to get ready with everyone coming and going. Papa dropped in regularly to prepare for his first service on Sunday, and several people had stopped by to meet the new pastor.

"What this town needs is a separate schoolhouse." Emma went to the front of the room where her desk was pushed back against the wall.

Connie walked to the front pew, which also served as a desk, and took a seat. She removed her gloves and set them on the desk next to her Bible. "There's no money to build one. Some former teachers have made the same request, but they're often met with resistance from the citizens of Hartville, so they don't pursue the idea."

"Resistance?" Emma gathered several Texas history books she had been studying and took her reticule from the top drawer. Just like all the other times people came to pray, Emma felt it best to leave. It caused a great deal of interruption in her daily routine, but the building was first and foremost a church.

"People in Hartville have a hard time changing," Connie explained, "or giving up their hard-earned money when they already have a perfectly good building for the school."

"But don't they understand how inconvenient it is for everyone?"

Connie raised her delicate shoulder. "I can't say."

Emma hugged the heavy stack of books in her arms. "I plan to speak to the superintendent of the school and see what can be done."

"I thought you were planning to go back to Minnesota in March."

"I am, but I can do something for the children before I leave." Emma's parents had hoped she'd stay in Texas, but she was already homesick for her work with the Ojibwe Indians. She would fulfill her teaching contract in Hartville and go home at the end of the winter term. "Surely, I can make a difference in that amount of time."

Connie offered an encouraging smile and then lifted her Bible.

"I'll leave you to your prayers." Emma walked to the back of the church and let herself out quietly.

Hartville teemed with activity on this second morning of 1874. The dusty streets and dry land around the town were nothing like the countryside of her beloved Minnesota. Back home, the lakes and rivers would be frozen over, the land would be covered under a blanket of snow, and the branches of large elm, oak, and maple would be bare against the pale winter sky. Ice skating, sledding, snow-shoeing, and hot cocoa around a fireplace were but some of the things she missed.

Emma crossed the road toward the blacksmith's shop where Mr. Cochrane, the school superintendent, had entered every day at this time.

The history books were a bit cumbersome in her arms, but she didn't want to take the time to carry them to the parsonage, which sat just behind the church. Instead, she passed through the open doors of the smithy and inspected the interior.

The ringing of hammer against anvil met her ears, and she was surprised to find several men in the building. It appeared to be a popular meeting place. Many of them doffed their caps at her, and she nodded a cordial greeting.

Mr. Cochrane turned and smiled, his large mustache touching the bottom of his nose. "Miss Longley, it's nice to see you again. Looks as though you've got your hands full."

"Yes, I just came from the church—school." She stood awkwardly. "I actually came to speak to you about the school."

"Oh? Can't it wait until the school board meetin' next month?"

"I'm afraid not." She had very little time in Hartville, so she must make the most of every moment.

Mr. Cochrane glanced at his fellow companions. Many of them gave him good-natured grins. "I'm about to start a game of cribbage with these men. Make it quick."

She cleared her throat. The heat and smoke from the blacksmith's fire made her eyes water. "I'd like to discuss building a new schoolhouse."

"A what?" Mr. Cochrane's bushy eyebrows came together in a V.

"A schoolhouse—one separate from the church. It's extremely inconvenient to share the school with the church."

"You haven't even started teaching yet, and you're inconvenienced?"

Mr. Cochrane looked to his companions, who nodded agreement. "The church has served us quite well until now."

"I haven't taught—yet—but I've been there every day this week, and I can already surmise the complications that will ensue."

"Big words for such a purdy lady," a man with white whiskers said. He turned his head, and a stream of brown tobacco juice flew from his mouth into a spittoon.

Emma tried not to gag.

"We have one of them highfalutin' women on our hands again, Jake," said another who was tall and spindly. "Nothing's good enough for them."

"That's not true." Emma's cheeks warmed at the accusation. "I simply want what's best for—"

"Miss Longley, this is a modest town," Mr. Cochrane said with a deep drawl. "We don't take much, and we don't ask for much. We make do with what we have."

"But a schoolhouse is necessary for the advancement of civilization."

"There she goes again talkin' all fancy-like." The man with white whiskers wiped his mouth with the back of his sleeve.

"A schoolhouse would cost a lot of money to build," Mr. Cochrane added. "Money we don't have."

"The only people in town with money are the Harts," said a younger cowboy who leaned against a dirty worktable. "Why don't you go ask G.W.?"

"Mr. Hart?" If he was anything like his son, she'd rather not make his acquaintance—besides, the town needed to raise their own money and take ownership of the school. It was everyone's responsibility. "I'd rather not ask him."

"I can't help you," Mr. Cochrane said. "There's not enough money for a new school building."

"What if I raise the money myself?"

The white-whiskered man whistled under his breath. "Fancy and rich? Where were you when I was younger?"

"Hush up, Willie." Mr. Cochrane turned back to Emma. "You're telling me you've got enough money to spare?"

"No. I thought we could hold a fundraiser."

Mr. Cochrane snorted. "If you think you can raise enough money for a school in this town, be my guest."

The other men laughed.

Emma repositioned the books. "Then I have your permission?"

Mr. Cochrane spread out his arms. "Permission granted."

"You'd save yourself some time if you just ask G.W.," the young man said.

Emma glanced at the men, frustration strengthening her determination. She would raise enough money for a school, and she wouldn't need to ask Mr. Hart.

"Good day, gentlemen." She left the building—but paused when she saw the poster Hays had tacked up near the entrance to the blacksmith's shop. With a sigh, she maneuvered the books to one hand and removed Hays's poster off the wall.

Her books toppled out of her grasp, and she clumsily tried to save them. "Oh, dear," she said as they fell into the dirt.

She bent to retrieve them just as a shadow loomed overhead. Emma looked up into the laughing eyes of Hays Hart. His charming grin threatened to make her knees weak, but thankfully, she was already near the ground.

CHAPTER 2

*H*ays squatted and lifted the first book within reach. *A Comprehensive Survey of Texas History.* The tome was surprisingly heavy, and it was only one of several Miss Longley had been carrying.

"Believe you dropped something," he said.

Without looking at him, she took the book and then proceeded to stack the rest in an organized pile, largest to smallest.

His torn poster was on the dirt next to her. Without another word, Hays stood and removed an extra poster from his back pocket. He unfolded it and tacked it in place. "Good thing I had one left over."

Miss Longley sent a frustrated look in his direction and then finished arranging the books.

"Here." He scooped up the stack in an effortless sweep of his hands. "I'll be happy to carry these for you."

"That won't be necessary." She rose and tried to take them, but he stepped out of her reach.

"Are you heading back to the church?" he asked.

Her hat was askew, and a dark tendril of hair hung over her eye. She blew at it, but it refused to leave her pretty forehead alone. "I am going to the parsonage—and I can carry my own books."

"I'm sure you can, but a gentleman always helps a lady in distress."

"I am not in distress." She rearranged her hat. "And you, sir, are no gentleman."

Hays laughed. He couldn't help it. He'd flustered her well and good. "Don't bother leading the way. I know where the parsonage is." He began to walk toward the south end of town.

Miss Longley set her shoulders, the daintiest scowl present on her forehead, and followed.

"Hays!" A woman's voice called to him from across the road near the church. "Hays Hart!"

Evelyn Palmer stood in a stunning gown, with lace and ruffles in all the right places. Her tiny waist was made tinier by the large bustle at the back, and her stylish hat tilted at a jaunty slant on her blond curls. Next to her was Miss Spanner, the new seamstress in Hartville.

Hays halted, torn between ignoring the notorious flirts—and introducing them to the new schoolteacher.

Evelyn rushed across the road, Miss Spanner on her heels. It looked as though he would have no choice.

Evelyn pointed to the new poster he'd hung at the church after Miss Longley had left. "Hays, darling, are you seriously looking for a bride?"

Miss Longley's gaze followed Evelyn's pointed finger, and her mouth parted in surprise—or anger, he couldn't tell.

"Yes." He nodded, wishing now he had ignored Evelyn.

"You silly man." Evelyn took a step closer, and he could smell the expensive perfume she wore. "You don't have to advertise for a bride. You know how I've always felt."

Hays swallowed, and Miss Longley's cheeks blossomed with color. "Miss Palmer and Miss Spanner, I'd like to introduce you to our new schoolteacher, Miss Longley."

Evelyn and Clarice Spanner inspected Miss Longley, their friendly smiles growing stiff.

"I'm pleased to meet you," Miss Longley said in a pleasant tone.

"Miss Spanner is the seamstress in town," Hays said.

Clarice extended her gloved hand to the teacher. "I prefer to be called a modiste."

Hays tried not to roll his eyes. "And Miss Palmer is—"

"My father is the president of the First National Bank," Evelyn said. "As well as the head elder of the church."

"How nice." Miss Longley smiled. "It was a pleasure meeting you, but I must be going." She held out her hands toward Hays. "If you'll give me the books, I can manage the rest of the way on my own."

"No need." Hays gripped the books tighter and looked at Evelyn and Clarice. "It was a pleasure seeing both of you, but I must help Miss Longley take these to her home."

"I'll pay a call to El Regalo soon." Evelyn practically purred. "It's been ages since I've seen the ranch."

Miss Longley squinted as though she was devising a way to grab the stack of books.

"I look forward to it." Hays dipped his hat to the ladies.

He directed Miss Longley toward the parsonage with his hand on the small of her back, eager to be done with Evelyn and Clarice.

A white picket fence enclosed the small yard. Overgrown lilac bushes crowded the front porch, and a two-person swing blew gently in the breeze. Gabled eaves, oriel windows, and thick vines graced the white house. It wasn't large, but it was quaint and had been a place of warmth to Hays his whole life. "Your father replaced a very kind man," Hays said. "Pastor Darby was loved by the whole town."

"We've heard good things about him."

"He used to come to El Regalo—our ranch house—for dinner on Sunday afternoons." It was Hays's favorite day of the week when most of his brothers gathered around his father's dining table.

They stepped onto the porch, and she reached for the doorknob.

"Look." Hays put his hand on her wrist.

Her startled gaze met his.

He pulled his hand back and grew serious for the first time since meeting her. Somewhere under all the manners and quiet hostility, she seemed to be a nice woman, and he wanted more than anything to set things right. "I'm sorry we got off on the wrong foot. Is there any way I can make it up to you?"

Before she could answer, the front door opened, and a middle-aged man stepped out. He stopped short when he saw them standing there. He had kind blue eyes and dark brown hair streaked with a bit of silver at the temples. "Hello."

Hays took off his Stetson with his free hand. "Howdy, sir."

"Mr. Hart, this is my father, Reverend Longley."

Hays slipped his hat on again and extended his hand. "It's a pleasure to meet you, Reverend. I'm Hays Hart."

"Ahh." Reverend Longley opened the door a bit wider. "Emma didn't tell me she had met one of the Harts."

Emma. It suited her.

"Are you G.W. Hart's son?"

Hays nodded. "One of them."

"I've been meaning to get out to the 7 Heart Ranch and introduce myself. I'm afraid I've been a bit busy since we arrived."

"My pa is eager to meet you." A new idea began to form. "In fact, we'd love for your family to join us for dinner after church on Sunday." Surely, Pa wouldn't mind if Hays extended an invitation.

"We'd be happy to—"

"Papa," Emma interrupted. "It's your first Sunday preaching, and you might be—"

"Nonsense," Reverend Longley said. "Tell your father we'll be there."

Hays couldn't hide the pleasure from his voice. "I will."

Emma turned to Hays and extended her hands. "Thank you for carrying my books."

Hays handed them over, and she bent slightly from the weight. "It was my pleasure. I'll see you Sunday, Miss Longley."

She barely acknowledged him before she stepped over the threshold and past her father.

Reverend Longley watched his daughter for a moment, curiosity in his steady gaze. "Thank you for seeing her home."

"It was my pleasure. Good day, Reverend."

"Good bye, Mr. Hart."

Hays stepped off the porch and quickly retraced his steps to the livery, where he'd left Gage to get their horses. He couldn't stop smiling.

Gage sat atop his gelding, lazily waiting for Hays. "Where'd you go?"

Hays took the reins of Bella, his dark-brown Morgan, and effortlessly mounted. "I walked Miss Longley home."

Gage nudged his horse into motion. "I don't imagine that was pleasant."

Hays set his spurs to Bella's flanks, his heart pounding hard. "I think I've found the one, Gage."

"The new teacher?" Gage's voice was filled with doubt. "Have you lost your mind, Hays? She doesn't like you."

"Maybe not now." He grinned. "But she will."

Gage offered him a dubious look.

"There's something special about her," Hays continued. "She's nothing like the others. If we had met under different circumstances, I know she'd like me."

They had gotten off to a rocky start, but he could change her mind. And he'd do it when her family came to dinner at El Regalo.

~

*E*mma sat in the back of the surrey nestled between her sister, Hope, and her young brother, David. Papa held the reins, and Mama shaded her eyes as she shook her head. "My, my. Would you look at that?"

"It must be El Regalo," Papa said. "I don't imagine there are any other houses like it for miles around."

"Emma, do you see?" Mama turned her pretty face toward Emma. Green eyes, the exact color of Emma's, blinked at her from a face that looked too young to belong a mother of grown daughters.

Emma bent in front of her brother to get a better look as they pulled up to a beautiful Victorian mansion. Two stories tall, with a flat roof, it was made of a sand-colored brick with darker brown brick accents around windows, doors, and corners. A three-story tower rose up from the structure with a blunted iron-railed widow's walk.

Eleven-year-old David whistled. "I bet you can see clear into Hartville from the top of that tower. I wonder if Mr. Hart will let me climb it."

"Oh, David." Mama sighed. "Please remember your manners—and do not ask to climb that tower."

Disappointment clouded his gaze. "Yes, ma'am."

Hope leaned across Emma as she, too, tried to get a glimpse.

Emma had inherited their mother's green eyes and their father's dark hair, but Hope had been blessed with the opposite. She had eyes as blue as Papa's and hair the same honey-colored hue as Mama's. She was only a year younger than Emma and was as opposite in personality as she was in looks. Mama always said Emma tended to be serious and astute, but Hope was lighthearted and as changeable as the weather. Emma knew exactly what she wanted in life, but Hope was blissfully content to let each day flit away with little direction. The only two things her sister was truly passionate about were playing piano, which she did every Sunday in church, and seeking a husband so she wouldn't be an old maid—though she was only eighteen.

"I've heard all the Hart brothers are tall and handsome," Hope said breathlessly. "And not one of them is married. Papa said Hays Hart brought you home the other day."

"I'd rather not talk about Hays Hart." Emma would rather not face him again either. She had glanced at him in church earlier that morning, but she had spent the rest of the time avoiding him. It wasn't hard to do, since it was their first week at the new church and everyone wanted to meet the Longley family.

"Would you like me to talk to Mr. Hart about donating money for the new school building?" Papa asked Emma as he secured the reins to the dashboard.

Emma shook her head. "No, thank you."

"It's up to you." Papa exited the surrey to help Mama. "But I believe you could save yourself a lot of time and effort if you simply ask him."

It would be simple, but in the end, it wouldn't be the best thing for the town or the school. The citizens of Hartville needed to take owner-ship of the school, and the best way to do that would be to raise their own money. Not rely on the family that seemed to be involved in every other aspect of the town.

David helped Emma step down from the surrey and then offered his hand to Hope.

The front door opened, and Hays strode out to meet them, his dimpled grin flashing. "Welcome to El Regalo."

Emma steadied herself with a deep breath.

A cowboy appeared from around the corner of the massive house, and Emma recognized him as the man who had helped Hays hang posters.

"Gage, please see to Reverend Longley's horses," Hays said to the blonde cowboy.

The young man nodded and stepped into the surrey and drove it away, but not before catching Hope's eye. She waved at the cowboy and watched until he disappeared from the direction he had come.

"My father and brothers are waiting for you in the parlor," Hays said as Emma and her family followed him through the front doors, past a small vestibule, and into a long, narrow grand foyer.

Emma blinked at the magnificence of the interior. She had not expected something so fine. Rich walnut trim, plush carpeting up the wide stairs, extravagant chandeliers dangling from the tin ceiling—everywhere she set her gaze, she was rewarded with opulence.

"We meet every week for Sunday dinner." Hays spoke to Mama as he motioned to a door on the right. "It was a tradition my mother started years ago when she was a young bride. Even though she's been gone over twelve years now, Pa is still faithful to her memory and the tradition."

"How nice," Mama said. "I hope we're not intruding on your family meal."

"Not in the least." Hays offered her his elbow. "Sunday dinner almost always includes guests. Another thing Ma insisted upon."

Hays pushed open two heavy doors, and a beautiful parlor came into view.

G.W. Hart stood near the fireplace. When the Longleys entered the room, he walked toward them and extended his hand to Papa. "Welcome to El Regalo."

Emma had been introduced to him at church earlier, but here, in his impressive home, he seemed larger than life and every bit the king of his domain. His white hair was cut short, and a well-trimmed beard lined his weathered face—but under the wrinkles and whiskers, Emma caught a glimpse of the younger man. His blue eyes, so much like Hays's, were filled with determination and purpose, and his gaze reflected a keen observation.

Four other men rose from their places around the room. It was obvious these men were brothers. They all shared the same dark hair and a variation of blue or brown eyes—yet their similarities went deeper than their looks. Maybe it was a sense of confidence or the same determination evident in G.W.

All but one of them had been in church, though Emma hadn't realized they were Hart men.

"Reverend and Mrs. Longley, I believe you met most of my boys today," G.W. said, "but let me introduce them to the rest of your family."

"Yes, of course." Papa stepped aside to allow everyone into the room.

G.W. gestured to the first one on his left. "This is my oldest son, Austin."

Austin nodded a greeting and shook Papa's hand, his light-brown hair falling over his forehead at the motion. "It's a pleasure to meet you. I hope you've found Hartville to your liking."

There was a round of acknowledgement from her family, but Emma remained silent. She missed Minnesota more and more with each passing day. Even if she had liked Hartville, she still wouldn't be content in Texas.

"This is my second eldest, Bowie." G.W. indicated the man standing to his right. He was the tallest of all the men, and he had a full beard. His hair was long, and when he tipped his head forward, it covered a black patch over his left eye. Emma glimpsed a scar and black markings on his face before he turned away from her perusal. He had a commanding, if not brooding, countenance. He hadn't been at church. If he had, she would have recalled seeing him.

"This is Travis." G.W. nodded at the man standing next to Austin.

"Dr. Travis," Hays said with a light punch to Travis's arm.

"Travis will do." He gave his brother a good-natured punch in return. "Welcome to Hartville."

Where Bowie was rough and withdrawn, Travis Hart was gentlemanly and hospitable. His brown eyes and brown hair were much darker than the others, and he had an easy, caring smile. He caught Emma's eye, and she smiled in return.

"My next son, Houston, is out in California. But this is Crockett." G.W. indicated the man beside Bowie.

Crockett nodded a warm greeting, and Emma instantly liked the handsome man with the bright clothing. He also had dark hair and brown eyes but wasn't as polished as Travis. "It's a pleasure to meet you. If there's anything you need, don't hesitate to ask."

"Boy number six is Chisholm," G.W. said with a tinge of pride in his voice. "He's a Texas Ranger."

"And this scoundrel," Travis said, putting his arm around Hays's shoulder and roughing his hair up a bit, "is Hays."

"The baby of the family," Austin chimed in with a wink.

G.W. chuckled and shook his head. "You've already met my youngest. Seems he knows everyone."

"We've had the pleasure," Papa said with a smile.

Hays elbowed Travis in the side, and when his brother dropped his arm, he made a show of straightening his dark hair. "The pleasure was all mine." Hays glanced past Papa and offered Emma another grin. "I had the good fortune of meeting Miss Emma Longley when I was tacking up one of my posters."

"By the way..." Austin crossed his arms and frowned. "I had to explain to Meribeth Mortenson at the mercantile that those things were a joke."

Hays hung his thumbs in the pockets of his denim pants, clearly ready to defend his actions—again. "No joke."

"Did anyone actually answer the advertisement?" Travis squinted at Hays as he studied his younger brother.

"Not yet."

Austin looked at Emma with a pained expression. "My apologies, Miss Longley. Our brother has very little tact. Apparently, he doesn't mind that the entire town knows about Pa's...interesting edict."

G.W. Hart cleared his throat.

"Miss Longley is the new schoolteacher," Hays said quickly.

The abrupt change in conversation caused all eyes to turn to Emma.

She offered a polite smile, but thankfully, a middle-aged woman entered the room and saved her from the attention.

"Señor Hart." The Mexican lady addressed G.W.

"Yes, Perla?"

"*La cena está servida.*" She glanced at the Longleys and dipped her head with a kind nod. "Dinner is served."

"Shall we?" G.W. motioned toward the door.

Everyone followed Perla out of the parlor and into the dining room.

A long walnut table was set with fine china and thick crystal. Dark walnut wainscoting graced the walls, and walnut beams crisscrossed the ceiling. Between the beams, gold-plated tin added yet another texture, and dark-green paper covered the walls.

The dining room was just as stunning as the rest of the house.

G.W. went to the head of the table, and his sons spread out on either side, with Bowie to his right and Austin, Travis, Crockett and Hays to his left. Each stood by a beautifully hand-carved chair bearing initials. Their monograms?

Three engraved chairs sat vacant, and the magnitude of their emptiness wasn't lost on Emma. Two were positioned near Bowie, and one was at the foot of the table. She assumed they were for Victoria, Houston, and Chisholm. A stunning portrait of a dark-haired, dark-eyed beauty sat above the fireplace. It could be none other than the late Victoria Hart.

Hays quickly pulled a chair from along the wall and placed it between him and Crockett. "Miss Emma, I'd be honored if you'll sit beside me."

Crockett rolled his eyes in a playful manner and then turned his amused face toward Emma. "We'd both be honored."

David and Hope were given chairs beside Bowie, and Mama and Papa sat on either side of G.W.

Perla disappeared behind a silk screen, and when she returned, she held a steaming tureen of soup. The delicious aroma met Emma's nose before she glimpsed the contents.

"This is *menudo*." Perla ladled the dark beef-and-bean soup into each person's bowl and then nodded for them to eat.

G.W. said a prayer before they partook of the savory soup.

The flavors were new to Emma, but she enjoyed them very much. Hays's banter with his brothers kept her entertained, especially as he brought her into the conversation several times. He was confident and lighthearted. It was evident he enjoyed making his family laugh. And they enjoyed teasing him right back.

G.W. spoke almost exclusively with Mama and Papa, and Hope prattled on with Crockett, who sat across the table from her. David had learned that Bowie raised Catahoula cur cattle dogs, and he asked dozens of questions, which Bowie answered quietly.

Perla arrived to clear the bowls, and when she reached Hays, she frowned. "You have not finished your soup."

"That's because he talks too much," Travis said with a laugh.

"Eat, Señor Hays." Perla put her free hand on her hip. "I do not work in the kitchen all day for nothing."

Hays gave her a good-natured smile and obediently finished his soup before she took the bowl away.

"A schoolhouse?" G.W.'s commanding voice rose above the others, and Emma lifted her head to find his blue eyes assessing her. "You plan to build a schoolhouse?"

Emma's father sheepishly inspected his dinner plate.

"I do." Emma nodded. "I spoke with Mr. Cochrane, and he gave me permission, provided I secure my own funding."

The other conversations came to a halt, and once again, Emma felt all eyes on her.

G.W. wiped his mouth and set his napkin aside. "I think it's high time this town had a proper school. I'd be happy to donate whatever is needed."

Heat gathered under her collar. She didn't want to appear ungrateful, but she couldn't accept his offer.

"This is called guacamole." Perla was suddenly at her side again and showed her the creamy green dish.

Travis leaned around Crockett. "I think you'll enjoy it."

Emma allowed Perla to place the foreign food on her plate and then met G.W.'s penetrating gaze once again. "Thank you for the offer, but I think it would be best if the community raised the funds on their own." She glanced at her father for support, then back at G.W. "You've been a generous benefactor to Hartville, but I believe the citizens, especially the children, would have a greater sense of ownership if they all pitch in and build the school together."

G.W. didn't say anything for a moment, but then a half smile appeared on his face. "I like your spirit, Miss Longley. I think you'll do just fine here."

"I think she'll do better than fine," Hays said beside her.

The heat crept up Emma's neck and blossomed in her cheeks.

"Don't mind my youngest. He's barely housebroken." G.W. chuckled. "We're still trying to tame him."

"An impossible task." Austin sent a grin toward his brother.

A round of smiles filled the table, and Emma relaxed. She had expected something far different when she arrived at the Hart home, but she was pleased she had been wrong.

"I wish you great success, Miss Longley," G.W. said. "And if there's anything we can do to help, please let us know."

Emma nodded, though she was certain she would not ask the Harts for a thing. They had already done enough for the town, and it was time the town did something for itself.

As she began to eat the next dish Perla presented, Emma caught Hays Hart looking at her.

The heat had begun to fade from her cheeks—but then Hays winked at her—and it blossomed again.

CHAPTER 3

*H*ays set his napkin on the table, fully satisfied with the meal but unsatisfied with his progress. He wanted to get Emma alone and away from his family.

"Thank you for the delicious meal," Reverend Longley said to Pa.

"It's our pleasure." Pa stood. "Let's head on into the parlor for Perla's coffee. There are a few things I'd like to discuss."

Chairs were pushed away from the table, scraping the wood floor as everyone followed his lead.

"Miss Longley," Hays said to Emma, "would you like to see the ranch?"

"That's a good idea." Pa turned abruptly, his countenance a bit heavy. "I'd prefer to speak privately with Reverend and Mrs. Longley."

Hays didn't miss the troubled glance Travis shared with Austin.

"Why don't the rest of you take a tour of the ranch?" Pa said to his sons.

"I'd like to see your dogs, Mr. Bowie." David looked up at Bowie with wide eyes. "May I?"

Bowie had been making a quiet exit, but he froze at the request and dipped his head until his hair covered his scars. "If you like. But they're workin' dogs, not pets."

"May I go, Mama?" David ran back to his mother and bounced from foot to foot.

"You may." Mrs. Longley adjusted the bowtie around his neck. "But mind your manners, and please don't be a bother."

"Yes, ma'am." David sidled up to Bowie, pulling the tie away from his throat. "How many dogs do you have? How long have you been breeding them? How much does one cost? Do you think I could have one someday...?" They disappeared out the doors, and David's voice trailed away.

Emma's sister stood smiling coyly at Travis. "Will you come on the tour with us, Dr. Hart?"

"I wish I could." Travis checked his pocket watch. "But I'm afraid I need to make a house call. It's been a pleasure meeting all of you." He left the dining room before anyone could protest.

"I should go see about the new colt," Austin said, following Travis.

"And I promised Perla I'd fix that leaking pipe in the kitchen," Crockett said, right behind his brother.

"I won't hear none of it." Pa's stern voice stopped Austin and Crockett in their tracks. "You two go with Hays and show these young ladies around the 7 Heart." He held the door open for Emma's folks and then showed them into his office without waiting to see if his sons obeyed.

Emma and her sister stood in the dining room with Hays, Austin, and Crockett.

Maybe Hays could still get Emma alone. "Do you enjoy riding, Emma—?"

"Would you like to see the new colt?" Crockett spoke at the same moment.

The two of them stopped and stared at one another. Austin stood off to the side as if he wasn't quite sure what to do with himself.

Emma looked between them and then nodded. "I do ride—and so does Hope."

Hope grinned. "Only sidesaddle, mind you."

"We still have my mother's old sidesaddle." Crockett motioned to the door. "Shall we?"

Without invitation, Hope circled her hand around his elbow and sashayed down the hall.

Hays turned to Emma. "I hope you don't mind spending the afternoon with me."

Her eyebrows tilted. "As long as I don't find more of those posters hanging around."

Hays put his right hand over his heart. "You have my word."

They moved through the hall and out onto the porch, with Austin following.

Emma was quiet as they walked, her eyes scanning the property. Hays tried to see it from her perspective. Directly behind El Regalo, a large barn, low bunkhouses, and a spacious corral with some of the best horses spread out before them. Pride in the 7 Heart Ranch made him stand taller.

Crockett left Hope at the barn door while he went in to help Gage saddle the horses. Austin paused outside the door, looking from Hope to the sanctuary of the barn—but her incessant chatter prevented him from going inside. Her conversation flitted around the barnyard like the sound of a little bird, and Austin could only stare. Emma didn't follow her sister but walked toward the corral and leaned against the fence, her eyes focused on the far horizon.

It was the opportunity Hays had been waiting for. He joined her and lifted his boot to rest on the bottom rail.

There was something pensive in her gaze—and it made Hays pause. Ever since he was a child, he hated to see people sad. Some of his earliest memories were of his pa's melancholy when his oldest sons left for the war, and the deep sadness after Mother died. Hays didn't want to add to the pain, so he had learned how to make his pa laugh. Sometimes it meant that Hays had to cover his own grief and laugh through the hard times, even when he didn't want to.

He stood silently as one of the mares strolled over to the fence and nuzzled up against him, looking for a treat in his pocket, no doubt.

Emma smiled at the playful horse, and Hays used the opportunity to speak. "You seem a little sad." He caught her eye. "I hope it's not because you're forced into my company."

She reached out and ran her hand down the mare's long nose. "Being forced into your company doesn't make me sad." She turned to face him. "Frustrated, irritated, and annoyed maybe—but not sad."

Hays's grin disappeared, and for a moment, he didn't know how to respond—until a faint smile tugged at the corners of her lips.

He dropped his foot and leaned against the fence, smiling at Emma as he crossed his arms over his chest. "You're a great mystery to me, Miss Longley."

"Oh?"

"Most ladies I know are quite easy to figure out—"

Hope let out an exuberant squeal, and Hays jumped. The mare bolted and joined a group of horses grazing in the corral.

Crockett stood near the entrance to the barn holding the reins of a beautiful horse, and apparently, Hope had been pleased. With Austin's assistance, she tried to pull herself up into the sidesaddle, but her dress made it difficult, and she began to giggle. Austin attempted to help her, while Crockett retreated into the barn.

Emma met Hays's gaze, and he continued. "Like I said, most ladies are quite easy to figure out." He refrained from making an example of her sister. "But you, on the other hand, are not so easy."

There was no guile or pretense in her gaze as she studied him. "I'm not sure if that's an insult or a compliment."

Hope hopped around on one foot while her other was stuck in the stirrup. She giggled so hard, she couldn't lift her body into the saddle. Austin tried to assist her, but there was nothing he could do. His hands fumbled about, as if he didn't know where to put them, and his lips had flattened into a thin line.

"It's a compliment," Hays assured her, "of the highest order." He tried to ignore Hope as best he could. "It makes me want to get to know you better."

Emma turned away from Hays and ran her hands along the top rail, not meeting his eyes. "I'm leaving Texas soon, and until I do, my attention will be focused on the school. I won't have time for anything else."

Emma was leaving Hartville? She couldn't leave, not before they'd had a chance to get to know one another. "When?"

"As soon as the winter term ends. My parents were missionaries in Minnesota until my father was called to Texas. I came at his request, knowing a teacher was needed, but I find I miss my work with the Ojibwe Indians far more than I thought possible."

"I had no idea." He suddenly understood the sadness behind her eyes—she was homesick. It didn't take much to imagine how she felt. He'd be miserable if he was uprooted and forced to leave Texas.

Hope continued to make a fuss about the horse, and Emma's attention was snagged away from Hays again—but he wasn't ready to give up his time with her.

"I understand that you miss your old home—but if you give Texas a chance, you might learn to love it like Minnesota."

She gave him a skeptical look. "I highly doubt it."

"I don't." He leaned against the fence again, his arms lazily crossed over his chest. "I can guarantee you've never seen anything like a sunset over the Sabinal River or a blanket of bluebonnets in the Hill Country. And there's nothing prettier than a Texas sky at night, or the sight of a newborn longhorn come spring." He chuckled. "But, best of all, the winters aren't as cold."

She wrapped her arms around herself as if remembering the freezing temperatures she had left behind. But it didn't deter her from smiling with confidence. "And you've never seen anything until you've gazed across the endless blue waters of Lake Superior or ridden a canoe down the Mighty Mississippi. You can't imagine the crystal-clear lakes or the delicacy of a Lady Slipper in a cool forest. And I can guarantee a Texas sunset has nothing on the crackling Northern Lights in the heat of summer."

Hays bowed his head in deference to her statements. "Can we agree that each state has a beauty all its own?"

"I suppose."

"Then may I offer you a challenge?" He leaned closer to her, loving the way she looked at him.

She didn't move away as her eyes took on a sparkle. "I'm always up for a challenge."

He wasn't surprised. "In the next two months, try not to compare Texas to Minnesota, and see if you don't fall in love with the charm that only Texas has to offer."

"Texas's charm? Or the charm of her people?" she asked with a faint smile.

He couldn't help but grin. "Both."

She studied him for a moment. "It seems like a fair challenge."

"And may I add one more suggestion? Allow me to be your guide."

She pulled back, and he feared he'd crossed a line, but then she offered a simple nod. "It's a valid suggestion—one I'll consider."

Hays couldn't stop himself from grinning. "Shall we start now? I'd be happy to take you to see the Sabinal Ri—"

"Oh, my!" Hope cried as she fell from the saddle onto the hard ground. Her left leg was still twisted in the stirrup, and her skirts became tangled around her legs. She frantically tried to disengage her boot, stirring up dust.

Emma rushed to her sister's side while Austin and Crockett lifted her onto her foot. Hays arrived just in time to grab the horse's reins and keep the mare from spooking.

"Whoa." Hays rubbed the mare's nose. "Steady, girl."

"My ankle," Hope cried as Emma helped extract her foot. "It's broken!"

Emma knelt and took her sister's foot into her hands. She probed while her sister continued to cry out in pain.

"I don't think it's broken," Emma said in soothing tones, "but you probably sprained it."

Austin glanced nervously toward El Regalo. "I'm sure Travis is long gone by now."

"Crockett..." Hays indicated the road leaving the 7 Heart Ranch. "Go after Travis and tell him we need his assistance."

"I could go," Austin said quickly.

"I need you to help with Miss Hope."

Crockett left without a second look back.

"What should I do?" Austin stood awkwardly, watching Crockett's retreating form

"You'll have to help me get Miss Hope into the house," Hays said.

Hope's cheeks filled with color, and she straightened her dress, suddenly looking a bit embarrassed. "All this trouble for me?"

"Do you think you can walk without assistance?" Austin's hopeful expression made Hays want to chuckle.

"Of course." Hope tried to take a step, but she buckled, and Austin quickly lifted her into his arms.

Her eyes grew round, and then they softened, and she suddenly looked quite pleased. "Oh, my," she said again. "I don't believe I can, after all."

Austin's face became grim as he rushed her toward the house.

"I'm sorry," Emma said to Hays with a sigh. "Sometimes my sister can be..." She didn't finish her statement.

"No need to apologize. I have six older brothers. I understand completely."

For the first time since they had met, Emma offered Hays a genuine smile—and he carried the memory of it for the rest of the day.

~

The next afternoon, Emma stood on the top step of the church and waved one last time as little Sadie Sue rounded the corner near the blacksmith's shop and disappeared from sight. Emma let out a contented, if somewhat exhausted, sigh. The first day of school was finished, and it had gone better than she had expected—if she didn't ponder too long on the older boys' rowdy behavior, the teasing Sadie Sue received because of her lisp, or the general cramped quarters they had all endured.

"Hello, Emma," Connie Prescott called as she approached the church. Like before, she wore a black mourning gown, but today she didn't carry her Bible. She had come to help Emma plan the fundraiser.

"Hello." Emma held the door open for her friend. "You're right on time."

"I couldn't stay home a moment longer. My father has a cold, and he's been more demanding than usual."

Good thing Connie had agreed to help with the fundraiser. It allowed her to get out of the house and take her mind off her troubles.

"I hope you don't mind..." Connie moved past her into the school. "I've asked a few other people to help."

"Mind?" Emma closed the door. "I'll take all the help I can get."

The door opened again, and Emma moved aside.

Hays Hart stepped over the threshold, the ever-present grin on his face. "Am I late?"

Emma clutched the doorknob. "What are you doing here?"

"I've come to help with the fundraiser." Hays took off his Stetson and greeted Connie. "Thanks for telling me about the meeting."

Connie's eyes twinkled with mischief. "It's my pleasure."

Before Emma could close the door, two young ladies entered, and both immediately noticed Hays.

"Emma, may I present Miss Ruby Brown and Miss Julia Brown? Their father is Giles Brown, the carpenter." Connie indicated the newcomers. "They're here to help as well."

"How nice. Won't all of you have a seat?"

The sisters sent several glances at Hays, but he didn't pay them attention as he walked across the room.

"Are we waiting for anyone else?" Emma asked Connie.

Connie shook her head. "I'm afraid not."

"My sister, Hope, had planned to help." Emma took her notes off her desk, trying not to notice Hays as he folded his long legs under the small desk. "But I'm afraid she's suffered an injury." Heat rose in her cheeks. Her sister had made such a fuss about her ankle. After Austin deposited Hope in Mrs. Hart's old parlor, he never reappeared. Only Hays stayed close to see if he could be of assistance. "She and the rest of my family will help where they are needed."

Hays turned his full attention on Emma, and for some reason, her stomach filled with butterflies. She tried not to let him see her reaction as she took a seat and looked down at her paper. No man had ever unsettled her before, and she wouldn't let one do so now—especially not this one. She cleared her throat.

"Thank you all for coming. As you know, I would like to raise money to build a new schoolhouse. I've gone to the lumberyard and the hardware store, and I believe I have come up with a realistic budget for this project." She found the sheet of paper with her calculations and handed it to Connie. "It's approximately five hundred dollars."

Connie glanced at the paper and then handed it to Ruby. "What kind of fundraiser do you have in mind?"

"I thought we could have a bazaar during the day and finish it with a street dance in the evening."

"I like the idea of a dance," Julia said with a grin.

"During the dance," Emma continued, "I'd also like to hold a bachelor auction."

"A bachelor auction?" Hays sat up a bit straighter.

"Yes." Emma tried not to sound nervous as she shared her idea. "I've heard they're quite popular in the East. My cousin went to one last summer, and it was very successful."

"How do they work?"

"We ask several bachelors to volunteer," Emma explained, "and each one is auctioned off to dance with the woman who pays the highest amount. He becomes her escort for the evening."

Hays leaned back in his seat—as much as he could, given the confines of the desk.

"The bachelor who is auctioned for the highest amount will lead the first dance of the evening," Emma said, "with the lady who paid for him."

Ruby and Julia whispered back and forth, their cheeks turning pink.

Hays leaned forward, his blue eyes filled with interest. "Do you really think the women in Hartville will pay to dance with the bachelors?"

Ruby turned to Hays with a dazzling smile. "I'll start to save my money now."

"I know several young ladies who would pay to dance with you," Julia said with a giggle.

An uneasy feeling settled inside Emma. Between his poster advertising for brides and the way the women in Hartville responded to him, he was surely not the kind of man she should spend time with—even if his offer to show her Texas had sounded appealing.

"The bachelor auction is only one piece we need to plan," Emma said, bringing the conversation back around. "I would like to hold the bazaar and dance on Saturday, February seventh. That will give us about a month to plan. Everyone will work on a subcommittee, and we'll meet back here each Monday after school until the event." If they raised enough money, she would have one month after the fundraiser to oversee the building of the schoolhouse before she returned to Minnesota. "Who would like to help me with the bazaar?"

"I will." Connie lifted her hand. "I know several people who would volunteer to host booths and sell baked goods."

"Wonderful." Emma wrote Connie's name on the list. "Now, who would like to be in charge of the street dance?"

"I would," Ruby said. "My uncle is the conductor of the town band, and I'm sure they'd be happy to play."

"I play the fiddle," Hays offered.

"I know." Ruby batted her eyelashes. "But you won't have time to play your fiddle when you're dancing with me."

"Thank you, Ruby," Emma said quickly.

"I'll help with the dance too." Julia smiled. "I'm sure our pa would be happy to build the stage and dance floor."

"I think that's a good idea." Emma looked at her list. "That leaves advertising—" She stopped. "I have a feeling you'd be good at that, Mr. Hart."

Hays spread his hands wide. "I'll do anything you ask, Miss Longley."

"Anything?"

He gave her a disarming smile—the one he used to flirt with her. Was that why he had come? She refused to be another conquest in his long line of blushing admirers. The three in the room were more than enough —and there was no telling how many more lived in Hartville.

"I'd like you to be in charge of the bachelor auction." Emma looked down at her paper. "Please find at least a dozen bachelors willing to go up for auction."

"Only a dozen?" he teased.

"Feel free to get as many as you'd like." Emma stood, suddenly feeling more confined within the church than she had all day. "I think that's all for now. Everyone work on their projects, and let's meet back here after school next Monday. Come by any time if you have questions or need help."

Conversation filled the room as the ladies also stood—but Hays remained in his seat. "Do I have to wait a whole week before I see you again?"

Warmth filled Emma's cheeks, and she didn't miss the looks Ruby and Julia sent her way.

Emma walked to the door, hoping he would take the hint. The three ladies gathered their things and filed out, one by one—and still, Hays stayed at the desk.

Connie said goodbye and closed the door behind her. Emma stood for a moment, unsure what to do. Finally, she walked to her desk and began to organize her things for the next day, as if he wasn't there.

He didn't say a thing.

Emma's heartbeat picked up speed, and her hands began to tremble.

She lifted an arithmetic book, but it slipped from her grasp, dropping to the floor with a thud.

"Mr. Hart." She spun to face him, her hands clasped at her waist. "Why are you still here?"

Hays sat with his arm draped over the seat back next to him, relaxed and carefree. "I'm not ready to leave."

She crossed her arms. "Why not?"

He leaned forward. "Isn't it obvious?"

Emma swallowed. In all her life, she had never met a man like him. She couldn't decide if she liked him—or detested him. Did he take pleasure in making her uncomfortable? If he did, she wouldn't give him the satisfaction.

She straightened her back and dropped her arms to her sides. "I'm not sure why you decided to volunteer for this fundraiser, but if you did it in hopes of turning my head, you'll be disappointed. I have no romantic interest in you, or—or anyone else."

Hays grinned. Again.

She lifted her chin. "I don't know why you think this is funny. You seem to disregard anything serious."

He left the desk and lifted his Stetson into his hands. He sauntered toward her, his spurs ringing in the small space. "Forgive me, Emma." He set his hat on his head and tipped the brim at her. "I've never been more serious about someone in my life."

Emma's breath stilled.

"I like to joke about some things, but I'd never joke about my intentions toward you." Hays turned and walked to the door. He opened it and then paused. "I look forward to seeing you at church on Sunday. In the meantime, I'll go find you those bachelors."

He stepped out and closed the door softly behind him.

She stood for several moments, staring at the door, and then rushed over to the window to watch him ride out of town.

Just before he disappeared, he glanced back, but she didn't bother to hide.

Hays Hart was full of surprises...and for some reason the thought made her smile—until she glanced at one of his *wanted* posters fluttering in the wind across the road at the general store. Was he pursuing her because he genuinely liked her, or was he pursuing her to fulfill his father's wishes and secure a bride for his inheritance?

The obvious answer left her feeling sadder than it should.

CHAPTER 4

*H*ays squinted as he tipped his head back and gulped from his canteen. The day was unseasonably warm, and even if it hadn't been, his impending conversation with Gage was making him sweat. Overhead, the afternoon sun hung in a cloudless sky, and underfoot, the brown grass crunched beneath the horses' hooves.

Gage sat next to him, carelessly crossing his gloved hands over his saddle horn, his gaze on the herd of cattle grazing nearby. "Looks like it'll be a successful drive up to Wichita come May. We've never had a better herd."

The herd was remarkable this year, but it was the last thing on Hays's mind. It had been four days since Emma had asked Hays to find bachelors for her auction—and nine days since his pa's unexpected edict. He wanted to please both Emma and his father, and to do so, he would have to find a way to make the auction a success.

"I've got a strange request," Hays said. "And I don't rightly know how to bring it up in normal conversation."

Gage slowly turned his head, his eyes shaded under the brim of his hat. "You've made more strange requests than anyone has a right to."

Hays had gotten him and Gage into a lot of trouble over the years— unintentionally, of course—but this was different. "It's for a good cause."

Gage gave him a skeptical look. "What kind of cause?"

"A schoolhouse."

"You mean it's for Miss Longley."

"You can look at it how you want. I just need volunteers for a street dance."

"I'm listening."

Hays shifted in his saddle. Usually, he could make light of most situations and ease his way through difficult tasks, but for some reason, seeing how upset Emma had been at his carefree attitude after the meeting, he wanted to take this job seriously. "Emma plans to hold a bachelor auction during the ball, and she asked me to find at least a dozen bachelors who would—"

"A what?"

"A bachelor auction. Each bachelor will stand on stage, and the women bid for the chance to dance with him."

Gage stared at Hays, his mouth tipped down at the edges. "You've got to be joshin'."

"I thought it sounded a bit strange, too, but the ladies at the meeting seemed eager to bid."

"What happens if you stand up there and no one bids?" Gage shook his head. "Nope."

"Come on, Gage. I've always been able to count on you."

"Not this time." Gage gripped his reins and touched his spurs to his horse. "Ask your brothers. They're more desperate than I am." He was gone before Hays could call him back.

His brothers? They were the last people Hays wanted to ask. He was still set on finding a bride before the rest of them, though none of them had shown any interest in the prospect of marriage, even after Pa's declaration. But beyond that, he couldn't imagine them in an auction. They weren't the type of men that liked to be on display.

Hays rode back to El Regalo, where Travis's buckboard was parked out front.

He hated asking his brothers for help, but the only way to prove to them that he wasn't a child was to find a bride and move onto his spread of land.

And the only way to get his bride was to find her a dozen bachelors. What better place to look than the 7 Heart Ranch?

Hays strode toward the back of the house, where Perla would be in the kitchen. Even before he opened the door, the spicy aroma of steaming tamales carried to his nose. His stomach growled as he walked inside.

"Perla." He groaned. "Are you gonna make me wait for supper?"

Perla stood at the stove with a large apron wrapped around her red skirt. She glanced at Hays, and the wrinkles around her eyes deepened when she smiled. "When have I ever made you wait for my tamales, Señor Hays?" She lifted a spoon from the pot she had been stirring.

He took two giant steps to her side and tasted the filling. The meat fell apart in his mouth and mingled with the spices. "Mmm. *Me encanta sus tamales, Señorita.*"

She patted his cheek. "I know you love them."

Hays tried to take another spoonful, but she swatted his hand away. "You can wait for more." She laughed and went back to her work. "What brings you into the house?"

"I need to talk to my brothers."

"The only one here is Señor Travis. He is in the office talking with your papá." She added more spice to the pot and continued to stir. "The others are out working."

"I saw Travis's buckboard and thought I'd talk to him first. If I can persuade him, then the others might follow."

Perla didn't bother to look at Hays. "I won't even ask what trouble you are planning now."

"Good." He bent and kissed her wrinkled cheek. "Make sure you set aside the biggest tamale for me."

She winked at him. "I always do."

Hays left the glorious smells in the kitchen and walked through the dark hall.

Travis was just closing Pa's office door. A frown puckered his forehead until he glanced up at Hays's approach. He cleared the concerned look from his face. "Hays."

"Is everything all right?"

"Everything is fine." Travis took his pocket watch out of his vest and glanced at it before he tilted his head toward the front of the house. "Walk me out. I told Widow Hanson I'd stop by to check on her this afternoon."

They passed through the front hall and into the vestibule, Hays trying to keep up. "I came to ask you a favor."

"I'll do what I can."

"I'm helping Miss Longley raise funds to build a new school, and she's put me in charge of a bachelor auction." Hays followed Travis onto the front porch. "I need to find at least a dozen bachelors to auction off on the night of the street dance."

Travis stopped on the top step and turned to face Hays. "You want me to volunteer to be a part of the auction?"

"Would you?"

Travis studied Hays for a moment, a glimmer lighting his brown eyes. "I thought you might be sweet on Miss Longley."

"This has nothing to do with—"

"Of course, it does." Travis grinned. "And I'm not surprised."

"Will you do it?"

His smile fell. "I don't know, Hays. I hardly have time for a decent meal, let alone to attend a dance. I don't remember the last time I went to a social gathering."

Hays hated to beg, but he was running out of time. He only had a few days before the next meeting, and he needed to show Emma he was serious about helping her. "Please. For me." He knew his brother was busy, but he also knew that Travis had a hard time saying no to his family.

Travis sighed. "I suppose. But I'm not doing it just for you. I'm also doing it for Pa."

"Pa?"

Travis set his hand on Hays's shoulder. "He's serious about seeing his sons get married. I'm afraid I'm too busy to look for a wife, and besides, my life isn't conducive to a family. You, on the other hand..."—he squeezed Hays's shoulder—"would make a good husband."

It was the first time one of his brothers had recognized him as a man. "Thank you, Travis."

"Good luck convincing the rest of your brothers. You'll need it." Travis turned and walked down the steps toward his buckboard.

It would be impossible to convince Bowie, so Hays wouldn't even try, but with Travis's involvement, Crockett and Austin might say yes.

And there was still the matter of convincing Gage.

~

On Saturday morning, Emma stood outside the post office holding the packages she had picked up for Mama at the mercantile, as well as the letters that had just arrived from Minnesota. One in particular held her interest. It was addressed to Emma from the director of the Belle Prairie Mission, where Emma's parents had served for years, and where Emma had grown up. Emma had written to inquire if there was a teaching job available. Would Mrs. Greenfield want her to return? Emma was almost certain the answer was yes, but there was only one way to find out...though she couldn't bring herself to open the letter here on the street.

She slipped the envelopes into her reticule and turned left to head back to the parsonage.

Her mama would be eager to hear the news from home. Minnesota held mostly good memories, though there were a few events in Emma's life she'd rather forget. But it didn't pay to dwell on the past—not when she had so much to look forward to.

Downtown Hartville was alive with activity. People greeted each other as they went about their business, horses kicked up dirt on the dusty street, and the sun cast short shadows across the dry earth. In Minnesota, she would have been bundled up on this January day, happily shuffling from store to store—

She halted her thoughts, remembering her promise to Hays that she would stop comparing Texas to Minnesota.

She closed her eyes and took a deep breath. When she opened them, she looked at Hartville with a fresh perspective. At first, it looked just as it had before, but then she started to notice the quiet hum about the town. It was punctuated with the drawl of the local citizens, the scents of spicy food wafting out of the hotel restaurant two doors down, and the ring of spurs on the wooden sidewalks.

An older cowboy passed by, tipping his hat at her with a kind nod before continuing down the street. His leathered skin suggested a lifetime of hard work under the Texas sun. What story could he tell her about life in Texas? By the contented look on his face, she sensed he wouldn't exchange it for anything.

A gentle smile found its way to Emma's lips as a soft breeze ruffled her hem and tossed the tendrils of hair against her cheeks. She felt as if she had dipped just beneath the surface of the town, and it felt strangely refreshing.

"Looks like you're in need of a hand." Hays suddenly appeared on the boardwalk. "I'd be happy to help carry those packages for you."

Her heart sped up at the sound of his voice, and she couldn't stop herself from smiling—but she didn't meet his gaze. "I'm rarely in need of help, Mr. Hart."

"Maybe you're not in need of help, but I'm in need of helping someone. I haven't met my quota for the day."

Emma finally looked at him, and she swallowed the flutter of awareness. She hadn't seen him since the meeting on Monday, but he had never been far from her thoughts.

Today, his face was freshly shaved, and his blue eyes sparkled with mischief. He wore a buttoned shirt tucked into fresh denim pants, and tall boots. Surely, it wasn't possible, but every time she saw him, he looked more handsome than the time before. "How gallant of you—but I'm afraid you'll have to keep looking elsewhere."

His lazy grin appeared—the one she didn't realize she missed until she saw it again—and he held out his hands. "Please let me help you, Emma."

She loved hearing her name on his lips...and she no longer wanted to say no to him. Sweet anticipation raced up her spine when she thought of spending a few minutes in his company. What would he say or do next? The prospect was...strangely exciting.

Emma offered him her purchases. "I'm heading back to the parsonage."

Hays took the packages, a satisfied smile lighting his face.

"Do you know...I don't think I've ever met anyone who smiles as much as you."

His grin widened. "I try to always be happy."

Emma started toward the parsonage—slowly. "It's impossible to always be happy."

"Maybe—but I try."

"Why?"

Hays shrugged, and his gaze drifted to a far-off place, almost as if he was lost in the past. "My childhood was filled with a lot of sadness. I didn't want to add to anyone's sorrow, so I found ways to stay happy."

Empathy squeezed Emma's chest at the look of pain in his eyes. "Trying to make other people happy is a heavy burden to carry."

He looked back at her, his eyes focused on the present. "Sometimes, yes, but when you love them, it's a burden you're willing to carry."

Emma glanced down at the packages he had offered to carry for her. It wasn't the first time he had tried to ease her load, and it likely wouldn't be the last. Was that why he had offered to help with the fundraiser? To shoulder her burden, even though it wasn't his to bear?

For a fleeting moment, she wondered who carried his burdens.

"I came to town looking for you," Hays said. "I stopped at the parsonage, and your mama told me where to find you."

What must Mama think of Hays showing up to see her? Hopefully, she didn't think he was romantically interested. "Why did you come looking for me?"

"I couldn't wait until Monday to tell you the good news."

"Monday?"

"The fundraising meeting."

"Oh." Emma's curiosity was now piqued. "What's the good news?"

"I have secured over twenty bachelors for the auction—and I have a feeling there will be plenty more."

"Twenty?" Emma stopped in front of Travis Hart's medical building.

Hays also stopped. "It was the strangest thing. Once word got out about the auction, I had cowboys from several neighboring ranches show up to volunteer, not to mention those from the 7 Heart Ranch— and a few townies, to boot." He chuckled. "I don't think we'll have trouble where the bachelor auction is concerned."

"No." Emma glanced around Hartville at the heavily male-populated town. "My concern now is that we won't have enough women to do the bidding."

"I think I have that covered too. I've already spoken to several women, securing their promise to bid. Our cook, Perla, was the first to agree."

Emma quickly calculated how much money twenty bachelors could bring in for the fundraiser—but then studied Hays for a moment. "Why are you helping me?"

"I want to make you happy, and if that means helping you build a school, then I'll do what I can to make it happen." All teasing had disappeared from his voice.

"You hardly know me."

"Something I'd like to change if you'd let me."

Emma started toward the parsonage again, and Hays followed. She was silent for a moment. "I'll be leaving Texas in a couple of months."

"You told me."

She looked over the town. "So why take the time to get to know me?"

He put his free hand on her elbow, helping her around a broken board. "Because everyone benefits from a friendship, even if it only lasts a couple months."

His hand stayed on her elbow, and Emma liked how it felt. "Thank you, Hays."

She would allow him to be her friend...but nothing more. In less than two months, she was leaving Texas, and she wanted no regrets to follow her.

CHAPTER 5

*H*ays rode into town and headed straight for the church. He hated to be the one to tell Emma, but someone had to do it.

It had been over a week since he had met her outside the post office, and in that time, they had spent several hours working together on the bazaar. Just yesterday, after church, he had met with Emma and Connie to design the posters that he would hang all over town to advertise the fundraiser.

He hated to think all their hard work might be for nothing.

It was midafternoon, and the children would still be in school. It was too early for their weekly fundraising meeting, but there was no time to wait. Hays jumped off Bella and wrapped her reins around the hitching post outside the whitewashed church. He took the steps two at a time but then paused when he put his hand on the knob. Her voice was muffled through the wood door.

Slowly, he turned the knob, and the door popped open. She must not have heard because she continued to teach. He stood outside, but the opening allowed him to hear her perfectly.

"Now that we've studied the general history of Texas, we'll move on to local history. Many of you know Mr. George Washington Hart, but not all of you know his father's name was Benjamin Franklin Hart. Benjamin and his wife Mary Ellen were part of the 'Old 300,' the first white settlers in Texas. They came here with their four children, George Washington, who you know as G.W., John Adams, William Penn, and Martha Abigail Hart."

There were surprised murmurs in the room, and Hays himself was amazed at how much Emma knew about his family's history.

"In 1824, the settlement of Austin began, but Benjamin Hart ventured farther west than most of the Austinites. Here he established the Hart ranch and set aside a portion of his property to start the town of Hartville."

"Miss Longley?"

"Yes, Adam?"

"Why do all the Hart brothers have strange names?"

Hays's laugh was drowned out by a round of giggles, until Emma successfully quieted them.

"They might sound strange to you," Emma said with a smile in her voice. "But for anyone who has studied their Texas history, they know all the Hart brothers are named after important Texans."

Again, the murmurs.

Hays used the opportunity to push the door open all the way and slip into the back of the church.

Emma looked up, and her cheeks blossomed with color. "It looks as though one of those strange-named men has come for an unexpected visit."

Dozens of eyes turned to Hays, and several of them looked at him with new admiration—some with downright awe.

"This particular Hart is named after John Coffee Hays," Emma said, keeping the attention on him. "Colonel Jack Hays, as he's known, is still alive and lives in California with his family, but when he was a young man, he was a heroic Texas Ranger, leading several campaigns against the Comanche Indians. Even though he fought the Comanche, they had great admiration for him."

Hays took off his hat and nodded at Emma, though he spoke to the children. "You have a smart teacher. She knows more about my name-sake than I do."

The children giggled, and Emma smiled. "I doubt that."

"Still...I'm impressed that you did your research." Had she researched all his brothers' namesakes...or only his?

He held her gaze for a moment before she glanced down at her lapel watch. "We're about out of time, children. Class is dismissed for the day."

The children cheered and quickly gathered their things. Hays ruffled David Longley's hair as he passed by.

When the last child had left, Hays walked to the front of the room where Emma stood waiting.

"I'm surprised to see you so early," Emma said. "Is something wrong?"

He clutched his hat and motioned to her chair. "You should probably take a seat."

The welcoming gleam left her eyes. "Is it that bad?"

He let out a long, weary sigh. "I'm afraid it is."

Emma walked around her desk and slowly lowered herself to her chair. "Go ahead."

"Perla was in town this morning. She went to Mortenson's Mercantile, and Meribeth Mortenson told her that there's a petition going around town to try and stop you from building the school."

"A petition?" Emma's eyes grew round as she rose from her chair. "But why? Who?"

"I don't know, but Meribeth said there were already dozens of names on it."

Emma's face grew pale, and she dropped into the chair once again. "If there are dozens of names, how will we get enough people to attend our fundraiser?"

Hays's thoughts exactly. He hated that there were people in Hartville who didn't want Emma to succeed.

"Emma." Hays circled around the desk and squatted in front of her. "We can't let these people win. I want to see that school built as much as you do. People are just afraid of change, that's all."

She didn't seem to hear him. "All this work wasted."

"It's not wasted. We'll still get that school built."

"How?" She finally looked at him. "If we don't raise enough money, it will be an impossible task."

"My pa made an offer the first time you met, and I know the offer still stands. He'd be happy to donate whatever you—"

"No." Emma stood and passed around Hays. "I won't let your father give yet one more thing to this town."

"Why not?" Hays also stood. "We owe them a lot."

"Because your grandfather founded the town?"

"Yes."

"If anything, they owe you."

"Why does it matter so much?"

She walked to the window and wrapped her arms around her waist. "They need to be loyal."

Hays frowned. "Loyal to what?"

"I want the citizens of Hartville to be loyal to the children and to each other. If you don't have loyalty, what do you have?"

He crossed the room. "Emma, what are you talking about?"

She turned, disappointment lining the edges of her mouth. "It's nothing."

"This isn't 'nothing.'"

She twisted her hands together and returned to her desk, putting space between them. "When I was a little girl, my family was forced to spend three weeks inside a stockade when one of the Ojibwe chiefs threatened to attack the white settlers."

Hays joined her by her desk, his heart heavy for her. "I can't imagine what that was like."

"It was horrible, but what hurt the most was that the people I had lived with, our Ojibwe friends and neighbors, had become disloyal to us. Or, at least, that's what I believed for a long time." She let out a weary sigh and met his gaze. "Loyalty means everything to me."

"That's why this fundraiser is so important?"

"Yes. It may seem insignificant—"

"I don't think it's insignificant at all."

"So then you understand why I can't accept your father's money?"

Hays scratched his chin. He didn't understand that part, not fully. "I suppose."

"What will we do?"

He paced away from her, thinking about their options—which were few. "If you aren't willing to accept Pa's money, are you willing to accept some other kind of help?"

She frowned. "What do you mean?"

"What if he made an announcement encouraging people to attend the fundraiser? Would you allow him to do that?"

Hope sparked in her gaze. "Do you think he would?"

"If you ask him."

Pa wouldn't turn down Emma. He had taken quite a shine to her after Sunday dinner.

In the meantime, they would continue to plan the fundraiser, and Hays would track down that petition and find the scoundrel who started it.

~

*E*very moment of Emma's spare time was dedicated to the fundraiser. It was exactly what she needed to keep her mind off her growing attraction to Hays. The only trouble was, he came into town almost every day to help.

Emma glanced out the window of the parsonage on Saturday morning as Hays helped Papa and David build a table for the bazaar. The three of them worked well together, and Emma often found Papa and David laughing at something Hays had said. Even now, Papa was standing straight, his hammer in hand as he listened intently to whatever it was Hays was saying as he sawed a piece of wood. Just as she expected, Papa bent over in laughter while Hays grinned.

"Your father and brother really like Hays," Mama said, entering the parlor from the kitchen.

Emma let the curtain fall back into place. "Oh?"

Mama's eyes twinkled with merriment. "You hadn't noticed?"

They were two weeks away from the bazaar, and everyone was busy doing their part to help. Last week, G.W. had stood up after church and invited the whole town to attend the fundraiser. Yesterday, Hays had located the petition and finally destroyed it, though he hadn't found the person who started it. And right now, Mama, Hope, and Emma were sewing quilts for the raffle. If all went as planned, they would have three made before the bazaar.

"Has Hope finished binding the red, white, and blue quilt?" Emma changed the subject as she moved away from the window and settled at the Singer sewing machine.

"Yes." Mama set a pile of fabric squares on the worktable next to Emma and then took a seat on the settee.

Hope came down the stairs, a beautiful quilt hanging over her arm. She still limped on her tender ankle, but it had healed enough for her to get around without assistance. "I just finished." She laid it over the back of a rocking chair near the front door. "I can start quilting the next one as soon as you finish piecing the squares together."

Emma surveyed the stack of squares, and a sigh left her lips before she could stop it.

"What's wrong, Em?" Mama asked, picking up a set of shears.

Emma stood and paced back to the window where the cloudless blue sky beckoned her. "I don't know."

"Why don't you take a break?" Hope took Emma's place at the machine. "You've been working day and night for weeks now."

"There's still so much to do."

"Hope and I can manage without you for a while." Mama glanced up from her work. "The men would probably enjoy some refreshment. Why don't you take some cold water and sugar cookies out to them? And who knows?" She cut another square. "Maybe you and Hays could take a little walk."

"Mama." Emma crossed her arms and paced away from the window. "You know how I feel about Hays Hart."

"I know what you've told me," Mama said, sharing a quiet smile with Hope. "But what someone says and what they feel are sometimes two different things."

Emma continued to pace. "We're only friends."

"And getting friendlier every day." Hope inspected the sewing machine to make sure the bobbin was full.

Emma ignored her sister's comment. It was true she and Hays had grown fond of each other, but that didn't indicate romance.

"For what it's worth to you," Mama said, "I like Hays, and so does your papa. He's a nice young man."

"And he lives here in Hartville," Emma added for her. "Not Minnesota."

"It's no secret we'd like you to stay in Texas." Mama spoke gently. "We hate to think of you fourteen hundred miles away...but if that's where God is calling you..."

The letter from Mrs. Greenfield had been everything Emma hoped and more. Not only did they want her to come back to the mission and teach, but they asked her to be the lead teacher for the entire school. Emma had been certain when she first arrived in Texas that God was calling her back to Minnesota, but now she wasn't so sure. Her determination to build this school had curbed her homesickness and given her something to look forward to. The thought of leaving it all behind didn't appeal to her as much as it had in the past.

At the same time, she ached to see her old friends in Minnesota and return to her work with the Ojibwe children. She also missed the lakes and rivers. It was a place she felt closest to God. Since coming to Texas, she had longed for the refreshment the cool water gave her.

"Maybe I will go for a walk." Emma needed to get out of the house and simply enjoy the outdoors.

"Will you ask Hays to join you?" Hope peeked over her shoulder.

Emma didn't bother to answer as she took her shawl off the hook. But she paused as she thought of Papa and Hays working hard on the tables for the bazaar. "Maybe I will take them some refreshments first."

Her mother and sister didn't say anything as she crossed the room and entered the kitchen, though no doubt they would have much to discuss after she left. Emma quickly put everything on the tray and then opened the back door.

"Invite Hays to stay for supper," Mama called as the door closed behind Emma.

The day was a bit cool, but the brilliant blue sky and warm sunshine made up for the lack of heat.

Papa, David, and Hays were working in the churchyard. Hays had his shirtsleeves rolled up, and the muscles in his forearms rippled as he sawed. He was listening intently as Papa spoke about his work as a missionary in the early years, when Minnesota was still a territory, before he had met Mama.

Hays was so engrossed in Papa's story that neither man noticed Emma's approach.

"I was a determined man, even back then," Papa told him. "Emma's a lot like me in that way."

"I admire her determination," Hays said, the depth of his respect evident to Emma. "I have a feeling she accomplishes everything she sets her mind to."

Papa flashed a grin. "I have a feeling you're quite similar."

"I usually don't have a problem getting what I want, if that's what you mean."

Papa laughed. "That's exactly what I mean, but I sense you've met your match."

"I have, indeed." Hays glanced up then, and a smile lit his blue eyes when he saw Emma.

Her heart skipped a beat.

Papa also looked in her direction. "Hello, Em."

"Are those Mama's cookies?" David asked, reaching for one.

Emma had a hard time finding her voice, so she simply nodded and extended the tray.

Papa took one. "I married Sarah before I knew how good her cookies were. I would have married her simply for that reason alone."

Hays laughed, though Emma had heard the joke so many times, all she could do was smile.

But it gave her time to compose herself. She set the tray on a finished table. "Mama is roasting a chicken for supper. You're invited to stay, Hays."

"Will you?" David asked. "Could you show me how to lasso? Could I help with the spring roundup if I know how? Do you think I could learn how to brand the cattle too? Mr. Bowie said I—"

"That's enough, son." Papa set his hand on David's shoulder. "Let's let Hays answer the first question before you ask him another."

Hays finished chewing a bite of cookie. "If Mrs. Longley's roasted chicken is as good as her sugar cookies, I'd be a fool not to stay."

"Her chicken is good." David rubbed his belly.

"Emma is lucky her mama taught her everything she knows," Papa added.

"Are you a good cook?" Hays asked Emma.

"My food is passable."

"Don't let her modesty fool you." Papa winked at Emma. "She's the second-best cook I know."

Hays's admiration shined from his face. "Yet another reason to like you."

"I'm going for a walk," Emma said quickly. "I'll be back before supper."

"We'll be here building tables," Papa said.

"All right." Emma started off toward town, and Hays made no motion to follow her.

Soon the sound of their tools and companionable conversation found its way to her ears.

Emma pulled her shawl closer around her body and tried not to feel disappointed that Hays hadn't insisted on joining her.

CHAPTER 6

It was the last day of January, which meant they were only one week away from the fundraiser and one month away from the end of the school term. Hays inspected his reflection in the hall mirror before reaching for his Stetson.

He was on his way into town to see Emma again, but this time, he wasn't going to help with the fundraiser. There was something far more enjoyable he had in mind for today.

Courting.

"Hays?" Pa's voice reached Hays from inside his office.

"Yes, sir?"

"Come here, son."

With a sigh, Hays set his hat back on the hook. He hadn't told Emma he was coming, though Reverend Longley knew of his plans. He hated to be late, but he also hated to disappoint his pa.

Hays opened the door leading into the office. The room had always impressed and intimidated him. It was one of the largest in the house and boasted a brilliant view of the ranch from its six floor-to-ceiling windows. A large longhorn bull head was mounted on the wall above a commanding fireplace, and hundreds of books lined the remaining walls.

Pa sat in his large chair, his feet propped up on his desk, as he watched Hays enter. "Have a seat, son."

Hays took the leather chair he often occupied while visiting with his father, but he didn't settle in like usual. "What can I do for you?"

"Are you off again?"

"Yes, sir."

"Into Hartville to see Miss Longley?"

Hays nodded. It was no secret that he had been spending all his free time at the parsonage.

Pa dropped his feet and put his hands on his desk, a surefire sign that he was about to get serious. "Austin's been in here complaining that you've got your head in the clouds and you're not gettin' your work done around the ranch."

Hays couldn't deny the claim. "I'm not doing it on purpose. I've been helping Emma with—"

"None of that matters," Pa said, studying Hays. "I'm only concerned about one thing."

Hays frowned. "The ranch?"

"Your marriage prospects."

"My what?"

"Are you making progress with Miss Longley? She's the one you're pursuing, isn't she? 'Cause if not, you're wasting time."

"Pa!" Hays stood, unable to stay in his seat.

"What?" Pa looked up at him. "I laid down the law a month ago, and you're the only one takin' me seriously. Are you makin' any progress?"

"Pa," Hays said again. "These things take time and patience."

Pa shook his head. "If I was thirty years younger, I'd show you whippersnappers how to go about courtin' proper-like."

Hays grinned. "I remember Mother said she was the one who had to pursue you."

"That's because I was a knot head like your brothers." He propped his feet up on his desk, longing in his voice. "If I had to do it all over again, I would've been a lot smarter."

"I'm trying—I just wish Emma wasn't so reluctant."

"I like her," Pa said. "And I like that she's making you work for her hand. She's a keeper."

"She is." Hays tilted his head toward the door. "Can I go to it?"

Pa nodded. "Don't worry about Austin and the ranch. Courtin' is more important right now."

Hays couldn't agree more. He left his pa's office, grabbing his Stetson on his way out the front door. He had no time to lose. In less than four weeks, Emma would get on a stagecoach and leave Hartville for good. The thought caused him to sprint to the barn.

Hays hitched the team up to a buggy and drove into town as quickly as he could. When he arrived at the parsonage, he jumped out of the buggy and strode to the front door to knock.

Even though he had come to this house every day for the past three weeks, he stood a bit stiff, more nervous than he'd ever felt in his life. It was a humbling experience to stand on a young lady's front porch and risk her rejection.

The door opened, and Mrs. Longley stood wiping her hands on her white apron, a knowing smile on her face. "Hello, Hays."

"Hello, Mrs. Longley. Is Emma at home?"

"She's in the backyard binding one of the quilts. You're welcome to join her."

"Thank you, ma'am." He left the porch and walked around the cottage to the back of the house. It was a cozy backyard with a hedge enclosing the space to offer privacy. Two large pecan trees stood in the middle, offering shade.

Emma sat beneath the trees on a wrought-iron bench. She wore a yellow skirt and white blouse, and her dark brown curls were gathered at the nape of her neck in a yellow ribbon. Her head was bent over a beautiful patchwork quilt lying on her lap, a needle and thread in her right hand. She looked so serene, with little wisps of hair playing about her cheeks in the gentle breeze. For a moment, Hays contemplated leaving her in peace, but the thought of walking away without seeing her smile was a prospect he didn't want to consider.

She must have sensed his nearness because she looked up from her work and rewarded him with the smile he had been seeking. Her green eyes sparkled with welcome, and her cheeks turned a pretty shade of pink. "Hello."

In that moment, Hays realized his attraction to her had grown into something far more serious than friendship. He had come to admire her deeply. She was loyal, honest, and above all, she had a heart to serve. The fundraiser had faced several setbacks, but each time, she had found a way to persevere. She was patient with her students, faithful to her family, and she was a good friend to Connie during her time of grieving. Yes, Emma was stubborn and strong-willed, and she was often more serious than necessary—but even those qualities could be strengths when she chose to use them wisely.

Above all, Hays liked Emma. More and more every day.

"Howdy." He sauntered toward her, enjoying the high curve in her cheekbones, the fullness of her lips, and the silky white softness of her neck.

She lowered the quilt and offered him her full attention. "I didn't expect to see you today. I thought you'd be busy catching up at the ranch."

"I thought it might be nice to do a little something different today— with you."

She picked up the quilt again. "I wish I could, but there are so many things to do before next Saturday."

Hays took a step toward her and put his hand over hers. "Emma."

She stopped and looked up at him.

"It's only one afternoon." He studied her, trying to understand her thoughts. "I'd like to show you something."

Her mouth parted as if she was going to refuse him, but something flickered in her gaze, and she nodded. "All right."

Relief and disbelief shifted within his chest, and he smiled. "Would you like to know where we're going?"

Emma snipped the thread and put her needle inside her basket. She stood and wrapped the quilt into a neat bundle. When she looked at him, there was a hint of mischief in her eyes. "Surprise me."

He liked her answer.

They walked across the backyard and entered the house. Mrs. Longley and Hope were in the small kitchen peeling potatoes. Both ladies lifted their gazes when Emma and Hays entered.

"Mama, Hays has asked me to go on a ride with him," Emma said, setting the quilt on a worktable.

Emma missed the pleased glance her mother and sister sent each other—but Hays didn't.

"Hays!" David ran into the kitchen. "I thought I heard your voice. Can you take me to the 7 Heart? I want to keep practicing my roping for the spring roundup. Is Mr. Bowie at the ranch? Do you think Clara will have puppies soon? Could you take me to see?"

"Not today, Davey. I'm taking Emma on a ride."

"Can I come?" David glanced at his oldest sister with bright eyes.

Emma began to respond, but Hays beat her to it, afraid she might say yes. "I'll take you out tomorrow after church if your parents agree."

David turned his freckled face to his mother. "Can I, Mama?"

"May I," Mrs. Longley corrected him. "And I'll ask your papa when he comes home, but I don't think there will be a problem."

"Whillikens!" David gave a little hop. "That'll be fun."

"David." Mrs. Longley frowned. "Please refrain from using slang."

"Ah, Mama."

"I'll grab a shawl," Emma said to Hays. She leaned over and kissed her mother's cheek. "I'll be back before supper."

"Where are you going?" Hope asked.

"It's a surprise," Emma said.

Hope sighed and went back to peeling her potatoes.

"Have fun," Mrs. Longley called as Hays followed Emma out of the kitchen and into the sunny front parlor.

She reached for a white shawl, but he grabbed it before she could. "May I?" He settled the shawl around her shoulders and rested his hands there for a moment. Before she could pull away, he reached for the door and opened it for her. "After you."

She passed by, and he caught the delicate scent of lavender. He wanted to pause and savor the smell, but he followed her out the door and closed it behind them instead.

"I can't quite believe I'm outside enjoying such marvelous weather at the end of January." Emma accepted his hand as she climbed into the open buggy. "Back home—" She paused and quickly looked at him as if she had said something wrong.

He climbed into the buggy as she settled into the seat. "Back home, what?"

"Nothing. I remember you asked me to stop comparing Minnesota to Texas."

Hays dipped his head to look her in the eyes. "That doesn't mean I don't want to hear about where you grew up, Emma. I'd like nothing better."

It seemed as if a weight was lifted from her shoulders, and she began to tell him all about her life in Minnesota. She spoke almost nonstop from the center of Hartville all the way to the edge of the 7 Heart Ranch and the section of land Pa had promised to Hays when he married.

She spoke about her work with the Ojibwe Indians and how her parents had married at the Belle Prairie Mission when they had only known each other for a week. "My parents worked for the American Board of Commissions for Foreign Missions, and they were required to be married to serve on the mission field. My father was a hundred and fifty miles up the Mississippi serving at Red Lake, so he got into a canoe and went to Belle Prairie because he had heard there was a single female missionary there." She laughed and Hays chuckled, imagining Reverend Longley as a young man pursuing a wife.

"When he got off the canoe," Emma continued, "he learned there wasn't one single lady—there were four, my mother included, and they were all looking for husbands." Her voice held a hint of awe. "Somehow my father knew she was the one, and they fell in love in seven short days. They've never regretted their decision once."

"Do you think it's possible to fall in love so quickly?" Hays asked quietly.

Emma gazed at the passing countryside and nodded. "How could I not? But I think it's very rare."

They were now on Hays's property, and just over the little rise, they would see his favorite place on earth—the banks of the Sabinal River. There was one place in particular he loved. It was where the tree roots were exposed along the riverbank from years of erosion, and where the canopy of leaves furled out above the water to create a little sheltered haven.

Hays stopped the buggy in a clearing and took a deep breath, inhaling the fresh air. He would save the best for last. "What do you miss the most about Minnesota?"

Emma sat with her hands clasped in her lap, a faraway look in her eyes. "There are so many things. I miss the dense forests that open onto tree-rimmed prairies. I miss the vibrant green in the summer and the blinding white of the winter. I miss our Ojibwe friends and our mission family." Her voice filled with longing. "But most of all, I miss the water. The endless lakes and the rushing rivers. I miss the Mississippi, which brought my father to my mother."

"I thought you'd say that." Hays slapped the reins against the horses' backs, and the buggy went into motion again. Emma had mentioned the Mississippi several times in the past few weeks, and from the first mention, he had wanted to take her to this place.

The buggy pulled up to the little rise, and the Sabinal came into view. The sunlight made the water sparkle and the green leaves shimmer. It wasn't really a river, but rather, a wide creek. In the summer, it was often reduced to little more than a trickle, but at the moment, it was running strong.

Emma inhaled and grabbed Hays's arm.

The touch made Hays pause. Most likely, she didn't realize what she was doing, but he didn't mind in the least.

~

The view mesmerized Emma. "It's...it's breathtaking."

The horses followed a gentle path worn into the soil.

"I thought you'd like it." Clearly, Hays was pleased with himself.

His voice brought her out of her reverie, and she realized her hand was on his arm. She removed it and clutched her hands in her lap. "I'm sorry."

"I kind of wish you'd do it again." He chuckled, and she couldn't help but smile.

Hays pulled up to the river and stopped the horses. He climbed down from the buggy and then reached up for her. "We can stay as long as you like."

She took his hand and climbed out of the buggy. When her feet touched the ground, she briefly closed her eyes and inhaled. "I could stay here forever."

"Me too."

He let her go, and she moved toward the water. "It's so clear."

"I'm afraid it isn't the Mississippi."

Emma glanced at him. "No, but it's the next best thing."

Hays joined her at the river's edge as she slowly turned in a circle, inspecting the entire area. "If I were going to stay in Texas, I'd want a house right there." She pointed to the top of the hill. "Where I could see the river every day."

"I'm glad you like it."

She looked back at him. "I do, very much."

"Good, because this is my land."

"Your land?"

"We're on the 7 Heart Ranch. My father sectioned off a portion of the ranch for each of his sons, like a wagon wheel, with El Regalo in the center. This is my portion, closest to Hartville." He turned her to face the little rise in the land again. "And that's exactly where I've always planned to build my house."

"It's perfect."

"There's only one problem." His voice grew serious as he turned her back around to look at him. "My pa won't let me build on this land and take possession of it until I have a wife."

Emma swallowed the sudden nerves that bubbled up. Was he pursuing her just to secure his land? She studied him closely. "Why did you bring me here, Hays?"

"I wanted you to see one of the reasons why I love Texas so much." His voice softened. "I thought you might like it too."

She wanted to believe him—no, she did believe him. She had seen how all the girls liked Hays. If he wanted to find a wife, simply to secure his land, he could have chosen anyone. But—he'd chosen to pursue her.

Perhaps he really did like her.

"I haven't felt so at home since we left Minnesota." She gazed up at him, and words failed her as she stared into his brilliant blue eyes. Even though he liked to tease, and sometimes he didn't take things as seriously as she'd like, in the past three weeks, he had proven he was dependable, hardworking, and passionate about the school. No matter what she had asked, he had gone out of his way to do. Everywhere they went, people respected Hays, and not just because his last name was Hart, but because he truly cared about his neighbors. He knew almost all of them by name, and he made them happy.

"Thank you for bringing me here," she whispered.

Her heart was so full, she wanted to show him how much she appreciated his thoughtfulness—not only now, but in the past few weeks.

Without giving it much thought, she rose on her tiptoes and placed a kiss on his cheek. She intended the kiss to be quick, but when her lips touched his face, she paused. His skin was warm and smelled of a spicy cologne.

Suddenly, she didn't want to pull away.

His arms went around her waist, and he turned his face until his lips were hovering near hers. His sweet breath warmed her mouth, yet he hesitated.

Her heart longed to be loved, and her lips yearned to be kissed, but her head warned her it was foolish. She was leaving in a month, and even if she wasn't, could she trust Hays with her heart?

Yet she wanted to savor the feelings he stirred in her and dive deeper until she was fully submerged under the refreshing waves of emotion. They made her feel carefree for the first time in years. It both exhilarated and frightened her.

"Hays." It was the only thing she could think to say before his lips covered hers.

She melted into his embrace. His hand came up to her cheek, and his thumb caressed her skin just under her eyelashes. The featherlike touch sent a delicious thrill up her spine and made her deepen the kiss. She wanted him to hold her tighter, but he was gentle as he kissed her back.

One of the horses snorted behind her, returning Emma to the present.

She pulled away from his embrace, her cheeks burning and her heart thumping hard.

"Emma." He reached for her hand, his eyes glowing. "You said it's possible to fall in love in seven days, and I think you're right."

She shook her head, realizing what she had just done. She had given him false hope—had given herself false hope.

"My pa said I need to be married by this time next year, or I'll lose my inheritance," he said. "Truth be told, that's all I thought about the day I met you—but now I want to get married for a far better reason."

"No." She took another step back, pulling her hands free. "Please don't, Hays." She didn't want to reject him. She liked him far too much to hurt him that way.

He moved toward her, his eyes serious. "I want you to know—"

"I wish you wouldn't. I'm leaving in a month. Mrs. Greenfield is expecting me at the Belle Prairie Mission. I've promised to teach the Indian children." She bumped into the buggy, feeling desperate to make him understand.

Hays put his hands around her waist to stop her. "Emma, I know you feel something for me too. You wouldn't kiss me the way you just did if you didn't."

She took a deep breath and lifted the hem of her skirt to step into the buggy. "I want to go home." To Minnesota. To a place that made sense and where she was in control of her thoughts and emotions. She hated feeling topsy-turvy, unsure what to think or believe about Hays, about Texas, and about herself. She prided herself on knowing exactly what she wanted and how to get it. This uncertainty made her panicky.

He stood for a moment, looking as though he might try to convince her to stay. Instead, he let her go and slowly walked around the buggy.

The ride back to Hartville was quiet. Hays sat stiff beside her, but Emma had nothing more to say to him. She refused to allow her heart to give way to fickle feelings. She knew what she wanted, and she knew what she needed to do to achieve her goals.

They had nothing to do with Hays Hart and his family's town.

CHAPTER 7

$\mathcal{M}$ ain Street had never looked as festive as it did the night of the street dance. Dozens of people trickled into town wearing their Sunday best as they mingled in the dying light.

Hays stood on the makeshift dance floor with over two dozen nervous bachelors waiting for Ruby and Julia Brown to arrive and give them instructions for the auction.

Evening had settled on Hartville, allowing the stars to canopy across the dark sky. Paper lanterns had been strung over the street from Mortenson's Mercantile to Collingsworth & Henderson's Hardware. The tables Hays and Reverend Longley had built lined either side of the street, with the dance floor between. A stage had been erected nearby, and the Hartville band sat there tuning their instruments.

"How do I look?" Gage pulled his collar away from his neck. "If I don't suffocate first, I might survive this horrible experience."

"You'll be fine," Hays promised. "Connie said she would bid on you if no one else does, so you have nothing to fear."

"I almost fear dancing with someone more than I do standing up there alone." Gage nodded at the stage, his face pale.

Ruby and Julia appeared in fancy gowns, their cheeks glowing. They swept onto the dance floor as if they had no cares in the world, but Hays knew better. They had done a good job planning the street dance, and they should be proud. He hadn't been sure they would pull it off, but they had. He was grateful they had stepped forward to help Emma.

"Gentlemen," Ruby said, drawing all eyes to her. "We will begin the auction in one hour, at exactly nine o'clock. We'll have everyone stand near the stage, and we'll call you up one by one."

Several of the men shuffled their feet, and some, like Gage, adjusted their collar yet again.

Hays tried to pay attention, but he was watching for Emma to arrive.

He hadn't stopped thinking about her all week. They had parted awkwardly when he brought her home after kissing her, but they had seen each other several times since then and had mended their tenuous relationship. She refused to be alone with him, though, but he wasn't deterred.

The kiss had solidified his feelings for her, and he was more determined than ever to win her heart—and her hand.

Connie appeared on the edge of the crowd wearing a beautiful pink gown. It was the first time since her mother's death that she had worn anything other than black. She looked lovely—but concerned. Her gaze landed on Hays, and she tilted her head toward the bank next door to Mortenson's Mercantile.

Hays nodded and wove his way through the growing crowd. "Is everything all right?" he asked when they finally met.

"No." She pulled him deeper into the shadows near the building. "I can't find any of the money we made at the bazaar."

"What do you mean?"

"Emma and I counted the money after the bazaar ended, and it was just over half of what we need to build the school. We put the money in the church safe and then went home to prepare for the dance." Connie's eyes filled with panic. "When I stopped at the Longleys' on my way here, Emma handed me another envelope full of money that had been donated after I left. She asked me to put it in the safe. But when I went into the church, the safe was open, and all the money was gone."

"Did Reverend Longley remove it?"

"No. When I was at their house, he said we'd leave the money in the safe until Monday morning when we would take it to the bank."

Hays surveyed the crowd, suddenly too warm in his evening suit. "Does Emma know?"

"No." Connie's voice was low. "I didn't have the heart to tell her. I want her to enjoy herself this evening. She was so proud of the bazaar and all the hard work everyone put into the event."

"Good. I don't want her to worry." She had worked harder than anyone and deserved to have some fun tonight. "Who do you think could have done it?"

"It was someone who has access to the safe combination because it wasn't broken."

"But who would have access?"

"The only people who know the combination besides the Longleys and me are members of the elder board."

Another thought began to plague Hays. "What if the auction doesn't make enough money?" Emma would be heartbroken, and whoever had done this would win. Was it the same person who had started the petition? If only he had discovered who that was.

"What can we do?" Connie asked, her eyes troubled.

An idea came to Hays, one that would work. "Connie, we need to make sure the bachelor auction makes enough money to pay for the school."

"How can we do that?"

"You're going to bid on me. I'll go last, and you can calculate how much money the other bachelors brought in. Whatever is needed at that point is how much you'll bid. My father offered to help pay for the school, but Emma refused. Surely, he will give me the money for this."

Connie's eyes grew round. "You want me to pay that much money for you?"

"Yes."

"But what will people think?"

"Does it matter? Emma needs that money."

The Longleys approached from the south, Reverend Longley leading the way along the boardwalk with Mrs. Longley on his arm. Emma and Hope followed.

Hays's attention immediately went to Emma. She wore a stunning green gown. It was tight in front, accentuating her small waist, and pulled back into a generous bustle. Her curls were piled high, with ringlets teasing her cheeks. She scanned the crowd, but when her eyes fell on him, she stopped searching.

His heart did a funny little flip, and he wanted nothing more than to cross the street and tell her how beautiful she looked.

"I'll do what I can." Connie drew his attention back to her and the problem at hand. "I just hope Emma doesn't suspect..."

"She won't." He offered Connie his arm. "Let's go say hello to Emma —and remember not to tell her about the money. I want her to have fun tonight."

They walked toward the Longleys, but Hays paused. "One more thing... After you bid on me and win, would you offer me to Emma for the first dance?"

Connie squeezed his arm. "Of course."

Hays was already looking forward to holding Emma again.

~

*E*mma sat with her family and G.W. Hart at a reserved table near the dance floor. A gentle breeze whispered across her skin, and the evening stars sparkled overhead. Warmth from the success of the bazaar earlier in the day, and now the success of the bachelor auction and street dance, cocooned her.

Loyalty. It felt good to find it in this community.

Hays stood at the end of the line, waiting to be auctioned. He had been watching her all evening—and truth be told, she had been watching him as well. Though she had been busy all week, nothing could keep her from forgetting the kiss they had shared near the Sabinal River. Every time she recalled the pleasure of the stolen moment, she had to remind herself it was a mistake.

If only her heart would believe her and let her forget.

Emma's cheeks warmed at the memory of the kiss—and then she noticed Mama and Papa watching her. Emma pretended as though nothing was amiss as she looked down at her reticule and counted her money once again.

"Our last bachelor of the evening," Ruby Brown said from the stage, "is Hays Hart."

Emma had to bite her bottom lip to stop the wide grin that wanted to make an appearance on her face. The last thing she needed was for her parents to suspect what had happened between them.

Hays stepped up to the stage, his carefree, confident grin fixed in place. Up and down the street, women cheered and clapped louder than they had for anyone else.

"Have you been waiting to bid on Hays?" Hope leaned over to whisper to Emma. "I think several women have. Good thing I got my bachelor early."

Emma glanced at Gage, who sat next to Hope, his hands clasping and unclasping in his lap. The poor man. He looked as though he had been lassoed and awaited the sting of a branding iron to claim ownership.

Some ladies, like Hope, had bid on the bachelors with romantic intention, but the majority had bid for the simple pleasure of helping the school. Hays's brothers had been bid on by Perla, who claimed Crockett, and the waitress Tillie, who claimed Austin. Old Widow Hansen had put her claim on Travis and now had the man all to herself—talking his ear off, pointing at various joints, and no doubt complaining of rheumatism or some other malady.

But here stood Hays in all his evening finery. Gone was the sense of good-natured competition among the women. Several narrowed their eyes with intent. One was Evelyn Palmer. She sat at a table with her father and Miss Spanner, wearing an elaborate gown.

"I believe Hays needs no introduction," Ruby said, though she had introduced each bachelor before. "He is well known by many young ladies in this town."

Emma knew what Ruby had meant, but still, the insinuation left her feeling uncomfortable...and jealous. Her heart thudded an irregular rhythm. Who would win the pleasure of his company for the rest of the evening? Surely, with so many vying for his attention, the paltry ten dollars she had in her reticule would not compete.

"Who will start the bidding?" Ruby asked.

Nerves bubbled up in Emma's stomach, and she took a deep breath. "I'll start—"

"I'll start the bidding." A young woman spoke up.

Emma spun and looked into the wide-eyed, nervous face of... "Connie?"

Connie gave Emma a wobbly smile, and then she looked up at the stage. "I'll bid two hundred dollars."

Gasps filled the air.

Two hundred dollars?

Emma swung back around to look at Hays.

He was now watching Connie.

Emma had to swallow the pain of disappointment. Why was her friend bidding on Hays? But, then, why wouldn't she? Emma had no claim on Hays, and it was clear Connie had always admired him. It made perfect sense that she would bid on him—but why the exorbitant amount of money? All the other bachelors had gone for five or ten dollars. Widow Hansen had spent twenty on Travis, and that had been the highest bid all evening.

"Two hundred dollars?" Ruby asked from the stage, her voice high. "Are you sure?"

Connie stood, her head raised, though Emma noticed the tremble in her hands. "Yes."

Emma turned her attention back to Hays, but he didn't look her way. The sudden realization that she wanted Hays's attention left her disconcerted.

The emotions that had been swirling inside Emma for the past few weeks culminated in that moment. Somehow, despite her best attempt at preventing it, she had fallen in love with Hays Hart.

Did he feel the same for her? She had thought so, but the way he looked at Connie now, with admiration and relief—she wasn't so sure.

Would Connie become the answer to his need for a wife?

"Are there any other bidders?" Ruby asked with uncertainty.

The townspeople looked at one another with stunned expressions.

The only person who was talking was Evelyn. She pulled on her father's arm, whispering something in his ear. But the older man shook his head, vehemently opposing whatever she was suggesting.

"If there are no other bids," Ruby said with less enthusiasm than she had exhibited all evening, "then I believe Constance Prescott has won the right to the first dance with Hays Hart."

For a moment, everyone was silent, and then a robust cheer rose from the crowd.

"Uncle Henry?" Ruby waved at the man who sat at the back of the stage. "The dance will now begin."

Uncle Henry nodded, his jowls wiggling, and set his beefy chin to the fiddle. "We'll begin as soon as the young lady claims her partner."

Emma looked down at the unused money in her reticule as Connie moved away from the table to meet Hays on the dance floor. Emma couldn't bring herself to watch her friend dance in his arms. Maybe she could excuse herself and leave—

"Emma." Connie tapped Emma's shoulder.

Emma's head jerked up, but she couldn't find the words to speak. Connie stood with Hays by her side—and this time, he was looking right at Emma.

"As a way to say thank you for all the hard work you and Hays have done for the school and the community," Connie said, "I'd like the two of you to lead the first dance together."

Hays extended his hand. By rote, Emma accepted it, though she didn't have the wherewithal to think about her actions as he drew her to her feet and led her onto the dance floor. The band began to play "The Blue Danube," and Hays bowed before Emma.

She offered a shaky curtsy, aware of everyone watching them.

He took her into his arms, and for a brief moment, they stared at one another. Slowly, the street and all the people of Hartville faded away. It was just the two of them as he twirled her around the floor in an exquisite pattern of movement. Never had she danced with a man who was so surefooted and graceful. It almost felt as if they were gliding on ice, something she missed desperately from home.

"Where did you learn to dance?" Her voice betrayed her awe.

"My mother. She insisted we learn."

"My thanks to your mother."

His blue eyes twinkled, and he wore his heart in his smile, as always.

The formality of the dance kept them at a distance, but ever so gently, Hays pulled her closer, despite their audience, and they waltzed on in beautiful silence.

The song ended much too soon, but it had been perfect. The whole day had been more than she had hoped.

Ruby called the other couples to come onto the dance floor, and soon Hays and Emma were surrounded by the bachelors and their ladies. Even Travis led Widow Hansen toward them, though they moved slowly through the crowd.

Hays held Emma's hand and didn't let it go. He was breathless as he said, "Emma, I'd like to speak to you—alone."

For the first time since he had brought her to his property along the Sabinal River, she wanted to be alone with him again. "All right."

"So it seems the Hart family ended up paying for the school, after all." Evelyn Palmer pushed her way through the dancers, her voice rising above the instruments.

Emma frowned. "I think you're mistaken." She squeezed Hays's hand. "It was Connie who paid for Hays—"

"At least that's what you think." Evelyn's cool gaze bore into Emma with triumph. "It's my understanding that Hays gave Connie the two hundred dollars to pay for that disgraceful dance we just witnessed."

"What?" Emma looked toward Hays. "What is she talking about?"

Hays frowned at Evelyn. "How would you know something like that?"

"I overheard you through the open window." Evelyn motioned across the street where her father's bank stood proudly next to the mercantile. "Really, Hays, you've never been one to deceive a friend."

Several dancers stopped nearby to listen.

Heat climbed up Emma's neck as she studied Hays. "Is it true?"

"Yes, but what does it matter?" He shook his head as if it was of little consequence. "Someone stole the money from the bazaar, and instead of ruining your evening and all your hard work, I thought this would be the best way to make sure there was enough money to still build the school."

"You knew I didn't want to take your father's money—"

"You worked hard, had a good turnout, and earned all the money you needed for the school. Whoever stole the bazaar money will have to live with their guilt, but we all still get what we want."

"What we want?" Emma gaped at him. "What I wanted was loyalty from this community, including the person who stole the money—but especially from you."

All the dancers had stopped now, and the band had come to a halt. What must all these people think of her carrying on this way? Embarrassment flashed hot. None of this was their fault, and they had all paid to enjoy their evening. "Please, continue the dance," she said, "and have a lovely time." She managed a weak smile. "Thank you all for your support of the school."

She turned, catching G.W.'s troubled gaze, and walked through the crowd toward the parsonage.

It was more obvious to her than ever that she and Hays were not well-suited for one another. How could she love a man who didn't have the decency to respect her wishes? She had explained to him why she didn't want the Hart money—yet he had tried to deceive her into taking it.

He wasn't serious enough for her—had never been, but she had allowed herself to be charmed...and to fall in love.

That thought alone made the tears finally come.

CHAPTER 8

*H*ays left the dance floor and caught up with Emma near Travis's medical building at the end of Main Street. The cloudless night offered a brilliant view of the starry sky, but there was no moon in sight. This part of Hartville was strangely quiet.

Emma brushed her hand across her cheek. Was she crying?

"Emma?" He put his hands on her shoulders to stop her and turned her around. The scant light revealed her tears, but she refused to look at him.

Guilt shot through Hays like a bullet, straight to his heart. He never imagined his actions would hurt her so deeply. He thought he was fixing the problem and sparing her pain—yet here she stood, crying.

"Emma, I'm sorry. I had no idea that you'd be so upset. I thought I was helping."

"I know—oh, Hays." She pulled away from his hands and wiped at the tears. "Don't you see? You tried to help by shielding me from the pain you thought I couldn't bear. Yet the disappointment over the stolen money is nothing like the disappointment in knowing that you betrayed my wishes."

Again, her tears fell, and he stood there, helpless to stop them. It was a horrible feeling, and it left him powerless for the first time since he was a child. He reached for her. "Emma—"

She took a step back and shook her head. "No. I'm sorry." She waved her hand between them. "I don't think any of this is a good idea. I've known it since we met. We're two very different people. It wouldn't work."

Again, the helplessness. How could he make this right? How could he restore her happiness? How could he recapture what they had felt at the Sabinal and dancing together just now?

"What can I do, Em?"

A single tear slipped from her eye. "Nothing."

Emma turned and walked away—and Hays didn't have the power to stop her.

He couldn't sleep that night, though he lay in his large bed and relived all the moments that had led up to Emma's departure.

As the hours ticked by, his mind wandered back to when he was a boy David's age. Most of his brothers had left the ranch, and then his mother had died. Hays thought long and hard about those difficult years and how they had shaped him into the man he had become. Truth be told, they had shaped all the Hart brothers—each in their own way.

Hays had wanted to have control over a world gone mad. Pain and sadness were two things he felt helpless to command—but joy, that was something he could produce with a few quick words, a big grin, and a helping hand—until this night, when it had all gone wrong with Emma.

Before the sun rose, Hays was out of bed. He couldn't handle any more thoughts. He needed to stay busy.

He left the house before his family woke up, and he went to the barn to saddle Bella. He spoke in soft tones as he led her out into the yard.

"Morning, Hays." Pa stood near the corral fence, quietly watching the sun rise above the eastern horizon, a steaming cup of coffee in his hands.

"I thought I was the only one awake."

"Did you sleep at all last night, son?"

It didn't pay to hide the truth—not from his pa. "No, sir."

Pa hitched his foot onto the bottom rail of the fence. "Did things go bad between you and Emma?"

Hays walked over to the fence and tossed the reins around the top rail. "Yes, sir."

"Over that money?"

"Did you hear?"

"I think everyone heard."

Hays closed his eyes briefly, embarrassed all over again by the whole situation. He couldn't imagine what Emma was feeling.

"Why'd you do it?"

Hays leaned against the fence, putting his forearms on the top rail, lowering his head to allow his Stetson to cover his eyes. "I was just trying to make her happy. I knew she'd be heartbroken if she found out there wasn't enough money to pay for the school building."

Pa was quiet for a moment, and then he sighed. "There's something you and I need to get straight. Something I've put off for too long."

Apprehension snaked its way up Hays's spine, until he was standing straight.

Pa's blue eyes were locked on Hays's face. "Son, you can't fix the world."

"I know that—"

"Do you?" Pa took a slow drink of coffee. "I've known you all your life. You think you can shield your loved ones from pain, but sometimes the only way to learn a lesson is to struggle through the hurt."

"If it's in my power to stop it, why shouldn't I try?"

"There have been times when I saw you and your brothers walking toward trouble, but I had to let you do it." Pa pointed out a mesquite tree sitting next to El Regalo. "See that tree?"

Hays nodded.

"Do you know what makes it so strong?"

"No, sir."

"Storms. When the wind blows against it, the tree is strengthened. If there were no storms, the tree would be weak and wouldn't stand up straight." He looked back at Hays. "We get strong by enduring the storms of life. If we're always sheltered, we'd be too weak to stand. Emma is no different. She's a strong woman, and she doesn't need you to protect her from the things she can bear on her own."

"But what if something is too hard for her to withstand?"

"That's when you need to stand beside her and lend her your strength—not by taking away the storm, but by holding her up through it."

Hays let out a long sigh.

The sun peeked above the horizon, tinting the land in shades of pink. What Pa said was true, though it wouldn't be easy.

"I think I'll mosey on into the kitchen and see if Perla has started breakfast." Pa took another sip of coffee and turned toward the house.

"Pa." Hays put his hand on his father's arm to stop him. "I respect your desire for me to marry, but I need you to know that I've made up my mind about something."

Pa studied Hays. "Go ahead."

"I love Emma and I plan to ask her to marry me." Hays paused and took a deep breath. "But if she won't, then I'll have to forfeit my inheritance."

"You're willing to give it all up for her?"

"I won't marry someone I don't love just to hold onto a piece of property." He swallowed, realizing all he'd give up if Emma rejected his proposal.

"You've loved that land all your life, yet you've only known her for a couple months. Are ya sure?"

The ache in Hays's chest wasn't from fear of losing the land—it was fear of losing Emma. "I've never been so sure in my life."

A smile lifted Pa's whiskered cheeks. "And you've never made me prouder." He pulled Hays into an embrace. "I love you, son. You have my blessing to do whatever you need to do to be happy."

Hays squeezed his pa close, his throat tightening with emotion. "I love you too."

~

*E*mma sat on the wrought-iron bench in her parents' backyard, her head bent in prayer as the midmorning sun climbed higher in the eastern sky. She had a lot to think about on this Sunday morning as her father's sermon drifted out the open windows of the church. Papa hadn't asked her if she was coming to the service. He knew she needed time alone.

A sparrow sang in a nearby tree, drawing Emma's attention to the dry, barren land just behind the hedge. What she wouldn't give to sit by the Sabinal River right now, under the canopy of trees, and let the soothing water carry her troubles away.

The thought made her pause. Until now, every time she had craved the peace of a river, she had yearned for the Mississippi. This was the first time she had yearned for the Sabinal.

It was the one place in Hartville that she felt truly at home—but whether it was because of the river, or because of Hays's company and the tender kiss they had shared, she couldn't be sure.

Thoughts of Hays made her sigh and turn again to prayer. She had come to respect Hays more than anyone she'd ever met, which made his decision last night all the harder to bear. The money wasn't the real issue. It was the feeling of dishonesty behind his act, and the sense that she didn't know if she could trust him, especially where her heart was concerned. Was he being dishonest about other things? Like his desire to marry her for love, and not to claim his land.

The final hymn came to an end, but it would be some time before her family came back to the house.

Emma closed her eyes and imagined she was sitting on the banks of the Sabinal under those glorious trees.

"Miss Longley?"

She opened her eyes and sat up straight at the sight of G.W. Hart standing in her parents' yard.

"Mr. Hart." She began to rise, but he lifted his hand to stop her.

"Please don't get up on my account." He crossed the yard and indicated the spot next to her on the bench. "May I?"

Emma nodded and then looked around him to see if Hays was nearby.

"Hays stayed out at El Regalo." Mr. Hart sighed as he took his seat. "I told him to take a nap since he didn't sleep last night."

Emma didn't know what to say, so she simply watched Mr. Hart and waited for him to tell her why he had come.

G.W. looked around the backyard, apparently in no hurry. "I've always liked this little house."

She had to admit it was a beautiful home, perfect for her parents. The whole family had enjoyed the pleasant cottage. "It's been very comfortable for our family."

"Did you know my father built this house?"

Emma's gaze drifted from the house to the man beside her. "I did not."

G.W. nodded. "After he built his own home and sectioned off a corner of his property for this town, he built the church and this house and invited Pastor Darby to come be the minister."

"My father is only the second pastor in Hartville?"

"He is. Pastor Darby was a young man when he came, and for the first little while, my family was the only congregation."

"I've heard good things about Pastor Darby. Many people miss him."

"He was a good man—none better. He impacted this community more than anyone else. You know he almost left Hartville that first year. He wanted to go back to Boston. I don't think he liked Texas much." G.W. gazed toward the church and Main Street. "I don't know what this town would be like if he hadn't stayed on."

A smile tilted Emma's lips as she began to suspect the reason for G.W.'s visit. "Why did he choose to stay?"

"He fell in love."

"I thought your family members were the only people in town."

"They were. Pastor Darby married my sister Martha. Did you know that?"

Emma shook her head.

"She was the first teacher in Hartville, and she taught in that little church, just like you." He chuckled. "'Course her only students were her brothers those first couple months, but the four of us rode into Hartville every morning for our lessons, and we went home every evening when they were done. At home, we could call her Martha, but in school, we had to call her Miss Hart."

Emma made David do the same thing.

"When Pastor Darby married Martha, she moved into this little house, and I used to come here and visit her. She made the best chocolate cake, and she always added extra icing just for me."

"I can tell you loved her." Emma paused. "But I thought Pastor Darby was a single man without children."

G.W. gazed at the little cottage with a sad smile. "Martha died on their first anniversary trying to birth her baby boy. The baby died too. Darby never married again, but he stayed on here." He ran his hand down his mustache. "I guess he finally saw it through Martha's eyes. He never regretted the year he had with her, even though he spent the rest of his life alone."

Tears sprang to Emma's eyes. "I'm so sorry."

G.W. patted Emma's knee. "I didn't mean to tell you this story to make you sad, my dear."

She wiped at a tear as it slipped down her cheek. "It's a beautiful story."

"It taught me something important." He studied her closely. "Loving somebody is a risk. But true love is always worth it, no matter how long it lasts."

Emma clasped her hands on her lap, unable to meet his penetrating gaze. The sparrow continued to sing, and the breeze blew across her face as she thought about his words.

"I suspect you're thinkin' on leaving Hartville," G.W. said, "but I'm asking you to stay and give our town a second chance. Who knows, you might fall in love with it like Darby did."

Emma glanced at the church and the town beyond, believing for the first time that it could be possible.

G.W. stood with a grunt. "I should probably get home. Perla is making enchiladas for lunch. Have you ever had enchiladas?"

Emma also stood. "No, I haven't."

"There's always a place at our table for you." He winked. "I'd even have a special chair monogramed with your initials, if you'd like." He patted her cheek. "Goodbye, Emma."

Emma blinked several times before she realized what he meant. "G-goodbye, Mr. Hart."

He walked across the yard, but just before he strolled out of hearing range, he looked back to her. "For what it's worth, whatever mistake you think Hays made last night, he did it because he loves you—of that, I'm certain. I can't fault him for that." He dipped his hat. "Goodbye."

Love? Emma stood in the middle of the backyard for several minutes watching G.W.'s retreating form.

Had Hays told his father he loved her?

Warmth cascaded through her, and she hugged her arms around her waist. If it was true, then he hadn't been pursuing her just for his land. Maybe his actions the night before weren't out of disloyalty. Maybe it was the only thing he could think of doing because he loved her and wanted her to succeed. She had been so overcome with emotion and pain from the past, she hadn't listened to him.

She owed him an apology.

The wind fluttered the kitchen curtain, and Emma could almost see Martha standing there icing a chocolate cake for G.W. The little cottage had taken on a new charm for Emma, and instead of sadness, she only felt joy thinking about the couple who had made it a home for twelve short months.

Maybe G.W. was right. True love was worth the risk...always.

CHAPTER 9

*P*a had suggested that Hays stay home from church and take a nap, but instead, he had come to his property along the Sabinal River. He hoped to keep his mind off Emma, but she was the only thing he could think about.

Hays laid on the banks of the river, his hands behind his head, and closed his eyes. His mind wandered to the day he kissed her, and instead of pushing the thought away, he allowed himself to bask in the peace and happiness the memory gave him.

Bella grazed nearby, nibbling on the dry grass while the river gurgled over rocks and roots. The sun shimmered through the canopy of leaves, offering short bursts of light on his face.

There really was no place on earth like this little spot of land. He hated to think that it might not be his.

Bella lifted her head, her ears twisting forward as she looked up at the rise of land.

Hays swiveled his head to see what had caught her attention—and his heart leapt.

"Emma." He scrambled to his feet as she nudged her horse down the path he'd worn in the soil and followed it to where Bella stood.

She stopped her horse, her gaze fixed on Hays.

Neither one spoke for several moments. Finally, he reached up and placed his hands on her waist and then lowered her to the ground.

She came willingly, and when he set her on her feet, she placed her hands on his upper arms, her green eyes searching his.

He smiled, and all the love he felt for her was harnessed in the simple expression. "What are you looking for, Em?"

Whatever it was, she must have found it, because she stopped searching and offered him a smile that matched his in intensity. "I'm looking for love."

His heart pounded hard as he took her hands and put them on his chest. "You've found it."

Tears shimmered in her eyes. "I've been so blind, Hays. Is it too late?"

Joy burst inside his chest, and he shook his head. "Never."

"I owe you an apology—"

"No. I owe you one."

She shook her head and he laughed.

They looked at one another for a moment, and then finally, she spoke. "May I offer you a gift for all your troubles, then?"

He pulled her closer, melding her curves into his. "What kind of gift did you have in mind?"

Emma stood on tiptoe, and like the last time they were by this river, she gave him a kiss—but now she placed that kiss on his lips instead of his cheek.

It was sweet bliss to hold her in his arms again, and this time, she stayed willingly and didn't pull away.

He finally broke the kiss, only to say, "That's the sweetest gift anyone has ever given me."

"Oh!" She giggled, a bit breathless. "That wasn't the gift. I got distracted and couldn't help myself for a moment."

Hays tilted his head back and laughed again. "You can get distracted anytime you'd like." When his laughter subsided, he grew more serious. "If that wasn't your gift, what is?"

It was her turn to take his hands in hers. She brought them to her lips and kissed his knuckles and then laid his hands against her cheeks. "My gift to you is my heart, in exchange for yours."

"Em." He pulled her close again, reveling in the way she fit perfectly against him. "It's all yours."

This time, he kissed her.

~

MARCH 7, 1874

*I*t was hard to believe a month had passed since Emma stood on the banks of the Sabinal River and accepted Hays's marriage proposal. Today she waited in the bedroom she had shared with Hope these past three months as her mama fussed over her gown and veil. The ensemble, as Miss Spanner called it, was more than Emma had ever imagined a humble pastor's daughter would wear on her wedding day, but G.W. had insisted on the very best for his first daughter-in-law, and Miss Spanner had agreed. It was a gift she couldn't refuse.

A knock at the door made both women pause.

"Who is it?" Mama dropped the veil over Emma's warm face.

"It's the father of the bride," Papa said from the hallway.

Mama and Emma exchanged a tender glance, and then Mama went to the door and opened it wide.

The look on Papa's face brought tears to Emma's eyes.

"The last time I saw such a beautiful bride was the day I married your mama." He entered the room and held out his hands. "You're lovely, Em."

She offered a nervous laugh mixed with tears as she took his hands. "Thank you, Papa."

"I'm happy I was able to get a minister to fill in for me today." He wiped at his cheek. "I don't think I could perform your marriage ceremony without choking up."

"We'll be late if we don't hurry." Mama grabbed Emma's bouquet of bluebonnets off the bureau and handed them to her.

Emma grasped the beautiful flowers, delivered earlier by her groom-to-be, who had picked them just that morning. He told Mama to tell her they were from the little rise above the river where their new house was under construction.

Emma lifted them to her nose, inhaling their fragrant scent, awaiting the day she could gaze upon them from her kitchen window.

Papa offered his elbow, and Emma lifted the train of her gown with her free hand.

They left the little cottage and walked through the yard to the church. Emma glanced across the road where the new schoolhouse was just completed. Two days after the street dance, the money had mysteriously reappeared in the church safe, and the construction had immediately begun on the building. They might never know who took it, though they both suspected Evelyn. She had access through her father on the elder board—but none of it mattered any longer. Come Monday, Hope would take over the new classroom, which pleased Emma very much.

But the schoolhouse couldn't hold Emma's attention today—not when Hays was waiting inside the church to marry her.

Papa stopped at the top of the steps and looked over at Emma. "Are you ready?"

Emma nodded, and Mama opened the door for them to enter.

Hope sat behind the piano at the front of the church, and the moment the door opened, she began the wedding march.

Everyone in the church stood and turned to look at Emma.

Sunshine streamed through the windows and washed the inside of the building with a golden glow.

David met Mama and offered his arm like a gentleman. He walked her to the front of the church and showed her to the pew on the left.

Papa squeezed Emma's hand, and they began to walk down the aisle.

Dozens of familiar faces greeted Emma—friends, neighbors, and students.

Connie straightened Emma's train and veil and then followed behind to act as Emma's maid of honor.

As they drew closer to the front, Emma had her first glimpse of Hays —and the smile on his face was unlike anything she'd ever seen. It radiated, making his blue eyes shine brighter than ever. Beside Hays was Gage, who would act as the best man.

G.W. Hart stood in the front pew at her right, with Austin, Bowie, Travis, and Crockett beside him. The only two missing were Chisholm and Houston, who could not be reached in time to come home for the wedding. Both brothers would be dearly missed, but Emma looked forward to the day she would finally meet them. For now, the rest were there to welcome her into the family.

The visiting minister was a young man who rocked nervously from foot to foot. When Emma and Papa finally reached the front, he asked, "Who gives this woman away in marriage?"

"I do." Papa lifted her veil and placed a kiss on her cheek before he rested her hand inside Hays's.

Hays laced his fingers through hers, his eyes filled with the promises his lips would soon confess.

He drew her close, and they faced the minister to pledge their hearts one to the other.

AUTHOR'S NOTE

First Comes Love was originally published in the Seven Brides for Seven Texans novella collection, released in 2016 from Barbour Publishers. It was the first of seven novellas, each following the story of one of the Hart brothers, who needed to get married by the end of the year or lose out on their inheritance. Each novella was written by a different author.

The collection was so much fun to write and collaborate on with the other authors. Each brother was unique, and their story was one of a kind. Although we don't explore those stories in this stand-alone novella, rest assured that they all had their own happy ending.

Thank you for coming along on another journey! I hope you've enjoyed this novella. Be sure to look for the others in the collection.

ABOUT THE AUTHOR

Gabrielle Meyer lives in central Minnesota on the banks of the upper Mississippi River with her husband and four children. As an employee of the Minnesota Historical Society, she fell in love with the rich history of her state and enjoys writing fictional stories inspired by real people, places, and events. You can learn more about Gabrielle and her books at www.gabriellemeyer.com.

THE HEART OF TEXAS

LORNA SEILSTAD

CHAPTER 1

MARCH 1874
BRADY CITY, TEXAS

$\mathcal{C}$aro Cardova lifted the shotgun to her shoulder and trained it on the *hombre* before her. She flicked a glance toward her poncho-clad cousin. He sat on horseback beside her with a noose around his neck. She wasn't a great shot, but with a gun full of buckshot, she didn't need to be.

She used the tip of her shotgun to indicate the direction she wanted the leader of this vigilante band to exit. "Step away from Señor Alvarez."

"Lady, we don't want to hurt you, but we will." The man spoke as if he was tolerating a naughty child. "This man's a rustler."

"Señor Alvarez is not a rustler. You have my word."

"Your word?" The man beside the leader laughed. "One Mexican covering for another. Slade, she's probably in on it."

Good heavens. They called him Slade. Slade McCord? Owner of the Mesquite? The most powerful man in the county? Or were there other Slades around? But if it was him, what was he doing here on the Walking Diamond?

"Let's get this over with." No sooner had Slade McCord spoken than one of the cowboys grabbed her from behind and disarmed her.

"You dogs!" she shouted. "Release me!"

"You heard the lady."

Caro turned to take in the man with the deep baritone voice that broke through the mayhem. A broad-shouldered stranger sat high on a buckskin quarter horse. The Winchester he aimed at the men seemed as at home in his hands as the Texas Ranger's star on his chest.

"There'll be no hanging here today." The Ranger sounded convincing, and she sent up a prayer that this lawman was right. "Release the lady."

The man holding Caro gave her a hard shove, and she fell to the ground. Her hands hit the rocky soil, and she winced.

"Near as I can figure, Ranger, there's one of you and six of us." Slade's hand hovered near his pistol.

"You might kill me, but not before I shoot you first." The Ranger didn't flinch. "Besides, who says I'm alone?"

The vigilantes peered into the trees surrounding them, but the dusk prevented them from seeing through the shadows. A hill blocked their view to the south, so they couldn't see who might be waiting there either. One man tugged on his collar. "Let's get out of here, Slade. Rangers travel in groups. We can take care of Alvarez later."

Slade glared at Ricardo Alvarez and then the Ranger. "I assume you'll take him in."

"If he's guilty"—the lawman nodded—"I certainly will."

Slade waited a few long moments and stepped back. From what Caro had heard, the man liked to win—at everything. A true Texan, he wanted the biggest and the best and wouldn't settle for anything else.

The men slowly mounted their horses and turned to leave, but before they were out of sight, the Ranger secured his weapon, hurried to her, and offered his hand. "Are you all right, miss?"

"I don't need your help now, and I didn't need it before." Caro swatted his hand away. "I had it handled."

"Sure you did. What were you going to do next?"

"I would have thought of something. I always do."

He frowned. "So this happens often?"

"No...no, of course not." She narrowed her gaze at him. She scanned the mesquite trees. Had any of them doubled back? "You took a big chance taking your eyes off those vigilantes so soon."

"My partner has them covered." He gave her a gorgeous dimpled grin, and she fought the urge to slap the handsome *gringo*. "Trust me."

Trust him? She didn't trust anyone, but especially a man with a badge who didn't have the sense to watch gun-toting thugs until they were out of his sight. And now he acted as if he'd saved the day to boot.

"I'm Texas Ranger Chisholm Hart, and the Ranger approaching is my partner, Whit Murray." He pulled a Bowie knife from his belt and sliced through the binding on Ricardo's wrists. "And you are?"

"Señorita Caro Maria Cardova Valenzuela, and this is Señor Ricardo Alvarez."

"Miss Valenzuela." He tipped his hat.

"Cardova."

"But you said—"

"My father was Hernando Cardova. Valenzuela is my mother's name. By American customs, I would be Caro Cardova, but I prefer both surnames."

"I see, and I apologize." He turned to Ricardo. "Sir, I know you've been through an ordeal, but I'm going to have to ask you some questions. It's my duty."

Duty. The word drove a spike in Caro's heart. Why did men always think they had to do their duty? Duty had killed her father, and at some point, would most likely kill this handsome, know-it-all gringo with dimples as deep as canyons.

Ricardo wrung the brim of his worn hat in his hands. "I understand. Come back to the Walking Diamond with us. I'm sure our boss, Señor Reynolds, will want to speak to you both. Perhaps Caro can make you supper to say thank you for your assistance in saving my neck. It's the least we can do. Right, Caro?" When she didn't respond, he nudged her arm. "Right?"

The Ranger sucked in his cheeks to keep from smiling. Did he actually think she would thank him? If so, he'd be waiting an eternity. Other women might fall at his feet when he came to their aid, but she knew better. This egotistical man needed to be taught a lesson.

Ignoring the lot of them, she mounted her horse, and a plan formed in her mind. She would most certainly make this interfering, dimpled Ranger supper—a supper he'd never forget.

◆◆◆

Chisholm eyed the man and woman riding in front of him and then cast a glance at his partner. After working side by side for over a year now, he and Whit didn't need words to communicate most things, and one look told him that Whit didn't trust Ricardo any more than he did. While Ricardo seemed gregarious to a fault, the way he fidgeted and avoided eye contact put Chisholm on guard.

Spring rains and warm temperatures had brought a lush green to this part of central Texas, southwest of Brady City. It brought a sense of nostalgia to him. Down south, at the 7 Heart Ranch, it was probably even greener.

The wide front porch of the Walking Diamond's homestead welcomed them. Well, at least the house seemed glad to see them. Miss Caro Cardova was about as warm as a rattlesnake and probably as deadly.

But she was a beauty. Her dark hair, secured with a strip of leather at the nape of her neck, hung down her back and bounced with the rhythm of her horse's gait. And even though he couldn't see her face now, he had no trouble recalling her eyes. Dark like molasses with a vivid ring of fire tucked deep inside.

Chisholm forced his gaze away from Caro and back to the house. While a far cry from El Regalo, the enormous 7 Heart ranch house at Chisholm's home, the Walking Diamond's hewn-log home sported two floors, three dormer windows on the front and three on the back, and a summer kitchen. He glimpsed a smokehouse out back and a barn and large corral to the east. Just the kind of spread he'd like to have someday.

The group dismounted in the yard, and a barrel-chested man with more salt than pepper in his hair came out of the house. He glanced from Chisholm to Ricardo and frowned. "Rangers, is there a problem?"

After introductions were made, the ranch owner, Hank Reynolds, dismissed Caro to her duties in the kitchen and asked the Rangers to join him in the house. Inside, it didn't take Chisholm and Whit long to explain the situation they had happened upon. "I can't thank you enough for what you did." Reynolds leaned on the edge of a walnut desk in the corner of the parlor. Whit and Chisholm sat across from him in wide, leather-clad chairs. "So you're here to address the cattle-rustling problem we've been having in these parts?"

Whit nodded. "We've been assigned to get to the bottom of the situation. What can you tell us about this man Slade?"

"Slade McCord's the owner of the Mesquite. His ranch has been hit hard by the thieves, and he's the kind of man who'd use someone like Ricardo to teach others what happens if you mess with him."

"So you don't think your Ricardo is in on any of this?" Chisholm asked.

"It's doubtful. Ricardo gets into his fair share of trouble, but he's never done anything illegal." Reynolds glanced up when a woman came to the doorway. She seemed to be an older version of Caro, only more serene. Her eyes were filled with kindness, but her demeanor spoke of a quiet strength.

"Eat! Eat!" She waved her hand toward the table.

"Gentlemen, I think you'll find Maria and Caro's food a treat."

The men took the seats Reynolds indicated, and Caro brought out three heaping plates balanced on a tray. Scents of seasoned pork filled the air, tugging on Chisholm's heart and reminding him of home. Caro placed the first plate in front of Chisholm, but he passed it on down to Whit.

"No, no, señor. That's for you." She smiled for the first time since they'd met, and his suspicions rose. What was this beautiful spitfire up to? Still, he took the plate back and thanked her.

Without saying grace, Reynolds untied the string around the cornhusk. "Caro, why don't you and your mother join us at the table tonight? We have so few guests, it would be pleasant for all of us to celebrate. Grab some plates and sit down."

Some disgruntled conversation carried from behind the door, but then the two women emerged and sat down in the empty seats. Both Caro and her mother bowed their heads in prayer before placing their napkins in their laps.

Caro lifted her head and again smiled in Chisholm's direction. "I do hope you like your food."

"I'm sure I will." Chisholm untied his cornhusk and forked a bite of the dough-wrapped pork. He blew on his fork, then slipped the morsel between his lips. Flames exploded on his tongue. Sweat beaded on his upper lip, and heat crept into his cheeks.

Boy, howdy, this was delicious! He closed his eyes and savored the sensation. It had been so long since he'd enjoyed a meal like this.

When he opened his eyes, Caro was staring at him, mouth agape. It was his turn to grin. "My compliments to the cook. I haven't had food like this since I left home and signed up to become a Ranger. Our cook, Perla, is known for her fine Mexican table, and this is every bit as good as hers. It's the kind of food I grew up on. I think even she'd admit it was excellent."

"But. . ."

"I like things spicy, Miss Cardova." He fought the desire to add a wink. "Guess you should know that."

He'd ask Whit later how hot his tamale had been, but Chisholm guessed it wouldn't come close to the fiery concoction Caro had made for him. She certainly had a creative way of making her point of how welcome he was and how thankful she'd been for his assistance. Watching her squirm throughout the rest of supper brought him more satisfaction than it should. He'd have to ask God to forgive him.

Whit blotted his napkin against his mustache and pushed his plate away. "So I'm assuming y'all discovered your missing stock after spring roundup. Have there been any more recent losses?"

Hank Reynolds set down his water glass. "Slade claims he's lost some recently, but that's not easy to confirm yet. My men say we're short some more too."

"We'll need to visit the other ranchers in the area," Chisholm said. "Can you possibly spare a man to show us around? It would save some time."

Reynolds leaned back in his chair. "I'm afraid with these rustlers around, I need all my men right now to keep watch over my herd, but Caro can show you the way to the other ranches. She knows this area as well as anyone." He flicked a glance in her direction. "And, of course, you gentlemen are welcome to stay in our guest rooms as long as you're in the area. It's an honor to have Texas Rangers around, and if I'm lucky, it will keep the rustlers away from my stock."

"Thanks. We'll take you up on that offer." Chisholm looked at Caro.

The embers in her dark eyes now flashed as hot as the peppers in his meal.

Apparently, Miss Caro Cardova was not happy with this arrangement. Oh well, it served her right. And the more he thought about it, the more he suspected he might actually enjoy some time in her fiery company.

CHAPTER 2

Caro dropped a pile of tin plates into the washtub, and suds splashed out. She'd add a soaked dress to the list of things that were the Texas Ranger's fault. She stuck her hands in the water, and they stung from her fall earlier today. That was his fault too.

"Caro Maria Cardova Valenzuela, what has gotten into you?" Her *mamá* slipped on an apron. "And how many peppers did you put in that poor man's tamale?"

"Enough." Caro rubbed the plates harder than necessary, rinsed them, and set them on the drain board.

"Enough to do what?" Her mother handed her a pot from the stove. "Give him blisters on his tongue?"

She immersed the pot in her washtub. "I wanted to teach him a lesson."

Her mamá chuckled and picked up a dish towel to dry the plates. "It seems that it was you who was educated."

"He makes me so angry." She scrubbed harder on the pot. "Why do men crave the praise of others? Why do they think they can march in and take over and that we should be grateful for their every effort?"

"Oh, Caro." Mamá sighed. "Are you sure that is what is bothering you?"

"What do you think it is?"

"Your *papá* loved you dearly, but he was a soldier, and he had a duty to do."

Caro hefted the washed pot onto the drain board and reached for a towel. "He was an anarchist. He didn't *have* to fight. He *chose* to fight. He wanted other people to applaud his great efforts more than he wanted to be with us. He wanted to be a hero."

"Caro! You will not speak ill of your dear, departed papá." Mamá carried the plates to the cupboard.

"He thought he could fix everything, but what did it get him? Nothing. What did we lose? Everything."

Mamá cupped her cheek. "He fought for us. The government was corrupt. He was willing to give his life to do what was right. Someday you will understand."

"I'm sorry, Mamá. I don't want to hurt you." Caro swiped a tear from her eye. "I know he was a good man, and I don't know why this Texas Ranger has brought up these feelings."

"Only God knows that answer." Her mamá smiled. "I've been praying for you. Take all of these feelings to the Lord and ask Him to help you sort them out."

"I do not think God wants to hear me rant."

"Don't be so sure. He is big enough to handle your hurt and your anger." Mamá kissed her cheek. "And try to be kind to the Ranger. Perhaps he's part of God's plan to bring you healing."

"I'll pray, Mamá, and I'll be as kind as I can, but I draw the line at that." She hung her apron on a hook. "The sooner that know-it-all Ranger is gone, the better."

◆ ◆ ◆

Sitting in Reynolds's spacious parlor, Chisholm patted his shirt pocket. He should've taken the time to read the letter from home while they were on their way to the heart of Texas. But correspondence from his pa or his six busy brothers was infrequent at best, so he cherished each missive. When he finally got time to read this letter, he planned on giving it his undivided attention and savoring every word. An ache rose in his chest. He missed his family more and more every day.

He glanced at Hank Reynolds and Whit playing chess a few feet away. Did Reynolds have family? No feminine items or portraits of any kind were in sight in the parlor. Had he never married? Was that why he'd hired Caro and her mother, in hopes of claiming a wife? If so, which woman did he hope to win?

"Checkmate." Reynolds moved his queen into place.

"Well played." Whit leaned back in his chair. "Maybe we can have another match before we leave."

"It would be my pleasure." Reynolds rang a little bell. "I'm sure y'all are both tired, and you have to get an early start. I'll have Caro show you to your room."

Caro didn't hide her frown when she was once again directed to help the two Rangers. They followed her up a wide staircase. Chisholm ran his hand along the worn, rustic pine handrail. Nice workmanship. He'd always loved woodworking. Maybe he'd have a chance to make a handrail for his own place once his Ranger days were over. His father had always promised him a piece of the 7 Heart Ranch, and he'd spent many hours on horseback passing time by imagining his spread.

He and Whit followed Caro down a short hallway until she stopped by a door on the right. "Here is your room. There are two beds, and there's water in the washstand. Since I have to go with the two of you tomorrow, breakfast will be at daylight."

Whit trekked inside and let out a low whistle. "This sure beats sleeping on the ground. You ladies have made this downright pretty."

Chisholm set his bag down in the hallway and turned to Caro with a grin on his face. "Thank you again for the delicious supper, Miss Cardova."

She crossed her arms over her chest. "It won't work."

"Excuse me?"

"Using your Ranger charms on me." She met his gaze. "You men of duty want everyone to think highly of you. You like to be revered. You want us to believe we need you to save us, but I, sir, do not need you."

He stifled a chuckle. While her temper surprised him, he found it oddly endearing. "I'll try to remember that."

"Please do." With a huff, she stormed off. But in her haste, she tripped over Chisholm's bag.

Chisholm could have caught her, but he didn't. She twisted and landed solidly on her backside with a thud.

She glared at him, accusation in her eyes. "Why didn't—"

He shrugged. "You said you didn't need me to save you, so I didn't." Without another word, he retrieved his bag, went inside the room, and shut the door, leaving a flustered Miss Cardova in a heap.

Still chuckling to himself, Chisholm took a seat on the bed's multicolored quilt, tugged off his boots, and withdrew the envelope from his pocket.

Whit punched a feather pillow into his preferred shape. "I heard you two out in the hall, and Chisholm, I think I can say with all certainty that that lady does not like you."

"I reckon you're right." He studied his father's script on the front of the envelope.

"Well, you're having way too much fun annoying her, but I guess you deserve a little fun. She seems like a lady who can take it." Whit spread his lanky frame over the bed. "Are you going to read that letter or hold it all night?"

"Guess I'll read it." Chisholm rubbed his chin.

"'Bout time."

Chisholm unsealed the envelope and took out the paper. His chest squeezed as he read the words on the page. Fear and frustration grew inside him and tangled like two tumbleweeds in a dust storm.

Whit sat back up, his bushy brows scrunched together. "What's it say? Bad news?"

"Sorta." A weight settled on Chisholm's chest. "For some strange reason, my pa has issued an ultimatum." He stared at the words on the page. "He wants to see each of his sons married and settled. He's given us one year to find a bride."

"The whole lot of you? All seven brothers have to marry up in one year?"

Chisholm nodded. "Or we lose our share of the ranch." The words tasted bitter on Chisholm's lips. "I can't believe he's doing this. My pa is a reasonable man, but this isn't fair. I'm a Texas Ranger, and I took an oath to serve and protect. Between the Indians and the thieves, Texas is awash in miscreants. Who's going to make this a civilized place to live if we Rangers take off willy-nilly to go courting?"

Whit smoothed his thick mustache with his hand. "There are Rangers who have wives. Some have even traveled with us."

"I remember a few, but I can't drag a soft little lady into a life like that. It wouldn't be right, and I can't take a wife and simply put her up at the ranch while I go off to do my job. I'd want to be there to take care of her." Chisholm stuffed the letter back in the envelope. "I think I have no choice."

"What are you going to do?"

"I'm going to pray about it, but as near as I can tell, I'll have to give up my share of the ranch."

CHAPTER 3

*H*umming "Fairest Lord Jesus," Caro looked out the window of the summer kitchen. The sun was barely peeking over the horizon, pinking the Texas sky and swallowing the night stars. She gave the scrambled eggs a final stir before heaping the yellow curds in a serving dish and setting them on the tray. Besides the eggs, she'd made fresh biscuits and gravy. Too bad the two Texas Rangers would be eating a congealed blob, but it wasn't her fault she'd not yet heard a peep out of either of them. She'd told them breakfast would be at daybreak, and she always kept her word—especially today.

She hefted the tray into her arms and carried it through the summer kitchen's door and into the main house. When she found Chisholm standing there, she came to an abrupt stop. The dishes clinked and the tray nearly toppled.

Chisholm Hart grabbed the edge. "Here. Let me take that." He took the tray and walked through the house's regular kitchen and into the dining room. After setting the tray on the sideboard, he turned to her. "I'm sorry. I didn't mean to startle you earlier."

Caro nodded mutely. This tough Ranger apologized? She began unloading the tray and arranging the food. It was going to be hard to remember how much she didn't like him if he kept being so nice. "I didn't realize you were awake."

His rain-blue eyes lit up. "I've already spent some time with the Lord, and I've got Whit's horse and mine saddled. I'll hitch a buggy for you after breakfast."

"I don't need a buggy." She planted her fisted hands on her hips. "I ride as well as any man."

"I saw that yesterday, but I thought you might be more comfortable in a buggy." Chisholm poured a cup of coffee. "Whit will be down in a minute."

His consideration touched her. She stepped aside and motioned to the spread on the sideboard. "Eat up before it gets cold."

"Ladies first."

"But. . ."

"It's going to be a long morning, and you need to eat. Besides, we can discuss our plans." He picked up a plate and handed it to her. "Please."

Caro heaved a sigh. How did this man catch her off guard at every turn? And how was she supposed to continue disliking him if he was a God-fearing gentleman? She'd prayed as her mother had recommended last night. She begged God to heal her aching heart, and she'd asked for an extra measure of kindness to get through the day. Maybe making the Ranger extra nice was God's doing.

Whit thundered into the dining room as she finished filling her plate. He dropped into a chair and released a loud yawn. "The rooster isn't even awake yet."

"Coffee?" Caro held up the pot.

Whit ran his hand through his bed-tousled, sandy hair. "Just give me the whole pot."

Chisholm loaded his plate with scrambled eggs. "In case you couldn't tell, mornings and Whit aren't really on speaking terms."

Caro laughed and passed the newcomer a steamy cup. A few minutes later, she found herself sitting across from the two Texas Rangers, enjoying the flaky biscuits and creamy gravy she'd whipped up before the sun had made an appearance. The Rangers didn't know it, but she'd also packed biscuits and ham in a lunch basket for them along with cinnamon-and-sugar-dusted churros. Perhaps it would make up for her cruel act last night. She'd put so many hot peppers in Chisholm Hart's tamale that his mouth was probably still burning today. At the time, she

THE HEART OF TEXAS

felt like he deserved it, but later, guilt had poked at her for hours, making her toss and turn.

Perhaps her mamá was right. He reminded her too much of her father. Today she would be as helpful as possible. Besides, it was in her best interest. The sooner the Ranger solved the rustling mystery, the sooner he'd leave.

Chisholm pushed back from the table. "Whit, I've been thinking. I reckon we shouldn't remove Ricardo Alvarez off the list of suspects just yet."

"He is innocent!" Caro set down her cup so hard, coffee sloshed out. She bit her lip and chastised herself for not controlling her tongue, but these two men did not know Ricardo as she did. "You have my word. He is not involved."

"Miss Cardova." Chisholm stood and put on his hat. "If, as you said, Mr. Alvarez was not responsible for the rustling, why were those men so ready to lynch him?"

Caro stiffened, fear making her stomach tighten like a noose. "I have no idea." If she explained, it would only make Ricardo look guiltier, and she had to protect him at all costs.

Chisholm frowned. "I don't believe you."

"That, sir, is your choice." Tears burned in her eyes. She rose, gathered the plates, and swept from the room.

So much for getting along.

◆ ◆ ◆

Chisholm slipped Bullet, his golden palomino, a lump of sugar as Caro sashayed across the courtyard toward the buckskin mare Ricardo Alvarez had saddled for her. With her dark eyes and hair and wearing a bright yellow dress, she looked like a sunflower in full bloom.

Caro slid a shotgun into the scabbard, then leaned close and spoke to Ricardo. Was she telling him they still suspected he might be involved? Although Caro seemed genuine to the core, Chisholm couldn't help but worry she might be fooling them. It was the hardest part of this job—always suspecting the worst in folks—but he'd learned to trust his instincts.

"They look pretty chummy." Whit mounted Buckshot, his spotted pinto. "Guess you can check her off your list of possible brides."

"Caro Cardova Valenzuela? My bride?" Chisholm let out a hearty laugh, and Caro turned. "You'd better watch your back. I think she'd poison you for suggesting such a thing, and then shoot me for letting you think it."

Ricardo held the horse as Caro mounted and then led her over to them. "Take care, *mi prima*."

Prima? Chisholm racked his brain for the translation. He'd spent hours with Perla, the Harts' Mexican cook. After his ma died, she'd been like a second mother to him, and he'd learned to speak Spanish quite well from her. So why was the meaning of that word escaping him? Was it a term of endearment?

Ricardo turned to Chisholm. "Señor Reynolds suggested you start at the Mesquite. They've been hit the hardest by the rustlers. He sent word you were coming, so they'll be expecting you."

"Thank you." Chisholm nodded. "And don't worry. We'll bring Miss Cardova back safe and sound."

Ricardo shared a look with Caro. "She can take of herself, señor. It's you who should be careful."

Chisholm nodded toward Caro to lead the way, but inside, he chafed at the idea that the Mesquite Ranch's owner and hands had been forewarned of their arrival. If anyone there was involved, the advance notice would give them ample time to cover up their participation.

He rode alongside Caro on the dirt road with Whit bringing up the rear. The morning sun had claimed the day by the time they finally got on the road, but one thing was for sure. Caro had been telling the truth about her riding ability. Although he'd witnessed her skill the day they met, he was even more impressed today. Not only was her riding excellent, but when they asked her some questions, her knowledge of the area proved outstanding, and she was truly helpful. She'd explained that the Mesquite Ranch sat between Señor Reynolds's Walking Diamond and another ranch called Tall Trees.

For the next few hours, they prodded her with more questions about the land and the ranch hands in the area. From what she'd heard, Tall Trees had only lost a few head, while the Mesquite had been hit hard by the rustlers, losing over fifty head. Reynolds claimed the Walking Diamond was down about thirty.

Chisholm did a quick mental calculation. If these men drove their cattle to Wichita, they could make over twenty dollars a head, so that meant combined they'd lost well over $1,600. No wonder he and Whit had been sent here to capture the rustlers.

Whit scratched his head. "What about the layout of the land? Is there somewhere a rustler could hide eighty-plus longhorns?"

"The Mesquite has a lot of hills and valleys, but I can't imagine being able to hide that many cattle anywhere. The men are just finishing spring roundup, so there are cowboys out and about all the time." Caro kept her eyes trained on the road without meeting either of their gazes. She might be cooperating, but she seemed determined to keep a distance.

"I'm thinking we may have several culprits working as a team." Chisholm reined Bullet in when they reached a creek. "What do you say we get off this road and do a little sightseeing before we get to the Mesquite?"

Caro laughed as she dismounted. "This is Brady Creek. It runs between the Mesquite and the Walking Diamond, so you are already there, but we can go wherever you'd like."

Chisholm led his horse to the water. "You're cooperating?"

"For the moment." She smiled. "But I don't think Señor Slade will cooperate if you delay much longer."

"Whit, why don't you go on to Slade McCord's ranch while Miss Cardova and I check things out around here? We'll catch up to you at the ranch in a little while."

"Sounds like a plan." His stomach groaned. "Why didn't we pack any grub?"

"It's not even noon yet." Caro rolled her eyes and then dug into her saddlebag. She produced three bundles wrapped in linen napkins. "Perhaps you can leave for the Mesquite after your second breakfast."

Chisholm chuckled, and the three of them sat on an outcropping of rocks. Both men unfolded their napkins and started to dig in.

"Gentlemen," Caro said firmly, "there will be no heathens around me. I expect a proper grace even out here."

Chisholm's gut cinched. He should have thought of that, and did she really think him a heathen? He could set her straight on that when they left. For now, he took off his hat and offered a prayer of thanksgiving, making sure to add a thank you for Caro Cardova's thoughtfulness.

At the "amen," he looked up to see her smiling, but she tugged the frown back in place within a fraction of a second. She might love the Lord, but she wasn't about to let any joy into her heart.

He drew in a long, slow breath. He'd have to do his best to change that. After all, it was the Christian thing to do.

◆ ◆ ◆

Caro took in the man kneeling before her as he studied the prints they'd found in the mud. His rolled-up shirtsleeves revealed the hills and valleys of his muscular arms. Even though she'd seldom responded, he'd kept up a steady conversation while they'd been riding along the creek, and all the while, he'd never stopped scanning the area.

She took a deep breath and willed herself to relax. It had been a long time since she'd felt safe enough to do that. Chisholm's presence might annoy her unbearably, but his demeanor certainly made her believe he was able to handle almost any situation. And his dimples made it easier to tolerate anything that came out of his mouth.

They'd come nearly full circle when he dismounted to examine something.

"These are fresh." He stood and wiped his hands together. "But that doesn't mean much. Let's give the horses a break."

Caro dismounted and led her horse, Angel, to the nearest mesquite tree. She slipped the reins around a low branch and secured them.

Chisholm brought Bullet alongside. "Hey, you used a bank robbers' knot. I'm impressed."

"You didn't think I knew how to tie my horse?"

"Of course, I did. I just didn't think you'd know to tie it that well."

"Ranger Chisholm, I am full of surprises." She flashed him a little smile.

"Of that, I have no doubt." He pointed to a large rock. "I think we've earned a break too."

The stiff breeze had loosened several strands from Caro's braid, and she paused to tuck them behind her ear. When she turned, Chisholm was staring at her. The look in his eyes made her breath catch, but he turned away, like a boy who'd been caught stealing cookies.

He cleared his throat and sat on the boulder. "So, Miss Cardova, how many brothers and sisters do you have?"

"I am an only child."

"Must be nice." He chuckled. "I've got six brothers."

"Seven boys? Your poor mother." Caro couldn't imagine living in a house full of men.

"My mother died during the war, so except for our cook, we have a house full of men."

"I'm sorry that you lost your mother." The familiar hole in her own grieving heart throbbed.

"It's just you and your mother here, right? Where's your father?"

"He died in a rebellion." The pain and bitterness came out in her voice.

Chisholm adjusted the hat over his eyes, and he spoke in a solemn tone. "In Mexico? In a war?"

"No, there was no war."

"Then what was he fighting for? He must have had a good reason to leave you and your mother."

"Does it make a difference if his cause was just?" She swallowed hard, emotion clogging her throat. "Either way, it is the same for us. He is gone, and we are alone." She took a deep breath and squared her shoulders. "But we are strong, and we can take care of ourselves. We came to Texas to escape the effects of my father's choices, and we were blessed to find work at Señor Reynolds's ranch. God has taken care of us."

"And I'll pray that He continues to do—"

A shot echoed through the valley, and a bullet whizzed between them.

CHAPTER 4

Chisholm half dragged, half carried Caro behind the boulder. He covered her body with his own and drew his sidearm. Another shot rang out and sailed over their heads.

"Stay down!" He needed to get a look at where the shots were coming from, but did he dare trust Caro to remain behind the boulder?

He lifted his head and caught a glint off a rifle on the opposite hill. He could return fire, but a handgun wouldn't begin to make it that far. He lowered his head, pressing Caro's down as well.

"Get off me!" She shoved against him. "And why aren't you shooting back?"

For all her bravado, her body trembled against his chest, and he pulled her closer. "Too far. It would be a waste of bullets. We're pinned down for the moment."

Blood rushed in his ears, and he fought the urge to dive from their location. He chanced another glimpse in the shooter's direction. No shots. Where was the man now?

"Is he gone?" Caro whispered.

"I'm going to check. Keep your head down." Chisholm rolled to his side and eased out from behind their cover. He took off his hat and tossed it in the air. If someone was out there, they'd fire at the motion.

Nothing.

He climbed to his feet, his gaze never leaving the open area between the two hills.

"Is it clear?" Caro peeked her head over the boulder.

"If it wasn't, you'd be dead." He held out his hand, and to his surprise, she took it. Her wobbly legs betrayed her, and she'd have fallen if Chisholm hadn't caught her. "Easy."

Caro let him hold her for only a second before she yanked away, but it was a delicious second. The strong desire made his breath hitch.

She hugged herself. Was she as rattled as he was by the contact? Seeming to come to her senses, she shook the dust off her skirt. "Someone doesn't want us here."

"I got that message loud and clear."

"We can take a shortcut from here to where we saw the shooter perched. I know the way."

Chisholm retrieved his hat. "I'll come back later. It's my duty to find these criminals, not yours."

A stony expression fell over Caro's face, and all the progress he'd made with her seemed to wither. What had he said?

"Caro, let's get our horses and go meet Whit."

Well, he'd used her name again, and she hadn't slapped him, so maybe not all of the progress was gone.

"Ranger Hart, I realize it's not my *duty*." She said the last word as if it were bitter on her tongue. "But I suggest we investigate the area where the shooter was sitting before the trail grows cold."

"If you call me Chisholm, we have a deal."

"Then, let's get moving—" She paused. "Chisholm."

He liked the sound of his name on her lips. He blinked. Had he been staring at her lips? Good heavens. If he was attracted to Caro Cardova, only one thing was for sure: He'd been away from womenfolk way too long.

◆ ◆ ◆

Caro stomped her foot. She was a woman, not a child. Why had Chisholm changed his mind about seeking out the shooter as soon as they'd met Whit on the road?

"It's for your own good." Chisholm glanced at Whit, hoping he'd add his opinion, but Whit remained silent. "The more I think about it, the more I'm sure we should come back after we see you home."

"You're not familiar with the trails around here. You need my help." And if she didn't help them, the dimpled Texas Ranger would be around forever. "Besides, you said you believe whoever shot at you is long gone."

He scowled. "They shot at *us*, not just me."

"Look at this dress." She held out the sides of her yellow skirt. "If they were shooting at me and missed, then they are a very poor shot. I'm an easy target."

"She's right, and it will go faster if you let her help, Chisholm. Remember, you need to get on with that *other* job."

Chisholm's brows drew together. "Other job?"

"The one your dad gave you." Whit chuckled.

He shot a glare in his friend's direction and then climbed on his horse, silent for the first time all day. Apparently, the Texas Ranger didn't like to lose an argument. That was fine. Neither did Caro.

Whit reported that Slade McCord had said his wranglers had completed ninety percent of their roundup. He had no idea why the two ranches were targeted or where the stolen cattle could be hidden. His men, Whit said, seemed deeply loyal to Slade McCord.

"But I wasn't impressed with Mr. McCord. He's a hard man, and I had the feeling he'd do anything necessary to get ahead." Whit turned to Caro. "And he sure believes Ricardo is behind this."

"Slade McCord is a fool." Caro steeled her shoulders and pointed to the trail ahead. "I think the shooter would have taken this path."

Conversation ceased as they made their way along the narrow trail. When they neared the shooter's possible perch, the two men dismounted and examined the area on foot. Caro's stomach knotted every time they appeared to find something of interest. What were they looking at? As much as she insisted Ricardo was innocent, she wasn't absolutely certain. He was an excellent shot. Would they discover something that linked him to the cattle rustling—or worse, to the shooting?

At length, Caro joined the men. "How do you know what you're looking for?"

"Chisholm is a great tracker. It's what got him into the Rangers." Whit stood. "The rest of his brothers were on a cattle drive, but they left him home to keep an eye on the ranch. A Texas Ranger came looking for a murderer, so Chisholm used his tracking skills to hunt the man down and helped the Ranger capture him."

"How did you learn to be a tracker?"

Chisholm walked over to stand with them. "Pa found a wounded young Kiowa when I was a boy. He stayed at the ranch until he was better. I spent a lot of time with him and taught him enough English so we could talk. We became friends, and he taught me to see things that most people miss."

"Such as?"

"Come here. I'll show you." He returned to the area he'd been examining. Squatting, he pointed to a set of prints. "Tracking is like a story that's being written and unwritten every day. You have to look for the parts and put the pieces together. You can't learn it overnight. It's like learning to read. You start with the ABCs, the easy stuff, such as where the suspect was heading, then you work up to the hard stuff with hidden meanings, the suspect's mindset or intent."

She knelt beside him. "You can tell all that from a footprint?"

"Not just one, but yes, you can from a set of prints." He bent low and pointed to an area. "You see this grass? See how the animal—in this case, a person—pressed it down, and now the shiny side of the grass catches the sunlight? That shininess disappears in about two hours, and the grass will return to normal in a day, so that means someone has been here in the last two hours. Our shooter most likely made this track." He stood and held out his hand to assist her. They walked over to another set of prints. "See how far apart the prints are here? Our shooter was running. He mounted his horse here."

His knowledge was impressive, but his willingness to share the information with her, as if she was an equal, meant even more. "Anything else?"

"The man's horse has a loose shoe. Right hind. He headed toward the Mesquite."

"So the shooter is one of Slade's men?" She exhaled and said a silent prayer of thanks.

"Possibly. We can only know he went that direction." Chisholm wiped his brow with a blue kerchief. "I found a shell casing from his rifle but nothing else. The trail ended when the shooter went across that rocky area."

"So we can't follow them farther?" She shielded her eyes to scan the area. "Wouldn't his trail begin again on the other side of those rocks?"

Chisholm looked at Whit and frowned. "Probably, but we're taking you home before we look further. It's too dangerous. We don't know what we're walking into."

If she left, she couldn't be sure Ricardo hadn't been involved, so she hurried to her horse and quickly mounted. "The sun will set before you get back, and I want to see more of your excellent tracking skills. I will be careful and do as you say."

Whit chuckled and followed her lead, but Chisholm grumbled about doubting she'd do as he or anyone else said. He was most likely correct.

They headed up a hill, and he rode beside her, still grousing. She smiled in his direction. She needed him to believe she would keep her word, but he didn't return a grin. Too bad. She'd grown rather fond of his dimples.

Her cheeks warmed. How had Chisholm gotten her to thinking fondly about him or his dangerous dimples? She needed to focus on the task at hand and make sure this man left the area before she found herself admiring more about him than his dimples.

Whit reined Buckshot in and let out a low whistle. "Well, look at that."

CHAPTER 5

*C*hisholm's jaw tensed. Cattle grazed in the valley below them, trampling any hopes of following the shooter's tracks. Five cowboys rode lazily around the herd. Could one of them be the shooter?

Whit patted his pinto's neck. "Do you want to go speak with those men or just head back?"

"Let's go talk to them. Maybe they saw something." Chisholm led the group down the hill but stopped well away from the ornery longhorns.

One of the cowboys approached on horseback, his rifle across his lap. Chisholm guessed the man to be in his forties. His crooked nose and the scar on his cheek said he didn't mind a good fight. His worn Stetson told Chisholm the man was no stranger to the range. He seemed to zero in on Chisholm's badge and dipped his head slightly. "I'm Digger Harrison, range boss of the Mesquite. What can I do for y'all?"

"A man shot at us from up on that hill, then took off." Chisholm eyed the weapon Digger carried. A range boss would have an excellent aim. "Seen anyone riding through?"

"We saw a Mexican about an hour ago." Digger jabbed the rifle into the scabbard.

Chisholm slipped a glance toward Caro. "How do you know he was a Mexican?"

"Sombrero." He looked at Caro. "Probably that one she was protecting the other day. You should have let us lynch him."

Caro's face reddened. "Other cowboys wear sombreros!"

"I know, Caro. Take it easy." Chisholm turned back toward the foreman. "Did you notice anything else? The direction the man rode off, perhaps?"

He nodded toward the Mesquite Ranch. "Probably went that way to throw you off." Whit cleared his throat. "What about your wranglers?"

Digger leveled a gaze at Whit. "Been here all day."

Caro grabbed her saddle horn and leaned forward. "You'd swear to that? On a Bible?"

The man's eyes narrowed to slits. "Crazy woman, you calling me a liar?"

"Mind your tongue, Harrison, and she didn't call you anything." Chisholm nudged his horse between them. "We'll be going now. Thanks for the information, and if you see anything else, send word to the Walking Diamond. We're staying there."

"Watch your back, Rangers," Digger added, then turned to leave. "This country can be pretty unfriendly to folks who go poking around— especially with the likes of her by your side."

For the next half an hour of their ride, emotions fired inside Chisholm. Fury at the man's veiled threat directed toward Caro. Anger at her for stirring things up. Frustration at losing the trail and at the lack of answers, and gnawing concern that Ricardo might indeed be involved. Why had Digger suggested that having Caro around was dangerous? He knew about how she'd stopped the lynching, but had her outspoken tendencies caused trouble before?

He rubbed the crick in the back of his neck and swept the area for danger once again. Maybe they should abandon the road?

Caro seemed to sense his unrest and said little. Maybe the early-morning hours and long ride were taking a toll on her. Even her smart tongue seemed to be losing its edge. Only Whit kept a steady conversation going, mostly with himself. They stopped to water their horses and then hurried back to the road.

Without any further problems, they made it back to the Walking Diamond before sunset. Chisholm dismounted and went to assist Caro. To his surprise, she let him.

"I need to go help my mother." She paused. "I know you are angry. I'm sorry. I didn't mean to upset Mr. Harrison."

"I'm not angry with you."

She lifted her dark eyebrow and nuzzled Angel.

"Well, not really." He drew in a long breath. "I didn't like how he spoke to you."

She blinked. Once. Twice. Her gaze did not leave his own.

"Mi prima!" Ricardo came out of the barn, walked directly to Caro, and pulled her into an embrace. "You are back. Your mother is waiting for you in the summer kitchen. How did your day go?"

She looked over her shoulder as Ricardo directed her toward the ranch house. Was that appreciation he saw on her face, or was Chisholm simply imagining that he'd made a crack in Caro's ironclad armor?

◆ ◆ ◆

Morning prayers on the front porch brought Chisholm a renewed sense of purpose, a clear head, and a direction to follow. This case was about rustlers and not Caro Cardova. When they'd shared their day with the Walking Diamond's owner, Hank Reynolds, he'd said Digger Harrison wasn't the type who'd hurt a lady. Still, he recommended they leave Caro behind if they went into town.

Since they didn't have a lot to go on yet, Chisholm suggested that he and Whit would go into Brady City and ask some questions. Rumors in small towns were a lot like a ball of yarn. If you pulled the string of maybes carefully, you might finally get some honest answers.

Armor back in place, Caro handed them filled canteens and said they'd best be on time for supper as she had no intention of holding it for them. Still, something in her tone made him doubt she meant it. Somehow, she seemed a little softer, more bark than bite now.

By midmorning, they reached Brady City.

Whit tied his horse to a hitching post in front of the town's general store. "All I'm saying is, you're awfully protective of her."

Chisholm let Bullet finish drinking from the trough and then tied him as well. "I'd be protective of any woman, and you know it."

"True, but if you dig down deep, I think you'd see you might actually like that she-wolf."

"Same as I'd like a case of measles" Chisholm grunted. "You talk to the storekeeper, and I'll head down to the saloon and talk to the barkeep."

Chisholm's boots thudded against the boardwalk, the familiar jingle of his spurs calming the irritation Whit's words had caused. What was his partner thinking? Chisholm was a gentleman, and he'd treated Caro Cardova like any other female in Texas. But he had to admit, she was a puzzle, and he liked a challenge. Was there an inkling of truth in Whit's observations? Nah, he just felt sorry for her. She was alone, and the only man who cared for her seemed rather worthless. She deserved better than Ricardo.

He crossed the dirt street to the saloon and pushed through the swinging doors. Given that it was so early in the day, he was surprised to find several people already imbibing. He made his way to the bar, and the barkeep was quick to offer him a drink on the house since he was a lawman.

Chisholm put his foot on the brass rail at the base of the bar. "Make it a sarsaparilla, and we have a deal. But what I really want is some information."

The barkeep chuckled. "Not sure I have much of that. You might try the school."

"Oh, I imagine you know more about this area than most folks. For example, did you hear about the man who was almost lynched?"

"Ricardo?" The barkeep grinned, revealing a host of crooked teeth. He set a glass in front of Chisholm and filled it to the brim. "Even if he was innocent, it wouldn't have been a great loss if they'd done it."

Chisholm took a swig. "Do you think he's innocent?"

The barkeep shook his head. "He's not smart enough to do it alone, and he's usually not—"

A chair fell over behind Chisholm, and he whirled to find a man stumbling. Ricardo?

Here? Drunk before noon? Did Caro know?

"Hey! Give me back my sombrero!" Ricardo batted at the hat a man dangled just out of his reach.

Chisholm waited to see if the men in the group taunting Ricardo complied with his request. When they continued, Chisholm stepped forward. "Give it back."

"We're just funnin' him." A young redhead waved the hat again. "Why would a big, fancy Texas Ranger care about the likes of him?"

"Give it back." Chisholm kept his voice firm and low.

The redhead relented and tossed the hat to the floor. Ricardo scrambled for it, nearly falling in the process. Chisholm grabbed the hat and stuck it on the unsteady man's head.

The barkeep picked up a fresh glass and polished it with a white cloth. "Like I said, lately he's not sober enough to do it, Ranger. Waste of good Texas air."

Chisholm draped Ricardo's arm over his shoulder and led him stumbling toward the swinging doors. "Come on. Let's get you home."

He shouldn't judge, but what did Caro see in this no-account drunk?

◆ ◆ ◆

"You promised to stay near home."

Caro ignored her mother's pleading and wrapped a shawl around her shoulders. "*You* promised, Mamá. Not me. But I won't go far. I only want to ride out to see if the bluebonnets have bloomed. They are close, and they'd make a lovely bouquet on the table for our guests."

"Very well." Her mother kissed her cheek. "But I wish you'd wait for one of the Texas Rangers to escort you, or even Ricardo."

"He should be in the barn. If it pleases you, I'll ask him to ride with me."

Her mother smiled. "Thank you, my precious one."

Caro searched the barn, but Ricardo was nowhere to be found. Worse, his chores were not yet completed. Where was he now? If Señor Reynolds discovered Ricardo had shirked his responsibilities again, he'd be fired for sure.

She rolled up her sleeves and reached for a pitchfork. She had little choice. Instead of riding out in search of bluebonnets, she needed to muck out stalls.

Family or not, Ricardo would pay for this one.

◆ ◆ ◆

Chisholm fought the urge to give Ricardo a lecture all the way back to the ranch. Since the man wouldn't remember a word of it, it wouldn't do any good. He'd save their "discussion" until Ricardo was sober. He'd better wait until Whit returned from town, as well, because Whit could make sure Chisholm didn't haul off and hit the cowhand.

Where had the idea of hitting Ricardo come from? When Chisholm became a Christian, Pastor Darby encouraged him to stop using his fists to settle problems and start using the brain God had given him. It had been years since he'd truly wanted to pummel someone, but that desire was growing every time he looked at Ricardo.

Chisholm dismounted in front of the barn and hurried to assist Ricardo before the man fell. Caro would be furious if he let her beau get hurt. "How could you do this to Caro?" The words exploded from his mouth before he could contain them.

Ricardo gave him a lopsided grin. "Caro, mi prima." He muttered something unintelligible in Spanish.

Chisholm led the man inside the barn and stopped short when he spotted the back of a shapely woman in a calico dress, heaving manure out of a horse stall. Like Ricardo, she released a string of exasperated words in Spanish. Chisholm translated enough to know Caro was not a happy woman.

Ricardo made a retching sound, and Chisholm whirled to find him with his hand pressed against his mouth. Chisholm grabbed hold of his arm. "Oh no, you don't. Not in here."

CHAPTER 6

*C*hisholm dragged Ricardo outside and let the man empty the contents of his stomach beside a fencepost.

Behind him, Caro's skirt rustled. She laid a hand on Chisholm's arm. "Is he ill?" She appeared to catch a whiff of the air, and her face paled. "He's drunk again?" Skirting Chisholm, she faced Ricardo, who had yet to stand. She slapped the hat off his head. "You promised, Ricardo. No more liquor. Are you listening to me?" When he didn't answer, she picked up a tin bucket and banged it against the fence.

Ricardo winced. "Stop, mi prima. The world is spinning." He rubbed his brow. "I'm sorry. So, so, so sorry."

Chisholm slipped his hand under the man's arm. "Help me get him to his bed."

Caro didn't move. When she turned toward Chisholm, her eyes shone with tears. "I...I can't."

Her pain was palpable. First, her father and now the man who held her heart.

Another man had let her down. Chisholm made a silent vow to not be the next one.

Once he'd deposited Ricardo in his bed, Chisholm followed the scraping sound of the pitchfork, punctuated by Caro's rantings, to a stall in the far corner. He stilled the pitchfork with his right hand.

Caro pivoted, holding fast to the tool. Tears slid down her dust-covered cheeks.

Chisholm gently grasped her wrist. "I'll handle this."

She met his gaze defiantly, but like a milk bucket with a hole in its side, the fight seemed to seep out of her. When he gave the pitchfork a little tug, she released it.

What he'd give to take her in his arms and comfort her, but that was Ricardo's place.

Something the man didn't deserve.

He knew he shouldn't, but he couldn't help himself. In one swift movement, he slipped his free hand around her waist and pulled her into his arms.

Caro leaned into his embrace. Did he make her feel safe? Secure? As though she wasn't alone? He lifted his hand to stroke her hair.

She suddenly yanked away and raised her hand to slap him.

Chisholm caught her wrist. "What was that for?"

"For being a man."

"You're afraid you might like me, aren't you?"

Her cheeks bloomed with color, but before he could say another word, she whirled and marched from the barn.

What a little spitfire. But in those few moments he'd held her, he'd gotten a glimpse behind her ironclad armor. Caro was a woman who wanted to be loved, but it was going to take one fearless man to stay the course and find a way to her heart.

Chisholm shook his head and laughed. He might face down the worst marauders in Texas, but not even he was that brave.

◆ ◆ ◆

Chisholm had completed the work in the barn by the time Whit returned from town. After washing up, they went inside for supper, only to discover that Hank Reynolds was still out with his men.

Caro's mother set a covered serving dish on the center of the dining table. "Where are the flowers, daughter?"

"I didn't get any," Caro called from the other room.

"They are not yet in bloom?" Her mother laid a folded napkin at each place.

"I didn't get to the field to see." She pushed the door open, carrying a cast-iron pot. "Ricardo—"

Her mother pointed to the empty spot. "Ricardo?"

Caro set the pot on the table, then spotted Chisholm and Whit in the room. "Never mind, Mamá."

"She wanted to see the fields of bluebonnets," her mother explained, before slipping out to the summer kitchen. She returned with steaming cornbread. "I told her you said she should not go out alone, but she wouldn't be stopped."

"It doesn't matter, anyway, since I didn't venture beyond the barn." Caro motioned the men to their seats. "Señor Reynolds said for the two of you not to wait for him."

Whit pulled out his chair. "You aren't joining us?"

"It's hardly proper with Señor Reynolds not home." Caro wiped her hands on her apron. "And I'm sure you have much to share with one another. My mother and I will eat in the summer kitchen tonight."

"Caro, wait." Chisholm picked up his napkin. "Where are these bluebonnets you were heading out to see?"

"Not far. I would have been fine."

"That's not why I asked." He poured himself a glass of milk from a striped pitcher.

"The bluebonnet fields are in the south quarter."

"Good. That's exactly the area I wanted to search tomorrow." He smiled. "Will you show me the way?"

"If I must." But her words didn't match the upward tug pulling on the corners of her lips.

Caro and her mother left them for the rest of the meal. Chisholm found the shredded beef perfectly seasoned this time, with a pleasing amount of spice and heat. The rice and beans only added to the delicious supper. Whit ate so much cornbread slathered in butter that Chisholm had to remind him Hank Reynolds hadn't yet eaten.

Throughout the meal, they caught up on the events of the day. Whit said he'd learned that the current rustling problem wasn't the first time cattle had gone missing, but it was the biggest loss ranchers had had to rustlers. No one seemed to like Slade McCord much, so there wasn't much sympathy for his losses, but most people liked Hank and were sorry to hear he'd lost so many. One man mentioned a group of drovers who'd come through town about a month ago who seemed sort of suspicious, but no one had seen any of those men since.

Caro returned with a sweet custard flan for dessert and served each man a generous portion.

Incessant pounding on the front door brought Chisholm to his feet, but Caro reached the door before him. She opened it, and Slade McCord stormed in, shoving her in the process.

"Is there a problem, McCord?" Chisholm stepped between Caro and the man.

"I'll say. We lost another ten head today in broad daylight." He came toe to toe with Chisholm. "What are you doing to catch these men?"

"Easy, McCord." Chisholm glared at the man just as he'd seen his father do, until the man stepped back, then took a long pause before answering McCord's question. "For your information, we're investigating. How many head do you run, McCord?"

"About three hundred."

"Since it's calving season, how do you know those ten cows haven't wandered off to give birth somewhere alone? Or maybe your count is off?"

"You're a lawman, not a rancher."

"My pa is GW Hart, and I grew up on the 7 Heart Ranch of Hartville." He crossed his arms over his chest and watched McCord's eyes widen. "I can see you've heard of it. So you know we run a whole lot more than three hundred head."

McCord's jaw tensed. "Where's that no-account Mexican?"

"Ricardo has been here all day," Caro insisted.

"And I suppose you're going to be the one to vouch for him."

"No, I am." Chisholm took a deep breath. While he hadn't actually been at the ranch all day, Chisholm knew the man's whereabouts, and he'd been in no condition to rustle cattle. "I know you're frustrated, but that doesn't give you cause to bust into this house and treat Miss Cardova disrespectfully. I suggest you go on home. It's too late today to do anything, so Whit and I will be over in the morning to check things out."

Caro's lips thinned to a hard line, but her shoulders sagged. Was she growing weary of protecting Ricardo? Tired of him repeatedly disappointing her?

Like a Texas twister, McCord blew out as quickly as he'd come.

Chisholm turned to Caro. "I'm sorry about the bluebonnets, but I have to do my duty first."

"Of course, you have to do your *duty*." Caro's icy tone stung. She walked away, not leaving him a chance to discuss it further.

But no words would smooth it over, anyway. Judging by the pain in her eyes, he'd let her down, just like Ricardo. Chisholm hated it, but it couldn't be helped. Maybe skipping the bluebonnet outing was for the best. Not only was Caro Cardova taking up too much of his prime thinking time, she was in love with Ricardo Alvarez, and Chisholm had no business spending time alone with her.

◆ ◆ ◆

Caro needed to be alone. She went to the summer kitchen and filled a glass of water. The cool drink did little to stem the ache coursing through her. She'd handled Chisholm's news badly. If he just hadn't used the word *duty*—

She sat down at the small table and rested her head in her hands, praying. She asked God to forgive her bitterness and to soften her words. Her mother had often said her anger would be her undoing. Was she right? The Bible said, *Be ye angry and sin not*, but Caro hadn't mastered that yet. She pressed her hand to her roiling stomach. Could God help her find peace with men like her father and Chisholm? If she didn't, she could never marry. Would it even be possible for her to love? Why did it all hurt so badly?

At a soft knock on the door, she looked up to see her mother.

"Are you all right, Caro?"

"I needed to be alone for a while—to pray."

"I'm glad you're seeking the Lord." Her mother moved to the larder. "I just spoke to the bunkhouse cook, and he said a couple of the night wranglers didn't make it in for supper. The problem is, he forgot to save them some—what does he call it?—grub? I thought I would take them a basket of food."

"You?" Caro stood up.

"I'm still quite capable of riding, and I taught you, remember?"

"Yes, Mamá." Caro placed a napkin in the basket. "But I'll go. The sun has not yet set, so if I hurry, I can be back before dark. It will give me a little more time to think and pray."

Her mother placed the cooled shredded beef and the rest of the rice and beans in the basket, then passed the basket to her. "Be careful."

Caro saddled Angel, the horse Señor Reynolds let her use, and rode off at a gallop. The evening's breeze chilled her cheeks. Soon she felt at one with the horse beneath her. No hurtful memories. No worries. No anger. No bitterness. Only the joy of riding.

She rounded the bend in the path and headed to the flatland where the cattle were currently grazing. A solitary figure on the horizon caught her eye, illuminated by the mellow hues of the setting sun. Was it one of the rustlers?

She slowed Angel, but the man heard her approach and turned. Chisholm. Even in the dimming light, she recognized his solid build and confident movements. He motioned for her to join him. She rode up, bracing herself for a lecture about venturing out alone in the twilight.

Chisholm took hold of Angel's bridle and stroked the horse's neck, then lifted his gaze to Caro's face. "What brings you out tonight? Miss me?"

"Hardly." So much for controlling her tongue. She took in his tired features and softened her tone. "And I could ask you the same thing. I'm here to deliver supper to the night wranglers. The *cocinero* said the men didn't get any grub tonight."

"So you came alone?" But when she started to answer, Chisholm held up his hand. "I know. You can take care of yourself."

"I was going to say it was not yet dark, so I wasn't worried. Why are you out here?"

"I had some thinking to do." He rubbed his hand over his stubbled face. "You know, whoever shot at us knew we'd be on that road."

Caro frowned. "But only the men from this ranch knew that."

"No, remember Mr. Reynolds sent word to the Mesquite Ranch that we were coming." He looked up at her. "Whoever is behind this is from one of those two ranches."

"Someone is stealing from their boss."

He nodded. "Or we could be dealing with a crew. There could be people on the inside at either or both places."

"But where are the stolen cattle? They have to be somewhere."

"True. Finding the missing cattle is the key. Tomorrow afternoon, I want to start an exhaustive search." He paused, appearing to weigh his words. "Caro, when I found Ricardo, he kept saying how sorry he was. He repeated that to you. I know you and he are—close, but are you absolutely certain he isn't involved?"

Every muscle in Caro's body tensed. "He did not steal those cattle. You brought him home from town yourself."

"I agree, but do you think he might know more than he's telling anyone?"

An imaginary lasso wrapped around her waist and pulled tight. Did Ricardo know something? Only in the last month had he begun to drink. Was he drinking away guilt? No, she couldn't think that way. She had to protect Ricardo. Señor Reynolds had taken him off the herd because of his drinking, or so he said, and threatened to fire Ricardo if there were any more problems.

"Caro." Chisholm's voice was soft. "Do you think you could ask him if he knows more than he's saying?"

"And then tell you?" She couldn't keep the mica-hard edge from her voice. "I will not betray him for you or for anyone else. He and my mother are all I have left."

◆◆◆

Chisholm lay in bed, staring at the streaks of moonlight on the ceiling. His six-foot-three frame meant his feet hung over the end of the bed, the curse of being George Washington Hart's son.

Caro's words, *"He and my mother are all I have left,"* kept replaying in his mind. Did Caro allow Ricardo to court her because she thought she had no other options? Or was it out of a sense of duty to her mother?

He'd kept watch over her until she'd delivered the basket, and then, keeping his distance, he'd followed her back to the house. He'd upset her not once, but twice, in one night. He reckoned he was the last person in all of Texas she wanted to see tonight.

Raised voices outside put him on alert. He crawled out of bed and moved to the window. Pushing the thin curtain aside, he peered down into the yard below. Whom was Caro talking to?

He eased the window upward and immediately recognized the

second voice as Ricardo's. Guilt nudged him as he eavesdropped on their animated conversation, all in Spanish. Chisholm mentally translated as much of the conversation as he could. Ricardo seemed to wobble, and Caro steadied him. Had he been drinking again?

After Caro begged Ricardo to tell the truth, Chisholm sat on the bed and tugged on his boots. Ricardo muttered an answer Chisholm couldn't hear, but he didn't miss Caro's promise to protect Ricardo, no matter what.

That was it. Enough was enough. He stormed through the house and threw open the front door. Caro and Ricardo spun, but the quick movement sent Ricardo flailing. He landed on his knees at Caro's feet.

Chisholm marched toward her. "I know you love him, but why are you protecting him?"

"Of course, I love him." Caro reached to help Ricardo stand, then reeled to face Chisholm. "Don't you love your family? Wouldn't you do anything to protect them?"

"By all means." Chisholm sucked in a breath. "But he isn't your family. He's your suitor."

"My suitor?" Caro snorted aloud. "You are *loco*."

"Don't try to deny it. He calls you 'mi prima,' and I heard you beg him to tell me the truth."

"You understood that, but not 'mi prima'?"

"My Spanish is rusty."

"Apparently." She released a little giggle, which irritated him even more.

"Well?" Chisholm crossed his arms over his chest. "What does it mean, then?"

"*Prima* means *cousin*." She brushed the dirt off Ricardo's back. "And for your information, he told me nothing of which you would be interested. He's had too much to drink—again—and I got no answers to the questions you wanted me to ask."

"Ricardo is your cousin?" Chisholm needed to say the words aloud to confirm them.

How could a trained tracker miss those clues? "I guess that changes everything."

"Indeed." She slipped her arm around Ricardo's waist. "Go to bed,

Chisholm. There's no duty for you to perform here. I am perfectly safe with my cousin."

But Chisholm's boots seemed leaded as he watched strong, loyal... beautiful Caro usher Ricardo to his bed in the barn.

Her cousin. Well, that certainly did change everything.

◆ ◆ ◆

Caro laid down on her bed and sighed. After last night's escapades with Ricardo and Chisholm, she needed a little nap.

She awoke with a start only to find her mamá standing at the foot of her bed. She could not believe her own mother would help Chisholm, but one look at the freshly pressed shirtwaist in her mother's hands confirmed it.

"Chisholm said he wants to look at the area near the bluebonnets after lunch, so he needs you to show him the way." She set the shirtwaist on Caro's bed. "I did this up for you, since the one you're wearing is smeared with jelly and is not presentable."

"I didn't say I'd go with him."

"No, but I did." Her mamá folded her hands in front of her. "And I am as stubborn as you, but more sweet about it. You'll learn this someday. Now, hurry. He'll return soon."

Mouth agape, Caro watched her mother stroll out of the room. Caro had taken extra care to avoid Chisholm Hart this morning, and now her mother was thrusting the man into her day. But she knew better than to fight with Maria Valenzuela. Her papá had called her mamá a silent warrior and said she won every battle by sheer will. Over the years, Caro found his words to be true. She could only pray to be more like her.

Caro changed into the clean shirtwaist, then removed the leather thong from her hair. She gave the waves a quick brushing and then braided a thick ponytail. After twisting the ponytail into a bun, she secured it with pins, which the wind would probably dislodge in minutes. If her mother wouldn't think it scandalous, she'd allow all her curls to hang loose.

Chisholm was waiting when she came into the parlor. He flashed her a dimpled grin, and her knees weakened. No man should be so attractive.

"I saddled Angel. She's outside."

"Good. I was afraid she was in the dining room." She released a little giggle and pulled on her leather riding gloves. "We should get going. I need to be back in time to help Mamá with supper."

Her mamá walked into the room with a basket. "No need. I'll handle it. And in case you are delayed, here is a supper for the two of you to share."

Chisholm took the basket and thanked her mamá, then held the door for Caro. She brushed his arm as she passed by, and a tingle rippled through her. Did Chisholm notice? And why did this outing seem so different than the other times they'd been side by side?

Somewhere in the last few days, Chisholm had gone from a Texas Ranger to a man who made her heart beat faster. She wasn't sure when it had happened, but today she was acutely aware of the difference.

As they rode, Chisholm filled her in on what they found at the Mesquite Ranch. About ten head were indeed missing from a small herd they had grazing near Brady Creek. Chisholm was disappointed to hear they hadn't gone out looking for strays, but he scouted the area anyway. Unfortunately, with all of the cattle prints, the tracks revealed nothing.

"I spoke to the Mesquite's wranglers, and they insist the only thing they saw was the Walking Diamond's cowhands and stock on the other side of the creek." He paused. "Unless Slade's boys are lying."

"How will you find out?"

"The truth always comes out eventually." Chisholm paused, seeming to weigh his words. "Listen, Caro, about last night, I'm sorry."

"You were eavesdropping, weren't you? How did you know what we were talking about? Do you speak Spanish?"

"Obviously not enough." Chisholm adjusted his position in the saddle. "I told you our cook, Perla, was Mexican. I picked up what I could from her. But I want to apologize not just for eavesdropping, but for making assumptions."

"I forgive you." Caro's heart softened at his genuine, humble words. Her father had been a proud man, and she didn't recall ever hearing an apology from his lips. "And I must admit, your assumption gave my mother a great deal of laughter this morning."

"And you?"

"To be honest, I laughed till I cried."

"Glad I could start your day off with a smile." He grinned and nodded toward a hill not far from them. "Are we close?"

"To the bluebonnet field, yes. To your rustlers, I have no idea. Race you to the top." Caro raised her eyebrows in challenge a second before she snapped the reins and Angel surged forward.

Chisholm gave a whoop and followed suit. Caro loved the excitement flowing through her veins. She had a bond of trust with Angel, and the horse responded to her every movement. She reached the crest of the hill first, but before she could rejoice in her accomplishment, the words were stolen from her lips. She reined to a stop at the scene before her. A carpet of violet-blue greeted them, cascading down the hill and into the valley below. Light-green leaves and dots of white accented gorgeous bluebonnet blooms. Her breathing stilled. Was there any sight in all of Texas as glorious as this?

◆ ◆ ◆

"It's breathtaking." Chisholm shifted from the bluebonnet view to the view of Caro, who was clearly filled with awe at the sight. All the sharpness of her features that came from remaining so guarded was replaced by the kind of uninhibited joy he'd seen on children's faces. He didn't want to steal a second of this moment from her, so he waited in silence.

Since he'd learned Ricardo was her cousin, he couldn't stop the undeniable attraction he felt for Caro from taking hold. It didn't make sense, but still, it was there. It was as if an imaginary wall had to be knocked down. He should run away as fast as he could, but something held him there. Was it the feelings he wanted to explore, or was it his father's ultimatum to find a wife?

Bullet whinnied, breaking the reverence of the moment. "Sorry. He doesn't have the best manners." Chisholm smoothed Bullet's glossy mane. "What d'ya say we give the horses a break while we bask in this view?"

Caro couldn't wait to soak up the sights and tuck them in her heart until next year. Once Angel and Bullet were enjoying a grassy snack, Chisholm spread the blanket from his bedroll on the ground and motioned for Caro to have a seat. He retrieved their supper basket and joined her on the blanket. He lay down on his side, propped his head on his hand, and stretched out his legs, but Caro was so enraptured by the bluebonnets that she barely acknowledged his presence.

He didn't blame her. The bluebonnet fields would stop anyone— man or woman— in their tracks. Only God could paint this kind of picture, but Chisholm was more enraptured by the view of her.

He forced himself to turn back to the flowers before them. "'Consider the lilies how they grow.'" Chisholm whispered the words from the book of Luke that came to mind. "'They toil not, they spin not; and yet I say unto you, that Solomon in all his glory was not arrayed like one of these.'"

Caro smiled at him with her soft, full lips. "Perfect scripture, Chisholm. Thank you."

"It seemed appropriate."

He cleared his throat. No more looking at her lips. "Hey, Caro, look." He pointed west.

She squinted against the sun. "Is that a calf by that bush? Right in the middle of the flowers?"

"Sure is. I wonder where her mama has gotten off to."

"Maybe she's lost."

"Then her mama will find her." He chuckled. "And by the way, she could be a he."

"Or she could be a she." She pulled off her riding gloves and tucked them in her waistband. "Can we stay here and make sure her mother comes? I'd hate for her—or him—to be left alone."

His gaze swept the area. "Sure. I see no reason to hurry. I'm pretty sure the rustlers aren't keeping that stolen stock out here in the blue-bonnet field. Any caves nearby?"

"None that I've ever seen."

"Good." He sat up. "I've done my duty. Let's eat."

Hurt flashed across Caro's face, and then her lips narrowed in a thin line. In an instant, the hedge around Caro's heart seemed to grow like the flowers in the field. Why? He hadn't done anything to put her off, or at least he didn't think he had. His pa told him once that a quiet man was usually thinking, but a quiet woman was usually mad. Hmm.

He set the basket between them like a shield. "What's got your hackles up? Everything was fine one minute, and then you became as cold as ice the next. What did I say to get you all rankled?"

She glared at him, her dark eyes flickering with anger. Was that how she kept folks at a distance? Scared them out of talking to her? Well, he didn't intend to back down.

He softened his tone, gentling her like he would a foal. "Talk to me, Caro."

"It's that word." She spit out her reply as though it pained her, then lowered her gaze and clutched the handle of the basket.

"What word?" When she didn't answer, he slipped his knuckle under her chin and lifted her face. "What word, Caro?"

Tears filled her molasses-colored eyes. "Duty."

"You don't like the word *duty*." He lowered his hand and chewed on the thought. "Does this go back to what you told me that first night I came? You think I want the people to praise me? That I'm a Texas Ranger because I want to be a hero?"

"I don't believe that anymore." Her voice caught. "You are a Texas Ranger because you love Texas and Texans. You take your responsibilities seriously. I know you aren't doing this for the glory." She dashed away a tear with her index finger. "My father was a man of duty."

"And he left you." Chisholm could see the pain in her eyes. He could think of a hundred reasons why her father might have felt he had to make that choice, but none of them would heal the vulnerable little girl inside the woman standing before him. What could he say to bandage those wounds?

"Caro, he loved you."

"Not enough to stay."

There it was. The crux of Caro's pain, and the truth of her admission throbbed inside him. If he let this seed of affection he was feeling blossom, he could never leave her—not even if Texas called.

CHAPTER 7

aro lifted the checkered napkin covering the food in the basket —meat- and cheese-filled empanadas and a glass jar of salsa she'd canned herself. She forced a smile. She needed to get this conversation back on even ground. "Chisholm, tell me about your brothers."

Chisholm released a long breath. Was he as relieved as she to return to a casual topic?

As she set out the food her mother had packed, he rattled off the list of siblings, and Caro tried to memorize each name and what he said about them. One brother was a storekeeper and one was a doctor. One had been badly hurt in the war. The youngest was twenty-one, and Chisholm said he was four years older.

"Are all of your brothers tall like you?"

"Some are. Some aren't. My pa and Bowie are six-foot-four, and I'm six-foot-three. I couldn't quite measure up, I guess."

Caro opened a tin of cookies. "Was it hard being the second to the youngest?"

"I think I'm a little like Hays. I was too young to help fight in the war, so in a strange way, I felt like I sort of missed out." He chuckled. "Guess I've wanted to live up to the things my big brothers did most of my life. Show them I can be something too."

"So you became a Texas Ranger?"

"That was probably part of it. At least at first." He tucked a napkin into his shirt collar. "Caro, I'm a good Ranger."

"And you're a good person." Heat rose in her cheeks. "We'd better eat now."

He offered grace, then snagged an empanada. Maybe it was the view, or maybe it was the way Chisholm prayed, but Caro felt as if God were sitting on the blanket with them.

Chisholm topped his meat pocket with salsa. Her mother had packed the hottest kind Caro made, but he didn't bat an eye at the heat. Apparently, he truly did like things spicy. If only she had sun-ripened tomatoes to make fresh salsa, it would be so much better. She set the bottle of milk aside that her mother had packed since Chisholm seemed accustomed to using his canteen.

Throughout the picnic supper, they chatted about Chisholm's family ranch back home and about her years growing up in Mexico.

To her delight, the tense moment they'd shared evaporated and conversation now came easily. When they finished eating, he packed the basket and carried it to Bullet while Caro folded the blanket.

She looked down into the valley at the bawling calf and squinted. There was something in the bluebonnets she'd not seen earlier. "Chisholm, look at that calf from this angle. What's behind those rocks?"

He shielded his eyes with his hand. "I think we may have a problem." He grabbed his rifle and a rope and started down the hill. After he'd walked a couple of yards, he turned to her. "You coming?"

"But you always say—"

"So you're going to start listening to me now?" He laughed and held out his hand.

Don't take his hand. Don't take his hand. With each step closer to him, she repeated the words, but her body didn't listen. His hand felt so strong wrapped around her own. They strode through the bluebonnets toward the calf. The poor thing had bawled so much, she was hoarse.

As they neared, the speckled red-and-white calf skittered to the side, revealing the mother longhorn, lying in the bluebonnets behind a rocky outcropping. The calf looked at Caro with round, pitiful eyes.

"Is the mama...?" She couldn't finish the sentence.

"Yes, I sure think so, but let me go check. If she isn't, be ready to run." He winked at her.

"Now you're teasing me." She rolled her eyes. "And I do know that since I live on a ranch, but even I can tell that cow doesn't look up to much of a chase."

"True." He took a step forward, and the cow made no movements. He poked her with the barrel of his gun, then laid his hand on her side. "She's gone. She looks young. Maybe a heifer."

Caro joined him and spotted the mountain-shaped *M* branded on the cow's hip. "She's one of Señor McCord's. What are we going to do with the calf?"

"She's only about a day old. Since she's up and about, I'm guessing she got about a day's worth of feeding before the heifer died." In two long strides, Chisholm was beside the calf. He scooped the forlorn creature into his arms. "I'll carry her up to the horses."

They began the climb, but even under the load of the calf, Chisholm didn't seem winded. All along the way, he kept saying soothing things to the sweet little orphaned calf that made Caro's heart swell. Between the song of the birds and the carpet of bluebonnets underfoot, this had the makings of a perfect moment—if the poor calf hadn't just lost her mama.

"How much does Bluebonnet weigh?"

"Bluebonnet? I guess that name fits, but it hardly sounds like something Slade McCord would name her." He adjusted his grip. "And I'd say she only weighs about sixty pounds."

"I told you the calf was a she."

He chuckled as they reached the crest of the hill and set Bluebonnet down.

"She's probably hungry. I wish we could do something for her." Caro scratched Bluebonnet between the ears. "Wait. We have milk. Mamá packed it in the basket."

She started to move, but he placed a hand on her arm. "Stay there. I'll get it." He returned a few seconds later. "Now we just have to get it in her."

"I've got an idea." Caro pulled one of her gloves from her waistband. "Can I borrow your knife?"

Chisholm handed it to her and she cut a small *x* in the tip of the index finger. She held the glove open and directed Chisholm to fill it with milk. "Now what do I do?"

"Get her to drink it."

His dimples deepened but he didn't laugh. "You don't want to do it?"

He laced his fingers and cracked his knuckles. "As you always say, you don't need my help."

"I don't think this falls in that category."

"Then say, 'I need your help.' "

"Chisholm, truly?"

He hooked his thumbs in his pockets. "You aren't going to let this starving little heifer suffer because you're stubborn, are you, Caro Cardova Valenzuela?"

CHAPTER 8

"Well?" Chisholm glanced from the calf to Caro. He shouldn't tease Caro about asking for help, but he couldn't resist the opportunity. Exasperation looked absolutely beautiful on her.

Caro huffed. "This is ridiculous."

"Then just say it."

"If I must." She rolled her eyes. "Chisholm Hart, will you help me?"

"Of course." He straddled the calf to hold it steady. "Ready?"

"I'm going to feed her? I thought you were going to help."

"I am helping." He pointed to her hand. "Let's start with getting her to suck. I'll talk you through it. First of all, let her suck on your fingers."

Caro wrinkled her nose. "You want me to put *my* fingers in her mouth?" He nodded, and she bit her lip as she slid two fingers inside the calf's mouth. "Her tongue feels like sandpaper."

"Now squeeze a little milk out of the glove so she'll get a taste of it. Then slide the glove's finger in and slowly slip your hand out."

"She's not sucking."

"Lift her jaw straight up and squeeze the sides of her mouth a little." Chisholm rubbed the calf's side. "As soon as the milk starts to trickle in, I'm sure she'll catch on."

The calf 's sucking pulled on the glove, and Caro's face lit. "She's doing it! We did it."

"We make a good team."

The calf emptied the glove, and Chisholm held out the bottle of milk. "Refill?"

He poured the milk in and then stepped away from Bluebonnet, but the calf continued drinking from the glove. "We'll have to get going pretty soon if we're going to make it back to the Mesquite."

"Do we have to take her back to Slade's?"

"You know we do. Don't worry, though. It's in his financial interest to keep her alive. He'll either get a cow that lost her calf to adopt Bluebonnet, or she'll be a bucket calf. Either way, she should be fine." He filled the glove with the last drop of milk and passed it back to Caro. "You finish up here with Bluebonnet. I have one more thing I want to do before we go."

Chisholm returned a few minutes later, and Caro held up the empty glove. "She drank every drop." She narrowed her gaze at him. "What are you hiding behind your back?"

He withdrew the two honey-scented bouquets of bluebonnets he'd just picked.

"One for you and one for your mother."

Caro stared at the bouquets, her eyes wide. She looked at him with a strange wonderment, and his insides warmed.

Then came a sobering chill. As a Ranger, he'd learned to listen to his instincts, and everything in him told him to run away from this beautiful lady. She might fascinate him. She might make him want to protect her. She might definitely make him want to kiss her, but if he stayed, someday he would break her heart.

She didn't want a man of duty, and he was nothing but that. But how did he stop the pull between them and still catch the rustlers?

◆ ◆ ◆

Caro arranged the bluebonnets from Chisholm in the basket's milk bottle. It seemed fitting, and the flowers looked perfect on her nightstand. The ones Chisholm had picked for her mother adorned the dining room table, but Caro wanted her bouquet close. It was the only gift she'd ever received from a man, and she wished she could keep them forever.

But they'd be gone soon—just like Chisholm.

She tugged one of the flowers from the vase and sat down on the edge of her bed. She fingered the velvety bloom and lifted it to her nose. So fragrant. So sweet. So lovely. Exactly like the day she'd had. Saving the calf, working side by side, and learning about Chisholm's family had all been so special. She could still picture how Chisholm had held the calf all the way back to the Mesquite. McCord's men had taken Bluebonnet, promising they'd tend to her, before she and Chisholm departed. She and Chisholm stopped to give the horses a rest at Brady Creek, so by the time they arrived at the ranch, the Texas sky was alight with diamonds.

But he'd not kissed her good night.

It was most likely her fault. Everything had been perfect except for that one moment. If only she hadn't brought up the subject of her father, but it had underscored an important truth. Her father and Chisholm were cut from the same cloth, both burdened by the responsibility to change the world.

She stuffed the flower she was holding back in the vase. Chisholm might have a noble cause, but no matter how charming, kind, smart, or strong he was, he would leave her. He had a duty to perform, and it would always come first. She needed to forget about picnics and posies and kisses and remember that fact. But why did it have to hurt so much?

She dropped to her knees beside her bed to pray and lowered her face into her hands. Tears soaked her palms as she asked for strength to resist her attraction to Chisholm and pleaded with God to allow Chisholm to catch the cattle rustlers so he could be on his way. The sooner he left, the better it would be for both of them.

Fitful sleep plagued her, so she rose early and had most of breakfast ready when her mamá entered the summer kitchen.

"You look tired." Mamá set out the copper tub to wash clothes later in the day. "Did you not sleep well?"

"Not really." Caro sat down at the worktable and took a drink of steaming hot coffee.

"The Ranger?" Her mother began to fill the tub with water. "Did he upset you?"

"No."

"Do you love him?"

"H...how could I?" Caro spit out. "We only spent one afternoon together. It's too soon and—"

"And he is too much like your father." Her mother smiled. "I saw it when he first arrived. Caro, being like your father is not a bad thing. I keep telling you that your father was a good man. I know you remember how much he loved you, but you refuse to recall that. You only see the end, when he left us."

"And Chisholm is a Texas Ranger. His heart is Texas. Even if he grew to love me, he'd leave like Papá." Hot tears filled her eyes, and she palmed them from her cheeks. "I don't understand it. Why do men feel such a great sense of duty?"

"What about you, Caro?" Her mother's voice was tender as she shaved soap into the pot. "What would your loyalties cause you to do? Protect Ricardo? Do something for me? Are you truly so different from the Ranger?"

Confusion filled Caro's thoughts. Loyalty. Fear. Love. Too many feelings to consider. How could she separate them?

"My child, your father wanted to make the world a better place for you." Her mamá placed her hands on Caro's shoulders. "Standing beside a man who was so easy to respect was my greatest joy, and I cherish every minute I had with him. Do not let fear steal away the joy God has planned for you."

Caro shifted so she could see her mother's face. "You think I'm afraid?"

"Aren't you?"

◆ ◆ ◆

Chisholm was afraid the rustlers had struck again. He led Bullet from the stables and watched Slade McCord ride in hard and come to a stop in front of the barn.

"What can we do for you, Slade?" Chisholm finished cinching Bullet, then glanced at Whit, who was putting a saddle blanket on Buckshot.

"I came to thank you." He pressed both hands to the saddle horn. "I wasn't there when you brought that calf in, but I wanted to express my gratitude. My men are bucket-feeding the calf. It took a while for her to catch on, but she's doing fine. Thought you might want to know."

"Yes, thanks. I'll tell Caro. She's the one who got the calf to take milk from her glove."

Slade seemed to ignore his reference to Caro. "Could you tell how the cow died?"

"There were no obvious reasons, but if I had to hazard a guess, I'd say it was a birth complication of some sort."

"Always sad, but it happens." Slade sighed. "Any news on the rustlers?"

Chisholm tugged on his gloves and mounted Bullet. "Whit and I are about to ride out to Tall Trees and ask around."

McCord scowled. "Tall Trees has hardly been hit at all. Shouldn't you be at my place, searching for clues or something?"

"We've already searched a lot of your ranch, but we'll be back at the Mesquite soon. You have my word."

"Guess that will have to do." McCord tipped his hat in farewell and rode off.

Whit looked over his horse's saddle at Chisholm. "Who was that man? Not the Slade McCord we've met the last few days. Maybe he wants us to think better of him."

"I guess anything is possible." Chisholm shrugged. "Stranger things have happened."

Whit pulled his horse alongside Chisholm's. "Speaking of strange things, what happened yesterday between you and Caro? She wasn't prickly or sassy this morning."

"She was quiet. Lots of women are quiet."

"Not her." Whit laughed. "Especially not when you're around. So what happened? You might as well tell me, because we've got a long ride, and I'll badger you until you spill. One of us should be having fun, and unfortunately, it looks like that someone is you."

"It was one afternoon, and there won't be any others."

"You didn't enjoy it?"

Chisholm cleared his throat. "No, I did. We had a great time."

"So?"

"So it won't work, and we have a job to do." He spurred Bullet into a gallop, leaving Whit in his dust. How could he explain to Whit that he couldn't see Caro because he did care for her?

CHAPTER 9

Caro entered the barn and looked around. Ricardo must have finished mucking the stalls because it smelled of dust and fresh sweet hay. She followed the clang of hammer against iron and found him behind the barn at the forge reshoeing Señor Reynolds's black roan. She paused to watch Ricardo work, mesmerized as he shaped a glowing horseshoe. Once the shoe was the way he wanted it, he used metal tongs and plunged it into a barrel of water. Steam rose with a hiss.

"Good morning, mi prima. What brings you to see me?"

She leaned against a pole. "Ricardo, it's time for the Rangers to move on. Don't you think?"

He nodded slowly. "But will they do that without finding the rustlers?"

"I don't think so, but if you help them—"

"I've told you before, Caro, I cannot." He lifted the roan's back hoof and held the cooled shoe against it.

Caro stepped forward. "But I think you know something."

"And if I did—note that I said 'if '—I must have a good reason for keeping it secret." He began to nail the shoe in place.

She waited until he'd finished and had released his hold on the horse's leg. "Then give me something I can pass on to the Rangers."

Ricardo stuffed the hammer in his back pocket. "Sometimes knowing things can be dangerous, mi prima. I won't put you in that position. It's for your own good."

Her throat tightened, and fear nestled in her belly. "Are you one of the rustlers?"

"No. You have my word." He wiped his brow with a kerchief. "But, Caro, you must stay out of this. It's for your own good, and if you care about the gringo Rangers, you'll get them to leave soon."

Her hand went to her chest, and her heart skipped a beat. "Would the rustlers hurt them?"

Before Ricardo could answer, Señor Reynolds rounded the corner of the barn. "There you are, Ricardo. Is my horse done?"

"Yes, señor." He handed the roan's reins to the ranch owner. "Ready to ride."

"Good, then you have time to run that errand I asked you to." Señor Reynolds turned to Caro. "And you can go back to work. I believe you've spent enough time away from your chores lately."

Caro stood dumbstruck for a moment. Usually gregarious, Señor Reynolds seldom spoke to her so sharply. And wasn't it his request that she help the Texas Rangers?

Perhaps he'd grown tired of the Rangers' interruptions, or perhaps Ricardo's recent mistakes had brought shame on their family.

Whatever the reason, she needed to be more mindful of her true responsibilities lest she, her mother, and Ricardo find themselves without a home.

◆ ◆ ◆

Chisholm heaved his saddle over the wall of the stall, then hung the rest of his tack on a peg. He reached for the brush and curry comb. Bullet deserved a good rub-down since he'd been working hard for days. Chisholm released a long sigh. Bullet wasn't the only one who could sure use a rest. Chisholm had barely slept a wink last night.

Whit brought Buckshot in and removed the cinch from the horse's girth. "I can't believe we went all that way just to find out that the wranglers miscounted the stock and they weren't missing any cattle."

"We still learned something." Chisholm drew the brush down Bullet's flank. "We now know only the two ranches are involved—the

Mesquite and the Walking Diamond. Whoever the rustlers are, they have a good operation going." He straightened and looked at Whit. "You know, we really need to wrap this up. We've been imposing long enough, and I think we're going to have to do something different. We need to catch the rustlers in the act—at night."

"You want to sleep under the stars?" Whit filled each of the feed boxes with oats for the two horses. "Which ranch?"

"Let's stay here tonight." Chisholm paused and looked at Whit over Bullet's back. "If we don't see anything, we'll move on to the Mesquite tomorrow. And, Whit, I don't want the cowboys to know about this."

"Are you going to tell Caro?"

"No, not even her." Guilt poked him in the gut. Caro would hate being left in the dark, but he had a job to do, and he couldn't risk anyone —especially Ricardo—finding out their plan. "We'll slip out after supper."

With the horses well cared for, Chisholm left the barn and headed to wash up at the pump. Whit followed a minute later. When his partner drew close enough, Chisholm splashed water in his direction. A melee ensued with water volleying back and forth, and soon they were both drenched from hair to boot. A little silliness was exactly what Chisholm needed right now.

He suddenly stopped and held up his hand. "Wait, something is burning." He turned and saw smoke billowing from the door of the summer kitchen. "Quick! Get some buckets from the barn!"

Chisholm bolted for the small building, praying Caro wasn't inside. He shouldered open the door. Thick black smoke poured out. He coughed and covered his nose and mouth with the wet kerchief from around his neck. "Caro! Maria!"

No answer. Fire from a pot licked at the beam above the cookstove. Chisholm grabbed a heavy rag rug from the floor and tossed it over the pot, smothering the fire. Whit appeared at the door with the buckets.

"Let's toss the water up there. That beam is smoldering." Chisholm coughed several times.

Whit tossed a bucketful of water at the beam, and droplets rained down on them. "Where's Caro?"

"Thankfully, not in here." Keeping the rug in place, Chisholm grabbed a towel and pushed the pot toward the back of the cooking area.

A shriek outside made the Rangers turn. Maria Valenzuela stood in the doorway with her hands pressed against her mouth. Caro stood beside her. "It's all my fault." Maria seemed near tears, and her voice shook. "I forgot the oil on the stove. I was going to make fried apple pies, but I had such a headache." She tipped her face upward. "Gracious *Dios*, protect us."

"It will be all right." Caro, her face pale, wrapped her arm around her mother's shoulder.

"But what if Señor Reynolds puts us out?"

Caro pulled her mother closer. "Señor Reynolds will understand. Come, Mamá. You need to lie back down. I'll serve supper."

Chisholm watched Caro usher her mother into the ranch house. The fear the two women felt hung in the air as thickly as the smoke. Would Hank Reynolds let Maria and Caro go over a fire like this? Perhaps if the damage were repaired, the ranch owner would be more understanding.

He turned to Whit. "That beam will have to come down. Think we can find a replacement around here?"

"Maybe." Whit rubbed his watery eyes. "You going to fix it?"

He nodded. "I'm a fair hand at building."

"And it might appease Reynolds?"

"Couldn't hurt." Chisholm picked up the chairs to clear the room. "From what we've seen, I don't think he'd put Caro and her mother out, but they didn't look so certain."

Whit drew his hand down his mustache. "Guess I better start looking for that replacement beam, then."

◆ ◆ ◆

Caro donned an old apron and rolled up her sleeves before joining Chisholm in the summer kitchen. Despite the diminishing sun, Señor Reynolds had not yet come home, and she wanted to have as much cleaned up as possible before he arrived. Soot and sawdust marred the cookware and dishes, but Chisholm and Whit had managed to splice a new beam in place above the stove.

Chisholm climbed down off the ladder and stuck his hammer in his back pocket. "Looks almost as good as new."

"Yes, it does. Señor Reynolds should be pleased." She set a kettle on the stove. "Where's Whit?"

"He went to wash up. Said his mouth tastes like soot."

She forced a smile. "How can I show you both my gratitude?"

"Consider it thanks for all of your help. We found everything we needed in the blacksmith area." He wiped his hands on his pants. "Thought maybe Ricardo and Mr. Reynolds would be home by now."

"They sent word there's a cow having trouble in a delivery. Ricardo may have fallen from Señor Reynolds's graces as of late, but he's an excellent *vaquero*—one of the best. If anyone can save the cow and calf, it's him." She picked up one of the buckets. "I'm sure you're tired. Your supper is on the sideboard. I want to do the cleanup in here while Mamá is resting."

Chisholm took the bucket. "I'll fetch the water while you stir the embers."

After he returned and poured water into the washtub, she insisted he go inside to fill a plate. He came back a few minutes later while she was shaving soap into the warm water. He dragged in a chair from outside and sat down. She loaded the washtub, casting an occasional glance at Chisholm, who devoured the meal. Poor man must have been starving.

As soon as he finished, he set the empty plate in the washtub and then carried the table and other chair back inside the summer kitchen. Next, he grabbed a towel and began to dry the clean dishes.

"You don't need to do that, Chisholm. You've done enough."

"I want to." He grabbed a pot from her drain board. "Caro, you said Ricardo had fallen from Mr. Reynolds's graces lately. Why is that?"

Caro hiked her shoulder. "I'm not sure. I thought he'd been caught drinking. Things seemed tense between them, but not so much anymore."

"Why?"

"Today I went to the barn. Ricardo was finishing shoeing Señor Reynolds's horse. When Señor Reynolds came in, he mentioned Ricardo running an errand for him. He was crotchety with me, but seemed amiable enough with Ricardo. Perhaps being around the house instead of working the cattle was some sort of privilege, and I read it wrong."

"Is that what you really think?"

"Maybe it's what I hope." The familiar bile of fear rose in her throat, and she wanted to tell Chisholm all about the rest of the conversation with Ricardo. Still, she held her tongue. She turned to get another pan, but instead hit Chisholm's solid chest as he reached for the same item.

Chisholm caught her arms, and his eyes locked on hers. He was so close, and he smelled of smoke, sweat, and masculinity. Had her heart ever pounded so hard in her life?

She noticed a scar beneath the corner of his right eye. How had he gotten that? Was he a boy or a man when it happened?

"I'm still a Texas Ranger." His voice was rough.

"I know." She shouldn't let this happen. He would leave her. But she could no more move than breathe.

His gaze dropped to her lips, and her tongue darted out to moisten them. He cupped her cheek, and she closed her eyes.

Just as the longing became unbearable, his tender lips met hers in the gentlest of kisses, making her wish this moment could last forever.

◆ ◆ ◆

Chisholm pulled away, but didn't remove his hand from Caro's face. His head said he shouldn't have kissed her, but his heart begged to disagree.

"Hey, Chisholm, why are—" Whit entered the doorway and stopped. "Oh, sorry."

Chisholm's hand dropped to her arm, but he maintained contact with her. "Your supper is inside on the sideboard, Whit."

"Uh, thanks, y'all." Whit hurried away.

Caro giggled. "Poor fellow."

"Don't feel too sorry for him. He'll get me back." Chisholm quieted, trying to form his thoughts into words. "Caro, I shouldn't have—"

"Don't say it. I'm not sure I can bear it." She pressed her finger to his lips. "I know. It can never work." Then she turned from his embrace and went back to her washtub, tears shimmering in her eyes.

A lump the size of Texas filled Chisholm's throat. *Dear Lord, what have I done?*

◆ ◆ ◆

Caro couldn't sleep. It seemed like a waste to lie there tossing and turning when there was more work to be done in the summer kitchen. She rose, donned her work dress and apron, and padded her way through the house. The mantel clock gonged eleven times, and she promised herself she'd work only an hour before trying to sleep once again.

She undid the latch on the back door and stepped into the moonlit, cool Texas night. Smoke still clung to the air, but she went ahead and drew in a deep breath. She wrapped her arms around her waist to stave off the chill as she listened to the cacophony of night sounds—frogs croaking, owls hooting, and insects chirping.

And hushed voices? She concentrated. Yes, voices in the barn. Had Ricardo returned? Or could the rustlers be right here?

If she went to wake Chisholm and it was nothing, she'd feel foolish. Surely, checking it out herself wouldn't be dangerous if she was careful.

She slipped across the yard, keeping her footfalls light. Lantern light leaked from beneath the barn doors. She peeked through the crack between the doors, and her heart plummeted.

Duty had called, and Chisholm was leaving.

◆ ◆ ◆

Chisholm shook out his bedroll and spread it on the hidden spot he and Whit had chosen overlooking the Mesquite Ranch's herd. Between riding most of the day, putting out the fire, and then splicing the beam in the summer kitchen, every muscle in his body ached for rest.

Whit had agreed to first watch, so Chisholm laid down using his pack for a pillow. He rolled to his side and punched the lumpy pack. He'd slept this way hundreds of times. Why was tonight any different?

He knew the reasons. The touch of Caro's lips still burned on his, but it was her words that plagued his sleep. "*I know,*" she'd said. "*It can never work.*"

His chest felt as if someone had set an anvil on it. Never work? He was a smart man.

Couldn't he figure something out?

He loved her.

The realization was mind-spinning. Here he was in the heart of

Texas losing his heart to a woman who couldn't stand him a week ago. Marrying her would let him receive his share of the ranch back home, but at what cost?

He flopped onto his back and stared at the stars dotting the sky, but no answers came to him. He prayed. Still nothing. He prayed some more, but it was no use. He was a sworn Texas Ranger. Even if he wanted to leave the Rangers, which he didn't, he couldn't do it right now, and Caro Cardova couldn't love him if he stayed. He might win her heart, but if he succeeded, what kind of husband would he be to leave her as her father had, even for a good reason?

Someday Caro might understand why her father had to go off and fight, but she wasn't there yet, and he had to accept that. She'd been through enough. If loving her meant leaving her for her own good and losing his share of the ranch in the process, no doubt about it, that's what he'd do.

◆ ◆ ◆

Sleep had eluded Caro most of the night, so when dawn broke, she welcomed the chance to go down to start breakfast. She dressed quietly, leaving her mamá sleeping.

When she reached the main floor, she stared at the hall tree. Señor Reynolds's boots and hat were not in their customary place. Had he stayed out all night with the herd? Maybe there'd been another cow that needed help, or worse, trouble with the rustlers. If Chisholm and Whit were still here, she'd ask them to go check, but they'd skipped out in the night. Why had they left without catching the rustlers? Had they received word from their superiors? It didn't make sense, but perhaps Ricardo would know something.

She crossed the yard to the barn and tugged open the door. The acrid scent that greeted her told her the stalls had not yet been tended. She made her way to the area that contained Ricardo's cot and personal effects. His bed was still made up. That was odd.

Her gaze landed on Ricardo's edged sheath knife. Its silver handle, inlaid with mother of pearl, made it hard to miss. Ricardo was never without the weapon. Ever. It had been given to him by his father, and he cherished it almost as much as his—

She whirled and looked above the doorway. Ricardo's rifle was there too. He knew too much about the dangers of Texas to leave either of the weapons at home. Even if he'd gone to town to drink, he'd have taken both weapons.

Fear inched up her spine, prickling her skin. Something was wrong, but what? If only Chisholm hadn't left when she needed him most.

CHAPTER 10

*R*ustlers could at least have the decency to show up when Chisholm and Whit gave up sleep to look for them. It sure would have made it easier. He and Whit could have arrested the miscreants and left the Brady City area without a second thought. Well, he'd have second thoughts about Caro, probably for the rest of his life, but at least she could move on.

They reached Brady Creek, which marked the separation of the two ranches. While the Mesquite herd was grazing a couple of miles away, the Walking Diamond's filled the plain. It was a good-looking herd. Bigger than Chisholm thought too. Hank Reynolds should be proud, and with the mild spring weather, the calves should be putting on weight in no time.

Three cowhands kept their eyes on the cattle, and a couple others were likely out looking for strays. Chisholm didn't see Ricardo's or Hank Reynolds's horses, so hopefully, the two men had taken care of the cow and gotten some much-needed sleep.

Bullet and Buckshot ambled toward the ranch house of the Walking Diamond. Neither Chisholm nor Whit felt the need to push their horses. There were no new leads, so what was the point?

Caro bolted from the barn, waving her arms.

Chisholm nudged Bullet to a gallop and hopped from his horse when he grew close. "What's wrong?"

Her dark eyes flashed with anger. "How could you leave?"

"We didn't leave. We went to look for the rustlers. I wouldn't leave without saying goodbye." He blinked. "Caro, what's going on? Why do you look undone?"

"Ricardo is missing."

"Are you sure?"

She glared at him and held up the sheathed knife. "See this? His knife and his gun are here, but he isn't. He would never leave his weapons behind. I'm telling you, something is wrong."

"Is his horse gone?" When she nodded, he went on. "Maybe he forgot them."

"He was almost lynched! If you were him, would you go anywhere without your gun?"

Chisholm rubbed his stiff neck. Caro had a point, but Ricardo was hardly a reliable person. He glanced at Whit, still on Buckshot, and knew his partner was thinking the same thing.

"I'm sure he's fine, but we'll go look for him. Where's Hank Reynolds? I'd like to talk to him first."

"And I didn't think of that?" Caro swung the sheathed knife in her hand as she spoke. "He is not here. He didn't come home, so he has no idea what's happening." Her voice broke. "What if Slade's men have come back and taken him?"

It was a possibility, but since he and Whit had been at the Mesquite, watching the herd, he found that doubtful. It was more likely that Ricardo was off drinking somewhere again.

Chisholm's stomach growled, but given Caro's state of mind, asking for breakfast was out of the question. Instead, he squeezed her arm and mounted his horse. "We'll find him."

They turned at the sound of the pounding of hooves. One of the Walking Diamond's cowboys rode in fast. "Twenty head went missing from the back quarter this morning. Mr. Reynolds said you should come while the trail is hot."

Chisholm looked from the concerned cowboy to a distraught Caro. He wanted to hold her and tell her everything would be all right, but instead, he had to do his duty. "Caro, I'm sorry. We have to check this out, but I'll go look for Ricardo as soon as I can. In the meantime, promise me you'll stay here. I can't look for him if I'm worrying about you."

◆ ◆ ◆

Caro hugged her waist as she watched the men depart. She'd always known Chisholm would choose duty over her, but the pain of it now made her stomach knot. What if Chisholm's duty cost Ricardo his life?

She wandered back into the barn and sat down on Ricardo's cot. Ricardo had volunteered to come with her mamá and her when they fled Mexico. Until recently, he'd been their rock. He'd taken care of them and made sure he found work at a ranch where the two of them could also be hired. And now he was in trouble. Where was he?

She'd promised not to leave the ranch, but she'd not promised not to look for Ricardo. Maybe one of the cowhands had seen him. After heading outside, she took the narrow path down to the bunkhouse and knocked at the shack's ramshackle door. No one answered. She nudged it open a crack. "Anyone home?"

When she didn't receive a response, she gave the door a push and entered. Bunk beds lined the walls, and the room smelled of unwashed bodies mingled with tobacco. She wrinkled her nose. Clearly, Ricardo wasn't here.

She turned to leave and spotted the branding iron by the door. She picked it up and studied it. The Walking Diamond's brand was two diamonds with stick figure feet on them. She drew the Mesquite's mountain-peaked M brand in the dust on the floor, then lowered the Walking Diamond's brand directly on top of it. A perfect fit. Could it be that simple? The Walking Diamond was rebranding the Mesquite's cattle while claiming they'd lost stock as well? No wonder they couldn't find them. Was this the truth that Ricardo had discovered?

Her heart drummed against her ribs, and her breath quickened. Chisholm needed to know. If Señor Reynolds was in on the rustling, then Chisholm and Whit could be walking into an ambush.

Still holding the branding iron, she hiked up her skirt and ran up the narrow path toward the barn. She considered filling her mother in, but there wasn't time. She set the branding iron aside, and in minutes, she had Angel saddled.

Taking hold of the bridle, she started to back Angel out of her stall.

"Where are you going, Caro?"

The deep voice made her blood freeze in her veins. She looked up to see Señor Reynolds in the barn's doorway. In his hand, he held an ebony-handled pocket revolver. "You know, don't you?" He looked from her to the branding iron. "I can see it on your face."

She tried to make her face a blank slate. "What are you talking about, señor?"

"Don't toy with me. I see the branding iron. You've always been too smart for your own good." He approached with the handgun and snagged a coil of rope from a hook. "Turn around, hands behind your back. And before you give me trouble, remember—you might be able to run, but your mother is not nearly as spry."

A heart-pounding, palm-sweating, mind-numbing fear consumed her. She had to protect her mother.

Caro slowly spun and did as he asked. *Lord, help me.* Her mind raced. She had to find a way out of this and warn Chisholm, but how could she risk her mother's life? Was this what Chisholm had felt? Torn between two impossible choices?

Once her hands were bound, Señor Reynolds lifted her by the waist and unceremoniously deposited her on Angel. He took the horse's bridle and led her out of the barn. "And remember, Caro, don't try anything."

He kept the gun trained on her as he mounted his roan.

She flicked a glance over her shoulder, hoping against hope Chisholm would return and save her.

So much for not needing him.

"Looking for the Rangers? I'm afraid they'll not be serving this great state much longer."

"And Ricardo?"

"Oh, you'll see him again." He gave her a rueful laugh. "I promise."

◆ ◆ ◆

With Bullet running at a gallop, Chisholm kept his gaze on the road ahead. A few miles from the ranch house, Whit had suggested he and Chisholm split up. Whit would handle the possible rustling, and

Chisholm would return to the ranch and look for Ricardo, just in case the man was actually in trouble.

Chisholm used his riding time to go over the rustling case. He tried to envision the tracks he saw on that first day out. He recalled the loose shoe. Loose shoes happened a lot on ranches, but Caro had mentioned that Ricardo had reshod Hank Reynolds's horse yesterday, and today Ricardo was missing. Could be a coincidence. But whoever shot at them that first day knew the route they'd be traveling.

Something wasn't adding up. They'd watched over the Mesquite's herd last night, and they'd seen the Walking Diamond's huge herd on the way home this morning.

Wait...

The Walking Diamond was supposed to have the smaller of the two herds, but that wasn't what they'd seen this morning. Hank Reynolds had a good hundred head more than Slade McCord. With all of his losses from the rustling, how could that be?

Unless...

He envisioned the brands of the two ranches. How had he missed it? The Walking Diamond's brand fit perfectly over that of the Mesquite's.

Chisholm spurred Bullet to a run. Maybe Ricardo knew too much about their operation.

He rode up to the summer kitchen. "Caro!"

Her mother emerged, her face full of anguish. "Oh, señor. She is not here. When I awoke, I saw her riding off with Señor Reynolds. Ricardo is gone too. Do you think he's hurt? Did the señor come and get Caro to help?"

Fear spiked in Chisholm's chest. Even though Caro had promised not to leave the ranch, she would go with the owner if he asked.

Maria wrung the towel in her hands. "I can see the worry in your face. Please tell me what is going on."

"I don't have time to explain." Chisholm fought to control Bullet, who, still full of energy, pranced in a circle, stirring up the dust. "But I'll find her, ma'am. I give you my word."

Nearing the barn, he reined in Bullet and dismounted. After wrapping Bullet's reins around a hitching post, he hurried toward the barn, careful not to disturb any prints. Inside, he immediately noted that Angel was missing. He studied the area. Caro hadn't been alone inside the barn. He leaned close to examine the prints in the stall. A man's boot prints left a clear mark in the dirt. Something lying in the straw drew his attention. He brushed the straw away and lifted the Walking Diamond's branding iron.

Blood drummed in his ears. Had Caro stumbled onto the same truth as he and confronted Hank Reynolds? If so, what would the cornered man do to her?

CHAPTER 11

*B*ranches slapped Caro's face as Reynolds forced her to ride through the trees with her hands tied behind her back. She'd prayed since the moment they left for a chance to flee, but with Reynolds holding Angel's reins, she had little choice but to follow. How could she leave Chisholm a trail to follow? He'd come for her eventually—if he could.

She closed her eyes and recalled the things he'd told her about tracking. He looked for things that others missed. Could she leave him some clues to follow without alerting Reynolds? She fingered the binds around her wrists and found a rough hemp thread protruding. She tugged on it and it finally gave way. She flicked it, praying it would land in the grass, though it was a long shot. She didn't even know if it was on the ground or stuck on the saddle's cantle.

The path they were on was packed hard. There would be few prints, but Chisholm could follow the marks along the path better. She'd spent hours training Angel on leg cues so she could direct her to the right or left without the use of reins. Nudging Angel's left side, the horse moved a bit to the right, stepping into the grass without Reynolds noticing.

Caro waited a few minutes before trying again. This time, she spotted a pecan tree to the north. Surely, a few of last year's pecans had fallen near the path. She urged Angel over and heard a satisfying *crack* beneath her hooves.

On and on she went. Broken blades of tall grass. Hoof prints in softer soil. Small broken branches.

And lots of prayer.

She urged Angel to the left.

Reynolds whirled around. "What are you doing?"

"Riding. Getting hit in the face by branches. Wishing I'd had breakfast."

His brows drew close. "Why can't that horse stay on the path?"

"Maybe because you won't let me have the reins." She shrugged. "Are we almost there? Have you hurt Ricardo?"

"You should be more concerned with your Ranger friends." He chuckled. "At least at the moment."

Fresh fear wound around her heart and squeezed the breath from her lungs. "What did you do to them?"

"They're getting too close."

"Why are you doing this? I thought you were a good man."

"People change." He sighed. "I never planned to hurt anyone. I thought if I let those Rangers stay at the ranch, then I'd know what they found, and I could throw them off my track if necessary."

"That was your plan all along?"

"Yep. Then Ricardo refused to help with the rebranding, but when I threatened kicking you and your mother out, he agreed to keep quiet." He glanced back at her. "Don't look so disappointed in me. You're the one who went nosing around. Too many people know too much. I have to take drastic measures to get it under control. I have no choice."

"You always have a choice." Her words sounded bitter, even to her.

"It's my duty to protect my men."

"Duty?" She could hardly believe her ears. "Duty is a moral obligation. It's knowing there are some things more important than yourself. I didn't realize it before, but I witnessed that in my father, and I see it in Chisholm. Duty is love in action, but there's no duty in what you're doing. Don't fool yourself. It's self-preservation, pure and simple."

Señor Reynolds grew silent as he slowed and they descended toward Brady Creek. Was he having doubts about his intentions? Caro prayed he was, indeed, but when he turned toward her, his eyes were granite hard with resolve.

He brought the horses to a stop, and Caro searched for a sign of Ricardo. Trees lined the swollen creek's bank. It must have rained last night to the north of Brady City for the water to be moving this swiftly. But where was Ricardo? She finally spotted him, his back to a tree. His hands, like hers, were bound behind him.

Señor Reynolds dismounted, then lifted her off of Angel. "Go say your goodbyes, but make it quick."

Tripping over her skirt, Caro hurried to Ricardo. She dropped to her knees in front of him. He looked at her, one eye bruised and almost swollen shut. When he tried to speak, his swollen lip wouldn't cooperate.

"He needs some water—now," Caro shouted to Señor Reynolds, who remained with the horses several yards away.

Señor Reynolds laughed. "Oh, he'll get plenty soon enough."

Caro opened her mouth ready with a retort, but Ricardo cleared his throat. "Don't, mi prima." He licked his cracked lip. "I tried to protect you. I'm sorry I failed."

"I know you did, and this is not your fault." She leaned closer. "Listen, Ricardo. We have to take care of ourselves. Do you understand? I don't know if the Rangers can come for us." Her voice shook at the thought of what Chisholm might be facing right now. As much as she wanted to go to Chisholm, she had to focus on saving Ricardo right now.

Señor Reynolds lumbered over to them, took out a knife, and cut the ropes that bound Ricardo to the tree. "Enough chitchat, y'all." He sheathed his knife and picked up his revolver. Its silver barrel glinted in a shaft of sunlight. "Hope you said your goodbyes. It's time to get this over with."

◆ ◆ ◆

Chisholm stopped to examine the crushed pecans near the trail. The faint imprint of a horseshoe left him no doubt that he was on the right track. So far, the clues had come at regular intervals, and he couldn't be more relieved at Caro's quick thinking.

He jumped back onto Bullet. The horse's strong muscles bunched, almost as if he sensed Chisholm's urgency. Chisholm headed to the top of the hill, praying he'd find Caro on the other side, safe and unharmed.

Keeping Bullet to a walk, he paused to survey the terrain. He spotted Caro, and his heart pounded so hard, it hurt to breathe. Reynolds stood with a revolver on Caro and Ricardo, prodding them toward the wide, turbulent creek.

Chisholm whipped out his rifle, but he was still too far to make a safe shot. What if he hit Caro or Ricardo? He stormed forward, praying he'd arrive in time.

Ricardo suddenly broke free from the rope, spun, and kicked the revolver out of Reynolds's hands. Reynolds dove at Ricardo, knocking him into Caro, who went flying into the creek.

Heart sinking to his gut, Chisholm pushed Bullet harder. Only a few more yards to the creek's bank, and he could get to Caro. Reynolds rolled away from Ricardo and spotted Chisholm. He jumped on his roan and drove his spurs into the animal's sides. If Chisholm didn't stop him, he'd get away.

But saving Caro was more important. Chisholm halted Bullet so hard, the horse reared. He vaulted from the saddle, dropped his rifle, and tore his boots off. Caro bobbed in the current. He jumped into the creek, and the shock of the cold water stole his breath. Lifting his head, he spotted her. It took only a few kicks to reach her. He grabbed the back of her collar and drew her against him. She struggled and kicked.

He crooked his arm beneath her chin. "Relax, Caro. I've got you."

She gave up the fight, and he swam back to the bank, where Ricardo was waiting to help her to solid ground. Chisholm scrambled up the slope and pulled her into his arms.

He sucked in a lungful of air. "Are you hurt?"

"I'm fine." But her shivering told him otherwise.

"Ricardo, get the blanket off my horse." His heart pounded. He'd almost lost her.

Caro pulled back and brushed a strand of wet hair from her face. She smiled, her eyes droopy with exhaustion. "The one time I wanted you to do your duty, and you let Señor Reynolds get away."

◆ ◆ ◆

Caro stood on the porch of the Walking Diamond's ranch house, watching for Chisholm to return. The sun would set any minute. Where was he?

As soon as he'd seen her back to her mother's care, Chisholm and Ricardo had ridden off to help Whit. He promised to return after they'd arrested Reynolds and his men and turned them over to the sheriff, and she hadn't stopped praying for his and Whit's safety since.

At least, she prayed continually while she was awake. After a warm bath, her mother had insisted she go to bed, and sleep had overcome her for most of the afternoon.

Now Caro sat down in a rocking chair on the porch and glanced around. Sadness filled her and she hugged herself. This ranch house had become her home. Ricardo, her mother, and she had no claim to it. They'd have to leave, and Chisholm would have to go on his way, as well.

The pounding of hooves sent her spirits soaring. Whit and Ricardo rode in first, followed by Chisholm. Something trailed behind Chisholm's horse, and she strained to see it.

Chisholm drew closer, and the other two men headed toward the barn. She could now see he had a little longhorn calf in tow. Chisholm laughed. "Don't look so confused. Don't you recognize Bluebonnet?"

"I thought it was her, but why is she here?"

"She's a gift from Slade McCord."

She descended the porch steps and knelt beside the calf. "It was nice of him to give you a gift for catching the wranglers."

"She's not for me. She's for us." Chisholm held out his hand and pulled her to her feet. He didn't release her but instead looked down into her eyes, his dimples impossibly deep. "Bluebonnet is a wedding present. She'll be the first cow in our herd."

Caro's breath caught.

"I know you can't marry a man of duty, so I'll resign from the Texas Rangers as soon as possible. I can live without them, but I can't live without you. I love you, Caro, and I'm asking you to marry me."

She bit her lip. How was she going to refuse him?

CHAPTER 12

A strange tightness seized Chisholm's throat. What was taking Caro so long to answer?

"I can't marry you"—she dropped her gaze to their joined hands—"under those conditions."

"Do you want to live here? I'm sure I can find a way to get this place. Reynolds isn't going to be needing it, but if I get married before the end of the year, then you can't believe the part of the 7 Heart Ranch I'll receive."

She jerked her head up, her molasses-colored eyes wide. "What?" He started to repeat himself, but she stopped him. "Chisholm, this isn't about where we'd live. You're a Texas Ranger—"

"Caro, I said I'll give that up."

"But I don't want you to." She pulled from his arms and turned. "It's who you are. You're fiercely loyal. You're a man who feels a responsibility for helping Texas, and the world needs men like you."

Chisholm shook his head. "So you won't marry me if I'm a Texas Ranger, and you won't marry me if I'm not?"

"Not exactly." She smiled. "I now realize that being a Ranger is part of what makes me love you."

His lips curled upward at her admission. "Go on."

"Like it or not, I've fallen in love with a man of duty, a Texas Ranger to his core, and the only way I'll marry you is if you promise to keep doing what you love as long as you like."

"But what about you? I can't hurt you every time I have to go away."

"I imagine Bluebonnet and I will do fine at the 7 Heart Ranch, waiting for your return."

What did she mean? This didn't sound like a refusal. "So you're saying yes?"

"*Sí, mi amor.*" She placed her hands on his broad chest. "Now stop standing there with your mouth hanging open and kiss me."

"Yes, ma'am." He removed his hat and pulled her close, branding the lips of the future Mrs. Hart with his own.

◆ ◆ ◆

Caro adjusted her position in Angel's saddle and glanced at Chisholm, who rode beside her. After five days driving nearly three hundred head of cattle from the Walking Diamond to the 7 Heart Ranch, she was ready for a bath and bed. Whit, Ricardo, Chisholm, and her mamá all seemed in a similar state. While she was glad Chisholm had hastily arranged purchase of the incarcerated rancher's stock, it had certainly made the journey longer. One look at Bluebonnet, however, made her glad the docile animals had joined them.

Caro looked down at her dusty skirt and sighed. She was not going to make a good first impression. Her hair refused to remain tied back, she reeked of horse sweat, and her clothes needed a thorough washing. She'd begged Chisholm to let them have a day to clean up before she met his family, but he'd pressed on, eager to be home.

She couldn't blame him. He'd not been with his family for months. He'd explained his father's ultimatum regarding his share of the ranch, and she couldn't help but tease him about having no choice but to marry her.

"Are we close?" Caro leaned over her saddle horn.

"We've been on the ranch for the last two hours, Caro." Chisholm chuckled and swept his arm over the area. "This will be Crockett's place. Ours is on the Little Bianco Creek southwest of El Regalo."

"El Regalo is your house? 'The gift'?" Caro tucked a loose hair behind her ear.

He nodded. "Pa built El Regalo as a gift to my mother. And, Caro, you can stop fussing. They're going to love you as much as I do."

The largest stone ranch house she'd ever seen came into view. In the front, a tower seemed to touch the sky. She gasped. "This is your El Regalo?"

"Yes, ma'am."

"Who has to clean it?"

"Not you." Chisholm laughed. "I wired my brother that I was bringing home a bride, and hopefully, they've already started framing our house, which will not be this large, in case you're worried."

"*Graçias.*" She looked again at the massive home in front of them. "Chisholm, what if your father doesn't approve of me? I'll understand, and you'll still have time to find another bride."

He flashed her a grin. "Nah. I've gone through enough roping you, so I reckon I'll put up a fight to keep you."

CHAPTER 13

Chisolm's face hurt from grinning. He stood in his old bedroom, adjusting the small cravat about his neck. It had been so long since he wore a frock coat and vest that he chafed beneath its constriction, but the discomfort was worth it. In a few minutes, surrounded by his family, he'd meet his bride in El Regalo's parlor.

The whole house smelled of Perla and Maria's spicy Mexican cuisine. Between the two women, his pa said he and Caro's wedding supper would be something no one would ever forget. He recalled the first meal Caro served him and smiled. He'd warned her that he liked things spicy, and Caro was all that and more.

His pa loved Caro. He said she had fire in her veins and in her eyes. His brothers loved her too. They'd said she was tough enough to handle ranch life, and they were surprised she fell for a weak fellow like him. Perla had kissed his cheek and said he'd brought her the best gift in the world—a daughter in Caro and a new friend in Maria. Emma, Hays's new bride, welcomed the first of what she hoped would be many new sisters.

Chisholm chuckled to himself. He still couldn't believe the youngest Hart had been the first to take a bride.

He picked up his Texas Ranger star and held it. Should he wear it today? Caro had said she loved all of him, including his sense of duty, but was wearing the star too much? He felt naked without it, so he opted for pinning it onto his vest.

A knock on the door sounded, and his father entered. "You ready, son?"

"Yes, sir." He tugged on the lapels of his coat.

In front of the fireplace, Chisholm took his place. Whit stood beside him. It only seemed right.

Caro took his breath away when she entered the parlor in her sunflower-yellow dress, carrying a bouquet of bluebonnets. A piece of fine white lace veiled her face. Rev. Longley said something about Adam and Eve and leavin' and cleavin', but Chisholm didn't truly hear the words. His pulse drummed in his ears as he said "I do," and soon he was being directed to kiss the bride.

He blinked and took a deep breath before lifting the veil and peering into Caro's eyes. Love shone on her face. This incredible lady was his wife. He bent to kiss her.

"Wait," she whispered. "Where's your star?"

He patted his vest.

Rumbles and chuckles could be heard from those gathered to witness the wedding.

She slipped her hand to his vest, removed the badge, and then replaced it on the front of his coat. "Now, Texas Ranger, you may kiss me."

And he did, soundly, leaving a promise of more to come.

One thing was certain. His loyalty might belong to Texas, but his heart belonged to Caro Cardova Valenzuela Hart.

ABOUT THE AUTHOR

Lorna Seilstad brings history back to life using a generous dash of humor. She is a Carol Award finalist and the author of the Lake Manawa Summers series and the Gregory Sisters series. When she isn't eating chocolate, she teaches women's Bible classes, runs a toy store, and is a 4-H leader in her home state of Iowa. She has three adult children and a Pyredoodle named Honey. Learn more about Lorna at www.lornaseil-stad.com.

THE TRUEST HEART

AMANDA BARRATT

CHAPTER 1

MAY 1874

*T*he Texas Hill Country, she had missed. The man before her, she—regrettably—had not.

Annie Lawrence found a smile for Brock Parker and stepped into his stiff embrace.

Her father's arms encircled her for the briefest of moments before he pulled away, surveying her from bonneted head to boot-clad feet. His eyes narrowed, his mouth firming into a dour frown. The sort of frown that spoke volumes. Words soon added to the equation.

"You're thinner than you were. You look older too. I would think you a staid matron of thirty-five, if I didn't know better. Where'd your bloom go, girl?"

When it came to expectations, far too often, her negative ones were met. No, exceeded. Especially where her father was concerned.

Drawing his attention away from her bloom, or lack thereof, she nudged Robbie forward. Her nine-year-old son seemed reluctant to leave the barricade of her petticoats and face the open fire of meeting his grandfather. Yet Robbie responded to her prodding, removing his straw hat and holding out his travel-grubby hand. As if Brock Parker were President Grant instead of a small-scale cattle rancher.

"Pleased to meet you, Grandfather. Ma's told me a whole lot about you." Robbie's cinnamon-hued hair riffled in the breeze, his brown eyes full of hesitant anticipation.

Annie's breath webbed in her throat. Her father wouldn't reject his only grandson. Would he? Not on their first meeting. Not when the boy had pinned so much hope upon this encounter.

"Has she?" Her father's Texas drawl was as smooth as maple syrup, though perhaps not quite as sweet.

Zeke, one of her father's few hands, sauntered across the dusty yard of the Parker ranch, toward the bunkhouse, a pail of water clutched in one fist. He paused in his jaunty rendition of "Arkansas Traveler" to aim quizzical glances in his boss's direction. No doubt the middle-aged cowhand scarcely remembered her. It had been nine years since she left, and she, a mere slip of a girl then.

Annie turned her gaze back to her son.

"Oh yes, sir." Robbie nodded vigorously. "She's told me all 'bout how you own lots and lots of cows, and how I'd get to come help you rope 'em, and brand 'em, and you'd learn me everything there is to know."

Instead of looking pleased, her father only glowered. "Teach, boy."

"Huh?" Robbie scrunched his nose. The wide look in his eyes gave warning that he was about two shakes of a lamb's tail from seeking refuge behind her gray traveling skirt.

"*Teach* you everything there is to know. Not *learn*. And if you're the sort of dunce who utilizes bad grammar, I doubt there will be much I can do on any account." Her father swiped at a fly, the impatient flick seeming to dismiss Robbie as well as the insect. "Of course, I blame it entirely on your mother. She never was one to put much stock in education."

Annie bit her lip. Suddenly, all she had done seemed like a terrible mistake. Leaving Galveston, the quiet gentility of life with Stuart's mother, Mrs. Lawrence. Never mind that Galveston was a bustling city, giving Robbie no chance to run and play outside, as she'd done in her girlhood. But at least there her son hadn't been ridiculed for the slightest misuse of grammar.

And if all she remembered about her father proved to hold correct, things were only going to get worse.

A young woman opened the ranch house door and hurried outside, crinoline swinging, fashionable coiffure already askew. A genuine smile appeared on Annie's lips this time. With quick steps, she met her sister halfway and crushed her in an embrace, breathing in the rosewater and love that emanated from Josie Parker like a glow.

"You're here. At last," Josie whispered, still clinging tightly to Annie. "You don't know how happy I am to see you."

"Believe it or not, I do. I've been counting down the days, begrudging the hours." A little laugh escaped as she repeated what the forever dramatic Josie had written in her last letter.

"And wishing every minute would skedaddle along just a little bit faster." Tears spilled down Josie's cheeks, but they were of joy, not sorrow as they'd been at their parting. She pulled from Annie's embrace with a giggle. "Now, where's the young gentleman whose acquaintance I have been longing to renew for such a great while?" Josie peered in Robbie's direction with a welcoming smile.

Annie motioned her son forward. Robbie left his grandfather's side with an alacrity that didn't surprise her. Her son's reluctance only reminded her of herself, twelve or so years ago.

"Are you my aunt Josie?" Robbie gazed at the beautiful young woman with eyes that flickered with hesitation only a moment, before warming to instant adoration. Little wonder. The word *beautiful* hardly did her sister justice. Golden ringlets. Warm blue eyes. Skin that seemed to stay forever the color of strawberries and cream, a blush in just the right places. The added years had only enhanced Josie's prettiness. While Annie's looks, on the other hand, had diminished. Painfully so.

"I am. And you'll not find a lady in all of Texas happier to be an aunt than I." Josie's smile could have fueled a dozen candelabras.

"She likes me, Ma." Robbie looked up at Annie, smiling shyly. Annie wrapped her arm around her son's shoulders, hugging him close. Her greatest treasure, this boy of hers.

The only truly good thing that had come out of her marriage to Stuart.

Josie sent a furtive glance in their father's direction, but Brock Parker was deep in conversation with Mr. Wade, the ranch foreman. She cut her voice low. "Father didn't give you much of a welcome, then?"

Annie raised her brow. "Did you expect him to kill the fatted calf for the return of his prodigal daughter?" Despite her best efforts, sarcasm wormed its way into her words.

Josie shrugged, her sigh all the answer that was needed. "Well, everyone else will be glad to see you. Especially Mrs. Miller. Her son stops by most every other day to ask if you've come back yet."

"Is she still seeing patients?" Annie followed her sister toward the house. Though the siding had gained a coat of grayish-white paint, little else about the single-story building had changed. Still the same unkempt shrubbery growing 'round the foundation, the same splintered doorframe. The same beaten-down look of disrepair, as if the house had lived too long and was dead tired of doing so.

"Yes, but she'll be happier than a cowboy with his first Stetson for you to take over. She's getting up in years, and babies are being born more and more these days. That's the reason she invited you to return and take over her responsibilities. You can ride to town tomorrow and get a list of her current cases." Josie pushed open the door and stepped aside to let Annie and Robbie into the blessedly cool entryway.

"Any news of Hartville that I haven't already heard?" Annie drew in a breath of beeswax and freshly starched curtains. Her travel-weary body ached for a hot bath and clothes not covered in grime and dust.

Josie flashed a mischievous grin. "As a matter of fact, there is. Two of the Hart boys have recently tied the knot."

The mention of that family still had the power to pull the breath from her lungs. She forced a casual tone. "Oh. Which ones?"

Josie laughed, her keen eyes no doubt sensing her sister's discomfort. "Not Travis. *He's* still single. Of course, that wouldn't matter a bit to you, now, would it? Come on, Robbie. Let's see if we can rustle up some corn bread and milk." Their footsteps clattered across the wood floor.

Annie dragged in a ragged breath. Why, oh why, did the very syllables of his name still have the strength to unravel her? As if she were an ancient tapestry, able to bear up under any strain but that.

Josie said his single state wouldn't matter much to her.

Nor would it. Too much had happened since those days, far too much. Why, they probably wouldn't even recognize each other if they passed on the street.

Never mind that she had kept every line of his face, every shadow of his smile, hidden deep within her heart. As if their past was some long-ago burial mound, each bone carefully preserved.

Best left to molder in silence.

~

*W*asn't he supposed to be deriving some sort of pleasure from this long-awaited holiday?

Travis Hart ran his gaze across the hotel dining room. Crystal chandeliers. Cream linen tablecloths and napkins folded into odd-looking fan shapes. Black-jacketed waiters serving slices of iced cake, tall glasses bubbling with champagne.

And, of course, the bride and groom. One mustn't forget them.

The happy couple, along with their families, sat at a long table at the head of the room. The groom, Matthew Wellington, leaned forward and placed a kiss against the lips of his bride, Eliza Littlefield. The young lady giggled and wrapped her arms around her new husband's neck, both heedless of propriety and the indulgent smiles of their family and friends.

Fiddling with the silver fork next to his untouched plate of wedding confectionary, Travis looked away.

All he seemed to do was attend weddings these days. First, his youngest brother, Hays. Then his other brother Chisholm. Today he'd witnessed the nuptials of his friend from the army, Matthew Wellington.

Of course, since Pa's edict five months ago, weddings seemed to be the main topic of everyone's thoughts. At least where the Hart family was concerned.

Not that Travis disliked marriage. Quite the reverse, in fact. He was happy for Matt and Eliza. The pair had endured more than their share of hardships in the years following the war, a war that both Matt and Travis had entered as first-year med students and ended as men who had seen horrors that ought to belong only in nightmares. Only...

All right, he'd admit it. Every bride walking down the aisle, pretty and aglow in white, every groom waiting for her at the front of the church, every joining of hearts, lives, futures, lanced the wound he tried so hard to keep bandaged and out of sight.

Annie Parker.

It'd been too long since he allowed himself to think her name. Yet here, at this festive event, it entered his mind, demanding to be heard. Like a pain ignored until the agony became too great to allow for any course of action other than dealing with the source.

Even now, he saw her face, bright against the canvas of his mind. Even now, he could hear her voice, feel her hand brushing his. How beautiful she'd been, with that strawberry-blond hair, those ever-changeable eyes that could only be described as hazel. Her smile wasn't an ordinary one, a mere turning up of the lips. No, it transformed her face, turned it aglow, and the room with it. . .

Enough. She was gone. Out of his life. For good.

He was at the wedding of his good friend. He *would* enjoy himself, even if he had to struggle through the doing of it like a new med student watching his first operation and trying not to keel over. Other women populated the world. He could still have a chance at fulfilling his father's demand.

Travis stood, pushing in his chair, leaving the cake and champagne behind. In the flurry following the ceremony and the short drive from the church to the hotel reception, he hadn't properly wished his friend well. He wove his way through the clusters of tables, narrowly avoiding a collision with one of the waiters, who bore an alarmingly large tray of more cake.

Matt and his bride were oblivious to all else around them, his hand on her waist, her lifting a champagne glass to take a sip, then putting it to her groom's lips. Travis hesitated. Should he intrude? Yet after making the seven-hour trip from Hartville to San Antonio, he at least wanted to say a few words, give some good wishes.

Travis put his hand on the back of his friend's chair.

Matt turned, a grin stretching his mouth. "Well, if it isn't old Trav Hart. Why didn't you come over earlier? I didn't even know you were here."

Travis smiled. "Looks as though you've been pretty well occupied."

Matt chuckled. "Pretty well? I still can't believe my good fortune." He sent a long and loving look in Eliza's direction. "For a man to have a woman such as this to walk through life with is a blessing that only God, in His great mercy, could provide. You should try this business of marriage one of these days, my friend. You might find it suits you."

"It obviously suits *you*. So tell me, Mrs. Wellington—do you have a lasso ready to keep my friend in line? If not, you'd better let me rustle one up. Matt here can be quite the—"

Thud.

In an instant, Travis shoved past Matt. Eliza's portly mother had fallen facedown onto the table. Supporting her head and shoulders, Travis assessed the woman. Still breathing. Pulse fast but not dangerous. A faint. Nothing more serious, as far as he could tell. But until she awoke...

Matt crouched at Travis's side, both working as the team they had once been. Travis undid the buttons securing the top of her too-tight collar. Matt left his side, returning seconds later with a bottle of salts volatile.

Travis uncapped the bottle and waved it under the woman's nose. Within a couple of minutes, a slight movement of the eyelashes told him she was reviving.

"Oh...my..." Mrs. Littlefield stared up at Travis with a dazed expression.

"Are you all right, Mother?" Eliza's eyes were wide and worry-filled.

"I...I believe so." Mrs. Littlefield's fingers fluttered to her collar. Her hand shook.

"You're perfectly fine, Mrs. Littlefield. You fainted. How much water have you drunk today?"

"Well...what with the wedding and the preparations and the guests... not nearly enough, I'm afraid." She took the tumbler proffered by Matt and managed a few swallows. "How can I ever thank you?" Mrs. Littlefield's voice became stronger, her face turning a more normal shade of pink.

Travis smiled, gently releasing his hold upon the woman. "I'm a doctor, ma'am. It's my job to help people."

"You're just fortunate Dr. Hart responded so quickly. If it had been something more serious..." Eliza shuddered and buried her face against her groom's chest.

"God's timing is always perfect." Travis patted the older woman on the shoulder. "My advice to you would be to drink several glasses of water per day, especially in this heat. And wear less constrictive attire."

"Oh, I will. I will." Mrs. Littlefield bobbed her head. "Thank you so much again, Dr. Hart."

"Now, if you all will excuse me, it's time for me to start heading home. I think I can safely release you into the care of your more-than-competent son-in-law." Travis said his goodbyes to Matt and Eliza, then exited the opulent dining room.

It had been a relaxing couple of days, a chance to visit some of his San Antonio colleagues and attend the wedding of his friend. But he would be glad to see the road to the 7 Heart Ranch and even gladder to return to his patients.

Helping people, healing them, was his life's work. Hadn't the past few minutes proved that? After the years of war, his profession gave him security. A calm consistency to his future. One that didn't need marriage to be brimful with purpose.

His father's edict notwithstanding.

CHAPTER 2

*I*t might have been midnight. Or one. Whatever the hour, no matter the weather, the passing seconds filled Annie with a mix of exhilaration and dread. Every fiber of her body focused on one goal—arriving at the home of the mother-to-be.

The road, dark and unlit as a graveyard at night, lay uncharted before her. She gripped the reins of her mount, one of her father's dappled gray mares, as the animal stumbled over some obstruction. A rock, perhaps.

Beside her, Mr. Tatum urged his horse to move faster with a whip of the reins. A universal thing, that. No matter if the expected baby was their first or eleventh, good fathers were always anxious. Always eager to return to their wives' sides with a midwife to aid.

A stream of light glimmered up ahead, casting dark and shapeless shadows. As they drew closer, Annie made out a farmhouse, middling size with a wraparound porch.

Mr. Tatum dismounted first.

Annie flung her legs over her animal's side and landed on the ground. She grabbed her saddlebag and rushed to the door.

Blinking at the sudden wash of light, she made her way down the hall, following the sound of groans she had come to recognize as oncoming labor. The two Tatum children stood at the foot of the stairs, sleepy-eyed and nightshirt-clad. She gave them a quick smile and then hurried onward.

Candles lit the room. A woman in her late twenties lay on the bed, legs drawn up, face damp with perspiration. Annie had met Helen Tatum once before, when she'd visited each of Mrs. Miller's patients to inform them of the switch in caretakers.

She placed her saddlebag on the chest of drawers, just as the sound of Mr. Tatum's heavy boots clunked down the hall, and he stepped into the room. He stared at his moaning wife, hands hanging helpless at his sides.

"Hot water. Lots of it. Towels, clean ones. Now, scoot!" Annie washed her hands in the basin and pitcher that sat atop the chest of drawers and tied on her apron. At least this family had a standard of cleanliness. She'd seen a thousand times worse.

"Are your pains often?" She dried her hands with the coarse towel and laid out her supplies atop the bureau. String to tie off the cord. Surgical scissors to cut it. Binding sheet for bandaging the cord stump. Remedies like castor oil and a tin of specially concocted herbal tea.

Helen didn't answer, her features contorting as she gasped, panting.

Stethoscope in hand, Annie waited until the contraction passed. She bent low, moving the instrument across the woman's distended middle, ears straining to locate the fetal heartbeat.

Her own breath quickened, pulse hammering. Annie laid aside the stethoscope and gently probed Helen's abdomen.

No. It couldn't be. Her first case as the midwife of Hartville, and the baby was presenting breech. A scenario she'd only seen twice. Twice!

God, please. Protect this woman and her unborn child. Give me strength and knowledge.

She couldn't, in good conscience, deliver this baby without a doctor's supervision. Had they been miles from medical help, she would have done her best. But Hartville was only half an hour away. What if forceps were needed? Only doctors were trained in the use of the instrument, something she and Mrs. Campbell, the midwife she had worked with in Galveston, thought ridiculous.

More boots clomping. Mr. Tatum entered with an armload of towels —far more than needed.

Annie explained the situation in a few quiet words, passing lightly over the possible dangers so as not to alarm the man overmuch. He listened, jaw tense with anxiety, then bolted down the hall to fetch the doctor, like a racehorse at the final stretch. The slam of the front door reverberated through the house.

She returned to Helen's bedside, performing an internal examination, which only confirmed the breech presentation.

"Everything all right?" Helen shifted on the bed.

Annie gave a quick smile. "There's nothing you need be alarmed about. But your baby is presenting breech, which means we're going to have to move you a bit."

"You mean my baby's coming out wrong end first?" Helen bit her lip, sucking in a breath.

She nodded. "I'm afraid so. We're doing this together, Helen. I'm going to work with you every second of the way. Now, I'm going to help you scoot down to the end of the bed, with your legs hanging off just a little. That will help when it comes time to push this baby out. Ready?" Annie supported Helen's shoulders, the woman's weight making her own back ache.

After Helen was in the proper position, Annie did another examination. Between contractions, Helen gasped out that her waters had broken two hours ago.

Annie's throat went dry. This baby wasn't about to wait for any doctor. The buttocks were already in sight.

Helen's shrill cries smote the air like gunfire. Writhing and moaning, the woman obviously wanted to push.

"Slow pushes, Helen. Not too hard. On your next contraction, I'm going to hook my fingers under the baby's legs and bring them out. I need you to remain completely still and try to relax." Annie's voice shook as she positioned her hands in time for the next contraction. Perspiration dripping down her face, she reached inside the birth canal, carefully sliding out first one leg, then the other.

Helen wailed. "Make it go away! Please, just make it go away."

Annie gave an encouraging smile. Helen's pain was no doubt a good deal worse than a normal third-time delivery. Poor woman. "You're doing wonderfully, Helen. In just a few more minutes, your baby will be born. Pant now."

Footsteps came up behind her. Annie scarcely heeded them. Another couple of pushes and the rest of the body emerged. Only the shoulders and head remained inside the birth canal.

Someone handed her a towel. She took it, not bothering to see whether it was Mr. Tatum or the doctor. The latter, probably. Mr. Tatum likely didn't know the first thing about the importance of these next moments, the risk of asphyxiation if the baby gasped due to an onslaught of cold air.

"Nearly over now. You'll get to hold your baby, Helen. Keep thinking about that." Midwives could produce encouraging smiles on command, and Mrs. Campbell had trained Annie well.

Helen only groaned as Annie turned the baby a quarter circle. On the next contraction, the shoulders slipped out.

It seemed to take an eternity for another contraction to arrive. It came, finally. Annie grasped the towel-wrapped baby as the head was born.

A moment later, the little girl emitted the sound that was music to every mother and midwife—a hearty cry.

Annie repositioned her hold on the baby. She had been kneeling on the floor for what seemed like hours—in reality only less than two. How would she ever manage to get to her feet? No matter. She'd marshal her legs later. The cord. It needed to be tied off.

A hand produced scissors and string. She tied and cut the cord, then passed the baby to Helen. The woman cradled the infant in her arms, tears of joy replacing those of pain.

Annie's hands and the front of her apron were in need of a thorough scrubbing. She clambered to her feet with the grace of a drunken barkeep.

A man stood just behind her. In an instant, the space of thirteen years vanished with the speed of winter twilight.

Rumpled dark hair. Liquid brown eyes, flecked with gold. A face that had brought her to tears, haunted her dreams, lingered in so many memories.

Travis Hart.

~

*I*n all his imaginings about their meeting, he never thought it would happen like this. Travis had been roused from his bed in the middle of the night by a frantic Andy Tatum. He'd thrown on some professionalism, along with a few clothes, and stifled his yawns on the ride to the Tatum residence.

He expected to find Mrs. Miller.

And instead encountered the woman he'd been powerless to forget.

The years had changed her. When he'd seen her last, thirteen years ago, she'd been a slight girl. Beautiful then. Even more so now. She was still thin, but some of her slender fragility had vanished. Erased by the war and the years after, no doubt. Circles ringed her hazel eyes. Stains from the evening's events covered her apron, her gray skirt creased and wrinkled.

He'd yet to see a sight he found lovelier.

"Annie."

"Y-yes..." She stared at him as if he were an apparition from the grave.

A thousand questions raced through his mind like unbridled horses on a stampede. *Why are you here? How could I have not known you were in Hartville? Have you even once thought of me?*

Yet his tongue cleaved to the roof of his mouth, mobile as cement.

The infant's mewling cries snapped him to reality. There was the afterbirth to be delivered, the baby to be cleaned and checked over.

Annie seemed to come to the same conclusion. Instantly, she became the professional midwife; he, the dedicated physician. They worked in silence, passing instruments back and forth, changing the bedsheets. Annie cared for Mrs. Tatum, while he washed and assessed the baby. The newborn girl kicked tiny feet, her lips puckering. Holding an infant during its first moments on earth had always seemed to him a miracle. Proof of God's goodness, His hand on every season of life. Tonight, that miracle was twofold. The woman he never expected to see again had come back into his life.

Would he once again be forced to let her go?

Travis placed the clean, swaddled infant back into the mother's arms. Helen gave a sleepy smile of pure contentment.

"Thank you both for everything," Mr. Tatum said.

"We're—I'm glad to be of help." Annie placed the last instrument in her bag and closed the clasps. She'd worked with greater efficiency than most doctors, setting both mother and room to rights in very little time. Admiration filled Travis. "I'll come by tomorrow to check on you and your baby, but for now, everything seems to be in order."

"Thanks so much, Doc." Mr. Tatum stuck out his hand, and Travis smiled. "Sorry to come tearin' to your house so late. Hope I didn't wake your pa."

"Don't worry about it. My father will be glad to hear of your wife and child's safety."

After final farewells, they made their way out of the house and into the cool night air. Annie went down the steps first, Travis following.

Overhead, stars winked in the inky sky. Silence wrapped around them, uncertain as the wind.

"You did a fine job in there. It wasn't an easy task." He found a smile and added it to the words.

She wrapped her arms around herself, gazing up at him. Sweet Texas thunder, he'd forgotten how the depth of her eyes could snatch his breath.

> And all that's best of dark and bright
> Meet in her aspect and her eyes:
> Thus mellowed to that tender light
> Which heaven to gaudy day denies.

His brothers had always teased him about his penchant for Byron's poetry. Yet if he'd scrounged his brain a million years, he'd not have found better words to describe the woman before him.

"I was terrified. I've never dealt with something so complicated on my own."

"You're a midwife?" That she was seemed painfully obvious. Yet he had to say something. He couldn't let her get on that horse and ride away. Not so soon.

She nodded. "I trained while living in Galveston. I've only been in Hartville three days."

"You're staying at your father's ranch?"

"Yes. Robbie and I both." She lowered her gaze. "Robbie is my son. Of course, you probably know that."

His knowledge of her life in the past thirteen years was about as limited as table scraps at a Hart family dinner. He knew of her marriage to Stuart Lawrence. Of Stuart's death in battle. Her son's birth. Her move to Galveston. He'd even heard rumors that she'd gotten remarried to a Galveston lawyer. From the moment he'd first heard the news, he'd despised the man, whoever he was.

"I've never met your son."

She smiled, slow and soft. "He's my greatest joy. The only true family I have except Josie and Father."

So she hadn't remarried, after all. Relief billowed over him.

"And you. You're a doctor now. Dr. William Travis Hart."

He liked the way she said his name. Probably too much for his own good.

"I went to school in Louisiana after the war. Since then, I've been practicing right here in Hartville."

A shaky laugh drifted from her lips. "Who would've thought it? A couple of kids who bandaged up stray animals out of pity. Look at us now."

"I'll never forget that cat."

"Kitten. Yellow-and-white-striped."

"You snuck out to the barn and slept in the hay all night, just so she wouldn't be alone."

"And awoke to find you beside me, with cocoa and biscuits."

"I thought you might have caught cold during the night." Though that wasn't the only reason he'd returned to check on his "patient." No, the main one had been to see her, twelve years old, long braids trailing down her back, forehead scrunched in concentration as she cared for the wounded kitten. He'd been sixteen. Always poring over medical books. Annoying his brothers by diagnosing their every bump and graze.

They'd been the perfect match. Until Stuart Lawrence had entered the picture, annihilating their secret hopes. For good, he thought then.

Now Travis Hart, the analytical, calm practitioner, didn't know what to think, feel, say.

As he lost himself in Annie's eyes, rational thought began to matter less and less.

CHAPTER 3

*H*ad she not succumbed to the sleep of exhaustion, Annie's eyes would have been hard-pressed to close in slumber after the previous night's events.

Travis Hart had grown from an attractive youth to an even handsomer gentleman. He possessed the family's good looks in spades, and he wore them well. Wide shoulders, wavy hair black as a raven's wing. His eyes still held those mesmerizing flecks of gold, his smile still curved into the slightest hint of a dimple.

Enough. In her thoughts, she was behaving every inch the seventeen-year-old. Betraying her husband's memory in death, as she had betrayed her marriage during his life. Though Stuart had not often been kind to others, he'd cared for her as much as he was able. Cared for her in a way some might prize a new riding horse or a set of fine china. Yet there had been those moments before his departure to the front. Moments when he'd treated her far better than she deserved. In those moments...she'd failed miserably.

And Travis Hart was not hers, nor would he ever be. She didn't deserve his love. Did not deserve even to be thinking of him in such a way as this. He would be her colleague and nothing more. They had worked well together last night and could continue to do so. She would toss aside her romantic fancies and focus on the reasons she had returned to Hartville. Building a life for her son. Mending her relationship with her father. Taking Mrs. Miller's place and helping the women of the Texas Hill Country birth new life into the world.

She jabbed a final pin into the messy chignon at the nape of her neck and smoothed the front of her tan-and-black riding outfit. She'd altered the skirt so it resembled a pair of bloomers, though when not atop a horse, it remained discreetly modest. In Galveston, her calls had been made using a buggy. Here, all would be undertaken on horseback.

Robbie bounded into her bedroom, Josie at his heels.

"Ma! There's a man to see you downstairs."

"It's Travis Hart," Josie supplied, a knowing gleam in her eyes. "The doctoring Hart brother. You feeling all right today, Annie? Maybe he's here to pay a house call."

A flush doused Annie's cheeks. "I'm feeling just fine, thank you. Dr. Hart is probably here to discuss a patient. Wash your face, Robbie." She ruffled her son's tousled hair. "You're as sticky as if you'd bathed in the syrup bottle." She gave him a push toward her washstand and descended the stairs, supply bag in hand.

What business did Travis have with her? Was something amiss at the Tatum household? Her pulse kicked up a notch as voices carried from the parlor—because she was a midwife concerned for her patient, not because one of the voices was deep, rugged, and decidedly Texan.

Travis stood in front of the fireplace, conversing with her father. Brock Parker lounged in a leather chair, hardly the picture of a ranch owner intent on work.

"Annie." A smile edged Travis's mouth.

"Dr. Hart." She made a slight nod, gripping the handle of her bag.

"I was wondering if you'd like to accompany me to check on Mrs. Tatum. Seeing as you're the one who oversaw the delivery and all."

"Don't you have more pressing calls in need of your attention?" The last thing her foolish heart needed was to be alone with him again.

He fingered the rim of the Stetson in his hands. Today, he seemed more ranch hand than doctor. Light-blue shirt, gray vest, tan trousers, and sturdy boots. "Not right now. I thought it prudent for me to have a look at things, seeing as the delivery was complicated."

She was going to have to start treating him as her colleague, and she might as well begin today. "Very well, then. I just need to saddle my horse."

"No need. I brought my buckboard. I thought it might be a nice change."

"Won't returning me home take up too much of your time? I don't have all day to waste tagging along on your calls." She lifted her chin a notch.

He didn't even blink. "I'll bring you back in plenty of time to do whatever it is you need to do."

She waited for him to precede her out the door, but he gestured for her to go first. "After you." Another steady smile.

Soon they were driving away from the Parker ranch, heading in the direction of the Tatum residence. The warm May air teased her senses, clean and pure. This was the Texas she had missed—endless blue skies, grazing cattle, dusty roads. Memories lived here, as crystal clear as if she'd written them in a diary. Memories that danced between apple-pie sweet and crabapple sour. Memories of two men. . .

Both didn't bear thinking about right now.

"I didn't get the chance to meet Robbie. Mind if I do when we get back?" Travis shifted the reins in his hands.

"I guess not." What did it matter if he met her son? Hadn't she wished during her confinement that Travis had been the father? A wicked, evil wish she'd long since banished from her thoughts.

"There've been a lot of changes around El Regalo lately. Hays is married. Fell in love with a nice young lady by the name of Emma Longley. Guess he liked the idea of settling down better than flirting after every skirt that comes along."

She remembered Hays Hart. Josie had always thought him extremely handsome and devastatingly charming.

Annie had eyes only for Travis.

Travis kept his gaze on the road. His Stetson tipped a bit, obscuring his eyes. "Then there's Chisholm. He recently returned with his new wife, Caro. I've never seen him so happy. I think he'd sit and stare at her all day, if he could. I guess love has a way of bringing even the most determined wanderers home."

Annie fixed her gaze on the pale blue sky, on the hard-packed ground, on anything other than his face. She didn't want him talking about love, not when their own past lay so raw between them.

So she merely said, her tone rather tart, "The younger Harts are putting the older ones to shame. When Austin and Bowie decide to follow their example, the ranch may very well go to rack and ruin, what with all that love going around, and no one having a mind to work."

She expected her words to make him angry, but he only chuckled. "My father would see the ranch run, even if everyone else stayed starry-eyed. He loves that place. Loves it more than anything else on this earth, except his children and his wife. Bit by bit, he's sharing it with us, our part of his legacy."

They reached the Tatum farmhouse. Travis jumped down and tied the horses to the hitching post. Annie grabbed her bag and moved to descend. Before she could collect herself, he wrapped his hands around her waist and lifted her down. Though she wore both jacket and corset, the warmth of his hands seared her like twin coals.

She headed toward the house.

Love has a way of bringing even the most determined wanderers home.

She'd come home, there was no denying that.

But love would have nothing to do with it.

～

*E*ither he'd offended her in some way, or Annie Lawrence had changed more than a chameleon. She didn't chatter. She scarcely smiled. She behaved as if Travis's very existence was a bane to her.

And here he'd thought their flame of a romance might catch tinder once more.

"Mrs. Tatum seemed to be in fine health." He had to say something to fill the silence. Some of his brothers—Bowie particularly—might be content to sit like a corpse while in the company of a lady. To Travis it seemed impolite.

"As well as can be expected, given the circumstances of her labor."

There. Finally, some words. She didn't meet his gaze, though, fixating instead on the trees and hills they drove past.

"I still can't believe that was your first breech delivery. You handled it well."

"I do what I must." A reddish-blond strand came loose from her upswept hair and blew in the gentle wind. He stared at it, as transfixed by the fluttering ringlet as a boy watching his first kite take wing.

They reached the Parker ranch, and Travis whoaed the horses. Chico and Cyrus had daily practice obeying his low-spoken commands, and the two black Morgans halted immediately.

"I'll help you with your bag." He jumped down and rounded the wagon.

"There's no—" Annie began.

Josie Parker rounded the corner of the house, heading straight toward them. "Oh, thank goodness you're back!" Her breath came in the short, ragged pants indicative of hyperventilation.

"Is something wrong?" Annie scrambled out of the buckboard.

"It's. . ." She bent double, heaving for breath. "Robbie. Accident. Quick. By the big oak tree."

It was wartime all over again. Someone was bleeding to death, would die if Travis didn't get there quick enough. After grabbing his bag, he ran at a speed that would've made his cowboy brothers proud, Annie just behind him.

A cluster of ranch hands circled the tree. Travis shoved them aside. A small boy—Robbie—lay on the grass, his left arm bent at an awkward angle. Travis dropped to his knees.

"Hey, there, young man. Took a spill, I see?" His breath whooshed out in relief as he surveyed the injury. No compound fracture. Just a simple break. But it would need to be set.

"Ma." Robbie reached his dirt-covered right hand toward his mother, who knelt on his other side. Annie grasped her son's fingers, clutching tightly, her other palm stroking his tangled hair. "It hurts, Ma."

"I know, darling. But I'm going to stay right here with you the whole time. You're going to be all right." Annie's tone resonated with total calm.

"I'll need two boards for a splint." Josie and one of the ranch hands scattered to do his bidding. Travis turned to Annie. "We're going to have to set this. You understand?" He tried to convey with his eyes what he didn't want to verbalize. Setting a broken bone could be painful, even for a grown man.

Annie nodded. "Yes, Doctor."

Josie and the adolescent ranch hand returned with two straight, thin pieces of board.

He found the bandage strips, then placed his hand on Robbie's forehead. "Listen to me, son. I'm going to fix your arm, but I'll need you to help me out here. You'll need to keep very still, and be real brave, just like a soldier."

Robbie sniffled. "I'll try."

"Good. You're doing fine already." He pulled a linen-wrapped dowel from his bag, handed it to Annie. She placed it in Robbie's mouth.

"Ready?" He met Annie's eyes.

She nodded, her face chalk-white.

In a swift movement, he maneuvered the bone back into position. Robbie screamed.

One of the ranch hands helped Travis splint the limb, wrapping it firmly with bandage strips. Annie held her son's hand the whole while, humming softly. Though the music didn't seem to calm Robbie, it loosened the tension tugging at Travis's nerves while he worked.

"There, now. The worst part is all over. We'll carry you inside, get you all nice and comfortable, and then you'll get a treat for being such a brave patient."

With the ranch hand's help, Travis carried Robbie into the house. Annie preceded them, and when they entered the only lower-floor bedroom, they found the quilt cast aside and the sheets turned down. As gently as he could, Travis laid Robbie atop the bed. He reassessed the splint, making sure all remained secure. Josie entered the room and handed Travis his bag.

"I've seen generals put up more of a ruckus than you, Robbie Lawrence. You're a fine man already." He pulled two peppermint sticks from a special compartment and passed them to the boy. "They might not be a medal of bravery, but they sure taste a lot better."

"Thanks." Robbie smiled weakly. "Did you doctor soldiers, sir?"

Travis returned the smile. "I sure did. I knew a lot of soldiers, young man. When I come to check on you tomorrow, I'll tell you about some of them." He handed a bottle of laudanum to Annie. "I don't have to tell you how to dispense this properly. You know what to do."

She nodded. As her fingers closed over the bottle, he noticed the tremble passing through her hands.

"Give him some right now. It will help him rest more comfortably. I'm going outside to make sure my horses are all right." He exited the room. For a moment, he stood outside the door, listening to Annie's gentle words as she tucked the blankets around her little boy.

He'd wanted to meet Robbie, though not under these circumstances. Still, a rush of affection for the boy welled through him. Annie's son. Just like her, too, with the same finely chiseled features and messy reddish-blond hair. The fear in her eyes as she'd knelt by her boy's side had made him want to swallow her in his arms and hold her close until her worry ceased...

It was all foolish thinking. She shouldn't be becoming so much a part of his thoughts, after so short a reacquaintance. The *if only's* crowded into his mind. If only he had never gone to war. If only she had never married Stuart. If only her heart might turn toward his once again. If only. If only. For now, *if only's* were all they were.

And all they would most likely become.

CHAPTER 4

"This is what comes of women gadding around the countryside, when they should be at home. You've been gone from this part of the country a long time, daughter. Pity your intelligence hasn't improved in the interim."

Annie lowered her head, not wanting her father to glimpse the tears needling her eyes. Wasn't witnessing her son's pain enough rebuke? Must he rub it in, salt on an already burning wound?

"A cat mothers its kittens better than you do your son. Whoever thought you were a fit person to bring infants into the world, I haven't a clue." Her father had returned home just minutes after Robbie was settled and had commenced with a verbal flailing ever since.

Her chin lifted ever so slightly. Brock Parker stood in front of the parlor mantel, his bulky frame and angry eyes menacing. Suddenly, she was seventeen all over again, begging to be allowed to live her own life...

"You will do as I say." Her father's voice was harder than granite, and just as unyielding. The same tone he'd used time and again for every decision Annie tried to have an opinion on. "You're only a woman, with no intelligence worth mentioning." A phrase uttered countless times, reducing her to nothing more than an automaton.

Something within her shattered. Her reserve, her docile obedience, broke like glass, and the physical shock of it nearly catapulted her to the floor. She gripped her hands together, ignoring the pain.

"Don't you even care about me? I don't love Stuart. We wouldn't be happy together. Why should you care who I marry as long as he loves me and I him? What about what I want?" She was screaming, something she would never have done before, but now it hardly fazed her.

The blow that followed nearly threw her to the floor. Annie stared at her father, one hand pressed against her scalding cheek. Tears stung her eyes.

"It's Travis Hart, isn't it? You imagine yourself in love with him."

She looked down so her eyes wouldn't betray the painful truth.

"What a stupid schoolgirl notion. He's probably buried in enemy territory this very minute. Stuart is here. He is willing." Her father grasped her shoulder with an iron grip. "And you will accept him!"

"You can't even carry a conversation without dazing off. I don't want to know what it was you were thinking about just now."

Father's words vaulted her into the present. Her hands were slick with sweat, her knees shaking.

"For once in your life, Father, just leave me alone. Please." She rushed from the room, down the hall, and into the empty dining room. There, she crumpled to the floor, hands pressed to her eyes, hot tears leaking through her fingers.

God, help me. I know I've sinned. I don't deserve happiness, but would a morsel of stability be too much to ask? Or have I gone so far as to be undeserving of that too?

What had induced her to come home? She would have been better off to have never left Galveston. Maybe it would be better to return once Robbie was well enough to travel, though leaving would mean reneging on her promise to Mrs. Miller to take over the town midwifery responsibilities.

Or perhaps she should start over somewhere new. A place where there weren't memories hiding behind every door, where shadows of the past didn't whisper in her ears.

"Annie." This voice wasn't full of her father's gruff rebuke. Although it was deep and masculine, it didn't resemble her father's at all. The single word, her name, held kindness. Enough tenderness to bring her to her feet, with the help of a hand on her shoulder. And when he stood, he didn't take his hand away, nor move backward. Instead, Travis Hart drew her into his arms, letting her rest her head against his chest, and sob out the anxiety of the past hour.

He was strength and gentleness all at once. She closed her arms tighter around his waist, her senses awash with soap and leather and sun-warmed cotton. His hand rubbed soothing circles across her back, and she let herself cry, feeling no shame in it. Truly, there was no shame in allowing emotion, though her father had always told her the opposite.

She pulled away, raising tear-blurred eyes to meet his. "Robbie. I must go see to him."

"No. Josie is with him. *You* must sit down and tell me what it is you're crying about." He pulled out a dining room chair, and she sat. Taking the one beside her, he placed his hands atop hers. "And that's a doctor's order." His smile ruined the effect of his commanding words.

"Robbie is so precious to me. I'm always afraid of losing him." She drew in a long breath.

"Broken bones, especially a clean break like Robbie's, are generally not fatal, given proper treatment." His brown eyes didn't hold even the tiniest hint of chiding.

"I know that. But that doesn't stop a mother from worrying. Foolish, isn't it? I'm a trained midwife, yet I fall to pieces at something so slight."

"It's not foolish. Though I've known your son less than an hour, I can already tell he loves you greatly. You're a good mother, Annie Lawrence. It's natural that you would be concerned about Robbie's welfare. I've treated countless patients, and I've found that those who care most feel the most anxiety when it comes to their loved ones. I guess it's one of those truths of life. As my father always says, 'With love, there's always the risk of loss.'"

She smiled slowly, his words taking root within her heart. "For a man who spends his days stitching people up, you possess quite the poetic streak, Dr. Hart."

"Much to the exasperation of my brothers. They never took well to Keats on roundup days." A dimple appeared, turning his smile so magnetic, she found herself unable to drag her gaze away. "But it works wonders to distract the patients. Once I launch into *Hamlet*, they're too diverted by my less-than-Shakespearean recitation skills to even care that I'm sticking a needle in their appendages."

She laughed. After her bout of tears, the joy of the sensation welled up and sent her into another spasm of giggles. He joined in, deep chuckles reverberating through the room. Had anyone stood outside the door, they might've thought she and Travis had taken leave of their senses. Perhaps they had. Perhaps finding laughter in the midst of such a tense day was as off-kilter as it seemed.

Or perhaps, it was the cure she'd so long needed.

~

Though Hartville wasn't a booming metropolis by San Antonio standards, the town suited Travis just fine. He knew everybody, cared for them in times of illness. Helped them through births and deaths alike. After the long, hard years of war, healing others had healed him in the process. He'd seen so many good men die, powerless to offer them more than the barest comforts, powerless to give them pain relief while he severed gangrene-infected limbs from their bodies.

Now he could concentrate on enjoying life, on helping others live theirs in good health.

He waved to Michael Mortenson. The young man paused from sweeping the walkway in front of the mercantile to return the salutation.

His glance fell on Collingswood & Henderson's Hardware, a business next to the post office that was rumored to be going on the market soon. His thoughts turned to Houston. His favorite brother had been away for so long. Would he ever come to his senses and make Hartville his home? Like Travis, Houston didn't share the Hart passion for ranching. That little old hardware store would be perfect for a businessman like Houston. Now, if only he would make up his mind to come home...

Past First National Bank and Virginia's Hotel lay Travis's favorite building in town. Unlike the ranch, which belonged to the entire Hart family, the tiny, wood-sided building was his alone.

WILLIAM TRAVIS HART, MD, read the neatly painted shingle.

He unlocked the door, flipped the sign from *Closed* to *Open*, and stepped inside. He didn't much regret not keeping steady office hours. Families in the outlying areas needed his care. Many didn't come to town often. Besides, in an emergency, everyone knew to send word to the 7 Heart. Usually, one of the ranch hands or Perla, the family cook, had some inkling of where to find him.

The clean smell of soap mingled with the pungent aroma of some of his herbal remedies. Had Mollie Olson been poking through them again? He'd hired the fifteen-year-old to clean the place, not stick her nose into jars.

The bell above the door jangled only moments after he'd sat down at his desk in the back room to update some patient files. He pushed back his swivel chair, stood, and stepped into the waiting area.

Miss Spanner, Hartville's attempt at bringing Eastern fashions to the Texas Hill Country, adjusted her showy silk skirts and stepped into the waiting area.

"What can I do for you, ma'am?"

The longtime spinster held up a bandage-wrapped thumb. "I was in the midst of sewing Chantilly lace onto Miss Palmer's new mauve silk when I nearly hemmed my thumb to the fabric. I bandaged it, but the pain still lingers, three days later."

"Why don't you come through, and I'll take a look?" He motioned for her to precede him.

Once Miss Spanner had seated herself on his examining table and unwrapped her thumb, she gave her usual opening line. "Did you hear the news?"

He busied himself with collecting supplies from one of the cabinets—a clean cloth to wash the wound, comfrey salve to help with healing.

"Not today," he answered, as was his custom.

In less than three seconds flat, she pounced on the invitation like a tabby devouring a crock of cream. "Annie Lawrence arrived in town last week to take over Mrs. Miller's patients. Already, she saved Helen Tatum's baby's life, went into the mercantile and bought a yard of white cotton, and dined at the Hartville Hotel with none other than Hartley P. Burton himself. Imagine that! And her away so many years. What in heaven's name are you putting on my finger?" Apparently, he'd momentarily diverted her attention by opening the pot of strong-smelling, green ointment.

"Comfrey salve. It's well-known for its healing properties. I'm going to give you some to take home, and if you keep applying it, the wound should heal in no time at all."

"Mm-hm." Lips clamped together, Miss Spanner sounded as if she were chewing on the very needles that had wounded her finger. "So what do you think of my news, Dr. Hart?"

He smiled, applying the salve to her outstretched finger. "You gave me four pieces of information. The first two, I know to be correct, as I was there. The third, possible. But the fourth, I know to be completely untrue, as her son broke his arm just last night. She wasn't anywhere near the Hartville Hotel."

"For someone who professes to know little of the doings of the town, you know a lot about the doings of Mrs. Annie Lawrence. Do I have the hope of stitching yet another wedding dress to be worn by a new Hart bride?"

Maybe the jar was slippery. Maybe his grip hadn't been tight enough. All Travis knew was that it now lay smashed in a hundred tiny pieces, a glob of the greenish mixture adorning his shoes.

"I'm so sorry." Thankfully, he'd finished using the salve on her finger. He wrapped it with a fresh bandage, trying to ignore the glass crunching under his feet. "I don't know what came over me."

Miss Spanner's thin lips formed a feline smile. "I do. What sort of dress would your bride prefer? Does she care for silk?"

He knotted the bandage, glad to be finished with the task, simple as it was. "I'm not getting married, ma'am. At least not anytime soon. And I'd appreciate it if you'd not mention Mrs. Lawrence in connection with me."

The middle-aged woman pouted like a child. "But you'd make such a fine husband, Dr. Hart. Out of all your father's sons, I've always thought you the best marriage material. Not that I'd tell anyone else, mind you. Some of those brothers of yours are so...wild. You're much steadier. And wouldn't you make a fine father to that son of hers?"

Her words probed at him, small scalpels needling his insides. The sight of Annie Lawrence had revived something he long thought relegated to the dustiest corners of his mind. In the handful of hours he'd spent with her, she'd made him feel new again. As if, instead of merely helping others live their lives, he could have one of his own. The moment his father had issued his command that each of his sons wed, it had seemed an impossibility. Travis wouldn't find a wife in order to hold on to something as concrete as land. It would be wrong, going against everything he believed.

But now? Now this woman, this beautiful conglomeration of sweetness and strength, fragility and determination, had come back into his life like a flame newly lit.

Lord, help me. Because I'm not sure if I could endure letting her go a second time.

CHAPTER 5

*W*hat would laying eyes upon Travis's home do to her after so long? Memories were embedded into El Regalo's walls, of growing up alongside Travis and the Hart family. Running away from young Hays Hart as the little prankster tried to steal her bag of gumdrops. Seeing GW come into the room and staring at him with unabashed, girlish awe. Trading smiles with Travis and indulging in rose-tinted dreams of someday taking his name and sharing his house with all those happy, loving people.

Now she was returning, Robbie at her side, squeezed between him and Travis on the hard-backed buckboard seat. She fought the urge to squirm. Every time the wagon hit a bump, she found herself pressed all too tightly against Travis's side. Though she wore skirts and crinoline, the layers didn't keep her from acquainting herself with his muscled thigh as it brushed against her. And wasn't there some sort of law against smelling so fine—all soap and leather and undeniable maleness? A hateful blush burned her cheeks.

"You're gonna let me see your old rope, aren't you, Doc Travis?" Robbie wriggled enough to put a hooked fish to shame. After nearly a month, his arm had healed almost totally, though he still wore a sling. This trip was Robbie's long-awaited reward for being a good patient and obeying doctor's orders.

"Yes, sir. I sure am." Travis smiled. "But you can't have it till your arm is better."

"You mean I can have it, then?" Robbie's eyes lit.

"Why not? I don't do much roping these days. Getting too old, I guess."

Old? Him? Not in a thousand years would she call this vibrant man beside her old. He had a few lines in his face, particularly around his eyes, but the broad width of his shoulders and the strength in his stride gave him the appearance of someone who could rope and ride with one hand tied behind his back. Well, perhaps that was a bit of an exaggeration, but still...

"Hear that, Ma? Doc Travis says I can have his old rope! I'll be a real cowboy in no time." Robbie grinned, his hair already wind-tousled. A stubborn cowlick flipped up on one side, and Annie smoothed it with her fingers.

"That's very kind of Dr. Hart. What do we say when people do kind things for us?"

"Thank you, Doc Travis. You're real nice. Can you sing that cowboy song again? The one you taught me when you was checking on my arm."

Annie suppressed a smile. Travis, sing? She must've not been within earshot when that was going on. She made a mental note to eavesdrop when Travis next spent time with Robbie.

"Not right now. We're almost there. You'll be meeting some cowboys in just a few minutes."

"Come a ti yi yippee, come a ti yippie yay!" Robbie pumped his fist in the air.

Travis glanced at her, amusement in his gaze. "Don't tell me he learned that in Galveston."

She grinned. "You know very well *you* taught it to him."

He chuckled. "Guilty as charged, darlin'." He accentuated his Texan drawl, prompting giggles from Robbie. Though it was meant as a joke, the endearment rooted itself in her mind. It would be easy to think of herself as this man's darling. Easy to imagine the three of them together, not just for the afternoon, but for tomorrow and every day after.

Far, far too easy.

The moment El Regalo came into view, it became easier still. Framed against the backdrop of gently rolling hills, the Hart ranch house could be termed only one thing—a mansion fit for royalty. Built of sandy brick, enlivened with ornately designed windows, it ought to have seemed out of place in this land she'd always thought of as wild. Yet it fit somehow. A tribute to George Washington Hart's years of work, and most of all, a testimony to his abiding love for his beloved late wife. Annie's breath caught.

"This ain't no ranch. It's a castle!" Robbie exclaimed. The moment the horses stopped, he jumped down.

"Isn't," Annie corrected. Her son had hit the nail on the head. When compared to the grandeur of El Regalo, the Parker ranch seemed like a rotting hogshead.

They made their way to the door. Before Travis could lay a hand on the door handle, it swung open. A tall, roguishly handsome man stood just inside. His face split into a grin, dimples emerging that could melt the heart of any Lone Star State gal.

"Well, well, look who's come for a visit. My all-too-absent brother. Who's the pretty lady, Travis?"

Was she mistaken, or did a hint of a flush creep over Travis's face? "You remember Annie Lawrence, don't you?"

"Of course. How could I forget? Heard you were back in town, Miss Gumdrops." He grinned.

So this was Hays. Annie returned the smile. "Haven't they tossed you in the clink for your thieving ways?"

"Still evading capture. My wife's been keeping me close to home lately, and she's pretty enough to beat general store candy ten times over." He squatted down until he was eye level with Robbie. The boy gaped at Hays's genuine cowboy attire of checkered shirt, brown vest, jean work pants, and tall leather boots.

"You must be Annie's boy. How do you like this part of Texas?"

"Fine and dandy. Just give me a rope, some cows, a horse that ain't lame, and I'll be ready and rarin' to go." Robbie said this with such gravity that the three adults were hard-pressed to stifle their laughter.

"Sounds like a plan." Hays matched Robbie's serious tone. "Looks like you got a sore paw, partner. You'll need plenty of grub to gain back your strength. Why don't you come on inside. Don't tell her I told you so, but our cook makes the best blueberry pie around. And if we sweet talk her just right, I'll betcha she'll let us have a piece. But first, let's say howdy to the rest of the family."

They made their way into the vestibule, Hays and Robbie keeping up a steady stream of chatter. Annie smoothed her hand down the front of her dove-gray silk dress, hoping her hair hadn't suffered too much in the dust and wind.

A mix of male and female voices drifted from the parlor. Annie swallowed hard. She'd grown up amongst these boys, so there was no need to be nervous. But they were grown men now. The war had no doubt wrought changes, some more obvious than others. Still, this was Travis's family. And he didn't seem the least bit uncomfortable as he followed his brother into the room.

Mercy, what a sight...

Claret-colored wallpaper. Walnut wainscoting. Ornately woven rugs. Plush sofas and comfortable-looking wing chairs.

And the people. A lovely, brown-haired young lady wearing a lavender skirt and white blouse sat on a sofa, Hays claiming the empty seat beside her. A broad-shouldered, dark-haired man leaned against the mantel, his jaw set into a hard line. Annie startled slightly at the man's missing left eye and burn-scarred face. A couple with their arms around each other seemed oblivious to everything else—probably Chisholm and his new bride.

Beside a wingchair that seemed a child's plaything next to his taller-than-tall height stood George Washington Hart. Though his hair had whitened and he looked a bit thinner, little else about the man had changed. He immediately advanced, grasping his son's hand.

"Haven't seen you in a couple of days, Travis." His tone was deep and unmistakably Texan. "Been keeping busy with all those ailing people, I bet. Who's this you brought with you?" He turned his clear-eyed gaze on Annie.

"This is Annie Lawrence, Father. Annie, you've met my father, GW Hart."

Though he wore no Stetson, the man tipped a nod. He smiled, the corners of his eyes crinkling. "Welcome back to El Regalo, Mrs. Lawrence. We heard of the loss of your husband, and our deepest sympathies go out to you. He died fighting for a fine cause, ma'am, as I'm sure you already know."

Annie returned the smile. "Thank you kindly, Mr. Hart. I'm very pleased to have returned to Hartville. I enjoyed my stay in Galveston, but it's good to be home."

"My sentiments exactly, ma'am. There's no place I'd rather be than here in this most beautiful country. No offense to any other part of Texas, of course." He looked down, as if noticing Robbie for the first time. "Let me guess. You're the new ranch hand. Am I right?"

While Robbie had warmed instantly to Hays, he seemed a bit taken aback by this giant of a man. He took a step behind Annie.

"Say hello to Mr. Hart," Annie said quietly, though she hardly blamed the boy. She'd always been a little frightened of Travis's father as a child. Who wouldn't be? He seemed to tower over even the trees.

"Come now. I expect any ranch hand of mine to know how to talk." GW looked on the verge of a smile.

Robbie hesitated, hung behind Annie's skirt an instant more, then stuck out his hand. "Howdy." An endearing grin stole across her son's face. "I'm Robert Stuart Lawrence. Ma says I'm too young to be a ranch hand but that I can start practicing real soon. She's dead set on making me learn to read and do my sums, but I'd a sight rather ride the range. Everybody says your ranch is the finest around these parts, and I've been real anxious to see it. Can I? Can I see your cows, Mr. Hart?"

"Well, now." GW cocked his head as if in deep consideration. "I suppose that could be arranged. Provided you don't give your ma any fuss next time she wants to teach you your numbers. I won't have ignorant ranch hands on my land, so you'd best study hard if that's what you're aiming for."

"I won't make a lick of a fuss. Honest."

"Then why don't you and Hays go outside? He'll show you 'round, won't you, Hays?"

At Hays's mournful glance toward the pretty lady at his side, GW said, "And don't you fuss none about leaving your bride. She won't run off. Will you, Emma?"

The lovely woman exchanged a smile with her new husband. "Not a chance." She crossed the room and stood by Chisholm and Caro.

GW turned back to Annie. "Now, come on in and sit yourself down, Mrs. Lawrence. You, too, Travis."

Annie allowed Travis to lead her to the sofa vacated by Hays and

Emma. Unlike the newlyweds, they sat on each end, a respectable distance apart.

A perfectly respectable distance that frustrated her far too much.

~

They belonged together. He'd sensed it when they were young, and he knew it now. Sitting beside her at El Regalo, the sleeve of her dress brushing his arm, her laughter soft, like a dozen butterfly wings, had given him such a sense of being alive that he could almost taste the exhilaration. With his father's announcement hanging in the air, might this be God's way of opening the door to Travis's future? Though Annie was unaware of the edict, such a thing wouldn't stop her from caring for him. It couldn't. Not when it mattered so little to himself.

The bodice of her dress rose and fell with gentle breaths as Annie bent over some sewing in her father's parlor, candles lighting the room with soft-etched shadows. A strand of hair spiraled from her hapless bun, falling downward and landing against the creamy skin of her exposed neck. His fingers ached to follow the ringlet's path, to touch that tempting swath of pink-tinged skin. Was it as soft as it looked? Did it smell of violets like her hair?

Could he dare hope she might give her heart to him? He wouldn't rush her to marry, only a courtship for now. Then someday, a wedding like Hays and Emma, Chisholm and Caro.

The ring resting in his top bureau drawer seemed to call to him. He'd seen it at a shop while on leave, soon after enlisting in the army. From the first moment of glimpsing it, he'd known it was meant for Annie and no other. After the war, it had lain beneath a pile of shirts, unworn and rarely touched. He'd taken it out once or twice, but before Annie had reentered his life, the pain of even looking at it had been too great. Could it be possible that now, after all these years, both he and the ring had a second chance?

"Annie?"

She raised her gaze from her work, laying it aside. Robbie had been worn out upon his return from El Regalo and had promptly fallen asleep, curled up on the rug beside the family's shaggy black dog. Mr.

Parker had gone outside half an hour ago to check on a problem in the stables. Leaving the two of them alone.

"Yes, Travis?"

He swallowed, his mouth suddenly dry. "It was a fine day, wasn't it?"

She nodded, candlelight dancing across her features. "A day to remember. I can't recall when I've laughed so much. Your brothers...my goodness. And your father seems so pleased with his family, with all they've achieved. He seems especially proud of you."

Yes, well... "What about you, Annie? What do you think of the life I've built here?" He waited, his breath and hopes hanging on her answer.

Her gaze fluttered to the carpet. Seconds—or was it hours?—passed before she spoke. "I think what you've accomplished is a thing to be proud of. I'm proud of you, Travis Hart. The war stole so much from so many. Not everyone has managed to regain all they lost. You're one of them. As for myself..." Finally, those ever-changeable eyes met his. "Stuart was so young when he died, with so much of his life ahead of him. He never got to see his son. Not once."

"But you never cared for Stuart. Wasn't it your father who coerced you into marriage?" Since the day he'd first clapped eyes on Stuart Lawrence, Travis hadn't held favorable feelings for the young man a few years his senior. Callous, often uncaring, he treated the world as if he held it in his beefy palm, goaded by his banker father. Stuart had been accepted as Annie's intended since their adolescence. Travis hoped the war might have changed that. But when he'd heard of their marriage in a letter from Houston, all hope had died, there on the battlefield like so many men.

It had come to life again. And in a few more minutes, that hope might take its first mewling cries, as Annie pledged her promise.

I haven't stopped loving you, Travis. I would be honored to allow your courtship.

Annie's soft voice brought an end to his musings. "I never gave Stuart the chance he deserved. How I behaved toward him is something no husband should have to experience." Her words, as well as the tears glimmering in her eyes, doused him like a bucket of ice water. What did she mean, the chance he *deserved*? She'd been a mere seventeen years old, and forced into the deal by her money-hungry father. "The two days we were together as husband and wife should have been the most joyous of Stuart's life. Instead, I made him miserable." Sorrow choked her words. "He tried to be kind and loving. He wanted to be a groom to his bride. And all I could think of was my foolish, selfish dreams." She stood, her sewing landing on the floor, and paced the carpet, her back to him.

Travis sat, as still as if rigor mortis had set in.

"I still remember the last words he said to me, just as he was leaving. 'I'll be home soon, Annie. And maybe, when I return, you'll find it in your heart to think kindly upon me.' I should have kissed him."

She spun around, her skirt swirling. "But no. I just stood there, not even extending so much as my hand in farewell. He wrote to me after that, a few letters in much the same fashion. He told me he wanted me to love him and that he'd do his best to love me. But he never came back. Sometimes I wonder if it was my indifference that killed him. If I'd treated him as I should, perhaps he would've fought harder to live. If I'd written and told him I was carrying his child, he might not have let himself die. So you see, Travis, I'm not proud of the life I lived then. But I will be proud of the one I live now. I was not a good wife to Stuart while he walked this earth, but I've been true since I learned of his death." She sank into her chair, palm pressed against her mouth, silent tears falling down her cheeks.

He drew in a fortifying breath, pain lancing his heart at the shadows of guilt this woman dwelt under. *God, help me to make her see the truth.*

"Annie, Stuart is gone. No amount of sacrifice on your part will bring him back. I...I...care about you very much. I—"

The look she gave him—well, it would've been better if she'd punched him in the gut. "How can you say that after what I just told you? Didn't you hear anything I said? I don't deserve to be cared for, Travis. Can't you see?"

"Then what do you deserve?" Every fiber of his body ached to take her in his arms, show her exactly what she did deserve. Love. A second chance. So she'd made a mistake. She'd punished herself for nine long years, lashing herself over and over with ropes of guilt and condemnation. Wasn't that enough, even in the eyes of God? Didn't He promise forgiveness, if one presented a contrite heart?

"Nothing." Her face was a cold, hard mask, beneath which simmered a layer of raw pain. "Please leave, Travis. I'm grateful for your friendship, but don't expect anything beyond that. Not from me. Not ever."

CHAPTER 6

She wasn't sure where the storm brewed most. Within or without. Outside, rain mercilessly pounded the roof, the torrent punctuated by a sudden flash of lightning.

Inside Annie's heart, the tempest blew with equal fury. Four days had not lessened its blast, nor softened the remembrance of Travis's expression as he'd strode from the room and out of the house, not once looking back.

The taste of her words still lingered in her mouth. She'd confessed it all—leaving out only the identity of the man whom she'd centered her thoughts upon during her marriage to Stuart. Travis Hart had been the cause of her sin. Not his fault, only hers. She couldn't blame him for his charm, that dimpled smile. How strong and warm and perfect his hand felt, twined within hers.

She turned in bed, punching her pillow with a ferocious thump. Sleep had become a stranger, night a prison.

"Oh, Travis. I didn't mean to wound you. How could you have hoped —thought—that there could ever be anything between us again?" The words were muffled against the well-worn fabric of her quilt. A wedding ring pattern, done in her favorite colors, lavender and white, given to her by a friend upon the occasion of her marriage to Stuart.

God, turn my thoughts from Travis. Help me to think only of Stuart, the man I have wronged. Help me to right the past, so guilt no longer haunts me. Thank You for Your faithfulness. And for forgiving such a wretched sinner as I. Amen.

The prayer salved her soul, and sleep finally came. Yet after what couldn't have been more than an hour, a knock on the front door shook her awake.

Only one reason why anyone would knock on a midwife's door at such an hour in such terrible weather. Dressing took only moments. Her bag found its way into her hands, and she hurried down the hall, creeping carefully so as not to wake Robbie.

The door open, she looked into the face of a drenched young man, water sluicing off the brim of his hat like an absurd sort of fountain.

"You the midwife?"

Annie nodded.

"Come quick! It's my Rachel. She's in a terrible state."

Thankful she'd never been squeamish about a soaking, Annie followed the man to the barn, where he assisted her in saddling her horse. They headed in the direction of town. Despite her shawl and bonnet, Annie's teeth chattered.

As was often the case, the house of the laboring mother was the only residence with a light shining. Annie dismounted, landing on the ground in a bone-jarring instant, splattering herself with mud. She headed inside, mentally going through her list of patient notes about Rachel Monroe. First-time mother. Three weeks ahead of due date. Young woman of only twenty. Pregnancy normal. Last visit two weeks ago.

Upstairs she went, heading in the direction of the moans. A single candle sputtered out its last breaths and left the room in darkness. Annie hastened to light another. In the dimness, Rachel's features were startlingly young. Everything in the room was new, from the shiny dresser to the polished brass bedstead. A sure sign of a newlywed couple, married barely a year. With a single sweep of her arm, Annie removed the coverlet. No sense spoiling that, seeing as it was white and lace.

"I'm so glad to see you." Rachel's eyes were huge, terrified blue discs against a complexion that was probably peaches and cream but at the moment blanched whiter than the comforter. "I never thought it would hurt like this. I'm scared. I wish my ma wasn't in San Antonio. She's supposed to visit next week. Why won't the baby wait till then?"

Rachel groaned as another contraction took hold. Suddenly, wetness doused the bed. Rachel began to cry. "I don't want to die. I'm only twenty. Bill told me he was going to take me to Austin next year for my birthday and take me to the theater. I don't want to die before I've done that." The girl sobbed.

Annie smiled reassuringly. "I've been doing this a long time, Rachel. You won't be dying. Not as long as I have anything to say about it. But crying won't help things and shall only make you feel worse. Now, I'm going to change the sheets and help you into something more comfortable."

Usually, her words calmed anxious mothers. Rachel only cried louder.

Bill flung the door open. He dropped to his knees beside his wife's bed, clutching her hand. His face paled. "Why is the bed wet? What's going on?" He raised frantic eyes to Annie's. "Something isn't right. My Rachel wouldn't be crying like this if everything was all right." He shot to his feet, looking like a little boy confronting another on a schoolyard. Far too young to be thinking of fatherhood. "My wife's in danger! You're too young to help her. I'm gonna get someone else. Stay with her till I get back. Don't leave her!" He flung the words over his shoulder as he raced from the room.

Had she been in any other profession, Annie might have been insulted. She was six years his senior. At least. Yet no one ever behaved like themselves in a delivery room. Whom would he fetch more competent than her?

There was only one person. And she didn't want to think about Travis Hart right now.

"Where'd he go? Where'd Bill go?" Rachel stared in the direction of the door.

"He'll be back. Don't concern yourself with him right now. You must put all your concentration into bringing your baby into the world." Sometimes it paid to put a bit of sternness into her tone. "You want to keep your baby safe, right?"

Rachel nodded.

"Of course, you do. Then you must stay calm." Annie found a set of clean sheets in one of the drawers. She made short work of changing both them and Rachel's nightgown, then performed an internal examination. The girl quieted, and her cries during each contraction held less hysteria and more concentration. Outside, rain still pelted the roof. Having nothing better to do, Annie sat beside the mother to wait out the duration of this stage of labor.

And to hope against vain hope that Bill Monroe would bring anyone but Travis Hart to the delivery room this night.

~

*A*s a practicing physician for over six years, his hands shouldn't shake during house calls. Though his concern wasn't due to the situation of the patient—a laboring first-time mother.

It was due to the other person Travis would find inside.

He climbed the steps, rain leaving a puddled trail in his wake, an anxious Bill Monroe at his heels. "She'll be all right, won't she, Dr. Hart? You can save her, my Rachel?"

Travis turned, placing a hand on the young man's damp shoulder. The boy's—for he hardly looked a man—throat jerked.

"She'll be fine, Bill. But *I* won't be, if someone falls and breaks their neck on these slippery stairs. Get a towel and wipe this mess up." He continued up the stairs toward the keening noises coming from behind the closed door. He opened it and stepped inside.

The second their gazes met, Annie's breath faltered for the briefest of instants. Overwhelming need swept through him. To pull her into his arms, soothe away that haggard look in her beautiful eyes. Reassure her that all her fears were for naught, that he would wait as long as it took for her to forgive herself. As long as he could be sure that in the end, the prize of her heart would be his.

But for now, she was the midwife. He, the doctor.

Both must work together to help this young woman bring forth a new life.

"Contractions are every two minutes. Waters broke over an hour ago. I'd say delivery is imminent." Hair straggled down Annie's face, and dark circles haunted her eyes. Yet as she knelt beside the mother, her expression was brimful of passion and purpose.

"Good." Travis washed his hands, noting the perfect order of Annie's instruments. "We're right here with you, Mrs. Monroe. Just do exactly as Mrs. Lawrence says."

He only half listened as Annie helped the girl into the proper position for delivery, intent on sorting through his own bag. Forceps, but only if they were absolutely needed. Surgical thread, in case of tearing.

Then he knelt beside Annie, and together they worked with Rachel Monroe as her little boy slipped into the world. Face like a wrinkled old man's, crying lustily. Perfect in everyone's eyes.

Annie handed the baby to the beaming Rachel. As she turned to Travis, sorrow flashed across her tired face. Of course. What person, having witnessed this moment, could not help but wish it for themselves? And not only Annie. He wanted to be in Bill's place. The anxious father, bursting into the bedroom, hearing his child's cries for the first time.

He wanted to experience these defining moments. As a man with something at stake, instead of the shadowy figure of attending physician.

Shared with no other but her.

After the baby was washed and wrapped, the couple cooed over their new addition, while Annie sat, watching with an absent expression.

He couldn't take her silence any longer, and once she moved to clean her instruments, he stepped behind her. "Do you like apple pie?" Thunder in Texas, how inane could he be?

Surprise lit her eyes. "Apple pie? I guess so. Why?"

"Good. You see, I had some fine apple pie last night at the Hartville Hotel. And I think we owe it to ourselves, after the night we've been through, to have some again...say, tomorrow evening?" Not exactly a sweep-the-gal-off-her-feet kind of proposal, but it would do for now.

For the longest moment, he anticipated her "no." Could hear it ringing in his ears, even. Yet a small smile found purchase on her lips, and she gave a little laugh. "I've heard of celebratory drinks before...but never apple pie. Might be fun."

Fun? Spending an hour in her company? Letting himself look his fill upon a face that held so much sway over his jumbled emotions? Fun was being seven years old, sneaking ice cream on the back porch with Houston. Apple pie with Annie?

Pleasurable torment.

CHAPTER 7

"So that was that. A little boy. Bill and Rachel overjoyed. And, I might venture to say, a bit more grown up after the experience." Annie cupped her hands around the cup of coffee, the comfort of Mrs. Miller's parlor wrapping around her like a well-loved blanket.

The longtime midwife nodded, a smile creasing her wrinkled cheeks. "Becoming a parent has a way of turning flighty girls into careful women. And fancy-free boys into hardworking men." Her chair creaked as she rocked back and forth, knitting needles keeping time. "Of course, you know that from experience, my dear."

Annie looked down, steam clouding up into her face. She took a sip of the warm beverage before speaking. "Yes. I never thought I could love anyone as much as I do Robbie. He's become my whole life. He and my patients, that is."

"Careful, Annie. The moment we say something has overtaken our lives is usually the moment the Almighty decides to give us more. And doesn't He always know best?"

"What if I don't want more?" The words had slipped out before she'd fully contemplated them. Although, if she'd been totally honest with herself, she would've admitted her true reason for riding over to Mrs. Miller's. Not to discuss patients, midwife to fellow midwife. But to gain the comfort she always received when in the woman's presence.

"Why? Don't you think the Lord has anything else in store for you? Contentment is one thing, child. Complacency another. You have such a giving heart. Do you think the Lord intends for you to love only Robbie for the rest of your life?"

"Would that be so bad?" A sigh whooshed from her lips. She was a Benedict Arnold to her own determination. Why had she agreed to Travis's invitation? It must've been fatigue. A chill from the rain.

Or a girlish desire to stay caught up in her own emotions.

It was tonight. And her thoughts shifted from backing out to keeping her promise with as much variance as the Galveston tide.

"I don't think I'm the person to answer that. I don't even think you are." Mrs. Miller laid aside her knitting.

"I'm only being realistic. I'm twenty-seven. A widow. And in my current profession, I doubt I'll be meeting throngs of eligible men. Nor do I wish to." Because there was only one man she could ever have. She'd already married him. And he'd already died.

"I don't think realistic expectations are holding much sway with you." Mrs. Miller's clear brown eyes seemed to delve deep inside Annie's mind. "I think you believe you don't deserve any more happiness than what you've already been given. Am I right?"

Annie didn't answer.

"The thing about God giving out blessings is that we don't deserve a lick of them. Life isn't about getting what we deserve. It's about getting what He, in His love, chooses to give us. Sometimes what He chooses isn't always easy. Sometimes it's full of so much pain that it leaves us aching. And other times, God smiles down and throws so much joy into our laps that we cannot help but rejoice at the beauty of it. I'm not going to make any attempts to grasp His path for you. But I will say this. Don't let guilt over something that happened years ago determine the way you face your tomorrows. God isn't like that, Annie. If He were, think of all those people in the Good Book who wouldn't have made a thimbleful out of their lives. I know you married your husband because it was what your father wanted. Whether that was right or wrong, well, there's no going back. But you don't have to let that decision affect the ones you make now."

Tears pricked Annie's eyes. She wanted to believe her friend's words. Wanted to trust that they held the truth she'd sought for so long. Still... "Isn't there such a thing as being punished for our wrongs?"

Mrs. Miller nodded. "If Robbie were to disobey, you'd give him consequences, right? God does the same. But it is not up to His children to choose those consequences. Doing so is putting ourselves in the Lord's place. And we humans surely don't belong there. Just keep that in mind as you go through the rest of your life." Mrs. Miller smiled, a look of total peace giving her features a glow that not even Galveston's most celebrated beauty could surpass.

"I'll try." Annie picked up the discarded knitting. The cranberry-colored wool was in the process of becoming...something. She couldn't tell what. "What are you working on?"

"A blanket." She gestured to a box in a corner of the room. "There are more in there. Just because I can no longer be the first one to hold those babies doesn't mean I can't make lovely things to wrap them in. It's a fine thing I did all those years, but that doesn't make what I'm doing now any less fine. It's all in how you look at the world. And I aim to do so through His eyes.

"Now, if you'll step on out into the kitchen, there's a plate of cookies just begging to be sampled. Nothing better this side of heaven than a cookie and a cup of coffee. Long as you're sharing them with the right people, that is."

Annie stood. But instead of moving toward the kitchen, she crossed the room and wrapped her arms around the frail old woman. "You don't know how much I've missed you while I've been away," she whispered.

"And I, you. God's got a fine purpose for you, Annie child. I can't wait to see how He's going to work it all out."

~

*N*ew beginnings could be made under these stars, the endless skies of Texas brimful with them tonight, crystals against black velvet.

Travis ran his hand down the front of his suit jacket. Thankfully, the Hartville Hotel was nearly empty tonight. He'd already chosen seats in the most secluded corner to be found. All that remained was for Annie to arrive.

The fresh, balmy scent of the night air wafted over him as he stood on the hotel steps. He drew in a long breath, accepting the calm it offered, as well as the fragrance.

Give me strength tonight, Lord. Help me to sort things out between us. I care for her so much. Let this not be a mistake.

As if in a glorious vision, she rode down the street—sidesaddle tonight. She stopped in front of the hotel and dismounted, tying her horse to a hitching post.

Sweet Texas thunder...

He'd thought her beautiful when she was younger, with those pretty eyes and that long, often unruly hair. She'd been a girl then. Was a woman now. A woman wearing a dark green dress that hugged her waist, revealing curves in all the right places. A woman with the faintest touch of sunburn on her nose and the smallest of smiles dancing across her cherry-hued lips.

How could he help but love her?

"I haven't dined out since before the war, so I wasn't sure what to wear." She climbed the steps, skirts held daintily just above her ankles.

"You look perfect." The words came easy. "Shall we go in?" He let her walk in front of him. The hand-on-arm gesture used by courting couples would only make her uneasy.

The elegance of the Hartville Hotel seemed a perfect backdrop for the evening of his dreams. The walls boasted walnut wainscoting and dark blue wallpaper. Linen and china adorned the circular tables.

Since he'd already made arrangements with the waiter, Travis led the way to his chosen table. He pulled out Annie's chair. As she sank into it, he caught the scent of violets lingering in her hair. It was heady stuff, a fragrance he would have gladly inhaled the whole night long, until he became as unaware of the world as a man under the effects of ether.

"I don't know how you did it, but ever since last night, I've been dreaming about apple pie. Robbie got mad at me. Said I was starving him with all my talk." She laughed.

"Where is Robbie tonight?"

"Playing with Josie. Apparently, there was some grand plan to make a batch of fudge and eat it all before I returned."

The waiter came and took their orders. Coffee for Travis. Tea for Annie. Apple pie for both.

Another couple took the table nearest. Travis scarcely noticed who they were. "You never used to be one for sweets. After school, when all the children ran to the store to splurge on penny candy, you and Josie always went straight home."

"Father only occasionally gave us money for treats. He said it was a waste of hard-earned cash and would ruin our digestion. Considering how much some of those children consumed, he was probably right." She rested her hand on the tablecloth, fingers toying with the folded napkin.

"Do you follow that principle with Robbie?"

She shook her head with another laugh. "No. Robbie has a sweet tooth the size of Texas. But I only let him eat Rhode Island quantities."

Travis chuckled. "You've done a fine job raising your son." His tone turned serious. "He's a blessed young man to have a mother who cares so much."

A sigh escaped her lips. "Father accuses me of not caring enough. Says I spend too much time traipsing the countryside. He's never understood my passions. Any of them."

Travis's heart sped up. Did she mean him, the passion they had shared? If her father had not interfered, he could be Annie's husband this very moment. Permitted to hold her in his arms. Love her, with a license to make it legal.

It went against everything the Lord taught, but at this moment, Travis loathed Brock Parker.

"Well, he can't stop you now. You belong to no one." Conviction filled his tone. It was true. She could give herself to whomever she pleased. He hoped it might be him.

The time passed in minutes all too fleeting. He could've sat with her for hours, studied her smile as diligently and as often as he had old anatomy textbooks.

But he'd kept her long enough as it was. So after he paid the bill, they made their way outside, past the hotel, and toward the secluded road heading away from town.

"Thank you." A chill stole over the night, and she wrapped her arms around herself with a slight shiver. "I needed that. It comforts me to know that we can remain friends. We can still work together and enjoy each other's company. You don't know how glad that makes me."

He could only smile. And wrap his coat around her shoulders, his fingers skimming her collarbone, the warmth and softness of her skin almost more than he could bear. His gaze fell to her lips, to the gentle pulse beating in her throat. She looked up at him with the wide eyes of the girl he'd fallen for first.

What was a man to do? A man who had waited, wanted for so long?

He pulled her to himself, like the day when she'd cried in his arms. This time, he let himself press his lips against hers. She jolted in his arms, but like a particle of ice laid upon a scorching fire, melted quickly, molding against him as though this kiss was their thousandth instead of their first. Her lips tasted of sweet apple pie, of desperation and regret. Losing himself in their sweetness was the easiest and at the same time the most difficult thing he'd ever done.

A soft moan escaped her lips as she tunneled her fingers in his hair. Then she stilled, became a statue in his arms. Before jerking away and putting a foot of space between them, eyes wide with shock.

His heart pounded in his ears. This time, he would speak first. This time, he would make his feelings known. Come what may. He sucked in a breath.

"That kiss was an accident. But I've dreamed of a moment like this for so long... I may not be as decisive or as reckless as some men, but this I know. I love you, Annie Parker-Lawrence. I've loved you since the moment I saw you in that barn, that kitten in your lap. All throughout the war, I loved you still, even though you were married to somebody else. But that somebody else is gone now, so there's nothing to stop me."

Her breath came in jagged gasps, her body trembling like a frightened colt.

In a single stride, he had his hands on her shoulders, gaze meeting gaze, though hers shone with tears. "Nothing to stop me from loving you. From wanting you. From fighting for you. And even if the man I'm fighting with is dead, I'm not quitting. So get used to it, Annie Lawrence. Get used to knowing there's a man who loves you. One who is very much alive and well and longing to cherish your heart till the end of our days."

CHAPTER 8

"*G*et used to knowing there's a man who loves you. One who is very much alive and well and longing to cherish your heart till the end of our days."

The sun beat down upon Annie's head, her gloved hands expertly holding the reins as she steered her mount in the right direction. By all outward appearances, she was collected, calm. Inwardly, her heart cried out in answer to Travis's words.

Get used to it, Travis Hart. I love you too. But that's as far as it will ever go.

When their lips had met, every thread of her being soared skyward. Every beat of her heart sang out with the pure sweetness of holding and being held.

At least, she could hold tight to that memory, though guilt would always nip at its heels.

Once again, she'd been a failure to Stuart. Broken the promise she'd made before God during her wedding vows, and to God when she'd returned to Hartville, determined to start afresh.

Perhaps it would be best to flee from this temptation and return to Galveston. Never mind that she'd be running away like a pup with its tail between its legs. Never mind that Robbie thrived in the wide-open spaces of Texas. Never mind that she loved her patients, bringing their children into the world.

Travis would never leave Hartville.

And she must leave Travis.

She pulled her horse to a stop in front of the ramshackle cabin belonging to Abe and Karen Sandler. She'd never made a house call this far out of town, but she needed the excuse today. A long ride, even in the name of professionalism, had done wonders for her peace of mind. And Karen Sandler needed to be checked on.

After tying her horse to a forlorn pine tree, she wound her way through tall, unkempt grass and rapped on the splintered wooden door. No answer, either by footsteps or voice.

"Mrs. Sandler. It's the midwife. I'm just calling to check on you. May I come in, please?"

Creak. Groan.

The door opened. Karen stood inside, ragged blue shawl around her shoulders, graying brown hair in straggles around her face.

"How are you today, Mrs. Sandler?" Annie gave a professional smile. "I'm just here to see how you're doing. Make sure you're feeling all right and so forth."

The woman smiled, the upward turn of her lips accentuating the hollowness in her cheeks and lack of luster in her eyes. "I've been having twinges all day. 'Spect that's just me gettin' old. A forty-five-year-old woman ain't got no business havin' a baby. Abe's so excited, though. Guess that makes it all worth it."

"Of course it does."

Karen stepped aside, and Annie entered the one-room cabin. Her stomach gave a momentary lurch. Of course, she'd seen women bear children in less-than-pristine living conditions before, but this... Dirt floor. Rumpled bedlinens atop a cornhusk mattress. Food-encrusted dishes lying scattered on a crude log table. Something scurried toward the corner of the room. Mercy, was that a rat?

"How have you been feeling? Anything I should be aware of?"

Karen's only answer was to pale and clutch the edge of the table. Concern welled through Annie.

"Why don't I help you lie down, and we'll listen to the baby's heart?" Supporting Karen's arm, Annie helped her onto the sagging mattress.

It only took a simple examination for fear to rise hot in Annie's throat. She swallowed hard. "How long have you been like this?"

Karen pulled down her threadbare dress. "A day. Abe went out hunting a few hours ago, and I was glad for him to be away. He doesn't like to see me hurting. 'Spect it reminds him of the war. Why?" Her faded eyes searched Annie's. "Is something wrong?"

"My examination shows me...I mean, it appears that...you're in the early stages of labor." Three months too early, she didn't add.

"That's bad." Karen's eyes took on a frantic gleam. "I ain't ever had a baby before. Will it be all right?" The woman placed a protective hand over her abdomen, as if to hold back the child from entering the world. Another pain seized her, and she ground her teeth.

"Let's concentrate on getting you settled." Annie pressed her fingers to the woman's pulse. High. Too high. And her skin...feverish.

Help. She needed help. A first-time birth three months early meant almost certain death for the child. All she could do was save the mother. A forceps delivery would be best. But Annie wasn't a doctor.

"Do you know when Abe is expected to return?" *Lord, please let it be soon.*

Karen shook her head. "Maybe in an hour. Maybe tomorrow."

Annie drew in a long breath. She couldn't leave Karen. Not for the time it would take to ride back to Hartville, even at a gallop. No. She would do the best she could alone.

Hours dragged by. The contractions strengthened. Karen's fever worsened. She writhed on the mattress, screaming, her body fighting against itself.

"Breathe, Karen. Don't fight the pain." Annie pressed a cool cloth to the woman's sizzling forehead.

Lord. Please send Abe. Soon. I need Travis's help. I can't save this mother alone.

"Just help my baby! Please, save my little girl." A strangled cry rose from Karen's throat.

Tears formed in Annie's eyes. How could she tell this woman the truth? How could she face Karen once her baby was born dead?

"I'll do my best." The words sounded brittle in the dank air of the cabin. "We'll both do our best."

The end came quickly after that. Heartbreakingly so. Annie placed the tiny blue body in a blanket and laid it on the table. She rushed to Karen's side again. The mother was all that mattered. She felt the woman's pulse. Low. Dangerously. Karen's breath came in short, weighted gasps.

"How's my baby? Is it a little girl?"

Annie nodded. "You were right, Karen. A little girl." She lifted the sheet to examine the woman.

Her heart slammed against her chest. Blood pooled on the dirty linen.

A hemorrhage.

No. Please, God, no.

Karen's heart rate dropped. The metallic scent of blood overpowered the air.

"Abe. Where is he?" Karen's voice came out in a gasp.

"Still not back." Annie prepared a dose of ergot, one of the few remedies she'd seen work in cases like these. The afterbirth needed to arrive, fully intact, for the hemorrhage to stop.

"Why won't he come? I need him. He needs to see the baby. Do him so much good...see his little girl."

The gush of red continued. A convulsion racked Karen's body. It was at moments like these, Annie felt exactly what she was. Totally powerless. Powerless to save the baby. Powerless to stop the bleeding.

Powerless to keep Karen Sandler from passing from this world into the next.

~

*N*ever before had he laid his emotions out, bare, raw, and bleeding to another living soul. Yet he'd done it now, confessing his love, offering himself, his heart.

Annie had rejected him. With her eyes, which spoke volumes more than any words. There'd been those too. Apologies. Tears. She'd said how sorry she was for her unladylike behavior.

A dry smile crossed Travis's lips, and he gave a furious scrub at the examining room floor. If the passion she'd shown in her kiss was what she considered unladylike conduct, then let propriety hang!

It was over between them. He wouldn't force his affections on her. That would only make the both of them miserable.

No. He must say goodbye to Annie Lawrence. The Annie who had lived in his memory for so long, taking up far too much space with her beautiful brightness.

In doing so, he might as well give a hearty *bon voyage* to his inheritance. He wasn't about to marry another woman, and he wouldn't ask his father to make an exception and grant one of his sons his share of the land without a wife.

Not that he cared all that much. Medicine, not cattle and horses, had always been his passion. He would still have a comfortable life without his place at the 7 Heart.

Who was he fooling? He did want his inheritance, to take his place beside his brothers and work the land and livestock his father loved so much.

He chucked the soapy rag in the bucket with more force than necessary. Sudsy water splashed everywhere, including all over his shirt and trousers.

A word his mother would have cringed to hear him use sizzled from his mouth before he could check himself.

Two losses, one after the other. Annie. His inheritance.

God, why? Is there sin in my life preventing me from being blessed? Annie is a free woman again, so there's no wrong in our being together. I love her. How am I supposed to quit? Love isn't like a fire in a furnace that can be doused at a moment's notice. You can't turn it on and off so easy. Is that what You expect me to do? Quit loving her? I might as well tell myself to quit walking. Or breathing.

A knot lodged in his throat, making it ache. What was it the chaplain had said during that wartime service? Something about God giving strength to bear all trials, no matter how great? Well, the Almighty had him all wrong. Because Travis wasn't sure if he could endure seeing Annie again without the knife thrust of rejection slicing him clean through each and every time.

Yet God had never failed him before. Not during the war, when he'd seen men fall only inches away from his face. Not throughout the long years of medical school, when he questioned his destiny and considered walking away without a degree. Never once had His hand not been evident in Travis's life.

Still, the doubts rolled in. What would his brothers think when they heard of his failure? Bowie would understand. Houston too. But happily married Hays and Chisholm would think him a type of deserter. They wouldn't say it out loud, of course, but Travis couldn't fault them for thinking it. In their position, he might do the same. Like Shakespeare said, anyone could master grief but him that bears it.

A price he must pay. To stay true to himself. To remain a man of honor.

God, be my guide as You've been so many times before. Help me to find fresh meaning in life, even a life that's not the way I've been picturing it. And be with Annie. Keep me from...

Loving her? It was what he needed to say.

But it was the last thing he could bring himself to put into words.

CHAPTER 9

*L*ess than ten minutes after Karen Sandler breathed her last, her husband entered the room. Annie couldn't imagine the emotions that went through him as he took in the scene. A baby lying on the table, blue and lifeless. Blood saturating the mattress. His wife, cold and ashen, in the midst of that blood.

Abe Sandler's face betrayed nothing. For the space of several seconds, he just stared. As if unwilling to believe the truth his eyes told.

Annie forced her shaking legs to support her and crossed the cabin floor. Far too soon, she stood in front of Karen's husband.

Lord, how am I to tell him?

"Your wife went into labor soon after you left. The baby was premature and did not survive. After the delivery, your wife suffered a severe hemorrhage. I did everything I could... I'm so desperately sorry." Her words faltered, tears blurring her vision.

Abe shook his head, a slow, back-and-forth motion of disbelief. His face might have been hewn in granite, it looked so hard. "No!" That simple word pierced the close air like a knife-thrust. "No. Karen ain't dead. The child ain't dead either. You save 'em. That's what you're paid for."

"I'm sorry." With effort, she blinked back tears and straightened her shoulders. The midwife she'd trained with had taught her to remain calm during cases like this, and she wouldn't forsake that training. "I did everything in my power. She needed a doctor, and there was no one here to fetch one. There was nothing more I could have done."

"No. You save my wife." Though his words were wooden, the twist of his wrist as he pulled a pistol from his pocket was lightning quick. He aimed the barrel at Annie with a steady hand. "You make Karen better. And if you can't, you're a killer, not a midwife. I'll just save the court the trouble and do you in myself. Now, I'm goin' outside. If you step even one foot out of this door, it better be 'cause she's all right."

A chill traveled from her shoulders down to her feet. "You can't do that to me. Childbirth is a dangerous ordeal. There is no guarantee of a woman's survival. I did my best. Your wife was ill, undernourished, and living in deplorable conditions. None of that was my fault."

With a ram of his fist, Sandler shoved her against the cabin wall. Pain jolted down her spine. He leaned in, his words low, breath fetid with liquor. "Shut up. I don't want any more words out of you." He pulled back abruptly and stormed out the cabin door. The slam of wood against wood shot terror deep through Annie's bones.

She'd only met Sandler once before. But Mrs. Miller had told her about him. The man had fought in the war and come back alive. Though according to rumor, it might've been better had he not. Even Karen had told her—in hushed whispers—of Abe's terrible nightmares, how the slightest thing set him off like a powder keg with a single spark.

Now Karen was dead; Annie, miles from help of any sort.

She chanced a look out the single cabin window. Sandler sat, his six-foot frame barring the door, pistol gripped between his hands.

Her gaze swung back to Karen. Annie had closed the woman's eyes, but the glassy orbs had reopened and appeared fixated on the ceiling, as if the woman were simply deep in thought.

Though a trail of perspiration slithered down her spine, Annie shivered. Perhaps if she waited until Sandler fell asleep, she could make an escape. But if he awoke and caught her... The cold steel of the pistol filled her vision.

God, what now?

She sank to the dirt floor, hugging her arms around her knees. Hours passed. As quietly as she could, Annie cleaned the cabin, washed Karen and the baby, and covered them with a blanket. Her throat tightened.

Karen had cherished so much hope for the new life inside her. The first time Annie had met the woman, her faded eyes sparkled, a smile on her lips. Now she would never smile again, never hold a squirming infant in her arms.

Dear God, why?

Sandler still sat outside, unmoving, except to take a swig from an amber bottle now and then. Would anyone realize her absence and start to investigate? Her father probably wouldn't. He himself had said he never expected her back for days on end. Who else would care? Robbie and Josie, but would the concern of either be taken strongly enough to warrant a search?

What if Sandler did kill her? Her life would end. Robbie would lose his mother. Tears trickled down her cheeks. She hadn't even said goodbye to him this morning, wrapped up in her own turmoil. What a terrible mother she was. Now would she ever have a chance to be a better one?

Another face filled her memory, creeping in at the edges before consuming the whole. Travis. She'd rejected him. It had been a chance at a new start, and what had she done? Ruined it.

No. She'd been right. She didn't deserve a new start.

"Don't let guilt over something that happened so many years ago determine the way you face your tomorrows."

"I don't know if I can, Mrs. Miller. I've carried this guilt around for so long. I don't know how to let it go. Or even if I should. Don't I deserve to be punished? I broke a commandment. I committed adultery in my heart when I was married to Stuart."

No condemnation to them which are in Christ Jesus.

The verse she had read only yesterday flashed through her thoughts. Then the words seemed empty, meant for others, not her. But now, as she sat alone in this cabin...

"God, I need answers. If You have truly forgiven me, help me to see it. I'm tired of feeling guilty about the past. I want Your blessings. Not because I deserve them...but because You love me. I know others have been given grace. I want to know that whatever happens, whether I walk through this door and return to my family, or whether I die here, that I'm forgiven."

No condemnation.

"Truly, Lord?" She raised her gaze to the ceiling.

No condemnation.

"And about Travis? My heart craves marriage. I don't want to be a widow for the rest of my life. I want babies and a family. Can I have those too?" Though exhaustion weighed heavy on her body, her heart had never been so at peace. Perhaps the enemy had been using guilt to steal this intimacy with her heavenly Father. Intimacy she desperately longed for.

The answer rose up, the cleansing waters of truth washing away the built-up grime of lies.

No condemnation, daughter. Rest in My love.

~

aking the afternoon off to visit the Parker ranch had to be one of the stupidest things Travis had ever done. All because he'd promised to give Robbie his old Stetson.

Then promptly forgot after the boy's mother broke his heart.

He slowed his horse as he reached the end of the drive. If anything, the ranch looked in worse disrepair than it ever had. Weeds grew in tangled abandon. A few shingles had blown off the roof and lay littered on the ground.

Not that it mattered much to him. He only wanted to see Robbie, give him the hat.

And steer clear of Annie.

He pulled the hat out of his saddlebag, climbed the steps, and knocked once on the door. A couple of minutes passed before it opened.

"Dr. Hart." Instead of giving her usual flirty smile, a wrinkle formed in Josie's brow.

"Miss Parker. I just came by to see Robbie. Is he around?"

Josie nodded. "Yes. He's sort of upset right now, though."

"Why?" Travis fingered the battered Stetson, meeting her gaze.

"It's Annie."

The simple mention of her name, coupled with the edge in Josie's voice, kicked his pulse to a dangerously high rate.

"She hasn't been back since yesterday. I've been trying to convince Father to go looking for her, but he won't listen to a word of reason."

"Do you know where she is?"

Dear God, please let her be all right. Please let us find her whole and well, not...

"She went on her rounds. I don't know her patients who might be close to delivery." Josie bit her lip, the troubled look in her eyes so like Annie's, Travis forced himself to look away.

"She didn't mention anything?"

Josie tilted her head. "She said she wanted a good long ride to clear her head. And she took an apple and a slice of bread from the kitchen, so I figured she knew she'd be gone for some time."

He mentally ran over a list of the expectant women who dwelt in the surrounding area. Emma—Hays's wife, but Annie wasn't at the 7 Heart. Margaret Foster, who lived just outside of town. Beth Perkins—she had to be at least eight months along, and the Perkins homestead was several miles away. Karen Sandler. Wife of Abe Sandler, a man known for his strange behavior, brought on after the war. The Sandlers lived the farthest out of anyone.

"I have a couple of ideas." He turned sharply and strode down the steps. "Don't worry, Miss Parker. I'll find her."

He'd do so quicker if he had help, and with a passel of brothers around, he easily found that. Hays had been preparing to take a ride, and he offered to assist Travis by going to the Perkins' place and checking some of the back roads.

Travis decided to take Bowie with him to the Sandler cabin.

Bowie wasn't much for needless conversation, so the brothers rode in silence. Travis was glad of it. Gave him time to think, time he sorely needed. Without a second thought, he'd volunteered to search for the woman he loved. Guess the Almighty hadn't given him much help in getting over her.

Or maybe, just maybe, the Lord had other plans. Plans that involved growing closer instead of further apart to the beautiful woman who had caught hold of his heart.

No. He couldn't go there. A man could only take so much disappointment.

"What are you fixing to do when you find her?" Thankfully, Bowie hadn't said *if.*

"I just want to find her first." He'd content himself with seeing her safe and well. Even if she looked at him as she had during their last meeting, he wouldn't flinch. It would be enough to know no harm had come to her.

As they neared the Sandler cabin, foreboding shadowed Travis like a ghostly specter. Bowie seemed to sense it, too, his posture tense, his gaze constantly roving.

The holstered pistol pressed tighter against Travis's hip as they drew into the clearing. Travis sucked in a breath. Sandler sat in front of the cabin door, swigging from a bottle. For the moment, he appeared not to have noticed them.

The brothers dismounted, tying the horses to a tree near the woods.

Travis kept his tone low. "Whether she's in there or not, Sandler's drunk. How much, I can't tell. Let's just act as if we're paying a friendly visit."

Bowie gave a quick nod.

They stepped into the clearing. Travis forced an easy smile. "Afternoon to you, Abe."

Sandler looked up. His eyes had the look of a hunted wolf. "Get off my land." His tone was clear, evidencing he wasn't as drunk as Travis had first suspected.

"Haven't seen you in a while. Do you mind if I go inside and say hello to Karen?" Travis resisted the urge to finger his pistol.

"I said get off my land. You're not welcome." Sandler stood, his six-foot height surpassing Travis by a couple of inches. Bowie was taller, though. Good thing they'd come together.

Thank You, Lord, for giving me foresight. And tall brothers.

Travis took a couple of steps closer, gaze on the window. A flash of movement from inside caught his attention. His heart pounded. Annie. She was in there. Had to be.

"I just want to give something to Karen. I need to make sure she and the baby are doing all right. I'll only be a minute." He kept his tone soothing, speaking slowly and clearly. This tone had worked to calm soldiers, five-year-olds, and little old ladies. Hopefully, it still had the right effect.

Without warning, Sandler crumpled to the ground. He curled into a ball, shoulders shaking. Travis was no stranger to the cries coming from his lips. He'd heard them on the battlefield and in field hospitals. Even once or twice from down the hall at the Hart house, coming from the room where Bowie slept.

His brother crouched beside the man, relieving him of his weapon. Travis couldn't tell what Bowie was saying, but a second later, his brother looked up. "Go get her."

Travis didn't waste another second. He stepped around Sandler and unlatched the cabin door.

In a swift glance, he took in the scene. Karen Sandler on the bed, a tiny baby in her arms. Both were stiff, their faces gray with death. A fire smoked and smoldered in the hearth, the scent of burning cotton imbuing the air.

Oh, Annie. What kind of torture had she lived through since yesterday?

She faced him now, her face pale, her dress filthy. Yet the sight of her whole and unharmed filled him with more joy than if he had beheld the most celebrated beauty.

"What are you doing here?" Her eyes widened.

"Searching for you." He reached forward and grasped her hand in his. In a sudden movement, he lifted her hand, pressing it to his lips. Her skin was as soft as he remembered, each of her fingers delicate in their strength. All that remained to make them perfection was the item he'd carried with him throughout the years of war. The question remained, would she take it? Yet that answer would wait. For now, savoring this moment was more than enough.

His chest tightened at the sweetness in her smile.

"I was running away, Travis." Her words were barely audible. "Not literally, but in a way. I don't want to run again." She took a step closer, her breath coming fast. "You've found me now. Please..." Tears shimmered in her eyes. "Please, don't ever let me go."

He kissed her hand again, hope drenching his heart in a waterfall of promise.

"Never."

CHAPTER 10

"*I* thought I'd have to get a crowbar to pry your arms from around that Hart boy yesterday." The censuring bite in her father's words greeted Annie as she entered the parlor the morning after her rescue. She seated herself, folding her hands properly in her lap.

"He was helping me down off the horse." Annie leafed through a stack of correspondence.

"Oh, so that's all it was?" Her father smirked. "You must have needed an inordinate amount of help."

Annie drew in a deep breath. The girl she'd been would've ducked her head and rushed from the room. The woman of only a few days ago would've done the same. But much had changed since then. No longer would she allow her father's angry opinions to bathe her in shame. God had freed her from that, and she wouldn't become enslaved again.

"No, Father. That's not all it was."

"Mind explaining?" Her father folded his arms across his wide chest.

She stood, mimicking his commanding stance. "If you'll actually listen, then no, I don't mind one bit. When I was seventeen, I allowed you to force me against following what my heart told me to be true. I've changed since then, and I won't let myself be persuaded to go against what I believe the Lord's will is ever again. God is the only One whose opinion matters to me, and I feel His peace about this. I believe Travis

242

Hart still cares for me. And if the Lord wills, it would be my joy and privilege to accept his offer of courtship." She dropped her arms at her sides. "I love you, Father. I will do my best to honor you. But I will not allow you to demean me or make me feel unworthy of happiness ever again."

Her father said nothing. Annie tried for a small smile. What she wouldn't give to have experienced a different relationship with the only parent she remembered. To have enjoyed father-daughter confidences, basking in mutual affection.

But life wasn't perfect. There would always be gaps, scars, missing pieces.

Lord, thank You for always being willing to fill them.

Robbie raced inside. Her son's smile widened, revealing the tooth he'd lost in her absence. A smaller version of a Stetson covered his mussed hair. "Ma! I gotta show you something. It's outside."

"Excuse me, Father." Annie followed her son into the hall. Robbie hopped up and down, eyes beaming with excitement. "What is this all about?" She laughed. "Did you get one of the ranch hands to help you build a tree house?"

Robbie grinned, opening the door and pulling her outside. "You'll see."

In the next moment, her gaze collided with Travis's. He stood beside his buckboard, looking finer than she'd ever seen him. A charcoal-colored suit coat encased his wide shoulders, his usually tousled hair slicked back.

Her breath faltered. With shaking hands, she smoothed her simple gray dress.

Mercy, he looked fine. A flush heated her cheeks, one *not* caused by the Texas summertime.

"I gotta go help with the horses." Robbie bounded away.

Travis stepped forward, offering her his arm. She let him lead her across the front lawn.

"Feeling all right?" Concern filled his eyes. "Any dizzy spells? Nausea? You looked incredibly pale when I left yesterday."

She smiled. "I've never felt better, Dr. Hart. Why are you so dressed up? Going somewhere?"

He faced her, taking both of her hands between his. "Maybe." That mesmerizing dimple flashed as he smiled, his eyes crinkling around the edges.

"What do you mean by that?"

"I mean...we might be going somewhere, but first, there's something I'm going to say."

Her heart skipped a beat.

And increased to double-time as he knelt on one knee, both of her hands still clasped in his. Maybe he'd better ask about her health again. Because right now she felt dizzy. With anticipation.

She drew in a jagged breath. Was he going to...propose? Stuart had never done so. Their parents had arranged everything.

A proposal. It was the moment every girl dreams of, the moment when the man she adored dropped to one knee, looking up at her as if his heart belonged to her and only her. As if, were she to refuse, the very fibers of his being would crumble and turn to ashes.

And it was a moment meant to be cherished.

"Annie Parker-Lawrence." Though this man had performed operations requiring skill and complete steadiness of hands, his shook slightly as they held hers. She smiled at it. Brave, calm Dr. Hart, nervous. Over her.

"Yes?"

"There's just one question..." He cleared his throat.

"Yes?"

"You may think this sounds a little crazy."

"Yes."

"I've already asked Robbie, and he's in complete agreement."

She laughed. "Just say what you want to say, Travis."

He chuckled. "All right, then." His eyes darkened, so much hope, so much love in their depths, it stole her breath. "Marry me, Annie. You don't know how often and for how long I've wanted to say this. You are truly the most precious woman I've ever known, and I would consider it the greatest of honors to walk through the rest of my life with you at my side."

Tears spilled down her cheeks, not the girlish ones of sorrow and desperation sobbed into her pillow late at night, but tears of joy. Giddy. Overwhelming. She nodded.

Perfect. Joy.

He handed her a handkerchief, and she gave an embarrassed laugh as she dried her eyes.

"If you keep crying like that, you won't be able to see the ring." He slipped it on her finger.

"Oh..." A simple gold band, a small but flawless diamond at the center. Beautiful.

Yet at that moment, Travis could have given her a rusty horseshoe to put around her finger, and she still would've wept with happiness.

"Do you like it?" He stood, hesitation in his gaze. "I picked it out myself. If you don't, we could always—"

"Oh, Travis," she whispered, wrapping her arms around him. "It's perfect. And this...is even better." She pressed her lips against his, giving him her answer in her kiss, needing to show how much she loved, wanted him. He tasted of peppermint, of the future ahead of them.

She stepped back, breathless. A knot formed in her throat. "I don't want to wait another minute to be your wife. There've been so many years lost. They're gone, Travis. Gone. We didn't get to share them."

"None of that matters now." He leaned her head against his chest, holding her close. Overhead, in the sky of grand old Texas, the sun shone, warm and bright. As if to offer with its beaming rays a picture of the life they would now lead. "All that matters is tomorrow."

"Our tomorrows. I like the sound of that." She smiled, loving the way he held her. As if protecting her, leading her, cherishing her. And she knew beyond a shadow of a doubt that as long as Travis Hart drew breath, he always would.

"Me too." He kissed her again. "Ours. Always ours."

ABOUT THE AUTHOR

Amanda Barratt is the bestselling author of numerous historical novels and novellas including The Warsaw Sisters, Within These Walls of Sorrow, and The White Rose Resists. Her work has been the recipient of the Christy Award and the Carol Award, as well as an Honorable Mention in the Foreword INDIES Book of the Year Awards.

Amanda is passionate about illuminating oft-forgotten facets of history through a fictional narrative. She lives in Michigan and can often be found researching her next novel, catching up on her to-be-read stack, or savoring a slice of her favorite lemon cake.

To connect with Amanda, visit: www.amandabarratt.net.

A LOVE RETURNED

KELI GWYN

CHAPTER 1

Twelve years was a long time to wait for a tamale. Sam Houston Hart forked a bite and savored the spicy taste.

Travis, who had met the stagecoach earlier that day, watched from his place at the massive dining room table opposite Houston. "Are they as good as you remember, Huey?"

"Better. Perla outdid herself." He'd thought about the meal that awaited him when he reached El Regalo several times during the long ride from California. The tamales the family's cook had prepared in the days before he'd left home back in '62 were delicious. These were an explosion of flavor well worth the wait. "I hope the rest of you aren't too hungry, because I plan to tuck in my fair share—and then some."

"Thanks for the warning." Hays reached for the platter in front of him and plopped another tamale on his plate.

His lovely wife, Emma, patted his arm and smiled. "Be nice."

Hays feigned surprise. "I am nice." His exaggerated expression gave way to a grin. "But I'm hungry too. Can't let Houston get my share."

Chisholm took the steaming dish his wife, Caro, passed him and added another tamale to the mound on his plate. "It's every man for himself around here. You have told your son that, haven't you, Trav?"

Nine-year-old Robbie, seated beside Travis's new bride, Annie, piped up. "He didn't have to. I've watched y'all and learned to grab what I want the first time around."

Laughter erupted. Although Houston had enjoyed his time in California, he'd missed sitting around this table with his family. His brothers were all there, with the exception of Crockett, who was out on the cattle drive. They were older, of course, but there were other changes too. Austin wore his authority as the oldest with more confidence. Bowie, left scarred due to war injuries, had retreated behind a wall. Travis, now a doctor, possessed an air of calm competence. Rough, rugged Chisholm did the Texas Rangers proud. And Hays, a carefree boy when Houston left, now overflowed with optimism.

Pa sat at the head of the table looking larger than life and as formidable as ever. When it came to men getting what they wanted, he was a prime example. George Washington Hart had set out to expand his father's cattle empire into one of the largest in south-central Texas, and he'd succeeded. The herd this year had been the biggest ever, a fact Austin had announced with pride. His brother had contributed to that success, unlike Houston himself. He'd left days before his eighteenth birthday, eager to leave this life behind—along with his inability to measure up to his father's expectations.

But he was back now, and he had plenty to prove. Folks in Hartville had sent curious glances his way when he'd emerged from the cramped quarters of the stagecoach. Some had been disapproving. Travis had warned him in his letters that there were those who thought Houston should have stayed and fought, as his three older brothers and Crockett had. But Houston hadn't. He'd left, and there were those who weren't all that excited about his return.

Was Coralee among them? Perhaps he'd find out Friday night, when the family was holding a barbeque to celebrate his homecoming. His former sweetheart never missed a social gathering, so she was sure to be there, whether he was ready for their reunion or not. He was curious to see her, of course, but nothing more. He'd proposed, eager to take her to California as his bride, and she'd turned him down. He wasn't about to risk rejection a second time.

The meal passed pleasantly enough, with the usual talk of cattle, the drive currently underway, and plans for the future. Pa was always looking ahead to bigger herds and larger profits. With three of Houston's brothers now in possession of their shares of the ranch, they exchanged friendly banter about besting one another as they strived to emulate their father's success.

If all went well, Houston would find a woman willing to be his wife, claim his share of the 7 Heart, and earn his father's approval. Not an easy task. Ranching ran in his brothers' blood, but not in his. They enjoyed spending hours in the saddle. He didn't. Although he sat a horse as well as any man, he preferred running a business over riding the range. His hardware store in California had done quite well, enabling him to carry out his dream of—

"So, Houston," Austin asked, "what are your plans? Are you going to rope yourself a filly and claim your share of the ranch, or is this just a visit?"

Their father leveled a probing gaze on Houston, one eyebrow raised. "Yes, son, what *are* your intentions?"

He sidestepped the question, responding with a humorous tone. "That remains to be seen, since I might not be able to find a woman willing to put up with me."

Several of his brothers laughed, but Pa's lips formed a thin line. Only one answer would have suited him, and Houston wasn't ready to give it in front of the others. This was between his father and him.

Ten more tense minutes passed before the last tamale was eaten. Pa stood, and the others followed suit, heavy chairs scraping on the wooden floor. Three of his brothers greeted him on their way out of the spacious dining room, welcoming him back. Bowie gave a curt nod accompanied by a grunt of acknowledgment, but Pa left without a word.

Houston, alone in the room, paused to admire the letters *SHH* carved into the crest rail of his chair. All these years, his place at the table had sat empty, a silent reminder of his absence. No wonder Pa's reception had been cool. Not that Houston had expected a warm welcome. He'd made it clear when he left that he wanted to make his own way in the world.

And he had. Alone. It wasn't supposed to be that way. He'd dreamed of taking Coralee with him. She'd been sweet on him for years, and he'd finally wised up enough to see it. The Southern beauty was everything he'd wanted in a wife, but she'd turned him down. He would never forget the shocked look on her face when he'd asked her to marry him, head to California, and lead a life free of their families' expectations. He was ready to leave his, but she'd said she couldn't leave hers. What she'd meant was, she *wouldn't*. If she'd loved him as much as he'd loved her, she would have put him first. But she hadn't.

Enough! Dwelling on that gut-wrenching scene did no good. He was sure to see Coralee at some point, but he wasn't about to give her the satisfaction of knowing that her rejection had nearly brought him to his knees. She'd gone on with her life, and he'd done the same. His might not have turned out the way he'd envisioned, but he'd done well for himself—without any help from his family.

But twelve years was a long time. When Travis's letter with Pa's edict arrived, Houston had fought an internal battle. He didn't particularly want a share of the 7 Heart, but he did want to be part of his family again, and the two went together. His brothers might have trouble believing he wanted to embrace his Hart heritage since he'd been so eager to leave, but he would show them. He'd work hard, and in time, they'd see that he was serious about being a rancher.

Pa could be harder to convince. Their parting hadn't been pleasant. So far, their reunion hadn't been either. Houston could understand his father's wariness. The 7 Heart meant everything to him, and Houston had turned his back on it. But he was older and wiser now. If accepting his share of the ranch was what it took to earn Pa's approval, so be it. Mother would have been glad her middle son was willing to make his peace with his father, provided that was possible.

Mother. The very word brought with it a flood of memories. He glanced at the life-sized portrait of Victoria Elizabeth Hart over the mantel. As always, her beauty struck him, but remorse caused him to tear his gaze away. His sweet mother was gone, and he hadn't been here to say goodbye.

Houston made his way to his mother's parlor upstairs, drawn there by a force so strong, he was powerless to resist. He opened the door, stepped inside, and closed it behind him. Unlike the dark, masculine rooms throughout the rest of house, her room was feminine, with green and gold furnishings and pretty knickknacks throughout. Being there brought a rush of memories—her sweet smiles, her soft hands that had caressed his face with such tenderness, her floral perfume. For a moment, he was sure he smelled it, but then he spied the vase of roses.

There were dance lessons too. She'd insisted on teaching each of her boys how to handle themselves on a dance floor. He'd treasured those times when it was just the two of them, with his petite mother guiding him through the dance steps as she looked up at him with love and acceptance. Pa might not understand him, but she had.

His announcement that he was leaving for California had created a ruckus, with his brothers all talking at once. Pa had scowled, but Mother, seated at the end of the table opposite him, had caught Houston's eye and nodded once, a dip of the chin so slight, he suspected no one else had seen it.

When he'd hugged her before heading out, she'd raised up on her toes and whispered in his ear. Her floral scent wafted around him, and her words sank deep into his heart. *"You're a fine man, Sam Houston Hart. I hope you find what you're looking for out West and trust you'll return when you're ready. You'll be in my prayers, son."* She'd brushed a kiss on his cheek and stepped back to stand beside Pa, ever the supportive wife and mother.

Houston gripped the arms of her favorite chair, the fabric smooth against his work-roughened hands, and gazed around the room. Nothing had been moved, although she'd passed on eleven years before. Her presence seemed to linger in her parlor.

He closed his eyes, remembering her lovely voice and how she'd sung one song after another to him when he'd waged his battle with measles as a boy. She'd had a way of making him feel like he was special. And what had he done? Headed off to California, where he'd been when she passed on.

He picked up the framed photograph sitting on the round table beside her chair, taken not long before he'd left. His parents stood side by side, unsmiling, but his mother's eyes appeared to shine. It was all he could do to force the words out of his throat, which had grown thick. "Goodbye, Mother. I'm sorry I wasn't here for you, but I'm back now. I'm not sure I'm ready for what lies ahead, but I'm committed to making this work. I just hope Pa comes around."

The door handle jiggled, and his father entered. "I heard voices. What are you doing in here, son?"

"Thinking of Mother."

"Good place to do it." He lowered himself into the large green armchair, the only man-sized piece of furniture in the room. She'd had it made especially for Pa, all six feet, four inches of him. Everyone looked up to his father, especially Houston, who at five feet, ten inches was the shortest of the Hart brothers. Another way he didn't measure up.

Houston set the frame back on the table. "The news of her passing was such a shock. If I'd known she was ailing..."

Pa stared at the image of the woman he'd loved with a Texas-sized love. "It wouldn't have made any difference. The Lord was merciful and took her quickly."

"Even so, I wish I could have done something, but I was so far away."

"You did." He opened the small drawer in the table, pulled out a piece of paper, and unfolded it. "You sent this."

Pa had kept his telegram? The sentimental action seemed quite unlike him. "It was the least I could do. I loved her."

His father stared at the telegrapher's swirled handwriting, stark black against the white page. "She knew you'd come back. I reckon she had more faith than I did. But here you are." He folded the telegram, returned it to the drawer, and closed it with a bang, causing the strings of Mother's pianoforte to vibrate.

Pa pinned him with a piercing gaze. "Travis told you the terms of the inheritance, didn't he? You have to get yourself hitched by year's end."

"He did."

"Good." Pa stood. "There will be plenty of single gals at the barbeque come Friday. You'll recognize a few, but there are new fillies in the corral. I expect to see you on the dance floor that night getting acquainted."

The orders had begun already, had they? It appeared Pa was as iron-fisted as ever. "I'll meet them." But he wouldn't dance with a lady unless he wanted to.

An image of Coralee in a sapphire-colored gown, ringlets swinging as he swept her around the floor years ago, flashed before him. She'd been light on her feet and prettier than a field of Texas bluebonnets.

Houston shoved the memory aside. Miss Coralee Culpepper was the last woman he would take in his arms Friday night—or anytime, for that matter.

CHAPTER 2

"It's a beautiful summer's day, Daddy, with plenty of sunshine, so it's sure to be hot." Coralee stood at the open window of Beauregard Culpepper's second-story bedroom in the family's white clapboard ranch house and reported the sights below, as she did every morning. "There are two scissor-tailed flycatchers having a disagreement." Surely, he could hear the birds' sharp, squeaky calls, provided sounds were able to penetrate the fog he lived in. She wasn't sure, but she persisted in talking to him even though he'd ceased to respond with intelligible words.

In years past, when her father still recognized her and wasn't yet bedridden, he'd spent hours sitting at this very window bird-watching. He'd taught her the names of the various species he spotted in their backyard. Some referred to the long-tailed birds currently waging a territorial battle as birds of paradise. No matter what they were called, they were best known for their long tails. She liked the splash of salmon pink beneath their wings, a sharp contrast to their gray bodies and black wings.

If only Daddy had more color. His pallor of late troubled her. She'd have to mention it to Travis Hart when he came for his weekly visit. The kindly doctor was sure to have some idea what was behind her father's pasty complexion and what she could do about it.

She summoned a smile and moved to her father's bedside, where he was propped against three fluffy pillows. Although she saw him every day, her heart pinched when she looked into his eyes. His vacant stare had her wondering if he even knew she was there.

Not that it mattered. He was her daddy, and she would care for him and treat him with the respect he deserved all his days. That was Momma's dying wish, and Coralee, barely fifteen years old, had promised to honor it. Little did she know at the time what that would cost her.

No! She mustn't think like that. If Houston hadn't loved her enough to ask her why she couldn't marry him, instead of storming off to California, she was better off without him. She had a good life here. Daddy needed her, and so did her brother.

Calvin lacked their father's business sense. She offered as much assistance as her older brother would accept, although he wasn't as willing to listen to her opinions as she would like. Not that she had a head for figures either. She much preferred dealing with people. Which reminded her... She would have a parlor full of ladies shortly, so she'd best get on with her day.

"Let's get you a drink before I go downstairs." She reached for the water on her father's bedside table, held the glass to his lips, and tipped it. He made no effort to swallow, so the liquid dribbled down his chin, dampening his bedcovers.

She laughed. "You're being ornery today, are you? Fine. We'll do it your way." She dipped a spoon in the water and offered it to him. His lips closed around the handle. He swallowed, opened, and held the position, which she'd learned meant he wanted more. She repeated the action until he clamped his mouth shut after she'd removed the spoon.

His eyes locked with hers for a brief moment, and she savored the sense of connection. He might not know who she was, but he trusted her.

"I have to go now, but I'll be back as soon as my meeting is over and will sing 'Jesus, Lover of My Soul' for you." Before his mind began fading, Daddy had chosen that hymn as his favorite. Grieving the loss of Momma, he'd embraced the idea of flying to the Lord's bosom and being reunited with his beloved wife. Theirs had been a love so deep that he'd sunk into a depression after her passing, from which he never resurfaced.

She knew the thrill of giving your heart to another freely and completely. Houston had been the keeper of hers—until he'd shattered it.

One day, the good Lord willing, she'd know what it was like to be loved in the selfless way Daddy had loved Momma, putting her happiness before his. At twenty-eight, the possibility seemed unlikely, but the longing persisted, despite her attempts to fill her life with meaningful activity.

She pressed a kiss to her father's forehead, turned, and nearly bumped into Sally.

"Whoa there, Miss C. I was just coming to check on our dear man. How is he?"

"It's a good day. He actually looked at me, although he wouldn't drink from the glass." Coralee sent an indulgent smile his way. "He does love to exert his independence."

Sally chuckled. "That he does."

Bless the dear woman. Not once had their longtime maid questioned Coralee's attempts to act as though Daddy were still with them. He was, of course, in body, but the father she'd known and loved had drifted further and further away, until only a shadow of his former self remained. But she couldn't dwell on that. Any minute now, the ladies would arrive, and she must be ready to greet them.

As if on cue, there was a knock on the front door. Coralee cast a lingering look at her father. She'd tried hard to sound positive, but his wan appearance was troubling.

Sally fluttered a hand toward her. "Go on now. He'll be fine. I'll sit by his side while I do some mending and tell him all about the delicious dinner Olive has planned. You know how much he enjoys her cooking."

He used to, back when he had an appetite. These days, his diet consisted of soups, puddings, and other easy-to-swallow foods. She would ask Olive to prepare a cup of cocoa. That was sure to tempt him. He loved his chocolate.

Coralee dashed down the stairs, opened the door, and greeted her guests. "Welcome, ladies. Won't you come in?"

They retired to the parlor decorated in her late mother's favorite colors of burnt orange and butterscotch, sipped lemonade, and ate generous slices of Olive's moist sponge cake while chatting for a few minutes before their meeting began.

Clarice Spanner, a spinster with gray hair swept into an elaborate style, monopolized the conversation. Hartville's new dressmaker relished passing on bits of information she'd learned about the various residents. Velma Duke, a motherly figure with a knack for organization who served as president of Hartville's Confederate Widows and Orphans Fund committee, joined Coralee in tactfully but firmly cutting off the pinch-lipped gossip and steering the conversation in new directions.

The clock on the mantel over the rock-faced fireplace chimed twice. Velma cleared her throat, a signal that their social time was over. Their secretary, Dorothy Allen, with pencil and tablet in hand, was ready to record the minutes.

"The July meeting of CWAOF is called to order." Velma opened her leather journal. "We haven't received any new requests for assistance, but Giles Brown has taken care of the repairs to Widow Foster's barn that we'd discussed at our last meeting. He did a fine job." The competent woman smiled at Giles's wife, Patty, who had suggested her carpenter husband for the job.

"Giles was happy to help."

Velma pulled out a loose sheet of paper tucked between the pages of her journal. "Here's what we paid him for his labor and the supplies. We received a reduced rate, thanks to our association with him." She handed the list to Meribeth Mortenson, their treasurer and Coralee's longtime friend. Meribeth and her husband, Michael, who were expecting their first child, ran Mortenson Mercantile. She kept the ledgers for their business too.

Record keeping was something Coralee had no desire to do. She'd looked at Calvin's books once and could make no sense of them. While Meribeth's figures were fairly easy to follow, her brother's smudged and crooked columns were anything but.

Meribeth examined the numbers and nodded. "This is a significant reduction, indeed. It's twenty-five percent lower than what we'd allocated."

"We have even more good news." Velma looked from one member of the committee to the next, building the suspense. Her gaze came to rest on Coralee. "Our gracious hostess will tell you about it."

A surge of excitement rushed through Coralee. "As most of you know, I'm also a member of the committee that plans the annual Christmas Eve Ball. This year, the committee has chosen the CWAOF as the charity that will receive the proceeds. We're expecting a wonderful turnout. Last year, we had guests from as far away as San Antonio. With the plans the committee has, this year's event might rival those of the early Christmas Eve Balls put on by Victoria Hart herself."

Joyous exclamations filled the room.

Patty Brown brought her hands together with a loud clap. "That's marvelous! This donation will enable us to continue our work for years to come."

Clarice brushed a crumb from her ample bosom. "Your relief is understandable. I heard your primary benefactor has ceased making contributions."

Velma's jaw went slack. She caught herself and brought her teeth together with a clack. "I'm not sure where you got your information, Miss Spanner, but that is speculation. Nothing has been confirmed. When it is, Meribeth will apprise us of our financial situation. Until then, we'll continue to operate as we have. I, for one, trust the Lord to provide for our needs, as He has so faithfully done since our group was formed."

Clarice ran a hand over the skirt of her amethyst gown, a silk creation that showcased her talents but put undue strain on the jet-black buttons of her form-fitting bodice. "That's not all I heard. Young Hays Hart was in town this morning spreading the word that everyone is invited to a barbecue at the 7 Heart tomorrow evening to celebrate his brother's return."

The news hit Coralee like an icy blast, chilling her to the bone. Chisholm's visits to El Regalo between his Ranger assignments were a regular occurrence, and Crockett wouldn't return from the cattle drive for another three weeks. That had to mean—"Houston's here?"

"I believe that was the name I heard, yes."

Meribeth, bless her, chose that moment to drop her ledger. On Miss Spanner's toes. "How clumsy of me! I'm so sorry. Would you mind getting it? I would, but..." She patted her rounded abdomen.

Miss Spanner bent over to retrieve the book. Meribeth took advantage of her well-timed *accident* to telegraph her concern to Coralee. She managed to produce a smile, but it felt wobbly.

Houston was back. She'd wondered whether he might return someday, but to have him here was...unsettling. She was sure to run into him at some point, which could be awkward. Twelve years had passed since he'd walked out of her life without a backward glance. Seeing him again could cause the feelings she'd experienced to come rushing back. She couldn't allow that.

She wouldn't. Sam Houston Hart-breaker didn't need to know what his failure to put her before his desire to leave Texas and make his fortune in California had done to her. How she'd cried herself to sleep for weeks after he left. Her younger self had been devastated to lose the man she loved, but she was a woman now, strong and capable. She refused to let his return upset her.

Velma tactfully steered the discussion back on track. "Coralee, would you please tell us more about the ball?"

Gladly. Anything to keep thoughts of Houston from flooding her mind. "Because the CWAOF is the recipient of the proceeds from the Christmas Eve Ball this year, I asked if our members could help with the planning and preparations. My offer was readily accepted, so if any of you would like to volunteer, let me know, and I'll pass on your interest."

Miss Spanner splayed a hand against her chest. "I'm not one to boast, but I do have an artistic eye and would be delighted to head up the decorating committee."

Coralee nodded. "Very well. I'll let them know."

The next few minutes passed in a blur, with the other members discussing ways they might be able to help. Velma brought the meeting to a close. The ladies thanked Coralee for hosting it, bid her farewell, and headed to the carriage they'd shared.

All but Meribeth, who lingered on the porch. "I'll be along shortly. I have a private matter to discuss with Coralee."

Velma smiled. "That's fine, dear."

Meribeth waited until the other women were out of earshot before speaking. "You didn't know he was back, did you? What are you going to do about it?"

"Nothing."

Her friend's voice was laced with concern. "Are you going to his party?"

"Certainly not. Why should I?"

"I don't think it would be wise, actually, but I thought you might be curious to see if he's changed."

Was she? Perhaps. But that didn't mean she would go running to see him at the first opportunity. Their paths would cross at some point, they'd exchange a few polite words, and then they'd go their separate ways. Live their separate lives. "I'm sure Calvin will attend, but I'll stay here with Daddy. Are you going?"

"I'll be at home with Michael and my footrest. My poor ankles are more swollen than the Sabinal River after the rains. But if you change your mind, stop by when you're in town and tell me all about it. How you're immune to his charms now." Meribeth narrowed her eyes. "You are, aren't you?"

"Of course. Houston Hart means nothing to me now."

And he never would. She'd learned her lesson.

CHAPTER 3

A quick search for Calvin the following afternoon found Coralee standing outside the pen where he kept his prize bull when it wasn't out grazing. Her brother slipped through the rails to stand beside her. He removed his Stetson and fanned himself with it. "What's up, sis?"

She told him about Houston's return, the welcome-home barbecue they'd been invited to, and her intention to remain at home with their father.

Calvin put his hat back on. "I'm going, and so will you. How would it look if you didn't show up?"

As though she had no interest in seeing Houston again. Which she didn't.

"I know things between you two didn't end well, but the Harts carry a lot of weight around here. So whether you want to go or not, I'm counting on you to be there."

She placed her hands on her hips and lifted her chin. "I'm not a child for you to order around, Calvin. I'm a grown woman, in case you hadn't noticed."

"I've noticed, all right. I also know you're headstrong, but that's good. You can show Houston you've moved on with your life."

She hadn't thought about it that way. Her absence might send the message that she was afraid to face him, but if she was there and gave him a wide berth, he'd see that he'd ceased to mean anything to her. "Fine. I'll go, but I won't stay any longer than I have to."

"Good. And if Houston gives you any trouble, let me know. I won't have him upsetting you again."

Her brother's protectiveness warmed her. She could fend for herself, but it was nice to know Calvin cared.

Two hours later, Coralee sat at her dressing table. She draped a ringlet over her shoulder just so and studied her reflection in the looking glass. The time Sally had spent with the curling wands had resulted in springy spirals, just the way Coralee liked them. The blue silk she'd chosen complemented her fair complexion and dark hair. "What do you think, Sally? Will I do?"

"You look real fine, Miss C. You can be sure that as purty as you are, Mr. Houston will notice. He'll like what he sees too."

Coralee puffed out a breath. "I did *not* dress to please him."

"I should hope not. That boy done burned his bridges years ago."

He'd done more than that. He'd cut too deeply into her heart, leaving a wound that refused to heal. There was now an impassable chasm where the road to his friends and family once lay. He was on one side, she the other. And that's how it would remain.

Sally pulled the curling irons from the stove to cool. "It will serve him right to see what he could have had if he'd treated you like the gem you are."

Although Coralee appreciated the loyal maid's support, she'd worked hard to forgive Houston. She still had a ways to go, but there was satisfaction in knowing she wasn't the impressionable young girl he'd left behind, apt to be swept away by a few compliments, should they come her way. "You're a dear. You know that, right?"

The kindly woman chuckled. "I just says what I think."

Coralee chose a necklace from her jewelry box, held it up to her throat, and studied the effect in the looking glass. "I think these will do, don't you?"

"Nicely. Let me help you with that, child." Sally took the string of pearls and clasped it around Coralee's neck. "Every time I see these lovely beads, I think of your sweet momma. She was mighty happy with your daddy. I know she'd want you to find yourself a fine feller like she done. It's high time you did. Take your old Sally's advice. Don't let what happened with Mr. Houston all them years ago stand in the way of your happiness. If some rugged ranchers ask you to dance tonight, then dance."

"I don't plan on staying that long. I'll be back to see to Daddy as soon as I can."

Sally took Coralee's face in her hands. "I've knowed you since you was knee-high to an armadillo, my precious girl. You have a good heart and have been the best daughter a father could ask for. But I knowed your daddy long before you did. He wouldn't want you missing out on life on account of him. He'd want you to march up to El Regalo with your head held high and have yourself some fun. So go do that. I'll see to him."

Coralee stood, slipped a handkerchief inside her sleeve, and scooped up her fan. "I don't know what I'd do without you, Sally. It's not easy watching him travel this path. He was such a strong man."

"You're strong too. Now, skedaddle." Sally waved her off with the back of a hand. "And don't you show up back here too soon, or you'll have me to deal with, you hear?"

"Yes, ma'am." She gave Sally a mock salute and dashed downstairs to wait for her brother in the entryway. Her boot heels clicked on the marble tiles as she paced.

Five minutes passed with no sign of Calvin. Coralee checked his room, but he wasn't inside. She headed outside, lifting her skirts to keep them from getting dusty, and found him in the pen with the bull. Again. "You said you'd be ready."

Calvin thumped the longhorn's side. "I meant to, but this fellow appears to be ailing. I'll finish up with him and ride over to the Harts' place as soon as I can. You can take the buggy. I had Gene get it ready for you."

"You insist I go, and now I have to show up alone?" She feigned irritation. "Fine brother you are."

He grinned. "I'm your favorite brother."

"You're my only brother."

They'd tossed the same words at each other many times over the years, but the game never grew old. Calvin could be a mite irritating at times, but he'd been her rock when the world around her crumbled. She was still mourning Houston's choice to put his dreams and aspirations before her when Daddy began forgetting things. She'd often wondered if Momma had suspected that he wasn't himself, prompting the promise Coralee had made to Momma as her earthly life drew to a close.

The trip to the 7 Heart passed quickly. The steady *clop* of the horse's hooves on the hard-packed road and the rustle of the grasses swaying in the breeze kept her company. In order to rein in her thoughts, which had an annoying tendency to turn toward a certain gold-chasing fortune seeker who preferred California to the Great State of Texas, she concocted a possible menu for the Christmas Eve Ball. She could almost taste the delicious desserts.

She reached the ranch and stopped in front of the huge barn. A ranch hand rushed out to help her. He surveyed her with appreciation. "Evening, Miss Culpepper."

Had she met the man before? She couldn't recall. "Good evening, Mr. …"

"Call me Cody." He smiled, his blue eyes twinkling. "Everyone does. I'll park your buggy and water your horse."

"I would appreciate that. I'm sorry you're stuck here with the animals when everyone else is having fun."

He held out a hand and helped her from the buggy. "Some of the other fellers and I are taking turns. When my shift is over, I'll come find you and whisk you onto the dance floor. I'm light on my feet. I'll be light on yours, too—when I step on them, that is." He winked.

She laughed. It had been ages since a man had flirted with her. She shouldn't encourage the cocky cowboy, but this could be her opportunity to show Houston that even if he'd walked out on her, she was still able to capture a man's attention. It didn't matter that Cody seemed the kind of fellow who would dance with anyone in a skirt. "I think I could survive one number. My boots are sturdy."

"I'll see you later, then." He doffed his hat, grabbed the bridle, and led the horse away.

Coralee tugged the hem of her jacket into place, brushed the dust off her skirt, and steeled herself for what lay ahead. *You have nothing to fear. He's just a friend from your past.* At least, he had been her friend.

The scent of barbecued steaks beckoned her to come closer. Not that she was hungry. Her stomach felt a bit queasy. No doubt from the heat, or perhaps it was the interaction with the blond, blue-eyed ranch hand to whom she'd promised a dance. Despite having enjoyed whirling over the dance floor when she was younger, she hadn't done so in quite some time. On the rare occasions when she attended a ball or a barn dance, she tended to keep busy serving refreshments. But she was here now, and she intended to enjoy herself.

She reached the yard where the festivities were taking place. Conversations buzzed all around her as people ate from plates heaped with side dishes prepared by the Harts' excellent cook. She was pulled into one group after another. Some of the women, members of the committees on which she served, had heard the news about the Christmas Eve Ball and wanted to know how they could help. A few folks asked after her father, and she gave them the usual vague responses, protecting his privacy as he'd begged her to when he was still somewhat lucid. But not one person mentioned Houston's return, which was odd, given that the party was being held in his honor.

And there he was, standing on the porch with his father on one side of him and Travis on the other. She froze. Houston stopped speaking and stared at her with parted lips. She licked hers and struggled to breathe. The moment went on and on, rendering her powerless to move. Heads turned, looking from Houston to her and back again.

"Aha! I knew it." Clarice Spanner's grating voice restored Coralee's senses.

She turned and responded with practiced civility. "Miss Spanner. How nice to see you."

The busybody's eyes shone with satisfaction. "When I mentioned the invitation at our meeting yesterday, you went as white as your blouse. There's a special connection between you and Houston Hart, isn't there?"

"I knew him before he left, but so did many of the people here."

"He hasn't looked at anyone the way he just looked at you. If I'm right —and I usually am—you two were sweethearts at some point. But things didn't work out, did they? A romance with a tragic ending, I suspect."

"Oh, look. There's Patty Brown. She had an idea for the ball she wanted to tell me about. If you'll excuse me..."

Miss Spanner caught Coralee by the arm. She resisted the urge to shake the woman off. "I know there's a story there. I have a nose for sniffing out such things."

Of that, Coralee had no doubt. "If you must know, Houston and I went to school together. He left town. He's back. That's it. Now, I really must speak with Patty. Enjoy the party."

Coralee made her escape and wove her way through the crowd until she reached the carpenter's wife. "Good evening. I thought now would be a good time to discuss your ideas for the ball, if that's all right with you."

"I quite agree." Patty cast a disapproving glance in Miss Spanner's direction. "That woman might be a talented seamstress, but she's a nuisance. But enough about her. We've more important things to discuss. If you'd like, we could do so over dinner. The scent of those steaks on the barbecue has my mouth watering."

The food was delicious, what little of it Coralee was able to choke down. Her appetite had long since vanished. She had enjoyed the company of Patty and her husband, Giles, but the moment they shoved their plates back, she excused herself.

As though drawn by some invisible force, her gaze scanned the crowd until it landed on Houston, seated between Travis and a young boy who had his full attention, presumably Travis's new son. Houston removed his hat and placed it on his nephew's head, causing the young fellow to beam.

Coralee hid behind a large shrub and studied Houston. The years had been good to him. He'd been attractive enough at eighteen, but at thirty, he was tall, dark, and more handsome than ever. His shoulders were broader, his hair longer and slightly mussed, which she found strangely appealing.

His clear blue eyes hadn't changed. His gaze was as penetrating as ever. She'd done her best to appear calm and unmoved when he spotted her earlier, but those few moments when their eyes had locked stirred feelings long buried. Love, anticipation, and exhilaration. She'd felt them all back then.

But they'd been followed by disappointment, confusion, and a pain so intense that she'd vowed never to give Houston the opportunity to hurt her again. Calvin didn't have to worry about that happening, because she wouldn't let it.

The sound of musicians tuning their strings brought her back to the present. Since she had no desire to dance, she started for the barn. She'd come to Houston's party, talked with his guests, and let him know she was here. Having fulfilled her obligation—and satisfied her curiosity—she was free to leave.

She'd taken two steps when she felt a tap on her shoulder.

"You weren't thinking of slinking off, were you?" The cocky cowboy who'd helped her with her buggy grinned. "I hope not, because you promised me a dance, and I'm holding you to it." He held out his arm. "Shall we?"

Cody had thwarted her escape. Since she had led him to believe she'd accept his offer, she might as well enjoy herself. She slipped a hand around his elbow and smiled. "My leather-reinforced toes and I are ready."

They reached the dance floor as the lively strains of the first number filled the air. He took her in his arms and set off. Contrary to his warning earlier, he was an accomplished dancer. Not as good as Houston, but—

What was she doing thinking about him? He was back, but that changed nothing. For all she knew, he didn't even want to be here and had only come to get what was coming to him. Since he'd shown that he was only out for himself, that made sense.

Cody led her in a turn. As she twirled around, she caught a glimpse of Houston wearing a scowl the size of Texas. So he didn't like her dancing with someone else, did he? That wasn't her problem. He should have considered the consequences when he'd made his choice all those years ago.

She looked up at her dance partner, who'd fired off another of his quips, and laughed.

CHAPTER 4

*J*aw clenched, Houston leaned a hand on the table where he'd eaten his meal with Travis and his new family and watched as Coralee glided over the dance floor, laughing and having a grand ol' time. She wore a dress as vivid a shade of blue as the darkening sky. Puffy white sleeves peeked from beneath her elbow-length jacket. A perky little hat rested on her upswept hair. Several springy chocolate-brown curls trailed over her shoulders.

He hadn't seen such an impressive display of ringlets since he'd left Texas. The hardworking women in the small California town where he'd lived had opted for more serviceable styles. He hadn't realized how much he'd missed seeing Coralee's curls—and the comely woman herself.

The brown-eyed beauty obviously hadn't missed him. The dancing had only begun, and yet she was out on the floor in the arms of a presumptuous ranch hand. He shouldn't be surprised. She'd always favored men who spent their days tending cattle. He could imagine what she thought of him out in California running a hardware store. Not that her opinion mattered. He'd made a success of the business, and he'd done it on his own. If he could do that, he could make ranching work out too. If he wanted Pa's approval, he had to.

Pa joined him. "Do you plan to stare at her all night, son, or take action?"

Houston forced himself to remain calm. "I have no intention of dancing with her."

"Why not? She's still good to look at."

"She turned me down."

Pa nodded. "She did, but she hasn't said yes to anyone else."

He'd wondered about that. A woman with Coralee's many attributes could have had her pick of the eligible bachelors. Maybe not during the war, but after. There was no shortage of single ranch hands around now, one of whom had already claimed a dance with her. "What Coralee and I had no longer exists."

Pa grunted his acknowledgment and rubbed a thumb over his weathered jaw. "If you want your share of the ranch, you need to find a wife, right?"

"Right."

"The way I see it, no woman here would consider taking up with you if they think you've come back to mend your fences. If you act as skittish as a colt around Coralee, they're likely to think that's what you're up to. Haul your hide out there and prove 'em wrong."

As much as it galled him to admit it, Pa had a point. Six months of the year he'd given his sons to fulfill his terms were gone. Three of Houston's brothers were already married. If one dance with Coralee could put an end to the speculation and give him a shot at finding a bride of his own, perhaps it would be worth it. Provided Coralee didn't humiliate him in front of everyone. "I'll consider it."

"Don't take too long. The clock's ticking." Pa clapped a hand on Houston's shoulder and left.

The music faded, and the couples flowed from the dance floor. Coralee stood a respectable distance from her partner, said something to him, smiled, and made her way through the crowd. Houston lost sight of her for a few moments. She emerged at the edge of the gathering and strode toward the barn.

He took off after her, not so fast that he would draw attention, but fast enough to catch up to her before she reached her destination. "Corrie!" His pet name for her had slipped out.

She came to an abrupt stop. Her hands fisted at her sides. Not a good sign. She turned around slowly and waited until he reached her before speaking. "Good evening, Houston. What do you want?"

"Dance with me. Just once."

She blinked several times, her mouth agape. "Why should I?"

"Because I'm the guest of honor, and I asked you." He didn't like pressuring her, but people had gathered and were watching them. If he was to show everyone that things between Coralee and him were over, he needed her to agree.

She inclined her head and looked at him with narrowed eyes. "Your father put you up to this, didn't he?"

"I make my own decisions."

"You can't fool me, Houston. You've evidently come back to secure your share of your father's ranch. And in order to do so, you'll need to take a wife, won't you?"

"What gave you that idea?" Did the whole town know about Pa's proclamation?

"I'm observant. The Hart brothers, who've had nothing to do with women for ages, are suddenly marrying up with remarkable speed. It stands to reason you're here to find a bride too. Or did you find yourself a wife out in"—she spoke through pursed lips, as though the word tasted bitter—"California?"

"I'm not married." Yet. If he wanted to claim his share of his father's ranch, he would have to be by New Year's Eve, but he'd never considered any woman before other than Coralee. Not that he had any intention of renewing his offer. If getting her to dance with him was this much of a challenge, he'd be an utter fool to think about asking her to do anything more.

"I hope you don't consider me a candidate, because if that's the case, you're sadly mistaken."

"No. I don't. I mean..." He removed his hat, raked a hand through his hair, and mashed the Stetson back in place.

Coralee said nothing, just watched him with a puzzled expression on her face.

"Why did you come?" he asked. "Evidently, you weren't even going to talk to me."

"I was being neighborly." She moistened her lips the way she had earlier—soft, supple lips he'd kissed a number of times in his youth.

Focus, Houston. "Then how about sharing a neighborly dance? Just the one. You can go home after that, and I won't trouble you again."

She startled. "Calvin was supposed to be here by now, but I haven't seen him. Have you?"

He shook his head.

"His best bull was ailing. That must be what's keeping him. A man can't leave an animal in distress."

"Does he need any help? I could send someone over if he does."

"He'll be fine. My brother is quite capable of tending his herd."

Coralee had never been this prickly before. "I'm sure he is. I was just *being neighborly.*"

"Shh." She cast a glance at the growing crowd of onlookers. "People are watching."

It had taken her that long to notice? "I'm aware of that. If you'll do as I asked, we can satisfy their curiosity about where things stand between us. They'll go on about their business, and we can go on about ours—separately."

"They think we're together?"

"I'm sure they're wondering. But we can let them know otherwise. So how about it? Shall we share a neighborly dance before you storm off?"

Indignation straightened her spine. She spoke in a heated whisper. "I was not storming off. I'd done my duty."

"I'm sorry if attending my welcome-back barbeque was such an onerous task."

"It wasn't. The party actually gave me an opportunity to visit with a number of folks and discuss plans for the Christmas Eve Ball." She paused, her eyes wide. "Oh. I hadn't thought about how difficult it must have been to come home after your loss. My condolences. Your mother was a sweet woman. She was also quite talented. The other members of the committee and I have done our best to host balls on par with those she organized."

Coralee might want nothing to do with him, but her consideration of others was bone deep. "It's different not having her here, but Pa seems to be doing all right."

A flicker of pain clouded her dark brown eyes, but it passed quickly. She gave a single, decisive nod. "One dance, Houston, and then we'll part as...friends." The way she'd uttered the word with her mouth tense and her voice firm said she considered them anything but.

"Very well. After you." He held out a hand toward the dance floor.

They reached the edge of the wooden surface that had been laid out and waited for the dance in progress to end. She stood next to him but left several inches between them. With her arms folded and her upper body angled away from him, anyone looking their way would have no trouble figuring out that she wasn't enjoying his company.

Her stance gave him the opportunity to study her without her knowledge. She'd been sixteen when he left and prettier than any girl he'd ever set eyes on. Now a woman, she was more beautiful than he could have imagined. But she'd changed. Instead of the free spirit with whom he'd spent many fun-filled hours, she seemed subdued. She wasn't any happier to see him than he was her, but there was more to it. Her zest for life wasn't there anymore. What had happened to rob her of the joy that used to bubble over?

The final notes of the lively number faded, and the couples left the floor, laughing and smiling. Coralee dropped her arms to her sides. Her shoulders rose and fell as she drew in a deep breath and released it. If he'd known how much she dreaded dancing with him, he might have reconsidered asking her. But they were committed now.

Mrs. Brown let go of her husband's hand and approached Coralee. She leaned close, glanced at Houston, and directed her attention to Coralee. "Are you all right?"

Coralee produced a halfhearted smile. "Yes, Patty, thank you."

"If you need anything, let me know."

"I'll be fine."

He hadn't spent much time around women, but it wasn't hard to see that Coralee's friend was concerned about her. Perhaps people weren't wondering whether he and Coralee were a couple as much as why she would consider taking up with him again. Some of the looks being sent his way weren't the friendliest. Did the distrust of him run deeper than he'd thought? The musicians readied their instruments, sparing him the need to ponder the question.

"Shall we?" He offered his arm to Coralee. She stared at it a moment, wheeled around, and made her way onto the dance floor, leaving him to follow. This was going to be the longest dance of his life.

They joined the others forming a line for a reel.

"Not so fast," the head musician hollered with a laugh in his voice. "Thought we'd play a waltz for y'all this time so you can get cozy with your partners."

A waltz? Houston stifled a groan. In years past, he would have welcomed the news, but Coralee had enjoyed being in his arms then. She stood as stiff as a branding iron now.

She closed the distance between them, faced him, and looked into his eyes. Even in the fading light, he could see the challenge hers held. The message was clear. If he pulled her too close, he was likely to feel the heel of her boot come down on the top of his.

The music began. He placed his right hand below her shoulder blade and cupped her right hand in his left. She rested her free hand on his bicep—if you could call it resting. It felt more like hovering. Her touch was so light, he could barely feel it. She held her head high and jerked it to the side so he could only see her profile.

"Relax, Corrie."

"Please, don't call me that again. You lost that right years ago."

"Fine, Coralee. If that's what you want. Or is it Miss Culpepper now?" He led her into the swirl of couples circling the floor, waiting for a response.

He'd almost given up hope of receiving one when she spoke. "Thanks to you, it's still Miss Culpepper, but I suppose you may call me Coralee. All my *friends* do."

"Thanks to me? What do you mean? You're the one who turned me down!"

"Yes. I did. And you left. But you're back now. At least for a time."

He changed direction to avoid a collision with another couple. "What's that supposed to mean?"

"I know about your hardware store out West. You didn't give it up, did you?"

"My partner's running it."

"You don't intend to stay, do you? I suppose that's to be expected. After all, you don't really want to be here, right?"

"I've been away a long time and done a lot of thinking. This is where I belong, working alongside my brothers."

She frowned, drawing her delicately arched eyebrows together. "But you were so eager to leave."

Not really. He'd felt forced into his decision by circumstances he was unable to change. "I enjoyed my time out West, but I learned a valuable lesson. You can take a man out of Texas, but you can't take Texas out of the man."

Skepticism pinched her fine features. "So you expect us to believe you're a Texan at heart, after all? The Texans I know didn't run off to California to strike it rich. Some of them left, yes, like your brothers, but they went to fight for our rights."

It appeared Coralee didn't trust him either. He had more to prove than he'd thought. He could prove his loyalty if he was willing to make his private affairs known, which he wasn't. What he'd done was between him, the Lord, and the precious few whose assistance he'd required. "I have great respect for those who served and sympathy for those who lost loved ones."

"Miss Culpepper!" A ranch hand shoved his way through the crowd.

She tore herself away from Houston and slipped between the dancers, not stopping until she reached the winded man, Houston on her heels. "What is it, Gene?"

"It's your brother. Calvin tangled with that sick bull and got tossed. Do you know where the doc is? We're gonna need him."

She gripped the fellow's arm. "How bad is it?"

"He thinks some ribs might be broke."

"I'll get Travis, and we'll hightail it over there." Houston started for the table where he'd last seen his brother.

"No!" Coralee jumped in front of him. "We don't need your help."

"With all due respect, Miss Culpepper"—Gene stepped into her line of vision—"it'll take two men to get him upstairs. I was the only hand still at the ranch. The rest are here. I'd go back, but I rode hard, and my horse is spent. I'd need to borrow one."

"I see. Um, thank you. Could you get my buggy ready?" She turned to Houston. "I was wrong. Please. Go. Quickly."

He took off.

CHAPTER 5

Because Travis had to run inside to get his doctor bag, Houston reached the Culpepper ranch before his brother.

Houston rounded the far corner of the barn moments later and spied Calvin sitting against the back wall, a few feet from the bull's pen. He sprinted over to the muscular rancher, who clutched his midsection and grimaced.

Houston crouched beside the injured man.

"What are you doing here? Gene was supposed to get your brother."

"Travis is right behind me. He'll be here soon. What happened?"

Slowly, cautiously, Calvin inclined his head toward the huge longhorn nearby. "Turns out Toro has a temper. I've been doing my best to help him, but the ornery fellow slammed me into a fencepost. I managed to crawl out of the pen, but when I tried to stand, I nearly passed out. I think the brute busted my ribs."

"And you've been sitting here ever since?"

"Since I sent Gene to get help, that only left Sally and Olive. I couldn't ask two older women to drag me upstairs." Calvin scanned the area behind Houston. "Where's Coralee?"

"She was with me when Gene showed up. He was going to get her buggy for her. She'll be along soon."

Calvin scowled. "What was she doing with you?"

"Dancing."

"I warned her to steer clear of you. Apparently, she didn't listen, so I'll make sure you know exactly what I mean. Stay away from my sister, Houston. She's suffered more than enough on your account."

Coralee had suffered? That didn't make sense. She was the one who'd rejected him.

Hoofbeats pounded the ground, coming to a stop several feet away. Travis slid from the saddle, whipped his reins around a fencepost, and rushed over to them, black bag in hand.

Calvin attempted a smile, but it faded quickly. "Howdy, Doc. I didn't mean to drag you and the guest of honor away from the shindig, but I'm glad you're here."

"Let's see what's going on, shall we?" Travis had Calvin lie on his back. "I'll start by having you take some deep breaths while I check for grating, which would indicate broken bones. Go ahead and breathe as deeply as you can."

Calvin's chest rose and fell, the effort causing him to wince. Travis moved the bell-shaped end of his stethoscope over the area, listening intently. Before long, he removed the earpieces.

Houston's curiosity got the best of him. "Did you hear anything?"

"Nothing definitive." Travis shifted his attention to Calvin. "I'm going to press on each of your ribs in turn. Tell me if my probing causes you any pain or tenderness."

"You mean more pain than I'm already experiencing, right?" Calvin attempted a laugh, but the movement of his ribcage transformed the sound into a strangled gasp.

"Exactly." Travis set to work, moving his hands methodically over Calvin's chest.

Perspiration beaded on Calvin's forehead. Just when Houston thought all was well, Calvin yelped. "In case you didn't notice, that spot's sore, Doc."

Houston smiled at Calvin's humorous response, but Travis kept a straight face. "I suspected as much."

The examination concluded moments later, following two more muffled cries from Calvin as Travis completed his examination. He straightened and stood with his arms folded, looking down at Calvin, who had returned to a sitting position. "Your diagnosis is correct. From what I can tell, three of your ribs are broken."

"That's not too bad, is it, Doc? I'll be up and around again in no time, right?"

Travis shook his head. "What you're experiencing is a serious injury. You'll need to be on bed rest for a good four weeks or more."

"No! I can't do that. I've got a ranch to run."

"I understand, but you'll have to find someone to take your place. Right now, Houston and I are going to help you up to your room. Once we have you settled, I'll wrap a band around your chest to help keep the ribs immobilized. I'll get his left side, Huey. You take his right."

With Sally's help opening doors and pulling down the covers, Houston and Travis got Calvin upstairs and into his bed. The weary man closed his eyes.

"I should probably get back since it's my party," Houston said to Travis, "unless you need anything else, that is."

Calvin's eyes popped open. "I don't want to worry Coralee. She has enough to do as it is. If you could find a ranch manager to oversee things here while I'm laid up so she doesn't feel obligated to step in, I'd be grateful."

Calvin's concern for his sister spoke well of him, even if that included warning Houston to stay away from her. "Travis might be the better one to ask. I've only been here a couple of days."

His brother pulled a roll of white cotton from his leather bag. "No one comes to mind."

"In that case, I'll ask Pa. He or one of our brothers is sure to know of someone." Houston wished Calvin well and left.

A moaning sound coming from the bedroom two doors down stopped Houston. He peered inside. An elderly man occupied the bed. He slipped a bony arm from under the sheet and motioned to Houston.

"Did you want something?"

The man didn't respond—not in words, anyhow. He just waved and grunted.

Houston stepped into the room, which smelled of honey and almonds. A quick survey of the items on the bedside table revealed the source—a jar filled with some kind of cream.

He reached the bed, and his breath left him in a *whoosh*. The wizened man must be Coralee's father. Once a robust rancher like Pa, Beauregard Culpepper was a shadow of his former self. "It's me, Houston Hart."

There was no sign of recognition in Mr. Culpepper's eyes. He tapped his fingers against his lips.

"Are you thirsty?" Houston lifted Mr. Culpepper's head with one hand, picked up a glass of water with the other, and pressed it to his lips, tipping it until a trickle of liquid flowed into his mouth. He swallowed. Houston repeated the motion five times, stopping when the water dribbled down the older man's chin. Houston set the glass on the table, eased Mr. Culpepper back into his pillows, and dabbed at his wet front with a cloth.

A gasp from the doorway caught Houston's attention. Coralee stepped into the room, her mouth agape. She staggered backward until she bumped into the doorframe, clutched it for support, and stared at Houston with eyes as big and round as barrel rings. "Wh-what are you doing in here?"

"I... The door was open. Your father called to me as I went by. I figured out he was thirsty. He drank several sips of water."

"You shouldn't be here. Get out!" She jabbed a finger at the hallway.

He crossed the room, faced her, and fought the urge to pull her in his arms and offer what comfort he could. She'd obviously been dealing with her father's decline for a long time. "Corrie—I mean, Coralee—I was only trying to help."

"I don't want your help, Houston. I want you to leave. Now."

He stared at her, trying desperately to make sense of her outburst. Questions bombarded him. He asked the first one that came to mind. "What happened to him?"

She drew in a series of shallow breaths and held up her hands below her chin, palms forward as though shielding herself from him. "Please, just go."

"Fine. If that's what you want. I'll go, since Travis is still here to take care of things. Or are you going to send him packing too?"

He didn't wait for an answer but turned on his heel and descended the stairs two at a time. The sooner he got away from Coralee, the better.

~

*H*ouston knew.

Coralee fought to regain her balance, but the floor still seemed to be moving. For years, she'd protected Daddy's privacy. He'd had two requests when he realized his memory was slipping away—that she and Calvin care for him at home and that they keep the truth confined to as few people as possible. Although they couldn't hide the fact that he was ill, since he'd ceased appearing in public years ago, he preferred having people speculate about consumption and other possible diseases rather than believing him to be mad. Which he wasn't.

When Gene had found her at the barbecue and delivered the news of Calvin's accident, her only thought had been about getting her brother the help he needed. It wasn't until she'd raced up the stairs and heard a man's voice in Daddy's room that she realized Houston was inside. In the rush to care for Calvin, Sally must have forgotten to close Daddy's door.

Seeing Houston giving her father a drink wasn't as shocking as the way he'd spoken to Daddy. Houston had been kind and compassionate, treating Daddy with the respect he deserved.

And what had she done? Sent Houston away.

She dashed down the stairs and out the door, not stopping until she was a few steps behind him. "Houston! Please. Wait."

He stopped, but he didn't turn around, nor did he say anything. Not that she could blame him. For all he knew, she was going to hurl even more harsh words at him.

She stepped in front of him.

His features were set, his lips pressed into a thin line.

"I appreciate you coming to help Travis with Calvin. And about the other. I, um..." Words failed her. How could she express what she was feeling when she couldn't begin to sort out the tangled mess of her emotions? "Thank you."

He opened his mouth as though he was about to say something but clamped it shut. His gaze bounced around. After several excruciating seconds, he looked her in the eye. "I'm not as coldhearted as you seem to think, Coralee. Your brother and your father needed help, so I helped them, but my job here is done. I won't darken your doorstep again."

She couldn't let him leave. Not yet. He had to understand. "About Daddy. Very few people know."

"You think I'm going to flap my jaw about what I've seen, don't you?" He scoffed. "I thought you knew me better than that, but clearly, I was mistaken. Good day, Miss Culpepper." He didn't wait for a reply but strode off, mounted his horse in one graceful movement, and headed for the 7 Heart.

She watched as Houston put distance between them. The chasm was wider than ever. Why that troubled her, she didn't know, but it did. He'd accused her of not knowing him. Perhaps she didn't—not as well as she'd thought, anyhow. She didn't have time to ponder that. Her family needed her. She headed back inside, dragged herself up the stairs, and entered Calvin's room.

Her brother looked up from where he lay, propped up against his pillows just as Daddy was in his room down the hall. Calvin sent her a lopsided smile and spoke in a slurred voice. "Howdy, sis. Sorry about this." He swept a hand at his chest, the bulky bandage around it visible through the cotton of his nightshirt.

"I'm sorry for you. That Toro is a troublemaker."

"Yep." Calvin chuckled and winced.

Travis snapped his leather case closed. "No laughing for you for a while, Calvin. You need to heal, and that's serious business."

"Whatever you say, Doc. Right now, I need...to take...a siesta." He closed his eyes and was asleep before Coralee and Travis reached the hallway.

She closed Calvin's door and accompanied Travis to the upper landing, where she asked the question that had been on her mind ever since hearing the news. "How is he?" She dreaded the answer. Calvin's injury was serious. A ranch hand had been run over by a wagon when she was a girl, and a number of his ribs were broken. He'd died a week later.

"The dose of laudanum I've given him will help ease the pain, but keeping him down won't be easy. If he's to heal properly, he has to stay in bed the next four weeks. You can help by seeing that he does."

A month? What was she to do about the ranch? Since Calvin had dismissed his foreman the year before and taken over his duties, there was no one to fill that role while her brother was laid up. "I'll do what I can, but he'll be chomping at the bit to get back to work."

"Houston is going to ask Pa if he knows of someone who could fill in."

"That's kind of him." He hadn't mentioned that when she'd talked to him outside. "Oh. In all the excitement, I almost forgot. I'd like you to take a look at Daddy. His lack of color concerns me."

"Certainly." Travis followed her into her father's room and performed a quick examination. He pulled the sheet back into place and nodded toward the door. "If you'll see me out, I'll tell you what I think."

She led the way to the entryway below, clutched the edge of the narrow console table, and braced herself for the news. "He's failing, isn't he?"

"I don't see a marked change, but it does appear his circulation has become even more sluggish. You've been completing the arm and leg lifts regularly, haven't you?"

"Yes. Morning, noon, and night, just as you said. Sally and I stretch his palms and rotate his ankles the way you showed us too."

Travis glanced from Daddy's room to Calvin's. "I know you'll be busy tending to your brother's needs, as well, but if you could increase your father's sessions to six a day, that would help to stimulate his blood flow and might result in better coloring."

"I'll do whatever he needs."

"I'm sorry, Coralee. You've been doing a fine job, but it just got harder. My family will do all we can to help. You can count on that."

Travis meant well, but there was one Hart who wouldn't set foot on the Culpepper ranch. Not that she wanted him to. She didn't need Houston throwing her world out of balance any more than he already had.

CHAPTER 6

Sweat trickled down Houston's brow. He removed it with a quick swipe of his sleeve. He'd forgotten what hard work stacking hay was. His work cutting firewood to sell in his hardware store out West had kept him in shape, but haying used different muscles. Several of them were protesting now. At least the temperature wasn't a problem. He'd dealt with heat in California. The humidity in south-central Texas was another story. He wasn't accustomed to it. But he would readjust.

He scanned the field, a testimony to his efforts. Austin hadn't thought Houston could get the entire field to this point before Perla had lunch ready, but he'd succeeded. He'd passed his first test—with plenty more to come.

The scent of roast beef greeted Houston as he walked into the dining room at El Regalo a short time later and took his place at the table. "Roast beef sandwiches. My favorite. You're going to spoil me, Perla."

The family's longtime cook chuckled. "Sí, Señor Houston. I will try."

Hays reached over Houston's shoulder and grabbed a sandwich on his way to his chair. "When can I expect my favorite dish, Perla?"

"Tonight. Tomorrow." She fluttered a hand. "You have so many favorites, Señor Hays, that there is usually one at every meal."

Pa entered and took his place. "You boys aren't starting before we've said grace, are you?"

"No, Pa," Houston and Hays said simultaneously.

"That's good. Now pass me those sandwiches. I need one."

Perla picked up the platter, walked to the head of the table, and put two sandwiches on Pa's plate. "Here you go, Senõr Hart. You need *mucho* energy if you're going to bark orders at your boys." The laughter in her voice as she headed for the kitchen took away the sting of her jest.

Houston filled his glass with milk from the nearby pitcher. "Looks like she's still keeping you in line, Pa."

"Don't think that's possible. I'm as ornery as ever."

Pa was joking, of course, although he was as tough as rawhide and could be hard to please. Houston knew all about that. He'd spent the first eighteen years of his life attempting to live up to his father's expectations.

Several others made their way to the dining room. The meal passed with the usual jesting, laughter, and comparisons of which brother had worked hardest that morning. Houston knew better than to enter the friendly competition since he was on trial.

Austin wiped his mouth and tossed his napkin on the table. "I took a look at the field you cut as I rode past, Houston. Nice job."

"Thanks." He hadn't expected the compliment, but he appreciated it.

Pa leaned back in his chair and studied Houston. "But will you be able to move tomorrow, son?"

The pressure to perform up to his father's standards never ceased. "I'm sure I'll be fine."

In no time, the room emptied. Houston followed his father to the large library lined with floor-to-ceiling bookshelves that doubled as his office. "If you have a minute, I've got a question."

Pa waved him in. "Fire away."

Houston entered and stood in front of Pa's massive desk. "Since Calvin Culpepper is going to be laid up for a few weeks, he's looking for someone who could fill in as his ranch foreman. I told him I'd see if you knew of anyone. Do you?"

Pa propped an elbow on the arm of his oversized desk chair and leaned his cheek on his fist. He rubbed his closely trimmed salt-and-pepper beard and stared at Houston for so long that he became aware of the ticking of the grandfather clock in the corner.

He didn't need to be kept waiting. He had plenty of work to do. "Do you, or don't you?"

"I reckon I do." Pa folded his arms across his broad chest and nodded. "Yes, sirree, I know just the man."

Houston's irritation grew. "Who?"

"You."

"What? You can't be serious. I'm liable to get a backside full of buckshot if I set foot on the Culpepper ranch."

Pa slapped his palms on his desk. "Hogwash. Calvin asked for your help last night, didn't he?"

"Not exactly. I was there when Coralee got the news that her brother had been injured. Travis needed another set of hands, so I rode over too."

"And Calvin threw you out? That doesn't make sense."

"It, um"—Houston cleared his throat—"wasn't Calvin. It was Coralee."

Pa drummed his fingers on the desktop. "I know Coralee's got a burr under her saddle when it comes to you, but it's high time she got over that."

Houston hadn't expected his father to come to his defense.

"You've got some fences to mend, too, son. Grab this opportunity by the horns and make the most of it."

So much for Pa taking his side. "Your plan is to send me into hostile territory?"

"My plan is for you to gain some valuable experience, here as well as there."

Perhaps Pa's idea had merit. Neither he nor Austin were about to hand over the reins of the 7 Heart. Houston would answer to them. At the Culpepper place, he would have freedom to do things his way for the most part.

"I'll consider approaching Calvin, but even if he agrees"—which was doubtful, since he'd already warned Houston to stay away from his sister —"Coralee might convince him otherwise. Supposing they go along with it, though...I have my conditions. I'll work here in the mornings and the rest of the day at the Culpepper ranch. And I don't want to be treated like a greenhorn when I'm here. I want to be assigned the same kinds of tasks my brothers are."

"I accept your terms, son. But if I'm only getting half a day's work out of you, it had better be good, hard work."

"I've never been a shirker. That's not about to change." He would work harder than ever before if it meant gaining Pa's respect. Perhaps Coralee might even be persuaded to see him as more than a disloyal fortune seeker too.

~

The rap on the front door couldn't have come at a worse time. Coralee juggled the stack of soiled bedding on one arm and a pail of dirty dishes over the other and made her way down the stairs with slow, careful steps. All they needed now was for her to take a tumble and be put out of commission with a twisted ankle.

Whoever was at the door repeated the summons.

"Hold your horses," she muttered under her breath. "I'm coming!" she called.

She reached the entryway, managed to turn the latch, and opened the door. "Houston!"

The pail crashed to the floor, followed by the breaking of glass, and the armload of laundry fell at his feet.

Concern shone in his bright blue eyes. "Are you all right?"

She nodded.

"What are you doing dealing with such things, anyway? Why didn't you ask Sally?"

"She's busy helping Daddy."

"Let me get them for you." He stooped to pick up the soiled bedding and grabbed the handle of the bucket filled with broken dishes.

"Please don't." She wasn't about to let him carry the foul-smelling load.

"Don't what?"

Don't be so caring. Don't confuse me. "Don't feel like you have to help."

He shook his head. "I'm going to be spending a good deal of time around here, Corrie, so you might as well get used to having my help. Now, where would you like these?" He lifted one arm and then the other.

"Spending time here? What do you mean?"

"Calvin asked me to find someone to help him run the ranch while he's laid up, and I did. Me."

"No. You're not..." He wasn't at all the person she'd expected to take her brother's place, but she had asked the Lord for a man who could handle the record keeping. That, more than anything else, seemed to be on Calvin's mind. He'd been mumbling about his ledgers in his sleep. Since Houston had run a successful business out in California, he should be well-versed in such things. "Fine. If my brother accepts your offer, I suppose I have no choice."

"I appreciate the warm welcome." His smile had a hint of merriment about it, as though he found her amusing. "I'll just take these things to the kitchen, then." He set off.

She hurried after him, her mind and stomach whirling at the prospect of having Houston around. How would she handle seeing him every day? Their first encounter had been hard enough. He'd looked good in his Sunday clothes, but he was even more appealing in his ranch wear. His broad shoulders and muscular arms did a fine job of filling out his work shirt. She tore her gaze away from him.

He greeted Olive, who rushed over to relieve him of his load. "Welcome, Mr. Houston. This is a surprise. If I'd known company was coming, I'd have made something special. All I have are some snickerdoodles. You're welcome to them." The Culpeppers' longtime cook, her arms filled with the laundry, leaned her head toward the plate of cookies on the table.

"I'm actually going to be working here until Calvin is back on his feet, unless he objects, of course."

That wasn't likely. Her brother's sole concern since his run-in with Toro was the ranch.

"So you'll be dining here?" Olive sent Coralee a questioning look.

The sooner she accepted the situation, the better. She needed to get back upstairs. Sally could use her help with Daddy. "Yes, he will. How many meals a day should we plan on, Houston?"

"I'll be here for lunch and dinner, but I'll have breakfast at El Regalo."

"Very well. Olive will see that there's plenty to eat. Now, if you'll follow me, I'll tell Calvin you're here."

Houston said nothing on the way up the stairs, which suited her. She'd fielded a number of changes since yesterday and taken them in stride, but this one unsettled her. How was she to deal with having him around when he looked so handsome and was being so helpful? She couldn't let those things sway her.

They reached Calvin's room. At her brother's request, she showed Houston inside. "Close the door on your way out, will you, sis?"

Clearly, she wasn't to be a party to this discussion, which was just as well. The less time she spent with Houston, the better.

She paused, listening to the rumble of male voices. Her brother's was softer than usual, but Houston's had a deep, rich quality. Not that she could make out what either of them was saying. That wasn't a problem. She wasn't one to eavesdrop. But was that her name she'd heard?

A sound from her father's room sent her scurrying. She hurried to his bedside.

Sally's back was to the door. She held one of Daddy's arms, putting it through the exercises. "Was that Mr. Houston I heard?" Wariness creased the maid's brow.

"Yes. He's going to be helping out."

"I see. And how do you feel about that?"

Coralee dipped her fingers in the jar on the table and slathered some cream on Daddy's arm, rubbing it in. She inhaled the soothing scent. "I'm grateful to him, of course, but I'm not happy about the situation."

"If that boy hurts you again..."

"I won't let that happen. I'm older now. And stronger. I know better than to trust him."

"I'm glad to hear that. It about broke my heart to see you crying your eyes out after he left."

The door to Calvin's room opened. Houston's footfalls heralded his approach. He stopped when he reached Daddy's room. "May I have a minute, Coralee?"

She sighed. "You might as well come in. Sally is like family, so say what you have to say."

He stepped inside. "Calvin has accepted my offer. I'll be starting immediately. My plan is to work at the 7 Heart every morning and arrive here in time for lunch. I'll spend the rest of each day here, dividing my time between working outdoors and seeing to the books."

"Very well. Let me know what you need. Sally, Olive, and I will see to it that you get it."

"Other than the meals, nothing. I can bed down in the bunkhouse and return to the 7 Heart at sunup."

"That won't be necessary."

Sally's eyebrows shot toward the abundance of gray curls peeking from beneath the bright red bandana attempting to corral them.

Coralee forged ahead despite Sally's shock. "There's a small bedroom downstairs that's unoccupied. You may use it."

"I appreciate that. I'll get to work, then. Unless you need anything first, that is."

Why must he be so helpful? "I'm fine."

"Very well." He nodded cordially and left.

As soon as the front door had clicked shut, Sally spoke up. "Do you reckon having him stay here in the house is wise? You're more likely to run into him that way."

"I can't exactly ignore him." Although she would avoid him as much as possible. "We'll just have to make the best of it."

She would have to guard her heart, as well, because Houston was proving to be as kind and caring as ever, two of the things she'd loved about him. She'd just have to remember that he'd failed to take her needs into consideration the day he'd walked out of her life.

CHAPTER 7

$\mathcal{T}$he fragrant scents wafting from the display of Meribeth's homemade soaps in Mortenson's Mercantile drew Coralee like a bee to a flower. She'd come to get some items Olive needed, not to get anything for herself, but she couldn't resist sniffing the various bars. She picked up one with a purple ribbon around it and a big floppy bow. _Mmm_. Lavender. After caring for both Calvin and Daddy the past week plus doing her best to avoid Houston, she deserved a treat. She put the bar in the wicker shopping basket.

"Coralee. I thought that was you." Meribeth waddled along behind the glass front cases, stopping when she reached the artful arrangement of her handiwork. She rested a hand on her rounded belly. "I'm sorry to hear about Calvin. How is he doing?"

"Being laid up is testing his patience—and mine. He's so fidgety, you'd think there was a scorpion in his bedsheets. Having Houston filling in for him has helped some. Calvin feels like things are under control."

"I can't believe it! Houston is working for your brother? Why? Calvin knows what Houston did to you, and he was none too happy about it."

Coralee grabbed another soap bar, brought it to her nose, and took a whiff. "This one's soothing. What's in it?"

"Chamomile and calendula petals. I answered your question. How about answering mine? Why would Calvin hire Houston, of all people? And what's more, why would Houston want to work for him? He has to know what Calvin thinks of him."

She'd done her best to change the subject, but Meribeth was known for her persistence. "I'm not sure. All I know is that the two of them have been spending an hour or so every evening holed up in Calvin's room. They seem to be focused on his ledgers. My guess is that since my brother's not as good with figures as you are, he's asked Houston for some pointers. That makes sense. His business out in California has been quite successful, from what I hear."

Meribeth picked up a soap bar and tied a bow that had come undone. "There are those who think he'll return to California once he gets his share of the 7 Heart. Some even hope he does. They didn't take kindly to him leaving when there was a war going on."

She'd heard that too. But Houston could do what he wanted as far as she was concerned. If he left, she wouldn't have to deal with the jumble of emotions she experienced each time they spoke. She had to remind her traitorous heart that he was the one who'd shattered it. She did hope, though, for Calvin's sake, that he would stay until her brother was on his feet again.

If only Calvin hadn't asked her to be more cordial when it came to Houston. Being around him was hard enough without having Calvin pestering her, and yet yesterday he'd asked her to take some lemonade out to Houston. Why she'd agreed to do it, she didn't know. Since Houston had been out felling trees for some odd reason, she'd had to ride all the way to the north pasture and back, taking a big bite out of her afternoon.

Although it didn't make sense, given Calvin's warning for her to keep her distance, she'd gotten the impression that his opinion of Houston was changing. That might be, but she'd have to be careful not to spend too much time with him because she was starting to enjoy his company far more than she should.

~

*S*tepping into Collingswood & Henderson's Hardware swept Houston back in time. The familiar smells of axle grease, linseed oil, and kerosene combined, creating a unique scent that filled him with a sense of nostalgia. With the two elderly proprietors busy assisting customers, he was free to explore.

Moving methodically through the shop, he took note of the inventory, from shovels and hayforks to washboards and scrub brushes. He couldn't resist shoving his hand into a bin of fencing nails. He scooped up a fistful and slowly released them, enjoying the satisfying *pings* as they struck the sides of the metal container.

The small store, a third the size of his business out in California, offered a fair selection of the basics. If the owners were to rent the vacant building next door, they could double their space and increase their offerings. Their customers wouldn't be forced to head to Uvalde or San Antonio to get what they needed.

Mr. Henderson finished with his customer and strode over to where Houston stood behind a display of washtubs. "Do my old eyes deceive me, or is that Houston Hart?"

"It's me, sir."

"Good to see you again, young man. What can I do for you?"

"Actually, I was hoping I could do something for you. I've got some fine oak firewood chopped and wondered if you'd have an interest in offering it to your customers. Calvin Culpepper and I would be willing to give you a nice commission." Calvin could use the money. From what Houston had discovered in going over Calvin's books, he'd been fleeced by his erstwhile foreman. Houston was doing everything he could to locate the cheat and see that he was brought to justice. He'd even enlisted Chisholm's help.

Mr. Henderson shook his head. "I'm sorry we can't help you out, but Jonas and I aren't looking to expand our business. In fact, we've been searching for a buyer."

"Really? Has anyone expressed an interest?" The store had the potential to become a lucrative one as Hartville grew. If circumstances were different, he could see himself buying it.

The older gentleman's smile faded. "Not a single solitary person.

Jonas and I decided just last week that if we can't locate someone by the end of the summer, we're going to close up shop."

"I'm sorry to hear that. Hartville won't be the same without your store."

"Folks will make do. Many of them have been getting their supplies elsewhere, anyhow." The discouragement in the older man's voice prompted Houston to do what he could to help.

"I owned a hardware store out in California and faced similar challenges. Perhaps I could offer some suggestions."

"That's right kind of you, but Jonas and I don't have the vim and vigor we once did and are ready to move on. He's got an invitation to go live with his son up in Dallas, and I want to be near my daughter and her family in Galveston. My second grandchild's on the way." Pride lit the man's eyes.

Although the closure would be a loss for those who lived around Hartville, Houston could understand the pull of family. "I wish you all the best, then." He bade the man farewell and turned to leave.

"Wait!"

Houston spun around. "Yes?"

"Why don't you buy the business? You've got the experience and the energy."

"I wish I could, but I'm not in a position to become a merchant again. If my circumstances were to change, I'd let you know, though."

The only way that would happen would be if he gave up on securing his share of the 7 Heart, but how could he? Ranching his portion was the only way he could show Pa that he was as much a part of the family as his brothers.

He bid the elderly gentleman farewell and left the shop, the bell hanging from the doorknob ringing behind him. The door on the mercantile directly across the street closed with an answering chime. He recognized the striking woman walking to her horse tied out front immediately. Coralee was particularly fetching in the dark purple dress. It hugged her in all the right places.

She looked up, saw him, and smiled. As quickly as the smile had arrived, it faded, replaced by a firm set to her lips. He'd seen the same thing happen several times over the past few days. It was as though she was genuinely glad to see him but refused to admit it, even to herself. The fact that she was conflicted filled him with hope. Perhaps in time, she would trust him enough to let him back into her life. Only then could he tell her why he'd left. For some reason, explaining himself to her had become extremely important.

He took his horse by the reins and strode over to her. "If I'd known you were coming to town, we could have ridden in together."

"Perhaps." She shoved the first of two brown paper parcels she carried into one of her saddlebags.

"I'm done, and it looks like you are too. Care to ride back with me?"

"I suppose so."

He responded in a light tone. "You don't have to sound so excited about it. A feller might think you didn't welcome his company."

She walked around her horse, stowed the second package in her other saddlebag, and slid the strap through the buckle. She patted her mare's neck and swung her gaze around to Houston. "Did my brother put you up to this? It's rather convenient, you showing up in town when I'm here."

"Of course not. I had business to tend to, and this was the best time to take care of it."

"I see. Well, I'm ready. Are you?"

"Sure am." He mounted his gelding.

They got underway. Coralee said little. He didn't press her but enjoyed the surroundings instead. He'd missed this part of Texas, with its wooded canyons, brilliant blue skies, and stunning sunsets. The lowing of a cow in the nearby field drew his attention. She flicked her tail in an attempt to rid herself of the pesky flies that plagued the herd.

Something seemed to be bothering Coralee too. If he had to guess, he'd say she was no closer to trusting him than before. So be it. He'd keep doing his best, and in time, both she and Pa might see that he was determined to do a good job.

"Are you glad to be back?"

Her question took him by surprise. "Yes. Why?"

"Being a rancher is quite different from running a hardware store. Are you sure that's what you want to do? You told me you didn't enjoy riding herd as much as your brothers, but you certainly seem to enjoy bookwork. You've done an awful lot of it for Calvin this past week."

He'd confessed years ago that his heart wasn't in tending cattle—once. He wasn't sure she'd even heard him since she'd said nothing. He'd assumed she wasn't too happy to find out that he didn't share his family's passion. "I'm a Hart. Ranching's in my blood."

"Even so, I can't help but wondering if you'd be happier as a shop owner. I saw you come out of the hardware store. Did you know it's for sale?"

"I do, but that doesn't change anything."

"Perhaps, but you could think about it, couldn't you?"

"Why all the questions?" Hers had come as a surprise. Had he misinterpreted her silence? Was it possible Coralee could accept him for who he was, even if Pa couldn't?

"I suppose I'm curious what your life was like after you left. From what I've heard, you did well for yourself."

"It wasn't always that way. There were lean times, but I found ways to generate income. I felled trees, cut them up, and delivered the firewood during the winter months when mining, building, and the need for supplies slowed."

"Ah!" She nodded. "You like chopping wood. That's why you've been clearing the north pasture. I wondered. When you're done, we'll be set for firewood for years to come."

As much as he'd like to set her straight, he'd promised to keep Calvin's perilous financial situation between them. "I'm helping in whatever ways I can, the same as you do."

The rest of the ride passed quickly, with their conversation taking a lighter turn. Coralee relaxed at last, and they talked the way they had on the many rides they'd enjoyed in their youth. It was as though she'd opened the window to her former self, back when her life was her own and she wasn't busy putting others' needs ahead of her own. She worked hard and gave so much of herself. She'd deserved this time away from her duties.

They reached the Culpepper ranch, slipped from their saddles, and stood staring at one another. She was so close, he could smell the fruity fragrance of her perfume. His gaze dropped to her lips. If he wasn't mistaken, hers was focused on his mouth.

Expectancy hung in the air, but he wasn't about to act until he knew

Coralee would welcome his kiss. And that wouldn't happen until she'd grown to trust him.

She stepped back, handed her reins to a ranch hand, and donned her businesslike manner. "I have to go. Daddy and Calvin need me, and I know you have work to do, as well."

The curtains that had parted closed, shutting him out once again.

He could be waiting a very long time.

CHAPTER 8

*O*live cleared the plates after their dinner. Coralee had taken to eating her meals in the kitchen with the cook and Sally of late. It didn't make sense to create more work for Olive by insisting on using the dining room when she was busy concocting special foods to accommodate Calvin's and Daddy's needs and doing more laundry and ironing than ever before. In addition, she was still preparing meals for some of the war widows and their children when the need arose. Sally was out delivering one of them now.

Houston had been dining with Coralee and the household staff since he'd begun working for Calvin two weeks ago and didn't seem to mind the informality. She could imagine what those out at El Regalo would have to say about the arrangements. So be it. She didn't have the time or energy to think about that.

He scraped his chair back from the table. "If you ladies will excuse me, I'll head to the study."

As soon as he left, Coralee turned to Olive. "Daddy liked the custard sauce you made today. He ate several bites."

"I'm glad. He needs to eat."

"Thanks to you and your excellent cooking, he does." Not nearly enough, but every bite helped. "I should look in on him and collect Calvin's dinner dishes."

Coralee headed for the stairs but paused on the landing. The lantern light pouring from Calvin's study caught her eye. Houston worked hard all day, first at the 7 Heart and then here at her brother's ranch. Night after night, he spent hours hunched over Calvin's desk studying his ledgers dating back several years. Why Houston felt the need to go through so many of them was a mystery. She'd asked him about it a time or two, but he evaded her questions.

Despite her resolve to avoid being with him any more than necessary, she found herself looking forward to their interactions. Things had changed on their ride back from town the week before. She'd resisted talking with him as long as possible, but she enjoyed learning about people, hearing their stories. If she was honest with herself, she'd felt a burning need to know what Houston's life out West had been like and why it had held such appeal.

Their conversation had proven to be enlightening. Although he'd enjoyed running his hardware store in California, he'd quickly dismissed the possibility of buying one right here in Hartville. It seemed he had it in his head that if he was to fit into his family, he had to be a rancher here at home.

Considering the fact that GW Hart lived and breathed cattle, Houston's way of thinking made sense. His father had always been a taskmaster, expecting those who worked for him to put in a hard day's work. She could only imagine how much more he demanded from his sons. Houston was certainly pushing himself, beginning his day before the sun was up and keeping the lamp burning late into the night.

If they were as close as they used to be, she would have no qualms about expressing her concerns. But they weren't. He was the master of his plans, and although she didn't like to think about it, they could change at any time. If things didn't work out for him here, he was liable to return to California. Even though her resistance was weakening, she had to keep her distance, or she could end up getting hurt all over again.

She grabbed the railing with one hand and shoved the other in her pocket. A piece of paper crinkled, bringing her to a stop. How could she have forgotten?

Reversing course, she dashed down the steps and made straight for Calvin's office. She rapped on the door frame. "Houston?"

He looked up from the ledgers spread before him, a sea of figures that must swim before his tired eyes. "Yes?"

"This came for you today." She approached the desk and held out the envelope from the telegraph company. "The delivery boy brought it right after lunch. He said it's from California. I'd intended to ride out and give it to you, but I got busy with Daddy's exercises, and it slipped my mind. I'm sorry."

He took the envelope and pulled out the telegram. His shoulders sagged as he read it. He tossed the paper on the desk, leaned back, and gripped the horseshoe-shaped arms of Calvin's captain's chair so tightly that his knuckles turned white.

Her chest tightened. "It's bad news, isn't it?"

"It's from Peter, my partner out West. He wasn't able to come up with the money to buy the hardware store from me before I left, so he was going to run it himself. But he's changed his mind. A buyer has made a ridiculously low offer, and he plans to sell it unless..."

Unless he went back? Despite the heat of the summer's day, a chill raced through her.

He rested his hands in his lap and twiddled his thumbs. His gaze flitted over the pages of figures spread before him. He spoke more to himself than to her. "I can't believe Peter would do something like this. I'll have to figure out how to handle it. I might have to—"

A crash came from above.

"Daddy!"

Coralee took off, mounting the stairs two at a time. She reached her father's room and found him moaning and thrashing about. She raced to his beside, kicked aside the pieces of his broken water glass, and rested her hands on his shoulders, exerting firm but gentle pressure.

"No, Daddy!" She dragged in a breath and forced herself to remain calm even though her heart was slamming against her ribs. "It's all right. I'm here. Everything's fine. Lie back before you hurt yourself."

He fought against her, batting at her arms and muttering.

She felt a hand in the middle of her back. Houston.

"What can I do to help?"

"I'm not sure." Her mind was reeling, but she forced herself to think. "You could h-hold him while I get his medicine."

"You'll need to move."

"Yes. Of course." She stepped to the side so Houston could take her place, picked up the bottle of laudanum, and pawed through the numerous items on the bedside table.

He grabbed Daddy's arms and held them. Daddy arched his back and twisted his torso. His groans grew louder and more insistent. Houston glanced at her over his shoulder. "What are you looking for?"

"The spoon." She continued her search, moving every item and sloshing water out of the washbasin in her haste. She dropped a cloth on the worst of the spill. "I've got to find it. Where could it be?"

"Take a breath, Corrie. It's here somewhere."

"I wonder if he knocked it off too." She dropped to her hands and knees.

"Careful! The glass."

She made contact with a shard, sending pain shooting through the fleshy area below her thumb. She stood, yanked out the sliver, and tossed it aside. Blood flowed from the small cut. She pulled the handkerchief from her sleeve, wound it around her hand as quickly as possible, using her teeth to secure one end, and tied a knot. Daddy's cries rang out as she worked.

"Calvin has a spoon. I'll get his." She ran from Daddy's room into her brother's. Despite the commotion down the hall, he was sound asleep, no doubt due to the hefty dose of laudanum she'd had to give him after he'd twisted the wrong way earlier. If only she could get Daddy settled.

She sprinted back to her father's room, spoon in one hand, medicine bottle in the other. Daddy continued to flail. He'd taken to kicking at his bedclothes too. If they didn't calm him, he was liable to hurt himself.

Taking the cork stopper of the bottle between her teeth, she pulled until it popped out. She poured the brown liquid, wrinkling her nose at the strong alcohol scent.

She slipped in beside Houston, who was holding Daddy's arms and pressing him into the mattress. He continued to fight, jerking his head from side to side. She took his chin in one hand, doing her best to keep him from moving, and held the spoon with the other.

Her hand trembled as she moved it to his mouth, spilling the laudanum. The dark stain hit the white sheet, wicking into the cotton and spreading. "What's wrong with me? I've done this hundreds of times."

"You're doing fine, Corrie. Just try again."

She drew strength from Houston's words of encouragement, took a deep breath, and refilled the spoon. Although she reached Daddy's mouth without mishap this time, the moment she touched his lips, he clamped his mouth closed. "Please, open up. This will help you."

"You could force his mouth open and pour it in. Some of it's sure to get between his teeth. He'd have no choice but to swallow."

"Yes. That might work." She doubled the amount of laudanum on the spoon and squeezed Daddy's cheeks, which wasn't easy with him turning his head back and forth.

Determination drove her on. She managed to get his lips parted, and his head tilted back. He gritted his teeth, but she tipped the spoon and poured the medicine anyhow.

Daddy relaxed.

She let go of him and turned to put the spoon on the table.

Something wet struck her cheek. She wheeled around, and another spray of laudanum hit her right in the face.

Her beloved daddy was spitting...at *her*?

"No. Please. Stop." She blinked to clear her vision, which had grown blurry. Her body began to shake. "I was only...tr-trying to help."

Houston released one of her father's arms and rested a hand on her shoulder. "Are you all right?"

She stared at her father as he continued to struggle. Houston did his best to contain Daddy's arms with one hand.

"What am I going to do?" Her voice broke. "He needs that medicine."

"I'll take care of it. You need to stay back. I don't want you to get hurt." He guided her to the end of the bed.

Coralee clutched a column of the four-poster bed and watched Houston work. He poured the laudanum, took hold of Daddy's chin, and pulled on his jaw firmly but gently until his teeth parted. Despite being battered by his wildly swinging arms, Houston succeeded in getting the medicine into Daddy's mouth, tipping his head back and forcing him to swallow. Houston perched on the bed, rubbing Daddy's arms and speaking words of encouragement and support as the medicine took effect. Thankfully, it did so quickly.

Houston's compassion touched her deeply. Not once during the ordeal had he shown impatience or judgment. He'd treated Daddy with the dignity he deserved.

She sniffed and blinked rapidly, but she couldn't keep the tears from falling.

Houston was on his feet in an instant. Without a word, he pulled her into his arms. She pressed her face into his work shirt, soaking the cotton as shudders racked her body. He rested one hand on her back and stroked her hair with the other, twirling one of her ringlets around his finger the way he used to.

When her flood of salty tears finally stopped, he rested his hands on her upper arms and pulled back until he could look into her face. Even though it must be a splotchy mess, he gazed at her with a hint of a smile lifting his lips. Ever so slowly, he leaned toward her. Was he going to kiss her?

Her eyes slid shut as though of their own accord. Her senses heightened. She could hear Daddy's shallow breathing and Calvin snoring in the distance. A gardenia-scented breeze wafted through the open window, reminding her of the time Houston had plucked one of the fragrant blossoms and twined it in her hair. She waited, standing as still as the bedpost she'd been clutching for support moments before, each second an eternity.

At long last, she felt Houston's breath warm on her face and the brush of his lips on...her forehead? No. That's where he'd kissed her moments before asking her to marry him.

The memory of that horrible afternoon when he'd turned and walked away, leaving her alone and bereft, brought her to her senses. She stepped out of his embrace and swiped at her damp cheeks with the handkerchief wrapped around her wounded hand. What a fool she'd been to drop her guard and welcome his affections. If he'd kissed her on the lips, she would have been powerless to resist. He'd spared her further humiliation.

She hadn't cried in years, not since he'd broken her heart when she was sixteen. "I'm sorry to turn into such a fountain. It's just that I've never seen Daddy like this. He's had bad days before, but this was the worst."

Compassion filled Houston's eyes, a deeper shade of blue than usual. "I can't begin to imagine what you've been through—or all you've done."

"It's been hard, but when Momma was at the end, I promised her I would take care of Daddy, and I wasn't about to—"

She realized too late what she'd said. No one but Calvin knew about her deathbed pledge. Her brother understood, having seen the early stages of Daddy's forgetfulness even before she did, but other people might feel sorry for her. She didn't want their pity. What she'd done, she'd done out of love.

The trouble was that Houston had asked her to make an impossible choice that day. When she couldn't give him the answer he wanted, he'd put as much distance between them as possible.

As much as she'd appreciated his comfort and the feeling of closeness she'd experienced in his arms a minute ago, she couldn't trust him to be there for her. He could up and leave at any time, a possibility she didn't want to consider. She couldn't leave, even if she wanted to. Little did he know how much she'd wanted to do just that years ago. How deeply she'd loved him and wanted to be his wife.

Her promise had kept her here, though, and that was just as well. Houston might not have loved her enough to find out why she couldn't marry him and go to California, but her daddy had loved her. She loved him, too, and would be here for him, no matter what. She couldn't think about anything beyond that, because a life without her father *and* her one true love would be too much to bear.

CHAPTER 9

"Thanks for letting me beg off on the job, Austin." Houston gripped his reins and glanced at yet another field of grass ready to be cut. At least he had his father's assurances that tasks more suited to his abilities and in keeping with his standing as member of the family awaited him. "I'll see to the haying when I get everything sorted out." Between the situation with Calvin and his partner's ultimatum, Houston had a lot on his mind.

His oldest brother shifted in his saddle, the leather creaking. "I'm counting on that. I don't know exactly what you're up to with all those telegrams you've been receiving, but Chisholm assures me you've got things well in hand."

Houston set out for the Culpepper ranch, savoring the time to do nothing but ride over the rolling countryside during the cool morning hours, listen to the rustle of wind through the stands of live oak trees, and think. The past two weeks had been challenging and yet rewarding. He was adjusting to the physical demands he encountered each day, but the bookwork had kept him up until well after the sun set each night. At least he'd unraveled the cause of Calvin's mysteriously depleted funds.

The drain had been slow and steady, the evidence carefully disguised, due to the shady but shrewd foreman. Calvin, a trusting sort, hadn't wanted to believe he'd hired a swindler. When he finally admitted something was afoot, he'd fired the shyster. Unable to prove anything himself due to the mess his books were in, Calvin had figured all was lost.

When Houston learned about the situation, he'd offered to do some investigating. He welcomed the opportunity to put his skills to work helping a friend. The late nights he'd spent poring over records from past years had paid off. Wait until Calvin heard the good news.

Houston arrived at the Culpepper ranch just as the ladies were finishing their breakfast. He entered the kitchen to a chorus of surprised female voices. He focused on Coralee's.

"What are you doing here so early? Is something wrong?"

"Everything's fine. I have some news for Calvin that he'll be eager to hear."

She wrinkled her nose in the most adorable way. "You two have been up to something, haven't you? It wouldn't have anything to do with all those hours you've been spending in his study, would it?"

"Perhaps." Her perceptiveness came as no surprise. Coralee was as observant as she was bright. It was a good thing she wasn't fond of numbers, or Calvin might not have been able to shield the ugly truth from her. Her brother hadn't wanted to add to her burden, a choice Houston understood and appreciated.

"I won't keep you, then. The sooner Calvin knows, the sooner I can try to pry the news out of him." She grinned. "Besides, my dear daddy will be wanting his breakfast, so I'd best get up there." She grabbed the tray Olive handed her and set off.

He marveled at how Coralee could leave yesterday's ugly episode behind her and forge ahead with a smile on her lovely face. Her selfless concern for others was an inspiration. Caring for her brother while his ribs healed and meeting Beauregard Culpepper's many needs took much of her day, and yet Houston had heard tales all over town of the good she'd done and the people she'd blessed. She was a remarkable woman. But she had to be bone weary. If only he had the right to take care of her and help carry the load.

Watching her deal with her father's outburst the day before had caused Houston's stomach to pitch. She'd been pushed beyond the limits of her endurance. He'd done what he could to ease her pain, but a brotherly hug and a few soothing words seemed a pitiful offering. What he'd wanted to do was throw caution to the wind, crush her to him, and give her a kiss that conveyed the depth of his admiration, respect, and...love?

Truth kicked Houston in the gut so hard, it was a wonder his ribs didn't crack. He loved Coralee. Deeply. Twelve years had passed, and yet his feelings hadn't diminished. They'd grown. She'd been the one for him. He'd known it then. He knew it now. But would she accept what he had to offer, or would she reject him all over again? Could he take that risk?

He mounted the stairs, passed Beauregard's bedroom, where Coralee was feeding her now-docile father, and peered into Calvin's. "May I come in?"

"Houston! By all means." Calvin waved him in. "I didn't expect to see you until later. You must have news."

"Yes. And it's good." He closed the door and filled Calvin in on the latest developments.

"I still can't believe the varmint hornswoggled me and that so much of my hard-earned money filled his pockets. I was sure he was going to get away with his crime, but thanks to you, he's going to pay for what he's done."

"It helps to have a Texas Ranger for a brother. Chisholm knew whom to contact and how to go about getting the information we needed. He's kept the telegraph lines busy the past few days."

Calvin changed positions, wincing as he did so. "Once I'm up and about, I'll thank him too. Why, I'll be able to throw a party."

"Not right away. The scoundrel has to stand trial. I'm sure he'll be convicted, though. Embezzlement is a serious crime, and since it involved stealing cattle—even though his elaborate scheme was carried out on paper with falsified documents and bribes—that won't go over well in these parts. They'll liquidate his assets, including a saloon in Corsicana, and then you'll get a good portion of your money back."

"Things will be tight for a while, but I can manage. What about you? What will you do once I'm back on my feet?"

Houston outlined his plans, which had become clear minutes before.

Calvin nodded. "A man's got to do what a man's got to do. So when are you leaving?"

"I'll catch the next stagecoach. No sense putting things off now that I've made my decision. You can't say anything to Coralee just yet."

"She won't take it well, but I'll keep my trap shut. Until it's time for me to do my part, that is."

"Good." He'd taken care of things here. Now to return to the 7 Heart, finalize things there, and face his father.

~

George Washington Hart shoveled in his last bite of steak, rested his fork on his plate, and tossed his napkin on the table. The three Hart brides had retired to the parlor minutes before, along with Houston's nephew, Robbie, leaving Pa and his sons—all seven of them, now that Crockett was back—alone for the first time since Houston's return. Normally, they only gathered for Sunday dinner, but they'd all shown up that Thursday evening for a private celebration of the successful cattle drive. They would hold a dance on Saturday and invite their friends.

Pa stood and leveled his gaze on Houston. "I'd like to have a word with you before I retire, son. Meet me in your mother's parlor in five minutes, will you?"

Houston's chest tightened. "Yes, Pa."

"Good night, boys."

Pa disappeared through the open doorway, along with all of Houston's brothers except for Travis. The curiosity on his face was likely evident on Houston's, as well. "What was that about, Huey?"

"I have no idea." Houston had planned to talk with Pa in the morning, but it appeared he would have the opportunity to do so tonight. Not that he was ready, but Coralee had made a good point during their ride back from town after he'd visited Collingswood & Henderson's Hardware. If he wasn't honest with his father, he'd be forced into a job that could become a burden.

Travis clapped a hand on Houston's shoulder. "I wish you well. You can find me later and tell me what he wanted."

"I will. Before you go, I wanted to thank you for stopping in to check on Beauregard. He's calmer now."

"I'm glad to hear it. I admire Coralee. She's been taking care of him for over eleven years now—and not a word of complaint. That's loyalty for you. Anyhow, I'd best not keep you. Pa wouldn't take too kindly to that." Travis went to join his wife and the others.

Houston made his way to his mother's parlor. He walked around looking at the items, each one reminding him of her. Except for the vase of freshly cut gardenias on the table. Their fragrance brought images of Coralee to mind.

He'd caught a whiff of the memorable scent when he'd taken her in his arms the day before. She hadn't resisted—at first. She'd trusted him to be there for her in her hour of need, but could she trust him with her heart? Because of her encouragement, he'd found a way to stay—on his own terms. It meant letting his business in California go for a fraction of its value, but she was worth it. Would his choices be enough to convince her that he'd be here for her, no matter what?

Footfalls signaled Pa's approach. Houston braced himself for what was to come, whatever that might be. He stood with his feet spread and his hands clasped behind his back. "I'm here, sir, as requested."

"Relax, son. Have a seat." Pa held out a hand toward Mother's favorite settee and lowered himself into the green armchair reserved for him.

Houston sat poker straight, waiting for Pa to speak.

"When did you plan to tell me that you don't cotton to being a rancher?"

Pa's question robbed Houston of the ability to speak. He swallowed in an attempt to remove the boulder lodged in his throat, giving him a moment to think. If Pa had already figured out the truth, there was no sense denying it. "How did you know?"

"I suspected it when you were younger, but it wasn't until you came back that I knew for sure."

"What gave it away? I've been working hard."

Pa leaned back into the plush chair and crossed his legs, looking completely at ease—and not the slightest bit disappointed. Odd. "That's how I knew. You've been trying *too* hard. Out to prove you have what it takes to inherit your share of the ranch, were you?"

"That was my plan." But it had changed. He'd realized Coralee was right. Running a hardware store made him happy. Riding the range and tending to the many tasks on a ranch didn't. She deserved a husband who was using the gifts God had given him, not one pretending to be something he wasn't and growing more resentful by the day. If that meant losing Pa's blessing—and the promised inheritance—so be it.

"You don't have to convince me, son. I know you could run a successful ranch, if you put your mind to it, but I don't think your heart's in it."

The time had come to make his declaration, come what may. "Ranching is good, honest work. I thought it could be enough for me, but it's not. I'm a businessman."

Pa rested his chin between his thumb and fingers and studied Houston for several seconds. "From what Travis has said, your hardware store in California did quite well. Calvin Culpepper's singing your praises too. When I stopped by to see him this afternoon, he told me he could have lost his ranch without your help. A father's chest swells to hear his son praised like that." He thumped his soundly.

Houston couldn't believe what he was hearing. Pa wasn't prone to compliments. "Thank you. That means a great deal to me."

Pa glanced around the parlor, his gaze coming to rest on the photograph of Mother and him. "Of all my boys, you're the most like your dear mother, God rest her soul. She was bright, too, and as quick to help others as you are. Victoria made up for my blustering ways. She understood why you had to leave. I was going to forbid it, but she urged me to reconsider."

"She did? Why?"

"Your wise mother said the only way for you to find out who you were and grow into the man the Lord intended you to be was for us to trust you into His care. Letting you go was one of the hardest things I've ever done, but I prayed one day you'd come home. And you have." Pa cast Houston a quizzical glance. "You are here to stay, aren't you?"

"I am, but I can't meet your terms."

"Coralee's being obstinate, is she?" Pa chuckled. "Give her time. She'll come around."

"I don't understand."

"You need a wife, right? She's got a heart as big as yours. Might as well consider her." Pa relaxed into the armchair once again.

"Actually, I have. I'm not sure she'll take me, but I aim to try."

"Glad to hear that. So why the long face?"

Houston rushed out his answer. "I'm going to buy the hardware store in town and run it myself."

"Are you, now? I'm sure you'll make a success of it." Pa's eyes narrowed. "But why turn down your share of the 7 Heart? Run your store and your ranch too."

He couldn't believe what he was hearing. "Really? I thought I'd have to spend all my time ranching."

"Travis doesn't. He runs his medical practice and oversees things at his ranch, but he hires ranch hands to tend to the chores."

The shackles that had bound Houston fell off. The realization that he could run the store *and* claim his land sent a jolt of excitement through him. All he had to do was find a wife.

Hopefully, he'd been right about what he'd seen in Coralee's eyes and she would consider marrying him. He knew exactly how he would propose. The way he planned to go about it would leave no doubt of his intentions—or the depth of his love. He just had to take care of one important matter first.

CHAPTER 10

"*I* can't leave." Coralee completed her father's midmorning exercises and laid his arm on top of the sheet.

"We'll be fine, Miss C." Sally gathered the dirty dishes on the bedside table. "Your daddy's having a good day, and your brother is feeling a lot better. If Doc Travis would let him, Calvin would be out of bed and back in the saddle in two shakes of a calf's tail."

Sally was right on all counts. Daddy showed no signs of agitation. Of course, the fact that Travis had been by and said it was time to double the dose of laudanum had a lot to do with that. Seeing Daddy's glassy-eyed stare as he lay there as still as the hot summer air sent a stabbing pain through her.

The news on Calvin was encouraging, though. His ribs appeared to be healing nicely, and he'd shown no signs of pneumonia. Best of all, he was more cheerful than she'd seen him in a long time. Whatever Houston had said when he stopped by to talk with Calvin yesterday had a profound effect on him. She would have to thank Houston later.

She'd have to guard her heart, too, because she couldn't stop thinking about the way he'd helped her with Daddy. Houston had been firm but gentle, lending his strength when hers had failed. She'd turned into a blubbering mess, and yet he'd held her close and looked at her with admiration in his clear blue eyes. Due to her overwrought state, she'd mistaken it for affection at first. Whatever it was, she was finding it harder and harder to keep from falling for him all over again.

If only she knew for sure that he was going to stay, but she couldn't get that telegram from his partner in California out of her mind. Before they were interrupted, she'd been sure he was thinking about leaving. How she hoped she was wrong. Perhaps some time away to clear her head would be a good thing.

"Meribeth *has* been asking me to visit, and I do have those baby clothes I ordered. I'll make sure I'm back in time to help with Daddy's afternoon exercises."

"Take your time, child. Olive and I can see to things here."

Coralee enjoyed the ride to town, with the wind whipping her ringlets. She passed several live oaks teeming with purple martins. Their throaty chirps and clicking calls filled the air. They would be leaving the area soon, now that the chicks had left their nests.

Leaving. Was that all she could think about lately?

She lifted her gaze to the brilliant blue sky. *Lord, if it's Your will for Houston to stay, I trust You to work things out for him here. But if he decides to return to California and run the business he worked so hard to build, please help me let him go. It would grieve me to lose him again, but I want him to be happy.*

Meribeth was delighted to see Coralee and ushered her to the rooms over the mercantile where she and her husband lived. Her friend bustled about the kitchen, preparing the meal while Coralee set the table. The scent of fried chicken hung in the air, a promise of the tasty lunch to come.

"Do you realize how many times you've mentioned Houston since you arrived?" Meribeth repeated several of Coralee's comments in a too-sweet voice. "Please tell me you haven't changed your mind about him. Remember what he did to you."

"I do, but he's changed. Not that you have to worry about me throwing myself at him," she added quickly. A change of subject was in order. "I'm glad I listened to Sally. It's wonderful to see you again. You're looking so—"

"Big?" Meribeth laughed, wiped her hands on her apron, and picked up the baby clothes lying on the sideboard.

Her ploy had worked. "I was going to say radiant."

"These gowns are darling. Look at this lovely smocking." Meribeth carried the garments to the window and examined Widow Foster's excellent needlework in the bright sunlight.

She set the baby clothes aside and rubbed her lower back as she peered out. From her vantage point, Meribeth would have a good view of Hartville's main street below, which was a hive of activity that morning. "I'd heard a woman in my condition could find the final months a mite tiresome. I can attest to that."

"I'm sorry you're hurting. Do you think you'll feel like going to the Harts' barn dance tomorrow night? I hope so, because it wouldn't be the same without you and Michael." Friends from far and wide had been invited to help the family celebrate the conclusion of another successful cattle drive. She'd been looking forward to the event ever since she received the invitation. Houston might ask to take her for a spin on the dance floor. And this time she would say yes without delay.

"We plan to join the fun, but I won't be doing any danc—" Meribeth gasped.

Coralee was at her side in an instant. "Are you in pain? It's too early for the baby, isn't it?"

"Nothing's wrong. I just saw something unexpected. That's all."

"What?" Coralee stood beside her friend and scanned the street below, but nothing looked unusual. Clusters of people stood on the planked walkways visiting, while others entered and exited the shops. Fred Chambers hefted a large wooden trunk into the boot of his trusty stagecoach. "It looks like someone's planning to be away for quite some time. I wonder who that could be."

Meribeth backed away from the window, eyes wide, reached for her chair, and sank into it.

"Why do you look so shocked? It's not like it was the midwife or anything. Annie Hart isn't going anywhere."

Uncertainty filled her friend's eyes. "I didn't see Annie get inside the stagecoach. It was...someone else. Someone you care about—even though your best friend warned you not to."

The realization of what Meribeth had seen hit Coralee with such force that her knees threatened to buckle. "It's Houston, isn't it? He's the one who's leaving."

"I'm afraid so. I heard people in the mercantile say he's going to run his hardware store, after all. I'm sorry, Coralee. I was afraid this would happen when I heard he'd come back. You've always had a soft spot where he was concerned. And now he's hurt you all over again. It's a good thing he's leaving, because if he were staying here, I would give him a piece of my mind."

"It's all right. I'm fine." She wasn't, but she would deal with her pain privately. "So...tell me...have you and Michael decided on names yet?"

Thankfully, her loyal friend let the matter drop. They enjoyed a delicious meal, although Coralee scarcely tasted it. She bid Meribeth goodbye shortly afterward, resorting to the ready excuse of needing to get back home to check on her father.

Coralee had just unwound her mare's reins when Clarice Spanner burst out of First National Bank next door and rushed up to her. "You're just the person I wanted to see, Coralee. I was inside tending to my deposit and couldn't help overhearing a conversation between Velma Duke and Bernard Palmer."

Although what the president of the Confederate Widows and Orphans Fund and the bank president had been discussing was none of Clarice's business, such things didn't stop her. Coralee didn't want to encourage the gossip, but Clarice prattled on. "I thought you might be interested in hearing what they said since a familiar name came up. It turns out the mysterious benefactor who's been the CWAOF's primary source of income all these years is none other than your former beau, Houston Hart. Can you believe it?"

It took every ounce of restraint Coralee possessed not to show her surprise. She knew Houston was generous, but—

"That's not all." Clarice looked up and down the street, as though she was concerned someone might hear her, when, in all likelihood, she would be bending the ears of anyone who would listen as soon as she finished regaling Coralee with the news. "It turns out he sent money to the war department before that, supporting our troops until our brave boys came home. What do you think of that?"

"It's...interesting." She'd had no idea Houston had done so much to support Texas from afar. She'd even accused him of being a fortune seeker. How wrong she'd been. He might have gone away for a time, but it seemed he really had left his heart in Texas.

If that was the case, then why had he chosen to return to California?

If he wanted to run a hardware store, he could have done that right here in Hartville.

She knew the answer, painful though it was. Whatever she and Houston had shared was over for good. He didn't want her in his life, and she must accept that. She *would* accept that. But first, she had to get away before she broke down right in front of the most notorious spreader of tales in town.

~

"I can't believe Houston's gone." Coralee sat on the edge of her brother's bed the following afternoon and handed him a cool glass of water. By keeping herself busy, she'd managed to get through the first day after Houston's departure without shedding a tear. There had been times when she'd had to blink them away before they fell, but not a single one had coursed down her cheek. Of course, if she kept thinking about him...

Calvin took a sip. "You could have stopped him. Why didn't you?"

Because nothing had changed. She loved him, but he hadn't loved her enough to find out why she'd been forced to turn him down. Oh, she'd thought he had, but she'd been wrong. Not that she would admit that to her brother. "Two weeks ago, you were warning me to stay away from him. Now you want to know why I didn't stop him. That's quite a change."

"I was wrong about him. He did me a huge favor. If it weren't for Houston, I"—he swallowed, his Adam's apple bobbing—"I could have lost the ranch."

She inhaled sharply. "No! That can't be. What happened?"

Calvin took a sudden interest in his glass, swirling the water around. "I didn't want to tell you before, but the foreman I hired was a crook. He lined his pockets with my money the whole time he worked for me. I'd suspected him for a while, but it wasn't until last year that I found a couple of discrepancies. That's why I let him go. I had no solid proof, though. Houston's the one who figured everything out."

That explained the hours Houston had spent poring over Calvin's books and their talks every evening behind the closed door. "I knew something was going on, but I had no idea it was so serious. You said you could have lost the ranch. Does that mean things are all right now?"

He drained the glass and handed it back to her. "Houston has found out where the swindler is, and there are plans in the works to have him arrested. If all goes well, I'm going to get a good deal of the money back."

"Oh, Calvin, that's wonderful."

"Things aren't certain. The details are still coming together. In fact" —he stroked his chin—"I was supposed to have heard from Chisholm Hart by now. Would you mind riding over to see if he has news for me?"

"Really? You're asking me to show up at another Hart celebration when I could just get the message tomorrow?"

"I wouldn't ask if I didn't have to, but it's a timely matter. We can't keep the other lawmen waiting."

"Fine." She huffed out a breath. "I'll do it. But I hope Travis lets you get up and about soon because I'm tired of being sent over there."

She made short work of changing into her favorite blue dress with the frilly white blouse. She checked on Daddy, mounted her horse, and headed for the 7 Heart. She'd find Chisholm, get the note, and get back home as quickly as possible.

The strains of a lively tune reached her as she neared El Regalo. She reined in her mare and studied the stately ranch house, silhouetted against the setting sun. Made of stone, with its majestic tower scraping the clouds and its wealth of windows, the massive structure resembled a castle, more imposing than inviting, although the Hart family itself was the embodiment of hospitality. So why did she feel so out of place?

Coralee rode to the stable, where a ranch hand took her horse. She searched the crowd for Chisholm. Tall, like all of Houston's brothers, he wasn't hard to find. He stood beside his father. She wove her way toward the two men, slipping through the crush of people surrounding the dance floor. The festivities had gotten underway early and would continue well into the night.

Chisholm saw her and smiled. "Welcome, Coralee. We've been expecting you."

"Good. Then you have the message for my brother?"

George Washington Hart answered. "There'll be time enough for that later, young lady, after you've enjoyed some good old-fashioned Texas food and fun. But first, let me welcome you." He yanked off his

Stetson, waved it over his head, and offered her a gentlemanly bow with his hat pressed to his chest. The lively number ended rather abruptly, and the musicians launched into a waltz.

GW nodded. "That's more like it. I've been hankering after a dance, but I need a partner. Would you do me the honor?"

She couldn't very well turn down the patriarch of the family, even if he intimidated her. "Yes, sir."

He escorted her onto the wooden dance floor. In deference to their host, the couples parted, allowing GW to guide her to the centermost spot. He took her in his arms and guided her in slow, easy circles.

"I heard the drive was a huge success."

"It was."

Their conversation was cut short when a gentleman with his hat tugged low and his face turned away tapped GW on the shoulder. "May I cut in?"

Coralee recognized the voice at once. "Houston! You're here?"

CHAPTER 11

*H*ouston's father released Coralee and grinned. "She's all yours, son."

It took all the restraint Houston possessed not to kiss Coralee then and there, but he reined himself in. His plan had gone smoothly so far—aside from having been spotted leaving town—but he was far from certain how she'd react to the next step.

Houston and Coralee assumed the waltz position, and off they went, swirling about the dance floor. He drew in a breath of her floral-scented perfume and gazed into her beautiful face. "You look lovely."

His compliment didn't even seem to register. She was still overcoming the shock. Perhaps his plan to take her by surprise wasn't a good idea, after all, but it was too late to change things now.

"I can't believe you're here. I thought you'd gone."

"I wouldn't leave without telling you."

"But you did. Meribeth saw you board the stagecoach yesterday, and I saw Fred load your trunk with my own eyes."

He led her through a crush of dancers with a series of deft moves, narrowly avoiding a collision with a rather enthusiastic ranch hand and his lady. "The trunk wasn't mine. I was only going to San Antonio to make a special purchase, so all I took was a satchel."

"I thought you'd left for California."

"So I heard."

Coralee's chocolate-brown eyes widened, and her brow furrowed. "You knew, and yet you allowed me to go on believing that you were gone?"

"I'd hoped to keep my whereabouts a secret."

"Oh, they were, all right. I thought you'd gone off and left me like you did before. But you didn't."

Was the tremble in her chin a good sign or a bad one? At least she was here—thanks to Calvin, no doubt. Her brother had promised to say whatever it took to get her to attend the post-drive dance. Unlike her, Calvin was in on Houston's plan—and heartily approved of it.

Despite a stomach so heavy it felt as though he'd swallowed an anvil, he had to enact the next phase. Things would either go well, or they wouldn't. *Please, Lord, give me the courage to make it through this.*

Houston caught the eye of his nearest brother and nodded. Crockett raised his hat over his head, a signal to the musicians to stop playing, which they did. Houston released Coralee.

She looked around, obviously searching for answers. "How odd. That's two numbers in a row they've cut short."

"There's a reason for that. You'll see."

The other couples gathered at the edges of the dance floor. Crockett and the rest of Houston's brothers—with the exception of reclusive Bowie—strode onto the planked surface and formed a ring around Houston and Coralee. They were joined by Pa, the Hart women, and Houston's nephew, Robbie.

Coralee's eyes grew wider and wider. "What's going on?"

Houston drew in a deep breath and slowly released it. Moments from now, he would either be the happiest man in all of Texas, or he would be forced to take his miserable self back to California and carry on with a large part of his heart missing.

He took Coralee's hands in his. "I know how important family is to you. I have a wonderful one, and I want them to witness this moment. Coralee Culpepper, you're the best thing that's ever happened to me. I was a fool to leave you all those years ago, but I'm back, and I'm here to stay."

"Are you sure? Because I can't leave. I made a promise."

"I am sure, and I will help you honor that promise. We'll see things through together."

She pressed her fingers to her lips. "That's about the nicest thing anyone's ever said to me. And I know you mean it. You've shown me that."

The weight in his stomach lessened a bit. "And you've shown me that I can choose to be happy. Thanks to your encouragement, you're looking at the new owner of Hartville's hardware store. It used to be called Collingswood & Henderson's, but from now on, it's going to be known as C & H Hardware." He paused as two ranch hands held up a weathered plank with a *C*, a plus sign, and an *H* inside of a heart.

Coralee laughed. "That looks just like the heart you carved on the back of my daddy's woodshed when we were courting all those years ago."

"It is. You were my best friend then, just as you are now. But I want you to be more than that."

He dropped to one knee, pulled out a velvet-lined jewelry box, and opened it, revealing a diamond ring. She clasped her hands in front of her gaping mouth. "Oh, Houston."

"I love you with a love that's bigger than Texas and California combined. I hope that's enough, because I want you to be my partner as well as my wife. I know I don't deserve you, but I hope you're willing to overlook that. Will you marry me, Coralee?"

"Yes! I most certainly will."

He took her hand and slipped the ring on her finger. Several ladies sighed, and some of the men let out with whoops and hollers, his brother Hays among them.

Houston stood, and Coralee launched herself into his arms, holding him more tightly than she ever had before. He longed to kiss her, but surely, being the Southern lady she was, she'd never allow him to do so in public.

She tilted her head to look up at him. If he wasn't mistaken, her warm brown eyes held an invitation he wasn't about to turn down.

He took her face in his hands, pressed his lips to hers, and showed her how much she meant to him. She couldn't marry him soon enough, because he wanted more of her kisses. Lots more.

All too soon, he was forced to release her. His family gathered around them, showering him with congratulations and offering Coralee their best wishes.

Pa slung an arm around each of their shoulders. "So when can we expect a wedding? I'm thinking a week from today sounds good. What do you say, Coralee? Would that give you enough time to rustle up a wedding dress?"

Houston held his breath, fearing she'd want time to plan an elaborate event.

She nodded. "A week sounds fine to me, sir. I've waited long enough for this day."

Relief whooshed the air from Houston's lungs. Coralee was as eager to marry as he was.

"Very well." Pa raised his voice and addressed the crowd. "We'll continue with the dance now, but you're all invited back for the happy couple's wedding reception this coming Saturday."

He returned his attention to them. "You told Coralee about your store, son, but does she know that you'll be a rancher too?"

"She does now." He smiled at his finacée. "Pa helped me see that I can do both. I won't be roping and riding, but I will be—"

"Keeping the books." Coralee laughed. "You'll run a fine ranch, Houston."

"That he will." Pa gave him a sound thump on the back. "He'll be a fine businessman too. And, before too long, I hope, an excellent father."

Coralee's cheeks went pink, but she looked Pa in the eye. "I'm sure he will."

Pa left them, and Houston whisked Coralee off to the far side of the barn, out of sight of the others. He slipped his arms around her waist, claimed her lips once again, and held nothing back as he kissed her. She responded with equal fervor and was breathless when they finally broke apart.

"You've made me the happiest woman in all of Texas today, Houston."

"Well, I'm the happiest man."

She held out her hand and admired the ring, the diamond catching the last rays of sunlight. "I take it this is what prompted your trip to San Antonio. It's beautiful."

"I'm glad you like it. I'm sorry about the confusion, though. I would have told you I was going, but I didn't want to spoil the surprise."

"I'm glad you didn't. Finding you here was surprise enough, but then you proposed. I've never been as shocked as I was when you dropped to your knee like that. You must have been quite sure of my answer to ask me in front of your family and a whole host of our friends."

He took her hand and squeezed it. "The truth is, I was shaking in my boots."

"Oh, my darling, you didn't need to worry. I thought I loved you when I was young, but what I feel for you now is so much richer and deeper than that. I love you wholeheartedly and without reservation."

He treasured Coralee's emphatic declaration. "And I love you to distraction, which is why I'm glad you agreed to marry me so soon."

She smiled. "Of course I did. I don't think I could wait another day for us to be man and wife."

Neither could he.

ABOUT THE AUTHOR

Award-winning novelist Keli Gwyn is a California native who lives in a Gold Rush-era town at the foot of the majestic Sierra Nevada Mountains. Her stories transport readers to the 1800s, where she brings historic towns to life, peoples them with colorful characters, and adds a hint of humor. She fuels her creativity with Taco Bell and sweet tea. When she's not writing, she enjoys spending time with her husband and two skittish kitties.

FOR LOVE OR MONEY

SUSAN PAGE DAVIS

CHAPTER 1

September 1874

Crockett Hart loped his spotted horse along the easternmost boundary of the 7 Heart Ranch, looking for wandering cattle. The Hart family's herd grazed mostly on the range that comprised the large ranch. But sometimes strays wandered onto neighbors' property, and the Hart men and their ranch hands had to bring them back. Of course, the annoying converse was that their neighbors' stock often came over to the 7 Heart for ample grazing.

Still, the family ranch had made a profit nearly every year for the last two decades. If it wasn't for his father's recent edict, Crockett would think they were doing well.

Pa wanted to see all seven of his boys married. That was all well and good for some—like Hays. Though he was the youngest at twenty-three, Hays had been first to woo and wed a bride, Emma. Then Chisholm, next up the ladder at twenty-five, had made a surprise move while most of them were off on the spring cattle drive, and found his match in the fiery Caro Cardova. Travis and Houston were not far behind, and Annie and Coralee had joined the family.

Well, Crockett just wasn't ready. Maybe he would be, if there were plenty of suitable candidates in Hartville. The truth was, his work on the

ranch kept him so busy, he seldom got off it long enough to go looking
for a bride. But September had rolled around, and if Pa had his way, his
three remaining sons would fall in line and pick themselves wives before
the end of the year.

The smell of wood smoke hit Crockett's nostrils, and he jerked his
head up and scanned the horizon. Sure enough, off to the east, a column
of gray smoke rose above the trees and rolling ground between him and
the next ranch. The Haymakers were the closest neighbors in that
direction.

He studied the smoke for a long minute. He hated to ride over there.
They were probably just burning off brush, and old Boyd Haymaker
would just as soon run off a neighbor as parley. But Crockett wouldn't
feel settled about it if he didn't check to make sure everything was all
right.

He rode through the line of cottonwood trees that served as a wind-
break as well as a boundary line and then loped to what passed for a
road to the Haymaker ranch. The stench of burning grew more noxious,
and the gelding snorted and tried to break stride, but Crockett urged him
onward.

"It's all right, boy. I won't let you get too close."

He rounded a bend and pulled back on the reins. The Haymakers'
house was engulfed in fire. Flames had torn through the wooden frame.
As he watched, the shingled roof collapsed, and a flurry of sparks and
debris flew outward.

The horse squealed, and Crockett let him turn away from the sight
but held the reins short to keep him from bolting. He let the gelding
high-step another hundred yards away and then tied him to a tree on the
7 Heart side of the road and hurried back toward the blazing house. The
acrid smell of the fire overpowered all else.

The Haymakers had lost everything in their small dwelling, for sure.
The sagging barn was still standing, but flames licked across the front
yard toward it, and flaming brands had landed near it, starting smaller
fires of their own in the dry grass. One had hit the barn roof and smoldered there. If no one did anything, it would soon blaze up.

Where was Boyd Haymaker? And what about his two children, Jane
and Ben? As he cautiously approached the hole topped by a tripod of
poles that was their well, the heat of the fire baked his face. Crockett sent

up a prayer that the family had not been caught inside the burning house.

～

*J*ane pulled her roan mare to a halt at the foot of the hill path. "Get down now, Pa. Go up to the cave and wait there."

"What are you going to do, girl? Where are you going?" Pa slid off the horse's rump as he spoke and landed with an "oompf" on the rocky ground.

"To save whatever I can."

Jane didn't wait to see if he went up to the cave. She spun the mare around and kicked her forward. The horse didn't relish running back toward the fire, but Jane pummeled its ribs with her heels and slapped its withers with the knotted ends of her reins.

The smoke billowed up in huge puffs and hung in the sky in slowly dissipating clouds. She was glad there wasn't much wind today. With luck, she might save the barn. She probably shouldn't have bothered to get Pa away from the fire. But he was useless and would only get in the way, so she had made him climb up behind her saddle and quickly taken him a quarter mile away, where he would be safe. Her brother had left at dawn to trade work with a rancher ten miles away. He probably wouldn't know about the fire until tonight.

As she forced the panicky mare closer to the inferno, she glimpsed a figure moving amid the smoky barnyard. Ben? Or maybe someone else had seen the smoke and come to help.

She leaped off the mare and didn't try to stop her from wheeling and tearing across the range as fast as she could go. That horse wouldn't go far, and Jane would find her eventually. Right now she had to save whatever she could of the homestead.

The house was beyond help, with the roof caved in and the studs and clapboard siding reduced to smoldering black sticks. She pulled her neckerchief up over her mouth and ran toward the barn, her eyes stinging.

A man barreled out the door, clutching several burlap sacks, and nearly knocked her down.

"Hey! Sorry!" He dropped the sacks and grabbed her arms to steady her. His face was grimy, but she would have known Crockett Hart anywhere.

"We can't save the house." Her voice was raspy.

"I know, but there's a firebrand on the barn roof. I was going to try to climb up and beat it out."

"Boost me," Jane croaked.

Crockett hesitated but then nodded and led her to the place where the barn roof was lowest. He hunched down. "Get on my shoulders."

She didn't spare him, but she tried not to think about the pain she caused as she climbed onto his back and then stood on his solid shoulders in her worn boots. Grasping the eaves, she pulled herself onto the roof as Crockett straightened. Pa was a lazy man, and he hadn't pitched the roof as steep as some ranchers would. They rarely got snow here, and he figured a little slope was enough to run the rain off. She rolled onto the strips of wood Pa had used instead of shingles. Crockett tossed a feed sack up beside her.

"Here. I'll wet another one and bring it to you." He ran toward the well, carrying the other sacks.

Jane turned toward the slope of the roof. Above the ridgepole, a wisp of smoke rose, darker than the hazy air around it. She crawled, slipping and gasping, to the top. There was the charred stick Crockett had mentioned, in the crease where the main roof met the lean-to that sheltered the pigsty. She sat on the ridgepole and cautiously edged her way down toward it.

When she was close, she leaned over, swinging her sack, and almost tumbled off the roof for her efforts. She caught herself and studied the situation. Maybe she could ease down a bit farther and kick the firebrand off the roof.

"Jane?"

"Yeah, Crockett."

He was below her, at the side of the lean-to. "If I toss this up, can you get it?"

"Maybe."

He stooped for a moment. "All right, look out. I wrapped a rock in it to make it heavier. Here goes."

As the wet sack thudded beside her, the firebrand caught, and flames leaped up from the strips of wood on the roof below her.

"I got it," she said, "but let the pigs out. We may lose the lean-to roof."

She grabbed the sack, shook the rock out, and let it roll down the incline to land on the far side of the lean-to. Then she lay on her belly and inched down the steeper main roof toward the blaze. She let the rough shingles catch on her wool pants to slow her down. Within seconds, she was slapping at the fire.

"Hey." Crockett's soot-streak face appeared at the lowest edge of the roof. "You got it?"

"Not sure."

He heaved himself up onto the lean-to, and Jane felt it shudder. Would the feeble structure her father had built support both of them?

Crockett didn't stop to fret. He wriggled forward and vigorously pummeled the flames and then the smoldering wood. Jane joined him from the uphill side, and they developed a rhythm. *Slap, thwack, slap, thwack.* Droplets of water flew off Crockett's sack and sprinkled her face. They felt good.

Finally, he stopped attacking the roof. "I think it's out." He sat back and looked toward the ruined house. "There's not much left of your house."

"I could see that from the start." Jane pushed her singed hair back from her face. "I just figured if I could save the barn, we could make it."

"Looks like you did."

"*We* did," she said. "Thank you."

He nodded. "I doubt it will spread from the house now, but we'd better beat around the grass for a while to make sure."

"How'd you get up here?"

"Climbed up the pig fence and did some acrobatics."

She laughed but stopped quickly when pain scraped her raw throat.

"So what happened?" Crockett asked.

She coughed. "Beats me. Ben left early, and I rode out to look for a heifer that didn't come in last night. About an hour later, I'm coming back, and I see smoke. Big smoke."

He nodded.

"I galloped in and grabbed Pa. He was just standing in the dooryard, gawking at the house, and it was all aflame."

"Where is he now?"

Jane looked over her shoulder. "There's a cave up on the hillside. I dropped him at the foot of the path and came back to do what I could."

"Come on." Without further warning, Crockett jumped off the lean-to roof. "Slide down to the edge and jump," he called. "I'll catch you."

She could just picture that—her landing in the arms of the Hart boy she'd had a crush on for years. Except he wasn't a boy anymore. "Can't I climb down the pig fence?"

"I sort of wrecked it when I thrashed around, getting up here. Just jump, Janie."

He used to call her that when she was a kid. She hadn't heard it in years from anyone but Ben. She slid down, pulling her damp, smelly feed sack with her, and let her feet dangle over the eaves.

Crockett, with a wide grin on his filthy face, stood directly below. "Fly, little bird."

Jane pushed off and flew. Crockett caught her, but her momentum swept him off his feet, and they landed breathless in the dead weeds. He held her close to his chest for a moment.

"You all right?"

"Yeah." Jane pushed away from him and clambered to her feet, though she hated to. His arms felt good around her. How long since anyone had hugged her, even for practical reasons like this? Her brother Ben was the last, she guessed, and he wasn't much of a hugger anymore. Pa hadn't touched her for years, except when he was drunk and she didn't get out of his way fast enough.

Crockett rolled over and scrambled up. He snatched his sack from the ground and headed for the well with long strides. Jane hurried to keep up. Flames licked at the scraggly grass between them and the well, and they had to beat them down before they could get to the brink.

"Wet the sacks again." Crockett turned his attention to more flames that had strayed through the dry grass and began stomping them.

Jane quickly hauled up a bucket of water and soaked a sack. She carried it, dripping, to Crockett.

"I dropped some more sacks over in front of the barn," he said.

An hour later, Jane collapsed against the barn door. The flames were out, except for a few stubborn flare-ups in the remains of the house.

"Let me get you some water." Crockett's eyes were bloodshot above his bandanna, and his voice was raspy. He plodded to the well and hauled up another bucket of water.

For the first time all afternoon, Jane felt shame. Why couldn't Pa have built a stone berm around the well, or at least a well house over it? She'd seen the Harts' yard before. Their well had a round masonry wall wide enough that you could sit on it, and a little roof above. The rope coiled up neatly on a windlass. The Haymakers' well was a disgrace, as was everything her father had made.

Crockett pulled the bucket awkwardly out of the hole in the ground by the rope attached to the bail and poured some water over his bandanna. He wiped his face with it, smearing the soot and grime worse than before, then untied the bucket and carried it over to her. "Sorry, no cups."

"It's all right." She scooped water with her hands and brought it to her mouth. It bathed her fiery throat. "Thanks."

He nodded. "You'd best come stay at our place tonight."

"No, I can't."

"Jane." He fixed her with a stern look that said *be reasonable* and put his hands on his hips. "You have no house. Where will you sleep?"

"In the barn, I guess, or the cave."

"We've got room for you at the ranch. All of you."

She shook her head. "It's not that I don't appreciate the offer, but I should be here when Ben comes home. And Pa—" No, taking Pa to the Harts' homey, comfortable ranch house would not be a good idea. Jane was sure Crockett's father had nothing but disdain for hers.

Most people who knew Boyd Haymaker pegged him as shiftless and lazy. And they were right. Since Ma died, he'd gotten worse. Jane and Ben kept the place going, if the truth were told. Without their hard work, Pa would have starved to death—or wandered off to find an easier way to get his hands on some money. She was doing Texas a favor by keeping her pa on the ranch.

She hiked her chin up and met Crockett's gaze. "We'll be all right."

His eyes held hers for a long moment. "All right, then I'll head on home. But I'll be back later with some vittles and stuff. I warn you, your neighbors will want to help."

"I told you, we'll be fine," Jane said.

"Don't be stubborn. If nothing else, you'll need help rounding up those pigs. Now, I'll let you alone for a few hours, but I'm not going to let you starve. As my Ma would have said, don't deny your friends the blessing of helping you out."

She couldn't argue with that. Wouldn't it be sacrilegious or something? Besides, Crockett's ma was the sweetest, smartest woman she'd ever known.

He walked down the trail and unhitched his flashy paint horse from a tree. After swinging up into the saddle, he looked her way, raised his hat, and waved. Jane waved back, and he turned the horse and cantered away. She let out her pent-up breath and turned around. The black heap where the house had stood was still putting off wisps of smoke, reminder of loss.

CHAPTER 2

The sun was heading downward when Crockett drove the ranch wagon into the Haymakers' yard with two of his sisters-in-law on the seat with him. Another wagon sat before the barn. Jane, her brother, Ben, and two other men were poking about the rubble from the fire. Crockett recognized both men—the owner of the ranch beyond the Haymakers' and one of his hired men.

"How terrible," Emma murmured beside him.

"Yeah, they don't have much left."

Jane looked up and walked slowly toward them. "Hey."

"How are you doing?" Crockett asked.

She shrugged. "Ben came home a little while ago. He was pretty upset when he saw the mess. But Mr. Allen and Jerry were here, and they calmed him down some."

"Where's your pa?"

"Yonder by the corral fence."

Boyd sat on the ground, leaning back against the gate. His right arm was hitched up in a gray cloth—an attempt at a sling, apparently. "Is he hurt?"

"Some minor burns on his hands, and he says he hurt his arm bad."

Probably so bad he couldn't help with the work, but Crockett didn't say so.

"I don't know if you've met these ladies." He looked at his brothers' wives. "This is Emma, who's married to Hays now, and Annie, Travis's wife. Girls, this is Jane Haymaker."

"I remember Jane from school," Annie said.

Jane nodded. "Nice to see you."

"Hi, Jane." Emma offered a sweet smile. "I think I've seen you at the church once or twice. My father is the pastor."

Jane's face flushed. "We haven't gotten to services much lately."

Annie smiled ruefully. "I'm awfully sorry about the fire. We've brought you a few things."

"That's nice of you." Jane glanced toward the wagon bed, where they had packed blankets, food, and a few other items Crockett thought might be needed.

Crockett climbed down and helped Emma and Annie. Emma was in a delicate condition, but of course, nobody would talk about that. Still, he was extra careful making sure she reached the ground without mishap.

"Crockett said you wouldn't come stay at the house," Emma ventured. "Are you sure—"

"We'll be fine," Jane said. "But we appreciate what you've done."

Crockett reached for a bundle of blankets. "We'll do more than this. I'll speak to Mr. Allen, since he's here. I reckon we can get a bunch of neighbors to come help you rebuild."

"Oh, well ..." Jane looked around with huge eyes. "We won't be ready for a while."

"It will take you a while to get organized," Annie agreed.

Emma picked up a bundle from the back of the wagon. "We put in a few clothes, along with blankets and some food. I think the skirt Annie brought might fit you, and I put in a shawl and some other things." She cast a quick glance at Crockett, and his face heated.

"I'll see if Ben can give me a hand unloading." He hurried to the site of the house.

Ben turned to meet him. Ash covered his clothes and hands, and hair stuck to his sweaty face. "Crockett. Jane told me you helped her this morning. Thank you kindly."

"Glad I was able." Crockett shook his head. "I wish I could have done more, Ben."

"Well, that's just ... how it is. We ought to have known better than to leave Pa alone in the house for an hour with the stove going."

"Did he say how it got started?" Crockett shot a glance across the yard, but Boyd was still sitting against the fencepost, and his eyes had slid shut.

Ben sighed heavily. "Just that when he went to stir up the fire, it got away from him. Stuff happens to Pa." He looked bleakly at Crockett.

"Yeah. You get those pigs back yet?"

Ben shook his head. "I caught Jane's horse a little while ago. I turned her out after I took the saddle and bridle off. If we put her in the barn, she'll just breathe smoke and ash all night. I hate to even keep her cooped up in the corral."

"She might be better off out away from the house," Crockett agreed. "What about you folks? The invite to stay at our place still stands."

"We'll stay here, thank you."

"You'll breathe smoke and ash too."

Ben looked over his shoulder. "Jane thinks we ought to bed down up at the cave tonight. The air's a lot better up there. She took some sacks and blankets from the barn up to sleep on."

"We brought you some bedding." Crockett gestured behind him. "Maybe I can drive the wagon closer, and the girls and I can unload that stuff for you?"

"Sure. Or Jane could take it, if you want to look for the pigs."

"Be glad to."

Ben nodded. "Thanks. Them and two horses and a couple dozen steers is about all we've got."

"I'll keep my eyes out while I'm looking for the pigs and let you know how the cattle are faring."

"'Preciate it. The girls can drive your wagon close to the foot of the trail to the cave. And you can take Jane's horse to look for the pigs." Ben turned back to the ruins and poked a mass of charcoal with his hoe.

Crockett went to the corral and saddled Jane's thin chestnut. Jerry, the cowboy from Allen's place, joined him. It took them most of an hour to locate the pigs and figure out how to run them back to the homestead. Once there, Jerry guarded the gaps in the broken fence while Crockett mended it so they wouldn't get loose again. Of course, that was iffy with pigs. They were great at digging under fences, but he did his best.

When they were done, he walked over to where Ben and Mr. Allen had lined up the few things they'd salvaged from the ashes of the house.

"Find anything usable?" he asked.

"A few things. Pieces of hardware mostly. I was saving nails, but Mr. Allen says they won't be good to use again." Ben kicked at a charred tin.

"Did the girls come back yet?"

"Nope."

"Maybe one of us ought to ride out there and see if they need help."

Mr. Allen had gone over to the well and had Jerry pour water over his filthy hands. He soaked his bandanna and mopped his face with it. "Ben, you reckon you'll be all right tonight?"

"Yes, sir. We appreciate you coming over to help, you and Jerry." Ben nodded to the cowboy.

"I know you'd do the same if it was us." Mr. Allen straightened and put his hands to his lower back. "Bad business. You let us know when you need a hand putting up a new house. It won't take long to throw up a cabin the size of what you had."

"Thanks."

Ben said no more but watched them go to Mr. Allen's wagon and pull out.

"Come on," Ben said to Crockett. He walked to the corral and put a bridle on his dark bay gelding and swung aboard with no saddle.

"Pa, we're going to bring Janie and the Hart ladies in."

Crockett had forgotten all about the old man. He had mounted Jane's horse again, and he swiveled around to look for Boyd. He sat in the same place he had nearly two hours ago, and he lifted a languid hand in response to Ben's comment.

"Is he all right?" Crockett asked Ben in a low voice.

"He'll be fine." Ben took off at a trot, and Crockett followed him out the trail toward the hills. The sun was low, casting long shadows. Ben turned to look at him, and he brought his horse up alongside the bay.

"Pa wanted to stay up at the cave, but I wouldn't let him. I said even if he couldn't help, he could come down and watch other people pick over the mess he made."

"It was an accident," Crockett said.

Ben shook his head, frowning. "Accident. My pa breeds 'em."

They rode less than a mile to where Jane had parked his wagon, at the bottom of a path winding up the hillside. Jane, Emma, and Annie were sitting in the grass nearby.

"Well, hi, gentlemen," Emma called.

"Howdy." Ben eyed the empty wagon bed. "Guess you got it all unloaded."

"That was hard work, lugging all that stuff up the hill," Crockett said.

"It was," Annie admitted, "but we did it. And now we're taking a little breather before we head back."

Hopefully, they hadn't let Emma make the trip too many times. Her baby wasn't due for four or five months, but still …

Emma stood and brushed off her skirt. "We should have taken you up on your offer, Crockett. I had no idea how far we'd have to carry that stuff."

"Anything left to tote?" Crockett looked around.

"Nope," Annie said.

Jane stood. "Did you find the pigs?"

Crockett smiled. "We did. It took Jerry and me a while to figure out how to herd 'em, though. They're snug in the pen now."

"He fixed the fence," Ben added.

"Thank you."

Crockett nodded. "You all sure you want to stay out here?"

"The barn isn't fit to sleep in." Ben flattened his mouth.

He was right. The so-called barn was a sorry sight. It was more of a large, rickety shed than a barn. When Crockett had run inside to find something to fight the fire with, he'd found the dirt floor knee-deep in manure and old straw. One corner had been cleared and held a couple of barrels and a few worn tools. Any animal forced to sleep in there would be miserable.

"Yeah, the air's lots better out here," he said.

He let Jane take her saddle horse and drove the wagon back to the barnyard with Emma and Annie. The two young women didn't say much on the way back. No doubt, they were tired and didn't want to voice their reservations in Jane's hearing. But he'd probably get an earful about the cave on the way back to the 7 Heart.

When they returned to the site of the fire, Crockett climbed down and took Jane's horse from her. He led it toward the corral, and to his surprise, Jane followed him.

"I wondered if I could get a little advice from you."

He stopped walking and looked down into her solemn green eyes. "Don't know if I'm the best one to give advice, but I'll listen."

She looked over her shoulder. Annie and Emma had stayed in the wagon, and Ben was already letting his horse into the corral. "I found something in the cave."

Crockett studied her drawn face. This had to be serious. His first thought was a dead body, but Emma or Annie surely would have mentioned that.

"I didn't tell the others."

"All right. What was it?"

"Money."

Crockett blinked. He hadn't expected that.

"A lot of money," Jane added. "It was way in the back, in a little niche in the wall. I thought maybe the spot was big enough for me to spread my bedroll in, and I'd have some privacy from Pa and Ben."

"Makes sense."

"There was a pile of rocks and sticks. I had a torch, and I started cleaning them out."

"Carefully, I hope."

She nodded. "Didn't want to come eye to eye with a snake. But I found an old tin box underneath. I opened it, and there was money inside. Annie and Emma were out in the big part of the cave, arranging the foodstuffs, and I decided not to tell them." She reached into the pocket of her cotton shirt and brought out a bill, folded up small in eighths, and handed it to Crockett. "There's a bunch of these."

He turned so no one else would see what he was doing and unfolded it carefully. The twenty-dollar bill looked funny. "'First Bank of Louisiana,'" he read off the top. "This isn't federal money. It's an old Louisiana bank bill."

"Do you think it's worth anything?"

"I dunno." He frowned at it. "Any idea how it got there?"

She shook her head. "I don't want to say anything in front of Pa. Or Ben, either, until I know more. Listen, your brother Chisholm's a Texas Ranger. Could you ask him about it?"

"I guess I could. He might have some ideas."

She touched his hand. "You take it, then. I'll keep the rest hidden, and if you find out anything, you can let me know." Her wistful smile reminded him that he liked Jane. A lot.

"All right." Ben was approaching, so Crockett tucked the bill into his pocket.

Jane's brother tipped his head as he assessed them. "Anything wrong?"

"No, I was just talking to Jane about what you folks will be needing." Which was true, in a way. Right now, Jane needed advice.

"Thanks a lot for what you've done," Ben said.

"Think nothing of it. And I'll talk to some other people about doing a house raising for you. See if you can start getting things together." He nodded at Jane and walked to the wagon. As he drove the team out of the yard, he resolved to do everything he could to make sure Jane came out of this all right.

CHAPTER 3

Over the next few days, several neighbors came by. The men helped Ben and Jane slowly clear away the debris from the house. The women brought food and offered Jane clothing. The Hart wives even brought Jane an extra pair of trousers that fit her. They took away the Haymakers' sooty shirts and pants to wash and offered repeatedly to let them stay at their ranch. Jane and Ben always refused.

In private, Ben told her, "I wouldn't mind going over there once. Couldn't we go for dinner one night? I'd like to see all the books they have."

"Crockett brought you three to borrow. How many do you need?" Jane wouldn't look at him as she worked on their supper. She placed beans, chunks of beef, and several root vegetables the neighbors had brought into the kettle Mrs. Allen had insisted on giving her.

Ben watched and sighed. "I don't know. Hays said they have dozens of books. Like a library, only in their house. I'd just like to see 'em, is all."

Did the Bible say anything about coveting your neighbor's books? She couldn't find out now because Ma's old Bible had burnt up. She couldn't be cross at Ben, though. He had worked like an ox, cleaning up their place and chopping wood and hauling logs. He had planned to work for other ranchers all week, building up credit so they'd help him later on. Instead, he was slaving away at home, trying to retrieve what he

344

could from the fire and preparing to build a new house, something he knew nothing about.

"I wish we had a proper bed for you," she said. "It's awful hard to sleep good in the cave."

Ben shrugged. "It's what we've got. At least it's warm. If this had happened in winter, then we'd really have it bad."

"I wish Pa would help the others when they come." Jane scooped a dipper full of water out of the bucket on the ground beside her open fire.

"You wish a lot of things," Ben said. "And that's one that won't happen."

"He's not hurt that bad. And his burns are healing." Jane sent her brother a challenging glance and stirred the stew.

Travis Hart, the brother who was a doctor, had ridden out the morning after the fire looked over Pa's wounds. He had put a dressing on Pa's left hand and asked him a lot of questions about his eating habits and his breathing and if his chest ever hurt. Then he'd told Jane he guessed her pa was in as good shape as could be expected. Whatever he meant by that. Maybe that Pa was a drinking man, and drinking men were sick a lot.

She glanced sharply at Ben. "Has Pa asked for any liquor?"

"He asked the doc if he had any whiskey along, and the doc said no. He's probably asked some of the ranchmen, too, but so far as I know, none of them has brought him any."

"I hope they won't." Jane's face heated, whether from the cook fire or her thoughts. It would be too embarrassing to tell the neighbors outright not to give her pa any strong drink. She'd found a couple of jugs and a whiskey bottle in the cave when they first decided to sleep up there. Mercifully, they were all empty, and she'd been able to get rid of them before the Hart gals came to visit and help her arrange things in the cave.

She'd left the money she found where it was hidden. If Pa knew it was there, he wouldn't miss the one bill she had given to Crockett. That seemed the most likely explanation to her—after all, Pa had used that cave to stash his jugs. Crockett had told her today when he'd come by to help Ben haul logs to the sawmill that his brother Chisholm was away. He was the one who was a Ranger. That was all right. She could wait.

"That stew gonna be ready soon?" Ben asked.

"It needs to simmer another hour or so."

Ben nodded. "Guess I'll pack another load of burned wood."

They had decided to build the new house in a fresh spot, but even so, they needed to remove the debris or the smell and soot would continue to plague them. They might also still find a few usable things if they went through all the trash carefully. They had precious little money to spend on anything new. The future looked bleak, indeed.

~

*H*ays and Emma, along with Houston and Coralee, who had their own homes now, came to supper at El Regalo, the Hart family home.

Emma turned to her husband. "So you went to school with Jane Haymaker?"

"Yeah," Hays said. "She's really smart."

"Ben's smart too." Crockett spoke up. "He would have done well in college, but Boyd's got no money to send him to school."

"That's a shame." Emma pursed her lips.

Travis hadn't come home from town yet. Likely, he was making rounds of his patients.

Caro, Chisholm's wife, looked up from her meal. "Does Jane still need clothes?"

"I don't think she's got one dress." Emma shook her head. "Annie took her a skirt, but it's pretty short. I doubt mine would fit her..."

Caro looked toward her father-in-law, GW, who sat at the head of the long table. "Papa Hart, do you think we might give her some of Mrs. Hart's things? Your wife's, I mean. You still have a lot of her clothing in a trunk, I'm told."

Pa shot her a sharp glance. "I don't think that would be a good idea, Caro."

When hurt flashed on Caro's face, Crockett felt bad for her. Chisholm should be home soon, but without his solid presence, Caro might be feeling a little out of place. Her Mexican heritage set her apart from the rest of them, and her beauty and fiery personality intimidated some of her sisters-in-law. But she was a Hart now, and Crockett felt protective of her. His father had a way of making a person feel small.

"Pa, it might not be such a bad thing," he said. "Ma's been gone a long time, and that stuff is going to waste. Jane could make over a few things. Really, Pa, they have nothing."

His father hadn't been over to the Haymakers' place yet. He didn't begrudge the young people going so long as it didn't interfere with the boys' work on the ranch, but so far, he hadn't offered his own labor.

"I said no."

Crockett sighed and went back to his roast beef. Some of the girls had helped prepare it. They often helped the cook out, which was probably a good thing now that they had so many people to feed. The new potatoes and fresh chard went down especially well.

He didn't care to argue with his father, but this time, Pa was just being stubborn. Ma's things ought to go to good use, to help someone less fortunate.

He liked Jane. Always had. She had been in school with Hays until fifth grade, when Jane's mother died. Crockett felt a special empathy for her because he had lost his own mother at about the same age. He had wondered how she was doing after she left school but saw her only occasionally at church, in town, or on the range helping her father. She had grown into an attractive, hardworking young woman. He had even entertained thoughts of courting her, but her father was a huge drawback.

Boyd was well known in the community...and heartily disliked. Pa wouldn't like it a bit if one of his sons courted Boyd's daughter. That fact alone had made him dismiss the notion any time it entered his mind.

Still, Jane must trust him. She had told him about the money when she hadn't even told Ben. She must think Crockett had some good judgment. However, she had asked for Chisholm's help through him, not his own, so maybe she didn't so much respect him as see him as a way to get the help she needed.

Crockett scowled. The more he thought about it, the surer he was that he was just handy for her, not special. As usual, he was not the one who was noticed in this crowd.

After supper, he pushed back his chair. "Whoever made that pie, it was mighty good."

"Why, thank you!" Annie grinned at him. "I put by an extra one for the house raising on Saturday."

"We gonna have dancing that night?" Hays asked.

"Prob'ly so." Crockett slid his chair back.

"I'd better practice up a little on my fiddle." Hays smiled at Emma. "The only bad thing about it is, I can't dance with my wife while I'm playing."

Emma sighed. "I guess I'll have to settle for your brothers and the cowpunchers for partners."

Crockett laughed. "Don't worry, Emma. I'll make sure he gets a rest from playing for at least a couple of numbers. And chances are, one or two other fellas will bring their instruments."

"I'll take my banjo," Houston said as he folded his napkin.

Coralee smiled. "It'll be nice."

Emma laid down her fork and stood. "I wish I could give Jane a pair of my shoes, but we're not the same size. All she has is her working boots." She shook her head and went into the kitchen.

Crockett strolled out onto the front porch. He'd had it easy, really, despite the rigors of ranch life. He and his six brothers had never had to wonder where their next pair of shoes or their next meal would come from.

His father came out, stretching. "Where you headed?"

"Just thought I'd take a look at my paint horse. I rode him pretty hard today."

"You and the boys get those yearlings up to the north range?"

"We did." Crockett hesitated. "Pa, we could donate some lumber for the Haymakers' house. Make it easier for them."

His father grunted and leaned against one of the pillars that held up the porch roof. "I don't have a mind to do anything extra for Boyd Haymaker. The way I hear it, he's the one that burnt the house down. And we all know he's shiftless. Doesn't do any good to give a man like that a boost. He'll just waste it."

Crockett sighed and looked off toward the hills, where the sun was setting. "I know Boyd's lazy, Pa, and he doesn't take care of his place like he should. But think of Jane and Ben. They're good people. It's not their fault their pa won't carry his end of the load."

His father was silent for a long moment, then he scratched his chin through his short beard. "You're probably right. Those kids are smart. I always felt bad for 'em after their ma died. She was the only good influence they had."

"But they've got good neighbors. If we help them now, Jane and Ben won't forget it." His father stirred, and Crockett said quickly, "I'm not saying we should build them a complete new house. Just help out with a load of lumber and some elbow grease. Pa, those two could use a hand about now. Ten years from now, they might be leaders in the community."

"That's a stretch. But all right, I'll pitch in. Take 'em a load of boards if you want. Tell John at the sawmill to put it on my account."

"Thanks, Pa."

His father inhaled deeply. "And tell the girls they can look in Victoria's trunk for some things for the girl. I can't feature a woman running a ranch, but I guess she's doing a man's work."

"She works harder than I do."

"That's not sayin' much." His father laughed and slapped him on the shoulder. "Joshin', son. You don't think the brides will want that stuff of your mother's?"

"They all seemed willing to give something to Jane."

"Well, I guess that gal needs a dress if there's gonna be dancing Saturday."

Crockett grinned. "That's nice, Pa. I'll throw in a nice shirt for Ben."

"He might not want to wear your duds. Some of 'em are downright garish."

"I'll pick out one of the tamer ones. You going?"

"Oh, I suppose I'll go pound a few nails. I don't know as I'll dance. I'm slowing down these days."

Satisfied, Crockett nodded and ambled toward the corral.

≈

*J*ane did her best to keep up with Ben in peeling the logs, but her brother was faster.

"Are you sure it'll be all right to use green wood?" She glanced toward their father, who was sitting in the shade of the barn.

"It's better'n nothing, ain't it?" Pa said.

"Won't it shrink and crack when it dries?" Ben studied the wood in question.

"Might split some," Pa conceded. "Still better'n sleepin' in a cave, eh?"

"I suppose." Ben stood and squinted toward the road. "Looks like Crockett Hart comin'."

Jane also rose and put her hand to the small of her back. She'd be sore tomorrow from all this bending over. "It's him," she said.

Crockett always wore a bright-colored shirt and, often as not, a neckerchief of a different color. Who knew why he wore such flamboyant clothes? Perhaps he wanted to be noticed. She had no explanation for why he'd been over to their ranch nearly every day this week.

"Hey, Crockett," Ben called with a wave.

Crockett trotted his pinto gelding up to where there were working and jumped down. "Hi, Ben. Jane." He turned around and nodded at Pa. "Mr. Haymaker."

"Afternoon, Davy Crockett Hart." Pa tipped his head. "What brings you out here today?"

"Just wanted to tell you to expect a big turnout tomorrow and a load of lumber."

"Lumber?" Jane's eyebrows rose.

Crockett grinned and nodded. "My pa told me to order it from the sawmill. I'll be here bright and early with a wagonload."

"No need for handouts." Despite his grim pronouncement, Pa didn't stir from his spot in the shade.

Jane didn't usually agree with him, but this was an unusual situation. "You're doing too much," she told Crockett.

Ben put his hand on her shoulder. "Thank you, Crockett." He gave her a sidelong glance. "That's what Ma taught us to say, Janie. If someone does something nice for you, don't make a fuss. Just say 'thank you' and let them do it."

Crockett grinned. "You're welcome."

Jane shook her head, not quite able to believe all this goodwill from neighbors who rarely came by the place before this week. "I admit, I wondered how much we could do with the logs we've hauled. It isn't enough for a cabin."

Crockett pursed his lips and surveyed the logs they had peeled and the pile waiting for attention.

"You've done a lot, but you're right. Maybe we can use the logs for one end of the house and frame up the other. And the finished lumber will make it nice inside."

"How much do you think we'll get done tomorrow?" Ben asked.

Crockett shrugged. "If there are plenty of men, we can probably frame it up and get the walls covered. Might not get to the roof or set the windows in."

"Windows?" Jane blinked. "We can't afford windows, Crockett."

"Then hang a blanket over the holes until you can. But if we don't frame them in, you'll never put them in later."

"You're probably right." Although Pa would never go to the bother of it.

Ben took off his hat and wiped his brow. He walked toward the well. "You all want a drink?"

"Bring me one." When her brother was out of earshot, Jane leaned toward Crockett. "We do appreciate all this. I don't expect we'll ever be able to repay everyone, though."

"Nobody wants you to." Crockett turned and leaned against the stack of logs. "Look, I remember a little bit of what this place looked like before your mama died."

Jane's posture stiffened. "Ben and I do our best."

"I know you do. But you got to admit, it was homier then. Prettier. Of course, a burnt-out house is never pretty, but I think you know what I mean. It was that way at our place, too, when my mama died."

"Yeah?" She furrowed her brow.

"Oh, yeah. Just because we've got more ranch hands than you and a cook to keep the meals coming doesn't mean we didn't miss the feminine touch. It's hard growing up without a mother, Jane. I understand that."

She thought about his words for a moment. "Your pa didn't take it the way mine did."

"Maybe. He was plenty disturbed, but I guess you're right. He's got a different temperament than your pa."

Ben came over with a tin cup full of water and held it out to her. Jane took it and tipped it up, grateful for the liquid washing her raw throat, even if it wasn't very cold.

"You want some, Crockett?" Ben asked.

"No, thanks. I just came to drop off a few more things."

Jane started to protest, but Crockett raised both hands, palm out, to stop her. "Now, don't go gettin' all het up about charity and such. My brothers want to bring their instruments tomorrow, and we thought we'd have a little dancin' after, if you folks don't mind."

Startled, Jane looked at Ben. How long had it been since they'd attended any event that included dancing? She was pretty sure there had never been a dance at their ranch, at least not since she could remember. "What do you think, Ben?"

"I think that'd be real nice," Ben replied. "Maybe we should ask Pa."

Jane pulled in a deep breath. "No, I think we'll just tell him—after Crockett leaves. Less chance of him saying no that way."

"Whatever you think." Ben looked down at his filthy clothes. "'We'll have to wash every stitch we own."

"Well, that's part of why I'm here." Crockett shifted his weight. "The family wanted you to have something for the dancing. And my pa sent a pair of my mother's shoes for you, Jane, so you wouldn't have to wear your boots. And one of Ma's dresses. Annie said to tell you that if you need help altering it, she and Coralee could come over later."

Jane caught her breath. "That's ..." Her eyes filled with tears. "I'm sure it will be just fine, Crockett."

He shrugged. "Maybe a little out of style. My mama's been gone a long time."

"All of our ma's things burnt in the fire," Ben said.

"I figured." Crockett managed a smile. "Brought you something, too, Ben. A clean shirt and pants. And Austin threw in a shirt for your pa."

"You didn't have to." Jane had seen how even the nicest of the neighbors made it clear they were bringing food and household goods and spending a few hours working for her and Ben's sake, not for her father.

"I know," Crockett said, "but folks want to. It's the same when someone's sick, or when there's a funeral."

Jane frowned. She hadn't seen much of the neighborliness he was talking about.

He untied a bundle from behind his saddle and passed it to her. She couldn't resist opening the sack—a nice, well-washed flour sack she could use to make towels from—and peeking inside. Folds of blue cotton and some kind of shiny green material lay within.

"I'm sure this is more than you oughta do," she said. "But thank you. And tell the ladies they don't need to stir themselves. If the dress doesn't fit, I can fix it."

Crockett smiled—a nice, warm smile. "I'll do that. But they're all coming tomorrow. Except maybe Emma. If she feels poorly, she'll stay home."

"She ought to. I felt bad that she rode all the way over here the other day in the wagon. Tell her and the others we..." Jane glanced at Ben. "Well, we appreciate it."

"Yeah." Ben nodded.

"I will. Oh, Jane, there's one more thing." Crockett walked around his horse and worked opened the other saddlebag. He came back with a book in his hands. "If you've a mind to, I'd like to lend you this. It was my mama's small Bible. Pa has a big one that he takes to church, but Ma liked this one because it was smaller and easy to carry around. And it was hers."

Jane took the volume. The leather cover was worn on the corners, and the edges of the pages showed water stains. She had never seen a Bible so small.

"It's a little bunged up," Crockett said apologetically. "I take it with me sometimes when I'm going on roundup or up in the hills. Any time a new book came into the house, my ma would read it. She read lots of things out loud to us boys when we were young. But the Bible was always her favorite."

Jane nodded. "I recall she had a beautiful voice. I used to listen to her in church, when we'd sing the hymns."

"I haven't seen you at church lately."

She swallowed hard.

"We're usually too busy," Ben said. "This ranch is tough—it gets away from you."

"I know what you mean," Crockett said.

"Janie," Pa yelled from his nest near the barn.

"Yeah, Pa?" she called back.

"What you jawin' about? Get something on for dinner. I'm right hungry."

"Sure thing." She threw Crockett a rueful look. "Thanks. I guess we'll see you tomorrow."

As he bid her goodbye, she allowed the smallest stirring of anticipation.

CHAPTER 4

Crockett let his paint out into the pasture when he got home, and he took a second look at the horses inside the fence. Chisholm's favorite red roan was grazing along with half a dozen others. His brother was home from his Ranger duties. Quickly, Crockett stowed his gear and strode to the house. Chisholm and his wife, Caro, were drinking coffee at the table with Pa and Hays.

"Hey!" Chisholm stood, stretching out his full six-foot-three height, tall like all of the brothers and their father.

Crockett slapped him on the shoulder. "Welcome home! Everything go all right?"

"Sort of. We got things settled down, finally. These range fights are never good."

Crockett nodded. "At least you're in one piece."

"Amen," Caro said softly.

Perla came through from the kitchen with a coffeepot in one hand and a basket of molasses cookies in the other. "Thought I heard a new arrival. Coffee, Crockett?"

"Thanks, I'd love some." He sat down next to Chisholm.

"Well, we'd better get moving, Pa." Hays pushed his chair back.

"All right, all right." Their father clambered to his feet. "Let me get my hat."

When he and Hays were out the door, Chisholm frowned at Crockett, his gray eyes troubled. "Pa looks awful."

"I know. I don't think he feels good lately."

"He won't admit it, but I am sure you are right." Caro set down her cup and smiled. "I am going to help Emma with some sewing, so I will leave you two alone."

Chisholm laughed. "That's hard to do in this house." He slapped her backside playfully, and Caro's eyes sparked.

She leaned over and kissed him. "You behave."

He laughed again as she sashayed out of the room.

"Got yourself a wild mustang there." Crockett reached for a cookie.

"Don't I know it? So..." Chisholm eyed him with speculation. "I heard about the fire. Hays says you're spending a lot of time over at the Haymakers'."

"They need a hand." Crockett took a bite of the cookie and chewed the sweet, spicy confection.

"You going to join us in marital bliss anytime soon?"

Carefully, Crockett picked up his mug and sipped the hot coffee, then set it down. "What makes you say that?"

"You like Jane, don't you?"

"She's nice."

"Yeah, but ..."

"What?"

Chisholm smiled tightly and picked up his mug. "Nothing. Just... her pa."

"Oh, yeah, Boyd's something to consider."

"I mean, having him for a father-in-law..."

"You're gettin' a bit hasty," Crockett said and took another bite of cookie.

"Well, the year's waning."

Crockett eyed him keenly. "Why do you think Pa told us all to get married? Don't you think that's odd?"

"Sure, but it's not the first odd thing Pa's done. Bringing breeding stock over from Spain—everyone for miles around thought that was odd, when we've got so many cattle here to choose from. Pa spent a fortune on that. But it paid off."

"So what's the payoff for us boys getting married all of a sudden?"

"For Pa? Don't know." Chisholm ran a hand over several days' growth of beard. "I know I need to shave, though."

"Can you come to my room for a minute?" Crockett asked. "There's something I want to ask you about."

"Sure."

Crockett drained his coffee mug and stood. He and Chisholm headed upstairs, passing Annie on the way.

"Glad you're back, Chisholm," she called over her shoulder with a smile.

"Thanks, sis."

In his room, Crockett opened his bottom dresser drawer and took out an old biscuit tin. He opened it and rummaged among the fishing sinkers, odd coins, brass shell casings, and horseshoe nails to pull out the banknote Jane had entrusted to him. "Here we go. What do you think of this?"

Chisholm frowned and took the bill so he could study it closely. "Where on earth did you get this?"

Crockett hesitated only a moment. "You can't tell anyone, all right?"

Chisholm nodded.

"Jane gave it to me. She found it in a cave on their place, along with a whole lot more."

"How much more?"

"A total of five hundred dollars."

Chisholm whistled softly. "That'd make a big difference to the Haymakers about now."

"I know. But they can't spend it, can they?"

"Doubt it. Not in Texas, anyway. I don't know if it's still legal tender or not. Before the war, it would have been, but ..." He shook his head, looking at the creased twenty-dollar bill. "Did she say how it got there?"

"She didn't know, but she was careful not to tell her pa. I don't even think she told Ben. Just asked me to try to find out anything I could."

Chisholm's eyes took on a faraway look. "Well, the last I heard about any quantity of Louisiana Bank bills was when the chief Ranger told me about the robbery at the State Treasury in '65."

"I remember that." Crockett nodded.

"A lot of the stolen money was never recovered. Seventeen thousand was in coin, but there was also eight hundred in Louisiana banknotes."

"You don't say. And they never caught the robbers?"

Chisholm shook his head. "They shot one man that night, at the treasury building. The rest got away. But the Rangers were disbanded during the war, and the locals weren't up to tracking them down."

"What should I tell Jane? I mean, if Boyd knew about the money in the cave, this could implicate him in the robbery. And I don't know who else would put it there. He's owned that land at least twenty years, probably more."

"I'll ask one of the older Rangers."

Crockett's chest tightened as he imagined a posse storming the Haymaker ranch and Jane's reaction. "You won't tell them who has it, will you?"

"I'll be discreet."

"Thanks, brother. I might have known lazy old Boyd Haymaker was involved in something like that. But why didn't he spend the money?"

Chisholm held up one hand. "Wait a second. We don't know he was involved. Innocent until proven guilty, remember?"

"You're right. I shouldn't let my experience with Boyd color my thoughts on this money thing. But you should see him with the kids. He treats them like slaves. I wanted to paste him one this morning when he started ordering Jane around."

"Take it easy," Chisholm said. "I'll see if I can find out anything before the house-raising tomorrow."

Crockett shook his head. "You just got home. I don't want to put you to work again already."

"Maybe I'll go to town in the morning and join you afterward at Boyd's place."

"That sounds good. Thanks."

"And as to why he didn't spend the money over the last nine years, *if* he knew about it, well, anyone local would probably get suspicious if he tried to spend a banknote like that."

"True." Crockett eyed him, trying to sort out the implications. "If you find that Boyd was in on the robbery and word gets out about it, feelings will run even stronger against the Haymakers."

"I'm afraid there's no turning back, now that you've showed this to me. It's my duty to find out who put it in that cave." Chisholm folded the bill.

Crockett wanted the truth to be found, but it made him uneasy to see Chisholm put the banknote into a pocket inside his vest. Would he have to decide whether he would turn against Jane and her family?

No, not Jane. He would have to separate the money from Jane in his mind. She had nothing to do with it. Even if her father stole it, he would not desert her. And if the whole town turned on Boyd, he wouldn't let any of them badmouth Jane and Ben because of their father's deeds.

~

Jane carried the sack into the barn and pulled out the dress. She brushed her hand across the smooth green material. The tucks on the bodice and the dark-green buttons down the front were too pretty for words. She would have to try it on later and see if it needed altering, but the size looked about right.

The dress might be old and rejected by all of the Hart daughters-in-law, but it was far finer than anything she had ever owned. She had long since made over and worn out the three dresses her mother had left behind, and those much-mended garments had burned up along with the house. True, Annie had brought her a skirt, but it was plain and drab. She hadn't even worn it yet because trousers were better for the work she'd been doing this week.

Someone had added a petticoat to the sack. It looked fresh and crisp, so it was unlikely it had been in a trunk for eleven years, since Victoria died. One of the wives over at 7 Heart had sent it out of her own wardrobe. For some reason, just knowing that brought tears to Jane's eyes. She hadn't cried when she saw the smoke rising...or when she galloped into view and saw their house hopelessly engulfed in flames. She hadn't cried when she and Ben found Ma's china platter, blackened and cracked, in the rubble. But this—knowing someone truly cared about her loss? That touched a place deep inside her.

From outside, Pa yelled something. Noon would be here in an hour or so. He probably wanted his dinner. She slipped the Bible inside the sack with the other things and hung it on a nail near the bridles. When she came out, her father appeared to be sleeping in the grass near the fence. She walked over and watched his chest rise and fall for a few seconds, just to be sure.

"What you lookin' at?" he asked.

Jane snorted and turned away.

"Meal time comin'."

Ben had not returned to the log pile but was once more poking about in the ashes where the house had been. They had hauled away a lot of the charred timber and sifted through the ashes over and over. Jane went to the makeshift cooking area she had set up and built up the fire. When the blaze settled down to coals, she would cook something for lunch. She walked closer to Ben and stopped on the blackened grass.

"I think we've found everything useful that we're going to."

Ben leaned on the end of his hoe and gazed at her. "Probably. I'm just tired of peeling bark."

"Me too." Jane looked toward the pasture. "I guess the stock is all right."

He nodded. "Not much we can do for the cattle. I'm just glad they were all out when the fire started." He swiveled his head and gazed at the debris. "Are you sure you don't want the house in the same spot?"

"It would smell all the time if we built over the ash, don't you think?"

"I suppose, if we didn't dig it all out."

"Well, we can't do all that before tomorrow, and if we have the neighbors do it, it will take all day, and we won't get a house built. I don't want to ask them to come back another day. One day is pushing it."

"Maybe we should mark out the corners of where we want it, then. Where do you want your front door?"

She had already considered this and chose a flat area beyond where the old house had stood. She walked to it and stood facing the lane that came in from the road. "Here, I guess."

Ben came to her with a stick and a sledgehammer. He drove the stick into the ground right in front of her. "All right, you go start your beans or whatever you're cooking. I'll get some string and measure off where we think the corners ought to go. The Hart boys can help me make sure it's straight when they get here."

After Jane had dumped beans into the kettle, chopped up a turnip, and added some dried meat, she straightened.

"Make sure you put salt in," her father called.

Her lips tightened. She rooted through her tin box of foodstuffs and took a pinch of salt from the small sack. When she had added it to the stew and stirred, she set the wooden spoon on a rock and walked to where Ben was working, out of earshot of their father, hopefully.

"Hey."

Ben glanced up. "Can you hold the end of this string?"

She took it and said, "Pa sure is complaining a lot."

"I reckon his burns hurt." Ben frowned as he unwound several yards from the ball of string.

"It's been five days, and I don't think his burns were that serious to begin with."

Ben shrugged. "Pa uses anything he can to get out of working. You know that." He walked away from her backward, toward another stick he had pounded into the ground about ten yards away.

She had to admit it. Her father had always been lazy. It hurt to hear people say so, but they only spoke the truth.

"All right," Ben said.

She let go of the string and walked toward him. "I think we'll like the house here."

"Yeah, we probably will." He tied off the string and looked along what would be the front wall of their new home. "Those Harts are smart, and they'll bring a lot of tools. We'll make it square and true, Janie."

She smiled. The new house was the one good thing that had come out of all this. Well, that and having all the neighbors come around and treat them nice. Ben's mouth twisted in a scowl.

"What's wrong?" she asked.

"Sometimes I think we should go somewhere else and start over."

"Why do you say that?"

"I dunno."

"Yes, you do. Tell me." She touched his shoulder, and his gaze met hers. Ben had the same green eyes she had, inherited from their mother, but today, his looked troubled.

"When I was a kid, I hoped I could go to college someday. It was foolish of me, looking back."

"No, it's not. You're plenty smart, Ben. You could do it."

"That dream ended a long time ago. We could never pay for it. Now I just want to support you and me. That's all I can think about anymore."

She looked out at the view of the hills that never changed. Why couldn't they have a normal family? Some families thrived, even if the mother died. Look at the Harts! They had the richest ranch in the whole valley. But GW Hart was a workhorse, and he expected his sons and the men he hired to work hard too. Not Pa.

She looked at Ben. "No matter where we went, we'd have to take Pa with us. We couldn't just leave him here on his own. And even if we did, his troubles would follow us."

Ben said nothing, but his face was set in grim lines.

"Ben, you won't strike out on your own without telling me, will you?"

"I've thought of leaving," he admitted. "But I'd tell you."

Her stomach clenched. Maybe it wouldn't be such a bad idea for Ben to go work for another rancher. That would keep him away from Pa's influence, at least, but she didn't know how she could manage both the livestock and Pa without Ben.

"Before I knew about the fire, I was going to ask Mr. Leonard if I could work for him all the time."

"And stay at his ranch?"

"Yeah. I was seriously thinking about it. I could send my pay home, and I'd come visit once a month. You'd be better off, Janie."

She didn't know what to say. How would she go on without Ben here? "You—you won't do anything sudden-like, will you?"

"No. Let's get a new house built for you, and then we'll sort it out."

CHAPTER 5

$\mathcal{J}$ ane had no mirror, but she could tell when she put on her new dress in the morning that it fit her well. She had tried it on in the barn before sundown last night, after Pa headed for the cave with Ben. She'd told them she wanted to stay down here and use the daylight that was left to get her clothes ready. All she'd ended up doing was to turn up the hem a bit. The soft material hugged her in all the right spots, but not too tight. It swished when she walked.

She closed her eyes for a moment, imagining twirling to the sound of Hays Hart's fiddle. Would Crockett ask her to dance?

Her eyes snapped open at the sound of wagon wheels. They were here so soon, and she hadn't even made Pa's breakfast. She yanked on the new shoes and hurried to the barn door, pushing back her hair.

Crockett and his brother Travis. She ought to have known the Hart clan would arrive first. They were driving the wagonload of lumber Crockett had promised. Two of their ranch hands rode atop the load. Crockett pulled the team to a stop, and the men jumped down.

"Morning, Jane," Crockett called. His eyes flickered as he observed her dress from top to bottom and back up again. He grinned. "You look fine. Where are we building?"

She stepped forward, blushing. "Uh, over there. Morning, Travis."

Travis touched his hat brim. "Morning. How's your father?"

"He's all right. My brother put up some stakes and string where he thought we should build, unless you think it should be otherwise."

She walked toward the site, and the Hart brothers fell into step beside her.

"That looks good. Maybe kinda small?" Crockett arched his dark eyebrows at her.

"It's the same as the old house." She smiled sheepishly. "I guess it *was* kinda small."

Crockett laughed. "We'll make it however you want it."

At the sound of hoofbeats, Jane looked toward the trail. "Here comes Ben now. He and Pa are just getting around." Beyond Ben, Pa slowly rode her horse down from the cave.

Ben jumped down from his saddle and let his mount's reins trail. "Howdy, Crockett. Dr.—Travis. Thanks for coming."

Travis Hart grinned and stuck out his hand to shake Ben's. "Morning, Ben. Now, don't you start saying 'Mr. Hart' today, or you're likely to get six or eight answers. Let's us and the boys start unloading this lumber."

Things started happening fast—too fast for Jane to keep up. While the Harts and their men began unloading studs and beams under Ben's uneasy direction, another wagon pulled in. Mr. Allen had brought a load of planks and siding boards, along with four hired men and his thirteen-year-old son, Billy. Mrs. Allen, her two girls, and their foreman's wife followed in a buggy, bringing food. A few minutes later, three of the Hart boys' wives rolled up with more food.

Jane took a deep breath and greeted the ladies, thanking them for coming and for contributing.

"That dress looks wonderful on you," Annie said with a smile.

Self-consciously, Jane touched the buttons at the neck. "Do you think so?"

"I know so."

Jane helped them set up a makeshift table using sawhorses and boards that would later go into the new house, and then they arranged the food. It kept coming as more families arrived—stewed beans, rolls, cornbread, sourdough, biscuits, roast beef, fried chicken, roast chicken, smoked ham, meatloaf, burritos, carrots, sweet potatoes, collard greens, succotash, and pickles. And pies. Jane lost count of the pies.

The Hart wives seemed to know what to do with it. In fact, Jane had the impression that all of them were used to large gatherings and entertaining in general. She tried to push down her shyness and smile the way Coralee and Annie did when other people spoke to them. Mostly, people smiled back, and she began to feel that they were actually glad to be here. Maybe they were happy to have a reason to neglect their own chores for once.

Somewhere during the morning, Mr. GW Hart himself arrived with two more of his sons.

Pa browsed about, throwing out comments to the neighbors who had snubbed him in the past and filching food from the baskets and platters. He hadn't had breakfast, Jane reminded herself, and she refrained from scolding him. The visitors seemed to exercise restraint as well. She didn't hear one of them say anything scornful to her father. In fact, Emma Hart laughed gaily when she caught him sneaking a cookie from a basketful Mrs. Allen had brought.

Jane fought back the discomfort that came with having other folks notice her and do good deeds for her family. They would have a new house, and it would be clean. The roof wouldn't leak when these folks got done with it. When she saw a small wood-burning stove in the back of the Mortensons' wagon, she caught her breath. They needed a stove, for sure, but would the mercantile owner expect them to pay for it? That was a large gift.

Meribeth Mortenson walked toward her, smiling. Her blond hair looked soft and fluffy around her face. "Hello, Jane. I hope you don't mind." Meribeth smiled apologetically and waved toward the wagon where her husband and Crockett and Hays Hart were unloading the small box stove. "We used to have that thing in the storeroom, but we've got another now. Michael had stuck it out in the barn, but when Crockett told me you had to fix all your meals over a campfire, I thought maybe you could put it to good use."

"Oh, Mrs. Mortenson—"

"Meribeth."

Jane swallowed and nodded. "Thank you kindly. That's...that's quite a gift. Or...do you want it back later?"

"Heavens, no. You keep it as long as it's useful. If you get a cookstove one day, pass that on to someone else."

"Thank you." Jane's mother had always cooked in the fireplace, and

Pa had promised many times to buy her a stove, but there was never enough money. Odd that they got a stove after all their worldly belongings were burnt up. It didn't have a bake oven, but even so, her life would be a lot easier now.

She went back to help the others set out the food.

Annie Hart smiled at her. "Crockett said some folks had come around yesterday with some lumber and coffee."

"They did, and a lot of people said they'd come today." Jane smiled sheepishly. "Crockett brought us a couple of tin cups to go with the coffee, and I was so grateful. Emma and Hays had sent over a coffeepot, but I guess no one had thought about cups."

"Oh, my goodness. You should have mentioned it."

"We made out all right," Jane said. "I don't like to ask for stuff."

"Of course not, but—honey, is there anything else basic that you need?"

"I can't think of anything right off." There were so many things they could use, but making their needs known made Jane feel like a beggar.

"Well, if you do, you tell us. And when we go tonight, I'll leave a couple of those ironstone mugs we brought for the luncheon. We have way more than we need."

Jane could hardly imagine that, with so many people living under one roof at El Regalo, the huge house at the 7 Heart ranch. How could one have too many dishes for so many people? And the boys who had married were building their own homes, too, and would need dishes. But then, with the fortune GW Hart had amassed, they could probably afford whatever they wanted.

She gazed over to the site of the new house, where the framing for the walls was rising. Crockett and his brother Bowie—the long-haired, wild-looking one—were hefting a six-by-six beam from a wagon. Why would a man like Crockett care about a dirt-poor girl like her? When this project was finished, he would probably go back to being the rarely seen neighbor from the big spread that dwarfed the Haymaker ranch.

*C*rockett worked side by side with Ben most of the morning. The young man wasn't too sure of how they should commence building, or where the doors and windows ought to go. After a few rounds of advice from the more opinionated neighbors, they set to work on the outer walls. When they stopped for a break, the framework of the four walls was standing, as well as interior walls to separate the kitchen, the sitting room, and two bedrooms. Ben had insisted he would sleep in the loft over his father's bedroom. Even so, the house would be larger than what they had lived in before.

Caro brought them each a drink of lemonade, and they sat down on the end of the Harts' wagon. Crockett took a long swallow and savored the tart flavor.

"So, Ben," he said. "Jane tells me you might go work on the Bar L."

"Thinkin' about it." Ben sipped his lemonade.

"How would Jane and your Pa get on if you did that?"

Ben lifted one shoulder in a half shrug. "I know Pa's no help anymore. But if Janie could hold things together here, and I could earn some money ..."

"So you want to keep this ranch going for the long haul?" Crockett asked. "Not just cut loose and forget about it?"

"I wouldn't do that to Jane."

"Good." Crockett drained his cup and then looked at the young man. "If it was just you, though? What would you do if you didn't have to think about Jane and your pa?"

Ben gave a short laugh. "That won't happen."

"Seriously."

Ben met his gaze and sobered. "I'd sell this place and go to college."

"College?"

"Yeah. And medical school, if they'd take me."

Crockett gave a low whistle. He should have suspected the boy had thwarted ambitions. Probably Jane did, too, but they were stuck here on this run-down spread. He jumped down off the wagon. "Come on, let's help the crew get the roof framed."

He didn't get a chance to talk much to Jane—at least, not without half a dozen other people close by—until evening. If possible, the food for supper was even more diverse than lunch had been. The Hart women had been cooking for several days in preparation for the event, and it seemed a lot of the other women of Hartville had too. The men took over the barn, where a couple of them had cleaned out the main floor that afternoon as a place to wash up and don clean shirts before the meal.

Jane met up with Crockett as he left the barn. "Been waiting for you. I don't know how to thank you, but I wanted to try." Her eyes gleamed in the rays of the setting sun as she looked toward the new house, all framed and covered with board siding.

"It's what folks do when a neighbor needs a hand."

Jane shook her head. "Not for us. Not usually. I think most of them came because you asked them to—the Harts asked them to."

That made Crockett a little uncomfortable. His own family could have done a lot more for the Haymakers over the years, but his father had avoided Boyd like the plague. That attitude had rubbed off on him and his brothers to a certain extent, though they always thought the kids were all right.

"Well, I don't know about that," he muttered.

Jane's green eyes looked strained and almost fearful. Was she afraid they would all abandon her family once the dancing was over?

"Look, Bowie and Houston and I are set to come back Monday and help Ben get the shingling done."

She glanced away. "You don't need to."

"We know we don't, but you've got to have a tight roof before the next rain. The three of us will be here...and maybe a few others if we can hound them into it."

She was silent for a moment, then said, "I can see that's settled, so I won't argue. I'll just say thank you again."

"You're welcome." Crockett paused and gazed down into her face. Jane was so serious, and perhaps fearful. He needed a bride. Could she be the one? And what would his father think if he proposed to Boyd's daughter? His mouth went dry. "Would you—would you save me a dance, Jane?"

Her smile blossomed, and suddenly, he knew it could work. Boyd and his lazy ways didn't matter. Jane would work her fingers to the bone to make her ranch and her family succeed.

"I surely will." Her cheeks flushed a becoming pink in the twilight.

Crockett grinned and walked over to join his brothers. If he did ask

Jane to marry him, his goal would be to put that smile on her face every single day.

~

The empty barnyard came to light in the twilight with a bonfire at each end. While everyone finished up their dessert and the musicians tuned their instruments to Hays's fiddle, Jane helped the other women put away the leftovers and return the dishes to their owners.

When the music began, she looked around for Crockett, but she didn't see him. She pushed down her disappointment. He'd said *a dance*, not the first dance.

To her surprise, Chisholm was the Hart brother who approached her first. He doffed his hat and gave a slight bow. "Miss Jane, would you dance with me?"

"I..." She looked around and saw Chisholm's wife, Caro, dancing with her father-in-law, who seemed to be enjoying it immensely.

"I suppose so. Thank you."

She let him take her hand and lead her to the edge of the area where the dancers swirled. He put his hand on her waist, and Jane lightly laid her left hand on his shoulder.

"Thought it might be the best way to talk without anyone overhearing," Chisholm said softly as the music flowed about them.

"Oh." Jane felt her color rise and glanced about quickly for her father. He was over near the depleted refreshment table, talking to a couple of the ranchers. He held a tin cup in his hand, and he looked cheerful. Hopefully, no one had slipped in a bottle or a flask, but that was probably too much to ask in a mixed gathering like this. If Pa got drunk, she would just have to deal with him later.

"About the Louisiana banknotes," Chisholm said.

Jane whipped her attention back to him. "Right."

"You heard about the robbery at the state treasury in Austin?"

Jane squinted up at him. "Well, yes, but that was a long time ago."

Chisholm nodded. "Part of the money that was taken was in Louisiana banknotes."

"But...if one of the robbers hid it in our cave, why didn't he come back for it? Or spend it before now?"

"Too recognizable."

They moved with the music, and Jane took special care not to touch him more than was necessary. She stumbled a bit, and Chisholm grabbed her arm to steady her.

"All right?" he asked.

"Yes. Sorry. I'm not a very good dancer. I haven't had much practice." In fact, the last time she had danced was at an end-of-the-year school program, when she was fourteen and the pupils performed a quadrille for their parents and the townsfolk.

"Doesn't matter," he said with a grin. "I haven't told anyone else about..." They passed close to Mr. and Mrs. Mortenson, who were dancing much closer together than she and Crockett's brother were. Chisholm lowered his voice. "About what you told Crockett."

Jane nodded.

"Is it all right with you if I show the sample to my boss?"

The back of Jane's neck prickled, and her throat went dry. Why did this prospect scare her? Because if the money was from the robbery, the most likely suspect would be her pa. What if he was arrested? And if the word got out—which it would—their ranch might be overrun with people looking for more of the loot.

"If people find out..."

"I'll be discreet," Chisholm assured her.

"I...suppose you have to."

"It's the best and quickest way for me to find out more about it. If it *is* from the treasury robbery, it would be the first of the money recovered since that night. It could be important."

Jane's legs felt like sticks of firewood as she moved in time with the music. "I'll have to trust you."

"Yes. You trusted Crockett, and I hope you can do the same for me. I'll do all I can to make sure your family isn't hurt, Jane. If it does implicate someone local..."

"You mean my pa."

His mouth flattened into a sober line. "Well, yes. Or a neighbor. But it could be that someone who fled Austin stashed it there when he realized he couldn't spend it freely. It might be someone who's long gone."

The song ended, and they stopped moving and clapped.

Suddenly, Crockett was beside them. "Time for my dance, Janie?"

"Oh. Yes, I guess." She looked at Chisholm.

"I think we're done," Chisholm said with a smile. "Don't fret about this, Miss Jane. Let us handle it." He nodded to his brother and walked away, toward where his wife was standing with her sisters-in-law, fanning herself and laughing.

Crockett peered at her. "You all right?"

"I think so. It's a little off-putting."

He nodded. "If you don't want to dance, would you like a drink?"

"I'd love some of that lemonade, but then I'd like to dance, Crockett. If you can stand my clumsiness."

"I saw you dancing with my brother. You weren't clumsy."

"You lie, but I'll forgive you." There. She'd managed to flirt with a man, another first for Jane Miranda Haymaker.

"Time for a quadrille, folks," the caller, Austin Hart, announced from near the band. "Form your squares."

Someone threw more wood on the nearer bonfire, and Crockett's eyes reflected the flying sparks. "Let's get that lemonade, and then we'll show these folks how to dance."

She gulped down a half cup of the sweet beverage, and then he pulled her over to join a set. Ben was part of it with one of the Allen girls. He smiled across the square at Jane, seeming almost happy. Happier than she'd seen him in years. Jane smiled back and crooked her arm through her partner's, glad that her slow dance had been with the Ranger, not with Crockett. She might have crumbled into a pile of ash if she'd had to waltz with Crockett first thing. But maybe later, before this odd evening ended.

She found herself short of breath as she whirled around. The old moves from the school program didn't match up with everything Austin Hart called out, but somehow she managed to keep up. When in doubt, she followed Crockett's lead or imitated the other women in her set.

When it was over, she stood laughing and clapping with the rest, with the firelit night still spinning around them.

The music started again almost at once, this time slower, to let the dancers get their breath. Many of the dancers drifted to the sides of the crowd, but others joined them. Jane started to walk away from the makeshift dance floor, but Crockett seized her hand.

"Hey, won't you have this one with me? I know you can waltz."

She wasn't sure what to say. Wasn't he afraid other people would pair them up if they danced together twice in a row?

"Are you sure you want to do that?" she asked, still a little breathless.

"I'm sure."

He pulled her into his arms, and out of self-defense, Jane put her hand up to his shoulder. Crockett seemed to want to dance a whole lot closer than his brother had. Her face felt hot, but maybe that was from the exercise or the heat of the bonfire.

As they turned around with the flow of the music, she spotted Pa, heading inside the barn with one of Mr. Allen's cowboys. That couldn't be good.

"Everything all right?" Crockett asked.

"Yes. Well, no."

His eyes widened, but he didn't miss a beat of the music.

"I was wondering about Pa," she confessed. "I'm afraid someone's brought him some drink."

"If you'd like, I'll go check on him after this dance."

"Thank you." She couldn't talk after that. As shameful as her fears about her father were, it was also something of a relief that someone else knew and didn't judge her. She glanced up at him, and he smiled at her, causing such an odd lurch in her stomach that she looked down and tried to concentrate on her steps.

The song came to an end, and they stood apart and clapped. When Hays poised his bow over his fiddle again, Crockett said softly, "I'll check on your pa."

She glanced toward the barn as Pa staggered out the doorway and nearly fell on his face. "Never mind. There he is."

CHAPTER 6

*J*ane's cheeks heated again. Thank goodness for the semidarkness to hide her shame. Mr. Mortenson, who stood nearby, reached out to steady her father. Pa turned and laughed heartily at something the storekeeper said.

"Think he's all right?" Crocket asked quietly.

Jane looked down at the ground. "As all right as he'll be until morning."

"I'm sorry."

She sighed. "Not as much as me."

The music was gentle and soothing, and Crockett leaned close. "One more dance?"

"Thanks, but I think I need to rest."

"Sure. Come have a seat." He led her to some benches people had brought. After supper, the men had arranged them around the yard, outside the dancing area. Crockett steered her to one beyond the circle of firelight, away from the people.

"Thank you." Jane sat down, very conscious of him settling beside her.

"There's something I've been wanting to talk to you about," he said.

Jane peered at him, trying to read his expression. "You mean, besides the money?"

"Yeah. I, uh..." He cleared his throat, looked up at the moon, and then looked back at her. "I'd like to court you, Jane."

She swallowed hard, but a painful lump remained in her throat. "I don't know what to say."

"Say yes."

She wanted to. Very much. She had always liked Crockett, though he was a few years older than she was. And he'd been very kind to her and her family. He'd seen her father stumbling drunk, and he still wanted to call on her. But would he change his tune if her father was revealed to be a felon?

She swallowed again.

"Should I ask your pa?"

"You saw him. This probably isn't a good time to ask him anything." Or maybe it was a very good time. Pa probably wouldn't remember a thing tomorrow.

Crockett shrugged. "I'll ask him if you want."

"You don't have to. I make my own decisions now."

He looked into her eyes for a moment and then said, "I'm glad."

And now Jane felt hot all over. She wanted to spill everything, to tell him how hard it had been for her and Ben. How she'd come to the conclusion that if she didn't stand up for herself, no one would. How many times Pa had come home from town inebriated after her mother died. She and Ben had learned to hide, and when that failed, to defend themselves. They had poured out liquor and concealed his ammunition until he sold his rifle to buy more drink. How many times had she braved Pa's anger to keep him from beating Ben?

"I'm surprised you'd want to see me," she squeaked out.

His expression softened. "Why?"

"Because of Pa." Well, mostly because of Pa. She also wondered why he would choose her over other young women in the county. Women who had real families. Women who didn't spend all day doing ranch chores and trying to keep their drunken fathers from destroying the place.

"You think he'd object?"

"Probably not. He'd probably think I'd snagged me a good one. But he'd want something in return."

"I think I can handle your pa."

"Really?"

Crockett nodded. "My pa scares me a whole lot more than yours."

She started to laugh, but she saw that he was serious.

"I should probably tell you," he went on, "my pa's got this bee in his bonnet that all us boys should get married. Soon."

Jane frowned. "Is that why Hays and Chisholm and Travis and—and—"

"Houston?"

"Yes, Houston. Is that why they all got married this year?"

"Well, I'd like to think it was love in each case, but I'm sure Pa's order had something to do with it. He sees it as giving us all a kick in the pants to get on with continuing the Hart family."

"Oh."

He cocked his head to one side. "What?"

"Is that why you said that you want to...you know, court me?"

"Not really. This summer, I'd about made up my mind to ignore what Pa said. Just keep on the way I have been—and maybe even set out on my own if Pa didn't like it. And then I got to know you better. That and seeing how happy my married brothers are—well, it sort of made me feel Pa might not have such a bad idea. And I realized, I really do want my own place. Pa won't give me my share if I don't get married this year. I was feeling like that was a lot to ask of us, but now..."

She sat there a bit numb. She had no parlor in which to entertain a suitor. The idea of a suitor—and a strong, handsome man from a substantial family, at that—stunned her. Whatever did he see when he looked at her that made him want to get to know her better and possibly move toward marriage? Eligible women didn't exactly grow on trees in Texas, but there were scads prettier than her who would come into a marriage with a hope chest full of linens and such.

She pulled in a deep breath. "Then I say yes. You can see what you're up against."

He nodded, smiling. "I've got my eyes open."

"All right, then."

"I'll come Monday about the roof, and maybe we can take a walk after. Or ride out and check your stock together."

"You'll spoil me."

"I hope so." Crockett grasped her hand and pulled her to her feet.

~

*J*ane declined Crockett's invitation to dance again. "I shouldn't..."

Yes, he had monopolized her, but he didn't care. Of course, etiquette said he ought to dance with some other young women, at least with his sisters-in-law. A few of the ladies were starting to pack up the things left on the refreshment table.

"I'll go help with the cleanup," Jane said.

"All right. See you later."

But before she could reach the table, one of the cowboys from the Hart ranch intercepted her. Crockett couldn't hear what he said, but he led Jane over to join one of the groups forming for a square dance. Crockett ambled away, keeping to the edge of the activity as the party began to break up.

As he strolled along the fence, someone saddling a horse in the shadow of the barn caught his eye. He stopped short. Ben. Why would he be throwing a saddle on his horse now?

Crockett ducked through the rail fence and walked over to stand behind him. "Going someplace, Ben?"

Jane's brother whirled and blinked at him. "Oh. Crockett. Yeah, I... was going to ride out and see if I could get back to the Leonards' tonight. I might still be able to get in a few days' work there, and we need the cash."

"Does Jane know?"

Ben shook his head. "She'll understand."

"Will she?" Crockett eyed him carefully. "She needs you, Ben. There's a lot left to do here."

"The neighbors have all been so nice. I figured this would be the time to go, when folks are feeling kindly toward her. At least three people have told me tonight that they'll help us again if we need it. She'll be all right."

"Do you think she can handle your pa alone?"

Ben let out a deep breath. "I don't know. He's been drinking tonight. I think some of the boys from town brought whiskey. But we've put up with that for a long time. If she can get him to the cave—or even in the barn—he can sleep it off."

With the money in the cave, what if the Rangers came and took Boyd off to prison? Then Jane would be totally alone. She couldn't run the ranch by herself. "Can't you hold off just a little while?"

"Why? The longer I wait, the less chance I have of getting work."

"She might need you. More."

Ben's eyes narrowed. "What do you mean?"

Crockett hesitated. The story wasn't his to tell, and Jane had purposely kept it from Ben. "Just talk to Janie first. There's things you don't know, Ben."

Ben tipped his head. "What do you mean?"

"Please, just wait a day or two and talk to your sister."

"Talk to me about what?" Jane asked. Crockett turn to find her approaching them. She looked at the horse. "Where are you going?"

Ben said sheepishly, "Back to the Leonards' to see if they'd take me on again, even though I didn't come back all week."

"You said you'd tell me." Jane stepped closer to him. "I wish you wouldn't go just now. You can send a note to Mr. Leonard if you want and explain about the fire. But I..." She grimaced and turned her face away.

"What?" Ben prompted.

Crockett touched her shoulder lightly. "I was saying to Ben that you might need him these next few days. Maybe you two should talk."

After a moment, Jane nodded. "You're right. It's time."

"What's going on?" Ben asked.

Quickly, Jane told him about the money she had found in the cave and the bill she had passed along to Chisholm Hart.

"He thinks it came from the state treasury robbery, Ben. He's going to try to find out for sure."

"The state..." Ben stared at her. "That was years ago."

"Yes. You were ten or eleven, I'd say."

"But...what are you saying? You think Pa was in on that robbery?"

Jane shifted her weight. "I don't know."

Ben's eyebrows lowered. "Was Pa at home then?"

"I've tried to remember." Jane's brow furrowed. "We were young, and it's kind of blurry. I remember when I first heard about it. A boy came to school and told everybody. I don't know how his parents heard. Maybe they read it in the newspaper, or maybe his father heard it from the sheriff. Anyway, that might have been several days after it actually happened."

"It was right after the war," Crockett said. "Communication was spotty back then."

"Pa might have been away and we wouldn't remember," Ben agreed.

"What you all jawin' about?" The familiar voice made them jump.

CHAPTER 7

*J*ane startled at the harsh voice and turned around. Crockett drew in a quick breath. Pa was standing in the doorway at the back of the barn.

"Mr. Haymaker," Crockett said in his easy tone. How could he sound so calm? Her own heart was racing.

Pa took two steps down the ramp they used for the wheelbarrow and stumbled against the rough railing Ben had put up last year, after Pa tumbled off into the muck one too many times.

"It's all right, Pa." Ben hurried toward him and took his arm. "We were just talking to Crockett about the old days. You know, when we were all in school."

Pa looked Crockett over, his eyes squinty and harsh. His gaze fell on Jane next. She stood as still as she could. Then he noticed Ben's horse.

"You headin' out tonight?" He pulled his head back, birdlike, and stared at Ben.

Ben's mouth twisted, likely because he'd gotten a strong whiff of Pa's whiskey breath. "I was thinking about going back to the Leonards' to earn some money, but Janie said I ought to stay a while longer."

Crockett walked toward them. "My brothers and I will come back Monday morning to help finish up the roof on the new house."

"Pa, you ought to go to bed," Jane said.

"Now? We've got guests." Pa had a hard time wrapping his tongue around the *s* sounds in *guests*.

"They're fixin' to leave now." Ben nodded back toward the party. "Come on. Let's put you on Star, and I'll take you up to the cave."

"I ain't goin' up to that cave now." Pa squirmed away from him.

"In the barn, then. I'll make you a bed in the hay. It'll be nice and soft —softer than the blankets you've been sleeping on at the cave."

"Not 'til I say goodnight to ever'body."

"All right, we'll go out front and say goodbye. Come on." Ben took his arm again and turned him carefully to face the barn door.

"I should probably go out there too." Jane looked at Crockett, wishing she could stay out here in the corral with the manure smells and horses and wait until everyone else was gone. But her ma wouldn't have hidden from her guests, even when Pa embarrassed her.

"You go ahead," Crockett said. "I'll put Ben's saddle away."

"Thank you." She headed for the back barn door.

Pa was arguing with Ben, who was still trying to keep him from going out into the yard. The music had stopped, and people were moving about beyond the open front door. She decided to duck out on the altercation and went back out the rear of the barn. Crockett was sliding the saddle off Star's back.

"Beware," she said. "Pa's still fussing."

Crockett grinned. "I'll see if I can distract him. Go on, now."

Jane hurried to the fence and ducked through the rails. The refreshment table was nearly bare. As she approached, Mrs. Allen saw her.

"Oh, good, there you are, Jane. I'm leaving the last of my fried chicken and some cake for you folks. It's right here, in this basket."

"That's very kind of you." Jane gave a nod. "I'll make sure and get the basket back to you."

"No hurry. This was a very nice gathering, dear. You should come into town more often."

"Yes, ma'am." As if she had time to leave the ranch, or money to spend in town.

"Drop by the mercantile when you do," Mrs. Mortenson said. "If it's not too busy, we'll sneak upstairs for a cup of tea."

Jane smiled sincerely. "I'd like that very much."

Coralee Hart, Houston's new wife, came toward them. "Jane! I've got some cookies in here for y'all."

"Oh, thank you." Jane accepted a bundle made up of a napkin wrapped and tied around something lumpy.

Coralee bent close and kissed her cheek. "Don't be a stranger at the ranch, now, will you?"

"I..." Jane had no idea how to respond to that, but Coralee didn't seem to notice.

"We're heading home now. Emma's tired."

"Oh, it was so nice of her to come." Jane glanced around. "I need to thank her."

"Best hurry, then. Hays is putting her in the buggy now."

"Excuse me, won't you?" Jane said to Mrs. Mortenson.

"Of course. See you soon."

Jane dropped Coralee's cookie bundle into the basket and hurried beside her to where Hays was settling his wife on the buggy seat. Houston was bridling the horse that pulled the buggy.

"Emma, Hays, thank you so much for coming," Jane said.

"We had a grand time." Emma reached for her hand and squeezed it.

"I'm glad. But I hope you didn't wear yourself out."

Emma shook her head. "I enjoyed it. But I'll probably sleep all day tomorrow."

Jane stepped back so Coralee could climb up.

Houston stepped forward and gave his wife a hand, calling over his shoulder, "Got your fiddle, Hays?"

"It's in the boot."

"Thank you for playing," Jane said.

"You're very welcome." Hays threw her a dazzling smile. "Seems as though I saw you getting in a dance or two, Jane."

She pulled in a deep breath. There was no need to be shy around the big, loud Hart boys. They were friendly, and after all, Hays was an old classmate of hers. "Well, I did. A couple of your brothers were kind enough to ask me."

One brother in particular, who'd quickly become someone special.

~

*C*rockett rode over to the new house Monday morning, after the Hart family had eaten breakfast and cleared their plans with his father. The 7 Heart had plenty of cowpunchers to take care of the routine business at home, so Houston and Bowie joined Crockett for a day of roofing.

When they got to Haymakers', Ben and Jane were in the yard, tidying up from their breakfast. Boyd was nowhere in sight.

"All right to turn our horses out in the corral?" Crockett asked as he dismounted.

"Sure." Jane waved. "Ben's ready to help you."

Bowie drove up with several bundles of shingles in the ranch wagon. His long hair fell down by his face, partly hiding the scars on his left cheek, but nothing hid the black eye patch he wore. He'd helped work yesterday but had slipped away before the dancing began. Crockett was a bit surprised and very pleased that he had agreed to come help Ben again today. He pulled the wagon up as close to the new house as he could.

"Morning, Bowie," Jane called.

He looked her way and lifted a hand in silent greeting.

Crockett began working the cinch free on his saddle. "How's your pa doing?" he asked Jane.

"He's still asleep, yonder in the barn. Ben finally got him to lie down in the straw, and he stayed there all night. He was snoring away when I looked in a while ago."

"I hope our hammering doesn't wake him." Houston flashed a grin.

"Won't matter if it does." Jane lifted a shoulder. "I thought I'd take my horse up to the cave and start moving stuff down here to the house while y'all are working on the roof."

"Sure," Crockett said. "You can move right in. Do you care which part we do first?"

"Maybe get the kitchen done so I can cook in there and not worry about the foodstuffs if it rains?"

"That sounds fine." Crockett lifted his saddle off the horse's back and laid it over the top fence rail. They unloaded the shingles, and Bowie unharnessed the team and turned them out. The hot, arid weather of

August had dried out most of the grass, and he had brought some feed in the wagon to keep their horses contented while they worked.

Ben, Crockett, and Houston climbed the ladder they'd made the day before, to the bare rafters. They nailed a few boards in place on the rough sheathing to help them stay steady while they nailed on the shingles. Bowie carried the first bundle up, and they tore into the work. The next time Crockett paid any attention, Jane was standing down below the ladder with a bucket and dipper in her hands.

"Got a batch of switchel here, if you boys want a drink, and there's leftover cake from last night."

"Perfect." Houston headed for the ladder.

Crockett climbed down after him and Ben and accepted a tin cup of the molasses, vinegar, and ginger drink. Nothing seemed to quench thirst like switchel.

"Thank you, ma'am," Bowie said, taking his portion from Jane last.

"You're welcome. There's more in the bucket, and the cake's over there." She pointed to where she had set out the leftovers on the rough outside table. Looking up at the roof, she said, "You're making good time."

"Many hands..." Crockett offered her a smile. "We hope you'll be settled in tonight."

"Well, I brought down all the cooking things people brought us this last week. I'm going to start arranging the kitchen."

"We'll hook that stove up for you before we go," Houston said. "Brought some new stovepipe along."

"I didn't think about that. Thank you." Jane picked up a bulging burlap sack and walked into the new house.

Crockett sat down beside Ben on a bench in the shade of the barn eaves. "You'll be needing some furniture, now that you've got a house."

Ben swiped his sweaty hair under his hat. "We can get by."

"Let us know if you're lacking something. I'd think you'd at least need bedsteads and a table and some chairs. Maybe a cupboard or two."

"We'll manage."

Crockett smiled. "Ben, don't be so stubborn. I know you're pretty much the man of the house here, but you can't do everything yourself."

Ben exhaled heavily. "I just want to be able to earn enough so Jane doesn't have to work so hard."

"Is that all?" Crockett gave the young man's shoulder a bump with his own. "It's a pretty tall order."

Ben shrugged.

Crockett eyed him closely. At twenty, Ben was old enough to shoulder the responsibility. The trouble was, he'd carried it since he was about ten years old. He and Jane both had taken on adult roles too early. "You told me you wanted to be a doctor."

"Not much chance of that." Ben looked over his shoulder. Bowie and Houston had settled down for a rest on the tailgate of the wagon, sipping their switchel and talking in low tones.

"Why isn't it possible?"

Ben shook his head. "I used to think maybe someday. But now I know it can't happen. There'll never be enough money in this family for that."

"You shouldn't give up on your dream, Ben. You're smart enough to go to college and medical school."

"That's not enough." He looked at Crockett bleakly, and Crockett could almost read his thoughts. *Your brother Travis is a doctor...but your family's different. You've got money. You don't have a father who's a lazy drunk, or a sister who needs support and protection.*

Crockett leaned back against the barn wall. "What would you say to working at the 7 Heart?"

Ben stared into his eyes. "Your pa would hire me?"

"We always need men in the fall for roundup. We might not be able to keep you on over the winter, but I can pretty much guarantee you a spot on our spring roundup and drive."

"That sounds good." Ben flashed a smile. "I was going to ask Mr. Leonard, but your place is a lot closer."

"That's what I was thinking. You could keep an eye on your pa and Jane easier, and you could come home at least once a week on your half day off." Crockett chuckled. "You might even be able to come home nights, at least some of the time."

"That'd ease Jane's mind."

"You think about it. Our pay is good. And if you really want to go to medical school, you'll find a way someday."

"Sure doesn't seem like it, even if I have steady work." Ben gave a mirthless chuckle. "If that money Jane found was honest money, maybe we could make a go of it. The neighbors have been real nice, but—"

"Don't count on that money," Jane said bitterly. Crockett hadn't realized how close she was. She held out a plate with a slab of cake on it to each of them.

"Thanks." Crockett took one, and Ben accepted the other.

"What about the money?" Ben frowned at her. "Can't you keep it if they don't find out where it came from?"

She shook her head. "If it's not from the treasury robbery, it's from some other dishonest scheme."

"I wouldn't put it past Pa to have something to do with that robbery." Ben took a bite of cake.

"Oh, yeah?" Boyd screeched from the barn doorway.

They all three turned to face him, and Crockett sucked in a painful breath. How much had Boyd heard?

The old man charged toward them and grabbed Ben's shirtfront. His face flushed almost purple as he snarled in his son's face. "You ungrateful pup! I oughta throw you into New Mexico."

"Pa—"

Crockett leaped to grab Boyd, but he was too late. Boyd punched Ben hard in the stomach, and Ben doubled over, his eyes wide as he gasped for air. Jane gave a little squeak and jumped backward, watching her father with huge eyes.

Boyd growled. "Traitors, the both of you."

"Stop it!" Jane dropped to her knees at Ben's side, next to the piece of cake he'd dropped. "Breathe, Ben. Are you all right?"

Boyd took a step toward them, and Crockett grasped the older man's arm. "Take it easy, Mr.—"

Boyd turned on him, fists swinging. Crockett jumped back, avoiding the first blow. Boyd's momentum carried him forward, and the second punch hit Crockett in the ribs. He swung back and connected solidly with Boyd's jaw. The old man flew backward, arms outflung. His head hit the edge of the bench with a thud.

Crockett hauled in a breath, ignoring the pain in his side and his aching knuckles, waiting for Boyd to get up and come back for more.

The white-haired man lay still. Crockett's stomach began to roil.

Houston and Bowie ran over from the wagon. "What happened?" Houston demanded.

"Boyd lit into Ben," Crockett said.

"When Crockett tried to stop him, he started fighting him," Jane added.

Crockett made himself approach and stoop over Boyd, pushing back his collar to finger his neck, where the pulse should run strong.

"He's out cold." Jane knelt beside her father and looked up at Crockett. "He'll be all right, won't he?"

"I can't feel his heartbeat." Crockett went to his knees and lowered his ear to Boyd's chest. His shirt and overalls smelled of sweat, whiskey, and horse manure. Crockett straightened.

Ben came closer, hugging an arm across his abdomen. His green eyes held a panicky look.

"Crockett?" Jane had tears in her eyes. "He's not breathing, is he?"

Crockett couldn't speak. Not since the war had he known this feeling, as though he had fallen off a cliff, but no land rushed up to meet him.

Bowie pushed him aside and knelt by the old man.

Crockett straightened and moved closer to Jane. He wanted to touch her, pull her away or take her in his arms or just pat her shoulder, but he couldn't. Would she ever want him to touch her now?

Houston hurried to Boyd's other side.

Ben stood back, gazing anxiously toward his father's still form.

Houston and Bowie talked in low tones across the man's body, and Houston rose. "I'll go for the sheriff."

Good thing he'd offered. Crockett didn't want to leave Jane right now, and Bowie would avoid going into town if possible.

"The sheriff?" Jane took a step toward Crockett. She wobbled a little, and he grasped her arm to steady her. "What about a doctor? Your brother Travis?"

"It's too late for that." Houston's lips flattened. "I'm sorry, Miss Jane."

Ben's jaw dropped. He was still breathing hard from the blows he had received. "You mean Pa's dead?"

"I'm afraid so." Houston threw a troubled glance at Crockett.

"It's not Crockett's fault," Ben said quickly.

"Pa attacked Ben," Jane agreed. "Crockett was trying to help Ben, and Pa hit him."

Crockett studied Ben, who looked as though he would keel over any moment. "You might ask Travis to come out here if he can, to see Ben."

"What about you?" Houston asked.

"I'll be all right. Sore ribs and skinned knuckles is all."

"I'm fine." Ben shook his head. "I can ride with Bowie if y'all will stay here." Perhaps he wanted to get away from the sight of his father's lifeless body.

"Get your horse, then." Houston walked toward the corral fence and gave a piercing whistle. His gray gelding lifted its head and trotted toward him.

Ben went slowly into the barn for his saddle.

Bowie stepped over to Crockett and laid a hand on his shoulder. "Are you sure you're all right?"

"I'll be fine. I—I don't know how to handle this." Crockett looked at Jane, expecting anger or hatred in her eyes. "I'm sorry, Jane."

"I know you are," she said. "I don't know what to think, or how to feel. It's just...well, God knew this would happen, didn't He?"

"I suppose He did, but it's the last thing I meant to happen. I didn't want to hurt him, just knock him down so he'd quit fighting. I thought maybe once he was quiet, we could talk to him about that money, and maybe he'd give us some straight answers."

"What money?" Bowie asked.

Crockett sighed.

Jane lifted her chin. "It's some old money I found on this property. Your brother Chisholm took a sample and is looking into it for us."

"I see. Well, it's in good hands, then."

"It's just between us," Crockett told his brother. "Nobody else knows except Ben. Well, Boyd overheard us talking about it. I'm pretty sure that's why he tore into Ben."

Bowie nodded. "Just tell it all to the sheriff when he gets here."

"No fear." Crockett squared his shoulders. "I'll tell him everything I know."

"So will I," Jane said staunchly. She glanced at him and back at Bowie. "Crockett won't be in trouble, will he?"

"I don't think so. All of you saw what happened."

"Yes." She frowned and walked over to the fence, avoiding looking at her father's body.

Crockett deflated. How could their courtship move forward from this?

CHAPTER 8

*A*s Ben rode out with Houston Hart, Crockett and Bowie stood behind Jane, talking softly near the barn. She sniffed. In the last five minutes, her life had changed, but how? The sun still glared down on them. The skinny cattle grazed on what little they could find. The new house still had only part of a roof.

Would she actually live in that house? Would Ben stay, now that Pa wasn't here any longer? Would he ride off to find his own life now? And what about Crockett—would he still want to come courting, after what he'd just done to her pa? Too many questions crowded her mind. She closed her eyes and leaned on the fence.

Pa had made her life and Ben's miserable the last ten years. A thousand times, she had wished he would go off and not come back. She'd thought she and Ben could get along just fine on their own, without him. Maybe better than with him, since they wouldn't have to worry about whether he ate anything that day, or where he got the latest jug of liquor, or if he was going to draw off and hit them for no good reason.

But she hadn't wished for him to die.

Slowly, she turned. Crockett was sitting on the far edge of the bench, and his older brother was talking to him. She couldn't hear what Bowie said, but Crockett's face was sober. He'd killed a man. That must have brought him up short, but she couldn't help him now. They weren't talking about just any man. It was her pa. Could things ever be the same between them?

Bereavement settled on her heart, not just for Pa. She may well have lost Crockett, too, before he was really hers. She had dreamed of a life with him, and last night, he'd seemed to want that too. Could they look at each other across the breakfast table every morning, knowing he'd killed her father?

Jane hauled in a deep breath and looked toward the clean, new little house. How foolish she had been to think her life had taken a turn for the better.

She stood leaning on the fence. A half hour passed, and the sun didn't seem to have moved. She ought to think about fixing dinner for the men. Achy and stiff from hunching over the fence so long, she took a few steps toward them.

Bowie had covered Pa with a saddle blanket—at least, she assumed Bowie did it while she was turned away, with her face to the range. Crockett still sat on the wobbly bench. He stood when she drew near.

"Jane." His brown eyes were broody, and his face was creased with lines, which made him look much older. She couldn't talk to him now, not with all the contradictory thoughts that jabbed at her from all sides. Relief was the main one. Was that wrong? Guilt was a close second. Sorrow was somewhere down the list, but it would probably catch up later, when the full import of Pa's death became clear.

She looked away, unable to hold Crockett's troubled gaze. "I thought...I thought I should cook something."

"Don't bother. Not for us." He huffed out a breath. "We haven't even set up your stove. Should have done that first, I guess."

Jane shook her head. "I'll heat water for coffee over the fire, and there's cans of beans and a few things left from last night."

Bowie eyed his brother closely. "We could get up on that roof and get a little more done."

"They should be back soon," Crockett said.

Bowie shrugged.

"You go ahead," Crockett told him. "I feel like one of us should stay here with...with Boyd." He looked over at the blanketed body, and the creases on his brow deepened.

"Thank you," Jane said. "Thank you both. I'll bring you some coffee."

A few embers glowed when she stirred the debris in the fire ring, and she built up a blaze. The day was so hot, sweat beaded on her forehead. While she let the fire burn down to useful coals, she walked slowly to the doorway of the new house. Crockett had promised a sturdy door when the roof was finished. It had all seemed so full of promise. But he might be sitting in jail this afternoon.

She squared her shoulders. She and Ben had both seen her father's attack. Crockett did nothing wrong. Even so, he might have to go to trial. She had heard of men being charged with crimes they said they didn't do, or that weren't their fault, and having to go to court, anyway, and sometimes spend years in prison. Of course, being a Hart would help Crockett's case. Now, if Ben was the one who had accidentally killed Pa, would he go free? She wanted to think he would, especially with her and Crockett to testify for him.

Shaking off her troubled thoughts, she went back to the fireside. This week, her few pots had stayed in a crate nearby, and she pulled out the coffeepot and took it over to the well to fill it. The brew was beginning to steam when she heard hoofbeats on the road from town.

Ben, Houston, and Sheriff Watson came into view, and Jane stood motionless near the fire, watching their horses jog toward her. Bowie's hammering stopped. Crockett came silently and stood beside her. He didn't say anything, but Jane felt much stronger, just having the tall, lean man at her side.

The sheriff swung to the ground and let his chestnut horse's reins drop. "Miss Haymaker. Crockett."

"Sheriff." Crockett dipped his chin.

"I understand there's been a tragedy here."

"Yes, sir. Boyd's over there."

They all turned and looked toward the body. Bowie had come down the ladder and walked toward them.

Ben and Houston dismounted, and Houston took Ben's reins from him. "You go on with the sheriff. I'll tend the horses."

Ben nodded and led the way.

Jane looked at Crockett. He held out his arm, as if they were going into church. She took it, because her legs were a little shaky. They walked together to stand in the dust of the dooryard. The sheriff stood beside her pa's body, and Bowie pulled off the horse blanket. Ben waited off to one side, not watching, but looking off toward the hills and the cave.

The sheriff knelt down.

Jane walked over to Ben and put a hand on his shoulder. He glanced at her and then away. Her breath caught at the sight of tears in his eyes. She rubbed his shoulder lightly. "It's going to be all right, Ben," she whispered.

"Is it?"

She didn't have a real answer.

After a moment, Ben said, "They'd better not blame Crockett."

"I don't think they will."

Ben turned suddenly and scooped her into his arms. Jane stiffened a moment in surprise but then returned his embrace, comforted by his warmth and the fact that he had reached out to her. They'd had such little loving contact since their ma died. Once in a great while, they had hugged or held hands when they felt especially sad, usually when Pa had been drinking and they'd had to hide to avoid his beatings.

"Don't you feel guilty, Ben."

"I do," he said, his voice cracking.

"I figured." She held on to him a moment longer, then gently pulled away. She touched his cheek, and he looked full at her. "It's not Crockett's fault, and it's not your fault. Pa brought this on himself."

Behind her, the sheriff cleared his throat. She turned to face him.

"Crockett's given me his story," he said. "I'd like you both to tell me how it was. You first, Ben."

"Well, we were sitting on that bench talking, Crockett and me. I kinda forgot Pa was in the barn, sleeping." He glanced at Crockett. "Janie brought us some cake, and Pa all of a sudden came out of the barn. He heard something we said, I guess."

"Who said?"

"Jane and me, I reckon." Ben lifted a shoulder.

"And what were you talking about?"

The sheriff gazed steadily at Ben, and he lowered his eyes. "It was something private."

"Best tell me, son."

"It's all right," Crockett told him.

Jane stepped forward. "I found some money about a week ago in a cave." She pointed toward the hills. "It's up yonder, and we've been sleeping up there since the house burned. But Chisholm Hart is looking into it." She looked to Crockett for him to corroborate her story.

"That's right." Crockett stepped closer. "I asked Jane if I could show one of the bills to my brother, and he thought the Rangers might have some information on it. Maybe I should have told you first."

The sheriff was quiet for a moment. "Well, you and Chisholm are family."

"Yes, but I mostly wanted him to see it because it had been there a long time, and I thought maybe it had to do with an old case he knew about."

"I see." The sheriff rubbed his chin. How offended was he that Jane and Crockett had consulted a Ranger, rather than going to him?

"I'll ask my brother to stop by and tell you anything you want to know about it," Crockett said.

Was it too little, too late? Jane had the uneasy feeling the sheriff might hold it against them that they hadn't come directly to him. Maybe he would go harder on them because of that.

"This was an accident," she said. The men all looked at her. "Plain and simple, it was an accident. When Crockett hit my pa, he didn't intend to kill him."

Crockett nodded. "She's right. I wanted to slow him down so we could talk some sense into him. He was going after Ben pretty fierce."

"And Ben won't hit back when Pa does that," Jane added.

"Janie." Ben shook his head, his eyes not focusing on any of them.

"I'm sorry, but it's the truth." She put her hand protectively on Ben's shoulder. "Pa's been mean to us for a long time. Pretty much since Ma died. At first, I guess we were too scared to hit back. We'd try to hide and stay out of his way. But now...well, we kind of feel sorry for him. We wouldn't want to really hurt him. And he doesn't come at us as often as he used to."

Crockett's expression darkened, and she stopped talking. Her face heated. She ought not to have said so much. What would he think of her now?

The sheriff let out a long sigh. "That about right, Ben?"

"Yes, sir." Ben blinked hard and looked away.

The sheriff walked over and crouched beside the body. He spent half a minute or so looking closely—most likely, eyeing the bruises. Houston came back from the corral and stood by Bowie, waiting in silence.

At last, the sheriff stood. "So Boyd had been drinking?"

"I don't know about this morning," Jane said. "He had a snootful Saturday, when we had the house-raising. As Ben said, some of the men brought bottles. I'm afraid Pa got some off them, because Ben and I went to church yesterday, and when we came home, he was curled up in the barn with an empty one."

"I found a couple more out back." Ben gestured. "We thought he was sleeping it off this morning when we got to talking. But I guess he woke up and heard us. He came out here..."

"He came out here at the worst possible time," Jane said fiercely. "We were discussing with Crockett how that money could have gotten in the cave, and whether Pa might have..." She broke off and shook her head. "Best you talk to Ranger Hart about that, I guess."

"I'll do that." The sheriff looked at Crockett, then at Houston. "I don't think you boys need to worry much. I'll let it be known it was accidental. In fact, we might be able to keep folks from knowing it was a fight. He appears to have hit his head when he fell back, and that's what my report will say."

"Thank you, Sheriff," Crockett said sincerely.

Jane swallowed hard and reached for Ben's hand.

"Now, have you got a wagon?" The sheriff looked around.

"That one's ours," Houston said quickly. "We brought some shingles this morning."

"Where do you want him taken, Sheriff?" Crockett asked.

"Giles Brown can make you a coffin. I'll tell him to expect you. All right, Miss Jane?"

He looked toward her, and she nodded. Mr. Brown did carpentry work for people, including coffins when needed.

Houston walked over to stand in front of her. "Is there anything else we can do? Would you like me to ask Reverend Longley to do a service for Boyd?"

Jane nearly choked. Pa hadn't been in the church as long as she could remember.

"Pa wouldn't like that." Ben shook his head.

"Maybe at the cemetery." Jane ventured a sidelong glance at her brother. "For us, Ben. Not for Pa."

Ben shrugged. "I guess."

Bowie walked over to the corral and brought Sheriff Watson's horse to him.

"I can drive Boyd into town," Houston said.

"Fine by me." The sheriff mounted and fixed his gaze on Crockett. "If I need anything else, I'll come by your father's place—or will you be here?"

"If I'm not here helping with the roof, I'll be home."

Watson nodded and lifted a hand in farewell, then turned his horse and trotted off toward Hartville.

"While we load your pa, you might want to think about clothes for him," Houston said softly to Jane. "What he's got on is pretty dirty."

She hadn't thought about that. Of course, they couldn't bury him in the clothes he wore when he slept in the filthy barn. But he didn't have much else.

"He's got a shirt someone gave him up at the cave," Ben said. "I'll fetch it."

"I've got some extra pants in my room," Crockett offered.

Houston nodded. "I'll stop by the house and get 'em."

They settled a few details, and then the Hart brothers loaded Pa's body into the wagon bed and hitched up their horses. Ben returned with the extra shirt someone had given Pa and decided he'd better go into town with Houston and speak to Mr. Brown.

After they left, Jane didn't know what to do or say to Crockett and Bowie. She wanted to collapse, but she didn't have a bed or even a chair to sit on. She walked slowly over to the bench in front of the barn and sank onto it.

Bowie scratched the back of his neck. "I could lay a few shingles."

"If you think so," Crockett said.

Jane looked up at him. "You don't have to put good trousers on my pa for burying. Nobody will be able to see them, anyway."

Crockett stood still for a moment, his lips twitching. At last, he said, "It's all right, Jane. I don't mind. And it will be easier for Mr. Brown when he lays out your pa."

"He does all that?" She wasn't quite sure what the process involved. Washing, surely.

"He will, unless you want someone else to do it. My sisters-in-law might help you...and the pastor's wife."

Jane's lower lip trembled. She didn't want to touch Pa now. Didn't want to wash his body or peel off his filthy clothes or dress him afterward in someone else's clean, soft things that were better than anything Pa ever owned. But mostly, she just didn't want to touch his clammy skin.

Tears coursed down her face.

Crockett walked over and knelt in the dirt before her. "Jane."

She tried to blink back the tears, but there were too many.

He took off his bandanna and blotted her cheeks. "Janie, it's all right."

She shook her head. "Y-you must think we're the worst scum in Texas."

His mouth almost smiled, then went sober. "I would never think that."

Next thing she knew, she was in his arms. He knelt there by the bench, holding her, and she sobbed into his shirtfront. Ma would have fits if she saw her behave this way, but Jane couldn't stop crying.

"I'm s-sorry."

"Don't be," Crockett said.

She cried some more, and then slowly pulled away. Crockett stuck the bandanna in her hand, and she wiped her face. Over at the new house, Bowie was climbing the ladder.

"I didn't mean to make a fuss in front of you. Or your brother either."

"Bowie won't tell anyone."

A little laugh jerked out of her.

Crockett smiled. "There, that's better. I want to help you. I want to make this as easy as I can. I feel all kinds of guilty about what happened between me and your pa, and now I'll do anything to make you not hate me for it."

"I could never hate you, Crockett."

"You sure?"

She nodded and sniffed. "I don't blame you for Pa's dying. It was his own fault. But I've been thinking...that you'd think less of Ben and me after you saw all you've seen here."

"Not a bit."

"Even if I tell you I'm not sorry for what happened?"

Crockett's eyes narrowed. "You mean, that he's dead?"

"Well, not that especially." She grimaced. "But I'm glad you did what you did. Pa might have hurt Ben real bad. He has before. Broke his arm once, when Ben was twelve."

"I'm sorry."

"I'm not exactly glad he's dead, but I despaired of him ever changing his ways." She looked up at him. "Your mother's Bible... I've been reading it."

"I'm glad."

Jane couldn't help a tiny smile. "She underlined things."

"Yes, she did. I used to leaf through it and read the verses she thought were special."

"That's what I've been doing, and you know what I found?"

Crockett shook his head.

"It's in Isaiah. It says, 'When thou walkest through the fire, thou shalt not be burned; neither shall the flame kindle upon thee.' I don't think I'd ever read that verse before." She shrugged. "Anyway, it jumped out at me because of the fire we had."

"And the fire didn't hurt you," he said softly. "Not any of you. Just your house and your stuff." He took her hand. "I can't imagine how hard it would be if our house burned...and everything in it. But I know it would be a hundred times worse if even one person was harmed in that fire."

Jane sighed and looked toward the new house, where Bowie had started nailing down shingles. "Pa got out. He set that fire by accident, but he got out. And I'm glad Ben wasn't here. He'd have tried to salvage some of Ma's things. You're right—it's not worth it."

"And you were smart enough not to try to do that."

"I just hoped I could save the barn and the stock." She gazed into his dark eyes. "Why did Pa survive the fire and die a week later?"

"I don't know."

"I thought to myself the night after the house burned that it might have been better if he hadn't got out. And then I felt so guilty!"

"You don't need to. Your pa has caused you and Ben a lot of grief." He slid his arm around her shoulders. "I'm glad Ma's Bible has been a comfort for you."

"I'm sure it has a lot of things in it about forgiveness too. Did you hear the sermon yesterday, when Reverend Longley talked about forgiving seventy times seven?"

"Yeah."

"I guess that means I should forgive Pa for all the mean things he did to Ben and me."

"I reckon so," Crockett said. "Can you forgive me what I did today?"

Her face softened. "There's nothing to forgive."

CHAPTER 9

$\mathcal{C}$rockett and Chisholm rode side by side into the Haymakers' yard. The roof was now finished, and so was the stone wall around the well.

"The place looks nice." Chisholm hadn't been back since the house-raising two weeks earlier.

"Thanks," Crockett said. "Bowie and Houston helped Ben and me finish the roof, and Ben and I did the well this week."

"Real nice." Chisholm stopped his horse in front of the barn and swung down. "Think they're inside?"

Crockett eyed the plume of smoke coming from the stovepipe. "The stove's going."

They ambled to the door, and Crockett knocked briskly. Jane opened it a moment later.

"Hello. I thought I heard someone ride up." She looked past Crockett to his brother and nodded at him. "Chisholm."

"Miss Jane, I hope I have some good news for you."

"I could use some. Come on in." She stepped back. "I'm expecting Ben any minute for his dinner, and I've got coffee hot if you'd like some."

"That sounds good." Crockett followed her in and sat down at the small pine table the Mortensons had donated.

The kitchen smelled of gingerbread. Jane poked at a skillet of sliced ham and potatoes she had frying on top of the little box stove. Its heat wasn't overpowering, now that the weather had cooled toward fall temperatures.

"I was telling Crockett the place looks good, Jane." Chisholm sat down and stretched out his long legs. "Looks nice in here too."

She smiled as she brought over the coffeepot and two mugs. "Thanks. Ben and I have been trying to make things a little better. It's amazing what prideful feelings a spanking-new house stirs up."

Chisholm laughed. "Well, I like it. Pretty curtains, even." He nodded toward the muslin panels embroidered with a red cross-stitch border.

"Why, thank you. Emma and Annie helped me stitch those." Jane poured out the coffee. "Hope you don't mind—I'll keep on with my work."

"Go right ahead." Crockett lifted his mug for a sip.

"Thanks." She turned back to the stove. "What brings you out, Ranger?"

Chisholm chuckled and winked at Crockett, as if to say that girl was sharp as a tack. "It's the money. We've confirmed it's from the treasury robbery."

Jane turned around with a long-handled fork in her hand. "You don't say."

He nodded. "One of our Rangers took the sample to Austin and consulted with the treasury people. They've told me to recover the rest of the money. My boss will see that it gets to the right place."

"Good," Jane said. "I'll be glad when it's gone."

"There's something else."

"What?" Uneasiness crept into her eyes, but Chisholm smiled as he reached inside his vest.

"The state treasury has had a reward sitting in an account for nine years. None of the stolen money was recovered up until now, and the specie probably never will be. The coins, that is. Everyone figures it was spent long ago. But these bills could be verified as loot from the robbery. And the state sent along a part of the reward money in that account for you—a hundred dollars."

He held out a piece of paper. Jane took it and unfolded it.

"What is this?"

"It's a bank draft," Chisholm said. "You can take it in town any time you want and cash it at the bank. It's yours."

Tears sprang into Jane's eyes. "I didn't do anything."

Crockett reached over and touched her hand. "Yes, you did. You found it, and you told the authorities. A lot of people would have just kept quiet and maybe tried to spend it."

"You deserve it, Jane." Chisholm beamed at her. "I'm glad to see you get it."

The door opened, and Ben came in. He looked at the Hart men and paused. "Crockett. What's going on?"

Quickly, Chisholm explained to him about the reward. Ben took the slip of paper in his hands and stared at it. "A hundred dollars. Jane, we can get the feed we need...and maybe a heifer calf or two."

"Sure, you can," Crockett said.

Jane's tears spilled over and ran down her cheeks. "I didn't expect anything like this. But I think we should keep it in the bank for you, Ben. Start a fund for you to go to college."

"No, we can't do that." Her brother shook his head.

"Why not? It would be a start toward what you always wanted to do." She set her lips in a firm line. Crockett smiled at the stubborn set of her jaw.

"But we need so many other things if we're going to make this place pay."

"That will take time," Jane said.

"I know. But we can do it." Ben laughed and swept her into a hug. "For once, I'm not the one bringing home the bacon. This is three months' wages, Janie. More than that."

She pulled away from him and swiped at her tears with the back of her hand. "Can we put half of it away for college?"

Ben frowned. "I don't—"

"Maybe you two should think about it for a few days," Crockett said. "Cash the draft and put half in the bank for now. Get what you need right away, and see where you are."

"That sounds smart." Ben gave a nod.

Jane glanced at Crockett. "Well, I guess." To Chisholm, she said, "Thank you. If you're sure it's all right ..."

"It's more than all right," Chisholm agreed. "It's fitting. And now, I'd best get going. I'm supposed to be in town before noon. I'm heading out for a few days."

"We brought the money down from the cave for you." Jane took the cover off a crock and pulled out the small metal box. She handed it to Chisholm.

"Thank you. That will save me some trouble," he said.

Crockett stood and slapped his brother's shoulder. "Take care."

"I will. See you soon. Thanks for the coffee, Jane." Chisholm went out the door.

"Do you want to go to the bank today?" Ben asked.

"All right. Wash up. Let's eat dinner, and then we'll go. Crockett, you'll stay to eat with us, won't you?"

"If you've got plenty."

"I think we do. I'll put a few eggs on to stretch it out."

"Be right back." Ben strode to the door and outside.

Jane sighed and went back to the stove.

Crockett went to stand beside her. "Jane." His mouth was dry, but now was the time. He needed to know if she would share his future. He couldn't bear thinking about what he'd do if she said no. He didn't care what his father said—if Jane turned him down, he couldn't marry someone else in a hurry. Because Jane was everything to him now.

She glanced up at him, then at the pan of potatoes and ham she was stirring. "Yes?"

"I've been wanting to ask you something."

"What? Because I wondered if you really think we ought to spend that money on supplies and young stock. I don't know how much college costs, but—"

"This has nothing to do with the money." Crockett nodded at the spatula she held. "Can you put that down?"

"I've got to cook eggs."

"Forget the eggs." He took the spatula from her hand and laid it on the table, then took both her hands in his. "Jane, I want to marry you. Will you—will you be my wife?"

She stared up at him, no sound coming out for a moment. "You mean it?"

"Of course I do. These past few weeks, I've come to care about you, and—well, I'm pretty sure it's love, Janie. I told you my pa wants all of us boys married, and I can't think of anybody else I'd rather... Well, you're it for me. Unless you say no." He eyed her anxiously.

She swallowed hard. "I won't say no."

"So you'll say yes?"

"Yes."

Her breath rushed out of her as he pulled her into his arms.

~

*W*hen the door creaked open, Jane leapt away from Crockett. Ben stood in the doorway grinning.

"Well, it's about time." He strode across the kitchen and stuck out his hand. Crockett grasped it heartily.

"Thanks, Ben. Jane just agreed to marry me."

"Capital! When's the wedding?"

Crockett laughed. "We haven't discussed that yet. Soon, I hope."

A flush bloomed in Jane's cheeks, and she had never looked prettier.

"We'll have to talk about it," she said, fighting to stay calm. "Now, you fellows sit down and eat this food." She quickly cracked eggs into the pan and brought the ham and potatoes to the table. They sat down, and she looked across the table at Ben. "Pa didn't hold much with prayer, but I want to start again. Do you mind?"

"No." Ben shot a sideways glance at Crockett. "Just don't ask me to say the blessing with no warning."

Crockett straightened. "I will."

Jane nodded, pleased at his offer, and bowed her head.

"Lord, we thank You for this day and all that it brings," Crockett said. "We thank You for the food You've provided, and for Jane and Ben and the ranch they have here. We ask that You will bless our future. In Jesus's name."

All three of them said "amen" together, and Jane smiled as she opened her eyes.

"Thank you. I hope we can always have the blessing in our home." She looked shyly at Crockett, very aware of his gaze, and a new wave of heat washed over her face.

"How about two weeks from Saturday?" Crockett watched her closely.

"You mean..."

"For the wedding. There've been so many in our family lately, I'm sure nobody at the 7 Heart will think it's odd. Or too soon. What do you say?"

Ben frowned. "Let's see, that'd be the twentieth, Janie. Sounds good to me."

Jane made a face at him, but she wasn't angry. "You've got nothing to say about it. But I admit, it sounds good to me too." She stood and went to the stove, where the eggs were simmering.

"Wear that dress you wore to the dance," Ben said. "You haven't put it on since."

"I will." She scooped the eggs onto a plate and brought it to Crockett.

He forked a serving onto his plate. "Unless you'd like a new one."

"Oh, no," she said. "It's fine. I love that dress."

Crockett smiled. "That's settled, then. Once my sisters-in-law hear, I'm sure they'll want to have you over for a sewing party."

"Why?" Jane lifted her brows.

"They like you." Crockett passed her the plate while Ben helped himself to ham and fried potatoes.

"Besides," Ben said, "you'll probably want some more dresses if you're going to be a housewife now. You can't run around in those trousers all the time."

"Well, I'll still be doing ranch work." Jane gulped and looked at Crockett. "Won't I?"

"Only if you want to."

"Where will you live?" Ben's question made her hesitate.

"That depends." Crockett sat back from the table a bit. "I can build a little house for us on my land, if you want."

"Or you could live here," Ben said. "It's already built. And there's room for all of us."

"That's if you stick around, Ben," Crockett said.

Jane stared at him. "What do you mean?"

Crockett shrugged. "There's a lot of ways we could do things. I had told Ben we could hire him on at the 7 Heart once your house was squared away. But I'll have my own land now. Pa will give me my share as soon as I'm married. I wondered if you'd like to combine this ranch with it. Ben and I could work it together. Or we could keep your place separate and share work when we needed to."

"It would be a good-sized ranch then." Ben blinked thoughtfully.

"Yes, it would. And if you want to go to school, Ben, we could probably help you with that." Ben opened his mouth, but Crockett continued quickly, "You've got the reward money. I asked Travis how much it would cost for you to go to college for medical training. He said you can pay as you go, and I think we could do it. I have a small herd of my own, and I could increase it if I had the use of this land too. You think about it."

"I don't know what to say." Ben looked anxiously at Jane.

She took a deep breath. "Me either. But that's a fine offer, Crockett."

"If it's what you want, Ben," he added.

Ben took a bite of ham and chewed. They all ate in silence for a few minutes. Then Ben took a sip of his coffee and set the mug down.

"I've always wished I could go to college. Never thought I'd have a chance."

"You've got one now," Crockett said. "We'd miss you, but I think Jane and I would both like to do that for you."

"We would." Jane smiled at him. Indeed, this was the first thing they'd decided together, other than the wedding date.

"What about the ranch work?" Ben asked.

"Don't worry about that." Crockett laid one of hands open on the table. "If I need extra help, I'll hire a couple of men."

"You make it sound so...simple."

"I'm sorry." Crockett's forehead furrowed, as though he didn't want to sweep in and take charge. Jane and Ben had never been in a position to think about hiring ranch hands, but for Crockett, it seemed like an everyday thing. He went on, "It's just something to think about. You two hash it over, and if you're not comfortable with that...well, we'll do things however you want, Janie. Truly."

Jane looked at Ben. She knew what she wanted. Would Ben be able to let his future brother-in-law help plan his future too?

Ben cracked a smile. "At least you know he's not marrying you for your money."

Crockett guffawed. "All for love, brother."

Ben nodded, satisfied, and started eating again.

"All right." Jane gave a brief nod. "We'll talk it over."

"Take all the time you need," Crockett said. "But the date's still firm, right?"

Jane hadn't smiled this much in her life. "It better be."

When they had finished eating, Ben slapped on his hat. "I'll saddle the horses so we can go to town."

"And I'd best get home and put in some work today." Crockett rose. Ben was out the door, and he walked around the table as Jane stood. "I'll tell my pa first thing," he said softly.

Jane nodded, not saying a word, but she was still smiling. He reached for her, and she flowed into his arms.

"You tell me if there's anything you need," he said. "Anything at all."

"I will."

"Good. And expect some of the girls to pay a call real soon."

She looked up at him archly. "What about you?"

"Oh, I'll be back. If Pa doesn't need me tomorrow, I'll come over and help Ben with whatever he's doing. Maybe Caro and Annie, or whoever's available, will ride over with me."

"I should help with the cattle too."

"No, that's hard labor. I don't want the future Mrs. Hart tuckering herself out with that kind of work."

"You won't make me stay inside all the time darning socks and baking pies, will you?" She smirked at him.

"Of course not, although the pie part sounds pretty good."

"I'll help where needed."

"Agreed. May I kiss you now?"

Jane's face flushed again, but she looked straight into his eyes. "I was hoping you would."

ABOUT THE AUTHOR

Susan Page Davis is the author of more than 100 novels. She writes romantic suspense, historical romance, and mystery. She is a Maine native now living in Kentucky, and a member of American Christian Fiction Writers. Her books have won several awards including the Carol Award for her novel The Prisoners Wife; the Faith, Hope, and Love Inspirational Readers' Choice Award for The Prisoner's Wife and The Lumberjack's Lady (Maine Brides series); and the Will Rogers Medallion Award for her novels Captive Trail (Texas Trails series, 2012), The Rancher's Legacy (Homeward Trails series, 2022), and The Outlaw Takes a Bride (2016). Visit her website at https://susanpagedavis.com

MAIL-ORDER MAYHEM

VICKIE MCDONOUGH

CHAPTER 1

HARTVILLE, TEXAS
EARLY OCTOBER 1874

S tephen Austin Hart stood behind a parked wagon in the alley beside the blacksmith shop, watching the main road leading into Hartville. The stage was due in five minutes, although that didn't mean it would arrive anytime soon. Or even today.

Leaning back against the wall of the mercantile, he tried to stop the apprehension snaking through him. He hadn't been this nervous since his first few battles during the War Between the States. Something in his gut told him he was making a huge mistake, but what choice did he have after his pa issued that ultimatum—get married in a year or lose his inheritance?

He couldn't lose the land that represented his future—land that had been in his family going on three generations. Here he was the oldest of the Hart brothers and still wifeless, while all of his brothers were now married except Bowie. His youngest five brothers had hopped on the task of finding a bride like cats on crickets, and each one had met with success and was happier now than he'd ever seen them. He didn't begrudge their success or happiness, but he sure didn't like that his pa had forced them all to marry so quickly.

Would Pa really deny him his inheritance if he didn't marry? The huge ranch house that had been the family home all his life was supposed to go to him, as well as a big section of land due south of it. What if things didn't go as planned? Could he lose everything? If that happened, could he ride off like Bowie? Had his brother turned his back on his heritage, or did Bowie plan to return before the deadline?

Austin gritted his teeth. Regardless of what his brother had done, he wouldn't give up his inheritance without a fight. The 7 Heart Ranch was his home. His only option was to marry—no matter what.

Like any warm-blooded man, his eye had strayed toward a pretty woman when he encountered one, but he'd never thought much about marrying. He stayed too busy for that, trying to keep things in order and running smooth at the ranch. But soon he would be married. Wrapping his mind around that notion wasn't easy, especially since he'd never laid eyes on his future wife. But soon. . .

He pressed his hand against his vest pocket, feeling the familiar crinkle. He'd done something none of his brothers had thought to do—sent for a mail-order bride. His belly churned as if he'd swallowed soured milk. What if he didn't like her? What if she was plug-ugly? What if she took one look at him and hopped back on the stage?

Austin blew out a sigh. Character mattered more to him than looks, when it came down to what was most important in a long-term relationship. Hopefully, his bride felt the same. He could face a homely gal each morning as long as she was honest and faithful to him and God and her cooking was good. But knowing that didn't take the edge off his jitters. The most important thing was that he could not fail.

He had a feeling he was already starting off on the wrong foot since he had agreed to Jenny Evans's request to meet him and then to spend a few days getting to know one another before they married. What if she decided she didn't like him? His brothers had said plenty times he was too cranky. Too bossy. They didn't realize how hard it was to keep six rowdy brothers, such a large ranch, and thousands of head of cattle all moving in the direction of profitability. One bad year of drought or sickness could ruin all that his forefathers had worked so hard to build. And even though his father was still alive, somehow the load of it all rode on Austin's shoulders.

Throwing an unknown woman into the whole shebang wasn't something he could prepare for. But he had no other option. He'd made up his mind to marry—and he rarely changed it once he'd decided on which trail to take. But he still wondered what he'd do if she changed *her* mind, which he was learning from his five sisters-in-law was something women did a lot. He booted a rock. It rolled across the narrow alley and *thunked* against the far wall. He couldn't shake the worry that his bride would find him lacking.

He had to make her want to marry him.

But he had no idea how to do that.

A man and woman strolled past the alley opening, arm in arm. Austin ducked behind the parked wagon again so he wouldn't be seen. He felt more like an outlaw scoping out a place to rob than the well-respected grandson of one of Texas's first white settlers. He'd avoided his brothers the past week and dodged their questions about him marrying for a long while. The last thing he wanted was for his big family to show up when he was wooing Jenny.

The pounding of the horse's hooves made the ground tremble, and he heard the jingle of harness. Glancing behind him, for a split second, he considered riding for the hills, but he couldn't do that to Jenny. He pushed his feet forward, hoping he'd be pleasing to her. He may not be the youngest or best-looking man in town, but he was honest, hardworking, and faithful to God. That would have to be enough for her—at least, he hoped it would.

~

*R*ebekah Evans's heart sank as the stage pulled into the small town of Hartville. What kind of mess had her trouble-prone sister gotten herself into? There were no huge buildings, much less large houses, as Austin Hart had said he lived in.

She turned to face her sister and gasped. "Jennifer Jane Evans, button up your shirtwaist this instant! And where is your hat? We've arrived, and you must look presentable, or Mr. Hart may send us packing."

Jenny groaned, fanning her face with her hand. "Why is it so hot here? It's October, for heaven's sake. Shouldn't it be cooler?"

"I suppose it's because we're so much farther south than we're used to." She bent down and picked up her sister's bonnet, which had slid off

Jenny's lap onto the floor. Fortunately, her sister hadn't stepped on it. The stage pulled to a quick stop, nearly unseating her. "Hurry, now. Let me adjust your combs. It's of the utmost importance that you present a good first impression."

Jenny fastened the final button, then sat still while Rebekah smoothed her hair and placed her bonnet on again. Jenny's lower lip trembled. "W-what if I don't like him? What if he. . .stinks? Or is horrible ugly?"

Her sister was nervous, but it was too late for turning back. "It didn't sound as if he was from his letters." She grimaced. That sounded rather unconvincing since letters were so easy to falsify. "The most important things are that he's an upstanding citizen and that he can provide a good home for you."

The stage driver opened the door and held out his hand to Rebekah. "We've arrived in Hartville, ma'am."

Jenny's hand grabbed hold of Rebekah's arm, her fingernails digging in.

She glanced at her sister's pale face, then back at the driver. "If you don't mind, could you please give us another minute to collect ourselves?"

The cowboy smiled and touched the brim of his hat. "Sure thing, ma'am. We'll unload your baggage while you ladies get presentable."

Rebekah pivoted as well as her squashed bustle allowed. "Jenny, you have to get hold of yourself. I don't know what will happen if Mr. Hart refuses to marry you."

Jenny crossed her arms and glared at her. "I wouldn't even be in this fix if not for you agreeing to marry Herman Riggs."

Her sister was partially right, but they were both near destitute and had no other options after Jenny's indiscretion and Herman's declaration. "I'm sorry that Herman refuses to allow you to live with us after we're married."

"Why do you want to marry him, anyway? He's fat and old."

She couldn't deny her intended was overweight, but that was because he sat all day, working as a bank clerk. "He's not that old—thirty-six."

"Why, that's fourteen years older than us."

"Your Mr. Hart is only two years younger than Herman."

Jenny pressed her hand to her stomach. "I know. That's one thing that frightens me."

A handsome man walked past the stage, peered in, and then continued on. Her heart somersaulted, but she pulled her gaze back to her sister. "We can discuss this tonight. Right now, it's time to meet your groom." Providing he was waiting. She had no idea what they'd do if he wasn't.

Jenny moaned but said no more.

If only they had other options. The war between the North and the South had taken so many good men's lives. There were few men to choose from in their small Missouri town and so many women. She'd been fortunate that Mr. Riggs had taken an interest in her, even though he certainly wasn't the man she'd dreamed of marrying. He could give her a home and security—and hopefully a child, and with that she'd be content. She prayed God would bless Jenny and that she and Mr. Hart would be a good match.

~

*A*ustin moseyed around the front of the stage. He'd tried to get a peek at his bride, but he couldn't make out the features of the woman he'd seen in the shadows of the coach. There was more than one person inside—he knew that much.

"Hart! Catch." Austin looked up in time to see a satchel soaring through the air. He grabbed it and back-stepped to keep from falling, casting a scowl at the driver, Fred Chambers. The last thing he needed was to be flat on his back in the street when his bride debarked the stage. She might think he was a drinker.

Fred chuckled. "Here comes another one."

Austin quickly set down the bag and caught the next one. "You'd better not toss those trunks. Could be something breakable."

"I won't, but I'd appreciate some help with 'em."

They made quick work of getting down a small mountain of baggage, then Austin dusted off his hands. Why hadn't the women exited the stage? Had Jenny taken one look at the town—or him—and changed her mind? But then again, she had no idea what he looked like, and she wouldn't leave without all of her baggage. He eyed the stack again, hoping that most of them belonged to the other person in the stage. But then his bride had probably brought most of her worldly possessions with her since she was moving to Texas permanently—he hoped.

Fred climbed down and nodded his thanks. He grinned. "You're in for a surprise, I suspect." He hustled to the door and reached up, while Austin tried to decipher the driver's odd comment. A gloved hand joined Fred's. The first glimpse Austin got of his bride was the top of her dainty hat and a mass of dark-blue fabric. The woman stepped down, smoothed her skirts, then glanced up. Austin hadn't believed it when a couple of his brothers had talked about their hearts bucking when they'd first laid eyes on their future bride, but he'd be hanged if his hadn't done the same thing.

Jenny Evans was beautiful. Her eyes—almost the shade of the bountiful bluebonnets that painted the fields with color each spring—stood out against her fair complexion and dark hair. They seemed to look clear into his soul. He fumbled for his hat, yanked it off, and crushed it against his chest. His mouth suddenly went as dry as if he were riding drag on the summer trail ride.

God must have been smiling down on him to send such a pretty woman to be his wife.

The woman studied him for a long moment, but then she spun around, facing the stage.

Austin frowned. Was she going to get back on without even talking to him? Yes, she was much younger, but he had told her his age. He couldn't let her leave without at least talking to her. "Miss Evans, wait!"

He started forward but stopped suddenly. Fred helped another woman exit the stage—a woman wearing a bonnet identical to Jenny's and a dress the exact same color. She, too, wrestled with her skirts. Jenny adjusted the woman's bonnet and whispered something to her. The second woman nodded, then Jenny stepped aside, took the other woman's arm, and moved toward him in unison. Both women looked up at the same time. Austin's heart thumped. They were exactly alike. A matched pair. Identical twins.

It suddenly dawned on him that in the two letters Jenny had written, she'd said nothing about being a twin. She also hadn't mentioned bringing her sister with her. Austin glanced past them, wondering if perhaps his Jenny was still on the stage, but Fred had climbed onto the bench and was gathering the reins. Grinning wide, he winked at Austin and mouthed, "Good luck."

The women moved as one toward him.

It was obvious that Jenny hadn't told him everything. What else had she omitted mentioning besides her sister?

And which gal was his bride?

CHAPTER 2

*R*ebekah watched several different expressions shift across the man's features. Was he not Stephen Hart? She looked around behind him and over her shoulder but saw no other man focused on them. If he was Jenny's fiancé, why did he look so confused?

Jenny's steps slowed, but Rebekah all but dragged her sister forward. If he wasn't Mr. Hart, perhaps he could direct them to the man. She stopped a good six feet from him.

His gaze shifted from her to Jenny and back. Had he never seen identical twins before? That seemed unlikely, but it certainly would explain his perplexing behavior.

But if he were Mr. Hart, why would he look so befuddled? Unless. . .

She leaned toward her sister. "You did mention I was accompanying, didn't you?"

Jenny visibly swallowed. Then she lifted her chin, flashed a coy grin, and shrugged.

Rebekah's heart clenched. Jenny didn't tell him. What if he had no place for her to stay? A surprise like this certainly wasn't a good way to start off a relationship.

Quickly composing herself, she struggled for a friendly expression. She sure didn't want the man standing in front of her to think she was upset with him. He stood tall, wearing an air of authority. He hadn't worn a suit, but his white shirt and dark pants looked new and of a good quality. A thin layer of dust clung to his boots, but the shine from a recent polishing was still there. And this man was handsome, with his dark, assessing eyes and black hair. His shoulders looked wide enough to bear any woman's problems. If he was Stephen Austin Hart, Jenny was a fortunate woman. A shaft of envy pierced her.

The man smiled, albeit a tad bit wobbly. "Ladies, I'm Austin Hart. I'm sure hoping one of you is Jenny Evans."

Her sister stiffened, but she lifted her hand as if responding to a schoolteacher. "I-I'm Jenny."

Rebekah hated the way her sister's voice trembled. Hated that she had to leave her here when Jenny was so apprehensive, but it was better than them both being on the streets, trying to get by on their own. There were few decent jobs for women, and she was determined they wouldn't end up working in a saloon—or worse.

The man looked a tad bit relieved and slapped his hat back on his head. "A pleasure to make your acquaintance." He glanced at Rebekah again, his dark eyebrows dipping. "And you are?"

"Oh, my apologies. I'm Jenny's older sister, Rebekah Grace Evans."

"Older by only six minutes." Jenny mumbled her normal response.

Mr. Hart shuffled his feet. "I don't mean to stare, ma'am, but I didn't realize Jenny had a twin, nor was I expecting you—so forgive me if I seem caught off guard." He glanced toward their luggage. "I'd best move your things out of the road." He trod toward the pile of trunks and satchels.

Mortification marched through Rebekah again as he strode off. She spun toward her sister. "I find it hard to believe you failed to mention you were a twin, but you also omitted the fact that I was accompanying you? Jenny, that's unconscionable."

"I was afraid he'd say no if he knew there were two of us coming."

"But I'm not staying. Only until the wedding." Rebekah blew out a sigh, tired of having to fix Jenny's messes. From what her sister had read to her of the few letters Mr. Hart had written, he was in charge of a big ranch and a large family. She had a feeling he didn't like being unprepared for any reason. It made sense he'd appreciate knowing what he was up against.

She closed her eyes, once more searching for a thread of composure, then she turned and moved toward the big man who lifted one of their heavy trunks as easily as if it were a five-pound sack of flour and set it on the boardwalk. "I'm so sorry for the inconvenience, Mr. Hart. I'm sure I can find a place in town to stay." As long as the room was inexpensive—and food didn't cost extra.

He shook his head. "No need, ma'am. I've booked a couple of rooms at the hotel, and once we go home, our house has plenty of space. You're welcome there."

His kindness was quite generous and appreciated. She lifted her head, looking straight into Mr. Hart's deep brown eyes. Lines creased the edges of his eyes, as if he laughed a lot. The sun had darkened his skin to a pleasing bronze. A sudden dryness coated her mouth that she was sure was not related to the dust blowing in the warm breeze. She cleared her throat. "I don't want to be a bother."

A gentle smile lifted his lips. "It's no bother, ma'am. I didn't plan for two, but I will now that I know you're here."

She wasn't completely sure what he meant. The relentless sun beat down, heating her whole body. Jenny was right that the temperature felt much warmer here in southern Texas. The tiny bonnets that were popular in Missouri did little to shade them from the sun.

"I think I might swoon if we have to stand out here much longer." Jenny dabbed her face with her handkerchief.

"My apologies. Let's get you two inside." Mr. Hart swatted his hand at the pile of baggage. "Which of these are the most important? We can take them now, and I'll get the trunks later."

Jenny gasped. "We can't go off and leave our possessions unattended. Everything I own is in them."

Rebekah motioned to Jenny to quiet down. Her sister often made a mountain out of a molehill.

"Your belongings will be safe here." Mr. Hart motioned toward the building behind them. "The people in Hartville are good, decent folk. They won't bother your things."

"Well, I suppose it will be all right—if you're certain." Jenny looked less than convinced.

"I am." He nodded, his lips pressed tight together. Mr. Hart gathered their four satchels, two in each hand. "The hotel isn't far. Just follow me, and I'll have you out of this heat in a minute or two."

"Thank you, Mr. Hart. That will be nice." Rebekah started after him with her sister lagging behind. She glanced over her shoulder and motioned with her head for Jenny to join her. She obliged, but her expression had yet to lose its sour pucker. "Don't you like him?"

Though Jenny shrugged, her eyes were on her future husband's back.

"Jen-nyyy. He's a nice man—and quite good-looking," she whispered. "Don't you think?"

Jenny blew out a sigh. "I suppose—in a rugged sort of way."

"He doesn't look much different than the cowboys we saw in Missouri."

"But I wasn't expected to marry one of them."

"You're the one who accepted Mr. Hart's proposal." This had to work. She needed to see her sister settled in a home with a good man so she could return to Arcadia and her future. She'd pull out the big guns. "Besides, you don't want to end up working in Toby Nelson's saloon, with all those half-drunk men leering at you every night, do you?"

Jenny's expression instantly changed. "No. Of course not."

"Then paste on a smile and give your beau some encouragement before he changes his mind."

"Fine." Jenny lifted her chin as if strengthening her resolve. "I'll bat my lashes and win his heart, if that's what it takes."

Rebekah sighed. "Just be friendly. Talk to him."

Mr. Hart stopped at an open door to one of the larger buildings in town. "Here we go, ladies."

Rebekah turned into the hotel lobby, delighted to be out of the hot sun, although the temperature inside was only marginally cooler. If only they'd worn more summery clothing, but with it being October, she'd chosen their normal autumn wear. As her eyes adjusted to the dimmer lighting, she noticed the clerk staring at her and Jenny from behind the registration counter. She should be used to people's stares since she'd been a twin her whole life, but they still made her uncomfortable.

Mr. Hart strode past her and set their satchels down. "I had two rooms reserved, Hank, but I'll be needing a third, if you have it."

She rushed forward. "Jenny and I can share a room. We always do."

Mr. Hart turned toward her. "Are you sure? It's not necessary."

"Yes. Please. We'd prefer it, actually."

Something warm flickered in his eyes, but he faced the clerk again. "Just the two then."

The clerk slid one key across the counter. "I'll put the ladies in the room across the hall from yours, Mr. Hart. It's also at the back of the building, away from the street."

Did everyone in town know Mr. Hart? It made sense since the town was probably named for his family and they more than likely visited it regularly. She appreciated the fact that their room wouldn't face the street—not that the town was overly noisy. Just the opposite, from what she'd seen so far, but they had passed a saloon, so cowboys would probably fill the streets come evening.

"Would you ladies like to take a seat in the restaurant while I run your bags upstairs?"

"I can take care of the baggage, Mr. Hart." The clerk stepped out from behind the counter. "You tend to the ladies." The man actually chuckled. "I'm guessin' one of them pretty gals is your bride—or Bowie's. Or maybe both! Now that Crockett's wed his bride, you two's the only ones left unmarried."

Mr. Hart slowly turned toward the man and lifted one brow. He stared at the clerk until the man squirmed.

"Uh. . .sorry, Austin—I mean, Mr. Hart." He snatched a bag and grabbed a second one. "I'll just see to the ladies' baggage."

"There are a couple of trunks out front of my brother's medical office. If you have someone to assist you, I'd appreciate if you'd fetch them. If not, I can help you later, or maybe Travis and I can see to the task."

"Don't you worry about a thing. I'll take care of them."

Mr. Hart gave a brief nod, then held out his elbows to her and Jenny. "Shall we eat, ladies? I imagine the stage food hasn't been the best at times."

"That's an understatement," Jenny mumbled as she tucked her arm through Mr. Hart's.

Rebekah felt odd touching her sister's fiancé, but it would be rude to refuse his kind gesture. "That sounds lovely." She lightly reached her hand around his upper arm, unprepared for the jolt of awareness that bolted through her as she touched his muscular bicep. What was wrong with her? She'd never had such a reaction to a man before.

As they entered the dining room, the clink of silverware and soft buzz of conversation suddenly stopped as all eyes followed them to a table in the back of the room. Mr. Hart held out the chairs for both of them. He selected the chair at the end of the table, so that he sat next to her and Jenny. The room was deathly quiet. Jenny glanced at her, and then around the room.

Mr. Hart blew out a loud breath and stood again. He glanced from table to table, where four groups of people sat. "What's wrong? Y'all never seen twins before?" He swatted his hand in the air. "Go on back to your eating."

Almost as one, people started dining and quietly talking, although they still shot glances their way.

Mr. Hart sat again. "Sorry about all of that. People here are naturally curious about strangers, especially two pretty ones like yourselves."

Rebekah was thankful for the low lighting at the back of the room, which hopefully hid the blush that unwillingly rose to her cheeks at Mr. Hart's compliment. Very rarely had anyone said she was pretty, other than her father.

"I get the feeling there's more to their stares than curiosity about strangers." Jenny pursed her lips.

Mr. Hart fidgeted—she thought—but a heavyset woman hurrying toward them with a plate of biscuits snagged her interest. The woman set the plate on the table.

"Good to see you again, Austin. Welcome to Hartville, ladies. What can I get for y'all today? Our special is pot roast, but we have tamales, ham and beans, and chicken and dumplings too."

"Thanks, Tillie. Ladies, the food here is some of the best you'll ever eat, so don't be shy."

"I'll take the chicken and dumplings, please." Rebekah smiled at the friendly woman.

"I'd like the pot roast. I suppose there's more than just the meat?" Jenny stared at Tillie.

"Most certainly. There's potatoes, carrots, onions, and gravy."

Jenny nodded. "That sounds fine."

Rebekah wished her sister would be kinder. What would they do if Austin Hart decided he didn't want a persnickety wife? By his pursed lips, she'd guess he wasn't too pleased with Jenny at the moment.

He lifted his gaze and smiled. "I'd like some of your delicious tamales, please. And coffee."

"You're in luck. I still have a half dozen or so, even though luncheon is nearly over." She bustled away and into the back room.

Silence stretched uncomfortably, and Rebekah searched for something to say. "Can I ask what a tamale is? I don't believe I've ever heard of that."

Austin's gaze shifted to her. "It's a Mexican dish made of a cornmeal type of crust with seasoned meat in the center, all cooked inside a corn husk. They're quite tasty."

"It sounds delicious. I suppose since you're rather close to Mexico here, that must influence your food and customs some."

He nodded. "That's true, although as you heard from Tillie, we have regular food too."

"Isn't Mexican food spicy hot?" Jenny asked.

He shrugged. "It can be, but not all of it is. Depends on the cook."

Tillie scurried back to the table, carrying two glasses of water and a cup of coffee. Once she'd set them down, she looked at Jenny and then Rebekah. "I also have some sweet tea, if you'd care for a glass."

"I would love some." Rebekah smiled.

Jenny shook her head. "Water is fine for me."

After another minute of silence, Jenny shot her a "help" look, then mouthed, "Say something."

"Um. . .would you tell us about your family, Mr. Hart?"

"Sure, but call me Austin. There are eight *Mr. Harts*, and it will get confusing if you keep calling me that, as well as my brothers."

She felt odd calling him by his Christian name, but nodded, anyway. "Very well, Austin."

He smiled, loosing a mob of butterflies in her stomach. Oh, dear. This was not good.

"As I told Jenny in my letters"—he shot her sister a smile—"I have six brothers, all younger than me. My mother is gone, but Father is still alive and determined to see us all married before he dies. Five of my brothers have complied, but Bowie, the second oldest, and I are still unmarried—but not for long, I hope." He stared intently at Jenny, but her sister ducked her head, her cheeks beaming red.

Hopefully, he wasn't marrying Jenny just to please his father. That sure wasn't the basis of a good marriage.

"Where do all your brothers and wives live?" she asked as she buttered a hot biscuit.

He stirred a spoon of sugar into his coffee. "Most all of them have built houses on their own land, which surrounds the big house." He took a sip from his cup. "Think of the main house and land surrounding it as the hub of a wheel with my brothers' land as the spokes. Sometimes on special occasions, all my brothers and their wives stay overnight at the big house."

"Your home sounds lively."

"It sure can be at times, especially when everyone is there."

Rebekah liked the idea that Jenny would have other women near her, especially women who were newly wed, too—and to Austin's brothers. It would give them all something in common and make her sister feel less uncomfortable and alone. If only she had someone to make *her* feel that way.

A commotion at the front door drew her gaze. Three women glided in, all talking at once. Austin glanced over his shoulder, coughed, then turned his back to them. If she wasn't mistaken, Jenny's tough tanned cowboy had suddenly gone pale.

One lady pointed toward a table, then she glanced their direction and then away. Her eyes instantly flicked back toward them. She spun around and whispered something to the other two, who also stared. Rebekah's grip tightened on her glass as they turned as one in their direction and then hurried across the room, all the time staring with curiosity. They circled the back of Austin's chair as his head lowered.

"Why, Austin Hart. Fancy meeting you here."

CHAPTER 3

*A*s Austin shot to his feet as though a noose tightened around his neck. All his efforts to keep his bride a secret was for naught. He glanced at Jenny and Rebekah, both brimming with curiosity, then forced a smile and turned to face his sisters-in-law. "Afternoon, Coralee. Annie. Emma."

The ladies' gazes all focused on the twins. Austin rued the day his pa came up with the nonsensical requirement for his sons to marry or lose out on their inheritance. Life had been fine at the ranch when it was just the eight of them. No frills, tears, or emotion. Just eight steady, dependable men.

"Aren't you going to introduce us to your. . .um. . .friends?" Coralee, the smallest of the Hart women, batted her brown eyes at him.

Austin cleared his throat, wishing someone would start a shootout in the street so he'd have an excuse to leave. He actually glanced at the door, but honor held his feet in place. "Of course." He held out his hand toward the table. "This is Jenny and Rebekah Evans. They are new to town." He gestured at the trio standing beside him. "And these fine gals are three of my five sisters-in-law. Coralee, Annie, and Emma Hart. All of them are Harts." He realized how dumb that last sentence sounded as soon as the words left his mouth.

He glanced behind him to see the few patrons still in the dining hall were staring at him and the ladies. He glared at Pete and Stubby, two cowboys he knew from the Morgan ranch. Stubby ducked his head, but Pete grinned back at him as if knowing Austin was knee-deep in quicksand and enjoying the fact. The coffee he'd swigged down churned in his gut.

"Of course, we're Harts since we're married to your brothers." Emma's green eyes held a teasing glint as she stepped around him. "It's a pleasure to meet you ladies. I'm Emma, and I'm married to Hays. He's the youngest of the brothers."

Rebekah smiled at Emma, her gaze dropping to Emma's belly. There was no doubt any more that Hays would soon be a father. The shaft of jealousy that shot through him took him by surprise.

"As Austin so kindly stated, I'm Coralee Hart, married to Houston. He's the middle of the seven brothers." She tugged Annie forward. "And this is Annie. She's married to Travis, who's the town doctor."

Rebekah rose. "We're pleased to meet you. Won't you join us?" Her gaze shot to Austin's.

He nodded. There was no way out of this debacle. He just hoped the Hart women didn't scare Jenny off. After the trio sat, he perched on the edge of his chair. He'd never been alone with his sisters-in-law before and wasn't sure what to say. More than likely, they'd never notice if he didn't say a thing, but Jenny might.

Coralee's ringlets bounced as she told Jenny and Rebekah how she'd turned down Houston's first proposal. Austin stared into his empty coffee cup. How was he supposed to get to know his bride with those three magpies chattering?

He could head up a cattle drive with three thousand head of longhorns and boss his six younger brothers into doing a decent day's work, but he had no idea how to corral a passel of frilly skirts and yappy mouths.

"Don't you think so, Austin?"

Uh-oh. "What?"

"Don't you think your brothers are happier since they married?" Annie stared at him with honest hazel eyes.

"I reckon." Happier, yes. But those beguiling women had turned his hardworking brothers into late-sleepin', "yes, dear" nincompoops.

Rebekah stared at him with a concerned gaze while Emma launched into her tale of Hays's signs advertising for a bride and how she'd removed them as fast as he put them up. Rebekah held his gaze for a moment, as if sympathizing with him. He offered her a smile, grateful that someone had noticed he was still there. When she smiled back at him, something hitched in his gut. He looked at Jenny and found her engrossed in Emma's tale.

Tillie bustled toward him, carrying their food. She set each plate down, then glanced at the newcomers. "What can I get y'all?"

"More coffee," Austin said before anyone else started chattering.

Annie shook her head. "I think we should go and allow Austin and his friends to enjoy their meal."

"But..." Coralee closed her mouth as Annie stood and tugged her up.

"I think Annie is right." Emma rose and pushed in her chair. "It was a pleasure meeting you two, and I hope we'll learn more about you next time we meet."

"Oh, and if you should find yourself in need of a doctor," Annie said, "my husband is just down the street during the day. We're still living at the ranch, so he usually heads back around three."

As Annie and Emma tugged Coralee toward the door, she was still talking. "I thought we were staying for a glass of sweet tea."

The room was deathly quiet after the trio left. He glanced behind him, relieved to see they were finally alone.

Rebekah stared at the front window as his sisters-in-law scurried past. "I feel a bit like a cyclone blew through here. It must have been quite a change at your ranch going from seven unmarried men to having five women in your midst."

"No kidding." Austin grinned at Rebekah's comment. "I'm glad that most of them have their own homes now, but our family gatherings are quite an affair. Lots of good food, though."

"Do they all live near you?" Jenny asked.

"Not too far away."

"I'm surprised they didn't ask about us."

"I'm sure they would have if Annie hadn't had the good sense to let us be." He needed to thank her next time he saw her.

Jenny flicked the edge of her napkin with her finger. "Do you think they suspect that we're. . .um. . .talking about getting...married?"

Austin pursued his lips. "More than likely, they're gabbing about that very thing right now." He needed to get Jenny to agree before his pa found out and questioned him. "I wonder if you'd consider going straight to the ranch tomorrow instead of staying in town another day or two as we had planned."

~

*R*ebekah's heart lurched at the same time Jenny's eyes widened. Jenny had hoped to get to know Austin before meeting his family, but it was too late for that now. Those women were sure to tell their husbands about running into Austin and his two ladies. Judging by the stares they'd given them, they were curious.

Having met the women, though, she felt better about leaving her sister here. Surely, they would rally around Jenny and make her feel welcome as Austin's wife.

While they finished their meal, Austin told them his family's history and how they came to settle in Texas. He was fortunate to have such a rich heritage. Rebekah took a bite of her lunch, thinking how different their lives had been. Her father had been a pastor, and the family had moved from one church to another, every few years, until his death two years ago. Her mother and grandparents had all died when she and Jenny were young.

"So do you currently live with your parents?" Austin asked, pulling Rebekah from her thoughts.

Jenny shook her head. "Both of them are gone. We've been living with our aunt, but she recently passed too."

"I'm sorry for your loss."

"Thank you." Jenny looked at Rebekah as if asking if she should share more.

Rebekah gave a tiny shake of her head. Austin didn't need to know that the bank was repossessing their aunt's house at the end of the month, leaving them homeless and desperate enough that they both looked at marriage as the answer to their dilemma.

Tillie put a fat slice of peach pie in front of Austin and had cut the slice of apple in half that she and Jenny were sharing. Rebekah took a bite and closed her eyes. The sweet cinnamon flavor reminded her of the pies her mama used to make. "This is delicious. I'm half tempted to just eat pie for dinner."

Austin smiled. "No one bakes pies as good as Tillie's. It's why I usually eat here whenever I come to town." He took a swig of coffee, then set the cup down. "Speaking of supper, I'm going to let you ladies rest up from your travels this afternoon, and then I'll return around five to escort you to our evening meal. Does that meet with your approval?"

Rebekah almost grinned at his formal tone. Not much about this cowboy seemed formal, but she liked what she'd seen so far. As much as he hadn't wanted his sisters-in-law to join them, he'd been courteous and mannerly to them. She could understand his not wanting three more women to listen to, but something had seemed off. Had he not told them he was expecting a bride? He certainly hadn't mentioned Jenny was his fiancée when he'd introduced them.

Ten minutes later, Austin bid them farewell at the bottom of the stairs, then strode out of the hotel. Inside their room, they both flopped onto their beds.

Jenny yawned as she untied her balmorals. The boots thudded as they hit the floor. "I can't believe how exhausted I am after all the bouncing and rattling around in that uncomfortable stagecoach."

She watched as her sister reclined. "What did you think of Austin?"

"I suppose he's all right. He sure doesn't make my heartbeat speed up."

Rebekah nibbled her lip. Austin Hart made her heart rate take off like it was running a race—more than once. She liked his dark eyes, emanating with kindness, and the deep rumble of his voice. She sighed. She supposed it was a good thing she liked her future brother-in-law, but she didn't dare tell her sister that she'd trade places with her in a second. "Herman doesn't make my heartbeat increase, either, but that's not what's important in a marriage. Austin Hart is a good man. You saw how nicely he treated those Hart women when they barged in on us. I could tell he didn't want them to join us, but he never said an unpleasant word to them."

Jenny giggled. "He did squirm a time or two while they were there."

"You do realize those women will be your new sisters, of sort."

Jenny stared at the ceiling. "I hadn't even thought about that. They came and went so fast, and they talked the whole time. They never even asked about us."

Pulling the pins from her hair, Rebekah thought about the ladies. "You know, I wonder if they didn't realize as soon as they sat down that they shouldn't have intruded. It does make me feel better to know you'll have other women nearby. I'm sure they will help ease your transition and settle in."

Jenny didn't respond. Rebekah removed her shoes, then laid back, her mind still on Austin Hart. If she hadn't already agreed to marry Herman, she might consider staying in Hartville. After all, Austin still had another brother who hadn't yet married. Wouldn't it be wonderful if she and Jenny could marry brothers?

But then she might always be jealous of her sister for snagging Austin first.

~

"Are you certain you don't mind waiting here while Jenny and I take a walk?" Austin hated leaving Rebekah by herself, but he *had* to spend some time alone with Jenny.

"Of course not." She settled on the bench in front of the Hartville Hotel. "I'll just sit here and chaperone from a distance."

"Thank you. We'll stay in sight so you have no need to worry."

Rebekah looked him in the eye. "I don't think I'd ever have to be concerned about Jenny's welfare when she is with you."

Her compliment made Austin's chest swell. "That's mighty kind of you to say so."

She smiled, and for half a heartbeat, he wished she were the one he was escorting about town. He flung that thought from his mind and held out his arm to Jenny. She hesitated for a brief moment before looping hers through his. As they started off, Jenny glanced back at her sister.

"She'll be fine there. No one is likely to bother her." No one except for some of the cowboys who came to town in the evening to visit one of the saloons. He'd keep his eye on Rebekah to make sure nothing happened to her. "What do you think of our little town?"

"I knew the town was named after your family, but I didn't know about the hotel. It must be difficult to always have people staring at you because you're part of a famous family."

"I guess I'm used to it." He probably ought to tell her that the folks in the restaurant had stared because he was with two pretty women—strangers to town—and they were speculating if one of them was to be his bride. Everyone in town and the surrounding counties had probably heard about his pa's ultimatum by now.

He gritted his teeth, wishing his pa had never come up with his cockamamie plan, but then again, without it, he might never have gotten around to marrying. The idea was slowly growing on him, especially with a pretty gal by his side. Still, it would be nice if she'd show more excitement about marrying him. "Can I ask how you decided to become a mail-order bride?"

Jenny's gaze flicked toward his, and if he wasn't mistaken, concern laced her expression. What did she have to fear from him? "As I told you at lunch, my aunt died."

He tried to figure out what that had to do with her choice to marry but he failed to make a connection. He nodded at Ted Arnold passing by in his wagon and noticed how Ted's eyes latched onto Jenny.

After walking past several stores, Jenny looked her sister's way. He did also to make sure she was still all right.

Jenny exhaled a loud sigh. "I don't suppose there's any reason not to tell you the truth."

Austin's heart clenched. One thing he couldn't abide was a liar. Had Jenny not been honest with him about some of the things she wrote in her letters? Why else would she mention telling the truth?

"My aunt didn't have a lot of money." Jenny started wringing her hands and looked away. "In fact, we found out recently that she hadn't made any payments on her mortgage in several months. We got a notice that the bank is repossessing the house at the end of the month."

"And you have nowhere else to go?"

She nodded.

So he was her last option. The thought shouldn't disappoint him since he was being forced to marry, too, but it did. He'd seen the way his brother's wives looked at them with a twinkle in their eyes and unmistakable love. He and Jenny had barely met, but he had somehow unknowingly begun to hope for a woman who could love him. Maybe it would come in time, but if he were a betting man, he'd say his odds were low based on how Jenny was treating him. If only he knew something about wooing a woman. Flirting with one. Asking his younger brothers just seemed wrong.

They came to the end of town and circled around, heading back toward the hotel. Jenny had yet to ask him anything. "Do you have any questions you'd like to ask?"

She shrugged and was quiet a little longer, then she asked, "What's your house like?"

"Big." He chuckled. "There's a parlor as well as a library. Large kitchen with a separate dining room. Lots of bedrooms." He would've mentioned the indoor washroom if it would have been polite conversation.

"Will we live in the big house or have one of our own?"

"When Pa dies, the family house will belong to me, as the oldest son. I can't justify building us another one knowing that."

"I understand."

He studied her face but couldn't tell if she was pleased with his response or not.

Gunfire sounded at the other end of the street, along with loud yelling. Jenny jumped. He pulled her behind him and sought out Rebekah.

CHAPTER 4

*R*ebekah stared at the beautiful sunset. Pink and orange washed over a sea of darkening blue, bathing the clouds in beauty. Gunfire jerked her from the pretty view. Holding her hand against her chest, she looked in the direction of the commotion down the street. Two cowboys raced past her, hooting and firing their guns.

The tension flowed from her. Evenings here were probably similar to those in Arcadia. The local cowboys, excited to be off the ranch, often created a ruckus when they first arrived in town. Most were harmless. The duo charged past Austin and Jenny, still hollering.

Austin pulled to a sudden halt in front of the saloon. He quickly stepped in front of her sister, as if ready to defend her, but his gaze shot straight to Rebekah's. Her heart jolted at his concerned expression. The stiffness in his shoulders deflated, then he took Jenny's arm and started forward again.

"Don't worry about them. They're just happy to be off work and in town."

Rebekah glanced at the dandy who had exited the hotel while she stared at the rabble-rousers. "Cowboys in Missouri often do the same thing."

The dandy smiled. He was nicely dressed in a gray suit, which looked good with his black hair and moustache. "So you're from Missouri. What brings you to Hartville?"

She wasn't used to chatting with strangers, and she wasn't about to spill Austin and Jenny's news. "Oh, this and that."

The stranger glanced in the direction of Austin and Jenny, who had nearly reached the hotel. His head swiveled between her and Jenny several times, almost making her smile.

He twisted the corner of his moustache. "Say, that woman is an exact copy of you."

"That's a good thing since she's my twin sister."

He pushed his bowler hat back, revealing his thick brown hair. "Well, that's not a sight you see every day, especially in such a small town."

Rebekah was used to people commenting about her and Jenny. She watched her sister as Austin talked. Jenny didn't seem any more excited about marrying him now than she had before she met him. What would she do if Jenny changed her mind? Herman had made it clear he wouldn't allow her sister to live with them. If only she had a better option, but there were no jobs available for unmarried women in Arcadia or any of the neighboring towns. Becoming a mail-order bride had been Jenny's only option. If only her sister were willing to marry Herman...As if hearing her thought, Austin looked at her, his brow furrowed. Shame on her for thinking such thoughts. Why couldn't Jenny see what a nice man Austin Hart was?

The stranger tipped his hat to Jenny as she and Austin approached. "Good evening."

Austin nodded. "Austin Hart. And you are?"

"My apologies. I was so flummoxed at seeing two of the same lovely ladies that I fear I was tongue-tied for a moment. Elrod Hewgley. Of the St. Louis Hewgleys."

He said the last part as if it should mean something to her, but it didn't. She'd never known anyone with the last name of Hewgley.

When no one responded, the dandy scratched his chest, looking a bit put off. "My family owns the *St. Louis Ledger*."

Jenny giggled. "Austin Hart of Hartville."

Austin and Mr. Hewgley both cast her sister an odd look. Austin cleared his throat. "I was born on the 7 Heart Ranch, not here in town."

Mr. Hewgley's gaze snapped to Austin's. "You're one of the seven Hart brothers? I heard about your father's deal to marry you all off in a year and came to write a story about it. How about an interview?"

Austin shook his head. "It's getting late, and I need to see the ladies inside." He motioned for Rebekah to enter that hotel, then followed with Jenny still at his side.

Mr. Hewgley trailed behind them. "I can wait until you say good night to the ladies, or we could talk tomorrow, if it's more convenient for you."

Austin stared at the short man. "It's not. My pa isn't in the habit of airing the Harts' private business publicly."

"But—"

"No buts." He gestured toward the stairs, then touched the brim of his hat. "Ladies, I bid you good night."

Rebekah took the hint and started up the stairs, glad her sister followed. As they turned the corner and started walking down the hall to their room, Jenny giggled again.

"What's so funny?" Rebekah had been pleased with how Austin had put that snoopy reporter in his place, both efficiently and fairly politely.

"If one of the Hart women has a son named Hardy, his name would be Hardy Hart." She snickered. "Isn't that funny?"

"Hardy is a perfectly fine name." She was seriously beginning to wonder if her sister's last name would ever be Hart. "Well, how did your talk with Austin go?"

"Boring." Jenny yawned. "He told me about his family history again."

Rebekah unlocked their room and opened the door. "Did you ask him any questions about himself, such as what he likes to read or what he does on the ranch?"

Jenny shook her head as she dropped onto the bed with a loud sigh. "No, I didn't."

"Why not?" Rebekah locked the door and turned up the lamp.

"Because I don't really care what he likes to read or what he does."

Rebekah resisted shaking her head. "Well then, why didn't you ask something you did care about?"

"Because I find him boring. There's nothing I care to know about the man."

Rebekah set her reticule on the desk and sat next to her sister. "Mr. Hart seems like a very nice man. His family is obviously wealthy, and he could take good care of you. That's what's important. You need to think seriously about marrying him."

Jenny bolted up. "But what about my happiness?"

"I feel certain happiness will come once you're married and get to know him. Just look how delightful his sisters-in-law were. They all seemed quite happy."

"But they probably weren't forced to marry."

"I'm not forcing you. You're the one who accepted his marriage offer. And besides, we're out of options."

Jenny flopped on the bed again. "It's all so unfair."

Rebekah couldn't help agreeing. Life for a man was so much easier than for an unmarried woman, but as things looked to her, Jenny was by far getting the better deal.

~

*A*ustin drove the buggy into the ranch yard, anxious to see Jenny's expression. She'd quietly assured him at breakfast this morning that she still planned to marry him although she had requested at least another week to prepare for the wedding. He didn't understand what there was to get ready, but after witnessing five of his sisters-in-law prepare for their weddings, he knew women needed time. Something about Jenny's demeanor nagged at him. Maybe it was that she didn't seem excited to be marrying like the other Hart women had. But then those gals had met their intendeds and weren't marrying a stranger like Jenny was.

Since he hadn't told any of his family about Jenny, he felt the best thing was to take her and Rebekah to the ranch, where they could get to know one another without being questioned constantly by curious townsfolk and reporters, and his family could all meet them before hearing any rumors. Jenny had been fairly quiet on the way to El Regalo, other than asking him what types of books he liked to read and what tasks he did. Hopefully, once she got used to him, she'd talk a bit more. Not that he especially liked chatty women, but he wasn't all that much of a talker himself and hated the thought that their home might always be quiet, except when his family was present. He was used to a noisy household.

He studied his family home. What would the ladies think of it? He turned in the seat so he could see the women, although both had their eyes trained on the house. "Welcome to El Regalo."

"It's incredible!" The back of Austin's seat gave way as Rebekah leaned out of the buggy to get a better look. "My, but you have a lovely home. I never expected to find something so large this far south. I imagine you can see for miles from the top of that tower."

Austin smiled, proud of his family home. "You can see a good ways on clear days. I used to climb up there to get away from my brothers when they were small."

Jenny stared at the house, her eyes wide. Was she as enthralled as her sister? "I knew you had a big house, but I was expecting a wood cabin. Does the stone keep it cool inside during the summer?"

"Definitely cooler than standing out in the sun. Speaking of which, we need to get you ladies inside. It's been a long, hot drive." He climbed out of the buggy, then lifted his hand to Rebekah since she was closest.

As she pressed her hand against his palm, his heart bucked like a mustang with its first rider.

Her blue eyes snapped to his, as if she also felt the odd sensation. "What. . .um. . .does El Regalo mean?"

Austin had never reacted so much to a particular woman before. Sure, he'd been attracted to them, especially when he was younger, but to have such a physical response from just touching a woman... "It means 'the gift.' My pa built this house seventeen years ago for my mother."

"It certainly is magnificent," Jenny said, reminding Austin he still needed to assist her. How could one touch from a woman who wasn't his fiancée turn him into a mindless ninny?

He reached out to Jenny and helped her to the ground. Why did her touch not affect him like her sister's? It made no sense. He yanked two satchels from the boot of the buggy. It didn't matter. This morning, Jenny had assured him she was willing to marry him, and she was the one he intended to wed.

Cody jogged out of the barn and headed toward them. He pushed his hat back and suddenly stopped, staring at the ladies. As if remembering his manners, he pulled off the hat, revealing his blond hair. His blue eyes twinkled, and a slow grin spread across his face. "I do believe I'm seeing double, boss."

Austin glared at the cocky young cowboy. "The buggy and horses belong to the livery in town. Cool them down, then groom and feed them. Tomorrow morning, I'll have someone return them. But first, I need the ladies' baggage unloaded and set on the porch."

Cody nodded. "Will do, boss."

Austin didn't like the way Jenny smiled at the good-looking cowboy. He narrowed his eyes. Was she actually batting her lashes at him, or did she merely have dust in them? The cowboy paused and watched as she strolled around the front of the buggy to join her sister.

He walked up to Austin, his eyes still stuck on Jenny like a burr to a pant leg. "Whoo-wee, boss," he said in a loud whisper. "Is one of them going to be your bride?"

"Never you mind that. Just tend to the horses. Have you seen my pa?"

Cody nodded. "He went for a ride about an hour ago."

Austin hadn't said a word to his pa about sending for a bride. He was looking forward to surprising him for once.

Cody walked away several steps, then swung around. "So who's the other gal for?"

Austin lifted his eyebrows and stared at the ranch hand.

"Oh yeah. The baggage." Cody led the team toward the porch, but his gaze kept flicking back to the women.

Austin sighed. He sure was glad most of his brothers had married so he wouldn't have to battle them for Jenny's heart. They were all younger than him and nice-looking men. If given her choice, Jenny might have picked a different Hart brother. Not liking the direction of his thoughts, he pushed his feet forward. There was no sense in dwelling on the senseless. His brothers *were* married and not a threat, except for Bowie. But he was gone to who knows where.

As Austin stepped onto the porch, he was surprised to realize that he missed his cranky brother. Being the two oldest, he and Bowie had been closer to one another than their other brothers—at least until Bowie changed so much—a result of the war. *Take care of him, Lord. Heal his hurts, and bring him back home when the time is right.*

And now, Austin had a bride to woo...

CHAPTER 5

$\mathcal{J}$enny sucked in a soft gasp, and Rebekah had a hard time keeping her mouth from dropping open as they entered the Hart home. Shiny walnut wainscoting lined the walls, and the oak floors gleamed as the light from the open door reflected on them. Past the vestibule was a wide hallway with several other open doors, although the one to her left was closed. The place was fancier than any building she'd seen in a long while.

"I've never seen anything so lovely." Rebekah turned to Austin.

"Me, either," Jenny murmured.

"My pa doesn't like to do things halfway. That's something you'll learn quickly."

The strawberry-blond woman Rebekah had seen at the hotel bustled around the corner with a half-grown boy at her side. The woman halted suddenly. Confusion flashed across her face for a brief moment, before a smile replaced it. "Welcome to El Regalo, ladies. It's a pleasure to see you again." She turned to the boy. "Robbie, would you please inform Perla that we have guests?"

Rebekah waited for Jenny to respond to the woman's greeting, but her sister's eyes were lifted to the coffered ceiling. "I believe the pleasure is ours. This place is quite impressive."

"It certainly is. I remember being as equally amazed the first time I came here. I'm Annie, in case you didn't remember."

"I'm Rebekah Evans, and this is my sister, Jenny."

"Would you like to have a seat in the parlor while I have some tea prepared?" Annie looked at her for a moment, then shifted her eyes toward Austin.

He stepped around them. "Actually, I'd appreciate if you could show them to the bedroom at the back of the house, if you have time. I'm sure they'd like to get settled and rest before lunch."

"Of course. I'm happy to. I'll also confirm with Josefina that the room is ready for visitors and let Perla know we have two guests."

"Thank you." Austin glanced at Jenny and Rebekah. "I'll go ahead and set these bags in your room, then have the others brought in. Oh, and so you know, Perla is our cook and housekeeper. Josefina, her cousin, helps her at times. Both are like family to us."

Annie smiled. "Ladies, if you'll follow me, I'll show you to your room."

Rebekah could barely keep from staring at the lovely home as she walked down the main hallway, then turned right into a shorter one. Austin exited a room at the end of the short hallway empty-handed.

Annie rapped on a closed door to her right, waited a moment, and then pushed it open. "This is a washroom. You will have it mostly to yourselves, unless we get some rainy days. If so, the men may clean up here before venturing farther into the house, so be sure to knock when the door is closed." She moved past the open door into a room at the back of the house. "This will be your room for as long as you're here. It belonged to Houston before he and Coralee got married and moved into their own place. Remember, you met Coralee in town?"

"Yes, we remember. Thank you so much for your hospitality." Rebekah's gaze roved the big room. A large bed sat on the far wall, with a desk and chair on the right, a settee and wardrobe on the other walls. The décor was a bit masculine, but that made sense once she learned the room had belonged to Austin's brother. She walked over, looking out the windows nearest the desk.

Annie joined her. "The porch runs along this wall and in front of the washroom, so you might want to keep the drapes closed when you're dressing."

"That's good to know." Jenny peeked out the other window overlooking the porch.

Annie moved toward the door. "I'll let you get settled. Please let me or one of the other ladies know if you need anything."

"Thank you for your hospitality." Rebekah smiled. "Are some of the other Hart men and their wives living here?"

"Not at present. The only Harts who live here now are GW, father of the clan, Austin, and Travis and me, although our house is nearly complete, so we'll be moving in a week or two. Bowie, the second oldest, still lives here, but he's currently away. If I'm not around, Perla or Josefina will be happy to assist you."

"Thank you."

Annie nodded and left the room.

Rebekah turned to her sister. "Quite impressive, isn't it? I'll rest well knowing you are living in such a fine place. Can you even imagine having an indoor washroom?"

Jenny shook her head and sat on the wide windowsill. "No, I never dreamed the house would have one—or that the place would be so monstrous. I fear I'll be constantly cleaning."

"Did Austin not tell you about his home?"

"Not that I remember. His pa probably wants his sons to marry so there will be more women to tend this big house."

"I doubt that's true." Rebekah eased onto the edge of the large bed. Annie seemed so eager to leave El Regalo to move into her own home. "I fear if I lived here, I'd never want to leave."

Jenny leaned out the window, looking toward the front of the house.

"What are you doing? Searching for your fiancé already?" She waggled her eyebrows so Jenny would know she was teasing.

"Of course not."

She studied her sister's frowning face as she crossed the room. Jenny had relented and told Austin at breakfast that she would marry him, but something was obviously wrong with her. Was she still having second thoughts, even after their talk last night when Rebekah had listed all of Austin's admirable qualities, while Jenny's main argument was his age?

She pulled the pins from her hair. The breeze blowing through the open window, although still warm, cooled her sweaty head. Men were so fortunate to be able to wear short hair. She liked Austin's tidy, freshly shaved look, so unlike the cowboy who had come out of the barn and ogled her and Jenny. Oh, he was nice looking and much closer to their age, but when he pulled off his hat, his blond hair had fallen into his eyes. Something pinched her stomach, and she looked at her sister. Jenny had taken a very unladylike pose as she bent at the waist and leaned clear out the window.

"Jenny, get back inside before someone sees you. What are you doing?"

"Oh, nothing." She ambled toward the door. "I think I might take a walk instead of resting."

With a loud sigh, Rebekah sat up. "Let me repair my hair, and I'll go with you."

"No. That's not necessary. You go ahead and rest. I'll stay within sight of the house."

"You promise?"

"Of course."

"All right. Maybe you'll run into Austin, and he can show you around your future home."

Jenny scurried through the door. Rebekah reached down to untie her shoe, a bit uneasy. Her sister was up to something, but for the life of her, she couldn't figure out what. Her boots dropped on the floor, and she lay back with a sigh, ready for a short nap.

But she couldn't fully relax. Something nagged at her. Why had Jenny seemed so eager to leave her behind? Rebekah bolted upright as a thought intruded on her rest. Surely, Jenny wasn't looking for that cowboy.

~

*A*ustin leaned against the corral railing and watched Gage take a green broke horse through its rounds. The bay mare still flipped her head up and sidestepped when Gage tried to turn her around to go the other direction, but she had vastly improved from when she'd first taken the saddle. "She's looking good."

Gage reined the mare back toward Austin. "She still thinks she's boss like a brand-new bride, but I'll have her straightened out soon."

Austin grinned. His brothers bent over backward to please their wives. "From what I've seen, the women *are* the bosses."

Gage chuckled. "Don't let Gypsy hear you say that."

"Gypsy?"

Gage pointed at the mare, then looked up and focused on something in the distance. "Looks like GW is ridin' in."

Austin climbed onto the lowest railing, searching in the direction Gage had looked. "Yep. That's Pa." No more putting off telling him about his bride. Pa would be pleased.

If only Jenny seemed less hesitant about marrying him. Was she simply shy, or did she find him less desirable than she'd expected? He rolled his neck as tension knotted his muscles. He pushed away from the corral and strode toward his pa, rubbing his leg that pained him when he was tense or had overdone things. If he'd had his way, they'd have married in town before he brought her home. Maybe her unenthusiastic attitude was due to being a mail-order bride and the fact that she needed to marry. He clung to that idea because the thought that she found him lacking mutilated his manhood, and it meant it would make their marriage all that much harder from the start. He sure hoped his pa wouldn't think less of Jenny because theirs wasn't a love match like his brothers' had been. But then again, some of them had a hard time wrangling their brides at first too. He could only hope and pray his marriage turned out as well as theirs had.

GW Hart reined his big horse to a halt and grinned. "Glad to see you back, son. Where you been?"

"I had some business in town to tend to."

His pa's moustache danced. "It wouldn't have anything to do with getting a bride, would it?"

Austin's mouth fell open, and he watched the big man dismount. "How did you know?"

Pa shook his head, grinning. "Haven't you learned that you can't outsmart me yet?"

It had to have been Annie, unless Coralee or Emma had been to the big house since they were in town.

Pa slapped him on the shoulder. "I've known for a while that you were writing to a woman."

"How? I never told anyone."

His father chuckled. "I have my ways."

He sure did. Austin thought he'd done well to keep Jenny a secret.

"When do I get to meet my next daughter-in-law?" Pa squinted his eyes and twisted the end of his moustache. "You're not already hitched, are you?"

Austin shook his head. "No, sir. Jenny just got into town yesterday, and she wanted some time to get to know me and to prepare for the wedding."

He led his horse toward the barn, and Austin followed. "Have you set a date? We'll need to let folks know."

There went his hopes for a quiet wedding "Not yet, but I don't expect it will be too long. Her sister is here, too, so she can stand up with Jenny."

"Good. I look forward to meeting her also. That will just leave Bowie without a bride."

Austin found it hard to see his troubled brother falling in love. Too bad Rebekah was already engaged. Maybe she and Bowie could have gotten hitched. It would be nice for Jenny to have her close. He didn't like the idea of Rebekah leaving on the stage and never seeing her again. It was sure to make Jenny even more withdrawn.

"So...are they here or in town?" Pa walked his horse toward the barn, and Austin joined him.

"They're here." Feminine laughter from inside the barn made Austin's gut tighten. As he stepped inside, Jenny was standing a few feet away from Cody.

Pa frowned and glanced at him. "How come he has his woman here?"

Austin swallowed the knot clogging his throat. "She's not *his* woman —she's mine."

Jenny and Cody glanced up at the same time. Cody had the good sense to look ashamed, but Jenny—she just looked caught.

She smiled brightly and moved toward him. "There you are. I couldn't rest, so I decided to go for a walk. I thought I might find you here, but when I first came into the barn..." She held her hand to her throat and glanced behind her into the shadows, visibly swallowed, then turned back. "A mangy dog nearly attacked me and frightened me out of my wits. Cody chased it off and was nice enough to show me around."

Austin stared at the young ranch hand. Was the tale true or not? Cody couldn't be more than a year or two older than Jenny, and he certainly was more of a charmer than Austin. Had Cody caught Jenny's eye? He sure didn't want to think such a thing was true.

"I explained to Miss Evans about how Clara don't like strangers, but that she ain't dangerous." Cody hurried toward them. "Let me take care of your horse, boss." He held out his hand, and Austin's father passed him the reins, scowling.

"Bowie should've taken that dog with him too." Pa turned to him. "So are you going to introduce us?"

Austin moved toward Jenny. "Of course. Jenny, this is my father, George Washington Hart. Pa, this is Jenny Evans, my fiancée." At least, he hoped she still was.

Jenny's smile seemed a bit forced, but then, most folks were intimidated when they met GW for the first time. At 6'4" and broad shouldered, he was taller and more imposing than most men.

"I'm pleased to meet you, sir." Jenny surprised him by giving his pa a quick curtsy.

"The pleasure is all mine, Miss Evans. I hope you realize that my oldest son is the pick of the litter and will make you a fine husband."

Austin had heard that line more than once in reference to his brothers. so he didn't put much stock in it.

"Thank you, Mr. Hart. I haven't met any of your other sons, but I'm sure I'll agree with you." She smiled at Austin.

He tried to let go of the nagging feeling that something was wrong, but he couldn't quite do it. "I thought you'd be tired from the ride out here."

"I wanted to get more of a look at my new home, but now that I have, I think I will rest for a bit."

Pa held out his arm. "Allow an old coot the pleasure of walking you into the house."

"Thank you, sir." Jenny lightly took hold of his father's arm, and they started forward.

She glanced back, but instead of looking at Austin, her gaze shot past him. He turned to see Cody staring at her. He tightened his fists. Were things as innocent as Jenny would like him to believe, or was something else going on here?

∾

*a*fter watching the lovely sunset, Rebekah leaned against the porch railing, enjoying the coolness of the evening. Crickets serenaded her, but other than the lowing of a cow or an occasional horse whinny, all was quiet. She liked the slower pace of life here on the ranch and the peaceful evenings free of saloon music and men's laughter she could hear from her home on nights when the window was up. But there was also something scary about it.

So much unknown. And just beyond the safety of the porch, who knew what lingered in the darkness? Looking up, she smiled at the thousands of stars. "So pretty."

"It is, isn't it?"

Rebekah jumped and stared into the dark. "Who's there?"

"It's me, Austin." He moved closer. "Sorry if I frightened you...uh... Jenny?"

"No. It's Rebekah." She laid her hand against her racing heart. "What are you doing out here?" She could barely make out his image in the darkness.

"Checking for anything out of the ordinary before I turn in. Old habit, I suppose. What are you doing out here?"

"I couldn't sleep." She chuckled. "I probably should warn you that when Jenny first goes to sleep, she tends to snore." As soon as she said that, she wished she could snatch back the words. Talking with a man about her sister's sleeping habits was highly improper, even if that man was Jenny's fiancé. In fact, standing in the dark and talking to a man was just as inappropriate, but something held her in place.

Austin passed by in front of her on the other side of the railing, and then boots clunked on the wooden steps. "I'm glad to see someone using this side porch. It's been a while. Would you mind if I brought a lantern out?"

"Not at all."

"Be right back."

The door creaked softly as he stepped into the house. He returned quickly, holding the lantern Josefina had left burning on the hall table for her and Jenny to use if they needed to go to the washroom during the night. He set it on a small table that stood next to one of the two rocking chairs.

"Thank you." She should probably go inside but felt odd saying so now that he'd brought out the lantern.

"What did you think about my family? You're really fortunate we had a small group tonight."

"They're very nice. Annie has been quite gracious and very helpful in getting us settled. Travis seems nice, and your father was very gracious too."

A smirk danced on Austin's lips. "He didn't scare you?"

"He certainly is a big man, but I saw kindness in his eyes."

Austin's feet shifted. "Did Jenny have anything to say about them?"

"I think she likes them, but we didn't discuss them. As you know, Jenny retired to our room early. She wasn't able to rest this afternoon and was tired."

He thumped his fingers against the railing. "I have to admit, I'm having a hard time figuring her out. In the three letters I received from her, she seemed so lively, but she seems a different person here."

"I think she's missing home some. We've lived our whole lives in Missouri, and she had to leave her friends." What few she still had after the bad choices she'd made.

"That's understandable."

"How would you feel if you had to leave El Regalo, knowing you might never return?"

His fingers brushed across his chin, making a rasping sound she found intriguing. "I see your point. I've been on several cattle drives that last a couple of months, as well as business trips to purchase new stock, but I've always known I'd be coming home again. I can't imagine how awful I'd feel if I knew I'd never see my home again."

She took a step toward him and almost reached out before closing her hand and keeping it at her side. "Please give her time. She only met you yesterday. I think the idea of getting married needs to soak into her mind. I don't think it seemed real until she met you."

"I understand, but I would have thought she'd already made up her mind. That was the point in writing letters."

What could she say? She wanted to defend her sister, but more and more, she didn't want to see Austin hurt. He was a good man. She could tell Travis looked up to him as his older brother. And Jenny could be unpredictable.

"I'll be patient, but I have to be honest. I have a deadline to get married."

"What?" Rebekah stared at him. What in the world did that mean?

He rubbed his jaw again, and she noticed he seemed to favor one leg, even wincing when he put his full weight on it.

"I should have told Jenny before she came, but I was afraid she'd stop writing me." He blew out a loud sigh. "Pa gave all of us an ultimatum—get married by the end of this year or lose our inheritance."

A loud gasp slipped out before Rebekah could stop it. "Why would he do such a thing?"

Austin scratched his ear and stared out into the darkness. "I honestly don't know." He faced her again, looking serious. "I suppose he made the ultimatum because he wants to see his sons married and maybe even enjoy some grandchildren soon. He isn't getting any younger. I'll admit, we were all upset at first—well, maybe all but Hays. The crazy thing is that it's turned out better than any of us thought—at least for those who are married."

And he was the eldest brother and still not married. No wonder he felt the pressure to find a wife.

"It's even a bit worse for me than the others, but I stand to inherit this house and the surrounding lands, as well as another nice section of land."

She couldn't help reaching out and touching his arm. "Surely, your father wouldn't turn you away simply because you didn't marry."

"I can't take that chance. This land—this family—is all I have."

"That's not true."

He stared down at her, frowning. "I've lived my whole life here. I've never wanted to be anywhere else."

"I understand. But this isn't all you have. You have the knowledge of being a rancher, and no matter where you end up, that will serve you well. From what I've seen, you're a good, honorable man, and whether you live here or somewhere else, that won't change."

Her gaze locked with his, and her heartbeat escalated. What was she doing out her alone with Jenny's fiancé? She stepped back. "I...uh... should probably go inside."

"Let me tell Jenny about the ultimatum, if you will. She should know before we marry."

And Jenny had something she needed to tell him too. "I won't say anything. I promise."

"Good night, Rebekah."

"Good night." She rushed inside, her heart racing. It wasn't until she was back in her room that she realized she'd left the lantern outside. A light under the door told her Austin had returned it to the table. She felt her way around the room and dropped down into the chair, thinking of her conversation with Austin. Why had he told *her* about the ultimatum? Did he feel as comfortable talking with her as she did him?

She laid her head back, tears gathering in her eyes. Over the years, there had been many times she and Jenny had swapped places to play a prank on someone. For the first time in her life, she wished she could change places with her sister permanently.

CHAPTER 6

*A*fter a delicious breakfast, Rebekah followed Jenny back to their room. "I'm excited to see Annie's house, aren't you?"

Jenny strode to the window overlooking the porch and stared out. "I don't think I'll go. I didn't sleep well last night, and I'm still tired from traveling. I was thinking I'd stay here and repair the hem on my petticoat and maybe read for a while."

Rebekah pursed her lips. Why did Jenny have to be such a spoil-sport? "Annie has been so hospitable. I hate to disappoint her. It was very gracious of her to invite us to see her new house." When Jenny didn't respond, she sat down on the edge of the bed, sighing. She'd been looking forward to spending a little time with her new friend, but on the other hand, she and Jenny didn't have much more time together. As soon as her sister was married, she needed to return home. "Don't you think it would be a good idea to get to know her since you two will be related once you marry Austin?"

Jenny crossed her arms and turned. "I have all the time in the world to get to know the Hart women. Right now, I'm tired." Yawning, she dropped onto the edge of the chair, hiked up her skirt, and reached down to untie her balmorals.

With a loud sigh, Rebekah rose. "Very well. I'll tell her that we can't go."

"What?" Jenny's head jerked up. "You don't need to stay with me. I'll be sleeping for a while and then reading—or sewing. I'll be perfectly fine by myself."

"You know Austin won't return until early this afternoon."

"I heard him across the breakfast table just as well as you. He said something about checking on some horses. I might as well get used to being by myself. I imagine it will happen a lot."

Jenny didn't look too happy about the prospect of her lonely future. Maybe her children with Austin would help fill the void—if they had any. Rebekah studied her sister as she removed her shoes and felt a bit of remorse for Austin. Though Jenny could be obstinate and selfish, Rebekah loved her dearly. But her growing admiration for Austin made her wish her sister was more hospitable and helpful. How would he ever fall in love with Jenny the way she'd been acting?

If he already knew about her past and had forgiven it, then he should be able to face any problem with his new wife. But had Jenny told him? Rebekah was hesitant to bring up the topic that had been on her mind since she met Austin, but she had to know. "I don't suppose you've told him about...you know."

Horror engulfed her sister's face. "No! Of course not."

"It's only fair that he knows before you marry."

Jenny jumped to her feet, turning her back. "How do you suggest I broach such a dreadful subject? How do I tell the man I'm engaged to that I'm not a...virgin?"

Rebekah longed to cross the room and comfort her sister. "I know it's difficult, but it needs to be done, and the sooner it is, the better things will be between you. I'm sure you'll feel better, and I think Austin will respect you for telling him."

"If he doesn't send us packing."

Having heard about his father's ultimatum to marry, she doubted Austin do such a thing, but men could be stubborn about marrying a pure woman. At least Jenny wasn't with child. Things seemed so unfair at times that a man could carouse and spend time with bawdyhouse women and then were slapped on the back and congratulated. But when a man took advantage of a naïve woman, it was always the woman who paid the price, no matter the circumstances.

Rebekah hated leaving her sister alone after raising such a heavy topic, but sometimes with Jenny, it was the best thing. A nap might well put her in better spirits, and being by herself would give her time to compose her thoughts about sharing her dreadful news with Austin. At least Rebekah hoped it would. She muttered a quick prayer for both of them and that Austin would be forgiving and not terribly hurt by Jenny's revelation.

"You're certain you want to stay?"

Jenny nodded.

"All right, then. Annie said we'd be back in time for lunch."

Jenny smiled and waved. "Enjoy your ride."

"I will. You have a good rest." Rebekah picked up her bonnet and closed the door, hating that she felt glad to have a few minutes away from her sister. All too soon, many miles would separate them for the first time ever, and then she'd sorely miss Jenny.

Ten minutes later, she climbed into the buggy with Annie. "I'm sorry Jenny didn't feel up to coming."

Annie gathered the reins and smiled. "Think nothing of it. Our Texas heat can be hard to get used to. And to be honest, it's good for Jenny to be comfortable staying in the big house by herself since Austin will be out working most days. Not that she's totally alone with Perla and Josefina there."

"I have to admit that it pricked my heart a bit that Jenny didn't want to spend what little time we have left together."

Annie patted her hand. "That's understandable. It may take some adjustment, but I think your sister will love it here once she's lived at the ranch a while. The Hart men may come across as large and intimidating, but deep on the inside, they have hearts as big as all of Texas."

"I thought Robbie was going to join us today."

"When GW heard of our plans, he invited Robbie to go with him and Austin. I don't think I've seen such a big smile on my son's face since we arrived here."

"It's nice of the men to include him." She was learning that the Hart brothers were conscientious men. They had to be, to be willing to take a boy with them for the day. But then Mr. Hart had probably taken his young sons with him to work the ranch. How else would they know what to do now?

Once they were clear of the ranch, wildflowers dotted the landscape even though it was autumn. A roadrunner dashed across the road up ahead of them.

"It's a lot drier here, and there aren't nearly as many trees as in Missouri," Rebekah said, "but there's a beauty all its own."

"Except for trees like the mesquite, most tend to clump around the creeks and rivers. You should see it in the spring when the bluebonnets are in bloom. Whole fields of delft blue. It's breathtaking."

"I can't even imagine that. I would love to see them one day. Maybe I can return for a visit then." Doubtful Herman would be in favor of her taking another trip so soon, though. Being this far away from him made her wish things were different. If only she could stay.

"Jenny would love that, I'm sure."

"Could you tell me a little about Austin? He seems like an honorable man, but Jenny hasn't told me all that much about him."

Annie nibbled her lower lip for a moment. "Since Travis and I have lived at El Regalo for a few months, I've gotten to know him and Bowie better than the others, but I still don't know them well. I can tell you that all of his brothers look up to him and respect him. He tends to be quiet unless he's belting orders or talking about the ranch."

"He was quite kind and generous to us when we arrived in town. He even offered to get me my own room at the hotel."

"The Hart men are all that way." Annie clucked to the horse and slapped the reins against the horse's back, and it started trotting.

The breeze helped cool Rebekah. "I'm grateful the canopy blocks the sun."

"It takes some time to get used to the warmer weather here, but the Harts are far better off than most folks. The thick walls of El Regalo keep the inside cooler."

"I noticed that. I guess you don't get snow down here."

"No. Almost never." Annie smiled. "Can I ask what your plans are? Have you considered moving to this part of the country so you can be close to your sister?"

Rebekah watched a flock of geese overhead. "I'll return to Missouri where I'm to be married."

"Oh! Congratulations."

"Thank you."

"Is your future husband as handsome as Austin?" Annie wiggled her eyebrows in a teasing manner.

"Um. . .no." She thought of Herman's overweight figure and pale complexion. "Herman is a bank clerk."

"That's honorable employment."

Rebekah started giggling. "I think that's probably one of the few positive things you could have said about Herman." That and he was one of the few men willing to marry her after word of what Jenny had done had spread through town.

Annie cast her a serious look, then focused on the road again. "I've been around quite a few women in love and newlyweds lately, I don't sense the same excitement in you. I may be poking my nose where it doesn't belong, but can I ask why you're marrying him? Do you actually love him?"

"To be honest, I don't." Rebekah stared at the landscape, blinking as the wind whipped tears in her eyes. "It's sad to say, but there are few options for women to earn an income, and my sister and I will be homeless once the bank reposes our recently deceased aunt's house, where we've been living. Our only choice was to marry."

"I'm sorry for your loss." Annie turned in the seat. "But you have other options now. Come and live here. Half of the big house is empty. I'm certain GW and Austin wouldn't mind. There's plenty of room—and lots of men in Texas who'd love a pretty wife like you."

The thought of not marrying Herman was more pleasing than she could express. It relaxed the tension in her stomach and gave her a sense of freedom that she needed to consider. Could she live here? Be around Austin and Jenny every day? The thought of seeing her sister's handsome husband each day made her heart leap.

Shamed, she glanced down to her lap. That was her answer. Her senseless attraction to Austin was inexcusable.

There was no hope she could stay.

~

*A*ustin rode into the ranch yard alongside Pa, who rode double with Robbie, ready for a cool drink and a warm meal. He smiled at the boy. He'd done better today than Austin had expected, and the gleam had never left his eyes, in spite of the warm sun, dust, and long day.

"Isn't that your fiancée at the corral?" Pa pursed his lips and frowned.

Austin's gaze shot to the corral, where one of the twins was watching Cody ride a green-broke mare. "I can't say for sure, but I think it's Jenny."

Pa shook his head. "She needs to learn not to venture out to the corral and barn without an escort. Most of the men we hire are reliable sorts, but you can never know for sure how they'll respond when a pretty gal is around. It can do strange things to a man's mind."

"I'll have another talk with her." He was fairly certain it was Jenny since Rebekah would have better sense than to be so far from the house alone.

She must have heard them because she turned and waved. Her smile looked a bit forced, but then maybe it was the sun in his eyes. Had she been waiting for him? The thought stirred something in his gut that had laid dormant for a long while.

"There you are." She pushed away from the corral railing and walked toward him. "I wondered when you'd get back."

Pa shot a look at Austin that warned him to be cautious. But of what? Surely, he wasn't warning him of his future wife. Not for the first time, he wondered if he'd done the wrong thing in writing for a mail-order bride. But then he wouldn't be in this mess at all if not for his pa's ultimatum.

In front of the barn, Pa swung Robbie to the ground and dismounted. Austin slid down as Jenny approached him. Just past her, Cody was watching them. When Austin's gaze collided with his, he jerked away and turned the horse in the other direction.

"So how were the horses?"

"Fine."

Jenny glanced over shoulder, then back at him. "How many do you have?"

"Several hundred."

"Hundred?" Her blue eyes widened. "Why so many? I thought you raised cattle."

Gage walked out of the barn. "Can I take your horse?"

Austin nodded. "Yes. Thank you." He passed the reins to the wrangler.

He offered Jenny his elbow. "We need lots of horses to herd the cattle and patrol the ranch. It's a big place, and fresh horses are a necessity."

"I see. The only time I rode a horse was when I was about five."

He stopped and stared down, surprised at her comment. But then she'd lived in a town, and there probably hadn't been much need to ride. "We'll have to remedy that." When her eyes grew big again, he chuckled.

"Ma! I rode Grandpa's horse all day!"

"Oh, look. There's Rebekah and Annie." Jenny tugged away and hurried toward her sister.

Austin shouldn't feel jealous about her wanting to be with Rebekah, but he did. For the first time, they were actually talking a bit. He walked toward the buggy. Why hadn't Jenny gone with the women? Had she been down at the corral for long?

He blew out a sigh. Being suspicious of his fiancée was hardly the right way to start out a long-term relationship. He glanced up at the sky. *I could use some help, Lord. I realize I sent for Jenny without consulting You first. I probably deserve to have some problems, but I never expected things to be so difficult. Show me how to win the heart of my bride and to make her happy.*

Watching Robbie bounce alongside the buggy as he relayed the events of the day brought a smile to Austin's face. What would it be like when his brothers started having young'uns? He glanced at Jenny. Would they have children? He hoped so, but that possibility seemed far away at the moment.

Austin thought about heading to the house, but the polite thing would be to escort the women. Jenny was yakking with Rebekah, while Annie listened to her son. Rebekah suddenly looked up as if she knew he were there and smiled. She gave a little wave, much as Jenny had done, but her gesture made him smile. He reached up and tipped his hat to her, realizing he hadn't done the same for Jenny.

He strode toward the house. Why did he feel something warm when Rebekah looked at him but felt as if a cold bucket of water had been thrown on him when he was with Jenny? It wasn't right, and he didn't like the guilt he felt because of it, but what was he to do? He'd made a commitment to Jenny, and he intended to honor it.

CHAPTER 7

*R*ebekah turned over in bed and glanced at the window. She blew out a loud breath at not seeing any light yet. She had dozed on and off, restless for some unknown reason. Last night's supper had gone well, with Robbie regaling them on his exciting day. Travis and Annie had looked so proud and happy.

She had been thrilled when she returned from Annie's house to see Austin and Jenny arm in arm, but then her sister had left him as soon as she'd noticed them. She was having a hard time not feeling sorry for the big man. She knew he was tough, but she'd also seen his insecurities when he looked at her sister. He was having doubts about marrying Jenny.

Her heart quaked at the thought, and she bolted upright. What if he decided not to marry Jenny? What would they do then? It was far better for her sister to not return to Arcadia given the circumstances and the disparaging way people looked at her. There was only one thing to be done—she had to make Austin see Jenny's good points and convince him to marry her.

So why was her heart not in the task?

Because Austin deserved better.

What he deserved was a woman who could love him. She could no more trick him into marrying her sister than she could marry him herself. She glanced at the lump of blankets next to her. Her heart bucked again. Why didn't she hear Jenny's breathing?

She slid her hand over to the blankets and gently pressed down. They gave way. Where in the world was her sister?

Rebekah slid off the edge of the big bed, crossed the room, and reached for the window. Someone had drawn the drapes. As she pulled them open, the light of dawn filtered in so that she could see. Jenny was not in their room. She must be in the washroom.

She hurried out the bedroom door and paused in the hall. The lamp glowed dimly from the table, and the washroom door was open. Had Jenny gotten hungry and gone to the kitchen for food?

She should dress before venturing farther into the house, but she felt a strange sense of urgency. If only she'd brought her bed jacket, but she'd wanted to travel light and hadn't thought she'd need one. The cool flooring chilled her feet. While the days were still quite warm, the nights could be frigid. The big house seemed more intimidating in the dark of early morning, but she continued. She stepped into the kitchen, blinking at the brightness of the lanterns. A man stood at the window with his back to her—Austin.

Rebekah froze, realizing the impropriety of her state of undress. Jenny obviously wasn't here. She backed away, hoping to make her escape.

Austin suddenly turned. His eyes widened as he stared at her. And stared.

Her heart fluttered. "I. . .uh. . ." She folded her arms over her chest.

"Sorry." He spun around. "Did you need something?"

"I was looking for Jenny. Have you seen her?"

He shook his head. "Not today." He pivoted again, his brow furrowed. "I'm sure she's here somewhere. It's an easy place to get lost in."

His expression conveyed his concern more than his reply had. Did he worry that Jenny had gone out for another stroll by herself?

She couldn't see her sister doing that so early in the morning. "I suppose that's true. I'll check the parlor."

"I'll take a walk around and see if she might be outside."

"I would appreciate that." She whirled around, knowing her cheeks were blazing.

The parlor was empty, as she'd feared it would be. She knocked on the door to the library, and when no one answered, she peered into the dark room. "Jenny?" When she got no answer, she quickly walked through the empty room, then checked the dining room before heading back to her bedroom.

Worry nibbled at her composure. Where could her sister be?

Rebekah grabbed the lamp off the hall table, set it on the desk in the bedroom, and turned it up. She gasped at the sight of the disheveled room. With the room dark when she first got up, she hadn't noticed the disorder on Jenny's side. One of the quilts was on the floor, as were several pieces of Jenny's undergarments. She hurried to the wardrobe and found Jenny's side mostly empty. Horrified, Rebekah glanced down. Jenny's satchel was gone. What had her sister done?

~

*A*ustin paced around the house in the pale light of dawn, not surprised to find the porches vacant at such an early hour. Occasionally, he and Pa had their coffee on the front one to watch the sunrise and talk about what they needed to accomplish that day, but it had been a long while since they had done that.

The barn was barely visible. Pinks and oranges lined the skyline to the east, and horses and cattle grazed quietly on the hillside, but the scene failed to inspire him today. He felt a sense of urgency, but he wasn't sure why. He finished his trek around the house and walked to the front again. Songbirds serenaded him, and the cool air helped him to wake up. He always liked this time of day.

He turned to go back into the house just as Clara barked at him. He paused, gazing at Bowie's dog. Clara tended to shy away from the rest of them, so it was odd she'd bark at him. She'd never been overly friendly to him, but neither had she been mean. The men usually locked her in the barn at night, so someone must be down there already. Surely, Jenny hadn't gone back to the barn after his admonishing her not to go alone.

Clara barked again. Gritting his teeth, he strode toward the barn, ready to confront his bride. He had a good mind to throw her over his shoulder, haul her back to town, and put her on the first stage to arrive. That would show her who was boss.

Shaking his head, he chuckled. Who was he kidding? His brothers may think they ruled their roost, but he'd seen the way they capitulated to their wives. *Yes, dear. Whatever you want, sweetheart.*

At the barn door, Clara eyed him as if asking what had taken so long, and then she disappeared inside. Bowie's cattle dog was getting fat and lazy in his absence. Austin pushed the door all the way open to allow in some light, and listened. He couldn't see all the way to the end of the stalls, but if anyone had been working here, the lanterns would be lit. Other than a soft whicker and the stomp of horses eager for their breakfast, everything sounded normal. So what was up with Clara? It wasn't like her to bark for no reason.

Instead of heading back to the house, he strode over to the bunkhouse and walked inside. Several pairs of eyes turned his way from men in different states of dress.

Gage hitched up his suspenders and walked toward him. "Somethin' wrong, boss?"

One of the beds was empty. "Anyone seen Cody?"

The men glanced at one another and shook their heads. Austin turned to leave.

"Boss." Brody, a recently hired cowboy, sat up in his bed. "I went to the outhouse in the middle of the night and saw him. He was mounted and leading another horse. Said you'd sent him to town."

Austin's gut clenched. "What time was it?"

Brody scratched at his chest and sat up. "I reckon maybe one or two. I thought it was odd you'd send him out at that hour, but I don't question your orders."

Austin nodded. "I appreciate the information."

As he left the bunkhouse and headed back to the barn, he didn't like where his thoughts were headed, but as long as he'd been alive, two plus two had equaled four. In the barn, he lit a lantern and walked down the alley, checking each stall. Cody's bay was gone, as well as a gray mare that was one of their more gentle horses. He returned the lantern to its peg and stormed out of the barn. He dreaded telling Rebekah what he feared.

The front door opened, and she rushed out, staring at him. She hurried down the steps and met him halfway across the yard. "Did you find her? Perla and Josefina checked the whole upstairs, and I checked the lower floor. Jenny is nowhere to be found."

Gritting his teeth, Austin stared at the woman he'd started to care for. He hated to hurt her. Hated to give her such awful news, but she deserved the truth. "I'm afraid it appears that your sister ran away with one of my cowhands."

~

*R*ebekah gasped, her mind struggling to understand. "No! Surely not. Why do you suspect that?"

Austin narrowed his gaze, staring her straight in the eye. "I checked in the bunkhouse, and Cody is gone. One of my men said he saw him mounted and leading another horse around one or two this morning. It makes sense. I caught Jenny down near the barn talking to Cody twice." He ducked his head, regret pressing his lips into a firm line.

"I didn't want to believe it, but I think you're right. Most of Jenny's clothes are gone. I felt sure she couldn't have gotten far on foot, but if she had help, she could be anywhere by now." She reached out to touch his arm. "I'm so sorry, Austin. I never would have thought Jenny would do such a foolhardy thing."

He drew in a deep breath. "I had my suspicions that she wasn't happy after we met." He rubbed a hand across the back of his neck. "But I never expected she'd run away. It's hard to think I wasn't man enough to keep her."

"Don't say that!" She wasn't about to let him think this was his fault. "This is all on Jenny. She made a commitment to you, then broke it. That's unconscionable. Don't you dare think this is your fault."

He stared at her as if wanting to believe her. She could tell he was blaming himself and needed to hear more.

"You're a kind, generous man, Austin. Most women would be honored to be your wife."

A muscle in his jaw ticked, and he stared off. "But not Jenny."

She squeezed his arm. "I don't think Jenny's heart was ever in getting married—no matter who the groom was. Perhaps I pushed her too hard, but neither of us had a choice. With the bank repossessing our aunt's home, we'll be out on the street by the end of the month. We had no source of income, and there is precious little paying work for decent women. Our only choice was to marry." She didn't mention the fact that she'd sold the last of her aunt's furniture to fund her trip to Texas and had just barely enough to get back to Missouri. "You needed a wife fast, and Jenny needed to marry..."

She sighed. "I've never truly known what Jenny thought. In some ways, we were close, but vastly different in others. She's more spirited and independent." More stubborn and picky. Rebekah sighed, her heart breaking. Where was her sister? Was she safe?

Austin reached out to grip her shoulder, his gaze serious. "This isn't your fault either. So don't try to take the blame."

She nodded, but she still couldn't help wonder if she'd done her best to help her sister after their mother died. *Please, God, keep her safe.* "What do we do now?"

"I'll gather up the men, and we'll go after her."

"I want to go too."

Austin's lips pursed as he shook his head. "You'll slow us down. You don't know how to ride astride, do you?"

"I rode a few times when I was a girl. Please, Austin."

He took hold of her hands, sending delicious warmth scurrying up her arms, across her shoulders, and settling in the pit of her stomach. "I know you want to help, but our best chance to catch up with Jenny is to ride fast. We can't do that if you go."

She frowned but nodded. He was right, even if she didn't want to admit it. "When you find Jenny, are you going to bring her back?"

He shrugged. "I can't force her to return. She's a grown woman and able to make her own choices." He gazed past her, then motioned to someone, and she turned to see several of the ranch hands exiting the barn. One jogged up to Austin.

"What do you need us to do, boss?"

"We believe Miss Evans's sister rode off with Cody. We need to find them. Get the other men, tend to the most basic chores, grab some food, and then meet me at the house in say. . .twenty minutes."

"Right, boss." The man's expression darkened as he looked at her. "Sorry about your sister, ma'am."

"Thank you." She watched him trot back to the other men, say something, and they scattered in different directions.

"I need to eat, then get going." He started toward the house, and she hurried to keep up.

"I'll admit, I'm worried about my sister. This isn't the first time Jenny made a bad choice." But it was the first time she'd run off. She bit the inside of her cheek and looked at Austin for a moment. "Surely, you don't want to marry her after this."

He flicked a sideways glance at her. "I can't think of that now. Besides the fact Jenny ran off, Cody stole two of my horses, and in Texas, that's a hanging offense."

She hated to think of any man hanging, especially someone her sister might care for. Suddenly, her heart bucked, and she stared at Austin.

"What?"

"What about Jenny? Could she also hang?"

Austin's expression softened. "Not too likely. Texas hasn't hanged many women."

"But she stole your horse..."

"Brody said he saw Cody alone with the two horses, so in my book, he's the guilty party. I imagine Cody sweet-talked her into going with him."

"I'm so sorry for all the trouble we've caused your family."

"I'm the one who wrote to your sister first."

Rebekah stared out at the peaceful hillside where cattle and several horses grazed. How could Jenny have run off with that man when she was already committed to marry Austin? It cut her to the quick to think Jenny might have fallen for a man who had no qualms about stealing from the men who employed him. It sure didn't speak much to his character. Did Jenny truly have feelings for Cody, or was he just a way to get her out of marrying Austin?

She shook her head. What a fool her sister was to choose a poor cowboy thief over an honorable man like Austin. Her heart broke for him. It broke for herself because she didn't know if she'd ever see her sister again. She'd come to accept leaving her sister here, knowing she'd be safe and well cared for, but having Jenny riding off into the unknown was something else altogether different. What would become of her sister? Her hands quivered, and tears burned her eyes.

Austin stopped at the bottom of the porch steps and turned to her. "Hey, now, tears won't help a thing." His palm slid down her arm to grasp her hand. "Don't fret. I'll do my best to find her."

"Thank you."

The door opened, and Travis and Annie rushed out. "Perla told us that Jenny is missing."

Austin nodded. "*Gone* is more like it. She packed some things and rode out with Cody—we think."

"Cody! Why, that charlatan..." Travis's dark eyes flashed.

"Yep. He's not getting away."

A muscle ticked in Travis's jaw. "I can check in town since I have to go to my office, and I can keep my eye out for them in case they show up later."

"I'll ride with you. I want to see if they got on the stage." Austin's voice faded as the men entered the house.

Annie's sad expression almost made Rebekah cry. "I'm really sorry, Rebekah."

"I can't but help feel this is my fault."

"Why would you think that? Jenny is well old enough to know her own mind."

"I was so determined that we'd both find a husband before we were homeless that I didn't listen to my sister. She truly wasn't ready to marry, but since my fiancé had said she couldn't live with us, she didn't have a choice."

Annie took hold of her hand. "It would seem she did, and she found a way to get what she wanted."

Thoughts buzzed in Rebekah's mind like a colony of hornets whose nest had been disturbed. Had Jenny taken a fancy to Cody and decided he was the man she wanted? Or had she merely sweet-talked him in to doing what she wanted him to do? What would be the cost of his compliance? Her stomach clenched. Had her sister made another disastrous choice?

CHAPTER 8

*R*ebekah awoke from a troubled sleep. After lunch, Annie had insisted she stop pacing the front porch and rest. She tried, but disturbing dreams had haunted her—one where Jenny was on trial for stealing a horse. Rebekah's clothes stuck to her body, and she longed for some fresh air. She quickly rearranged her hair, smoothed down her hopelessly wrinkled dress, and went looking for Annie.

Women's voices drew her to the parlor. As she stepped around the corner, she took in the sight of five women, standing in the middle of the room. They hadn't noticed her yet.

"Well, are you going to keep us all in suspense?" A tall woman who looked part Mexican jiggled the arm of the chatty dark-haired woman Rebekah remembered from the hotel.

"I feel bad sharing it, all things considered."

"Please!" Ella—or was it Emma?—stood with her hand resting across her belly. She looked to be due to deliver in another month or two.

"Yes, do tell." Annie clapped her hands

The short woman nibbled her fingernail and nodded. "All right. I will only because I can't not tell you." She grinned widely, then took a deep breath. "I'm almost certain that Houston and I are going to have a baby."

Rebekah jumped at the squeals that filled the room. The four women bounced around Cora-belle—Cora-lou—Cora-something—

464

all chattering at once. After a long minute of everyone trying to talk over the other, the Mexican woman noticed Rebekah and whispered something. The women instantly quieted, and the soft swish of fabric echoed across the big room as they turned in unison.

Annie hurried toward her, a big smile on her face. "I'm sorry if we disturbed you, but Coralee just shared the most wonderful news."

Coralee. That was her name. Rebekah smiled at the short, dark-haired woman. "Congratulations. That is happy news. Please, don't allow my presence to put a damper on your excitement. I'm headed to the porch and was merely surprised to see so many ladies here."

Annie took her by the arm. "I know you've already met most of us, but let me introduce you again. Everyone, this is Rebekah Evans." She walked up to the dark-skinned woman, who was the tallest of the group. "This is Caro, and she is married to Chisholm."

Caro's coffee-colored eyes brightened. "It is a pleasure to make your acquaintance."

"Thank you. It's nice to meet you too."

Caro's expression dimmed. "I was very sorry to hear about your sister."

"Thank you." She smiled at the kind woman.

Annie turned her away from Caro to face the other Hart woman she hadn't yet met. The thin, green-eyed woman was only an inch shorter than Rebekah. "This is Jane. She's married to Crockett."

Jane smiled. "Happy to make your acquaintance."

Rebekah nodded. "Me too."

"And you've met the other ladies, Emma and Coralee. Emma is the wife of Hays, who is one of the three blue-eyed bothers, and the youngest. Makes him easy to remember."

"That, and his quick smile," Emma said.

"And if you remember, Coralee is married to Houston."

Coralee stepped forward, smiling. Her dark ringlets bounced as she moved. "It's such a pleasure to see you again, even though the circumstances aren't the best."

Rebekah felt taken aback by their warm welcome after all the trouble her sister had caused. Even now, their husbands were out searching for Jenny. "Thank you all for your kindness."

The women gathered around, each trying to talk, asking her questions.

Coralee cleared her throat loudly. "Ladies, please. I have a favor to ask." Her expression turned serious. "Houston and I don't plan to inform the men about the baby just yet. He agreed that I could tell y'all since I simply couldn't keep from it and had to tell someone. But we want to wait a little longer to announce our news to the men—possibly until Thanksgiving or Christmas."

Rebekah stepped back as the women assured Coralee they would keep her secret and talk returned to the baby. From Rebekah's viewpoint just inside the parlor, she noticed Perla come around the corner at the far end of the hall, carrying a tray.

She moved closer to the women. "Ladies, Perla is coming. Unless you want her to know, too, you might want to change the topic."

Coralee grasped her hand. "Thank you for the warning, and no, not yet."

Perla entered the room, and everyone quit talking. The older woman stopped and eyed them suspiciously, but then smiled. "I brought you some tea and gingerbread."

Comments of appreciation flitted around the room, and the ladies each took a seat. Annie tugged Rebekah down on the settee next to her, thwarting her escape outside.

Once Perla had left and they all had tea, Emma squealed. "I'm so excited that our baby will have a cousin."

Several of the women smiled. From what Austin had said, all of them were newlyweds. It wouldn't surprise Rebekah if there were more announcements of babies before long. A part of her wished that she could be there when it happened.

Talk turned to the Christmas Eve Ball.

"It's one of the highlights of the year," Annie said, her hazel eyes bright with excitement.

Footsteps sounded on the porch, and the room grew quiet. The front door banged open, and Robbie ran down the hall. The gangly boy skidded to a halt, barely able to keep from falling. His arm hit his hat, sending it rolling toward the door. He turned into the parlor, his cinnamon-colored hair flopping in his eyes. "Someone's coming!"

~

*T*he bell above the door of Travis's office rang as Austin walked in. His brother strode in from the back and slowed his steps when he saw him. "Did you find them?"

Austin shook his head. "They're not here. Our horses are at the livery, though. Seems Cody left them there with a note saying he'd only borrowed them."

"That's good that he returned them. At least we won't have to get the Rangers after him." Travis scratched his ear. "So what now?"

"I checked at the stage office, and Cody and Jenny were on the one that left just before we got to town."

"Are you going after them?"

He shrugged. "Don't know. Jenny left a note for her sister."

Travis leaned against the wall, arms crossed. "Did you read it?"

"No."

"Don't you think you should? It might determine whether or not you should ride after her and bring her back."

"I can't marry her after this." Austin sighed. "If I brought her back, it would only be for Rebekah's sake. But what good would that do? Jenny would probably only leave again."

"I'm sorry. I know that puts you in a real tight bind with Pa's deadline looming so close." He rubbed his hand over his jaw. "What about the other sister?"

Austin narrowed his eyes, not sure what Travis meant. "What about her?"

"Have you considered asking her to marry you?"

He had to admit, the idea sounded better than expected, but given the circumstances... "She's engaged. She only came here to be with Jenny for the wedding."

"That's unfortunate. What are you going to do? I can't believe Pa would actually turn you and Bowie out just because you didn't find a bride by the end of the year."

"I'm not willing to take the chance. I'll marry, one way or another."

Travis pushed away from that wall, crossed the room, and stopped in front of him. He placed his hand on Austin's shoulder. "I know how important the ranch is to you, but I can tell you honestly, the love of a good woman is far better. It's worth taking your time to find the right one."

"But if I do that, I'll have nothing to give her."

Travis pursed his lips. "Not nothing. You'll have yourself—and in the eyes of most who know you, that's a lot."

Austin barked a harsh laugh. "Thanks, but women want houses, security, not a man with empty pockets."

"Guess maybe it's time to take things to the Good Lord."

The bell chimed again, and Austin moved out of the doorway as Miss Spanner, the town gossip, entered, holding one hand in the other. She glanced at him, then at Travis. "I burned my hand on some hot grease."

Travis stood aside and gestured toward the rear of his office. "Come on back to my exam room and let me check it." He cast Austin an apologetic look.

Miss Spanner paused at the doorway and turned back. "Is it true your bride ran away with another man?"

~

*A*s Austin rode into the ranch yard, Miss Spanner's question still nagged him. If she knew about Jenny, the whole town—maybe even the county—did by now. He'd be the laughingstock of southern Texas before long. And except for Bowie, he'd be the only Hart brother who hadn't landed a wife.

Sighing loudly, he dismounted. He tied his horse and the two he'd picked up at the livery to the hitching post rather than heading to the barn, knowing Rebekah would be dying to hear news of her sister. He still hadn't read Jenny's note and wondered what it said.

The front door opened, and Rebekah rushed out. She hurried down the stairs and stopped in front of him, her eyes dimming. "You didn't find her."

"Not exactly, but she left this for you." He pulled the note from his vest pocket and handed it to her. "She and Cody left the horses at the livery and caught the morning stage."

Her hands quivered as she unfolded the paper and read the short note. Her chin wobbled. "It says not to follow her. That she wants to be with Cody. Then just the word *sorry*." She crumpled the paper and gazed up at him. Her miserable expression cut him to the quick. "What are we going to do?"

Several of his sisters-in-law were staring out the parlor window, and two others watched from the open door, looking concerned. "Let's take a walk." He held out his arm, and she took it without hesitation.

He headed toward the pasture where the cattle grazed. They'd be within sight of the others for propriety's sake but out of hearing range. Once they'd reached the fence, he stopped and turned to face her. "There's not much we can do. I can try to find her and bring her back, but from what I know of your sister, she'd be spitting mad and just leave again."

"I honestly can't believe Jenny would do such a thing. She's always been headstrong, but this is deplorable." Rebekah turned her sad blue eyes on him as she clutched his arm. "I'm so sorry for the horrible predicament this puts you in. What will you do?"

He had no idea. "I don't know. Need a little time to think."

"I should probably pack my bags and leave. My presence will only make everyone uncomfortable, all things considered."

The thought of her leaving created a crevice in his heart so wide it hurt. Was it possible he'd actually developed feelings for Rebekah? Or was it his desperation to marry causing the ache? "There won't be another stage today."

She nibbled her lip.

"It won't bother anyone for you to stay here, but if you'd be more comfortable, I can take you to town and rent a room at the hotel."

She looked as if she were fighting to not cry. "I truly hate to ask you to do that, but I think it would be for the best. My family has created enough trouble for everyone here."

Rebekah Evans was a kind woman who put others before herself. She was lovely, inside and out. If she weren't already engaged, he'd seriously consider asking her to stay. But she was, and he couldn't hurt another man like he'd been wounded, by stealing his bride. Austin nodded and held out his arm again. He'd take her to town, and then he needed to find himself another bride.

But his heart sure wasn't in the task.

~

*R*ebekah sat on the side of her bed in the lonely hotel room, staring at the floor. Her heart ached. But was it from her sister's abandonment or Austin's? He'd rented her a room, escorted her upstairs, and then said goodbye. Her chin trembled. She'd never see him again—the man she was sure now that she loved.

If only he'd asked her to stay. She would have with a happy heart.

But she was doomed to a loveless marriage with a man she could barely tolerate. A man who couldn't find it in his heart to take in her sister.

She thought of the happy faces of the Hart woman and longed for the joy they had. No, it was more than that. She wanted to be one of them. Part of the large, supportive family. She wanted to wake up every morning in the arms of the man she loved and to grow old with him. She wanted to be Austin's wife. She wanted to share in their excitement of the babies that were soon to come and the announcements of more on the horizon.

Tears burned her eyes, and she didn't have the strength to fight them. She despised feeling sorry for herself, but this time, she couldn't help it. Tears dropped in her lap, darkening the blue of her skirt.

What was she going to do? Could she return home and marry a man she didn't love? Live her whole life with Herman Riggs? The thought of it made her stomach churn. She could have settled for him before, but now that she'd met Austin and grown to care for him, she realized how dreadful her marriage to Herman would have been. No love and affection. Little happiness. It seemed wrong to marry Herman now.

She rose and walked to the window, looking out at the small town. Was there any hope she could find work here? If so, she would still be able see the Hart women at times and be friends with them. She shook her head. That would make things so awkward, especially if Austin never married and lost his land. Would he blame her?

The thought of it all made her groan. What a fool her sister was. Why couldn't Jenny see what a good man Austin was? How could she settle for a poor cowboy instead? Her only comfort was knowing her sister wouldn't hang for being a horse thief. But what if things didn't work out with Cody? What would Jenny do?

Worrying about her sister did no good. There was nothing she could do about Jenny now. Her sister had made her own choices and would reap the consequences.

Rebekah needed to decide if she was going through with her marriage to Herman. Now that she was alone, it might be possible for her to stay with a friend for a short time. Perhaps Leona or Thelma Lou wouldn't mind taking her in until she could find some kind of employment.

What she needed was some guidance and direction. She removed her Bible from her satchel and sat at the desk. She turned up the lamp and thumbed through the pages, hunting for something to encourage her and show her what to do.

After reading for thirty minutes with nothing jumping out at her, she decided to go downstairs for a bowl of soup. She probably couldn't eat much, but the nourishment would help her get through the long night ahead. Tomorrow the stage would take her out of Hartville and home to an unknown future.

CHAPTER 9

*R*ebekah gave Annie a farewell hug, then climbed into the coach. She was grateful most of the Hart women had come to town this morning to try to talk her into staying. Only Emma, the one with child, hadn't come. Rebekah waved goodbye, knowing she'd disappointed them. But staying simply wasn't possible. Still, she deeply appreciated that they had cared enough to try. Her friends gave a final wave, then walked down the street. Rebekah had promised to write to Annie, but she didn't see what the point was. She wouldn't return to Hartville or El Regalo.

The coach door slammed shut, and Rebekah settled back in her seat. Thank goodness, no other passengers were on the stage today. She wanted to be alone and ponder her future. Ponder what might have been.

She thought she'd be leaving here with her sister safe in Austin's capable hands, but instead, Austin's hopes and dreams had been dashed, as well as her own desire to see her sister happily married. She was returning home not even knowing where Jenny was, and that left a deep void. Would she ever hear from Jenny again?

She yawned, leaning her head against the window as the driver walked past. He winked at her, then shimmied up the side of the stage and settled on the bench seat. Her whole body felt heavy, as if right on the verge of sleep, but sleep had refused to come. She'd been restless most of last night. She'd doze for a few minutes, then jerk awake, and each time she'd awakened, she had prayed. Prayed for guidance and direction. For wisdom. But when morning dawned, she still had no answers.

Now she was headed home, while her heart stayed here in Texas. More than likely, Herman would meet her at the depot. What would she say to him? How would she find the words to explain why she couldn't marry him?

She hated hurting him just because she'd changed. But she wouldn't marry one man when her heart belonged to another. Maybe in time, what she felt for Austin would fade and she might be free to marry, though that probably wouldn't happen for a long while.

"Wait!" someone yelled. A man ran down the street toward them, waving a paper in the air. "Wait!" He paused on the boardwalk, breathing hard, and stared up at Fred, the driver. "Is a Miss R. Evans in there?"

"Yep."

"Got a letter for her."

Rebekah's heart jumped. Had Jenny written her again? "Here!" She leaned out the window and held out her hand.

"Whoo-wee! I just caught you in time." The man grinned and passed her the missive. "I heard you were leaving today, but I just stumbled across the letter a few minutes ago as I was sorting the mail." He tipped his hat. "Have a safe journey, ma'am."

"Thank you." She sat back, frowning at the masculine handwriting. Was the note from Jenny's beau? Had something happened to her sister? Her heartbeat thundered as she tore into the envelope and shook open the folded page.

Dear Miss Evans,

It has come to my attention that your sister has led a more immoral life than I had first realized. After discussing her improprieties with my mother, some of which I have just recently been made aware of, I have decided that I cannot in good conscience sully my family name by marrying you. While I do realize you are not at fault, the close connection with your sister casts suspicions your way.

Mother's heart is simply not strong enough to endure the gossip and scandal surrounding your sister's escapades.

Please accept this letter as a formal withdrawal of my marriage proposal.

No longer yours,

Herman Gilbert Riggs III

The stage lurched into motion, throwing Rebekah back against the seat. She gasped as she read the part about suspicions being cast on her. She'd done nothing to deserve them, other than perhaps not be stricter with Jenny, but then she wasn't Jenny's mother. Her sister had resented her trying to make her see reason.

She drew in a deep breath. Herman no longer wanted to marry her. The thought should upset her, but instead, it brought a freeing release she couldn't have explained if asked to. She may not have a place to live when she got back home, but at least she wouldn't be stuck with a man she didn't love for the rest of her life.

～

*H*e was a coward—no doubt about it. Austin had spent the night in town so he wouldn't have to fend off questions or sad looks from his family members. But attempting to sleep in a bed other than his own had been a waste of time. He'd tossed and turned all night and then paced since sunup, making the leg wounded in the war throb. Several times, he'd wanted to march downstairs, rap on Rebekah's door, and tell her that he finally realized he loved her. But he hadn't.

Instead, he stood there, watching out the window as the stage rolled out of town with the woman he loved on it. For the first time in his life, he felt brokenhearted. All his hopes and dreams were on that stage. It suddenly dawned on him that all the land in the world meant nothing without Rebekah.

And he'd just let her go.

A commotion came from the hall, and a loud knock at his door jolted him from his morbid thoughts. He didn't want to see anyone, so he didn't respond.

"Austin, we know you're in there, so open the door."

We? It sounded like Coralee. What did she want? Had something happened to Houston or maybe his pa when the men were out searching for Jenny? The knock came again, longer this time. With a loud sigh of resignation, he padded across the room in his socks and pulled open the door.

Annie, Coralee, Jane, and Caro stood there, each with her hands on her hips, four pairs of eyes flashing.

Annie stepped forward. "Are you just going to stand here and let her go?"

"Who?" He eyed the women, knowing exactly whom she meant. Emma was the only Hart woman not in the hall. She must have stayed home since her baby was due fairly soon.

"Rebekah, of course." Coralee swung her head, sending her ringlets flying behind her. They bounced up and down as they returned to their normal position.

"Yes, Rebekah. You cannot let her go." Caro stared solemnly at him.

Jane nodded. "She cares for you."

"She's engaged. There's no reason for me to go after her."

The man from the room across the hall returned from breakfast and stared at the crowd. He opened his door and stepped inside but then left it open two inches. Austin cleared his throat, drawing the man's gaze over the heads of the women. He narrowed his eyes. The man's Adam's apple lurched as he swallowed. He slowly shut the door.

"What if I told you that she loves you?" Annie lifted her eyebrows as if daring him to deny the fact.

His heart bucked. "Did she tell you that?"

"No, you dunderhead. We can tell by looking at her." Annie glanced at the other women, who nodded in unison. "It's clear she doesn't want to leave."

"She knows she can stay. I tried to get her to stay at the big house for a few more days, but she wouldn't."

Annie tossed her arms to the side, slapping them loudly against her skirts while Caro and Jane jumped at the sudden action. "Well, of course not. Think how awkward that would feel with you supposed to marry her sister who ran away with one of the ranch hands."

Austin narrowed his eyes and leaned against the doorframe. He didn't need them to rub in what had happened. "So what's your point?"

"Go after her." Coralee reached out and jiggled his arm. "Ask her to stay."

"But—"

Annie lifted her hand. "No *but*s. That woman is in love with you. Don't let her get away. You need her."

"She needs you," Jane said.

He forked his hand through his hair. "Are you sure?"

"Positive."

"Definitely."

"Of course."

"*Sí.*"

All four women responded at once. Could they be right? Was it possible Rebekah loved him? It was almost too much to comprehend. *How* had that happened? *When* had it? What did that matter if she truly did love him? A slow smile pulled at his lips.

Annie crossed her arms. "Well, I'm glad to see you're finally understanding things."

"You'd better hurry up if you plan to catch her." Coralee wagged a finger at him.

He spun and crossed to his bed. Sat down and tugged on each boot. He buttoned up his shirt and marched to the door. Annie handed him his hat, and Coralee held up his gun belt by two fingers. He snatched them as he headed out the door. Outside the hotel, he pulled up short at seeing Travis standing in the road holding Austin's saddled horse.

"Howdy, big brother. Looks like that posse of females made you see things clearly."

Austin grinned. "You could say that." He grabbed the reins, hopped up on his horse, and tipped his hat at the women as they walked out the hotel door.

Reining his horse around, he tapped his heels into its side. "He-yah!"

~

The sound of someone yelling jarred Rebekah from her sleep. She glanced around and moaned. She was still on the stage. Not that she'd been on it all that long, because they hadn't even reached the first town.

Now that she'd awakened, she didn't hear anyone, just the sound of horses' hooves pounding the dirt and the creaking of the stage. Had she merely dreamed someone was hollering at her?

"Stop!"

She jolted. There it was again. She scooted to the window and peered out, but all she could see was the landscape whizzing past.

"Halt!"

She clutched her bodice. Was the stage about to be robbed? She had precious little to hand over to a thief. Only her mother's cameo and the coins she'd planned to use for her meals. "Please, God. No."

"Fred! Pull over."

The voice came from the other side of the stage. She slid across the seat. Surely, they weren't about to be robbed if the thief knew the driver's name. Suddenly, a man flew from his horse and banged against the side of the stage. Rebekah jumped back. The door flew open, and the man ducked his head, showing only the top of his hat, and climbed in as the stage finally slowed.

Rebekah's heart nearly burst from her chest.

The man's head lifted as he dropped on the seat beside her.

"Austin? What are you doing here?"

He tugged off his hat and tossed it across to the other bench, his grin tentative. "I couldn't let you go without telling you how I feel."

Her heart, which had barely begun to slow, sped up again. Dare she hope? "How you feel about what?"

"You."

"Me?"

He nodded. "I tried to fight my feeling, knowing that you're engaged, but I can't let you go without a battle. Somehow, you sneaked in and stole my heart."

"I did?" Tears burned her eyes.

"Yes, ma'am. Do you think you could stay a bit longer and give me a chance to win your heart? I mean, I know it's not fair to that man you're engaged to, but I really do care for you, Rebekah."

"Is this because of your land?"

"What?" He blinked. "No! I don't want the land if I can't have you there to share it with."

Rebekah smiled. If he was willing to give up the land he loved for her, his feelings must be strong. "I care for you too. And I have something to show you." She pulled the crumpled letter from her handbag and handed it to him.

He smoothed it against his leg, read it, then glanced up, his expression sober. "The man is a fool. You're not at fault for the choices your sister made."

"That's true. Maybe in this instance, I'll benefit from her bad choice."

A wide grin spread across his handsome face. "That is my wish too." His sober expression returned. "Although, if I had loved Jenny the way a woman deserves to be loved, maybe I could have made her happy."

Rebekah touched his cheek. "I've spent a lifetime trying to make my sister happy and failed most of the time. It's not your fault. You did all that you could to make Jenny comfortable, but she wanted something you couldn't give her."

"What about you? What do you want, Rebekah?"

It wasn't a woman's place to mention marriage before the man did, but she wasn't about to let her one chance at love and happiness slip away. "I want to stay here and be your wife and spend the rest of my life making you happy."

Austin's grin returned, and he tugged her into his arms. His mouth pressed against hers, igniting her whole body with sensations. She wrapped her arms around his neck, returning his delicious kisses.

Someone cleared his throat. They jerked away from one another and stared at Fred. Rebekah hadn't even realized the stage had stopped. The driver leaned in the open door, grinning. "I take it that another Hart brother is about to get married."

"Close the door and drive." Austin sounded gruff, but the smile on his face belied his tone.

"Drive to where? Back to Hartville?"

"No. Take us to San Antonio."

"What about your horse?"

Austin leaned out the window and whistled. His black gelding trotted up to him. "Tie him to the back."

Fred nodded and closed the door.

Austin sat back in the seat and looked at her. Rebekah's heart still thumped a frantic beat. He took hold of her hand, brushing his fingers over hers.

"Why are we going to San Antonio?"

"I want a place where I can woo my bride without an audience."

"You don't need to woo me. I already told you how I feel."

He studied her for a long moment. "How would you feel about a quiet wedding with just the two of us?"

She could understand him not wanting all his siblings and their wives making a big fuss about him getting married. "If that's what you want, it's fine with me."

He nodded. "So, Rebekah Evans, will you marry me? Be my wife and the mother of my children?"

Her cheeks warmed at his pointed questions, but she couldn't help smiling. "I would love to."

The stage lurched as it started forward. Austin gave her a quick kiss, then wrapped his arm around her and pulled her close.

She sat back and closed her eyes. Could this really be happening? She'd come to Texas to attend her sister's wedding, but God had other plans for her. A verse from Jeremiah came to mind. *For I know the thoughts that I think toward you, saith the* Lord, *thoughts of peace, and not of evil, to give you an expected end.*

God had given her the happy ending she'd dreamed of but dared not hope for. Not the ending she expected, but rather, an unexpected one. At least in her mind. Perhaps her coming here had been part of God's expected ending all along. And if that were true, she could entrust her sister to God's hands. God would watch over them both.

She smiled at that thought and rested in the arms of the man she loved. After a few wonderful moments, she pushed up and looked Austin in the eye. She nibbled her lip, hating to ask for something so soon. "Could I ask one favor of you?"

His dark eyes sparkled with love. "Of course. What is it?"

"Could we perhaps stop at a store in San Antonio so I can buy fabric to make Emma's baby some gowns?"

He stared at her for a long moment, his gaze lovingly roaming her face. Then he smiled and said, "Yes, dear."

ABOUT THE AUTHOR

Bestselling author Vickie McDonough grew up wanting to marry a rancher, but instead married a computer geek who is scared of horses. She now lives out her dreams in her fictional stories about ranchers, cowboys, lawmen, and others living in the Old West. Vickie is the award-winning author of more than forty published books and novellas. Her novels include the fun and feisty Texas Boardinghouse Brides series and the Land Rush Dreams series. Vickie has been married forty-one years to Robert. They have four grown sons, one of whom is married, and a precocious ten-year-old granddaughter. When she's not writing, Vickie enjoys reading, antiquing, watching movies, and traveling. To learn more about Vickie's books or to sign up for her newsletter, visit her website: www.vickiemcdonough.com.

LOVE AT LAST

ERICA VETSCH

CHAPTER 1

SEPTEMBER 28, 1874

*B*owie Hart eased into the foyer of El Regalo and leaned his rifle against the hall tree, his chest heavy and mind preoccupied. Perla, the housekeeper, flashed him a smile as she disappeared through a doorway into the back of the house. She'd been in her element, what with all the recent engagement parties and weddings in the Hart family. The place had been in an uproar for months.

Bowie missed the quiet rhythm of the days before Pa's ultimatum.

Stonewall nosed his way past the front door, his nails clicking on the hardwood, tail wagging. Bowie rubbed the dog's head, making his ears flop. Perla always frowned on Bowie letting one of his cow dogs into the house, but she had a soft spot for Stonewall. Bowie had found the pup nearly drowned when his cruel owner had tossed him into a burlap bag and thrown him into the Sabinal River, and Perla had helped Bowie nurse the sodden pup back to health.

"Stay here, and don't chew on anything."

Stonewall dropped to his belly and rested his chin on his outstretched paws. For such a large and athletic dog, the Catahoula leopard obeyed well, trained to voice and hand signals into the best cow dog in Texas. Bowie bent and gave him another pat before heading toward Pa's office. It was well past the time he and Pa had a talk.

Five weddings so far, and Austin's most likely not far away. All six of his brothers married, taking up their inheritance just as their father wished.—Wished? Ha. *Commanded* was more like. Marry or be disinherited. Bowie's gut tightened every time he thought about it.

That would leave Bowie as the sole remaining bachelor...and likely to stay that way.

He moved down the hallway, the thick carpet muffling his steps. As he approached the heavy pocket doors, male voices drifted through the slight opening, and Bowie stilled, not wanting to interrupt.

"This year's worked out even better than I could've hoped. All you boys toppling like bowling pins. Five in nine months, and I expect you have a plan to find yourself a bride."

Pa. Bowie closed his eyes, picturing his father leaning back in his office chair, propping his boots up on the corner of his immense desk. Satisfaction colored his every word. And why shouldn't it? His sons had lined up and marched to his tune right on the beat.

"I'll admit, I was sore when you rolled out this plan on New Year's Day, but I can't argue with the results."

Bowie's older brother, Austin. He'd confided to Bowie that he had been kicking around the risky idea of sending off for a mail-order bride, a notion Bowie had considered for himself and discarded...quickly. Still, Austin would get something worked out before time ran out on the edict. Another party for Perla to plan. Seems they'd hardly gotten any ranching done around these parts all year. Bowie took a step toward the door but stopped when Austin spoke again.

"Pa, me and the boys have been talking it over, and we think you should let Bowie out of the marriage requirement."

Bowie sucked in a slow breath, and feathers of unease rippled across his chest. His brothers had been talking about him? His muscles tensed, and his hands had fisted at his sides.

"I mean, it's already near October, and he hasn't found a wife, and I don't think he's even going to try. Are you really going to take his part of the ranch away from him? Hasn't he been through enough?"

Bowie wanted to leave, but his boots stuck to the rug. Twin flames burned in the pit of his stomach, one of shame and one of hope. Shame that even his brothers recognized no woman would ever marry the likes of him, and hope that perhaps his pa would renege and let him out of the marry-or-be-disinherited clause of the will.

Pa's chair creaked. Bowie could picture him rubbing his chin, his eyes sharp as flint. "I'll admit, the thought has crossed my mind, but"—his hand smacked the desk—"he's got to at least try. Otherwise, he's going to spend his life alone."

"Maybe that's what he wants. And where is he going to find someone to marry him? If his battle scars don't put the ladies off, his surly disposition will. I heard in town that someone suggested starting a betting pool. Which of your sons would marry in what order, and they were offering some pretty tall odds on Bowie, but there weren't even any takers. I doubt there's a woman in the county who can even look him in the face to talk to—much less walk down the aisle with him. And it's nearly too late for a mail-order bride."

Bowie's skin prickled, and anger speared through him. Anger at the ignorant townsfolk who were looking on his family's private business as sport, at himself for caring at all what anyone thought, and anger at God for not letting him die on the battlefield at Gettysburg or in Elmira prison where he'd sat out the duration of the war. Anything would be better than being the object of his brothers' pity or the ridicule of the good people of Hartville, Texas.

"Gambling? On my sons?" Pa's voice rose.

"Don't get in a squawk. I put an end to the betting pretty quick, but still. It's all over town that nobody expects Bowie to find a wife. And if he doesn't, what are you going to do? Kick him off the ranch? Have him stay on, but working *for* his brothers instead of alongside them? That will go over real well."

Pa was silent for a while—no doubt, thinking it over. "Maybe you're right. I'll admit, when I thought up this scheme, it was Bowie I worried about the most."

Bowie reached up and touched the patch covering his left eye socket, letting his fingers trail down his puckered and shiny cheek...well, shiny except for where the black powder of the explosion that had taken his eye had embedded itself under his skin like a tattoo.

A freak.

A monster.

An embarrassment to his family.

He'd heard and thought them all.

Turning on his heel, he strode back down the hallway to the stair-case, treading quietly up the steps to his room at the back of the house.

Minutes later, he was packed. Saddlebags thrown over his shoulder, papers rolled and under his arm, gun belt wrapped around his waist, and a scrap of linen and lace that he'd kept for more than ten years tucked into his pocket. He clomped down the stairs, not caring if anyone heard him this time, snatched up his rifle from the hall tree, snapped his fingers at Stonewall, and left El Regalo.

He refused to look back. Either his plan would work, or he'd just keep riding.

The sun was setting as he rode into Hartville, and he was grateful for the concealing dusk as he headed down a back alley toward his brother Houston's hardware store. Stonewall trotted at his stirrup, nose raised to all the unfamiliar smells of town.

Houston opened the back door to Bowie's knock. His blue eyes took in Bowie and Stonewall, and then he glanced up and down the alley. "Trouble? Is it Pa?"

Bowie ducked under the door frame. "Pa's fine." *Fine and still meddling in his sons' lives.*

"Then what are you doing in town? You never come to town."

Coralee, Houston's new bride, swept down the shop, and Bowie turned so his right side was toward her, tipping his chin so his long hair swung forward. "I'm going away for a little while, and there's a couple things I need you to do for me while I'm gone." He dug into the inside pocket of his buckskin jacket, drawing out the folded papers.

"Going away?" Coralee twisted one of her ringlets around her finger.

"Yes, ma'am." Bowie shifted his weight, not looking at her. He'd known her for years, but now she was his sister-in-law. He was at a loss to know how to act around the bevy of females that had invaded his family, so he fell back on saying as little as possible.

She laughed, and he tensed, as he did every time a woman laughed. Was she laughing at him?

"When are you going to call me 'Coralee'? 'Ma'am' sounds so formal."

He jerked his chin to let her know he heard. Handing his papers to

Houston, he said, "Can you get started on this for me? On the rise above the Sabinal where Austin shot that big buck when we were kids. And can you put my horse up at the livery? He's tied out back. I'm taking Stonewall with me, but could you tell Travis to have Robbie keep an eye on Clara for me? I'm pretty sure she's going to whelp in about six weeks."

Houston scanned the pages, flipping through them. "A house?" Bowie could just about see the lists of needed items forming in Houston's head. Lumber, doors, windows, nails, shingles.

"Where did you get these plans?"

"Can you do it or not?"

"Of course I can. Just how long do you expect to be gone?"

"A while." *Maybe forever.*

"How soon do you want this done?"

"By the end of next month. Hire whoever you have to. I need to hustle to make the evening stage." He nodded to Coralee. "Ma'am."

Houston followed after him. "Wait, you want me to build you a house in not even five weeks? What are you planning? When will you be back? Does anyone else know you're leaving? What do I tell the family?"

Bowie kept on walking, Stonewall trotting at his side.

As he settled himself into the stage bound for San Antonio, he gripped his rifle barrel and took the scrap of linen out of his pocket, wondering if he was the biggest fool in Christendom and if he had the courage to take the next step in his plan. He rubbed the last few threads of the monogram that remained on the fabric. Stonewall sat on the floor between his boots, looking up at him as if questioning his sanity. Bowie couldn't blame the dog. He was wondering too.

Pa's demand that his sons marry hung over him like a sword, and his brothers' pity and concern twisted like a knife.

Marry or be disinherited.

There was only one woman he would ever consider asking to marry him, the only woman who had never recoiled at the sight of his ravaged face. He would track her down, propose if she wasn't already married, and if she refused, that would be it. His inheritance would be gone. He'd just keep going and never return to the 7 Heart Ranch.

"*Y*ou are undoubtedly the most addle-brained female it has ever been my curse to be saddled with. A three-legged, blind donkey could work the button punch better than you." Uncle Zeb towered over Elise Rivers at her station in the button factory, his hand raised.

She jerked her head at the last instant, but not quickly enough to avoid the slap altogether. Hot pain shot through the side of her face, and tears welled in her eyes in spite of her vow never to cry in front of Uncle Zebulon. The clack and punch of the machines around her and the sickening miasma of old seafood hanging in the air made her nauseous.

His rant continued as the women on the factory floor kept their heads bent to their work. Elise didn't blame them. To draw attention to oneself was to call down wrath.

"Look at these. Wasteful." Uncle Zeb held up a fistful of oyster shells, each pierced with many round holes. "It isn't enough that you're a charity case forced on me. Now you try to rob me? Look how far apart you've spaced these punches. And you're nowhere near the edges, leaving all this behind." He flung the shells at her, and she threw her hands up to protect her face.

Fear burned away, flaming into indignation. She stiffened her spine, knowing she would regret challenging him but unable to stop the flow of words. "You slapped me last week because a batch was returned as defective. You had us cut the buttons so close together, they overlapped and weren't round. And I *would* cut them closer to the edge where the shell is thicker if you'd ever sharpen the blades on the punches so I could get through the mother-of-pearl without shattering it. It's your own miserly fault we can't turn out a decent product."

One of the workers gasped, and Uncle Zeb's face reddened. He floundered for a moment, spittle flecking the corners of his mouth, his fist rising. "You ungrateful leech! When I think of how I took you in, fed you, clothed you, gave you a place to live and work, and this is how you repay me? Insolence, wastefulness, laziness. I'll teach you to backtalk me!"

Elise braced herself, her eyes slamming shut, already ruing her hasty accusation, though every word of it was true and she wouldn't take it back.

An odd squeak from her uncle had her eyes popping open. Elise sucked in a breath that snagged in her throat.

Silhouetted against the sunlight streaming in the open factory door, a massive man stood firm, his huge hand gripped around Uncle Zeb's fist. At his side, a muscular dog bristled and snarled, his eyes glowing hot.

"Touch her again, and I'll break you into kindling," the big man growled.

Where had she heard that voice before? Low and gravelly, making eddies in her middle. He stepped farther into the workroom, pressing down on Uncle Zeb's fist, forcing him to stagger back and drop to his knees. The women at the punches sat, open-mouthed and wide-eyed. Machinery stopped, and hands and expressions froze.

Buckskin fringe swayed along the big man's sleeves, and in one hand, he carried a long rifle. The other maintained its hold on Uncle Zeb with seemingly little effort. Zebulon squeaked again, his eyes wide, all the fight gone out of him.

Elise swallowed and half rose from her stool. She *knew* that voice, but from where? Then the man looked at her, his long, dark hair swinging back so she could see his face.

It wasn't the patch or the black-powder burns on his cheek and neck that she recognized. No, it was the single brown thickly lashed eye that she remembered. Watchful as a bird of prey, trained on her as she had moved through the hospital ward tending the broken bodies of men fighting for what they believed in.

"Captain Hart." The whisper came, not so much from her lips as from her memory, the heartbreak, the despair, the desperate longing to be able to do more for the wounded...

"Let go of me, you...you...brute. I'll have the law on you." Zebulon writhed, unable to loosen the captain's hold on his fist. The dog inched closer, his fangs bared by his curling lips. Zeb stilled, sweat globbing on his reddened face.

"Miss Rivers?" Captain Hart tossed her uncle aside like an old newspaper, snapping his finger to the dog that quieted but never took his eyes off Zeb. "I'd like to talk to you." He glanced at the workers, frozen at their stations, then at her uncle, stock still and rigid, held at bay by the dog. "In private."

"This ain't her break time." Uncle Zebulon barely moved as he spat out the words.

Captain Hart ignored him. He lifted his rifle and held it in the crook of his elbow, pointed at the ground, the very image of power under control. "Miss? Can I have a word?"

Elise pressed her lips together, wishing her mouth wasn't so dry. *Why on earth is he here? How did he find me? My uncle will thrash me proper if I leave my station.* And yet, when Captain Hart motioned with his head toward the door, she found herself wanting to follow him, curiosity winning over all.

"Yes." She wiped her hands on her apron and slid off her stool. As she edged around the dog, Captain Hart moved between her and her uncle.

"Heel, boy." The dog relaxed and came to his master's side.

Uncle Zeb pushed himself off the wall, rubbing his hand, scowling.

Captain Hart stepped out into the alley behind the factory and away from the door, his stride long and confident. Elise had never had the opportunity to observe him upright and healthy before, and his height struck her. He must be well over six feet. Near six and a half, maybe. And lithe as a cat.

The alley stank of discarded refuse, rotting cabbage, and old smoke. Grimy brick walls rose on either side, blocking out the sun. He turned to her, and behind him on the street, New Rochelle, New York, bustled and hurried, indifferent to the sadness and suffering around it, intent on its own purposes.

Elise stuffed a stray lock under the kerchief covering her hair and folded her hands at her waist. If only her apron was clean, at least. Sniffing and snuffling the plethora of odors and smells in the ally, the dog nosed from one pile of trash to the next. The captain looked down on her, saying nothing, and she forced herself not to fidget under his intent stare.

Finally, he spoke. "Is that man your husband?"

Elise blinked. "No." *As if I would marry such a contemptible tyrant, and twice my age or better?*

"But you live with him? He said he took you in."

"He's my uncle, though admitting it brings me no joy." She twisted her fingers at her waist.

"Are you married to anyone?"

She almost laughed. A spinster of thirty years whose uncle had long ago discouraged any man from courting her lest he lose his unpaid servant, she'd given up hope of marriage and family. Who would want *her* anyway, a penniless factory worker? It was a question with which her querulous uncle often taunted her. Old maid, plain as a slice of bread, useless hanger-on.

"No, sir. I am not married to anyone."

Something in him seemed to ease. He shifted his weight and adjusted the rifle in his clasp. "Do you want to be?"

Elise's hands went slack, and she raised her eyebrows. "Pardon me?" What kind of question was that, and to be asked so abruptly by a man she hadn't seen in ten years or more?

He sucked in a deep breath, expanding his already broad chest. The presses in the factory began their familiar thumping and banging, and Uncle Zeb's shout berating his workers pierced the fall air. "Is there some place quiet we could talk?" Captain Hart had to raise his voice.

She nodded, though her uncle would be watching the clock, ready to punish her for every second away from her work. Still, she might as well be hung for a sheep as hung for a lamb. Edging past Captain Hart in the dingy alley, she led the way out on to the street and down toward the waters of Long Island Sound. The small strip of green grass and trees that the city called a park was the only refuge Elise had when her life threatened to overwhelm her. Directing him to a bench, she looked out over the water, letting the lap and scrape of the waves against the rocky shoreline calm her.

The dog charged to the water's edge, scattering the gulls and barking, high-stepping along the shore, his tail wagging.

The captain took the near end of the bench, stretched his long legs out, and crossed his booted ankles. His rifle rested against the bench at his side. Elise paused before stepping over his legs to sit, smoothing her skirts, wishing she'd thought to grab her shawl as the brisk mid-October wind blew in over the water.

When he made no move to speak, she said, "I never thought I would see you again." Glancing up at his profile, she realized he'd put her on his right so the damaged side of his face was away from her. The last time she had seen him, weak and bandaged, he was being dragged from his hospital bed and shoved into a train car for the trip to Fort Delaware and the prisoner of war camp. He and so many of his fellow Confederates. Though she had protested their treatment, knowing many were still too sick and injured to survive the journey, the surgeon had ignored her, shunting them off like so many cattle to the slaughter. All she could do was press a few pieces of hardtack into his hand as he was shoved away from her.

"I prayed for you." She studied her hands in her lap, too ashamed of what had happened to him to look up. "I prayed you were still alive."

He stirred, as if uncomfortable with her whispered confession. "Miss Rivers, I promised myself at the end of the war that I would never come north of the Mason-Dixon Line again. I'd had enough of Northern hospitality to last me a lifetime—first the hospital here, then Fort Delaware, then Elmira."

He'd survived Elmira Prison? No wonder he never wanted to come north again. She couldn't blame him, and yet here he sat, not two miles from the hospital at Fort Slocum where she had treated his wounds and held his hand as he wandered in delirium, fevered and insensible, injured terribly at Gettysburg and shuffled from one hospital to another as those medical centers closer to the battlefield filled to overflowing.

"What brings you here now, Captain?"

His fine, narrow lips pressed together, the skin taut over his cheekbone. "Miss Rivers, I came all this way to ask you to marry me."

She couldn't have been more shocked if he had declared he was going to sprout wings and fly. "What? Why?"

"Because I need to get hitched, quick."

Had his war injuries addled his brains? She'd heard of that happening to some veterans.

"Miss Rivers, my pa has got hold of an outlandish notion, and there's nothing I can do about it. He says if me and my brothers want our inheritance, then we all have to get married, pronto. He gave us until New Year's, and confound it all, nearly every one of my brothers has up and found a woman to marry." He fisted his hands on his thighs. "I'm the last holdout."

Her hands went slack, and her jaw did too. "Why come all this way? Are there no women in Texas?"

"The war exacted a high price from me." He made a vague gesture toward his damaged eye. "The women in Texas are not inclined to look on my face favorably."

The more fools, them. Captain Hart had more than his fair share of handsome looks, scars and patch notwithstanding. There was a strength and dependability to him, and a vulnerability that called out to her and set her heart to racing. He had courtly manners and an ingrained chivalry she'd found sadly lacking in the men of her acquaintance. Of all the soldiers she had treated throughout the war, Captain Hart was the most memorable.

And now he had rescued her from her uncle's wrath, at least temporarily. She couldn't remember the last time someone had stood up on her behalf or shielded her from harm.

He whistled to the dog that had gone out onto the pier. "I remember your kindness in the hospital. During my imprisonment, that memory helped me survive. Most Northerners reserved their hospitality for Union soldiers."

Her heart warmed. "I was only doing what was right. Injury cares not for allegiances."

His long fingers curled around his knees, and he glanced at her. "You aren't married, and from the way your uncle is treating you, you aren't exactly prospering since the war."

A blush heated her cheeks. No, she wasn't prospering. He had probably taken note of her shabby clothes and battered shoes. She stared out over the water, unable to meet his eye.

"I propose a deal. I need a wife, and you need to escape your uncle. Marry me and come to Texas. I'll get my inheritance. You'll get freedom from that dumb-as-a-sack-of-hammers uncle of yours...and the protection of the Hart name."

My first marriage proposal. She tugged at her lower lip, wanting to laugh but feeling the prick of tears too. *I am nearly overwhelmed by the romance of it all.* A cold gust of wind whipped over the water, and she crossed her arms, hugging herself against the chill.

Then his coat was dropping around her shoulders, warm from his body, surrounding her with comfort and protection. The butter-soft leather smelled of sunshine and hard work and male. It was as if the captain had put his arm around her, so intimate was the jolt to her heart.

Such a protector by nature wouldn't be a bad risk as a husband, would he?

"You should know..." He spoke as if nothing out of the ordinary had happened. "This would be a paper marriage. I don't expect anything of you except for you to say the words in front of the preacher and come live at the 7 Heart. I'll provide for you, and you can have the running of the house. I won't put any other demands on you. All I ask is that you keep the terms to yourself. My family doesn't need to know that ours is anything but a normal marriage."

She buried her fingers in the fringe on the coat. A loveless marriage, but one of security, and on her part at least, regard and liking.

As opposed to her current existence on sufferance with a cruel relative.

It seemed an easy decision.

But did she have the courage to jettison her girlhood dreams of marrying for love and accept the captain's offer?

She snuggled into his coat and decided she did.

CHAPTER 2

*E*lise didn't feel any different from her old self as they boarded the train, except that she was relieved not to have to go back to the factory. She certainly didn't feel as she expected a new bride should, elated and giddy, eager to start a new adventure with the man she loved. Captain Hart—no, not captain, Bowie, as she'd learned at the hasty wedding ceremony—kept his hand on her elbow, guiding her through the crowds at the station as if he feared she might bolt.

She patted her handbag, feeling the crinkle of paper. The ink was barely dry on their marriage certificate, and here they were leaving New York for Texas already. Not that she had any long goodbyes to say. Her uncle had boiled, red in the face, then glowered and grunted a "good riddance" when she'd told him she was leaving. Of course, what else could he do with Bowie and the dog right there to protect her from his wrath?

The pastor of her little church had taken a long look at Bowie, his rifle, and his dog, and asked her in a hushed whisper if she was sure she wanted to do this. After she assured him she did, the wedding was done in a blur. All she could remember was how Bowie's hand engulfed hers, and how steady his voice when he repeated his vows.

Vows to love, honor, and cherish her.

And she'd promised to love, honor, and obey this man for the rest of her life.

There hadn't even been a wedding kiss.

As he handed her up the steps into the train, the enormity of what she was doing washed over her like an unexpected wave at the beach, threatening to topple her. She stumbled as her breath caught in her throat.

"All right?" His deep voice behind her made her jump.

"Yes. I'm fine." Her words sounded as weak and quavery as she felt.

The porter took her valise and Bowie's saddlebags, their only luggage, and frowned as the dog—Stonewall—leapt aboard.

"Livestock is not allowed in the passenger cars, sir." He looked down his narrow, hooked nose and sniffed.

"He's got a ticket." Bowie showed him the pasteboard, his face impassive. The man examined the slip, sniffed again, and held open the door.

"This way, ma'am."

Not "miss" but "ma'am." She pressed through her glove against the plain circlet of gold Bowie had placed on her finger. From spinster to bride, from miss to ma'am, in the space of an afternoon.

She followed the railroad employee, with Bowie and the dog coming along behind, and to her surprise, the porter continued past the bench seats in the passenger section to the end of the car and into a private compartment. "This is your berth." He stowed her bag in an overhead rack. "We'll be departing the station soon. Dinner service is in the forward car at seven p.m., and a porter will be around to pull down your bed at nine if that pleases you?"

"Fine." Bowie stepped aside to allow the man to leave, and Elise surveyed the little room. A private compartment all to themselves? Polished wood and glass everywhere, velvet seats. Such luxury. She felt as out of place as a tin cup at a tea party. Could Bowie really afford this?

He put a coin in the porter's hand, something large enough to make the man's eyes widen and for him to bob his head. "If there's anything you need, please let me know."

Bowie nodded and stepped inside the compartment. "Will this do?"

Stonewall jumped up on the seat and looked out the window, leaving a nose print on the glass. Elise took off her gloves, finger by finger, comparing the train accommodations to her uncle's cramped, mean rooms above the factory. "'Will this do?' This is the nicest place I've been in since..."

"Since?"

She took a steadying breath and swallowed. "Since my parents passed away." Removing her bonnet, she smoothed her hair.

"When was that?"

"During the war. A week before you were brought in to the Fort Slocum Hospital, actually."

He stilled in that way she'd noticed several times now, so still she knew he was concentrating solely on her. "So you were in mourning when we met." It wasn't a question.

"Yes." She sat on the bench across from the dog, testing the springs, running her hand over the burgundy velvet cushions.

Bowie took the seat across from her, resting his rifle against the bench, patting the dog. There wasn't much room in the compartment, and Bowie and Stonewall seemed to fill most of it.

"My parents passed away within two days of each other, of an illness. I was volunteering at the Fort Slocum Hospital, and after the war, most hospitals wouldn't take an unmarried woman as a nurse. It was one thing to help out in a crisis, but afterwards, the proprieties must be observed. There were many war widows who needed those jobs, anyway. My uncle is my only relative. I had nowhere else to go, and no money to get there, even if I had a place to go."

"That's how I found you. You mentioned the button factory once."

And he had remembered.

She studied her new husband from beneath her lashes. His dark hair fell over his shoulders, and he wore a full beard and moustache. On the side of his face that had been injured, the hair grew unevenly, but the black powder stippling blended in with his dark whiskers, hiding some of the damage. She remembered being so careful of his wounds the first time she had washed and shaved him in the hospital. His beard looked soft and nicely trimmed, but she missed the strong line of his jaw hidden beneath the whiskers.

He stroked Stonewall's gray-and-black coat, and he stared past the dog's head out the window, keeping his good side toward her. She well remembered the breadth of Bowie's shoulders, his solid frame, as she'd tended him in the hospital, changing his bandages and bedding, feeding him, holding his hand when the pain was too great or the nightmares stalked him.

It was one thing to be his nurse, something else altogether to be his wife, even if only on paper.

How did one make small talk with a new husband? She twisted her gloves in her hands.

"I didn't know your name was James Bowie. Not until you told Pastor Gates. I always knew you only as Captain Hart."

"My pa named all of us after famous Texans."

"Tell me about your family. I know some from when you were in the hospital, but I feel I need a refresher." And what she knew had come from the fevered wanderings of an injured man who probably didn't even know he was rambling. Once his fever had broken and he'd come to senses, he'd barely spoken, and then only to her.

The train whistle blew, and with a jerk, they were moving down the track. Her heart rate accelerated along with the train. She'd never been farther from home than a quick trip to Boston once when she was twelve. To think of traveling all the way to Texas...

"There are seven of us brothers. Austin's the oldest. Tough, a good leader. If things went according to his plans—and they usually do—he should be married by the time we get back to Hartville. Then there's me. After me is Travis. He's a doctor, and he married Annie Lawrence, who has a son, Robbie, from her first marriage. Houston is number four, and he's got a hardware store in town. He's married to Coralee Culpepper, a neighbor girl he was sweet on before he ran off to California for a few years. He's seeing to getting you a house built. Should be done by the time we get back."

Elise blinked. "You had him building a house before you knew if I'd accept your proposal?"

Bowie shrugged. "Figured you'd need a place to live if you said yes. Figured the family could rent it out or use it for a foreman and his family if you said no."

A house being built, just for her. What would it be like? Big? Small? Far from town? Near his brothers' homes? So many questions.

Bowie must've sensed her interest. "You can shop in Hartville for furniture and rugs and such, or order from a catalog. If you need to, there's always someone going to Santone. You can go along to shop, or send a list."

She nodded. Shopping for a houseful of furniture? Her. Elise Rivers...no, Elise Hart now. The ladies at the button factory wouldn't believe it.

"I'd love to go to town with you and choose things for the house." Her mind raced with ideas, wondering what his tastes were, if he liked heavy, dark furniture, or if he preferred things more Spartan.

"I don't go to town. Do as you like with the house. It won't matter to me." His flat tone told her to leave the subject for the time being. Such a curious man—kind one moment, cold as snow the next.

"Which brother comes after Houston?"

"Crockett." Bowie shook his head. "You'll know him when you see him because he's always wearing a loud shirt or bandana or both. As a kid, he was always getting into scrapes. He's settled down, a real steady hand, good rancher. Married Jane Haymaker, a neighbor."

"That's five." She held up one hand. "What about the other two?"

"Chisholm is number six. He's a Texas Ranger. Married a Spanish beauty named Caro. He's cool-headed in a fight." Bowie said this as if it was the highest praise he could offer.

"And number seven?"

A slight smile touched Bowie's lips—a rare occurrence, from what Elise could gather. "Hays. 'Fortune's Favorite' is what Mother used to call him. The ladies think he's charming—at least, from what I hear. He stole a march on all of us and married the new padre's daughter, Emma, way back last spring. They're expecting their first child sometime around Christmas."

"As an only child, I can't imagine having so many siblings. I hope I can keep everyone straight." She ticked them off on her fingers. "Austin, Bowie, Travis, Houston, Crockett, Chisholm, and Hays. And their wives. And one baby on the way."

"That I know of, anyway. Could be more. Harts are a prolific breed."

"Do all you boys look alike?"

His brows came down. "I suppose. We all have dark hair. I'm the tallest."

"What about your parents?"

"There's just Pa now. Like your folks, my mother died during the war.

I was rotting in Elmira Prison, and my family thought I was dead." Disgust rasped in his voice. "I'll always regret that. Mother dying thinking I'd been killed at Gettysburg."

"Your family thought you'd died?" Elise's heart broke. "How terrible for them. And for you. I wish I'd known. I would've written to them. I would've gotten a letter to them somehow."

The moment he spoke of the war, his face had hardened. "I'm going to stretch my legs." Levering himself up, he motioned for Stonewall to stay.

She stared at the door. Had she said the wrong thing? Done the wrong thing? Settling back against the squabs, she rested her head, watching the world slide by.

Lord, help me to be a good wife. I never thought I would pray those words, but here I am, a married woman. At least on paper. Reaching into her bag, she pulled out the marriage certificate, staring at the signatures that said she was someone's wife.

Elise Marie Hart.

Mrs. Bowie Hart.

It was the name of a stranger. Would she ever get used to it?

~

*E*lise barely saw Bowie, though they were confined to the same train for nearly a week. She spoke more with Stonewall than her husband. It was as if he couldn't bear to be in the same space with her. Where he slept, she had no idea. The porter came each night and made up her bed, and she climbed into it, Stonewall curling up on the end of the bunk and keeping her feet warm.

New York City, Pittsburgh, Cincinnati, St. Louis, Wichita. Miles and miles to think and wonder if she had made a huge mistake. Bowie checked in each day to see if she needed anything, and at each stop, he took Stonewall for a run. Her new husband didn't join her in the dining car, and she wondered if it was that he didn't want to be seen with her, or if he didn't want to be seen at all.

When they reached Wichita, she stepped off the train, greeted by a brisk wind and the smell of cattle. She wrinkled her nose and reached for her handkerchief. A young man broke from a group of cowboys and hurried to her side.

"Sorry about the smell, ma'am. The stockyards have to be close to the railroad. You staying in our town long? Are you looking for a hotel or rooming house? I'd be pleased if you'd consider having dinner with me tonight." He reached for her valise, not waiting for her to respond. Were all men here as forward as this one? A large hand reached around Elise and took the bag before she could even gasp at his boldness.

"She's with me." Bowie stared at the cowboy, the chill edge to his voice sending a shiver up Elise's spine.

The cowboy held up his hands, backing away. "Sorry, pard. I didn't know."

Bowie put his hand under Elise's elbow. "You shouldn't talk to strangers. Wichita's a wide-open town."

"I didn't say a word," she protested.

"A lady as pretty as you doesn't have to." He guided her down the platform steps.

He thought she was pretty?

Without giving her time to mull that notion over, Bowie led her along a boardwalk to a hotel. Cowboys in wide-brimmed hats and jingling spurs passed them, and ladies with bonnets that shielded their faces from the sun went in and out of the shops, baskets on their arms. Horses and wagons lined the main thoroughfare, and most of the buildings were made of wood. Dust blew in scudding puffs along the dirt street, and a donkey brayed nearby.

And over all, the biggest, bluest sky she'd ever seen.

Bowie held the door for her, and she smiled up at him, grateful for his protection and care in these unfamiliar surroundings. He went to the front desk. "When does the next stage for Dallas leave?"

"Tomorrow morning."

"Then I'd like a room for the night."

"For you and the missus?" The clerk leaned around him to nod to Elise.

"That's right."

"A dollar for the room." Putting his hands flat on the counter, the clerk raised himself on tiptoe to peer over at Stonewall. "The dog..."

Bowie dropped a five dollar gold piece onto the register. "The dog stays with us. And I'd like a bath brought up for the lady."

Elise almost cried at his thoughtfulness. A real bath after making do with quick washes in a basin aboard the train for a week.

"Certainly, sir." He handed over a key. "Room six, top of the stairs."

Elise followed Bowie up the wooden staircase. He unlocked the door and looked inside before he let her enter. The room must've met his expectations, for he leaned against the bureau and crossed his arms.

She removed her hat and smoothed her curly brown hair. "It will be nice to sleep in a bed that isn't moving."

A tap at the door, and a porter entered carrying a tin bathtub. "Be up in a jiffy with the water."

He was as good as his word, carrying in two steaming cans and pouring them into the tub.

"Thanks." Bowie flipped him a coin.

Just how much money did he have? It seemed he was tipping and paying and doling out cash every time she turned around.

When the porter had gone, Bowie straightened. "Go ahead and have your bath. I'll be back in a bit, and then we can find some grub." He handed her the key. "Keep the door locked. I'll knock."

Elise nodded, staring after his departing form, something she seemed to do often. What a complex man. He saw to her every comfort, but he kept himself at a distance. The only time he had talked at any length was when she asked about his family.

The bath refreshed her, body and spirit. Her only regret was that her one decent dress was limp and travel worn. She didn't relish putting it on again now, but perhaps tonight she could sponge it and hang it up, and hopefully, some of the wrinkles would come out before morning.

She was brushing her hair when a knock sounded on the door. Remembering Bowie's caution, she asked before she opened it. He entered, followed by Stonewall, and she caught the smell of soap and noted Bowie's damp hair. Her husband had taken advantage of a bath as well.

He rested his rifle against the foot of the bed and folded his arms across his broad chest, setting the fringe on his jacket to swaying. She was conscious of his stare as she coiled her hair and pinned it up. No one had seen her with her hair down since she was a girl, and to have him watching her so intently sent flutters skittering across her skin.

"The hotel restaurant opens in a couple of hours. I thought you might like to do some shopping in the meantime."

Shopping? Since she had exactly three dollars and forty-one cents in her handbag, this would be a short endeavor. She gathered her hat and bag. Still, it would be nice to get out. It had been a long time since she'd had the freedom to take a leisurely stroll along some storefronts. Window shopping would be a treat.

Bowie had other ideas. He held the door for her to enter a vast emporium, making the bell overhead jangle their arrival. When Stonewall would've followed, he snapped his fingers, motioned with his hand flat, and the big dog stayed on the porch, eyes soulful but patient.

Elise inhaled a kaleidoscope of fragrances. Vinegar, leather, coffee, tobacco, kerosene, peppermint. The store was so large, there were two center aisles and long counters down each side.

She could get lost in here.

"Afternoon, folks. What can I do for you?" The shopkeeper ambled over, a trio of new pitchforks on his shoulder. He stood them in a barrel near the door, clattering the tines together and dusting his hands. "Got everything from A to Z."

Bowie put his hand on the small of her back, and the warmth of his touch spread through her. "You sell ready-made clothes for ladies?" he asked.

"Sure, sure. Got a whole section, right there in the back. Got a room to try on things if you need." The storekeeper eyed Elise from her shoe tips to her hat brim. "Should be plenty to choose from in your size. Let me go get my wife. She can help you better than me."

As he trotted to the staircase that ascended one wall, Elise stood on tiptoe to whisper into Bowie's ear. At the last moment, he turned, as if startled to have her coming up on the damaged side of his face, and suddenly they were nose to nose.

Air clogged high in her lungs, and she blinked. They hadn't been this close since she had first peeked beneath his dirty, encrusted bandages in the hospital.

"Yes? Is there something you need?" It was a question he'd asked every day since he'd rescued her. He didn't move away, and she felt mesmerized by his dark-brown eye.

She eased back a step, her cheeks warm. "I thought we were just window shopping. I don't have money for new clothes." How could she explain that the wages her uncle should've paid her over the years had gone for her room and board?

He raised the eyebrow over his good eye and shrugged. "Money isn't a problem. Get everything you need. Dresses, hats, shoes." He touched her threadbare sleeve where she'd repaired a small tear months before. "You're a Hart now. You need to look the part."

Stung, she turned away, tears pricking her eyes. He must be ashamed of her appearance. He didn't want to return home with such a tatty-looking bride.

The storekeeper returned with a pretty blond woman in a lovely blue gown, all tucks and ruffles, the exact color of her eyes. She looked so stylish and up-to-the-minute, Elise felt worse than ever.

"Hello, I'm Janet Cloverton. My husband says you're looking for some new clothes?"

Was she? She cast another glance at Bowie. How kind he had been, having rescued her and seen to her every need the past few days. The last thing she wanted to do was embarrass him in front of his family.

Bowie nodded, keeping his face turned away from Mrs. Cloverton. "My wife needs a new wardrobe. A what do you call it when a woman gets married—all the clothes she gets?"

Mrs. Cloverton smiled. "A trousseau?"

"That's it. My wife needs a trousseau."

Elise let Mrs. Cloverton lead her toward the back of the store, determined to buy whatever she needed to meet Bowie's expectations.

And later, she would savor the thrill that hit her chest because he had called her his wife.

CHAPTER 3

*B*owie hadn't foreseen this turn of events.

The stage was so full that when he and Elise went to board, there was only one spot left. He had no choice but to take the seat and hold Elise on his lap. Stonewall took up most of the floor space between the passengers' feet, and Bowie anchored his rifle between his leg and the side of the coach.

Elise perched on his knee, and he put his arms around her waist as the stage jolted and moved forward. She jerked against his chest and then sat up, stiff as ironwood, her cheeks rosy.

"It's a long ride. You should try to relax." He whispered against her ear, marveling at the glossy texture of her hair, her delicate profile, and how smooth and fine her skin was.

She kept her eyes down, studying her hands. The five other men in the stage stared at her, and Bowie gave them each a hard glare, reminding them of their manners. They looked out the windows and at the floor, and slowly, Elise softened against him.

Before too many miles had passed, she laid her head on his shoulder, all but melting into him as she fell asleep. All those nights on the train when he'd waited until she was asleep before entering their compartment and taking up his spot on the bench to watch over her hadn't prepared him for this. Bowie savored the feel of her in his arms. He'd never held a woman like this, never been this close to one. He'd watched his brothers as one after another they met their wives, fell in love, and became a world of two.

And he'd never thought it would happen to him.

That brought him to his senses. He wasn't in love, and he and Elise would never have that kind of relationship. They were married, yes, but only on paper. Theirs was a mutually beneficial arrangement, nothing more. She had married him because she wanted a way out of her dead-end life, and he'd married her to get his inheritance. Love didn't come into the equation.

He couldn't resist rubbing his bewhiskered chin against the top of her head, inhaling her scent.

Jasmine.

She must've purchased some jasmine soap at the emporium. Along with some mighty pretty clothes. He hadn't thought to wonder what she'd bought specifically, merely settling the bill when she was done and toting the packages back to the hotel. When Bowie had come to her room this morning, she'd about taken his breath away, she looked so beautiful. He breathed in the jasmine once more, feeling sleep tugging at his eyes. He would be glad to get home...

The pain had been unbearable. White-hot, searing agony from his collarbone to his hairline. He remembered nothing from the moment the caisson he'd been crouching behind as he reloaded his pistol had exploded, throwing him down the hill toward the enemy lines, until the hospital orderlies dropped his litter on the floor of the makeshift prisoner's hospital at Fort Slocum.

For days, he had been in and out of consciousness, lying first on the battlefield, and then transported with the other wounded prisoners to area hospitals. He gripped the litter poles, gritting his teeth against the agony in his face and neck.

The scent of jasmine drifted toward him, delicate and elusive. After months of smoke and blood and horses and men, it was the first pleasant aroma, and he drew it in like a hungry man.

"Shhh, easy there, Captain." A woman's voice.

He opened his eyes...at least, he tried to...but he could see nothing. Panic clawed through his chest, making him gasp.

"My eyes!" Moving his lips at all sent another cascade of pain through him.

"Shhh." Her hand rested on his right shoulder, pressing gently. "You're safe in a hospital, soldier. I'll take care of you. Your eyes are bandaged for now. Just rest."

Her voice sounded low and sweet, the nicest thing he'd heard in months. A spoon pressed to his mouth, and he swallowed the laudanum.

"Who are you?" His voice rasped.

"My name is Miss Rivers. Elise. Sleep now. I'll watch over you."

When next he awoke, the pain was more bearable—that was, until she began to remove the bandages. As much as he wanted that, wanted to be able to see her face, to see *anything*, the pulling of the encrusted bandages awoke the searing agony once more.

"I'm so sorry. I'll be as gentle as I can." Cool water touched his skin, soaking through the wrappings. "I brought you a salve that my mama used to make up for burns. It will help, I promise."

Then she removed the last bandage, and he could see her face. Blurry at first, then coming into focus.

Lots of curly brown hair, and light-brown eyes, sweetly curving cheeks, and a pink mouth. As beautiful as she was kind. She wore an encouraging smile, and he decided his wounds couldn't look as bad as they felt, not if she wasn't shocked and repulsed.

But what was wrong with his left eye? Was it still bandaged? He lifted his hand, but she grasped it and pressed it down. "Don't touch your wound. You risk infection."

A man in a stained white coat blundered over, banging into the cot, sending a jolt of pain through Bowie. "Ah, he's awake, is he? Move aside, nurse."

A doctor. Bowie hurt so badly, he could barely concentrate on the man's words.

Lost the eye. Black powder burns. Lucky to be alive, but you'll be disfigured.

Blinded, scarred, mutilated.

A scream bottled in his throat—anger, fear, panic. Sweat formed on his face and neck as he strained to come to grips with the doctor's diagnosis.

No! Why hadn't God just let him die there on the battlefield at

Gettysburg? Cannons roared, men shouted, horses screamed, and bullets whistled as men fell all around him.

He couldn't breathe, he couldn't think, he couldn't escape the pain ravaging his body.

Then her touch was there, cool and soothing.

"Bowie."

The hospital receded, the sounds of battle growing faint.

"Bowie, wake up. You're having a bad dream."

He opened his eye. Elise cupped his cheek, her fingers brushing the hair away from his face. He gulped in a huge breath of jasmine and fresh air.

Her hand lowered to rest against his chest, his heart hammering as if trying to get out. The stage rocked and swayed.

"Are you all right?" Concern clouded her gentle brown eyes, just as it had in the Fort Slocum Hospital.

No one had touched him in years. He never allowed anyone to get that close.

"I am now." He took another steadying breath, and for the first time in a decade felt comforted.

~

*E*lise followed Bowie up the steps of the house he called El Regalo, butterflies bombarding her stomach. The place looked like a castle—big, stone, with ironwork railings and many, many windows. She began to get a new perspective on the change in her circumstances.

Horses and buggies stood tied up out front.

"Did you tell your family we were coming home today?"

Bowie shook his head. "It's Sunday. We all eat together on Sundays."

Elise gripped her gloves, trying to hold onto her nerve. She had known she would have to meet Bowie's family, but she hadn't anticipated she would meet them all at once.

Opening the massive oak door, Bowie ushered her inside, dropping his saddlebags and her valise onto a bench in the foyer. The livery driver brought her new trunk up the steps and set it just inside the door.

She tried to take it all in—the high ceilings, the plaster medallions, the papered walls and shining woodwork.

And the sound of voices.

"This way." Her husband held out his hand, and she swallowed hard as she placed her fingers in his. "They won't eat you. They're going to be glad, once they get over their surprise."

She nodded and let him lead her into the dining room—the most sumptuous dining room she'd ever seen, with ornate carved wood and a coffered ceiling, and what surely had to be the longest table in Texas.

"Afternoon."

Bowie's voice made every head turn and every conversation stop. Elise gripped his hand as if holding onto a lifeline. He drew her into the circle of his arm, snugging her up against his side, and she looked up at him in surprise. Public displays of affection were not something he'd done before. Then she remembered how he'd asked her not to let anyone know theirs was a marriage of convenience.

The gray-haired man stood from the end of the table. "Bowie. Good to see you. Who's that with you?"

"Pa, everyone...I'd like you to meet my wife. Elise, this is my family."

For a long moment, nobody moved or spoke. Mouths hung open, and forks remained half raised.

Then all at once, the room burst into action. Chairs scooted back, laughter rang out, and Elise and Bowie were surrounded. The men pounded Bowie on the back, and the ladies held out their hands in greeting. The knot in Elise's middle eased some, even as Bowie's grip on her waist tightened.

"Where have you been hiding *her*?" Hays—she thought it was Hays—asked Bowie.

"We've known each other a long time."

"Aren't you a sly one, keeping her under wraps?" Was that Chisholm?

"Welcome to the family." A pretty young woman—Emma? It must be Emma since she was obviously in the family way—leaned in and kissed Elise on the cheek. "I'm sure you must be tired from your trip, and then to meet all of us all at once..." She didn't have a Texas twang to her voice, but Elise couldn't place the accent. Definitely a Northerner, though, which made Elise feel better. At least she wasn't the only Yankee in the family.

"Let me meet this young lady." The gray-haired man parted the group, his moustache twitching. This must be GW, Bowie's father. Elise found herself engulfed in his embrace and then stood away while he studied her. She held her breath, waiting for his verdict.

Finally, he hugged her again and said, "Welcome to El Regalo. Come in and have a seat."

Chairs and place settings were procured, and Elise found herself seated at the massive dinner table. Bowie sat beside his father, GW, at the end of the table, and Elise sat on Bowie's right. From this side, it was impossible to see his scars or eye patch. Had this always been his seat at the table, or had he changed it after his return from the war?

Each of the brothers introduced themselves, and Elise covered her amusement at the pride the Hart men had in presenting their brides. There were fond gestures, a touch to the shoulder, a wink, a hand clasp under the table edge that made Elise wistful. Clearly, Bowie's brothers had all made love matches.

When the oldest brother, Austin, introduced his wife, Bowie straightened. "So the mail-order thing must've worked out fine? Congratulations."

The couple shared an amused glance, and Austin put his arm around his wife. "Not without some ups and downs, but yeah, I got the right girl for me." He laughed. "We'll have to tell you the story sometime."

Bowie ate his meal and listened to the lively banter around him but didn't join in, part of the group yet separate somehow. But something in him seemed to have eased. He was relaxed, not nearly as tense as he had been the entire journey from New York to Texas. Was it just that he was happy to be home? Elise felt at a loss, knowing so little about him compared to the people in this room.

Houston said from down the table, "You might be interested to know that the house is done except for the furniture and rugs and such. The workers finished the plastering and trimming out the doors and windows yesterday afternoon."

Bowie nodded. "Travis, how's Clara?"

Elise tensed. Who was Clara?

Travis—he was a doctor, Elise remembered that much—set his glass on the table. "She's fine, though she'll be glad to see you. She pined the whole time you were gone. Robbie checked in on her often, though." He leaned past his wife, Annie, to wink at his young stepson, a child of about nine or ten, Elise guessed.

An unfamiliar feeling trickled through Elise. Someone named Clara pined for her husband? Who was this woman?

"I, for one, am glad you're back, though," Travis continued. "I didn't want anything to happen to her with you away. I know how much you've been looking forward to a litter of puppies from Stonewall and Clara. Not to mention Robbie here and Emma's brother David lining up to get one. If Clara doesn't have at least three or four pups, there will be a lot of sad little boys."

Chagrin heated Elise's cheeks. A dog! She'd actually been...jealous... of a dog. She must be more tired than she thought.

Elise was overwhelmed by the time the meal finished. The exuberance of the Hart brothers, their vitality and masculinity, surged through the room. And the ladies were no less animated, chattering and laughing, clearly enjoying one another's company. As they moved into the parlor, Elise began to wonder when she could decently plead fatigue and find a quiet spot to get her bearings.

~

*B*owie noted the tiredness around Elise's eyes and the way she bit her lower lip as she watched his family. They were a boisterous lot, he had to admit.

But as they grouped together on the settees and chairs and settled around the tables for chess and checkers in the parlor, for the first time in a long time, Bowie felt the equal to his brothers. Scarred and battered, a helpless prisoner for most of the war, yes, but he'd fulfilled the letter of his father's command. Just like his brothers, he'd found a wife. He leaned against the mantel, arms crossed, watching her.

Elise sat between Coralee and Annie, Houston and Travis's wives, and a burst of pride shot through Bowie's chest.

She was his. His wife.

Her dark hair shone as light streamed in the tall windows. Though she had it all coiled and pinned up, he remembered how it had looked tumbling down her back and over her shoulders when he'd returned to the hotel room in Wichita. The sight had sucked all the wind out of his lungs and dried out his mouth.

She smoothed her skirts, and he compared her outfit to those of his covey of sisters-in-law. Yep, she fit right in. Another thrust of satisfaction shot through him. Buying her new clothes had been the right thing, and the least he could do to show his appreciation. After all, he owed her from way back, and he owed her now. He didn't want her to feel embarrassed or out of place amongst the Hart women.

He knew too well what it meant to feel out of place.

"You sure know how to keep a secret." Austin nudged him, coming up on his blind side. "Why didn't you tell anyone you were leaving?"

"I told Houston."

"Yeah, a few minutes before you lit out. You sure didn't tell anyone you were going to get a wife. Why not say something about Elise before?"

Bowie turned so he could see his older brother. "I don't recall interfering in the courtships of any of you boys. Why should I invite you into mine?"

"I'm not asking to be invited into your courtship, but you do have to agree, you dropped quite a cannonball into the water trough, showing up with a bride when none of us had a notion you even knew any unmarried ladies."

Bowie shrugged. "I've known her for a long time." Which wasn't a lie.

"Well? How did you meet?" Austin asked, never taking his eyes from Rebekah as she chatted with Emma.

How much should he tell his family about himself and Elise? Not that theirs was a marriage of convenience, for sure. That was nobody else's business. But he would have to tell them something.

"I met her during the war. She was a nurse at the Fort Slocum hospital after Gettysburg."

Austin stopped staring at his wife to finally look at Bowie. "That was more than ten years ago. Did you write letters all this time? How did I not know about this?"

"No letters. The last time I saw her, they were hauling me out of a hospital bed and shipping me off to prison." He'd nearly been undone by the loss, by the tears in her eyes and the desperate way she'd fought with the doctor to prevent them from taking him. "Until I showed up on her doorstep in New York."

"New York? How'd you even know where to find her? How'd you know she wouldn't already be married with half a dozen kids?"

"She talked about where she lived, that after the war was over, she'd be living with her uncle who had a button factory in New Rochelle. I figured I'd start there, but I didn't have to look far. She was working at the factory." Actually, she was all but enslaved there. The bruise on her jaw had finally faded, but Bowie's anger burned against her sorry excuse for a relative. Any man who would lift a hand against a woman was a coward who deserved to be beaten to shrapnel. "And I figured if she was already married, I wouldn't propose to her."

Austin laughed and clapped him on the shoulder. "Well, she's pretty as can be, and she's clearly taken with you. She watched you all through lunch, and she keeps peeking at you under those long lashes as though you might disappear."

Which merely meant she was playing her part well.

"Bowie, come over here. I have something for you." Pa came into the parlor, a long envelope in his hands.

A small cheer went up from his brothers, and Bowie couldn't keep back a smile. *At last.*

"Son, I'm pleased as punch to give this to you. I'll admit, I had my doubts, but you've proven up to the task. The first of November, 1874, and all you boys are married." Pa handed the deed over. "I hope you and Elise have a long and happy life together, as happy as your mother and I were, God rest her soul."

"Thank you, sir." Bowie held the envelope in both hands. He was the equal of his brothers in this too. He removed the papers and unfolded them.

"I took the liberty of penning Elise's name on the deed as well." Pa grinned. "Since it belongs to both of you now."

Austin gave him another nudge, as if to remind him that his bride should be a part of this.

How could he have forgotten? "Mi—" Bowie cleared his throat. He'd almost called her Miss Rivers. "Elise. Come and see." He held out his hand to her, and she rose, her cheeks glowing, her eyes shining. She crossed the room and took his hand, and he tucked her into his side as if he'd done it a thousand times. She fit just right and even put her arm around his waist to lean in and read the document.

Hays called from across the room, "I couldn't wait to kiss my bride when Pa handed over those papers, since she was the one who made it possible."

The knot of insecurity Bowie carried around with him tightened in his chest. He wanted to throttle Hays for his ridiculous comment. No woman would want his ravaged lips against her skin. How could he give Elise a graceful escape?

But Elise was a better actress than he'd thought. She turned in his arm, put her hand to his damaged cheek, her fingertips just grazing the edge of his eyepatch, and drew him toward her. Her soft brown eyes fluttered closed, and before he could draw a breath, her lips met his.

He felt as if he'd been struck with white-hot lightning. This was no quick peck to satisfy his family's expectations. Her lips moved under his, and his embrace tightened. A growl formed in his throat, and he barely smothered it as her fingers threaded into his hair. The smell of jasmine surrounded him.

Laughter broke through his senses, and he remembered where he was. Elise stepped back quickly, smoothing her hair and looking anywhere but at him. Male satisfaction at her flustered appearance swept over him until he realized his own heart was pounding and his breath was coming too fast.

His sisters-in-law clapped, and Hays let out a long, low whistle, while Bowie tried to pretend nothing unusual had happened. Pa beamed, and Austin gave Bowie a long, speculative look.

By the time evening rolled around, Bowie had had his fill of the talk and laughter. As much as he enjoyed his family, he needed to get away from people for a while to feel like himself again. His brothers and their wives departed, two-by-two, until only Austin and Rebekah who lived at El Regalo together with Pa remained.

Bowie carried Elise's new trunk up the stairs.

Perla bustled by, her arms full of linens. "One moment, Senor Bowie. I put fresh sheets on the bed after dinner, and here are clean towels." She opened the door to his room, already lamp-lit. Bowie paused, considering something he hadn't thought about until now. With Austin and Rebekah and Pa in the house—not to mention Perla—he and Elise would have to share a room to keep up the notion that theirs was a normal marriage.

He set the trunk on the floor at the end of the bed.

Elise stood in the doorway, her shoulders drooping. She straightened when Perla left, pausing to thank the woman for her kindness. The housekeeper smiled and closed the door behind her, leaving Bowie and Elise alone.

Perla had placed a bouquet of flowers on his bureau, something she'd never done before. Brown-eyed Susans, old man's beard, and purple horsemint in a blue pitcher, but he could only smell jasmine... whether he could actually smell it or was merely remembering it, he wasn't sure. His mind kept returning to that kiss, and he couldn't be certain about anything.

Elise sighed and leaned back against the door. "Whew."

"You did well today. It's a lot to take in."

"It is, but your family is delightful. They clearly care about you. Your father couldn't be more proud of his sons." She shook her head and removed the strings of her reticule from around her wrist. "Everyone was so nice. But I'll admit, I'm ready for bed. I didn't realize I was so tired until this minute."

"Elise..." How could he explain that his family would expect them to share this room?

"I had a hard time not laughing when you almost called me 'Miss Rivers.'" She sat on the side of the bed.

And I had a hard time remembering my own name when you kissed me.

"Elise, I really appreciate everything you did today. My family is satisfied that we're a happily married couple. But, the thing is..."

"They're going to expect us to share this room." Her gaze didn't flinch. "Of course they are."

Her calm acceptance of the situation surprised him. "You don't need to worry about anything. I'll sleep on the floor."

She grimaced. "Bowie, I realized something when I was surrounded by all your relatives, when I read my name next to yours on that deed, even more than when I saw it on the marriage certificate."

Was she sorry? Was she going to back out? Something akin to panic clawed its way up his chest.

"I realized that this marriage is permanent. Whether in name only or not, we are bound together. You can't sleep on the floor for the rest of your life. We can certainly comport ourselves with propriety. You can stay on your side of the bed, and me on mine, and we can both get a good night's sleep."

Once again, she stunned him. He needed to get out of here and sort this out in his mind.

"I thought I'd go check on Clara and Stonewall before bed. I imagine you'll be asleep when I get back."

She blinked and after a moment stood and touched him on the arm. "I'll say goodnight, then."

He carried her sweet smile with him as he descended the stairs and went outside.

Clara greeted him in the barn, wriggling and lapping at his hand. Stonewall didn't rise from his straw bed, merely lifting his head for a moment before curling up again. Bowie ran his hand down Clara's plump side. "Not long now, huh, girl? Tomorrow we'll get you moved out to our new place."

He inhaled the familiar scents of hay and leather and horses in the cavernous barn, grateful to be home. The crowded cities, the smoke and rattle of the train, the constant presence of strangers... He shook his head. He was a Texan, through and through, and now that Elise was on the 7 Heart, he couldn't imagine a reason he'd ever have to travel that far from home again.

But now he needed to travel back to the house, to that room, to that bed. Bowie didn't particularly relish sleeping on the floor or sitting up as he had on the train. But the thought of sleeping in a bed with Elise scared him.

Not Elise herself. No, it was the nightmares that kept him from sleeping beside his bride. It was that he couldn't remember the last time he'd slept the night through without waking in a cold sweat, reliving battles and prison and pain. It embarrassed him, but up to now, he'd been able to keep it to himself...until Elise had gotten past his defenses on the stagecoach.

But she didn't know that his nightmares were an every-night occurrence. He patted Clara once more, stepped outside into the moonlight, and forced himself to go back to the house.

CHAPTER 4

*E*lise wakened wrapped in her husband's arms.

She couldn't remember him coming to bed the night before, though she'd tried to stay awake. After donning a new nightgown, she'd brushed her hair, wishing she had a looking glass larger than the square shaving mirror tacked to the wall above the washstand. Still, she could understand Bowie not wanting a larger mirror, since he seemed so conscious of his scars. She slid into bed, wondering which side Bowie slept on and trying to quell the flutters in her stomach and the trembles in her legs at the thought of sleeping in a man's bed.

You are a married woman. Use some of that reason and logic you just gave Bowie and stop being so silly.

She yawned, her eyelids heavy. Would he come back? What if he stayed away all night and his family came to know of it? What would they think?

And then it was morning and she was waking up, snuggled against his side, warm and drowsy and safe. More comfortable than she could ever remember being. Her cheek rested against his shoulder, his arm held her close, and her hand lay on his broad chest, rising and falling, clocking his steady heartbeat. She had clearly crossed the centerline of the bed. And if he awoke, how was she going to explain that? But it felt so good.

Don't move. Hang onto this moment as long as possible.

Sunlight slanted across the bed, so it must be well after time to rise, but she couldn't make herself stir. His warmth and masculine scent wrapped around her, and she breathed deeply. It had been a long time since she felt this protected and cherished. Her life had been bereft of care and tenderness since her parents' deaths, and she'd been so alone all those years.

But now she had a husband, and an extended family, and a place to put down roots.

"Good morning." His voice rumbled under her ear, deep and raspy but tinged with humor.

How long had he been awake?

She pressed herself up on her elbow, looking at his face with a gasp, mortified to be caught cuddled up against him.

For the first time since she'd removed his bandages in the hospital so long ago, she saw him without his eyepatch. The place where his eye should be was just an empty socket, dry and healed. She felt a rush of pride that he had recovered so well...and that she had a small part in that recovery.

He tensed at her gasp. His face hardened, and he yanked his arm from around her, rolling away, slipping into his pants, reaching for the eyepatch on the bedside table, and securing it before turning around.

She put her fingers to her lips, chagrined at having been so bold as to move off her side of the bed, and even more scandalized that he'd awakened before she could sneak back onto her own. But she hadn't done it consciously. Should she apologize? Say it was an accident? If she did, would he believe her, and would it embarrass him further? Before she could say anything, he reached for his shirt on the chair back, his movements hurried and jerky.

"It's late, and we have a lot to do today." He stuffed his shirt into his pants and buttoned it up, looking out the window. He stomped his feet into his boots, his face hard—accusatory, even. "We're moving to the new house. I'll bring a wagon around to the back door. Pa's loaning us some things until you can order whatever furniture you want." The last words were said as he closed the door behind himself.

Elise dropped back onto the bed, feeling hollow and confused. Would she ever really know this complicated man? Would he ever be at ease around her? She hadn't meant to violate their agreement and make him uncomfortable, but she couldn't deny how bereft she felt without his arms around her.

When Elise came downstairs so late, the housekeeper, Perla, gave her a knowing smile. "I kept some breakfast for you. Do not be nervous. We have had many newlyweds here this year. Bowie has gone to get the wagon. I have been packing some things for you to take—dishes and food and such."

"Thank you." Elise's cheeks heated, but she was grateful for the housekeeper's prattle. She ate quickly, and within the hour, she was seated next to Bowie in the wagon and headed to her new home.

"I've arranged for someone to take you into town this afternoon, after you've seen the place, so you can start your shopping." Bowie flicked the reins.

Her eyebrows rose. "You won't come with me?"

He shook his head, his dark hair shielding his face. "I told you, I never go to town if I can help it. You'll do fine. I don't care what you buy."

Behind them in the wagon lay a bedstead and mattress, a table and chairs, and a bureau. The barest of necessities until new furnishings arrived.

They drove northeast along a two-track road. "How far is your property from the main house?"

"El Regalo sits in the center of the 7 Heart, and our portions are like spokes on a wheel. Houston built the house on a rise above the Sabinal River about five miles as the crow flies from El Regalo." He spoke as if reciting facts that had nothing to do with him or her.

Longhorn cattle grazed everywhere, the wind blew through the grasses and brush, and the sun shone happily. And yet, she was sad. Here she was riding to her new home with her husband, and the gulf between them yawned wider than ever.

Soon they approached a pretty white house with windows that gleamed in the sunshine. Two stories, with a wide front porch that wrapped around one corner. It couldn't have been more perfect if Elise had designed it herself. Everything looked new and ready for a fresh start.

Bowie leapt from the wagon and reached up for her, clasping her waist as she put her hands on his shoulders. He didn't look at her as he swung her to the ground, and a chill set up residence in her middle. She rubbed her arms, even though the temperature was quite warm outside.

Stonewall barked and leapt from the wagon bed, followed more slowly by his mate. Bowie had introduced Elise briefly to Clara, but she remained aloof. Stonewall sidled up and nudged Elise's hand for a pat. Elise obliged, grateful that someone seemed happy she was here.

Bowie held the front door open for Elise, and she walked into her new home, trying not to feel sad that there was no hope of Bowie behaving like a traditional groom and carrying her over the threshold. *Stop being silly. You know it isn't that kind of marriage. You knew what you were signing up for when you agreed to wed, and it's ridiculous to pine for something different now.*

But she couldn't shake the feeling of being cherished that she had awakened with, nor the thrill that had shot through her and stolen her breath when they had kissed yesterday. In those moments, she had allowed herself to hope, to dream a bit, that their marriage might someday be more than just a quiet agreement to co-exist.

"Parlor, kitchen, dining room down here, bedrooms upstairs." Bowie pointed to the staircase. Everywhere around them, the smell of fresh paint and plaster and newly sawn wood swirled. The rooms were large but not vast, and Elise could picture how inviting and cozy the house would look with rugs and pictures and books.

"It's perfect. I love it." She ran her finger along a smooth windowsill. "How is it that Houston knew just what kind of house to build?"

Bowie shrugged. "Before the war, I used to think I might want to be a carpenter or even an architect. Houston worked off some plans I drew up when I was a kid."

There were so many facets to this man. Would she ever know them all?

Stonewall and Clara nosed around the baseboards, investigating the house. She wasn't fond of dogs in the house, but she could put up with them as long as they stayed downstairs.

"The kitchen's this way." He led her to the back of the house.

She sucked in a breath, delighted at all the honey-colored wood. Cabinets and shelves covered one wall, a pump and sink sat under a wide window, and a massive black range stood in one corner. A door led out to a back porch where she could see trees along what must be the riverbank below the house. Everything was light and bright, and she could imagine a tin-topped work table in the center where she could roll out pie dough or knead bread.

"One of Perla's relatives, Josefina, will come out to clean house and do laundry and cook." Bowie opened several cabinet doors and drawers. "I'll say this for Houston—he hires the best. These drawers glide perfectly. I'll have to tell Giles Brown when I see him. Nobody beats his carpentry."

"I don't think I'll need a housekeeper or laundress, not with just the two of us living here," Elise said.

"You might be surprised how difficult things can be here in Texas. I think you should rest and take things easy. You had a long, hard trip just getting here, and you deserve time to recuperate. The shopping and decorating and such will keep you busy. Anyway, Perla's cousin needs the work."

What would Elise do to fill her time if she didn't have housework or laundry or cooking?

"I suppose I can plant a garden. I'm not sure what grows here or when to plant, but I can learn."

"Josefina's husband, Carlos, will take care of the gardening, the chickens, and the like. It's all been planned out."

Without consulting her.

And just like that, Bowie subtly reminded her that she wasn't really needed here beyond changing his marital status so he could inherit his land.

Footsteps sounded on the back porch, and a young man appeared in the doorway, snatching off his hat to reveal wiry blond hair. "Boss, I'm ready whenever your missus is." He bobbed his head toward Elise, an open, friendly smile on his face.

"Elise, this is Gage O'Reilly. He'll drive you to town and fetch and carry for you." Bowie looked out the kitchen window. "Looks like Carlos and Josefina are here too. They can get the wagon unloaded and some cleaning done while you're gone." With barely a nod in Elise's direction, he passed Gage on his way outside.

"Ma'am, GW asked if we could stop by the main ranch house on our way into town, if that's all right with you." Gage tapped his hat against his thigh.

"Of course. Let me make a few notes, and I'll be ready." Elise went to the wagon and got the tablet she'd packed for the purpose and went room to room, making lists. Furnishings, window coverings, kitchen supplies.

Upstairs, she peeked into the three bedrooms. Each was a generous size, but the one at the back of the house that overlooked the river caught her fancy. Lace curtains, a cheerful quilt on a four-poster bed, a beveled mirror on a stand. It would be quite charming when she was finished.

The other two rooms must've been planned for children—one for boys, one for girls. Her heart ached a bit as she thought of Bowie sketching his designs for a home, probably anticipating being a husband and father, having his family around him.

Now he had a "paper" wife and no plans for fatherhood.

Which meant she would be denied the opportunity to ever be a mother.

~

*B*owie hadn't slept so well in over a decade as he had last night. And it bothered him.

Waking up with his wife in his arms had been a surprise and a revelation. When he'd come in after checking on the dogs, Elise had been sound asleep on the side of the bed he usually used.

The blankets had slipped to the floor, and she lay curled on her side as if trying to warm herself. Her hair spilled across the pillow like a chocolate river. Bowie had touched one of the glossy waves, the satiny strands catching on his rough hand. He covered her up, and before he rounded the end of the bed, she'd rolled over and shed the blankets again.

He'd stripped to his small clothes and slid under the covers, careful not to jostle her. Stacking his hands behind his head, he'd stared at the ceiling. Within seconds, Elise had rolled once more and cuddled against his side like a kitten seeking warmth. Bowie had frozen, not even breathing. Her hair tickled his skin, and her breath fanned across his chest. Gently, he'd eased his arm down around her shoulders, and her hand came up to lie over his heart.

Letting out his breath slowly, he'd swallowed. She'd snuggled in as if she'd always slept this way, and he'd allowed himself to relax. She was sound asleep, but even so, she'd sought his protection and warmth. So much for each of them staying on their own side of the bed.

Yawning, he'd reached up and tugged off his patch, tossing it onto the bedside table and rubbing the skin around his empty eye socket. He would be sure to wake up first and put it on before she had to see his disfigurement. He didn't remember falling asleep—he just knew he'd remained asleep all night for the first time in years. No nightmare had stalked him. No raging battle, no despair, no regret. Just...peace.

And waking up had been a pure pleasure. Bowie had lain still for almost an hour waiting for Elise to awaken. He'd been so comfortable, he had forgotten he wasn't wearing his patch.

It still cut, the look of shock in her eyes as she'd stared at his ravaged face, at the hole where his eye should be. Why hadn't he gotten up and out of the house at first light? Why had he subjected her to the horror that was his visage when he knew how awful it was?

Bowie snapped his fingers as he strode toward the barn construction site, and Stonewall loped over, tongue lolling.

"Last night was a mistake," he told the dog. "One I don't aim to make again. Let's get to work."

Even as he made himself that promise, he knew it wouldn't be without cost. Holding Elise in his arms, he'd been the most content and at peace he had since well before Gettysburg. Shrugging, he joined the workmen.

He'd have to live on the memory, because it could never happen again.

~

GW greeted Elise on the front porch of El Regalo, inviting her to sit in the shade, offering her a glass of cider.

"Thanks for stopping by. I wanted a chance to talk to you on your own without the family bustling around." He tipped his chair back and hooked his boot heel over the stringer. "I can't tell you how surprised I was, Bowie showing up with a bride out of the blue like that, but I'm grateful."

Elise perched on the edge of her chair, wary, not wanting to say the wrong thing. "It all happened rather suddenly."

"Austin tells me that you knew Bowie during the war. That you were his nurse?"

"Yes, at the Fort Slocum hospital in New York." She told him a bit about volunteering there, treating the soldiers, and how in the days and weeks after Gettysburg, there seemed to be no end to the wounded being shipped in from the battlefield hospitals.

"My wife would've liked you, and she would've thanked you for taking care of our son. After Gettysburg, there was no word of him, not for years, and we all thought he was dead. My wife died thinking Bowie was gone. I like to think that when she got to heaven, God let her know he was all right."

"I'm sure she's at peace about that." Elise couldn't help leaning forward to touch his gnarled hand. He turned his palm to clasp her fingers and gave her a wink.

"First, his nurse and now his wife." He released her hand. "I'm glad he has someone to share his life with the way I did with my Victoria. Bowie needs someone to look after him and show him some tenderness, even if he doesn't think he does. Victoria understood him better than I do, I'll admit, but I have a notion that you understand him pretty well yourself. I could tell he cares a great deal about you, the way he kept watching you, kept checking to see that we didn't overwhelm you completely. And the two of you having a nice long lie-in this morning went a fair ways toward proving to me that you're the right woman for Bowie. I can't remember the last time he wasn't up before the rooster."

Elise blushed and he laughed. If GW only knew that Bowie watched her so carefully to make sure she didn't slip up and let on that theirs was anything other than a love match.

"My son has a great deal of love to give, but he keeps it to himself mostly, though he's the first one his brothers go to when they need someone strong to stand with them in trouble. But he rarely asks for help himself, so I'm glad he has you now." He smoothed his moustache. "I won't keep you, since I know you've got a lot of shopping to do. By the way, don't buy any silver for the table. I'd like that to be my wedding gift to you." He let his chair come to rest on the porch and levered himself up.

Elise rose as well, and she couldn't help but smile when he placed a whiskery kiss against her cheek. "You're a good girl, Elise Hart."

She thought about his kind words all the way into town. He was glad Bowie had someone to share his life with. But did Bowie, really?

At the time he had proposed, she had been grateful, thinking half a loaf was better than none, but now...now that she'd seen his happily married brothers, and the way Bowie protected her and saw to her every need, now that she'd seen how much he had to give, she wanted more.

She wanted a real marriage, with loving and sharing and caring.

Hartville had gone by in a blur the previous day on the stage, but now that she stood on the main street, she had time to study it. Gage had parked the wagon in front of H & C Hardware.

"This is Houston's place. You can get paint here, and wallpaper and such. And either of the mercantiles can order furniture and rugs and lamps and things. I'll be by to load up your purchases later. I'm headed to the blacksmith's, the livery, and the saddle shop for the boss. You can have tea or coffee at the restaurant in the Hartville Hotel up yonder, and I'll meet you there. That all right with you?" He seemed eager to be about his business, and Elise nodded, letting him go, trying not to feel set adrift in an unfamiliar sea.

Houston and Coralee couldn't have been nicer, and Coralee had fine taste, helping with paint and paper choices, as well as household items like pails and pitchers and washbasins. Both Houston and Coralee expressed their happiness for her and Bowie.

Elise couldn't help but feel a twinge of envy as she watched them together. Coralee had a pretty laugh and made Houston smile, and he was always touching her, his hand on her shoulder, brushing one of her ringlets off her cheek.

The Yost Mercantile at the end of the street was enormous, a warehouse of a place stuffed from baseboards to rafters with everything from aprons to zinc paste. Disorganization reigned, and Elise's heart sank as she stepped inside. How was she going to find anything in this wilderness of inventory?

"Yeah?" A man sitting on a stool behind the counter didn't so much as glance at her, speaking around a nasty cigar stub jammed into the corner of his mouth and reading a newspaper.

"Do you have a catalog?" Elise bit her lip and twisted her fingers at her waist.

"Sure. Got a great big one. But if you need something, I prolly got it on hand." Sighing as if he was annoyed to be interrupted, he laid down his paper and finally looked up. "You new in town?" Sliding off the stool, he leaned on his palms on the counter.

"Yes, I'm Elise Hart."

He yanked the cigar from his mouth and threw it behind the counter, offering her an ingratiating smile. "Hart, did you say?"

"Mrs. Bowie Hart." Though it felt strange to say, she got a thrill just the same.

"Well, well, Bowie got himself a wife, did he? Folks will be mighty surprised to hear that." He looked her over. "You said you wanted a catalog? Come to spend some of that Hart money already?" He cackled and slapped his thigh. "Guess it don't matter how ugly a man you are, if you've got cash, you can find a gal to marry you."

Her jaw dropped. How dare he? She skewered him with a stare. He stopped laughing.

"I believe I've changed my mind, thank you very much." She turned on her heel, making sure to slam the door behind her. She'd rather sleep on bare floorboards and bathe in a bucket for the rest of her life than buy anything in that store.

Things went much better at Mortenson's Mercantile up the street. Their place was bright and clean, and the proprietor, Michael Mortenson, was helpful and friendly. Elise spent a happy two hours selecting pieces for the house, ordering some from the catalog at the table in the back and choosing some from the extensive inventory. She was especially happy to see Mrs. Mortenson's selection of handmade soaps and picked up three jasmine-scented bars for herself.

"My mother said a woman should always have a signature scent. Roses, vanilla, cinnamon, lavender. I chose jasmine, but it isn't always easy to find." Elise smelled the floral soap, warmed by the memory of her mother.

"Now that I know you use it, I'll make sure to keep some on hand. Easy enough, since I make all my own soaps, and I have a jasmine vine at home." Meribeth Mortensen handed her baby to her husband and jotted down a note to herself. "Now, what else might you need for your new home?"

By the time she'd finished choosing furnishings for an entire house, Elise was weary and ready to sit for a while.

"I'll send this order out by telegram this afternoon, and it should be freighted from San Antonio within a couple weeks. I'll leave directions for it all to be shipped right out to your house." Mr. Mortenson totaled her purchases in his ledger. "And The Hartville Hotel? It's across the street on your left, beside Harley Burton's law office. Tillie will take good care of you there."

Elise entered the hotel and paused beside the screen that separated the lobby from the dining room, taking the time to smooth her hair and gather her courage. She once again wished Bowie was here. It had felt wrong to spend so much money, make so many decisions on her own, even though she was doing what he had asked.

A pair of young women swept in, laughing and chattering. When they saw her, they stopped, giving each other knowing looks and walking by, almost drawing their skirts aside. Elise frowned. Now what had caused that reaction? She was a stranger to them. What could they possibly have against her?

They took a table in the front of the restaurant by the windows, whispering and glancing over their lace gloves at her.

A large woman in a flowered apron came by, plates balanced in her hands. "Hi, honey, you take a seat anywhere you like. I'll be right with you." She sent a kind smile Elise's way, which acted like a balm to her frazzled nerves.

She chose a small table near a potted fern, mostly out of sight of the twittering duo by the windows. Before the waitress returned, a tall woman in rustling silk strode in, the brim of her hat drooping fashionably to one side. Her eyes, like the blades on a button press, bored through the room, stopping when they struck upon Elise.

"So you must be the newest Hart bride I've been hearing about from Mr. Yost."

The room went still. News traveled fast. "I am Mrs. Bowie Hart. And you are?"

"Miss Spanner. I am a *modiste*. My salon is across the street." She said it with a haughty lilt in her voice that told Elise she was a plain old dressmaker. It was the same way her uncle had used to say *entrepreneur.* "I was sorry to hear you had already married, since I was hoping for a chance to sew a wedding gown for a Hart bride." She looked Elise over, and her lips twitched. "Ready-made garments, I see."

Elise's happiness with the new clothes Bowie had purchased for her dimmed a bit.

"Still, I imagine you'll be coming by my shop soon. I heard you were in town already to spend some of that lovely Hart money. I don't blame you. At least the money will sugar the pill of being married to Bowie Hart."

The waitress returned, cutting in front of the outspoken dressmaker before Elise could form any thought beyond anger.

"Nice to meet you, Mrs. Hart. I'm Tillie, and I'll be looking after you. Can I get you some coffee or tea? Maybe a slice of apple pie?" She handed a menu to Elise with a smile. "Sure am glad to make your acquaintance, and I'm glad Bowie found himself such a pretty bride. He deserves a little happiness."

Miss Spanner sniffed and stalked away to join the two women near the window, and Tillie leaned close. "Don't you mind Veronica and Hattie over there by the window. Spiteful cats. They both wanted a Hart brother to propose to them, and they're jealous. And Miss Spanner and her airs. She's just a frustrated old woman who set her cap for Harley Burton, the lawyer here in town, and he isn't exactly coming up to the mark, shall we say? She gets spleeny because he runs away every time he sees her coming."

Elise nodded, but her heart hurt. No wonder Bowie avoided town. She had a feeling that given the choice, she'd avoid the place too.

CHAPTER 5

ithin a week, the papering and painting were finished, and Elise found herself at loose ends until the rest of the furnishings arrived. Josefina and Carlos did their best to ensure she didn't lift a finger inside the house or out, and her husband was absent much more than he was present. Bowie worked from dawn until dusk on the new barn and with training his horses and dogs, ate his meals with barely a word spoken, and every night, at the head of the stairs, she turned to go into her bedroom and he into his across the hall. And every night she felt more isolated and lonely. They co-existed amiably enough, but Elise found herself wanting more.

She wanted Bowie to let her into his life.

But how could she get him to open up to her? How could she get to the man who existed behind the walls he'd erected? She had glimpsed behind that protective barrier when they'd first met, when he was helpless in the hospital, out of his mind with fever, begging her not to leave him, refusing treatment unless it was by her hand.

She'd seen it again when they had kissed in front of his family, when he'd received the deed to his land. She was sure he had felt something. Not to mention the joy of waking up in his arms. What would it be like to awaken that way every morning? To be desired and cherished like that for the rest of your life? To be able to spend all the love she had been storing up in her heart on someone who would love her back?

Elise wanted that. And she wanted that with Bowie.

But how did she reach the man's heart?

What she needed was a plan to at least get her husband to spend time with her. That would be a good start. Then she could work on getting past his defenses. And the sooner she started, the better.

She waited supper that evening until well after the regular time, but Bowie didn't come inside. Finally, she sent Josefina home, saying she would clear up. Bowie had been late before, but not this late, and Elise found herself looking out the window and listening for his footsteps on the porch. Eventually, she went in search of him. She wrapped a shawl around her shoulders against the mid-November chill and headed toward the new barn. Bowie spent his days training a crop of young colts how to be cow ponies. Perhaps one of them had fallen ill. She'd check the corral behind the barn first.

But Bowie wasn't there. Six sturdy horses stood together, munching hay, swishing their tails, but her husband wasn't to be seen. Elise turned and started for the barn, but as she rounded the corner, she collided with Bowie. He put his hands out and grabbed her shoulders to keep her from stumbling.

"Something wrong?" His deep voice brushed against her hair before he set her back, sending a tremor through her.

"You didn't come in for supper."

"I was with Clara. It's her time. I was coming in to get you, if you wanted to see the pups born."

She smiled. He'd thought of her, wanting to include her. That was something, wasn't it?

Taking her hand, he led her into the barn and into a stall piled with hay. Under the manger on an old blanket, Clara lay on her side, panting and grunting softly. Bowie had lit a lantern, and a bucket of water and a pile of rags waited nearby.

"How long does it take?" Elise sat on some bags of grain he'd piled along one wall.

"This is her first litter, and it depends on how many pups are in there. She's bigger than I thought she'd be, so there might be quite a few, which is just as well, considering all the folks who want one." Bowie squatted on his heels, reaching out and running his hand down Clara's distended side. She turned her head and lapped his fingers. "Good girl. You're doing fine."

When the first puppy was born, Bowie handed it to Elise along with a piece of toweling. She rubbed the wet, trembling creature. "It's been a long time since I was a nurse."

He took the puppy, laying it alongside Clara. "You haven't lost the knack."

She swallowed and gathered her courage. "I was scared the whole time I worked at Fort Slocum. I think the most scared I ever was, though, was when I took your bandages off."

Bowie went still, his lips flattening. "Because you were afraid of how I looked?"

"Of course not. How could you even think that?"

"Because the other day, when you saw me without my eyepatch on, you were...repulsed."

"James Bowie Hart, that's the most ridiculous thing I ever heard. When will you believe that I'm not repulsed by your face?" A quiver went through her. "I gasped because I realized you were awake, and there I was, draped all over you when I said I would stay on my side of the bed..." Mortification ran through her from her hairline to her hem. "I was embarrassed that you caught me in such a way."

He blinked, and a bemused, wary look came over his face, as if he wasn't sure he should believe her explanation. If he only knew how badly she wanted to wake up in his arms again, he'd run for the hills.

"So if you weren't scared of what my face looked like, what were you afraid of back there in the hospital?"

"I was afraid for you, that you would be blind. I cried when you could still see, I was so happy. The rest didn't seem to matter compared to that. In fact, I miss seeing your face under all that beard. You have such a nice jaw. I remember from when I shaved you in the hospital. Have you ever thought of shaving your beard and cutting your hair?"

Bowie shook his head, no trace of a smile remaining. "I look bad enough now. Without the beard and long hair..." He shrugged. Clara gave a low moaning grunt, and he turned away from Elise, the subject closed.

Through the evening, Elise marveled at Bowie's gentleness, even as she longed for him to realize that the people who mattered, the people who cared about him, didn't see him as a monster at all. That a man's measure and worth weren't in his appearance but in his actions. "I wish, just once, you could see what I see when I look at you," she whispered, her heart aching.

By the time midnight rolled around, Clara was licking and nuzzling seven beautiful puppies.

"They're so helpless, and yet, they all know exactly what to do." Elise rubbed the last one with a bit of toweling before placing it alongside its littermates. "Even with their eyes closed and weak limbs, they find her and latch on." Pup seven was no exception, squirming and working his way toward his first meal.

"God is pretty amazing, the way He made His creatures." Bowie rubbed Clara's ears. "They just seem to know by instinct what to do most of the time. Which reminds me, I talked to Hays, and he and Emma will stop by day after tomorrow to take you to church. You missed last week, but nobody would've expected you to be there, being a newlywed."

Elise paused in washing her hands in the bucket, wishing her reason for missing church *had* been that she was still on her honeymoon. "Where will you be? I thought we'd go to church together."

"I don't go to church. Not anymore."

"Why not?"

He looked up at her. "In case you hadn't noticed, church is in town. I don't go to town."

"Not even to church? Where do you get your spiritual guidance from?"

Shrugging, he levered himself up. "Parson Longley comes out for a visit most weeks. We talk about spiritual things then."

"And he is fine with this arrangement?" Elise certainly wasn't.

"He's after me to come to church on Sunday mornings, but he doesn't press too hard anymore. I do my praying and Bible reading privately, talk to the preacher once a week or so, which is more than a lot of folks do, I imagine."

But how much you miss, cutting yourself off from people, from worshipping with fellow believers. And yet, if what she had experienced at the hands of some of Hartville's citizens was any example, could she blame him?

"I'll ride over and join you for Sunday dinner at El Regalo. Hays and Emma can bring you home after that."

"Actually," Elise said, grateful for the opportunity to put part of her fledgling plan into action. "I would prefer if you would bring another saddle horse so I could ride home with you."

"Ride?" He looked up quickly, his hair swinging back from his face, the long strands snagging on his beard.

"I am a rancher's wife now, aren't I? I should learn to ride a horse, and I want you to teach me. Surely, a short ride from El Regalo to home would be a good first lesson?" She twisted her fingers at her waist, praying he would say yes, that he wouldn't spurn her.

Bowie studied her, the lamplight illuminating half his face, the scarred half, so that she couldn't see his good eye. In the semi-darkness of the barn, the black-powder burns didn't show as much.

"I suppose it would be a useful skill. There's a sidesaddle in the tack room at El Regalo that used to belong to my mother. And I can scare up a gentle horse for you."

Elise was ready and waiting on the front porch Sunday morning when Hays and Emma drove up. Hays hopped down, grinning, and helped her into the surrey. He and his bride chatted all the way to town, including Elise in their conversation. Elise had to force herself to be cheerful, missing her husband, aching that he chose not to come. *I don't want to be a church widow for the rest of my life.*

And yet, it felt good to be back in church, worshipping with fellow believers. The Hart family took two-and-a-half rows, and Elise found herself sitting beside GW. He had a nice voice, and he sang every hymn with gusto.

Following the service, nobody seemed in a hurry to leave, and Elise was surrounded by townsfolk. GW introduced her as the newest member of the Hart clan. It felt strange being with so many people after spending so much time alone, but the parishioners were friendly, welcoming her to the community.

A pair of little boys laughed and chased one another around the pews, dodging between skirts and pant legs, shrieking and twisting. One bosomy older lady grabbed them both on the way by, hauling them up short.

"Christopher and Manuel, how many times do I have to tell you to take your hooliganism outside? This is a house of God, not a playground. I've warned you before what happens to naughty little boys. If you don't straighten up, Bowie Hart himself will sneak into your window some night and eat you in two bites." She gave them a shake.

Elise gasped. "How dare you use my husband as some sort of ogre to scare these children into obedience? My husband is not a monster. He's a good, kind man, loyal to his family, and a brave war veteran. If this is an example of the Christian love and charity practiced by this church, it's no wonder Bowie chooses to refrain from attending."

The woman gaped like a landed fish, her grip on the boys loosening. "Well, I never!"

"Then perhaps you should." Elise picked up her hem and strode out, her anger carrying her until she reached Hays' surrey. That awful woman. Elise took a few deep breaths, trying to get a hold on her temper and her dismay.

"Elise?"

She turned. Austin stood there, his face grim. Chagrin bowed her head. What a spectacle she'd made of herself on her first Sunday in church. The Harts must be thoroughly ashamed of her.

"Are you all right?"

The lump in her throat prevented her from speaking, so she nodded, blinking fast.

"I wonder if Bowie knows what a champion he has in you." Austin helped her into the surrey, keeping hold of her hand and pressing it in a reassuring, big-brotherly way. "Don't let Mrs. Mulligan's silly notions get to you."

"How can people be so ignorant and cruel? They don't even know Bowie if they can think such terrible things. He's kind and protective and intelligent and strong." She gripped Austin's hand. "He always puts the needs of others ahead of himself, and just because he's quiet when he's around other people doesn't mean he's hateful or scary or plotting how to harm them."

Chuckling, Austin patted her shoulder. "Bowie's a blessed man. It's as plain as day how much you love him. If you would've stayed inside, you would've seen a lot of church folks coming to your defense and his."

"I *do* love him," she blurted out, giving voice to the feelings that had been building up inside her since the moment she first saw Bowie in the factory doorway...or was it when she first held his hand and mopped his sweaty brow in the hospital? "Why do people have such a hard time believing he is worthy of being loved? I can't even convince Bowie of that fact."

"Bowie is proving stubborn? I'm stunned." He grinned and winked at her. "He changed after the war and distanced himself from all the people who love him. I think you might be just the thing he needs to bring him all the way back into this family."

~

Bowie joined his family in the parlor before Sunday dinner. Elise greeted him, rising from her place on the settee and holding out her hands to him, raising herself on tiptoe and kissing his scarred cheek above his beard. He blinked, trying to quell his surprise.

"I'm so glad you're here. I missed you." She tucked her hand into the crook of his arm and leaned against him. "Did you bring a horse for me?"

He nodded. "I did. Rode over to Coralee's brother's place yesterday. Calvin had a nice little dun mare that I thought would be a good mount for you, and he was only too happy to sell her to me. She's been ridden sidesaddle before, and she'll be used to a lady's skirts flapping." Bowie inhaled the fresh jasmine scent of Elise's hair. Would he ever tire of it?

His brothers and their wives laughed and chatted, waiting for Perla to announce that dinner was ready. Though Bowie had expected Elise to rejoin Emma and Caro, she stayed by his side. Pa came over, smoothing his moustache and grinning.

"Missed you at church this morning, son." He said the same thing every week. "Glad to see Elise there, though. She made quite an impression on the congregation."

Elise's grip on Bowie's arm tightened, and he glanced at her. She worried the corner of her lip, a small crease between her brows. She gave a small shake of her head to his pa. Had something happened at church?

Before he could ask, Pa said, "It's all set in the dining room."

Bowie nodded.

"Dinner is ready." Perla made the announcement, and everyone filed across the hall into the dining room.

Bowie kept Elise back, waiting to go in last. "Pa has a little surprise for you."

Near the head of the table, Pa waited, his hands resting on the back of a chair. "Elise, I'm pleased as can be that Giles finished this so quickly. Bowie, come help your wife get seated."

Bowie put his hand on the small of Elise's back and guided her down the long table. She gasped when she saw her own monogrammed chair, twin to his except for the initials. *E.M.H.* Elise Marie Hart.

"Do you like it?" Bowie asked.

He barely had time to brace himself before she threw herself into his arms, squeezing him tight. "It's perfect. Thank you." He didn't miss how her eyes shone as she released him and turned to hug Pa. "Thank you. Thank you for welcoming me into your family. I couldn't ask for anything more beautiful."

GW patted her shoulder awkwardly, grinning over top of her head at Bowie. "We're all mighty glad you're here."

A stab of guilt that he was deceiving his father and brothers about the nature of his marriage hit Bowie, but he quashed it. They'd be more horrified if they knew the truth. The details of his marriage were his business, anyway.

Elise took her seat between Bowie and Houston as if it had always been hers, and Bowie pulled out his chair beside her. Everyone joined hands, and Pa led them in saying grace. During the meal, Elise took every opportunity to touch him, leaning close, putting her hand on his thigh, smiling at him. It set his heart to racing. He tried to act as though it was no big deal, but he didn't miss the grins of his brothers. Austin watched him particularly closely.

Putting her hand on Bowie's arm, Elise leaned in. "I met a handsome young man just before church today. He said he was a friend of yours."

Bowie stilled and waited for her to continue. What young buck was chatting with his wife when he wasn't around? A cowhand from one of the ranches? Some townie? His hands fisted on his knees.

"His name is David Longley."

Bowie glanced down the table at Emma, David's big sister, feeling sheepish.

"He told me he is twelve, and he seems to think you are ten feet tall and can walk on water. I gather he's visited El Regalo before? He wants to be just like you when he grows up, and have lots of dogs and horses and carry a rifle everywhere. He even said he would find himself a pretty wife someday, just like you." Elise squeezed his arm, a saucy grin curving her pink lips.

Bowie didn't know what to think as a ripple of laughter went around the table. Usually, the town kids ran away when they saw him coming. No kid had ever said they wanted to be like him before. "He should aim a little higher than to want to be like me."

Elise took his hand, nestling hers into his palm, a serious light in her eyes. "Nonsense. I think he couldn't do any better than to aim to be like you. I told him all about Clara's new litter, and he can't wait to come out and see them. He pestered me to promise he could have one of the pups when they were weaned, but I told him he'd have to talk to you. I don't know how many are already spoken for."

She went on to tell his family about the puppies' birth, and she made him out to be the hero of her story. He hardly recognized himself. Evidently, he was patient and gentle and smart. And he wasn't sure how handsome entered into the whelping of pups, but she threw in hand-some too.

What was she up to?

His brothers grinned, and his sisters-in-law beamed. Then it dawned on him that Elise was merely fulfilling her part of the bargain, pretending theirs was a normal marriage. She was acting like his broth-ers' wives did around their husbands, in spite of the fact that none of it was true. A little of the shine went off the day.

After everyone returned to the parlor, Elise allowed herself to be drawn into the circle of her sisters-in-law. The talk seemed to center around babies. Emma was nearing her time, about six weeks away, and Coralee was due sometime in the spring. Bowie wasn't sure who was most proud—Hays, Houston, or Pa. They all went around with their chests puffed out as though they'd invented babies.

Elise sat in a winged-back chair, listening to Annie assuring both Emma and Coralee that she would be with them through their deliver-ies, and she would even bring Travis along to help. Though the girls laughed, Elise studied her hands in her lap, her expression sad and wistful.

A sharp jolt hit Bowie's gut. Because of their sham marriage, he had condemned Elise to never knowing what it was like to be a mother, never to hold her child in her arms.

Hays stood behind his wife's chair, his hand on her shoulder, and she reached up, clasping it. They shared a look, and Emma's other hand went to her rounded belly.

What would it be like if it was Elise having a baby...his baby? Bowie rubbed his palms on his thighs. He hadn't considered becoming a father, not since he awoke in the Fort Slocum hospital mangled and broken. But surely a child raised with him from birth would grow accustomed to his scars and eyepatch and not be terrified of him as most town kids were?

Of course, that would mean having a real marriage, something he had promised Elise he would never demand. He would never inflict his ugly self on any woman, much less one as beautiful and perfect as Elise. There was no chance he would ever be a father, none at all, and he should stop thinking such ridiculous things.

~

The riding lesson drove Bowie crazy. And all because Elise was so sweet and earnest.

"This is Sugar. At least that's what Calvin said he named her. You can change it if you want. I doubt it will matter to the horse." Bowie carried his mother's sidesaddle and bridle to the corral where he'd left the horses. His own horse, a brown gelding the cowhands had named Burlap for his raspy personality, trotted over and snorted, shaking his head and making his mane flop. Bowie liked the rangy horse, who wasn't much to look at, but who was smart and tireless and had forgotten more about cow work than most cowboys would ever know.

The mare sniffed Elise's hand and lowered her head for a pat on the neck. "She's lovely. Sugar is the perfect name."

Bowie entered the corral, pushing Burlap out of the way. "Wait your turn." He smoothed the saddle blanket on Sugar's back and placed the saddle atop it. "Calvin said she hadn't been ridden in a while, so I had Gage knock some of the dust off her yesterday. I would've done it myself, but she's not up to my weight."

He tightened the girth in stages. Sugar flicked her tail but submitted to the bridle.

"She's so pretty. I love her long lashes." Elise turned into the breeze, brushing a stray strand of hair off her cheek. She wore a dark-green riding habit, an outfit that Bowie hadn't seen before, and he admired the way it hugged her curves, flaring just right over her hips, reminding him once again what a beautiful woman he'd married. She must've brought the outfit with her to change into. Smart.

Sunlight glinted on her hair, pink rode her cheekbones, and she wore an expectant expression, as if setting out on some great adventure. How had she survived so unspoiled after so many years under her domineering uncle?

He made quick work of saddling Burlap and tied him to the corral fence.

"What do I do?" She tugged on a pair of brown leather gloves.

"Come here." He showed her how to gather the reins and then put his hands on her waist. "Ready?"

She nodded, and he lifted her easily into the saddle. "Put your left foot in the stirrup, and your right knee goes here, on the pommel."

Sugar stood rock still. Bowie grasped the reins near the bit. "I'll lead her around a little so you can get the feel of her. All right?"

Elise nodded.

"It's okay to grab some of her mane if you want. She won't mind." He led the mare in a slow circle. "Try to feel the rhythm of her movement. Relax and sway with her."

"It feels so odd. I've never been on a horse before."

Bowie tried to imagine what that was like, but he couldn't. Pa had taught him to ride almost as soon as he could walk, and he didn't remember a time when he didn't know how. He glanced over his shoulder at her. She was concentrating, her body moving with the horse. After two rounds of the corral, he let go of the reins and stepped back. "Lift your reins, cluck your tongue, and press your heel into her side a bit."

Sugar responded beautifully, but it was Elise's smile that shook Bowie. Pure happiness. As she directed the mare in a circle around the pen, she beamed. "I'm doing it."

Bowie went to his horse and swung aboard. "You ready to try it outside the corral?"

"As long as you're with me, I'll try anything."

He couldn't help but smile at her enthusiasm, and the warmth in her look sent sparks across his skin. "Let's go home."

The trip took much longer than it would've taken Bowie alone because he refused to let her go faster than a trot. "You're not ready to ride for the Pony Express yet. When you've mastered a walk and a trot and you can get your mount to go where you want to when you want to, then you can canter."

She made a face at him. "Then you'd better clear your schedule and make time for more lessons. I want to be able to ride out with you and go to town if I want to and visit your family, and I don't want it to take all day to get there."

"I didn't realize how determined you were. At this rate, you'll be riding like a Comanche in no time."

Their house finally came into view, and Bowie was a bit sorry. He wasn't ready for the lesson to end.

Gage stepped out of the barn, wiping his hands on a rag. "Evening, boss. Ma'am."

"Take Mrs. Hart's horse, Gage. Brush her down and turn her out in the small corral."

"Will do." He reached for the reins to hold the mare so Elise could dismount.

"Wait." Bowie nudged Burlap next to Sugar and reached for his wife, plucking her from the saddle and seating her sideways in front of him. She responded as he hoped she would, giving a small shriek and throwing her arms around him.

"What are you doing?"

He grinned as the smell of jasmine drifted toward him, and she nestled against him. "You said you wanted to go fast. Hold on." He wheeled Burlap and legged him into a canter. Bowie held Elise firmly about the waist, anchoring her safely, moving in rhythm with Burlap's stride, pleased when she caught the cadence too.

Her laughter filled the evening air, and instead of clutching him in fear, she twisted to face forward in his embrace, holding her arms wide as if trying to catch the wind. Her hair slipped from its pins and blew against his chest and face, tangling with his own as they raced across the Texas prairie into the setting sun.

She trusted him completely not to let her fall. Dead humbling. He couldn't keep himself from smiling, almost laughing at her joy.

At last Bowie turned his horse in a wide circle, heading back toward the barn. When they reached the corral, he pulled to a stop, dropping from the saddle and reaching up for her.

When he would've set her down, she clung to him, wrapping her arms around his neck, her feet dangling off the ground, her body tight against his. "Thank you." She stared into his eye. "I've never felt so wonderful as racing across our land with you."

She'd never looked so wonderful either. Her hair tumbled down her back in a riot of chocolatey curls, and the wind had colored her cheeks. This close, he could see the golden flecks in her brown eyes. For a moment, he forgot that theirs was a marriage on paper, that he was scarred, that she was too good for him. He slowly lowered her to the ground, but instead of stepping away, he kissed her.

His fingers tunneled in her hair, and his lips sought hers. Her eyes fluttered closed, and she cupped his face in her hands. She tasted of wind and sunshine, and she smelled of jasmine. He couldn't seem to gather her close enough. As he slanted his head to deepen the kiss, her fingers caught in the strap of his eye patch, dislodging it.

With a start, he remembered where he was—who he was—*what* he was, and he broke the kiss, all but shoving her away, making sure the patch covered his eye socket properly. Gulping, he tried to ignore the shocked look on her face.

"I'll put the horse away. You go on to the house." He grabbed Burlap's reins and stalked to the barn, calling himself all kinds of a fool. He'd taken advantage of her generous nature, and all because of some ridiculous notion that he was a whole man.

CHAPTER 6

"I don't know what you're so worried about. It's your family, and it is high time you had them over to your home. Thanksgiving dinner seemed to be the perfect occasion."

Bowie stepped back as Elise brushed past him, checking the place settings at the new dining room table. For the past two weeks, she'd pretended that nothing had happened, that he hadn't overstepped his bounds by more than a country mile, and he'd been walking on eggshells ever since. Why didn't she scold him and get it over with? Why hadn't she slapped his face when he took such liberties? It wasn't as if he could claim he was acting out a part in front of his family. There hadn't been another Hart for miles.

"I'm not worried. I just don't know why we have to have them all at once." He placed his rifle in the gun cabinet in the corner of the room.

Elise paused, her eyebrows raised, her face the picture of innocence. "I did it for you. I thought you'd rather have it all done in one evening instead of stringing out the invitations to the couples over a whole month." She returned to straightening silver and crystal. "I put a clean shirt on your bed."

He took her hint and tromped up the stairs, grouchy as a spring bear. The fact that she was right irked him. He *would* rather get all the entertaining done at once, though he wished he didn't have to do it at all. It was time spent with his happily married brothers and their wives that reminded him the most about what was lacking in his own life.

The new furniture that Elise had ordered had arrived, three big wagons full. He and Gage had spent a whole day moving settees and bedsteads and bureaus a few inches here, a few inches there, all under Elise's direction. Bowie had to admit, she'd chosen well. His only complaint was the small beds she'd ordered for the guest rooms. They were more like children's beds.

Of course, the bed in her room seemed to cover half of Texas. He shrugged out of his work shirt and washed up. In the new beveled glass mirror over the washstand, he studied his face. Nothing had changed. His patchy beard blended with his blackened scars, and his eyepatch covered the worst of the travesty. He shook his head at the shaving cup, strop, and razor Elise had put beside the pitcher and bowel. So she thought he had a nice jawline? The last time he'd had a shave, Elise had done it in the hospital. With his scarred mug, he'd rather appear in his long johns in church than show up anywhere with a naked face for people to gawk at.

The sound of horses and buggies came from the front yard, and he stopped mooning in the mirror, shrugging into the crisp white shirt Elise had left on the bed. She'd also laid out a dark suit coat and tie, but he left those behind. It wasn't like the governor was coming tonight. Just his family.

Dinner was a success by all accounts. Bowie felt odd to sit at the head of the table, and Elise was much too far away at the foot, close to the kitchen where she could oversee the serving of the meal. She looked stunning in a dark-blue gown with black glittering beads scattered over it. He was aware of her every movement, her every look. Candlelight glinted off her hair and made her eyes luminous, and something in his chest tightened every time he looked at her.

Pa nudged him with his knee. "You did well for yourself, son. I still can't believe all you boys did it. Seven weddings in a year...better yet, seven fine marriages that, God-willing, will see you all into a happy old age."

Bowie stabbed a forkful of turkey off his plate and said nothing. His brothers talked about plans for next spring's round up, how far down they should cull the herd, and whether or not to import some English blooded bulls to improve the stock on the 7 Heart, while the girls complimented Elise on the house, the furnishings, the wallpaper—just about everything. The meal was perfect, the house was perfect, her dress was perfect.

The only imperfect thing in her life was him.

Somehow he managed to get through the meal, but then they all moved into the parlor. Pa took a seat in the chair Bowie had occupied every evening for the past week, the one opposite Elise's, the one where he pretended to read the paper every night while he watched her knit or sew or read a book.

Austin brought in one of the dining chairs, since the parlor didn't boast seating for sixteen. "I ran into David Longley in town yesterday. He's hot after one of Clara's pups. I thought I'd never seen a kid so keen about getting a dog until I remembered how you were at his age. All you thought about were horses and dogs." He sat and rested his ankle on his opposite knee. "Guess you have more on your mind now." He nodded in Elise's direction. "All I thought about once upon a time was running this ranch and keeping you boys out of trouble, but now that I have Rebekah, my priorities have changed a bit. I guess marriage has a way of doing that to a man."

Bowie glared at his older brother. Why did he want to talk about marriage? Austin never said anything without a purpose behind it, so just what was he after?

Bowie steered the conversation onto safer ground. "The pups are growing fast. Their eyes are open, and they're fat as butter. They'll be ready to wean around Christmas time. Maybe, if you see the Longleys, you can let them know that if they want to give one as a Christmas present for David, there'll be one available. I already talked to Travis, and I'll bring one over to El Regalo on Christmas morning for Robbie." He kept his voice low so his new nephew wouldn't overhear. "I'll keep the rest for a while, see if I can spot a good cow dog or two to train."

Pa stretched out his boots to the fireplace and laced his hands across his stomach. In minutes, he was asleep. Elise rose and took a knitted blanket off the arm of her chair and spread it over him, smiling softly. Bowie shook his head, tamping down the homey feelings in his chest. When he was a younger man, especially during the war, before he was injured, he'd imagined evenings like this, where he had a wife to make a home for him, a place for his family to gather. Elise had done that, creating an inviting home, showing hospitality to his family. It was almost picture perfect. Almost.

Talk turned to the upcoming Hartville Christmas Eve Ball, an annual event held at the Hartville Hotel. Folks from as far away as San Antonio came for the party, filling the town, celebrating the season. Bowie's mother had begun the tradition years ago, using the proceeds from the event to fund various charitable functions in and around Hartville. This year, the funds would go toward the Confederate Widows and Orphans Fund, with Miss Spanner overseeing the decorations and details as only she could.

"I don't think I'll be doing any dancing." Emma shifted in her chair, pressing her hand to her lower back. "I might be home with a newborn by that time. But just in case, I ordered a new dress from Miss Spanner's."

Jane nodded. "Crockett insisted I get a new dress. He even went with me to pick out the fabric."

The boys spoke of previous Christmas Eve dances. Bowie had hated the dances as a youngster, mostly because he was so tall and lanky and ungraceful, tripping over his feet. By the time he'd grown into his legs and arms, he was a passable dancer, thanks to his mother's patient teaching. He'd never be as smooth as Hays or Austin, but he could get by without disgracing himself. Not that he'd ever go to a town dance again.

Elise came to stand beside Bowie's chair. She bent down and whispered in his ear, "A Christmas Eve ball? It sounds like so much fun, and a good cause. Should I order a new dress? Will you need a new suit?"

He shook his head. "Get a dress if you want, but don't get new clothes for me. I won't be going." When was she going to realize that he didn't go to balls or church or shopping? He felt bad having to refuse her, but nobody would thank her for dragging his ugly carcass to a town function. "Someone from the family will get you there and back."

Her lips tightened, and she blinked. Tears? He felt lower than an earthworm's belly, but confound it, she knew better than to think he'd go parading into town. He looked away from the hurt in her eyes.

"What are you going to wear, Elise?" Annie called from across the room. "There's still time to get a gown made. That shade of blue is lovely on you, but I think you would look fabulous in red."

Elise left his side and returned to her chair by the fire. "I won't be attending the ball, but I hope you all have a lovely time and raise lots of money for the cause." She held up her hands as protests began. "I've decided to steer clear of Hartville. I find I much prefer to keep to the ranch."

Though they tried to get her to change her mind, she remained adamant. Bowie said nothing, but he simmered. Even Pa, who woke in the midst of the debate, couldn't budge her from the notion of staying home from the biggest social event of the year.

The minute all this company was gone, Bowie would get to the bottom of things.

~

*E*lise was in for a battle, judging from the hard look in Bowie's eye, but she welcomed it. She was heartily sick of pretending she didn't love him—blast his stubborn hide. She was tired of being alone in her marriage. And she was tired of her husband acting as if he were some sort of pariah, even in his own family. As she said good night to their guests, she braced for the conflict.

Returning to the parlor, she found him leaning against the mantel, arms crossed, a scowl on his face.

"What's the idea of not going to the Christmas Eve Ball? And not going into Hartville? You have no reason to cut yourself off from town. You should go to the dance." His eye burned hotly, his face hard as he fired the first salvo.

"So should you," she shot back. "It's perfectly ridiculous that you hide out here, and I'm tired of it. Do you know how difficult it is for me to go to town alone? Or to sit in church by myself? As for a town dance...with all your family in attendance except you? Do you have any idea how humiliating that would be for me to be the only Hart woman there without her husband?" Folding her arms, she glared at him. "Well, I'm not going to do it any longer. If you won't go to town, then neither will I."

He paused, as if he hadn't thought of how difficult it might be for her to show up to social engagements alone. "You have my whole family at these shindigs. You aren't alone."

"Oh, right. And just which couple should I attach myself to? I have no desire to play gooseberry to your brothers and their wives."

"What do you want from me? I told you from the beginning that I didn't go into town. Now you're mad because I won't go?" Bowie paced the area in front of the fireplace, eating up the distance with his long strides. Frustration flowed from every line of his body, his muscles taut under the crisp white shirt she'd pressed so carefully earlier that day. But she was frustrated, too, and she found it all spilling out.

"When you first came into the factory and saved me from a miserable existence, I thought you were the answer to my prayers, that I had finally found someone who would care for me and that I could share a life with, but you don't want that, do you? You've walled yourself up in your fortress of pride and shame. You've cut yourself off from life, your family, and most of all, you've cut yourself off from me."

To her mortification, tears welled in her eyes. She tried to blink them away, but they tumbled down her cheeks, breaking the dam she'd formed and releasing her carefully restrained emotions.

At first, Bowie looked horrified at her tears, and then he threw up his hands. "I never pretended to be anything other than what I am. I don't know what you want from me. I've followed the absolute letter of our agreement. I gave you my name, my protection, a place to live. You've got money now and social standing as a Hart, for what that's worth." He jammed his fingers into his hair. "I *knew* this marriage was a mistake. I should've just kept on riding when I left the 7 Heart. It sure didn't take long for you to regret marrying me. I never lied to you about what I was proposing."

Elise bowed her head. He was right. He hadn't changed the rules. She tried to explain herself.

"At first, it was enough. I thought that I could do it, that a paper marriage, a platonic relationship would be enough for me. But it isn't. Not when I see how much you have to give, how happy we could be."

When he forgot to be ashamed or bitter, when they were flying across the prairie together on his horse, when he held her in his arms and kissed her senseless and she got a glimpse of how it might be between them, it broke her heart.

He was so bewildered, and she couldn't miss the hurt and confusion on his face.

"Right now, this marriage feels like a prison—only it's not me behind bars, it's you. You've locked yourself away, hoarding your love and affection, and you've lumped me in with all the people you think might hurt you. I don't know if I can go on in a loveless marriage. I need more."

"I don't have any more to give."

"Then where does that leave us?" Her heart broke anew, more painful than anything she'd encountered before.

He had no answer, and neither did she.

"I want you to go to the dance. It would embarrass my family if you weren't there."

"And there's nothing I can do or say to change *your* mind about going?"

"No. I've told you before. I don't go into town."

Shoulders sagging, she sighed, wiping the tears from her cheeks. "I'm sorry. You're right. You have been nothing but honest with me about your feelings. I'm sorry I overstepped. It won't happen again."

She lifted her hem and went upstairs to her bedroom, pausing on the landing to look into his room across the hall. The room she had thought might become a nursery one day, but now stood for all that was wrong in her marriage. Her efforts to get her husband to love her had come to nothing. The rest of her life stretched out before her, lonely and unfulfilled.

And she had nobody to blame but herself...and her stubborn husband.

~

*B*owie tightened the girth on his saddle. "Easy, boy." The colt he was training sidled and stomped his back foot. "There, that's not too bad." He untied the lead line from the corral fence and began a slow circuit with the bright chestnut, letting him get used to the feel of the saddle.

"He's coming along nicely. Think he's got any cow sense?"

Bowie halted, turning as Austin dismounted and tied his horse to the fence. "Too soon to tell. You never know about a horse's cow sense until you ask him the question, but he's got a good disposition. Calm and kind so far."

Austin raised the collar on his coat as a chilly wind blew, whipping up a cloud of corral dust. He crossed his arms on the top rail and rested his chin on his wrists. "I was hoping for a little snow for Christmas. It would make tonight's Christmas Eve Ball special."

"We almost never get snow this far south. You come for something specific, or just want to talk about the weather?" Bowie led the colt around one more circuit, stopping in front of his older brother.

"You know me pretty well." Austin smiled. "I had something on my mind."

"You usually do."

"Actually, I came to talk to you about Elise."

Bowie's muscles went taut. "What about her?"

"Rebekah tells me she's going to the dance tonight, after all. The girls all met up at Miss Spanner's for dress fittings and such, and Elise was there."

"That's right." Not that he got much satisfaction out of it. Elise had been so quiet and withdrawn since Thanksgiving night, as if someone had snuffed a candle flame and left the house dark. She didn't even want any more riding lessons.

"But you're still not going?"

"Nope." Bowie loosened the cinch. His temper was frayed. Not a good frame of mind for training colts.

"You're an idiot." Austin said it like it was a commonly held fact.

Bowie jerked the saddle off. "What did you say?"

"I said you're an idiot. It's one thing for you to cut yourself off from town, and to hold your family at arms' length, but why push Elise away? You do realize what a gem you have there, right? She's beautiful and kind and sweet and giving. Meanwhile, you're shutting her out of your life like a cutting horse keeping a calf out of the herd."

"Of course, I know what a gem she is. I married her, didn't I?" Grabbing a currycomb, he started in on the colt, his movements brisk. Who did Austin think he was, barging in here and poking his nose where it didn't belong?

Austin waited, a favorite tactic of his. Well, it wouldn't work this time. Bowie wasn't about to spill his guts to his brother and admit what a failure he was.

"I married her so I could get my inheritance. We have a paper marriage, not a real one. A marriage of convenience." The words were out before he could stop them. Great. It had worked. Even when he knew what Austin was doing, he still fell for it. Yet it felt good to unburden to someone.

"You mean you've never...?" Austin stopped, his eyes wide. "No wonder you're so surly."

"I'm not surly," Bowie snapped. "The whole thing has been a colossal mistake. I should've just gotten on my horse and kept on riding when Pa came up with this stupid plan. I should've known I couldn't be a good husband, not even on paper. If I had an ounce of sense, I'd head to town right now and have Harley Burton start work on annulment papers before I ruin Elise's life forever." He threw the currycomb into the box with force. "Nobody could be happy married to a freak like me."

"Don't you think ten years and more is enough time to feel sorry for yourself?" Austin reached into his coat pocket and withdrew a toothpick, jamming it into the corner of his mouth, his expression bland.

"What are you talking about?" Bowie slipped the halter off the colt and vaulted over the fence. He jammed his hands on his hips. He hated it when Austin acted superior, as if he knew everything.

"So you were wounded. So you have some scars. So what? I'd wager Elise doesn't even see them when she looks at you. I got shot, too, if you'll remember, and I have some nasty scars, but Rebekah doesn't care. She says they are marks of courage, not cowardice. So you were captured and spent time in a Yankee prison. Big deal. You weren't the only one in Elmira, were you? Were all those men failures? It's beyond time that you got over yourself. You've held onto your bitterness for too long, and you've made it an excuse to push people away." Austin shifted the toothpick in his mouth, staring at Bowie, his face hard but not without compassion. "We love you, Bowie. You're our brother and the equal of any of us, and that's a fact, scars and surly disposition and all. Elise loves you, too, and it's tearing her apart."

A tremor went through Bowie, and it felt as if someone was scouring out his chest with sandpaper. "You think she loves me?"

"Even a one-eyed man should be able to see that. She lights right up when you come into the room, and when she talks about you, I feel as if we should all bow before your royal highness. And don't even pretend that you don't love her. You care about her so much, it's eating you alive.

You want her so bad, it's like you're running a fever. She's the first thing you think of when you wake up and the last thing you think of before you go to sleep, and pretty much everything you think about in between. You'd do about anything to see her smile. And you're scared stiff that she doesn't feel the same about you."

Bowie sagged against the corral fence. "How do you know all this?"

Austin grinned. "Because I'm in love with *my* wife. I recognize the symptoms."

"I do love Elise." Saying it out loud terrified him worse than facing a Union charge. "But it's too late. I've ruined things with her. She'll never love me now, and it isn't about the scars." Bowie waved toward his face. "No, it's because she's found out the secret that I *am* an idiot."

"That's not a secret." Austin clapped him on the shoulder. "I've known it for years. But it's time for you to decide what you really want. If it's Elise, then you have to let go of the past. You're going to have to drop the armor and let yourself be vulnerable. You're going to have to trust Elise with your heart. If not, you're relegating both of you to a miserable existence, and yes, you should start the annulment proceedings, because Elise deserves better. What you need to realize is that you do too."

CHAPTER 7

*A*ustin helped Rebekah with her coat before turning to assist Elise with her cloak. Elise thanked him, smoothing the polonaise of her gown.

"Annie was right—red suits you beautifully." Rebekah checked her hair in the cloakroom mirror. Music drifted down from the ballroom on the third floor. Her own gown of ivory satin complemented her rose-petal complexion and brought out the blue in her eyes. Austin offered her his arm, grinning down at her with pride.

"I'll be the envy of everyone at the party tonight with two such pretty ladies to escort." He offered his other arm to Elise, who took it, wishing she was at home in her room.

Still, she had no right to dim everyone else's pleasure, so she put on a smile and allowed Austin to lead her upstairs.

Miss Spanner had done wonders. Garlands of ivy and mistletoe hung from every post, and the chandelier dripped with red bows and greenery.

Miss Spanner herself, resplendent in purple satin trimmed with black velvet, beamed, clutching the arm of Harley P. Burton, who had his hair slicked down and his best checked suit on. He looked bewildered, half proud, half terrified.

"She caught him at last," Austin leaned in to whisper. "At least for this dance. He looks as though he can't decide whether to brag or bolt."

The orchestra began a reel, and couples lined up. Each Hart brother led his bride out onto the dance floor, with the exception of Hays and Emma. Emma sat along the wall, her hand resting on her pregnant belly, and Hays brought her a cup of punch. Emma accepted it and nodded Elise's way.

Hays walked over, a friendly smile on his face. "Would you care to dance? Emma can't right now, and I'm itching to get out there." His smile reminded her of Bowie's—on the rare occasions Bowie ever smiled—and she blinked hard and nodded. It would be better than standing on the sidelines all night, a reminder to everyone that her husband wasn't here.

Hays was an excellent dancer, making it easy for her to match his steps. "A good crowd tonight. Should raise a lot of money for the cause." He looked up at the banner over the refreshment table. "'Confederate Widows and Orphans.' Miss Spanner outdid herself this time."

When that dance ended, Elise found herself not lacking for partners. The Hart men must've decided not to let her feel on the outside looking in. One after another, they claimed her for waltzes, reels, and two-steps. Between times, they danced with their wives and sisters-in-law, laughing and keeping the party lively.

Austin took Elise's hand from Crockett's, grinning, his dimples deep creases in his cheeks. Rebekah went into Crockett's embrace as the strains of a waltz filled the room. "My dance?" Austin asked.

"I've been watching you. Where did you learn to dance so well? All of you Hart boys are good, but you and Hays are the best." Elise looked up at him.

"We have my mother to thank. She insisted all her sons know how to dance with the ladies." He pivoted her in a perfect circle, making her skirts belle. "We hated the lessons, but I think we're all thankful now."

"So Bowie had to learn to dance too?"

Austin laughed. "And he was bad at it at first. All arms and legs, like a newborn colt. All I can say is, my mother had a lot of patience." He sobered. "I know it's not my place to ask, but how are things between you and Bowie? Any better? I sure was hoping he'd change his mind about coming tonight."

Elise swallowed against the lump in her throat and shook her head. "We're fine."

Her brother-in-law gave her a hug as the music ended. "You're a good woman, Elise, but a pretty poor liar. Maybe Bowie just needs more time."

He led her over to where GW sat. Soon they were surrounded by Harts, the men bringing punch for the ladies. GW patted the settee next to him, and Elise sat, grateful to be off her feet. "They'll be serving supper soon." He consulted his pocket watch. "Midnight's coming. It will be Christmas Day in another quarter of an hour."

Elise set her cup on a small table, loneliness sweeping over her, even in the midst of the crowd. Everyone around her was so happy, Hays and Emma and Houston and Coralee anticipating the births of their first children, Chisholm and Caro holding hands, Crockett brushing a quick kiss on Jane's temple, and Travis whispering in Annie's ear. Austin had his arm around Rebekah as if he never wanted to let her go.

She shouldn't be envious, but she was. She should be happy for her new family, but she couldn't muster any joy. She only felt empty inside.

Oh, Bowie, what are we going to do?

~

*B*owie field stripped his rifle, laying the pieces out on the low table he'd spread with newspapers and picking up the cleaning solvent. The clock on the mantel ticked loudly, and Stonewall snored softly on the rug in front of the fireplace.

His house was almost everything he'd dreamed it would be. Cozy, inviting, a safe haven away from the world. Elise had done all of this for him. His house lacked nothing, except it wasn't a home.

The clock chimed, and he studied the bland face.

What was she doing now? Who was she dancing with?

He'd deliberately stayed in the barn late so he wouldn't have to face her before her ride to the dance arrived. Coward that he was.

Since Austin's talk with him that afternoon, Bowie had thought of little else. Had he been holding onto his bitterness so he didn't get hurt? Was it possible that Elise could really love him? Not his name, not his protection, not his money, but him?

He knew he loved her. He had for some time. Maybe from the first time he smelled her jasmine perfume. He'd felt something for her the minute she'd taken his bandages from his eyes. He'd waited for her in the hospital every day, uneasy until she came into the ward.

And she'd fought so hard to keep him at the hospital, and she'd cried when they'd hauled him away. He reached into his shirt pocket and took out the lace-trimmed handkerchief. It bore her initials, and he'd carried it with him for more than ten years, through the long months in prison camps, on the journey home after the war, on cattle drives. Elise had dropped it one day in the hospital, and he'd snatched it up, inhaling the scent of jasmine. The lace was frayed, and the monogram stitching had almost all come loose. But he still had it, and if he hadn't wanted to lose this small link to her, why was he sitting here in his empty house risking losing her love?

Was he brave enough to be that vulnerable, to go to her with his heart in his hands and offer it into her safekeeping?

Maybe not, but he had to try.

He jumped up, startling Stonewall. Taking the stairs two at a time, he had no plan in mind other than to try to be the man Elise deserved. And that meant making some changes for her.

~

*E*lise needed to get out of there. The ballroom closed in on her, the laughter and music and movement. It all meant nothing when her heart was breaking, when she carried this great emptiness with her. GW was saying something, but she could only think about getting away. She gathered her skirts and stood, but before she could take a step, her heart shot into her throat.

Bowie.

She blinked, sure she was imagining things, but it was him.

He was so handsome, he took her breath away.

The crowd parted, everyone staring as he glided toward her, cat-like. He wore a black suit with a white shirt that showed off his tanned skin, and he had a determined gleam in his eye, but that wasn't the most startling transformation.

He'd pulled his hair back from his face and tied it behind his head... and he'd shaved off his beard.

No rifle, no dogs, no protective barriers to hide behind. The black-powder burns and shiny scars so easily visible did nothing to detract from his appearance, and his eyepatch was just a part of him.

He came to a stop in front of her, not touching her. His family encircled them, surprise and delight on their faces.

"My knees are shaking." He sounded hoarse.

Tears burned her eyes at the vulnerability in his voice. "Mine too."

"Elise Hart, I'm not good with words, and I know I don't deserve a woman like you, but I'm asking you to be my wife, for real this time. I love you."

Several of her sisters-in-law sighed, and she thought she heard Hays whistle. Elise was overwhelmed by the sacrifice Bowie was making, coming to town, exposing his scars for all to see, and all for her. All because he loved her. Her voice had deserted her, but she nodded, her eyes filling with tears.

"Well, go ahead and kiss her already. I'm hungry." Hays poked Bowie in the shoulder and everyone laughed.

Bowie held his arms open, and Elise went into them. She reached up and cupped his face in her hands, and a glimmer of fear shot into his eye, but she didn't stop. She caressed his lean cheeks, admiring the strength of his jaw and chin. Her arms went around his neck, and he crushed her close, bringing his lips down on hers. She kissed him back with all the love in her heart, hardly believing that he was here and that he really loved her.

The music started for the last waltz before supper, and Austin clapped Bowie on the back. "Dance with your bride already. She's been waiting for you all night."

"Thanks, Austin. For everything."

His brother nodded and turned to his own bride.

Elise went into Bowie's arms, and he held her much tighter than convention dictated. She didn't care a bit. She couldn't stop touching his face and hair. Friends called to them, welcoming Bowie to the dance, and no one mentioned anything other than Christmas greetings. Even Miss Spanner smiled as she whirled by with Harley Burton.

"This feels unreal," Elise whispered.

Bowie squeezed her tighter. "It's real. We'll make it real."

She didn't know if she could stand the joy pulsing through her veins.

When the song ended, Elise found herself standing under a ball of mistletoe. Bowie looked up, and he smiled, a broad smile that showed his teeth. "Coincidence?" He gathered her close, kissing her thoroughly until her corset felt too tight and her head whirled.

When he broke the kiss, he rested his forehead against hers, taking deep breaths. "I love you, Elise Hart. I have for a long time."

"I love you, Bowie Hart, and I will forever."

GW strode over. "I don't know what's been going on between you two, but whatever it is, I'm glad it's settled. And I don't think anyone will mind if you don't stay for supper. I remember my own newlywed days." He grinned and tucked his thumbs under his suspenders, heading into the dining room with the rest of the party guests. As he turned the corner, he looked back and gave them a broad wink. "Merry Christmas."

Bowie threaded his fingers through Elise's, laughing. "Well, Hart sons always listen to our pa. Guess that means I can take you home, wife."

She rested her head against his arm, still unable to believe how her night had changed from miserable to majestic in such a short time.

When they reached the house, Gage was there to take the horses and buggy, and the minute he was out of sight, Bowie scooped Elise up in his arms. She squealed and flung her arms around his neck, but he didn't stop, striding over the threshold, kicking the door shut behind them and heading up the stairs. "I'll have you know, I am never sleeping in that little bed across the hall again, and don't think I don't know what you were up to, woman, ordering such a large bed for in here and such short ones for the other rooms."

Elise laughed, kissed him on his scarred cheek, and said, "I was willing to try anything to get your attention."

"You've had my attention since the first time I smelled your jasmine perfume." He set her down beside the bed. "And I can prove it." He withdrew a scrap of fabric from his suit coat pocket.

"What is that?" She took it, frowning.

"It's one of your hankies. You dropped it more than a decade ago in the hospital, and I've had it all these years. Having it got me through some tough times." He trailed his finger down her cheek. "But having you is much better."

"Bowie." She wrapped her arms around him, clutching the handkerchief, overcome with love for him.

"I love you, Elise," he whispered against her hair. "I want to make you happy. I want to fill this house with kids and laughter and love. I don't want you to ever regret marrying me."

She thought she might burst with happiness, with all the love he was offering her. It was more than she'd hoped for and everything she'd dreamed. "I can't believe we've found love at last, after all these years."

Bowie reached out and shut the bedroom door, sealing them into a world of two.

EPILOGUE

*G*W sniffed and blinked hard, slowly walking through the dining room to stand in front of the portrait of his wife. The bundle in his arms squirmed and snuffled before quieting back to sleep.

"Well, Victoria, we did it." He eased the blanket back from the baby's face. "I'd like to present Edmund Jackson Davis Hart, Jack for short. Your first Hart grandchild." GW wiped away a tear with his shoulder. "Hays and Emma kept up with tradition. He's named after the governor of Texas."

GW angled his chair at the head of the table so he could see the portrait and sat, glancing down at Jack's full cheeks and head of dark hair, then back up at his wife's lovely face.

"I sure wish you were here to see him. He looks a lot like Hays. You always did have pretty babies, and it looks as though the next generation will be just as handsome."

He surveyed the long dining room table, set for the New Year's Day dinner. The number of chairs had doubled in the past twelve months. "Hard to believe it's been a whole year, but what a year it was. All your boys are married now. You'd like their wives, every one of them."

Going down the table, he relived each romance—Hays's whirlwind courtship of Emma, Chisholm's falling for a Mexican beauty, Travis reconciling with his sweet Annie, Houston winning the love of his childhood sweetheart, Coralee, Crockett doing a kind deed for his neighbors and ending up head over boots in love with Jane, Austin fixin' to marry one gal and falling for her twin sister instead, and Bowie realizing he loved Elise and her happiness meant more to him than his own insecurities.

"Yep, quite a year. Seven marriages, and a new grandbaby in twelve months. And another baby will be making his appearance soon. Probably another boy. Harts tend to throw boys. Though I wouldn't mind a girl or two, just to keep things interesting."

Laughter came from the parlor across the hall. "You raised some mighty fine sons, Victoria, and smart too. Travis guessed what was behind the codicil to my will, and he rounded on me pretty good for not telling him. He prescribed some new pills that he said should help with my heart trouble, and he said if I took it easy and did what he told me, I should last for quite a few years yet, Lord willing. Which is good, because while I'm looking forward to seeing you again when the Lord calls me home, I still have a lot to live for."

He rose, pressing a kiss against Jack's forehead, and went to rejoin his family.

ABOUT THE AUTHOR

Best-selling, award-winning author **Erica Vetsch** loves Jesus, history, romance, and sports. When she's not writing fiction, she's planning her next trip to a history museum. You can connect with her at her website, www.ericavetsch.com and you can find her on Facebook at **The Inspirational Regency Readers Group** where she spends way too much time!

Did you enjoy this book? We hope so!
Would you take a quick minute to leave a review where you purchased the book?
It doesn't have to be long. Just a sentence or two telling what you liked about the story!

Receive a FREE ebook and get updates when new Wild Heart books release: https://wildheartbooks.org/newsletter

If you love historical romance, check out the other Wild Heart books!

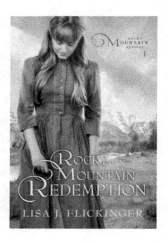

Rocky Mountain Redemption by Lisa J. Flickinger

She's a debutante with broken dreams...He's a preacher with an unsavory past...Both want to bury their secrets...

Charles Bailey's life has done a complete turnaround. He may still be a logging crew foreman, and he may still have a past that would make a godly man weep, but he's also a man with a changed heart and a mission to serve as pastor to a small logging community. If only walking the narrow path weren't so difficult. The last thing he needs is the temptation of the vulnerable—and beautiful—new cook's assistant. It's clear she needs a friend, but anything more than that is completely off-limits...

Disgraced and grieving, Isabelle Franklin is packed off to work in a logging camp's kitchen in the Rocky Mountains. Though feeding a crew of barbaric lumberjacks can't be further from her life's dream, she finds a small measure of solace in the beauty of the land. And in the unexpected kindness of the camp's foreman, who's broad shoulders and gentle eyes make her feel...almost safe. Is it too much to hope that her unspeakable past can stay buried?

But not even the great Rocky Mountains can hide a person's secrets forever—not when God means to bring them to light. When all the gritty truth is laid bare, two hearts are forced to decide what they truly believe about God's amazing grace.

~

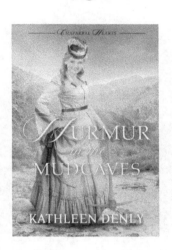

Murmur in the Mud Caves by Kathleen Denly

He came to cook for ranch hands, not three single women.

Gideon Swift, a visually impaired Civil War Veteran, responds to an ad for a ranch cook in the Southern California desert mountains. He wants nothing more than to forget his past and stay in the kitchen where he can do no harm. But when he arrives to find his employer murdered, the ranch turned to ashes, and three young women struggling to survive in the unforgiving Borrego Desert, he must decide whether his presence protects them or places them in greater danger.

Bridget "Biddie" Davidson finally receives word from her older sister who disappeared with their brother and pa eighteen years prior, but the news is not good. Determined to help her family, Biddie sets out for a remote desert ranch with her adopted father and best friend. Nothing she finds there is as she expected, including the man who came to cook for the shambles of a ranch.

When tragedy strikes, the danger threatens not only her plans to help her sister, but her own dreams for the future—with the man who's stolen her heart.

~

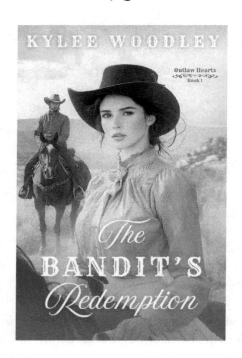

The Bandit's Redemption

A holdup gone wrong, a reluctant outlaw, and the captive she's sworn to guard.

Life in the American West hasn't been easy for French refugee Lorraine Durand. She has precious few connections and longs to return to her native land. So when the man who rescued her from a Parisian uprising following the Franco-Prussian War persuades her to help him with a deadly holdup, she reluctantly agrees. Despite his promises otherwise, the gang kidnaps a man, forcing Lorraine to grapple with the fallout of her choices even as she is drawn to the captive she's meant to guard.

Jesse Alexander must survive. If not for himself, then for the troubled sister he left behind in Los Angeles. At the mercy of his captors, he carefully works to earn Lorraine's trust, hoping he can easily subdue her when the time comes. But as they navigate the treacherous wilderness and he searches for his opportunity to escape, he realizes there may be more to her than he first believed.